BALANCE OF POWER

RICHARD NORTH PATTERSON'S eleven previous novels include seven consecutive international bestsellers. His novels have won an Edgar Allan Poe Award and the Grand Prix de Littérature Policière. Formerly a trial lawyer in Washington and San Francisco, Mr Patterson also served as an Assistant Attorney-General in Ohio and as the SEC's liaison to the Watergate special prosecutor, and now serves on the boards of several Washington-based advocacy groups dealing with gun violence, political reform and reproductive rights. He lives with his wife, Laurie, and their family in San Francisco and on Martha's Vineyard.

RICHARD NORTH
PATTERSON

BALANCE OF POWER

PAN BOOKS

First published 2003 by Random House Publishing Group, New York

First published in Great Britain 2003 by Macmillan

This edition published 2004 by Pan Books
an imprint of Pan Macmillan Ltd
Pan Macmillan, 20 New Wharf Road, London N1 9RR
Basingstoke and Oxford
Associated companies throughout the world
www.panmacmillan.com

ISBN 0 330 49083 4

3 5 7 9 8 6 4 2

A CIP catalogue record for this book is available from
the British Library.

Typeset by Intype Libra Ltd
Printed and bound in Great Britain by
Mackays of Chatham plc, Chatham, Kent

FOR PHILIP ROTNER

A well-regulated militia being necessary to the security of a free State, the right of the people to keep and bear arms shall not be infringed.

—*The Second Amendment to*
the United States Constitution

Characters

The White House

Kerry Francis Kilcannon, President of the United States
Lara Costello Kilcannon, First Lady of the United States
Ellen Penn, Vice President of the United States
Clayton Slade, Chief of Staff to the President
Kit Pace, Press Secretary to the President
Peter Lake, head of the President's Secret Service detail
Liz Curry, Director of Legislative Affairs
Alex Cole, Congressional Liaison
Jack Sanders, Chief Domestic Policy Advisor
Connie Coulter, Press Secretary to the First Lady
Francesca Thibault, White House Social Secretary

The First Lady's Family

Inez Costello, Lara's mother
Joan Costello Bowden, Lara's younger sister
John Bowden, Lara's brother-in-law
Marie Bowden, Lara's niece
Mary Costello, Lara's youngest sister

The United States Senate

Senator Francis Xavier Fasano of Pennsylvania, Senate
    Majority Leader
Senator Charles Hampton of Vermont, Senate Minority
    Leader

Senator Chad Palmer of Ohio, Chairman of the Commerce
Committee
Senator Paul Harshman of Idaho
Senator Cassie Rollins of Maine
Senator Frank Ayala of New Mexico
Senator Vic Coletti of Connecticut
Senator Macdonald Gage of Kentucky
Senator Dave Ruckles of Oklahoma
Senator Jack Slezak of Michigan
Senator Leo Weller of Montana
Senator Betsy Shapiro of California
Senator Kate Jarman of Vermont
Senator Hank Westerly of Nebraska

THE GUN LOBBY

Charles Dane, President of the Sons of the Second
Amendment ("SSA")
Martin Bresler, former President of the Gun Sports
Coalition
Bill Campton, Communications Director for the SSA
Carla Fell, Legislative Director for the SSA
Jerry Kirk, Vice President of the Gun Sports Coalition
Kelsey Landon, former senator from Louisiana and outside
legislative strategist for the SSA

THE LEXINGTON ARMS COMPANY

George Callister, President and CEO
Mike Reiner, Vice President of Marketing
Norman Conn, Manager of Quality Control

COSTELLO VERSUS
THE LEXINGTON ARMS COMPANY, ET AL.

Sarah Dash, co-counsel for Mary Costello
Robert Lenihan, co-counsel for Mary Costello

John Nolan, counsel for Lexington Arms
Harrison Fancher, counsel for the SSA
Gardner W. Bond, Judge of the United States District Court
    for the Northern District of California
Avram Gold, outside counsel to President Kilcannon
Evan Pritchard, counsel for Martin Bresler
Angelo Rotelli, Judge of the Superior Court for the City
    and County of San Francisco

OTHER VICTIMS AND THEIR FAMILIES

Laura Blanchard, a sophomore at Stanford University
Henry Serrano, a security guard
Felice Serrano, his widow
George Serrano, his son
David Walsh, a security guard

THE WITNESSES IN COSTELLO VERSUS THE LEXINGTON ARMS COMPANY, ET AL.

Dr. Callie Hines, trauma surgeon, San Francisco
    General Hospital
Charles Monk, homicide inspector, San Francisco
    Police
Ben Gehringer, felon, member of The Liberty Force,
    a white supremacist group
George Johnson, felon, member of The Liberty Force
Dr. Frederick Glass, expert witness for Lexington Arms
Dr. Larry Walters, expert witness for Mary Costello
Dr. David Roper, expert witness for Mary Costello

THE MEDIA

Cathie Civitch of NBC, interviewer
Taylor Yarborough of ABC, interviewer
Carole Tisone, *San Francisco Chronicle* reporter

THE LOBBYISTS

Tony Calvo of the U.S. Chamber of Commerce
Mary Bryant of the National Association of Manufacturers
John Metrillo of the National Federation of Independent
    Businesses

THE PRESIDENT'S FAMILY

Michael Kilcannon, Kerry's father
Mary Kilcannon, Kerry's mother
James J. Kilcannon, Kerry's brother and predecessor as
    Senator from New Jersey, assassinated while seeking the
    Democratic Presidential nomination

OTHERS

Elise Hampton, wife of Senator Chuck Hampton
Allie Palmer, wife of Senator Chad Palmer
John Halloran, District Attorney for the City and County of
    San Francisco
Marcia Harding, Chief of Halloran's Domestic Violence
    Unit
Caroline Masters, Chief Justice of the United States
    Supreme Court
Anna Chen, Lara's bridesmaid
Nakesha Hunt, Lara's bridesmaid
Linda Mendez, Lara's bridesmaid
The Reverend Bob Christy, Head of the Christian
    Commitment
Warren Colby, former United States Senator from Maine
    and predecessor to Senator Cassie Rollins
Leslie Shoop, Chief of Staff to Senator Rollins
Lance Jarrett, President and CEO of Silicon Valley's largest
    chip maker
Rep. Thomas Jencks, Speaker of the United States House of
    Representatives

The Prime Minister of England
The Prime Minister of Israel
The President of the Palestine Liberation Organization
Mahmoud Al Anwar, terrorist and leader of Al Qaeda

PART ONE

THE WEDDING

JULY 4 TO LABOR DAY WEEKEND

ONE

FEELING THE GUN against the nape of her neck, Joan Bowden froze.

Her consciousness narrowed to the weapon she could not see: her vision barely registered the cramped living room, the images on her television—the President and his fiancée, opening the Fourth of July gala beneath the towering obelisk of the Washington Monument. She could feel John's rage through the cold metal on her skin, smell the liquor on his breath.

"Why?" she whispered.

"You wanted him."

He spoke in a dull, emphatic monotone. *Who?* she wanted to ask. But she was too afraid; with a panic akin to madness, she mentally scanned the faces from the company cookout they had attended hours before. Perhaps Gary—they had talked for a time.

Desperate, she answered, "I don't want anyone."

She felt his hand twitch. "You don't want *me*. You have contempt for me."

Abruptly, his tone had changed to a higher pitch, paranoid and accusatory, the prelude to the near hysteria which issued from some unfathomable recess of his brain. Two nights before, she had awakened, drenched with sweat, from the nightmare of her own death.

Who would care for Marie?

Moments before, their daughter had sat at the kitchen table, a portrait of dark-haired intensity as she whispered to the doll for whom she daily set a place. Afraid to move,

Joan strained to see the kitchen from the corner of her eye. John's remaining discipline was to wait until Marie had vanished; lately their daughter seemed to have developed a preternatural sense of impending violence which warned her to take flight. A silent minuet of abuse, binding daughter to father.

Marie and her doll were gone.

"Please," Joan begged.

The cords of her neck throbbed with tension. The next moment could be fateful: she had learned that protest enraged him, passivity insulted him.

Slowly, the barrel traced a line to the base of her neck, then pulled away.

Joan's head bowed. Her body shivered with a spasm of escaping breath.

She heard him move from behind the chair, felt him staring down at her. Fearful not to look at him, she forced herself to meet his gaze.

With an open palm, he slapped her.

Her head snapped back, skull ringing. She felt blood trickling from her lower lip.

John placed the gun to her mouth.

Her husband. The joyful face from her wedding album, now dark-eyed and implacable, the 49ers T-shirt betraying the paunch on his too-thin frame.

Smiling grimly, John Bowden pulled the trigger.

Recoiling, Joan cried out at the hollow metallic click. The sounds seemed to work a chemical change in him— a psychic wound which widened his eyes. His mouth opened, as if to speak; then he turned, staggering, and reeled toward their bedroom.

Slumping forward, Joan covered her face.

Soon he would pass out. She would be safe then; in the morning, before he left, she would endure his silence, the aftershock of his brutality and shame.

At least Marie knew only the silence.

Queasy, Joan stumbled to the bathroom in the darkened hallway, a painful throbbing in her jaw. She stared in the mirror at her drawn face, not quite believing the woman she had become. Blood trickled from her swollen lip.

She dabbed with tissue until it stopped. For another moment Joan stared at herself. Then, quietly, she walked to her daughter's bedroom.

Marie's door was closed. With painstaking care, her mother turned the knob, opening a crack to peer through.

Cross-legged, Marie bent over the china doll which once had been her grandmother's. Joan felt a spurt of relief; the child had not seen them, did not see her now. Watching, Joan was seized by a desperate love.

With slow deliberation, Marie raised her hand and slapped the vacant china face.

Gently, the child cradled the doll in her arms. "I won't do that again," she promised. "As long as you're good."

Tears welling, Joan backed away. She went to the kitchen sink and vomited.

She stayed there for minutes, hands braced against the sink. At last she turned on the faucet. Watching her sickness swirl down the drain, Joan faced what she must do.

Glancing over her shoulder, she searched for the slip of paper with his telephone number, hidden in her leather-bound book of recipes. *Call me,* he had urged. *No matter the hour.*

She must not wake her husband.

Lifting the kitchen telephone from its cradle, Joan crept back to the living room, praying for courage. On the television, a graceful arc of fireworks rose above the obelisk.

TWO

PRESIDENT KERRY FRANCIS KILCANNON and his fiancée, Lara Costello, watched as a red flare rose above the Mall, bursting into a galaxy of falling stars which framed the Washington Monument.

For this rarity, an evening alone, they had left the annual party for staffers and retreated to the porch on the second floor of the White House. Spread across their table was a white linen cloth, a picnic of cheese and fruit, and a bottle of light chardonnay which cooled in a silver cylinder, a gift from the President of France. Lara took Kerry's hand.

"When I was six," she told him, "our father took us to the fireworks at Crissy Field. I remember holding his hand, watching all those explosions above the Golden Gate Bridge. That's my last memory of being with him."

Turning from the fireworks, Kerry studied the sculpted face—intense dark eyes, high cheekbones, pale skin framed by jet-black hair—which, to her bemusement, had helped Lara rise from a semianonymous political reporter for the *New York Times* to celebrity as a television journalist. Like many women, Kerry supposed, her self-concept had been fixed in adolescence: then she had not thought of herself as beautiful—though she surely was—but as the perfect student, the dutiful oldest daughter who must help her mother and sisters. It was the dutiful daughter who had achieved success, driven to make Inez Costello proud, to free her younger sisters from the struggle caused by their father's desertion. Even at thirty-two, Kerry knew, her family still defined her.

"What I was hoping you'd remember," he said, "is the scene from *To Catch a Thief*. Cary Grant and Grace Kelly in Monaco, watching fireworks from her hotel room."

Lara faced him with an amused, appraising look. "I remember that they lay down on the couch, and then the camera panned away. The fireworks were a metaphor."

"Uh-huh. Very 1950s."

Leaning forward, Lara kissed him, a lingering touch of the lips, then rested her cheek against his shoulder. "This is the twenty-first century," she told him. "No metaphors required."

Afterward, they lay in his canopied bed listening to the last, faint whistling of fireworks. One table lamp still glowed—making love, and after, both needed to see the other's face.

Smiling, she lightly mussed his hair. "You're not too bad," she told him. "At least as Presidents go."

As she intended, this elicited the boyish grin which lit his face and crinkled the corners of his eyes. There had been too little lightness in Kerry's life. Even his first success in politics, election to the Senate at age thirty, had been as surrogate for his brother, Senator James Kilcannon, assassinated in San Francisco while running for President. Lara had been nineteen then; she remembered watching the telecast of James's funeral, the haunted look on Kerry's face as he attended to his widowed mother. So that when, as a reporter for the *New York Times*, she had met him seven years later, the first thing she noticed was not his fine-featured face, incongruously youthful for a potential President, nor his thatch of chestnut hair, nor even the scar at the corner of one eye. It was the startling contradiction presented by the eyes themselves: their green-flecked blue irises, larger than most, gave Lara the sense—rare in a white male politician—of someone who had seen more sadness than most. Then, she had thought this an illusion, abetted by her memory of the funeral; only later, when Kerry shared the private history he had entrusted to almost no one, did she understand how true it was.

"If so," he answered, "you're free to take it personally. Tongue-tied Catholic boys from Newark don't usually get much practice. Lord knows that Meg and I weren't much good to each other, in any way."

If only, Lara thought, Meg could be dismissed so simply. But her existence affected them still—publicly, because Kerry's lack of an annulment had forestalled them from marrying in the Church; privately, because their love affair had begun while Kerry was married. Its secrecy had saved Kerry's chances of becoming President: only after his divorce and the California primary, when Kerry himself had been wounded by a would-be assassin, had they come together in public.

Now she touched the scar the bullet had left, a red welt near his heart. "*We've* been good to each other," she said. "And very lucky."

To Lara, he seemed to sense the sadness beneath her words, the lingering regrets which shadowed their new life. "Just lucky?" he answered softly. "In public life, we're a miracle. Rather like my career."

This aspect of his worldview—that good fortune was an accident—was, in Lara's mind, fortified by his certainty that gunfire had made him President: first by killing James, the deserving brother; then by wounding Kerry, causing the wave of sympathy which, last November, had helped elect him by the narrowest of margins, with California tipping the balance. But this had also given him a mission, repeated in speech after speech: "to eradicate gun violence as surely as we ended polio."

"Speaking of miracles," she asked, "is your meeting with the gun companies still a go?"

"A handful of companies," Kerry amended. "The few brave souls willing to help keep four-year-olds from killing themselves with that new handgun Dad bought for their protection. If you listen to the SSA, tomorrow will be the death knell of gun rights in America." Suddenly, he smiled. "Though in preparing for the meeting, I discovered that it's you who's hell-bent on disarming us."

"Me?"

"You, and your entire profession." Turning, Kerry removed a magazine from the briefing book on his nightstand; as he flipped its pages, Lara saw that it was the monthly publication of the Sons of the Second Amendment, perhaps Washington's most powerful lobby, and that its cover featured a venomous cartoon of Kerry as Adolf Hitler.

" 'Surveys,' " Kerry read, " 'have shown that most reporters for the major media live in upper-class homes, head and shoulders above most of us in fly-over country. Many took their education at Ivy League universities where they protested the Vietnam conflict, smoked dope, loved freely, and ingested every ultraliberal cause their professors threw at them.' " Pausing, he said wryly, "Truth to tell, they're onto something. What was wrong with *you*?"

Lara propped her head up with one hand. "My mother cleaned houses. So I was afraid to lose my scholarship. Besides, I missed the war by twenty years."

"It hardly matters—you caught up soon enough. Listen to this: 'Once they graduated, they faced the prospect of going to work. What better way to earn a fat paycheck and change the world than become a reporter for ABC, or CBS or NBC or CNN or write for the *New York Times*?'

"That's *you*," Kerry added, fixing her with a mock-accusatory gaze, and then continued. " 'Having become gainfully employed, these men and women from Yale and Harvard and Brown and Princeton brought their own biases with them. Many do not know anyone who owns guns. Their only exposure to firearms comes when they report on the carnage left by a deranged shooter going "postal" . . .' "

"How about knowing someone who actually got *shot*?" Lara interjected. "Does that count?"

"Oh, that? That just means you've lost your objectivity. Like me."

The rueful remark held an undertone of bitterness. This involved far more, Lara knew, than what his opponents claimed—anger at his brother's death, or his own near death. Kerry was sick of bloodshed, weary of meeting, year after year, with families who had lost loved ones, of trying to comfort them with the same empty phrases. For him, his failure was both political and deeply personal. And Kerry did not live with failure—especially regarding guns—well.

"Sooner or later," Lara assured him, "you'll get Congress to pass a decent gun law."

Kerry raised his eyebrows, exchanging bitterness for an irony tinged with good-natured frustration. "Before or *after* we get married?"

Lara smiled, unfazed. "That I can't tell you. But certainly before I find a job."

This was another blind curve on the road to marriage. Though she was developing a degree of fatalism, the resignation of a would-be First Lady to the limitations of her new life, Lara had always been independent, beholden to no one for support or a sense of who she was. That Kerry understood this did not change what she would lose by marrying him—her own identity. Already she had been forced to take leave from NBC: the potential for conflicts of interest, or at least their appearance—that a powerful network might profit by employing the President's fiancée —also applied to any other segment of the media. A brief flirtation with the presidency of the Red Cross—based on her high profile as a television journalist and experience in war zones—had floundered on the fear that major donors might want something from President Kilcannon. Other jobs had similar problems, and the best ones, Lara acknowledged, would take away from her public duties and her private time with Kerry. "I'm sorry," she said at last. "I was being a brat. It may not seem so, but you're actually more important to me than running the Red Cross."

Though he knew this, or at least should, to Lara his expression betrayed a certain relief. "Then your fate is sealed, I'm afraid."

"I guess it is," she answered dryly. "I'm a fool for love."

Once more he drew her close. "The thing is," he continued, "I'm forty-three. Even if we started tomorrow, by the time our first son or daughter graduates from college I'll be on Social Security. If there's any left."

"Tell that to the Pope."

"Oh, I have. I even mentioned that Meg couldn't stand the thought of children." There was a different tone in his voice, Lara thought; hand gently touching her chin, he raised her face to his. "And, at last, he's heard me."

She felt a tingle of surprise. "The annulment?"

Kerry grinned. "Yes. That."

Astonished, Lara pulled back to look at him. "When?"

"Yesterday."

"Why didn't you tell me?"

"I was in Pittsburgh." There was new light in his eyes, and he spoke more softly. "This just seemed like a better time and place."

Knowing how much he wanted this, Lara felt the depth of her love for him. This moment was the last threshold, she knew, before she entered the hall of mirrors which was the Presidency, the omnipresent, often merciless scrutiny which could change lives and warp marriages until even the most private act assumed a public significance. Briefly, she thought of her abortion, felt the familiar stab of fear. Then she thought of Kerry, and imagined their children.

"Is Labor Day too soon?" she asked, and kissed him.

Later, they turned to the practical. It began with her wistful comment, "Let's run away. Or at least have a private wedding—maybe at the Inn at Little Washington."

"Besieged by the media?" Kerry asked. "With helicopters circling? We'd look like Madonna—except that the public would hate us for it."

"Of course," she answered dryly. "How could I forget our stockholders?" She emitted a brief sigh. "I was thinking about us, of all people. And my family. You and I may be public people, but they're not used to this."

Quietly, Kerry pondered that. Her family, as he had learned, was as complex as most, their relations more fraught than many. But these realities lived beneath a surface which, for image-makers, was the stuff of dreams. For Kerry, there was no one left; two months before, quite suddenly, he had lost his beloved mother. But Lara had two sisters, a niece, and a handsome mother who, collectively, would be catnip for any Democratic media consultant worth his fees—the Hispanic cleaning woman who had raised three bright and attractive daughters, seen them through college, and who with the two youngest girls would now watch the oldest become the new First Lady. And though Kerry did not say this, Lara knew that his advisors would envision uses for her family beyond attending their wedding.

"I won't have them exploited," she said. "How many Presidential relatives begin by thinking it's all so wonderful, then find out too late their lives will never be the same."

She saw resistance in his face, the wish to believe—despite all he knew—that this time would be different. "That sounds a little dire," he answered. "For my part, I'll never let my people turn the Costello family into reality TV."

Faintly, Lara smiled. "Then you might begin with Clayton."

At this mention of Kerry's Chief of Staff, his closest friend and protector, Kerry smiled back. "Clayton? If he wants to be Best Man, he'll remember which one of us is President." Pausing, he assured her, "Seriously, I worry about them, too."

"I know you do."

The telephone rang.

Distractedly, Kerry picked it up. "It's midnight on the Fourth of July," he wryly told the operator. "Are we at war?"

Pausing, Kerry listened. His eyes grew hooded, his face sober. "Put her through," he ordered.

"Who is it?" Lara murmured.

Covering the telephone, Kerry met her gaze. "Your sister Joan. For me."

THREE

KERRY HAD BEGUN to fear for Lara's sister the previous November.

Until then, he had not met her family. Returning to California to thank supporters for his narrow victory, Kerry asked Lara to invite them for dinner at his favorite San Francisco steakhouse, Alfred's—Lara's mother, Inez; her youngest sister, Mary; and Joan, her husband, John, and their six-year-old daughter, Marie. But the dinner, while a great success with Inez and Mary, was marred for Lara by the absence of the Bowden family. Joan had food poisoning, she had told Lara that morning—they would all meet Kerry on his next trip out.

At dinner's end, Kerry and Lara dropped off Inez and Mary, and the black limousine, shepherded by Kerry's Secret Service detail, headed for their hotel. "I liked them," Kerry told her. "Very much. Your mother's a lot like mine was, but feistier and less reserved."

Lara was quiet. "Mom was embarrassed," she said at length. "All that chattering about Joan—she thinks Joan's lying."

In the darkness of the limousine, Kerry could not read her face. "Why?"

"Aside from being too 'sick' to meet my future husband, the President-elect, or see me for the first time in almost a year? So sick that John and Marie didn't come without her?" Lara turned to him. "This wasn't about bad fish. In the ladies' room, Mary admitted that they hardly see her now."

This touched a nerve in Kerry. "Is it the husband?" he asked.

Lara did not answer. "I'm going to see her, Kerry. Before we leave."

Joan and her family lived in a bungalow in the Crocker-Amazon district, houses snug together along the rise and fall of urban hillocks sectioned by the grid of city blocks. Though modest in size, the house was freshly painted, the drawn curtains frilly and neatly pressed, and the front porch brightened by pots of multihued geraniums. The door bore the label of a security service; rather than a doorbell, the button Lara pressed was for an intercom.

Lara waited for some minutes. When her sister's voice came through the intercom, it sounded disembodied. "Who is it?"

"Lara."

Once more there was silence. "I'm sorry, Lara." The delayed response, wan and uninviting, made Lara edgy. "I really don't feel well."

"Food poisoning's not contagious." To her chagrin, Lara recognized her own tone as that of the oldest sister, prodding the others to rise and shine. "Please," she implored, "I've missed you. I can't leave without at least seeing you."

Joan did not answer. Then, at length, the door cracked open. For a moment, Lara saw only half of her sister's face.

"I'm so glad you're home," Lara said.

Joan hesitated, then opened the door wider.

Her right eye was swollen shut. The neatly applied eyeliner and curled lashes of Joan's unblemished eye only deepened her sister's horror.

"Oh, Joanie." The words issued from Lara's throat in a low rush. "My God . . ."

"It's not what you're thinking," Joan protested. "I fell in

the shower. I got faint from the food poisoning, and slipped."

Pushing the door open, Lara stepped inside, then closed it behind them. She placed both hands on Joan's shoulders.

"I'm not a fool, Joanie. I've seen this before, remember?"

Her sister seemed to flinch at Lara's touch. "So you say. I was three when he left."

Lara stepped back, arms falling to her sides.

Her sister's face was plumper, Lara saw, but its stubborn defensive cast was the same. The well-kept living room, too, was much as Lara recalled—the polished wooden floor; a spotless oriental rug; immaculate white furniture; a shelf of neatly spaced family photographs. Spotting a formal portrait of Marie, dark and pretty, Lara paused to study it. More calmly, she asked, "Does Mom know?"

"She doesn't want to know." Brief resentment crossed Joan's face—at whom, Lara was not sure. "She likes John. You're the only one who thinks it's great for children not to have a father. That's what *I* remember—not having one."

"Then I envy you, Joanie. I remember him quite well."

"Don't patronize me, dammit." Joan's speech became staccato. "Everything worked out for you: great looks, perfect grades, famous friends, a multimillion-dollar contract – oh, don't think for a minute Mom didn't tell us about *that*. And now you're marrying the goddammed President-elect of the United States."

"All I need do for you to resent me," Lara shot back, "is exist." Fighting her own anger, she finished, "I'm marrying a man who treats me with respect. You deserve that, too."

Joan stood straighter. "We have a good life," she insisted. "He's good to Marie. It's not that often, or that bad."

"How often does it have to be, Joanie? How bad does it have to get?"

Joan's voice rose. "That's so easy for you to say. What does your life have to do with mine?"

"I'm your sister, and I care about you. We're not competing." Lara paused, speaking more quietly, "Don't take a beating on *my* account. Or Marie's."

Abruptly, Joan turned from her. "Please leave, Lara. This is *my* home. I didn't invite you here."

Gazing at her sister's back, Lara felt frustration turn to helplessness, then a piercing regret. Briefly, she touched her sister's shoulder.

Joan remained frozen, back still turned to Lara. After a moment, Lara let herself out.

"I'm worse than useless to her," Lara said sadly. "Proving me wrong is one more reason for her to stay."

In the thin November sunlight of midmorning, she and Kerry walked through a narrow valley in Marin County, headed toward a blue-grey ocean which flooded an inlet between jagged cliffs. Both craved exercise, escape from people and stifling rooms; on the road they scheduled an hour, when they could, to walk and talk and breathe fresh air. At a respectful distance, Secret Service agents walked in front and back of them; others watched above them, along steep hills, green from recent rains. As they continued, hands jammed in their pockets against the cold, Kerry gave her a searching look. "She resents you that much?"

"I'd forgotten quite how much. Perhaps I was hoping we'd outgrown it." Lara gazed ahead of them at the glint of distant waves. "Some working-class mothers might have knocked me down a peg, reminded me that I was nothing special. But Mom held me up as their example.

"They had to excel, like me. They had to go to college, like me, even if they couldn't get into Stanford, or win a scholarship." Pausing, Lara added with irony, "So I made things worse by paying their way."

This elicited, in Kerry, a faint smile. "Half the time," he told her, "I loathed my brother. Jamie was so damned good at everything—so untouchable, it seemed. He was entirely self-invented, I realize now, and very much alone. But then he was the last person on earth I'd ever feel compassion for. Or listen to."

Quiet, Lara moved closer, so that their arms brushed. At times she felt such relief at all they shared, a blessed release from the sense of solitude she had lived with for so long, that it overwhelmed her ability to tell him. "It's that," she finally said, "and more. Joan became the domestic one—helping Mom cook and clean, keeping track of things, not complaining. That was her value, the thing she was better at than me *or* Mary. When John Bowden came along, and wanted to enshrine her as the princess of a perfect household all her own, she was more than ready."

"What did *you* think of him?"

"Eager to please—a little too eager, I thought. He virtually courted our mother, as if to prove how helpful and considerate he was. I remember her telling Joanie not to let him get away." Lara's tone became soft. "Then they got married, and I moved to Washington for the *Times*. Marie was born about the time I met you. They were the ideal family, Joanie claimed."

Listening, Kerry heard more than the words themselves: that Lara felt she had been too caught up in her own career, and Kerry, to see the warning signs. "And then you went to Kosovo," he said. "How could you have known?"

This tacit reference to their own estrangement caused Lara to take his hand. "I do now, don't I."

They walked in silence until they reached the beach, a grey-brown skein of sand strewn with driftwood. A redwood log stripped of bark had washed up near the lapping waves; after Lara sat, wind rustling her hair, Kerry did the same. "When I started prosecuting domestic violence cases," he said at length, "I began to see this depressing, endless cycle. Kids who witness abuse and then grow up to be abusive—or abused. In time, Marie could become Joan."

"So how do I help them?"

"Someone should do something. But you may not be the one." Turning, Kerry faced her. "If you don't mind, I'd like to talk to Joan myself."

At once, Lara felt resistant. "This is *my* family. I know them. I'm not going to dump our problems on you."

"They're about to be *our* family." Kerry looked at her intently. "You already know about my own. Too often people treat this as a family matter, something private, and it just gets worse. We've both seen way too much of that."

Still Lara hesitated. Softly, Kerry asked, "What if he kills her, Lara?"

FOUR

THE NEXT MORNING, Kerry Kilcannon went to the Bowdens' home.

That this proved difficult reminded Kerry of the new strictures on his movement. Slipping the press was hard in itself; worse, Kerry was forced to wait in a nondescript Secret Service van while two agents introduced themselves to a startled Joan Bowden and asked permission to search the house. Kerry's only consolation was the certainty that her husband was not home; at his absolute insistence, the agents assigned to guard him agreed to wait outside.

When she opened the door, her swollen eye was no more than a slit. Kerry tried not to react to her disfigurement.

"I'm Kerry," he said.

Joan glanced past him as though worried he might be seen. Then she gave him a small, rueful smile. "I know who you are."

Kerry tilted his head. "May I come in?"

"All right," she said reluctantly, and then added with more courtesy, "Of course."

He stepped inside, hands in the pockets of his overcoat. The room was bright and orderly. But the visceral feeling he had on entering a home where abuse had occurred made the violence feel near at hand.

He turned to Joan. Whereas Lara resembled her mother—slender, with a certain tensile delicacy—Joan was rounder, with snub, placid-seeming features altered, on this day, by a wary, guarded look. "I've felt funny," Kerry told her, "having an almost-wife whose family I'd never met."

As Joan smiled, a polite movement of the lips, she seemed to study him. "It was strange for us, too. You and Lara came as a surprise."

Though he felt the irony of his own evasion, Kerry gave his accustomed response. "It even surprised me," he answered. "When I got shot, Lara awakened to my virtues. A hard way to get the girl."

Joan appraised him. Then, belatedly, she motioned him to an overstuffed chair, and sat on the couch across from him. Kerry resolved to be direct. "Lara loves you," he said simply. "And now she worries for you."

Curtly, Joan nodded, as if confirming her own suspicion. "So she asked *you* to come."

"No—*I* asked." Kerry looked at Joan intently. "I used to prosecute domestic violence cases. I've seen too many 'family secrets' go wrong, too many people damaged. Especially children."

That there was more to this Kerry did not say. But the purple swelling of her eye stirred all of the emotions his father had left roiling inside a frightened boy of six or seven—a hatred of bullies; a sympathy for victims; the sense of guilt that he could not protect his mother; the angry need to sublimate this powerlessness through action. Nervously, Joan glanced at the door, as if Kerry's presence would summon her husband.

"I'll be all right," she insisted.

"You won't be. And neither will Marie." He paused, choosing his words with care. "I know you're watching out for her. But in the end it's not enough. When he harms you, he harms Marie."

Joan hesitated. Kerry watched her decide how much to say, how far to trust this man—at once so familiar, a constant presence on the screen or in the newspaper, a subject of relentless curiosity among her friends—yet a stranger in her living room.

"It's not John's fault," she said.

"Perhaps not," Kerry answered. "But it's his responsibility. And yours."

Joan kneaded her dress, a nervous gesture which seemed intended to gain time. "John's life growing up was hard," she said at last. "I don't think his father beat him, or his mother—it was more like John was terrorized. If he violated a rule, no matter how small, his dad would lock him in his room—maybe for a weekend, with no escape except for bathroom breaks. And sometimes not for that." She gave a helpless shrug. "It's like John goes back there—like someone throws a switch which sets him off. Afterward he's so sorry I almost feel for him."

To Kerry, this sounded like the Stockholm Syndrome—where a captive begins identifying with her captor. Like John Bowden, the boy, must have done.

"Except now John's the father," Kerry told her. "The only difference is that he's violent. And that he abuses his wife instead of his child."

Stubbornly, Joan shook her head. "He doesn't want to be like that. When I first met him, he wasn't at all."

"How was he then?"

"Wonderful." The word seemed to fortify her; a look akin to nostalgia flickered in her eyes. "He was so responsible, so sure of himself, so determined to take care of me. He was unlike any boy I'd met—considerate, hardworking, and never drank a drop of alcohol. He was wonderful with my family, especially our mom. And I was the center of his world."

This was all too familiar, Kerry thought. "What about friends?"

"We didn't have that many—there really wasn't time." Her voice trailed off—the impact, Kerry guessed, of illusion crashing into reality. After a time, she added in a chastened tone, "He just wanted to be with me, he said. Sometimes he'd get jealous of other men, really for no reason. But he said it was because he loved me so completely he'd gotten too afraid of losing me."

As she paused, shoulders curled inward, Kerry felt certain she had never talked about this before. "And that felt right to you?" he asked.

She seemed to parse her memories—or, perhaps, to decide whether to respond. In a monotone, she answered, "Every day he sent flowers, or left notes on my front porch. I could hardly believe anyone loving me like that."

Though perhaps Kerry imagined it, the last phrase seemed to carry a faint shudder. Quickly, Joan glanced at the door again.

"When did he first hit you?" Kerry asked.

"When I was pregnant with Marie." Pausing, Joan briefly closed her eyes. "We were in bed, listening to an oldies station. Then they started playing 'The Way You Look Tonight . . .' "

The first few bars made Joan smile—at seven months pregnant, it was hard to imagine herself in Lara's white prom dress, altered through her mother's best efforts. Then she felt John staring at her.

"This song reminds you of *him*."

The accusation so startled her that at first Joan hardly remembered who "he" was. "God, John—that was high school. I couldn't say if he's still alive."

She could, of course—Mary had seen him at Stonestown Mall, with his new wife. In an accusatory tone, John said, "You're *lying*, Joanie. That was 'your song,' remember?"

It was so unfair: years ago she had trusted him with a

harmless scrap of memory, never imagining the ways in which he might harbor this inside him. "I'd *forgotten* . . ."

With sudden fury, John slapped her across the face.

She rolled away from him, stunned, eyes welling with startled tears. Rising, she took two stagger-steps, head ringing, and rested her hands against the white wicker bassinet he had brought home to surprise her. "*John* . . ."

His eyes were damp as well. "I'm sorry, baby. I'm so sorry."

The next morning he sent flowers.

"But he couldn't stop being jealous, until it was about any man I met or even might meet." Averting her gaze, Joan touched her discolored cheek. "Of the fifty-year-old mailman, because we spoke Spanish together. A twenty-year-old teacher's aide at Marie's preschool. Some man I talked to at a party. When I would see friends or family without him. Even when I mentioned maybe getting a part-time job. When he began drinking, it got worse."

Yes, Kerry thought—it would. "When did that start?" he asked.

"About a year ago. With problems at work, I think." Still Joan looked down. "He was very insecure about his boss. The first time John came home like that, there'd been some reprimand. After I put Marie to bed, John hit me."

"And the drinking just kept on."

"Yes." Joan's words took on a despairing rhythm. "He'd drink, and hit me, and apologize; drink and hit me and apologize; drink and hit me . . ."

Abruptly, her voice caught. "Drink and hit you harder." Kerry's voice was soft. "Like the more he hit you, the more he needed to."

She gazed up at him, lips parted in surprise. After a time, a tear escaped her swollen eye.

More evenly, Kerry asked, "And *this* time?"

She would not answer. "Marie was in her room," she finally said. "He always waits for her to sleep."

Already, Joan was exhausted, Kerry saw. Rising from the chair, he walked to the shelf with the formal picture of Marie. Studying it, Kerry was struck by a thought he knew better than to express—Joan's six-year-old was a replica of Lara.

Turning, he asked, "Who do you talk to, Joan?"

She shook her head. "No one."

"Why not your mother? Or Mary?"

"I suppose I'm ashamed." She gazed at the rug, voice low and despairing. "Once, when I drove my mother to the grocery store, John hid a tape recorder beneath the car seat. Even if I'd told her, she couldn't comprehend it. John's so responsible, so good to her. He sends her flowers on Mother's Day."

For a moment, Kerry fell as silent as she, absorbing the fissures beneath the surface of a well-intended family, the way in which silence served their differing needs, their disparate denials and illusions. "Is that all he does?" Kerry asked.

Once more, Joan averted her eyes. "John controls the money. He says he'll never let me take Marie." She paused, throat working. "Last week he bought a gun."

Kerry felt an instant hyperalertness. "Has he threatened you with it?"

A brief shake of the head. "No. But he says if I ever leave him, he'll kill himself."

Crossing the room, Kerry sat beside her, taking both her hands. "Joan," he said, "I'm scared for you. Much more than when I came here."

So was she, her eyes betrayed. He felt her fingers slowly curl around his. *"Why?"*

"Because he's getting worse. And now he has a gun."

Kerry paused, marshalling the words to reach her. "*Look* at him. Maybe his childhood explains him. But it's the adult who keeps choosing to be violent. And if he needs a reason to hurt you, he'll find one.

"Then look at *you*. Look at your reasons for staying — economic insecurity; fear of shame before your family; fear of Marie not having a father; fear of not having Marie." Clasping her fingers, Kerry gazed at her until her eyes met his. "*You're* scared for you—all the time now. And your only way out is to help John stop, or stop him yourself. Which could mean taking him to court."

Joan paled. "I *can't*," she protested. "I could never put Marie through that."

Kerry gave Joan time to hear herself. "Can you put Marie through *this*?" he asked.

Joan's face was a study in confusion—by turns fearful, irresolute, resistant, and imploring. He searched within himself for the words to reach her and realized, against his bone-deep instinct to seal off the past, that they could not be the words of an observer.

"I'm going to tell you something," he said, "that only three people know who are still alive—my mother, my closest friend, and Lara. It's about me. But it's also about Marie."

FIVE

KERRY KILCANNON'S clearest memory of early childhood was of his father bleeding.

It began as many other nights had begun—with the sound of a slammed door, Michael Kilcannon coming home drunk. He would teeter up the stairs to the second floor, talking to himself or to someone he resented, pausing for balance or to take deep, wheezing breaths. Kerry would lie very still; until this night, Michael would stumble past Kerry's and Jamie's rooms to the bedroom at the end of the hall, and the beatings would begin. Through his tears, Kerry would imagine his mother's face at breakfast—a bruised eye, a swollen lip. No one spoke of it.

But on this night, Kerry's door flew open.

Michael Kilcannon flicked on the wall light. The six-year-old Kerry blinked at the sudden brightness, afraid to move or speak.

Slowly, his father walked toward him, and then stood at the foot of his bed. Blood spurted from his forearm.

Terrified, Kerry watched red droplets forming on his sheets.

Michael glared at Kerry, his handsome, somewhat fleshy face suffused with drink and anger. "Look." His Irish lilt became a hiss. "*Look* at what you've done."

Kerry stared at the bloodstains, stupefied.

"Your *wagon*, you pissant. You left your fooking wagon on the path . . ."

Kerry shook his head reflexively. "I'm sorry, Da," he tried. Then he began to cry, trying hard to stop.

Mary Kilcannon appeared in the doorway.

Her long black hair was disarranged, her skin pale in the light. Kerry was too afraid to run to her.

Entering, she gave him a gaze of deep compassion, then placed a tentative hand on her husband's shoulder. Softly, she asked, "What is it, Michael?"

Throat constricted, Kerry watched his father's angry face.

"The wagon." Michael paused, and then gazed down at the sheets with a kind of wonder. "Sharp edges . . ."

Eyes never leaving her son, his mother kissed Michael on the side of his face.

"That'll need tending, Michael." Still trembling, Kerry watched his mother take his father by the hand. "We should go to the hospital."

Slowly, his father turned and let Mary Kilcannon lead him from the room.

Kerry could hardly breathe. Turning, Mary Kilcannon looked back at him. "Don't worry about your father . . ."

Somehow, Kerry understood she meant that he was safe tonight. But he did not get up until he heard the front door close.

His eighteen-year-old brother Jamie—tall and handsome, the family's jewel—was standing in the door of his bedroom. "Well," Jamie said softly, to no one, "they cut quite a figure, don't they?"

Kerry hated him for it.

It started then—the thing between Kerry and his father.

Two days later, the stitches still in his arm, Michael Kilcannon, with two tickets a fellow patrolman could not use, took Kerry to a Mets game. Michael knew little of baseball—he had emigrated from County Roscommon in his teens. But he was a strapping handsome man in his red-haired florid way and, when sober, a dad Kerry was desperately proud of: a policeman, a kind of hero, possessed of a ready laugh and a reputation for reckless courage. Michael bought Kerry popcorn and a hot dog and enjoyed the game with self-conscious exuberance; Kerry knew that this was his apology for what no one would ever mention. When the Mets won in the ninth inning, Michael hugged him.

His father felt large and warm. "I love you, Da," Kerry murmured.

That night, Michael Kilcannon went to Lynch's Ark Bar, a neighborhood mainstay. But Kerry felt safe, the glow of his day with him still.

His bedroom door opening awakened him.

Rubbing his eyes, Kerry looked at his father across the room, half-glad, half-afraid.

Michael staggered toward him and sat at the edge of the bed. Kerry kept quiet; his father was breathing hard. "Bastards." Michael's voice was hostile, threatening.

Kerry's heart pounded. Maybe if he said something, showed his father sympathy . . .

"What is it, Da?"

His father shook his head, as if to himself. "Mulroy . . ."

Kerry did not understand. All he could do was wait.

"I'm as good a man—better," Michael said abruptly. "But *he* makes sergeant, not me. They give it only to the kiss-ass boys . . ."

As she had two nights before, Mary Kilcannon appeared. "Michael," she said in the same soft voice.

Kerry's father did not turn. "Shut up," he said harshly. "We're talking . . ."

Fearful again, Kerry looked at his mother. Her words had an edge her son had never heard before. "Leave the boy alone."

Michael Kilcannon shrugged his heavy shoulders and

rose. With a slap so lazy yet so powerful it reminded Kerry of a big cat, he struck Mary Kilcannon across the mouth.

She reeled backward, blood trickling from her lip. Tears stung Kerry's eyes; watching Mary Kilcannon cover her face, he was sickened by his own fear and helplessness.

"We were *talking*." Michael's voice suggested the patience of a reasonable man, stretched to the breaking point. "Go to bed."

Gazing at Kerry, she backed into the hallway.

Michael turned from her and sat at the edge of his bed. He did not seem to notice that Kerry was crying.

"Mulroy," he repeated.

Kerry did not know how long his father stayed, mumbling resentful fragments. Kerry dared not fall asleep.

After this, Kerry never knew when it would happen. On some nights his father would come home and beat his mother. On others he would open Kerry's door and pour out his wounds and angers. Kerry learned to make some sound or comment so that Michael thought he was listening, to fight sleep or any sign of inattention that might set his father off. Michael never touched him.

As long as Kerry listened, he knew that his father would not beat Mary Kilcannon.

As deeply as Kerry feared his father, he loved his mother.

What Michael imposed on them at night was a shameful secret, never to be discussed. Kerry knew that his mother could not ask the police for help. Michael Kilcannon *was* the police: to tell his friends would shame him, perhaps make him even more brutal. Within the tight community of Vailsburg, where a quiet word from a policeman was enough to nip trouble in the bud, Michael treasured his reputation.

Every morning Mary Kilcannon prayed at Sacred Heart.

In the half-lit vastness of the church, Kerry would watch her rapt profile. Kerry, too, found the church consoling— its hush, its seventy-foot ceilings and beautiful stained-glass windows, its marble altar framed by a fresco of Jesus ascending. Sometimes they stayed for an hour.

One snowy winter morning, they wended their way home. They made a game of it, Kerry trying to walk in his mother's bigger footprints without making footprints of his own.

His prize was a cup of hot chocolate. As they sat at the kitchen table, his mother smiling at him, Kerry felt he would burst with love. But it was she who said, "I love you more than words can tell, Kerry Francis."

Tears came to his eyes. As if reading his mind, Mary Kilcannon said softly, "Your father's a good man when he's sober. He takes good care of us. He's only frustrated, afraid he won't succeed as he deserves."

The words were meant as comfort. But what Kerry heard was that they were trapped: from the long nights with his father, he sensed that the reasons for Michael's failure to rise were the same as for his abusiveness, and that this would never end until someone ended it.

Kerry squeezed his mother's hand.

But outside their home, Kerry knew, Mary Kilcannon would always be known as James's mother.

It began with how much Jamie favored her, so closely that only his maleness made him handsome instead of beautiful. By seventeen, Jamie was six feet one, with an easy grace and with hazel eyes which seemed to take in everything around him. Vailsburg thought Jamie close to perfect: he was student body president of Seton Hall Prep; captain of its football team; second in his class. Jamie's clothes were always neat and pressed, nothing out of place. Girls adored him. Like most obvious expressions of emotion, this seemed to amuse Jamie and, perhaps, to frighten him.

This was Jamie's secret—his ability to withdraw. To Kerry, Jamie seemed driven by a silent contempt for both parents, the need to be nothing like them. From an early age, Jamie was too successful for Michael Kilcannon to disparage. Because of Jamie's size and his attainments, their father came to observe a sort of resentful truce with his older son: Michael received praise in public, was reminded in private of his own inadequacy. But Jamie did not raise his hand, or his voice, to help his mother.

When Jamie left for Princeton on a full scholarship, he would not let his parents drive him there.

Jamie did well at college, played defensive halfback on the football team, became involved in campus politics. His much younger brother dimly imagined classmates thinking that Jamie did this easily. But Kerry knew that as he fearfully waited for his father to climb the stairs, he would sometimes hear his brother through the thin wall between their bedrooms, practicing his speeches, testing phrases, pauses . . .

Kerry never forgot the Christmas vacation of Jamie's second year away.

Jamie was running for something. He practiced a speech late into the night; sleepless, Kerry listened to his brother's muffled voice.

Michael Kilcannon came home.

Hearing his father's footsteps, Kerry wondered whether Michael would open the door or go to his mother's bedroom. He sat up in bed, expectant, as Michael's footsteps passed.

A moment later, Mary Kilcannon cried out in pain.

The only sign that Jamie heard was the silence on the other side of the wall. Tears ran down Kerry's face.

No, he would never be his brother James.

In school, Kerry became contentious, angry, picking fights with older and stronger boys who often beat him badly. And then Liam Dunn, his godfather, took him to the CYO to learn boxing.

Boxing became his salvation—what Kerry lacked in athleticism, he made up in resolve, and then self-discipline. He stopped fighting outside the ring; by seventeen, weary of his own violence, he stopped fighting at all.

By then, Kerry was as big as he would ever get: five feet ten, one hundred fifty-five pounds. He was a full three inches shorter than his handsome brother, the state senator, that much shorter and sixty pounds lighter than his father, the policeman. Beyond boxing there were not many sports for a boy who was neither big nor fast of foot nor a natural leader, let alone one who still lost his temper in frustration at his own lack of talent.

Finally, Kerry made himself a serviceable soccer goalie. "Serviceable" captured Kerry's senior year—Bs and Cs, no honors won, a slot the next year at Seton Hall University, a few blocks from his home. For the longer range, Michael suggested that Kerry go into the police department. "It's enough for a lot of us," he said, "and no point worrying about why you're not your brother. After all, who is?"

Kerry did not answer. His father's failure was etched in the deepening creases of his face, the bleary eyes, and the only relief he found beyond drink was abusing his wife and belittling his son. Kerry's mother seemed almost broken. Perhaps, Kerry thought, his father's women had been her final degradation.

Michael still sat at the foot of Kerry's bed, but often now

he talked of the women he met in bars or on the job, so much younger, so much more admiring. Quietly disgusted, inexperienced himself, Kerry simply hoped that this diversion would help Mary Kilcannon. But the beatings Michael gave her grew worse, especially after his second citation for police brutality: the time Michael had beaten a black man into a concussive state for trying to "escape." It brought him a reprimand, a month's suspension, and a dangerous self-hatred; the night after this happened Mary Kilcannon needed two stitches on her upper lip.

Kerry drove her to the hospital, despair and hatred warring in his heart. When she came out of the emergency room and into the night, Kerry simply held her, cradling her face against his shoulder.

"Leave him, Mom," he murmured. "Please. It can't be God's will that you should stay."

"It's only the drink . . ." Mary closed her eyes, adding softly, "Divorce is a sin, Kerry. And what would I do?"

The look on her once-pretty face, now so pale and thin, pierced him. When they came home, Michael Kilcannon lay passed out on his bed. For a moment, Kerry wondered how it would feel to kill his father in his sleep.

Mary watched his face. "I'll call the priest," she said quietly. "I'll call Father Joe."

It was far safer to call Liam, Kerry thought. Surely there were policemen who cared nothing for his father, prosecutors who owed Liam Dunn a favor. But the priest was his mother's wish.

"Yes," Kerry said. "Call Father Joe."

The next Saturday, the slender, balding priest came to the Kilcannons' home and spoke quietly to Kerry's father. His mother stayed in her room. For several hours his father sat still and silent and then, before dinner, left.

He returned after midnight.

Kerry heard his feet on the stairs, heavy, decisive—then

the ponderous breathing as Michael reached the top. He did not stop at Kerry's room.

Kerry's mouth was dry. He lay on his bed, dressed only in boxer shorts, listening for sounds.

His mother screamed with pain too deep for Kerry to bear.

For a moment, Kerry's eyes shut. Then he stood without thinking and went to his parents' room.

His mother lay in a corner, dressing gown ripped. Blood came from her broken nose. Her husband stood over her, staring down as if stunned, for once, by what he had done.

Kerry stood behind him. He felt so much hatred that he barely registered his mother's fear as she saw him.

The look on her face made Michael turn, startled. "*You,*" he said in surprise.

Kerry hit him with a left jab.

Blood spurted from his father's nose. "You little *fuck,*" his father cried out.

Kerry hit him three more times, and Michael's nose was as broken as his wife's. All that Kerry wanted was to kill him; what his father might do to him no longer mattered.

Kerry moved forward . . .

"*No,*" his mother screamed, and Michael Kilcannon threw a savage punch.

It crashed into Kerry's shoulder; he winced with pain as Michael lunged forward to grab him.

Kerry ducked beneath his father's grip and hit him in the midsection.

The soft flesh quivered. Michael grunted in pain but kept coming, eyes focused with implacable anger. Arms blocking Kerry's next punch, he enveloped him in a murderous bear hug.

Helpless, Kerry felt his ribs ache, his lungs empty. His father's whiskey-maddened face was obscured by black spots, then flashes of light. Kerry felt himself lose consciousness. With a last spasmodic effort, he jammed his knee up into his father's groin.

Kerry felt his father stiffen. His eyes were great with surprise. Panting for air, Kerry lowered his head and butted his father's chin.

Michael's grip loosened. Kerry writhed free, almost vomiting, then stumbled to his right and sent a flailing left hook to his father's groin.

His father let out a moan of agony, his eyes glazing over. His mother stood, coming between them. "*No*, Kerry, *no*."

Still breathing hard, Kerry took her in his arms and pushed her to the bed with fearful gentleness. "Stay," he commanded. "Let *me* finish this."

She did not move again.

In the dim bedroom, Kerry turned to his father.

Michael struggled to raise his fists. Kerry moved forward. *Whack, whack, whack* . . .

His father's eyes bled at the corners now. Kerry hit him in the stomach.

His father reeled back, mouth open.

Kerry brought the right.

It smashed into his father's mouth. Kerry felt teeth break, slashing his own hand. His father fell in a heap.

Kerry stood over him, sucking air in ragged breaths, sick with rage and shock and astonishment. His eyes half-shut, Michael spat tooth fragments from his bloody mouth.

Kerry knelt in front of him. "Touch her again, Da, and I'll kill you. Unless you kill me in my sleep." He paused for breath, then finished. "I wouldn't count on doing that. I'm too used to waiting up for you."

After that night, Michael Kilcannon never hit his wife again. His younger son never hit anyone.

*

Joan listened with downcast eyes. As Kerry finished, they closed.

"In some ways," Kerry told her, "my mother was lucky. So was I. But that wounded, angry boy still exists. Maybe he's the ruthless one I keep reading about." Kerry stopped, dismissing self-analysis or self-justification; as he had learned long since, a reputation for ruthlessness had its uses. Softly, he finished, "You won't raise a brutalizer, Joan. You'll raise a victim."

Joan was silent. Kerry sensed her absorbing all that he had said, yet struggling with the habit of years. He could not push further, or try to talk her, yet, into leaving.

"I'll leave my number," he said at last. "If you ever want to reach me, about anything, please call anytime. Once I'm President, I'll make sure the White House operators know to put you through."

Leaving, Kerry was startled by a slender, brown-haired man standing on the porch.

The man stared down at him. Even had Kerry not seen photographs, he would have known John Bowden from his look of fear and fury.

Kerry felt a reflex of hot, returning anger, then stifled it—to indulge this could do harm. Calmly, he stuck out his hand. "I'm Kerry Kilcannon," he said. "Your future brother-in-law."

Humiliated by his own impotence, the difference in their stations, Bowden did not move.

Kerry's hand fell to his side. Softly, he said, "You're wondering what she told me. Nothing. She didn't have to."

A red flush stained Bowden's neck. Still he did not answer.

"Get help," Kerry told him. "Or someday you'll go too far. And then, trust me, you'll be the one who suffers most."

SIX

KERRY SAT ON the edge of the bed, Lara beside him, listening to Joan Bowden through the telephone. The scene was so vivid that he could envision it—the darkened living room; the frightened woman; the husband passed out in their bedroom.

"It's bad," Joan whispered and then, haltingly, she told him what had happened.

"Where's the gun?" Kerry asked at once.

Lara turned, clutching Kerry's sleeve. Fearfully, Joan answered. "He still has it."

"Has he mentioned suicide again?"

"Not tonight." The despair beneath her whisper deepened. "Only if I leave him."

"What about threatening you. Or Marie."

Joan hesitated. "Just me."

"And the beatings are more frequent now."

"Yes." The word held weary resignation. "They're worse, because John's drinking more. He's worried about his job."

Kerry stood, fighting his own anxiety. "You have to get him out of there," he said with quiet urgency. "Or take Marie and go."

"How? Where?"

Kerry felt Lara at his back, her hands clasping his waist. "There's a drill for this," he answered. "Wait until he leaves for work. Then call the District Attorney's Office and ask for the domestic violence unit. I'll have spoken to them myself by then.

"Tell them what John did. They'll go to court for an

emergency protective order. It's called a kick-out order. They'll take his gun away, make him pack up and leave. Unless you go to a shelter."

The enormity of this induced an extended silence. Lara leaned her face against Kerry's back.

"No," Joan said at last. "I can't put Marie in a shelter. It's too much."

There was no time, Kerry thought, to argue. "If you stay at home," he said, "there are things you can do. Keep close contact with the police, and Mary and your mother. The order should ban John from coming there, cut off his visitation . . ."

"He'll go crazy . . ."

"He'll use Marie if you don't stop him." Kerry paused, lowering his voice. "How do you know he won't just take her?"

"*Take* her." Joan's voice was anguished. "Then how can I do this?"

"By protecting her. If John has to see her, it should be at a visitation center. Otherwise, the order should say that he can't go near her—at your home, her school, or wherever. Make sure her principal and teacher have a copy of the order. Then change your locks, and start looking for another place . . ."

"We'll help her," Lara whispered from behind him.

"We're here for you," Kerry finished. "Don't worry about money. And if you want Lara to fly out there, she will."

Once more Joan was silent. Though he was careful not to say so, Kerry shared her trepidation for reasons of his own: in Kerry's first domestic violence case, the husband had shot his wife to death on the eve of trial, in front of their young son. Joan and Marie were poised on razor's edge; she could not stay with him, and yet leaving was the moment of greatest danger—the time when a husband's violence, fueled by the desperate sense that control was slipping away, might turn lethal.

"We'll get John in a program," Kerry promised. "Each step of the way, I'll be with you."

Through the phone, he first heard quiet, then a sigh. "If you talk to them first," Joan told him in a choked voice. "I'll try."

Afterward, Kerry and Lara returned to the porch. The Mall surrounding the monument was silent now, the festivities ended. The air was moist but cooler.

Head bent, Lara touched her eyes. "I don't know," she murmured.

"About what?"

"Anything. Even me."

Watching her, Kerry waited until she spoke again. "I'm so damned scared for her. But it's all a tangle." She faced him. "This was supposed to be *our* night. Instead you've taken on my sister.

"I'm angry with her, God help me—why did she marry this man, why did she stay so long, why did she have to call tonight? And angry at myself. I can't even get her to talk about this, except through you." She gave a brief shake of her head. "I didn't say it was pretty."

But at least that was honest, Kerry thought. Wearily, he perceived that he had become part of a complex triangle in which Lara, despite her guilt over this, might resent both him and Joan.

"She's in danger," Kerry said.

"I know that. I can feel it from here." Her voice softened. "If anything happened to her or Marie it would kill me."

"I know that, too." Kerry reached for her hand. "So listen to me, okay?

"You've done so much for me. But you don't have to do *everything* anymore. Because there are also things I can do for you.

"It'll take some getting used to, for both of us. But some morning we may wake up feeling sheer relief at being able to lean on someone else." Pausing, Kerry saw that he was asking, at least in one sense, for a favor. "Protecting them means a lot to me. Please, let me help her. Who better, after all?"

Studying him, Lara took this in. Then, at length, she said, "Whatever you do, Kerry, I want to know before you do it. She's still my sister, and I can't let go."

SEVEN

"THE ARMY THINKS they've trapped Al Anwar," Clayton Slade told the President.

The two men sat in the Oval Office. Kerry had slept little, worrying about Joan. But the Presidency did not stop. It was his iron routine that at seven a.m., he and his Chief of Staff met to sort out their priorities, the endless list of choices a President must make.

So, as always, the first sight of Kerry's workday was an African-American with a round face, short, greying hair, clipped mustache, gold wire-rim glasses, shrewd black eyes and a laconic wit which cut to the core of whatever came their way. Since meeting as young prosecutors, Clayton had been Kerry's closest friend and, in politics, they complemented each other—Kerry was intuitive, at once "ruthless" and a romantic; Clayton was earthbound, pragmatic, deeply attuned to consequence and, at times, a brake on Kerry's impulses. Kerry relied on Clayton's judgment—between the two of them, he once had quipped, they might just add up to one reasonably decent President. But Clayton had learned—and this was the most delicate part of their relationship—that he could not act in Kerry's name.

Now their daily meeting was as integral to Kerry's comfort as the decor which made the Oval Office his — bookshelves filled with biography and poetry; busts of Robert Kennedy and Martin Luther King; the world globe on his desk, a reminder of his power and its limits; a table with photographs of Lara, his mother, his godfather Liam

Dunn, his brother James. All of them had helped define who Kerry was; only Lara knew him as well as Clayton did.

They had much to consider: the budget battle, in which Kerry was fighting for more social spending; a conference in Brussels to discuss expanding NATO; a goodwill visit to Lara's ancestral village in Mexico; this morning's event with gun manufacturers. But Clayton's reference to the terrorist Al Anwar erased all else. For Americans, Mahmoud Al Anwar was the newest face of terror: he had moved from kidnapping and executing Americans abroad to financing the two fanatics who, shortly after Kerry's election, had flown a private airplane filled with explosives into a football stadium, killing or maiming several thousand onlookers and scarring the national psyche. And so Kerry had inherited the hunt for a captive Al Anwar and his inner circle, now directed by the Special Forces through one of two warring factions in the Sudan.

"They've 'thought' that before," Kerry said. "How long until they know, I wonder."

Clayton shrugged. "It's bad terrain, and tunneled. It could be days, weeks, months. But suppose you get a phone call in an hour, and find Al Anwar on your hands?"

It was choices like this, Kerry reflected, that nothing could prepare you for—a fateful decision, made in a moral quagmire, with untold consequences. "If *that* happens," Kerry answered, "it's too late."

Looking past him, Clayton stared out the window at the Rose Garden, then sipped from his mug of coffee. "You'd have to put Al Anwar on trial, I expect. Except that he'd make a rotten prisoner."

Slowly, Kerry nodded. "Bad for hostages, you mean. His people could kidnap more Americans, demanding his return. And when I didn't cave, Al Qaeda would start mailing me their prisoners' severed limbs."

"You'd have to assume that."

"And the World Court?"

"Legalities aside, same problem—except that our allies would hate it. Imagine NATO once Al Anwar starts bombing Italian lovers in cafes, or blowing up Big Ben. We'd lose support for rolling up his network." Pausing, Clayton stared into his coffee cup. "And so . . ."

Kerry was silent. As often as he had imagined being President, the weight of lives in the balance felt heavy beyond his reckoning. At length, he answered, "We hope for the ideal outcome. Where there's nothing to decide."

There was nothing more to say. Clayton understood him well: tomorrow morning, perhaps, Kerry would learn that Al Anwar was dead.

"Guns," Kerry said.

The verbal shorthand was typical of them. "They'll be here at ten," Clayton answered. "Martin Bresler and five gun company CEOs."

"Voluntary safety locks." Kerry's tone combined wonder and disgust. "Thirty thousand deaths from guns a year, and this is the best we can do."

Clayton shrugged again. "If these folks don't get kneecapped by the SSA for doing *this*, maybe next time they'll help you keep guns away from criminals. That might actually save some lives."

"Amazing," Kerry said. "We pass a law requiring licensed gun dealers to run background checks so felons, wife-beaters and drug abusers can't buy weapons. But all you have to do is say you're a collector, not a dealer, and you can take your arsenal to a gun show and sell semi-automatic weapons to Charles Manson. A loophole big enough to drive Mahmoud Al Anwar through, courtesy of the SSA." Shaking his head, Kerry finished, "The 'right to bear arms.' The SSA thinks that means the right to arm bears, or anything old enough to pull a trigger."

Clayton's smile was thin. "How many pickup trucks did

you see last election with stickers like 'Ban Kilcannon, not guns'? For a lot of folks, guns are a symbol—the system's stacked against them, and now a city boy with no kids and a celebrity girlfriend wants to take their guns away. Or so the SSA keeps telling them in every fund-raising letter . . ."

"All this paranoia. When all I want is to keep innocent people from dying."

"Paranoia," Clayton answered, "is what the SSA has to sell. Gun owners voted against you three to one. But the people who worry about gun violence care about sixteen other things, too."

"Don't I know it," Kerry said with weary resignation. "Even school shootings have the half-life of a fruit fly. And so here I am, going hat in hand to gun companies, begging for scraps."

Clayton frowned. "They've got their problems, too," he pointed out. "Big tobacco has the highest cash flow in America, and they can export death to the third world like hell won't have it. But the gun industry is small and fragmented—dozens of companies struggling to get by. So the SSA has them by the balls—*they've* got the money, the scariest lobby in Washington, most of the Republican Party, more than a few Democrats, and half of these guys' customers. What do *you* have to offer them?"

"Decency. And survival." Kerry leaned back in his chair. "I swear I can make this issue work for us. Sometime, some where, there's going to be a tragedy so awful that people will wake up."

"And what will *that* be? It wasn't Columbine." Clayton's voice was quiet now. "Your brother was shot, then you. And nothing happened.

"I know how you feel, Kerry. But don't break your heart over this one. Take what you can get, and move on."

The remark, with its reminder that Clayton—and Clayton alone—called Kerry by his given name in private, also bespoke his friend's role as pragmatist. *Don't bet your Presidency on guns,* was Clayton's unspoken message. *You're still an untested President, who won by a handful of votes, searching for a comfort zone with the millions who doubt you. Look for your successes elsewhere.*

"I'll try to pull back from the precipice," Kerry said at length. "In the meanwhile, cheer up. I'm about to clean up my values problem."

"How? By adopting twins?"

"Not yet. But Lara's finally capitulated."

"A wedding date?"

Kerry grinned. "Yes. I guess she got tired of going home at midnight."

"Congratulations, pal." With a smile of genuine pleasure, Clayton added, "God knows you two have earned it."

"*I* thought so."

"Have you picked a date yet?"

"Labor Day, we think. Care to be Best Man?"

At this, Clayton was quiet, clearly touched. "Will I have to buy a new tuxedo?"

"Maybe blue jeans. We've decided to run away."

Above the smile at one corner of his mouth, Clayton gave him a probing, bright-eyed look. "You're joking, of course."

"Somewhat. But Lara would like a private wedding. Close friends and family, nothing like Charles and Diana."

"But you told her you knew better, right?"

Kerry smiled. "Do I?"

"Of course you do," his friend expostulated. "You barely won a bitter election. You rammed through your nominee for Chief Justice, a single woman, by one vote after she became the poster girl for 'partial-birth' abortion. Now your approval rating is stuck at fifty-three percent." Clayton held up a hand, seeking time to finish. "I'm not arguing for a political rally. But this is huge—a once-in-a-lifetime, nonpartisan opportunity to ensure that millions love you who don't now. You've got no right to squander it."

Now Kerry's smile was fractional. "Please mention that to my fiancée."

"Lara knows. She didn't make a zillion dollars on television by not knowing." Clayton's tone was that of a man reciting the obvious. "She's got a mother, two sisters, and a niece who, from the pictures, are all adorable. That Mom's a working-class Hispanic makes them the American Dream."

"To Lara, they're her family. And families, like the American Dream, can have their dark side."

Clayton raised his eyebrows. "How so?"

"The middle sister is also a battered wife. Last night, she called us."

As Kerry summarized the call, Clayton settled back. His expression, though empathic, became guarded.

"Get me the D.A.'s private number," Kerry finished. "As soon as I'm through meeting with the gun executives, I want him and his domestic violence person on the phone."

Clayton considered this. "Watch your ethics," he admonished. "If this was a federal prosecutor instead of a local, you'd probably be breaking a law or two. Presidential fingers on the scale of justice."

"These people don't work for me," Kerry rejoined. "I'm just going to walk them through this, make sure it all goes right."

"Maybe so. But this isn't a random phone call from a casual friend. This is the President calling."

"Which is why I won't have to call them twice." Kerry paused, voice level and determined. "This can't keep happening to her, Clayton. Not on my watch."

EIGHT

A T T E N O ' C L O C K, Jack Sanders, the President's Chief Domestic Policy Advisor, ushered Martin Bresler and five CEOs of gun companies into the Oval Office.

Collectively, the seven were an ill-assorted group. Slender, scholarly and intense, Sanders was a generation younger than the rest, a political scientist from Princeton. Bresler—small, dark, loquacious, and frenetic—headed the Gun Sports Coalition, an industry group formed to soften the image of gun manufacturers and, Bresler hoped, steer a middle ground between two implacable enemies, Kerry Kilcannon and the SSA. The CEOs were the first subjects of this improbable experiment: middle-aged and white, burly except for one, they looked as uncomfortable to Kerry as suspects in a lineup. Though respectful, they were reticent; Kerry was quite certain that none had voted for him. As Kerry greeted them, only George Callister, the CEO of Lexington Arms, returned his handshake with an unflinching gaze which bespoke a quiet confidence.

The White House photographer hurried in. Serially, each CEO posed with Kerry for the obligatory "grip and grin" shot; struck by the awkwardness of it all, Kerry idly wondered if any of these photographs would end up on a wall. Waving them to the u-shaped couch and wing chairs, Kerry amended his mental image of a lineup—they seemed more like prisoners on the wrong end of a firing squad.

The absurdity of this made Kerry smile—when all else fails, he thought, make an offering to the god of laughter. "Believe me," he told them, "I know how tough it is to be seen with me. But don't worry—right after the ceremony we're putting all of you in the witness protection program."

There was tentative laughter. Smiling, Bresler asked, "Are you telling our wives?"

"We already have," Kerry rejoined. "They all wish you guys a lot of luck."

The chuckles felt more genuine now. But even as George Callister joined in, Kerry felt Callister assessing him with genuine curiosity. With his grey crew cut, stocky build, broad face, and midwestern accent, Callister reminded Kerry of an engineer, the kind of man who worked with his head and hands. Instinctively Kerry felt that, among this group, Callister was important. Though careful to look from face to face, Kerry focused his attention on the CEO of Lexington.

"Seriously," he told them, "I'm grateful that you're here. Too many gunshot accidents can be easily prevented, too many involve young children. Look at cars—air bags, seat belts, and changes in design have all saved lives. So will this.

"To me, it seems so simple—by putting safety locks on all your guns, you're preventing needless tragedy. But I know you're bucking the SSA."

Bresler nodded. "We're willing to stand with you, Mr. President, and see where it goes."

"I appreciate that." Kerry leaned forward, hands clasped in front of him, looking intently from one face to the other. "Let me tell you where I hope it goes. Supposedly, our current laws prevent felons, wife-beaters, drug abusers, those convicted of violent misdemeanors, and the adjudicated mentally ill from buying handguns. That only makes sense—instead of locking them up *after* they've already killed someone, we run background checks to prevent the most dangerous among us from buying guns.

"But the SSA and its friends in Congress confined the

background checks to federally licensed dealers, exempting anyone who claims to be a so-called private seller." Pausing, Kerry focused on George Callister. "As one example, that means that someone convicted of a violent crime can go to a gun show, and buy enough semiautomatic handguns to arm the whole Al Qaeda network. Which makes no sense."

"Maybe to you, Mr. President," Callister responded soberly. " 'But what if your private seller's a bona fide hobbyist,' the SSA would say. 'Why should he wait three days for a background check to sell a handgun to a law-abiding citizen?' "

"Because law-abiding citizens," Kerry rejoined, "don't need gun shows to buy weapons. They can pass a background check and buy from licensed dealers.

"Look, George, we all know the realities. Gun shows shaft law-abiding dealers and put your guns in the hands of criminals who wind up killing someone. So you end up with terrible PR and a raft of lawsuits from people who think you should be held responsible for who gets guns that can fire ten rounds in seconds."

"But we're not responsible." Callister's voice was grim. "Let's be blunt. The man who shot you got a used Lexington gun on the street. We didn't know the seller, we didn't know the shooter. What would you have had us do?"

Kerry's gaze and voice were level. "I didn't sue you, did I? But here's what you can do: refuse to let *your* dealers sell *your* guns at gun shows unless the promoter runs background checks on every gun sold. The promoter will have no choice but to agree.

"We have to get this done. Or by next month, or the month after, we'll have that many more deaths on our hands. I doubt there's anyone in this room who wants them on their conscience." Pausing, Kerry focused on

George Callister. "I appreciate that the SSA is a problem. But I will be, as well. I'd like to think it matters which one of us is right."

Callister wore a skeptical frown: *"right" is one thing,* his expression said, *power another, and no executive of a gun company can overlook the difference.* Quietly, Kerry finished, "If all of you stick together, you can liberate your industry from your 'protectors' at the SSA. Saving lives will be a bonus."

There was an uncomfortable silence, and then Martin Bresler intervened. "One step at a time, Mr. President. We can't take too much excitement."

At this, Kerry smiled, standing. "Ready for the Rose Garden?" he asked. "I'll stick my head out first, and see who's shooting."

When Kerry returned to the Oval Office it was close to eleven-thirty, eight-thirty in San Francisco. By now, Kerry calculated, Marie would be in school, John Bowden on his way to work. It took a minute to track down the D.A. for San Francisco, one more to conference in the chief of his domestic violence unit.

"Mr. President," Jack Halloran began. "To what do we owe this honor?"

The D.A., Kerry thought, sounded dazed by more than hearing from him. A onetime student radical of dubious stability, Jack Halloran liked to drink too much. To Kerry, this threatened whatever clarity Halloran retained: it was Kerry's private theory that Halloran had rewired his brain with hallucinogens sometime in the 1960s, well before his bewildering reincarnation as a Democratic pol. At the very least, his judgment was impaired—Kerry only hoped that his deputy, a woman named Marcia Harding, was as capable as she needed to be.

"It's my future sister-in-law," Kerry said without preface, and tersely described Joan's call. "She's in trouble," he concluded. "And her daughter has seen far too much."

"Will Joan fill out a complaint?" Marcia Harding asked.

"Yes," Kerry said, and hoped that it was so. "Once she does, can you get a kick-out order before Bowden gets home tonight?"

"Sure." To his relief, Harding sounded unruffled. "After notice and a hearing, we'll go for an emergency protective order, finding that he's a threat to the safety of his wife and child, and barring him from stalking, harassing, threatening, or using force. We'll also ask for an order keeping him away from Marie."

"Can you get him into a program for batterers?"

"There's a backlog, Mr. President. But pretty soon."

"What about guns? This guy's a stick of dynamite."

"The cops will search the house, his car, anywhere he might keep a weapon. And the judge will order him to turn in any guns."

"That's all fine," Kerry told her, "but worry about Bowden buying another."

"We'll do our damnedest, sir. Once the judge issues the order, the cops enter it into our computer system. California law's much stronger than federal law—anytime anyone transfers a gun, like at a gun show, they have to run a background check. Bowden will come out denied."

"Then please, do me a favor, Marcia. Enter the order yourself." Standing, Kerry began to pace. "I used to do this work. Too often the guy at the computer is some bitter old cop with a bad arm, stuck with a menial task because he's disqualified for street duty." In a softer tone, Kerry added, "I'm sorry if I sound anxious. But this is Lara's niece and sister, and I know what can go wrong."

"Don't worry, Mr. President." It was Jack Halloran,

anxious to regain center stage. "I will *personally* enter this order."

Please, Kerry thought, *don't.* "If Marcia says she will," the President responded mildly, "that's probably best. Everyone knows you, Jack—if you do this yourself, it could hit the papers.

"That's the final favor I'm asking: please try to keep this out of the media. That could only inflame Bowden, and it would be humiliating for Joan. She shouldn't have to suffer because her sister's marrying the President."

There was a momentary silence. "I can't issue a guarantee," Harding answered. "But I've got no reason to tell anyone who Joan's sister is, or mention that you called me. Battering is battering."

Kerry sat again. "Thank you," he said with relief. "Lara will be grateful, too."

By late afternoon, the police had arrested John Bowden. The lead article in the *Washington Times* was "President, Gun Companies Announce Pact." Martin Bresler was quoted as hailing "a new maturity and moderation in the American gun community." The final quote was from the president of the SSA, Charles Dane: "No good can come to those who stand with Kerry Kilcannon."

NINE

"I've checked the Saturday of Labor Day weekend," Kit Pace said to Lara. "In terms of television, it might seem pretty good for a wedding—no conflicts with major sports events, no big network specials. But that's because the networks know better: who wants to be inside watching television on the last weekend of summer?"

With a sense of resignation, Lara looked at the others. They sat in the yellow Oval Room of the President's private residence: Kit, Kerry's press secretary; Clayton; Connie Coulter, a savvy young public relations expert Lara had asked to become her press secretary; and Francesca Thibault, the White House social secretary. Kerry sat next to Lara; the others, sworn to secrecy, were the planning group for their wedding. At Lara's insistence they had chosen Sunday afternoon—with its diminished scrum of reporters outside the West Wing—for their first meeting.

"It doesn't matter," Lara answered blithely. "We're planning on a two-line announcement: 'The President and his fiancée, Lara Costello, were married today. Ms. Costello plans to keep her name.' "

"Three lines," Kerry amended. "You can add 'The happy couple is honeymooning at an undisclosed location.' "

Kit's smile was tentative, as if she were worried that, beneath the levity, Lara was drawing a line. "Are you two planning on a second term?" she inquired dryly. "If so, to affirmatively include the country in your wedding would be absolutely unifying."

Lara managed to smile. "I'm all for unity," she said. "My

modest hope is for a wedding somewhat more subdued than halftime at the Super Bowl. Consistent with the wishes of the media, Kerry's political advisors, and the Democratic National Committee."

The wry edge in Lara's tone elicited, from Kit, a sympathetic shake of the head. "During the transition," she responded, "I had a meeting with my predecessor. He'd run a computer search to identify the subject on which he'd gotten the most inquiries. The winner—by over ten times more than the war in Kosovo—was the President's acquisition of Frisky, his Boston terrier. The questions included whether Frisky would get spayed, and the existence of protective measures to keep him from disemboweling the First Lady's pet Siamese.

"Your wedding, it goes without saying, is somewhat bigger than the acquisition of a dog . . ."

"I'll take that as a compliment," Lara interrupted with a smile.

"Lara," the President informed Kit, "is wondering whether Frisky at least got to keep his job."

Kit threw up her hands in mock dismay. "Welcome," she said, "to the theater of the absurd."

Dark, elegant, and dangerously thin, Francesca Thibault hastened to infuse a note of seriousness. "The challenge," she interjected, "is to have a public event which is true to who you are.

"This is not an old-fashioned society wedding. You and the President are the American meritocracy. So we can style it as a private event—scaled down, with a touch of informality; a wedding party comprised of friends and family; and a larger reception to include the guests we just can't do without."

"Can we 'do without' guests who actively hate us?" Lara asked.

"Not really," Clayton answered, deadpan, "but we can probably set a quota."

"Jokes aside," Connie Coulter said to Lara, "the composition of the guest list is important. It can't be so big that an invitation is meaningless or so political that it looks crass."

"But what is 'it'?" Lara asked. "A wedding, or our reception?"

"A White House wedding," Francesca Thibault answered firmly, "whatever the guest list." Turning to the President, she said, "The last time a President married at the White House was almost ninety years ago, and *that* was Woodrow Wilson . . ."

"A White House *reception*," Clayton corrected. "The wedding should be in a Catholic church."

Lara glanced at Kerry. "Clayton," Kerry told her baldly, "wants to clean up my problems with the Church. Until the annulment, I was a divorced, pro-choice opponent of prayer in public school, whose selection for Chief Justice is absolute anathema to the Catholic hierarchy. And, in particular, to Cardinal McKiernan, the archbishop of this diocese."

"It's not just the hierarchy," Clayton said to Lara. "Last November, Kerry only carried fifty-two percent of the Catholic vote. The bloodbath over making Caroline Masters Chief Justice—*after* she ruled in favor of late term abortion—has made those numbers even worse."

The lightness of spirit Lara felt had vanished. As the others did not, Clayton knew of her abortion: to the extent he could, he was trying to inoculate Kerry against scandal by cloaking their marriage in the blessings of the Church.

"What about St. Mathew's?" Francesca Thibault asked. "Where the President goes to Mass. It's a magnificent structure . . ."

"Which," Kit interjected, "would televise beautifully."

Lara glanced at the others, then at Kerry last, and saw his look of reflection. Clayton, too, looked at Kerry before speaking to Lara. "Cardinal McKiernan," he told her, "would see it as a tribute. So would Catholics nationwide."

"So would *everyone*," Kit told the President. "Suppose we have pool coverage only, and a stationary camera . . ."

"What's to keep them," Kerry interjected, "from treating it like the New Hampshire primary? While Lara and I are repeating vows, CNN is saying, 'Our instant tracking polls are showing that the President's numbers among Catholics are up seventeen percent.' Just how exploitative do we want to look?"

"We can set the ground rules," Kit answered. "We can even select the commentator. We've got the leverage here."

"What about still photographs?" Lara suggested. "Won't that be enough?"

"It's not the same," Kit insisted. "This isn't about show business, or even politics. It's a unique moment in American history, and Americans will want to share it. Please consider giving them that."

There was silence, and then Francesca Thibault spoke. "What about a small wedding at St. Mathew's?" she asked. "Televised with dignity. Then a larger but still manageable reception at the White House, with the White House photographer and perhaps our own video crew. Elegant tents on the South Lawn, dancing in the East Room."

"With a mariachi band?" Lara asked.

Only Clayton did not smile. "Actually," he said, "that's not such a terrible idea."

Connie Coulter gave Lara a quick glance. "We can only avoid a charge of elitism," she argued, "by including the American people. But we can't let in random tourists—in the age of Mahmoud Al Anwar, that would be a Secret Service nightmare. One could argue that televising the wedding is more intimate and meaningful than televised toasts and dancing."

Listening, Lara felt the wedding slipping away from her in the crosscurrent of advice. "Who would officiate?" Kit was asking. "Cardinal McKiernan?"

"My old parish priest," Kerry said promptly. "Father Joe Donegan."

Clayton raised his eyebrows. "Isn't that the cardinal's call?"

"I'm the President, Clayton. Vince McKiernan can pass out wafers."

Clayton smiled at this. "A simple nuptial mass," Francesca Thibault offered, "with tasteful liturgical music."

Kit glanced at Lara. "Who might be in the wedding party?"

"Beautiful people," Francesca suggested dryly, "without a hint of scandal."

"My college roommates," Lara said. "Anna Chen from NBC is one of my closest friends. My sisters, of course."

Kit gave an emphatic nod. "That's great. The media, including the Spanish language media, will want them before the wedding . . ."

"Oh, absolutely," Lara said with mock sincerity. "Hispanics and women carried California. And who better to help with Catholics than my family?"

"They're part of who *you* are," Kit answered. "It's your burden, Lara, to be more popular than the President."

"We're all proud of Lara's family," Kerry interjected. "But having them with us is enough. We don't want anyone to use them."

Lara touched his arm. "For Kerry's sake," she told the others, "I'll do my part. I'll learn to live with becoming 'Lara Costello Kilcannon.' I'll even consider television. But about my family, I want everything—and I mean that—to go through Connie and me."

"Of course." Clayton said this so quickly that Lara wondered if he and Kit had used her family as a cat's-paw, hoping for other concessions to political practicality. Like a televised wedding at St. Mathew's.

"Concerning the gown," Francesca Thibault suggested brightly, "this is a chance to put your stamp on contemporary fashion. But the designer has to be an American—perhaps Vera Wang or Carolina Herrera . . ."

When the meeting was over, Clayton asked to speak to them alone.

"About the honeymoon," he observed, "isn't Martha's Vineyard too much of a privileged enclave?"

"We like it," Kerry answered crisply. "Sorry, pal, no Yellowstone. Or pup tents with mosquito nets."

Clayton's smile came and went. "The other thing is Lara's sister. Joan."

"What about Joan?" Lara asked.

Clayton turned to her. "For a week now, the President's managed to keep her problems quiet. But once the media knows you're getting married, there'll be more focus on your family—including your brother-in-law. Your chances of keeping *that* from becoming public will diminish day by day.

"Imagine some tabloid story two days before the wedding—embarrassing your family, sapping some of the joy out of what, for them and all the rest of us, should be a wonderful day . . ."

Listening, Lara imagined Joan's sense of betrayal. "We're trying to protect her, Clayton."

"Then talk to her about a carefully managed disclosure, sooner rather than later. Perhaps softened with a broader message on combating family violence."

Lara stared at him. Glancing at her, Kerry said softly, "Remember my mother? You know how I feel about this."

Clayton was unflinching. "What happened to your mother ended twenty-five years ago. You're President now and the media's very different. You won't be able to control this."

"We can damn well try," Kerry told his closest friend. "Beginning with you."

TEN

STANDING IN HER KITCHEN, Joan Bowden held the telephone to her ear, one finger of her other hand resting on the replay button of her answering machine. Her throat was dry. The living room was filled with flowers; the answering machine jammed with messages. It was only two p.m.

"I didn't want to call you," she said to Kerry. "But it's been like this since I got the stay-away order. Deliverymen ringing the doorbell, John leaving message after message. He sounds more desperate every day."

"What does he say?" the President asked.

"Listen," Joan said, and pushed the button. Her husband's disembodied voice echoed in the kitchen.

I love you, Joanie. I know there's something wrong with me. But I can't change unless you help me . . .

"Did you talk to him?" Kerry cut in.

"Yes. I asked him to go with me to counseling . . ."

I don't need therapy, the recorded voice said. *I don't need anyone but you. We can fix it together . . .*

Joan stabbed the stop button. Wearily, she said, "He just keeps saying that, over and over . . ."

As Kerry listened, her words over the speakerphone sounded in the Oval Office. Their tension kept him taut and still. "Joanie," he entreated, "don't let John pull you back in . . ."

"His trial's coming up." Her voice became constricted. "I'm scared for him, scared for us. If he loses his job . . ."

"He's *trying* to scare you. It's emotional terrorism . . ."

"*Listen*," she insisted, and her husband's plaintive voice filled the Oval Office.

I can't go to work, Joanie. I can't even get out of bed . . .

"He managed to send you flowers," Kerry interjected. "To make phone call after phone call . . ."

You're destroying me. Bowden's tone approached hysteria. *You've taken my home, my daughter, my reason for living . . .*

"It's like he's in the room," Joan was saying. "I can *feel* him." Her husband's voice sounded muffled by choked tears.

Marie. I miss my little girl . . .

Softly, Kerry requested, "Please, turn him off."

There was a moment's delay, and then Bowden's pleading went silent in midsentence.

Kerry exhaled. "There's nothing new here. 'I'm the victim,' John keeps saying. 'Come back into my closed-off world, or terrible things may happen.' "

Kerry waited out her silence. Tiredly, Joan asked, "What if I just tried it . . ."

Hearing her despair, Kerry fought his worry and impatience. "Last week, Joanie, he put a gun to your head."

There was a knock at Kerry's door, and Clayton stuck his head in.

Switching off the speaker, Kerry picked up his telephone. "Hang on," he said to Joan, and stared at Clayton. In silent inquiry, Clayton raised his eyebrows.

"I'm on with Joan," Kerry snapped. "What is it?"

Clayton's brusque nod was, Kerry knew, meant to telegraph his concern about Joan Bowden. "Sorry to interrupt," Clayton answered, "but Martin Bresler's on the line, sounding close to suicidal."

Kerry frowned. While useful, Martin Bresler struck him as someone whose sense of disproportion might lead him to deem every internecine skirmish worthy of a President's attention. "Try Jack Sanders," Kerry instructed. "He's Bresler's contact person."

"I suggested that. Bresler says he has to talk to you. Do you want to just say no, or set another time?"

Pausing, Kerry thought of Joan. "How much time do I have right now?"

"The AIDS activists have been waiting for ten minutes. After them you've got the National Security Council."

Kerry glanced at his watch. "Tell the AIDS people I'll be with them in five, and put Bresler through."

Clayton briefly disappeared, giving instructions to Kerry's secretary. With fresh urgency, Kerry said to Joan, "Please, hang in there until the hearing. Keep calling to check in."

"Okay." She sounded unsettled and unsure. "It's just so hard . . ."

Distracted, Kerry motioned Clayton to take a seat. When Joan said a wan goodbye, he picked up his second line.

"Martin?" he asked. "What's up?"

"I'm sorry, Mr. President. The gun-show deal's off."

Bresler sounded jangled, like a man who had drunk too much coffee with too little sleep or food. "Why?" the President asked.

"They just *did* it." Bresler's speech was rapid. "I really can't talk about that. I just wanted to tell you myself. I was proud to work with you, Mr. President. But now I've got no job . . ."

"Is there something I can do?"

"No." Bresler's voice lowered. "You've got no idea how much they hate you."

Kerry did. But there was no point saying that to a man *in extremis*. "What if you expose what the SSA is doing . . ."

"That would ruin me, Mr. President." Abruptly, Bresler

summoned a belated dignity. "I just wanted you to know, and to thank you for your courtesies."

Feeling anger overwhelm his pity, Kerry repeated, "If I can be of any help . . ."

"I wish you could." With these last dispirited words, Bresler thanked him again and got off.

Kerry slammed the phone.

Clayton stood. "What is it?"

"The SSA. Somehow they got Bresler, though he won't say that directly. It's their message to anyone who tries to deal with me on guns." Belatedly, Kerry stood as well. "They must have put the screws to the gun companies. Maybe the antitrust division should take a look at this."

Clayton folded his arms. "Hardball's not illegal—if it were, you'd be in jail. Bring in the Justice Department, and you'll be the overreaching proto-dictator the right wing says you are."

"In my dreams, Clayton."

"Maybe in your second term. In the meantime, it's enough to try and conquer AIDS."

At this reminder, Kerry headed for the door. But he could not let go of his anger. "We'll conquer AIDS," he said over his shoulder, "before we ever stop slaughtering each other with guns. AIDS doesn't have the SSA behind it—at least officially." Opening the door, he turned and ordered, "Track down that guy George Callister, from Lexington Arms. I'd like to have a word with him."

ELEVEN

ON THE FOLLOWING SUNDAY, two days after the public announcement of Kerry's wedding date, the President met in secret with George Callister.

The date and place were carefully chosen. A weekend offered Kerry some relief from press vigilance, and a chance for seclusion; on this weekend, the prospect of a presidential wedding—setting off a spate of stories and a headlong competition for interviews with Lara, Kerry, or both—consumed the media's attention. Thus it seemed only natural that, on a balmy Sunday morning, the President would seek respite at Camp David. The press did not know that, an hour before, George Callister had arrived.

Among the White House staff, only Clayton and Jack Sanders knew of this meeting—Callister, as he assured the President, had told no one but his wife. "Unlike you," Callister observed dryly, "even the devil himself doesn't want to confiscate our guns." For Kerry's part, he had determined to go slowly—it was enough, in this first meeting, to take the measure of George Callister.

Now, in the wooded seclusion of the Catoctin Range, the two men toured Camp David. Hands in the pockets of his blue jeans, Callister stopped on the wooded trail to breathe in mountain air, cooler by degrees than in the flatlands of the capital. "I grew up in Minnesota," he told the President. "My father and I spent weekends in the woods, fishing and hunting. The things *his* father taught him."

Kerry did not miss this implicit statement of their differences. "I'm a city boy," he answered. "I grew up liking sun and ocean and beaches. Sometimes Camp David's so quiet at night that I imagine hearing the Manson family."

Callister looked at him wryly. "But it's secure. And very private."

"It is that. We're in the middle of a national park, with absolute restrictions on overhead flights and unauthorized visitors, surrounded by a double cyclone fence, attack dogs, sensors, concrete barriers, the Secret Service and at least one hundred Marines. We're safe from Mahmoud Al Anwar *and* the *New York Times*." Kerry paused a moment, adding, "Even the SSA."

Callister did not take the bait. "Still, you don't like it."

Kerry looked about him. "There's a lot I *do* like. There's so much history here—Roosevelt and Churchill planning the Normandy invasion, Carter brokering the peace agreement between Begin and Sadat." Pausing at a rise above the trees, Kerry pointed at the valley below, a sequence of rolling hills which softened in the distance of a sun-streaked mist. "It's hard not to appreciate views like that. The White House is a gilded cage—elegant, but hardly private. Here Lara and I can open the front door and walk out in the yard, or play a mediocre game of tennis completely unobserved." As they began walking again, Kerry added, "When I was a kid, I couldn't imagine having a vacation home of any kind. Even on loan from the government."

Callister gave him a sideways glance. "Neither of us had money, Mr. President. Like you, I worked my way through school."

Kerry nodded. "That's not all bad, of course. But law school was a little short on leisure time."

"Did you ever hunt?"

"Shoot Bambi? No thanks. To me, hunting is the only sport where your competition doesn't know they're playing. I've never even fired a gun, though my father wanted to teach me." Kerry stared at the trail wending toward his lodge. "He was a cop, I guess you know. He used to carry a Lexington Peacekeeper."

Kerry left the rest unsaid—that he associated his father's gun with mindless brutality, the questionable killing of a black man who had "resisted arrest." But Callister paused once more to look at him. "With respect, Mr. President, how can you understand a product you've never used?"

Kerry turned to him. "It's true," he answered in level tones. "I've never shot a gun. But I've been shot, and I've lost a member of my family. So have a lot of other Americans. We have reason, you and I, to try to narrow our differences."

After breakfast, they sat beside a swimming pool near Kerry's cabin. Once more Kerry was struck by Callister's midwestern solidity and unflinching gaze. A man not given to artifice or flattery, or saying what he did not mean.

Callister put down his mug of black coffee. "My industry isn't a big moneymaker, Mr. President. Most of us are in it because we know and appreciate guns and respect the craft of making them.

"I've been in this business twenty years. Of all the manufacturers, Lexington may have the proudest history—we've been arming our military and police going back to the Civil War. When I took this job six months ago, it wasn't to get rich but to help this company survive."

The President nodded. "I've got no quarrel with that, George. But Lexington makes weapons no law-abiding civilian needs, like handguns good only for killing people quickly. Cop-killer bullets, too. I'm wondering why."

Callister shrugged. "A gun, Mr. President, is only as good or bad as the man who uses it. But the weapons you're complaining about all preceded my arrival."

Pausing, he fixed Kerry with a steady, inquiring gaze. "Just how much do you know about the business of selling guns?"

"Not as much as you."

"Well, guns are like Singer sewing machines—treat them right, and they don't wear out. Some of our revolvers from the Civil War are still in circulation." Callister allowed himself a brief, sardonic smile, as if amused by the President's need for this tutorial. "In short, guns aren't consumable. There's no such thing as obsolescence. All we can offer is newer and better.

"Our problem is 'to whom?' The times are running against us—there are still hunters out there, and sport shooters, but fewer of them. Maybe women are becoming a bigger slice of the consumer pie, but not for us . . ."

"Unless you scare them to death."

Callister gave Kerry a keen look. "Yes, we market self-defense to women—to everyone. It's their right to protect their homes and families."

"Is that all you're selling? Self-defense for Mom and Dad? Or do they have to worry about criminals armed with even deadlier Lexington guns?"

Callister frowned again. "We can't be held accountable for a buyer's motives. Would you say that gun fanciers have no right to buy a semiautomatic handgun, or that someone with a deep belief in the Second Amendment shouldn't buy whatever weapons he wants?"

"The whole Second Amendment argument," Kerry countered with some impatience, "is senseless—this idea that the Constitution is a suicide pact, with the Founding Fathers hell-bent on arming private citizens to overthrow the government they'd just created. They thought that's what *voting* was for."

At this, Callister briefly laughed. "Please, Mr. President—say that in public. The four million members of the SSA will fill our coffers by arming themselves to the teeth. This may pain you, but the three weeks after your election were our most profitable in years. Every speech you give on gun control is worth hundreds of thousands in free advertising."

Kerry could not help but smile at the irony. "You're saying that my great crusade is more like 'rope a dope,' when Muhammad Ali let George Foreman punch himself into exhaustion. And that I'm George Foreman."

"Much slimmer, Mr. President. And certainly no dope." Callister's expression became serious again. "But that's the problem with this whole debate. Gun controllers aren't so much stupid as flat ignorant—they don't know the guns they're trying to ban, or see the consequence of what they're asking for. They pass a law banning so-called assault weapons and cutting magazine capacity to ten rounds, and help create by inadvertence a whole new market for hand-guns which can fire ten rounds in seconds . . ."

"Or in Lexington's case," Kerry cut in with a caustic edge, "take advantage of an SSA-created loophole allowing small, concealable handguns to accommodate the forty-round magazines Lexington made before the law was passed."

Callister frowned. "You've done your homework, Mr. President. But a lot of manufacturers did that."

"Well *that's* the problem, isn't it." Leaning forward, Kerry spoke with new intensity. "Lexington could have made guns safer, looked for ways to ensure a gun could only be used by its owner—not by his kid, or against him by intruders. But instead you made them more concealable and more lethal. Then told Americans they needed more and deadlier guns to protect themselves from all those other Americans with even more and deadlier guns. You can't credit me for that."

Callister met his gaze. "Guns aren't going away, Mr.

President. As for safety, why not teach it to kids? We wouldn't have half the accidents we do. But the gun controllers are like the folks who want to stop teen sex through abstinence education—teaching safe sex means fornication, and gun safety means more gun owners. Which is exactly what they don't want."

Silent, Kerry gazed into his coffee cup, then beyond them at the sweep of mountains. "We can debate this all day," he said at length. "At the end, on average, eighty more people will have died."

"If that's true," Callister replied, "they'd be dead regardless. If we're going to get anywhere, you'll have to understand how hard it is to get there. And why."

Kerry looked at him steadily. "I'm willing to listen, George. And then I may have a proposal for you. If you're willing to come back."

Callister considered this, eyes narrow, and then nodded. "I'm willing, Mr. President. But only if no one leaks it."

TWELVE

BENEATH THE overhead light in her kitchen, Joan Bowden sat at the table, staring at a stack of unpaid bills. Through the answering machine her husband blamed her.

I've lost my job. You've emasculated me . . .

Swallowing, Joan choked back tears.

Did you hear me, Joan . . . ?

John's inflection wavered between pleading and hysteria. Hand trembling, Joan reached for the telephone.

"John?"

His voice suddenly gained strength. "You've gone too far, Joanie . . ."

"What's this about your job . . ."

"I couldn't work." His timbre became high-pitched, as insistent as a child shifting blame. "I told you that. You've taken everything away from me."

Through her fears, she could feel his isolation. More quietly, she said, "I didn't want to. I was just so scared . . ."

"Why do I hurt so much? I hurt all the time now—physically, like a sickness . . ."

Impatience overcame Joan's guilt. "Why is it up to *me*, John? Why can't you help yourself? I keep asking you about counseling . . ."

"It's too late for that. I've got no family now. You're sending me to jail. There's nothing left to live for . . ."

"*Stop* it."

As if he were strengthened by her panic, John's voice calmed. "What's to stop me from coming to the house and blowing my brains out with a gun?"

Startled, Joan blurted, "Marie."

"I can't see her, remember? You've taken her from me. But I won't leave her to you, Joanie. That's what you want, isn't it?"

Joan sat down, trying to stay rational. "What do you mean?"

His tone retained its eerie calm. "I won't go by myself, Joanie. You'll go with me."

It was as if, Joan thought, she was caught in John's descent into madness. "Then Marie would be an orphan . . ."

"My parents could raise her."

"Your *parents*. How could you do that to her?"

"It would be your fault." The words mingled accusation with pity. "You never face your own responsibility, do you?"

Nerves frayed, Joan cried out, "This is crazy—you turn everything around . . ."

"You've turned my *world* inside out." His tone turned soft, ominous. "But now it's happening to you, isn't it. And you can't take it."

There was silence. The sound of the click, John hanging up, terrified her more than anything he had said.

Tuxedo tie dangling around his collar, Kerry glanced at his watch. As though she could see him, Joan interrupted her narrative.

"Is this a bad time?"

"There's a state dinner at seven with the Prime Minister of Canada. Tell me when this happened."

"Last night."

"He's threatening you, Joanie. Did you call the D.A.?"

Kerry heard her draw a breath. "There's more . . ."

*

Standing alone near the wooden play structure, Marie Bowden saw her father.

Her heart stopped. He stood at the edge of the playground, gazing at her. Her mother had said he shouldn't be here. But he looked so sad.

Almost timidly, he approached her. "Marie . . ."

She took two steps toward him. Then he knelt, holding out his arms.

Marie ran to him.

He held her tight, kissing her hair and neck. When he released her, taking both her hands, his eyes were bright and strange.

"It's okay," he reassured her. "I just needed to see you, one last time. Before I go away."

Marie held his hands tighter. "Where?"

"Far away." Leaning forward, he kissed her forehead, and then gazed into her eyes. "I wish I could take you with me, sweet pea."

Fear and sadness pierced her heart. Quickly glancing over his shoulder, her father cradled her chin in his half-closed hand. Then, without another word, he stood and walked away. At the fence, he turned to gaze at her.

Suddenly, her teacher was kneeling in front of her. When Marie looked up again, her father was gone.

Miss Suarez's eyes seemed as worried as her father's had been sad. "What did he say to you, Marie?"

Marie told her. Gently, Miss Suarez said, "I'll have to call your mommy," and Marie began to cry.

The bedroom door opened. As Kerry listened, Lara slipped into the room, wearing a simple black gown. Silently, she mouthed, "Five minutes."

Telephone to his ear, Kerry nodded. When Lara

approached, he cupped the receiver and whispered, "Joan . . ."

Lara became quite still. To Joan, Kerry said, "We have to call the D.A. For Marie's sake, and yours."

"But he'll only get more angry."

To stem her panic, Kerry kept his own voice patient. "If we don't, he'll only be more emboldened. What if, next time, John decides to take her?"

"God . . ." Her voice broke in anguish. "I wish I could be *sure* . . ."

"Trust me," Kerry implored her. "Please."

There was silence. As Kerry listened, he saw Lara's eyes fill with doubt and worry. "All right," Joan murmured. "I guess you know . . ."

To Kerry, this sounded more like exhaustion than assent. As she said goodbye, her voice was faint.

"What is it?" Lara asked.

Troubled, Kerry shook his head. "Help me with this tie, and I'll tell you."

Lara worked on the knot. As she finished, so did Kerry. "His pattern worries me," he told her. "Depression; hopelessness; anger about losing Joan and being cut off from his child; this 'life is no longer worth it' monologue, with threats of suicide and worse. And then bringing Marie into his psychodrama.

"He's panicking, becoming desperate. It's classic, and it's dangerous." Turning, Kerry plucked his tuxedo jacket off the canopied bed, shrugging into it. "Our job is to help protect them until he can get help, or at least accepts that Joan is gone for good."

"I agree," Lara said. "But the issue is how. I think Joan needs security, however we can manage it. I also worry you're getting drawn in too deeply—that it will boomerang somehow. Maybe we should find Joanie her own lawyer, and work through him."

Kerry reflected. "After tomorrow," he said, "we'll try to do all that. But we need to get the D.A. on this right away."

Pensive, Lara considered this. "All right," she answered. "But the sooner we find her help in San Francisco, the better. This isn't feeling right to me."

Together, they left the bedroom, Kerry trying to anticipate how Bowden might react to his arrest. At the top of the stairs, he paused to refocus on the dinner to come, hands resting on Lara's shoulders.

"Canada," he said. "It's north of here, I think."

Shortly after eleven, Kerry unknotted his tie, picked up the telephone in the office of his living quarters, and called Marcia Harding at her home in San Francisco. Lara stood beside him.

The Assistant District Attorney listened without interrupting. "It's not enough to bust this guy," Kerry finished. "Somehow we need to reach him."

"We'll pick him up tonight," Harding promised. "His trial's two weeks away, Mr. President. But when we bring him up tomorrow for violating the stay-away order, we'll ask the judge to put him in a batterers' program right away." She paused, her voice filled with concern. "We take these kinds of threats seriously. In over half our domestic violence murders last year, the murderer killed himself."

Kerry glanced up at Lara. "How many involved guns?" he asked.

"Again, well over half." Harding paused. "Don't worry, Mr. President. As soon as they arrest him, they'll do another search."

The black cop cuffed him; the red-haired cop began searching his efficiency apartment, going through the rental furniture and pressed-wood desk and end tables. Filled with impotent rage, John Bowden watched her.

There was nothing for her to find, barely anything his own. Men should be self-sufficient and resourceful; never weak or confused. But now he was in a strange room as sterile as a doctor's office, handcuffed, struggling not to scream or cry.

THIRTEEN

THE NEXT MORNING, before meeting with the Canadian Prime Minister, Kerry had Senator Chad Palmer of Ohio to the White House for breakfast.

The two men ate alone in the family dining room. For Kerry, the breakfast was both a pleasure and one of the harder things he had done. A Republican and a military hero, Chad had been Kerry's closest friend in the Senate despite their differences in philosophy and a clash of ambitions. Chad, too, had been considered a prospective President, and Kerry admired Chad's candor and independence, enjoyed his iconoclastic wit. Among politicians, Chad Palmer had always cut a dashing figure: his aura of unquestioned courage was accentuated by blond good looks so distinctive that his enemies on the Republican right had satirically dubbed him "Robert Redford." But the Palmer who sat across the table was far sadder and more subdued, his face newly etched with suffering.

That this in part had been Kerry's doing, however unintended, made this morning's task more difficult. When Kerry had nominated Caroline Masters, Palmer, then Chairman of the Judiciary Committee, had helped Kerry conceal from her opponents a private matter which they both felt should remain so. For both men, principle was commingled with complex calculations of political advantage; for Palmer, the decision had led to tragedy. Masters's secret was discovered, Chad's role in protecting her exposed. In reprisal, Palmer's right-wing enemies within his party had leaked a secret of his own—that his only child,

Kyle, had become pregnant as a teenager and, despite Palmer's public opposition to abortion, had terminated her pregnancy. Humiliated by her exposure, Kyle had become intoxicated and driven off Rock Creek Parkway to her death.

Filled with anger and remorse, Chad had played a decisive role in helping Caroline Masters win her narrow confirmation. Then, with his wife Allie, he had retreated into a reclusive, silent mourning. That this was Chad's first visit since the fateful dinner in which he had agreed to protect Judge Masters was, Kerry felt certain, no more lost on Chad than it was on him. And so, after observing the amenities, Kerry asked directly, "How are you, Chad?"

Palmer gazed at the white tablecloth, the silver service set in front of them. "It's been four and a half months," he said at last. "Some days I can forget it for an hour, mostly when I'm doing the job that killed her. Then, in an instant, Kyle's with me again—in a quiet moment, or maybe because some Senate page, a young girl, evokes her in the smallest way. And the ache is as deep, almost debilitating, as it was the day we buried her. I don't think that ever gets better."

The painful honesty of his words left the President without an adequate response. He recalled his mother, staring at the face of her murdered son before they closed the casket. "And Allie?" Kerry asked.

Chad looked up at him. "I have work. But Kyle was Allie's life. Now all she has is me."

To Kerry, this last quiet phrase conveyed far more than Chad's feelings of inadequacy. For Allie Palmer, it would always be Chad's world which had consumed their daughter, Chad himself who would remind her of all she loathed about public life. "What does she do now?" Kerry asked.

"Very little." Palmer toyed with his napkin ring. "She's too unselfish to ask me to retire—she knows the work she's come to hate at least serves to distract me. But we rarely go out. Some nights I find her staring at old photo albums."

Once more, Kerry wondered at the propriety of his request. "I wish," he said at length, "that there were anything I could do or say." He paused, choosing his words with care. "For me, it's complicated by the knowledge that—whether you want to or not—you'll always associate our friendship with Kyle's death."

There was a moment's silence, and then Chad looked at Kerry directly. "I've thought about our dinner a thousand times. So, yes, what you say is true. Because now I know what happened, and wish I'd never come.

"But you didn't know Kyle's secret. *I* did. *You* simply did what presidents do—play to win."

For an instant, Kerry thought of his and Lara's secret, their wish to believe that they somehow could avoid the humiliation, and worse, which had happened to so many others. No doubt the man across from him had once believed the same.

"It's far too high a price," Kerry said, "for winning."

Chad's smile was faint and bitter. "And yet we come here, knowing the rules: that our enemies don't simply want to beat us, but destroy us. That anyone close to us is fair game for a media which has no limits. We know that, and still we enter politics." Chad shook his head in wonderment and, it seemed to Kerry, self-disgust. "Some even want to be President. So what does that say about *us*, Mr. President?"

Kerry shrugged. "A lot of things, I expect. None of which justifies a culture which sees us not as fallible humans, doing our best in a complex world, but as targets of opportunity, accountable for every private mistake we ever made. Or which saw Kyle not as a lovely young woman, but as a pawn to use against you."

"Maggots." Chad's voice was quiet with contempt. "All

that breast-beating in the media. We'll see how much this town has learned from Kyle's death. If anything." He paused, seeming to redirect his thoughts through a sheer act of will, and then summoned a smile, which, while brief, appeared genuine. "Anyhow, I wish you and Lara all the happiness you deserve. Or, at least, can steal."

Kerry considered Chad across the table. "We have our hopes," he said at length. "Which brings me to what I wanted to ask.

"This comes with a lot of caveats. I know my timing's lousy. I know that being my friend makes *you* no friends among those who already think you're soft on liberals. But Lara and I hope that you and Allie will come to our wedding."

Chad looked honestly amused. "Attend a President's wedding? Is that what passes for courage these days?"

"Perhaps not in itself. But being *in* our wedding may." Though Kerry smiled, his eyes were serious. "Before Kyle's death, I'd have asked you without thinking. And there's no reason, on my part, to feel any differently."

Chad looked away, his thoughts unfathomable. Then, reaching across the table, he rested one hand on the sleeve of Kerry's suit coat. "We've been friends for thirteen years, twelve before you had this job. For most of that time you were stuck in an unhappy marriage—you never said that, I just knew. But now you've found this terrific woman. No matter what's happened, I'm happy for you. I wouldn't miss your wedding for the world."

For that moment, Kerry felt the shackles of the Presidency fall away, and he and Chad were young senators again, trusted friends amidst the tangle of ego and ambition which was the Senate. He could barely bring himself to speak.

Blessedly, he did not have to. As they had planned, Lara

appeared at the entry to the dining room, looking from Chad to her fiancé.

"Am I interrupting?" she asked.

At once Chad smiled, and stood. "You are," he answered, "just in time."

Lara crossed the room, taking his hand. "For me, too," she told him. "I just finished a meeting with Connie Coulter and Francesca Thibault. Connie had some numbers on which of the networks promises the biggest ratings for a prewedding interview; Francesca is picking an undisclosed location for us to audition wedding gowns in secrecy. I feel utterly ridiculous."

"You aren't," Chad assured her. "Just everyone else."

"Including Chad," Kerry interrupted with a smile. "He's agreed to take a leading role in this extravaganza."

As Kerry watched, Lara embraced Chad Palmer and then, on tiptoes, kissed him on the cheek. "You don't know what this means to Kerry. And to me."

Smiling, Chad gazed down at her. "Me, too," he answered.

Convoyed through sun-baked streets by the Secret Service and police on motorcycles, Kerry's limousine approached the White House, returning from a mid-morning visit to See Forever, a pioneer charter school for at-risk teens. On a secure telephone, he talked with Marcia Harding.

"We're looking at a bail motion," Harding told him. "Bowden's got a public defender. We'll bring additional charges, of course, and he'll get a lecture from the Court. But usually the judge will kick him loose."

"What if you oppose bail?"

"We could, but that would be unusual. Another problem's Bowden's lawyer. He knows Joan is Lara Costello's sister—if we come down on his client, he's likely to complain of prejudicial treatment, and splash this all over the papers. Bottom line we probably lose, and Joan's tomorrow's headline."

"What if Bowden does this again?"

"Then it's jail, I'm pretty sure."

Kerry felt his frustration boil over. "Assuming it's not too late. This guy could kidnap Marie, or do far worse to Joan."

There was silence, as though Harding felt stymied by her lack of ready options. "Hopefully," she ventured, "Bowden's night in jail has cooled him off. And his trial for battery is coming up—unless he agrees to a program, he'll likely get some jail time. Until then, the police will come as soon as anyone calls."

As the motorcade slipped inside the East Entrance, the guard waved at Kerry's limousine. The iron gate closed behind him. "Assuming they *can* call," Kerry said.

At a little past seven p.m., Clayton and the President sat on the balcony of Kerry's private quarters, reviewing the status of budget negotiations as evening shadows spread slowly across the South Lawn. Both were in shirtsleeves; Clayton drank bourbon, Kerry two shots of Bushmills on ice.

At length they turned to Joan. "The counsel's office checked this out," Clayton told Kerry. "By law, you can't use the Secret Service to protect Lara's family—you'd have to go to Congress for permission."

"And make it a cause célèbre."

"Exactly. You *could* call the mayor, request twenty-four-hour police protection. But then what happens when some ordinary woman in the Mission District gets shot by her deranged ex-husband after five or six calls to the police? The *San Francisco Chronicle* charges you and the Mayor with favoritism and misuse of public resources." Finishing his drink, Clayton put it down. "You're in this one too deep already. I understand why, but your position's like no one else's."

Silent, Kerry let the peaty burn of whiskey slide slowly down his throat. "I can't tell you," he remarked, "what a heady thrill it is to wind up another workday as the most powerful man on earth."

Clayton smiled. "That's why the Founding Fathers created the federal system, and then gave us a free press. To tax your ingenuity."

But Kerry did not answer, or even return his smile. By now his thoughts were far away; Joan Bowden's home was more vivid than the majestic scene around them. "I'll talk to Lara," he said at length. "There must be something we can do."

FOURTEEN

"What I don't understand," Kerry told George Callister, "is why CEOs of gun companies take orders from the SSA."

Three Sundays after their initial meeting, the two men had returned in secret to Camp David, and now sat at the table on Kerry's patio. Callister allowed himself a thin smile. "Is that a challenge to my manhood, Mr. President? Or a genuine question?"

"Both," Kerry answered bluntly. "One day Martin Bresler comes with you to the White House. The next day he's a leper, and none of you will touch him."

Callister took a swallow of coffee, eyeing Kerry over the rim of his mug. "Running a gun company," he said at length, "is like running a gauntlet between five competing forces. If you worry too much about one, another one will take your head off.

"Start with the public. Maybe twenty percent believe guns are sacred. Another twenty percent—which you seem to represent—thinks guns should be melted down and turned into manhole covers . . ."

"Remind me," Kerry interjected, "to propose that."

Callister did not smile. "The rest," he continued, "are all those folks in the middle, who go back and forth, swayed by events, and yet hold the balance of power.

"Next are the politicians, who need the people in the middle to keep their jobs. So every time some lunatic shoots up a day-care center, you Democrats take up the cry for gun control, hoping to convince enough mothers that some new gun law will actually protect their kids . . ."

Nettled, Kerry held up his hand. "If you're saying I'm cynical about this . . ."

"At least I'm not questioning your manhood." There was a glint of amusement in Callister's eyes. "I accept that you're different, Mr. President. You've certainly got reason to be. But I've learned not to trust a class of people whose first priority is self-perpetuation. And I sure as hell don't trust them to be fair.

"Frankly, I think a lot of your Democrat friends would rather keep the issue alive, and complain about the SSA, than pass a law. Others would rather take credit for passing a bullshit law which sounds good but does nothing. Because all they really care about is winning the next election."

Whatever quarrel Kerry might have with this, he had no doubt that Callister's bleak view of politics was deeply held. "So far," he said, "we've got the public, which is fickle, and the politicians who exploit them. What makes that problem unique to you?"

"The lawyers." Callister's voice combined disdain with resignation. "The plaintiffs' lawyers—your fervent supporters—are always looking for the next big thing. Five years ago it was tobacco: that's where they got all the money they keep giving to politicians who treat lawsuits as the American way. After tobacco, they decided to take a run at us.

"They dress it up in a lot of noble rhetoric, trying to make us out to be the moral equivalent of R.J. Reynolds. But these lawsuits all come down to a single bogus theory: that because guns can be used to kill people, we're responsible whenever somebody actually uses a gun to kill someone—particularly if they can call it an 'assault weapon' . . ."

"If the suits are bogus," Kerry interrupted, "why worry?"

"Bogus or not, they cost money. We have to hire our own lawyers, who keep sending bills and telling us we'll win. But by the time we *do* win, we've paid them millions, and taken a hellacious beating in the media. Because the plaintiffs' bar has used the press, politicians, and any other weapon they can to try to taint the jury pool by poisoning the public mind." Pausing, Callister sounded genuinely weary. "Most presidents of gun companies are middle-aged white guys like me, who aren't media-slick or even photogenic. We make pretty good villains—especially with our own lawyers advising us to shut up and keep our heads down. When was the last time you saw a gun company get a break on *60 Minutes*?"

Kerry nodded. "Being ambushed by Mike Wallace," he responded, "is worth avoiding."

"That's the fourth dimension—the media. They live off sensationalism, not enlightenment—off tragedies like Columbine and extremists on both sides. Why ask a boring guy like me about the realities of our business, when you can put on some Aryan supremacist or the president of the SSA?"

"You can complain about the skinheads," Kerry retorted, "but you've let the SSA speak for you. You've stood silent while they've gutted the laws, even though whenever someone who shouldn't have a gun kills somebody else, the gun companies share the blame. And now they've trashed Martin Bresler for trying to get you out of a legal and public relations mess the SSA has put you in. It's a joke."

"Anyone who controls your customer base," Callister replied, "is no joke. How do you think the SSA gets its power? By scaring the bejesus out of millions of people who buy and own our guns.

"For the SSA, you're the man who'll strip Americans of their gun rights, and only they can stop you. And so their members—our customers—vote how the SSA says to vote, and send the SSA the money it uses to fund your political opponents, or to scare the hell out of *them* as well. And *then* the SSA goes about scaring the hell out of the rest of America by describing all the criminals who'll be beating down their doors once you've snatched their guns away. You complain about Lexington marketing fear? Our ads are nothing compared to the six o'clock news and the SSA propaganda machine.

"I've got no way to reach my own customers, Mr. President. Let alone to reason with them." Callister stopped, his gaze holding Kerry's. "A few years ago, the president of our biggest rival was fool enough to say that he thought licensing gun owners was inevitable. The SSA didn't bother complaining to *him*: they used the media and their own magazine and e-mail list, and pretty soon our rival company found themselves on the wrong end of a consumer boycott which drove it to the brink of bankruptcy. Which is exactly what will happen to Lexington if the SSA finds out I'm here."

Kerry considered him. "Tell me about Bresler," he demanded.

Callister studied the table, then looked directly at Kerry. "Nothing pretty about *that,* not even a veneer of civility. They just put his head on the block . . ."—with a swift, chopping motion, Callister hit the table with the edge of a thick hand—"then mailed it to me."

"The SSA?"

"I can't prove that." Pausing, Callister spoke more quietly. "Whatever the SSA did, they did without me. But Bresler was a threat to them. As public relations, the safety lock agreement he made with you was brilliant— it was the first good media we've gotten in years, and maybe down the road it'll spare us lawsuits where some six-year-old kills little sis, with the gun Dad was too dumb to lock up. But the SSA lives off conflict, and the perception of its power: if we can compromise with you, and someone else can broker that deal, then the SSA is out of business . . ."

"So they got Bresler."

"That's what I believe. But all my fellow CEOs would say was that Bresler was too much of a self-promoter, that he was dividing the gun rights lobby."

Kerry shook his head. "Your fellow CEOs," he observed, "may have had their reasons. But they put me in mind of lemmings."

Callister turned, surveying the valley. "Someday," he said bleakly, "a gun company will be destroyed by a lawsuit based on some loophole the SSA and its surrogates in Congress created to protect the 'rights' of gun owners. But my colleagues can't look ahead that far, except to hope it won't be them. Because the SSA can destroy them here and now." He turned to face the President. "This may be hard for you to fathom. But I love this company, and I care about the folks who work there. I don't want Lexington Arms to be the one that goes."

Kerry stood, taking his turn at surveying the view around them. But his mind was on his next few words. "Then the only question," he said at length, "is how to ensure that doesn't happen." Turning, he gazed down at Callister. "Right now, you're like a man in a catatonic trance—perfectly aware that you could get run over, but unable to move, or even cry out for help."

Callister's smile mingled resentment with an acknowledgment of his dilemma. "What would you do?"

"Take control of my own fate, for better or worse." Kerry sat again, meeting Callister's gaze. "I'll think about all you've said. I'd like you to think about how to avoid lawsuits, and what Lexington needs to survive the SSA. The next time we meet, I'll have a deal to propose. If you're willing to listen."

For a long moment Callister studied him. "I'll listen to a President," he finally answered. "I don't need the SSA's permission for *that*."

FIFTEEN

"THE PRESIDENT'S WEDDING," Peter Lake said dryly, "must be the nightmare of the event-planning business."

The head of the President's Secret Service detail sat in Clayton's office with those summoned to review the security for Kerry's wedding and reception: Kit Pace and Francesca Thibault from the White House; Connie Coulter on behalf of Lara. There were smiles all around, and then Francesca Thibault allowed, "It is a bit more challenging than the Easter Egg Roll."

"Or pardoning the White House Turkey," Peter rejoined. "From a security standpoint, it's more like the wedding of Charles and Diana." Surveying the others, Peter sat back, a burly, even-tempered man with a law degree, a philosophical bent, a deep spiritual commitment to his Roman Catholic faith, and, above all, a total dedication to protecting Kerry Kilcannon. "It's a unique opportunity," he continued, "for high-profile mischief—terrorists, crazies, protestors of every stripe, malcontents wanting to make a point, anyone who thinks he has a grievance against the President. We're not only telling people like Mahmoud Al Anwar the time and place, we're offering them the cover of hundreds of guests, and thousands more hoping to get a glimpse of the President and new First Lady."

Francesca nodded. "What do you need from *us*, Peter?"

"Lists, for openers. Every guest for the wedding and reception—name; date of birth; Social Security number; how they're getting here; how they're leaving. We'll need all that to get them in . . ."

"Hopefully," Francesca interjected pointedly, "without offending them, or making the reception look like a detention camp."

"I understand," Peter replied. "But all of you know the problem: Kerry Kilcannon is a human lightning rod. And the angry and unstable are drawn to the myth of the Kilcannons like moths to a flame.

"James Kilcannon was killed, this President nearly so. There are a thousand copycats hoping to finish the job and secure a place in history. The President excites passions other politicians don't: pro-life fanatics hate him, and a lot of hard-core gun folks are convinced he's out to get them. And now he's taken on Al Anwar.

"Every time he goes somewhere, we go there knowing that a lot of people want him dead." Facing Clayton, Peter finished, "I realize his political people are hoping for the maximum exposure. But I'm not much willing to compromise when it comes to Kerry Kilcannon."

Clayton nodded. "I'll make the President conscious of your concerns," he answered. "As far as *he's* concerned, he's never had so much to live for."

The Chief of Staff's voice was bland. But the comment reminded Peter of what they knew that the others did not: that Kerry and Lara had been lovers in secret. During the California primary, three nights before Kerry Kilcannon was shot, Peter had let Lara into Kerry's room; the night after the shooting, Peter had assured a worried Lara that he would never tell anyone. Nor had he—not his superiors in the Secret Service, or even his own wife.

"What about media?" Peter asked.

Clayton glanced at Connie Coulter. "Lara's given in," Connie said. "The wedding will be televised. But nothing afterward."

This, Peter knew, was a concession—the Lara Costello he had come to know was intensely private. "Two nights before the wedding," Connie went on, "the President and Lara will do a live interview from the White House, on ABC. The night before there'll be a private dinner at the White House, for the wedding party and family." She glanced at a piece of paper. "On the eve of the wedding, Lara will move from her apartment to a suite at the Hotel Madison. Two hours before the ceremony a limousine with her family will leave the White House and go to her hotel. There'll be TV coverage of their departure and arrival at the Madison, but only the White House photographer will be allowed into the suite. From there, they'll proceed to the wedding."

"And the day after . . ."

"Lara will be taking her family out to Dulles Airport for the return trip to San Francisco. And then she'll meet the President at Andrews Air Force Base for the flight to Martha's Vineyard."

"Will the Costellos be doing any media?"

"Perhaps a few selected interviews, some with the Hispanic media." Pausing, Connie said wryly, "Very selected."

From this, Peter inferred that Lara was, as he expected, resisting the no doubt limitless requests that she offer up her family to the press. "I'll want their schedule," Peter told Connie. "Especially for whatever time they'll be spending with Lara."

"Absolutely," Connie answered, and then Clayton's telephone rang. With a puzzled expression, he rose from his chair and answered.

Placing the receiver down, he turned to Peter Lake. "As soon as we're finished, Peter, the President would like to see you."

When Peter entered the Oval Office, the President motioned him to a comfortable couch, and sat in a nearby chair.

"It's about Lara's family, Peter. I need your help."

This was said with a sobriety which suggested, to Peter's trained antennae, that the President was deeply concerned. This was underscored by the absence of the President's usual inquiries about Peter's own family, or even the casual greetings suitable to two men who spent much time together, one of whom saw the other in unguarded moments few other people witnessed. Peter Lake considered Kerry Kilcannon an extraordinary man, with a grace and kindness at odds with the cold-minded politician his enemies portrayed. The President had never asked for secrecy regarding his affair with Lara, and seemed to trust him utterly. That he also had never mentioned the nearly successful attempt on his life which had occurred on Peter's watch, but instead expressed great pleasure at Peter's assignment to the White House, only intensified Peter's determination that no harm would ever befall this President.

"Anything I can do, Mr. President."

"As much as you can, I'd like you to watch out for them while they're here—if not directly through the Service, through the D.C. Police." The President leaned forward. "They're not public people, and I don't want them harassed. Worse, they'll be targets of opportunity—for Al Qaeda or whoever else. I can't let anything happen to them."

This was more concern, Peter thought, than Kerry Kilcannon had ever shown for himself. "I'll make sure they're well protected," Peter answered, and then paused before adding gently, "And the First Lady–to-be."

With a faint smile, the President considered him. "I know that. But there's something else I need your help on, in confidence."

Peter made no answer. He did not need to.

"You'll remember the problems with Joan's husband."

The President steepled his fingers, eyes remaining fixed on Peter Lake. "Last month she got a court order that he stay away from her and their six-year-old daughter, and had the cops take away his gun. He's threatened suicide or even murder."

"And you think that's more than talk."

"It *could* be." Pausing, the President spoke in a lower voice. "This morning, he went to court on the battery charge. Joan told the court that—if he agreed to a program for batterers—she didn't want him jailed. So that's what the judge did.

"For a lot of men, these programs really help. But I can't assume that about John Bowden. The only thing I'm sure of is that he's free."

Peter considered this. "You can't be sure he won't try to get another gun. And he can always snatch Marie, with or without one."

"My problem is that I'm stuck." The President stood, hands in his pockets, as if his lack of power made him restless. "I can't ask the Service to protect them. And I can't ask the police to guard them without creating a lot of problems—including publicity, which Joan doesn't want and which might only make Bowden worse. The only recourse Lara and I seem to have is hiring private security, like everyone else. For whatever that's worth."

Briefly, Peter reflected. "There *are* things we can do," he answered. "If someone who might attract a violent person is in proximity to you or the First Lady, we take over. As for the rest, we can have our field office in San Francisco in touch with the police, monitoring her situation."

"I appreciate that. But it doesn't guarantee Joan's safety. Or Marie's."

"If you want to set up personal security," Peter said, "one of our ex-agents has a security firm in San Francisco. Anything you want—security monitors, twenty-four-hour protection for Joan, someone watching her daughter's school—my friend Tom Burns can do. It all depends on how much you want to spend."

At once, the President looked relieved. "Money's no object," he replied. "At least until this guy's calmed down."

At seven forty-five that evening, the President took a call in his upstairs office.

"Sorry I'm so hard to find," Robert Lenihan told him. "But I'm in the middle of a securities fraud trial, with close to five hundred million dollars in damages. Another corporate rip-off."

His tone was less apologetic than self-satisfied, tinged with the suggestion that Bob Lenihan's work approached in import the President's own. In recent years, his personal wealth swollen by millions wrested from tobacco companies, Lenihan and his trade association of plaintiffs' lawyers, Trial Lawyers for Justice, had become major donors to Democratic campaigns. Fueled by ideological passion and the desire for headlines—in Lenihan, Kerry had found, these motives were impossible to separate— Lenihan had recently launched a series of high-risk lawsuits against the gun industry on behalf of American cities, asserting that companies who marketed semiautomatic handguns were responsible for millions of dollars in costs incurred by public hospitals in treating the dead or injured. The kinship Lenihan felt this established with the President was only enhanced by two million dollars in television ads that Trial Lawyers for Justice had run in support of his nomination of Caroline Masters to be Chief Justice.

"You're a busy man," Kerry answered mildly, "so let me cut to the chase. With the understanding that this *cannot* hit the papers."

For Lenihan, Kerry knew, this request would only increase his self-esteem. "Absolutely, Mr. President."

"Clayton tells me you've got thirteen major lawsuits against gun manufacturers. Suppose I want to reach an agreement with one of the biggest, settling all of your lawsuits against it?"

This, for once, induced a momentary silence in Bob Lenihan. "In exchange for what?"

"Zero damages," Kerry said briskly. "Just a fundamental change in how this company does business—including how it sells its guns, and who it sells to." After a brief pause, Kerry added, "And, perhaps, your legal fees. Some modest compensation for time spent."

To Kerry's amusement, more silence followed. "To agree to that," Lenihan ventured, "I'd need the approval of all the cities."

"That shouldn't be hard. These suits are all uphill—and in a few states, the SSA is pushing legislation to bar them outright." Kerry's tone remained crisp. "The mayors of all thirteen cities are Democrats, and they need the assistance a President can provide. Besides, they filed these lawsuits claiming they wanted to reform the American gun industry. I'm proposing to help them."

Once more, Lenihan hesitated. When he spoke again, his tone was subdued. "You've taken me by surprise, Mr. President. I'll have to consult with my clients and cocounsel."

"You do that," Kerry said succinctly. "*I* need a breakthrough on guns. *You* need a President who looks as strong as possible. Especially for the next time the Republicans in Congress gin up some 'tort reform' bill to wipe out half your lawsuits against the corporations you sue, or cut the damages you can collect to zip."

This time, Kerry surmised, the quiet on the other line suggested not resistance, but calculation, the weighing of political costs and benefits. At length, Lenihan said, "I'll start making inquiries tomorrow."

"Thank you," the President answered politely. "This is delicate, and I don't have time to waste."

SIXTEEN

FOUR DAYS BEFORE the wedding, Lara's family arrived at the White House.

Lara had met them at Dulles; on a muggy late afternoon, the motorcade of black limousines eased through the East Entrance of the White House, accompanied by the Secret Service and D.C. Police, some on motorcycles. As Kerry emerged from the East Wing to greet them, television cameras and photographers with telephoto lenses, cordoned off by more security, followed him from a distance.

The President had cleared his schedule, determined to make this visit as warm and easy as Lara devoutly wished it to be. When Lara emerged from the limousine, he walked over briskly, and kissed her.

"How was the trip in?" he asked.

Lara smiled. "Noisy. Marie loved the sirens."

Inez emerged next. In her mid-fifties she retained the slender build she had passed on to Lara. Her handsome face, while careworn, was animated by spirited black eyes which conveyed warmth and intelligence. Her dress was simple, her grooming flawless. Once more Kerry was reminded of his own mother, Mary, an Irish immigrant who, despite her great surprise at finding herself mother to a President, had always maintained a dignity she felt appropriate to his achievements. He went to Inez and kissed her on the cheek.

She smelled of a spicy perfume, felt more fragile than

Kerry had recalled. Pulling back, Kerry smiled at her. "You," he said, "are the mother-in-law I had in mind."

Inez laughed softly, taking in the grandeur of the White House. "I'm Lara's mother, in any event." Though she had come to America as a child, her voice was lightly accented. "So *this* is where my daughter will be living."

"For seven and a half more years, I hope."

Turning, Kerry saw Lara's youngest sister, Mary. Neither as plump as Joan nor as pretty as Lara, Mary had crescent eyes, a wide mouth, and the tentative look of someone who was waiting to be invited to dance, but felt uncertain that this would happen. She was a kindergarten teacher: it was with children, Lara had told him, that her hesitant manner was replaced by an air of unflappability.

Kerry kissed her on the forehead. "Mary," he said, "it's terrific that you're here."

After a tentative moment, she hugged him. "To me, it's amazing that I am. But Lara's an amazing person."

To Kerry, Mary's comment had a faint and unintentional undertone—that Mary felt more awe for Lara than she found comfortable. Then he saw Joan standing behind her, and extended his arm. When Joan came forward, he gently pulled her closer, until she rested the crown of her head against his cheek.

"How *are* you?" he murmured.

"Better, for now." She leaned back; her liquid brown eyes were filled with a trust which reminded Kerry of how much he still worried for her, how deeply he had become enmeshed in the life of Lara's family. Quickly, Joan glanced down at Marie. "Thank you, Kerry. For everything."

Grasping her mother's hand, Marie was looking about her with the shyness of a six-year-old in the presence of a stranger. It struck Kerry that Marie, so much a part of his thoughts, had never met him.

Kneeling, he took both of her hands. "Hi, Marie. I'm Kerry."

She looked at him, head slightly angled away, as if to keep her inspection surreptitious. "You're the President."

Kerry smiled. "True. I'm also marrying your Aunt Lara. That makes me your uncle, believe it or not."

Marie gazed at him, as if torn between interest and suspicion. As her picture had suggested, she was so much like a miniature Lara that it pierced him, yet there was something harder to define, perhaps the set of her mouth and the apprehension in her eyes, which reminded Kerry of his encounter with John Bowden.

"At the airport," she informed him, "they took my picture."

"Yeah—they do that a lot. After a while you sort of get used to it."

Marie gave a fractional shrug. "I didn't really mind," she allowed, and then looked past him at the White House. "It's huge. My teacher said it would be."

At once, Kerry had the sense of Lara's family stepping through the looking glass—for reasons Marie could not truly comprehend, the world was signalling her that she had become a child apart. Even without this, too much had happened to her—a home life that must seem unpredictable and often dangerous; a mother who was fearful and confused; a father who, in his banishment, had become a frightening enigma. "It may be big," Kerry assured her, "but it's pretty nice inside. Would you like to see it?"

The little girl bit her lip. "Can you show me where Mommy and I are sleeping?"

Kerry heard the implicit plea: *please don't separate me from my mother.* "Sure," he answered with a smile. "It's called the Lincoln Bedroom. The bed's big enough for both of you."

Around them, the White House ushers came for the Costellos' luggage. Perhaps, Kerry thought, it was the presence of more strangers; perhaps it was that Kerry was a man, and that Marie Bowden missed her father. But when they entered the East Wing, the fingers of Marie's left hand rested lightly in Kerry's.

John Bowden sat amidst the wreckage of his life.

His clothes were flung over chairs and on the floor; there was nothing in the refrigerator but bagels, ice cream, and a chilled bottle of vodka. The red light on his answering machine was a message from his probation officer, asking why he had missed the workshop for convicted batterers, and warning that this was a parole violation. In his hands he grasped the framed picture of Marie; at his feet, on the front page of the afternoon paper, Joan and Marie stepped out of a limousine at San Francisco International, above a caption saying "Wedding Bound." From his television, CNN assaulted him.

"The arrival of the Costello family," the anchorman said, "begins a unique chapter in American history—the marriage of a President, the son of Irish immigrants, to the daughter of a woman who came to the United States from Mexico . . ."

In an act of will, John Bowden forced himself to look up.

Their backs were to the camera: four women, a man, and a little girl, entering the portals of the White House. But no one needed to identify President Kerry Kilcannon, or the child who held his hand in one of hers, her doll clasped in the other.

Tears filled John Bowden's eyes; outrage filled his heart.

Though Lara considered it a failing, Kerry was indifferent to what he considered the frills of history—which First Lady had procured what portrait, which President had been given a French Empire clock. But for Lara's family he had read up on the evolution of the White House, committing discrete chunks to memory.

Among those were the histories of each upstairs bedroom in which the Costellos were staying. Entering the Queen's suite, he told Inez, "This is where Queen Elizabeth stayed, along with Queens Juliana and Wilhelmina of the Netherlands, Queen Frederika of Greece, a gaggle of princesses, and even Winston Churchill. But not at the same time."

Inez eyed the room with the mock-critical gaze of a woman concerned that it met her standards of domestic order, her gaze resting last on the canopied bed. Then she turned to Kerry, touching his arm. "It's wonderful, truly."

"I'm still getting used to it myself," Kerry answered with a smile, and led them to the Lincoln Bedroom—Inez, Joan and Marie, with Lara and Mary chatting behind. "This was actually Lincoln's office," he explained. "But after he was assassinated, it was felt no one should work here." Turning to Marie, he said, "A long time ago, in this country, white men were allowed to own blacks as slaves. This is where President Lincoln signed what they called the Emancipation Proclamation, making slavery against the law."

And it was in this room, Kerry thought, where history became palpable for him. But it was not easy to explain to a six-year-old girl the ineradicable stain which slavery had left on our nation, the ongoing legacy of which remained one of Kerry's deepest concerns. Scooping her up in one arm, Kerry walked over to an oil depicting a cluster of slaves, hiding in a cellar as they gazed at a watch by candlelight, waiting for the hour of emancipation to strike. "These were slaves," he told her, and pointed to the worn face of an old man. "This man has been waiting all his life to be free."

For a long time, Marie gazed at the painting, doll held tight to her. Perhaps, Kerry thought, this reflected less a conscious understanding of slavery than of the fear and hope she read in the faces, the sense of hiding in the darkness. It was *that* sense, Kerry suspected, which Marie could feel as intensely as Kerry had at her age, listening to the sounds of his father's anger, his mother's cries.

"Come on," he told her. "I've got another room to show you."

This solarium was light and sunny—there was a television, and Lara had stocked it with children's books and the same games Marie had at home. To Marie, her mother exclaimed, "Oh, sweetheart, this is really nice." More softly, she said to Lara, "Thank you."

Quiet, Lara touched Joan's arm.

Perhaps now, Kerry hoped, things would change between them. If so, that would be a wedding present to Lara beyond anything else she could receive. Together, the adults watched Marie place her doll at a small wooden table.

The telephone rang. Glancing at the caller ID number, Kerry saw that it was Clayton Slade.

"Yes?" he answered.

"I'm sorry to bother you," Clayton apologized. "But we've got a problem, with the *San Francisco Chronicle*."

At once, Kerry felt hope turn to apprehension. "What?" he asked. "Did I lose the recount?"

"They're working on a story about Joan. And you."

SEVENTEEN

"CAROLE TISONE called me," Marcia Harding told the President. "From the *Chronicle*. She knew all about the stay-away order; Bowden's threats to Joan; his visit to Marie; his conviction. Even that he's in a program for abusive men."

Sitting in his upstairs office, Kerry glanced at the others—Clayton, Kit Pace, and Lara—as Harding's voice resonated from the speakerphone. "How?" he asked.

"Not from me." Harding's voice was flat. "Maybe from court files, or the cops. Maybe someone in the PD's office told somebody else—the only thing that isn't run-of-the-mill domestic violence is that Joan is Lara Costello's sister. Now that she's left for your wedding, her life has become a 'human interest story' . . ."

"What's the public interest in humiliating Joan?"

"I asked much the same thing. She started with some pieties about domestic violence being 'our most closely guarded family secret,' and how Joan's case was like Nicole Simpson's—a wake-up call that exposes the issue." Harding paused, then added with palpable reluctance. "Then she asked about your call."

At the corner of his eye, Kerry saw Lara's look of alarm. "There were only three of us on that call," Kerry said tersely. "You, me, and Halloran."

"I can only speak for me, Mr. President. I didn't tell a soul—no one in the office, not even the police."

"What did you tell the reporter?"

"Only that it was an internal matter, and that I didn't feel free to comment. I've got a call in to Jack Halloran—I haven't been able to reach him. So I decided to warn you myself. Whatever happens, Mr. President, I clearly can't *deny* you called."

Across the room, Kerry watched a series of expressions register on Kit Pace's snub features—disquiet, concern, calculation. More evenly, Kerry inquired, "What did this reporter want to know?"

"What we'd talked about. How many times you'd called. What you wanted us to do. Whether Joan got special treatment." Now Harding sounded annoyed. "As to that, I said no. Which is true—the only thing I did any differently is to personally enter the stay-away order in the computer, as you asked, in case he tried to buy a gun. And that was only to ensure the system works the way it should."

Listening, Kerry felt a moment's sympathy for Harding: she had been helpful and professional, and yet might be tarnished by having talked to him at all. "I'm sorry," he said, "if I've created a problem for you."

"Oh, I'm fine with how we handled this—I just hope it helps her. And him." Her tone became more cautious. "The thing I worry about is Jack. If he told someone, and that someone told the *Chronicle*, he'll probably have to admit it's true. And then I'll have to talk about it."

Kerry glanced at Lara. She stared fixedly at the floor, as though watching her hopes for these few days—a warm visit with her family; a healing interlude with Joan—evaporate. "If you have to," Kerry answered, "you have to—every conversation, everything I said or asked. Pass that on to Jack, as well."

Harding was briefly silent. "Thank you, Mr. President. I will."

*

To Lara, Kerry said softly, "You were right. I should have hired a lawyer at the beginning, someone to be a go-between. Not been so intent on fixing things myself."

Watching, the others seemed embarrassed. "You were protecting her," Lara answered in an even tone. "You know what can go wrong."

"Yes," Kerry answered. "This. We'd better discuss how to handle it."

Briefly, Kit glanced at Lara. "We don't have many options," she told Kerry. "Halloran probably had a few too many, and couldn't resist telling a crony about the phone call from on high. We can't expect him to stonewall this, and it might only make things worse if he tried.

"You know the classic rule: get the story out your way, and get it over with. That's all the more true when you've got nothing to hide . . ."

"Nothing," Lara interjected, "except my sister's private life. On the eve of our wedding they'll have a field day with this."

Kit grimaced. "That's why we have to make a public statement. Get ahead of this with dignity, and make a plea for Joan's privacy . . ."

"How do you put *that* genie back in the bottle?"

"You don't," Kit responded. "We can simply make it better, or worse."

Kerry stood. "How much time do we have?"

Kit sat back, eyes narrow with thought. "As long as it takes them to nail down the D.A., and call us—they'll have to do that. Figure a day, maybe two."

"Any chance of killing this?"

"An appeal for decency?" Kit answered in a dubious tone. "We can try. It might be easier if you weren't part of the story."

Kerry did not look at Lara. "And you?" he asked Clayton. "You warned me about this, after all."

"It's easy to give warnings," his friend answered. "If I were President, and one of my girls were at risk, I wouldn't delegate this to anyone."

It was a kind remark, Kerry thought. But he could feel Lara's unhappiness. Facing her, Kerry asked, "Do we try to kill it?"

"Of course."

He turned to Kit, eyebrows raised in inquiry. "When the *Chronicle* calls me," she told him, "I'll make as strenuous a plea as possible. But if it doesn't work, we'll have to move quickly. I'd suggest a positive message about protecting women and children, giving troubled families a second chance—maybe through an interview with Joan. That's much better for us than a President exerting influence."

Silent, Lara shook her head in wonderment. "And if that doesn't work," Kerry answered, "we'll decide what's next."

When the others had left, Lara said, "I blame myself. I should have never put this off on you—it's not fair to Joan, *or* you."

"I made the call," Kerry answered. "You didn't ask me to." Pausing, he felt his frustration boil over. "We can sit here beating ourselves up, or try to figure out what to say to your family and, if necessary, to the media. And how to make the next few days as happy as we can."

Lara inhaled. "For a long time, I've known how little privacy a President can claim. But you and I assumed that risk with full knowledge of the rules. Joan didn't. Instead, we helped drag this to her door."

"It was my mistake, not yours." Kerry went to where she sat, taking both of her hands in his. "If you don't mind, I'd like to tell Joan myself."

"To protect me?" Lara inquired coolly.

"To explain," Kerry answered. "And to apologize. She put her trust in me, after all."

Lara looked up at him, and then her gaze softened. "I'll tell my mother and Mary," she said.

They ate in the family dining room, by candlelight, with Marie and her doll sitting next to Kerry. Lara and Kerry maintained a plausible vivacity; based on his recent remedial reading, Kerry told Marie that this once had been a bedroom in which another child, Alice Roosevelt Longworth, had her appendix removed.

Marie took his hand. "Did it hurt?" she inquired.

"Maybe the doctor," Kerry answered. "Alice had a wicked tongue. She was known for saying, 'If you don't have anything nice to say about anyone, please sit next to me.'"

"Today," Lara added with a teasing smile, "we call people like that reporters."

With her child's ear for the literal, Marie gave her aunt a puzzled glance. "Lara used to be a reporter," her grandmother explained. "But she covered wars, not gossip."

"I remember your letters from Kosovo," Mary told Lara, "telling us not to worry. And all of us worrying like crazy, with Mom praying for you every day."

Lara smiled. "And here we all are," she said. "With me about to get married."

"Oh," Inez told her, "I prayed for that, too."

Amidst laughter, Kerry raised his glass to her. When dessert was done, and the others about to leave, Kerry asked Joan to visit with him awhile.

Even in candlelight, she seemed to pale. Her eyes filled with tears, as if at a sudden blow. Her voice choked with fear and humiliation. "He'll be furious. John couldn't stand the thought of people knowing. It was like he was more ashamed of being exposed than he was of beating me up."

Without much hope, Kerry ventured, "There's a chance that they won't print it."

Joan shook her head. More quietly, she said, "I can never talk about this. Not in public."

Nor, Kerry thought, had his mother. "If it comes to that, I can. Or Lara. But not before you tell us what you'd be comfortable with."

"Nothing." Disbelief lingered in her voice. "I have to trust you about what's best to do. But it all seems terrible to me."

"It is terrible," Kerry answered. "For Lara, too."

Joan's smile was faint. "*That's* hard for me to imagine. I can't remember her ever seeming scared, or overwhelmed, or even vulnerable."

Kerry nodded his understanding. "People as accomplished as Lara, and as driven, don't excite a lot of sympathy. They sure don't ask for any." He paused, gazing at Joan intently. "But she'll never feel right about her life if *your* life isn't good, or if your relationship isn't good. I can't tell you what hopes she had for this time with you, and how shattered she feels now."

Joan seemed to absorb this. When she smiled again, her gratitude was tinged with melancholy, perhaps the thought that, just as she had failed to fully see her sister, she had imagined seeing love in the eyes of the wrong man. Softly, she asked, "Does Lara know how lucky she is?"

"Every day I remind her," Kerry answered with a smile, and then his expression became serious. "*I'm* lucky to have all of you in my life. The Costellos are all the family I have, at least until Lara and I have children. I'm hoping for a daughter like Marie." Pausing, he added, "And, like Lara, I never want anything to happen to either one of you."

Shyly, Joan kissed him on the cheek. "We'll be fine," she promised.

Mary waited until Inez was tucking in Marie to take her oldest sister aside, speaking quietly. "You've always been the one to decide things," she told Lara. "But this isn't good."

They lingered in the hallway outside the Lincoln Bedroom. "What isn't good?"

"Anyone talking about John in public. He'll blame Joanie."

"We don't control this anymore. Especially the media."

Mary's brow knit. "But you control who talks to them. If *you* do it, he'll think that Joan betrayed him."

"I'm worried, too." Unsettled by Mary's new assertiveness, Lara touched her arm.

Mary stared at her, unmollified. "Don't put me off, Lara, or treat me like a child. You're not my mother."

"I know," Lara answered with renewed sadness. "Sometimes it must have seemed like I thought I was." Glancing at Marie's bedroom, she finished softly. "I can't tell you what will happen. But whatever we have to do, we'll protect them both."

Silent, Mary seemed suspended between resignation and frustration. Then, without saying good night, she turned and went to her room.

EIGHTEEN

THE NEXT MORNING, under the cover of showing Lara's family Camp David, Kerry again met George Callister in secrecy.

As Lara led the others on a tour, the President and Callister took a separate trail. Even in the Catoctins, the air was hot, dense, mosquito-ridden, causing Kerry to fear for the weather on his wedding day.

"Your immediate problem," Kerry began, "is lawsuits. Including thirteen already brought by cities against the industry, seeking to recover the cost to the public health system of treating gunshot deaths and injuries."

Hands shoved in the pockets of his jeans, Callister scowled. "Those deaths and injuries are caused by shooters we've never heard of. These suits are bullshit—political grandstanding combined with blackmail, meant to extort a settlement by imposing millions in legal fees."

As they entered a bright patch of light, Kerry put on the sunglasses hanging from the neck of his polo shirt. "So," he ventured, "if the federal government sued the industry for the costs of security in public housing, that would also be bullshit?"

Callister stood still, turning to the President with a look of controlled anger. "You'd do that?"

"In a heartbeat," Kerry said evenly. "And if some demented ex-felon slaughters a roomful of schoolchildren with one of your semiautomatic handguns, and the grieving parents bring a wrongful death action, would that be bullshit, too?"

"Yes," Callister snapped. "And for the same reason. Personal responsibility."

"But it's still costly, you'll agree. Plus you can't be sure that a jury won't choose the mother of a murdered six-year-old over a company which markets weapons whose only legitimate purpose is to slaughter human beings. And if anyone thinks the Republicans can pass a bill to immunize you from lawsuits, forget it. If I can't get thirty-four senators to uphold my veto, I shouldn't have this job." Facing Callister, Kerry placed his hands on his hips. "It seems that you're caught between the SSA and a pack of cynical pols and greedy trial lawyers. Settle, and the SSA will bankrupt you with a boycott; litigate, and you'll be bled to death by legal fees, or whacked with a jury verdict bigger than your whole net worth."

Callister emitted a harsh laugh. "If you're trying to scare me, Mr. President, tell me something new. Other than that you'll sue me, too."

"It's this. I'm also your only way out."

Callister folded his arms. "You may be the President, but you don't control thirteen city governments. Let alone megalomaniacs like Bob Lenihan."

"Every one of those cities," Kerry countered, "has a Democratic mayor. They need me. So do the trial lawyers. They're both already on board."

Callister's expression betrayed complete surprise. "You're putting together a package deal?"

"Yes. For the company brave enough to take it. The one thing they don't know is the company I'm meeting with."

Turning, Callister began walking again, gazing at the trail of light and shadow cast by overhanging trees. "I don't know what you're proposing. But the SSA would put us on the cover of *The Defender* magazine, with me as Neville Chamberlain." Pausing, he glanced sideways at Kerry. "They'd make Lexington an object lesson. Dealers would stop selling our guns, customers would stop buying them. They'd destroy my company and end my career."

"You're headed there already," Kerry retorted. "Lexington's owned by a British corporation. They can't be happy owning a wasting asset. When they decide to sell you, who'll want to pump more money into a company which promises endless legal fees, the worst PR this side of nicotine, and an excellent shot at insolvency?"

Taking out a handkerchief, Callister dabbed the sweat off his forehead, refolding the cloth with great deliberation before returning it to his pocket. "What do you have in mind?" he asked.

"Let's find some shade," Kerry answered. "It's too damned hot out here."

They sat in the relative cool of the patio. The steward brought ham sandwiches, iced beer mugs, and two cool green bottles of Heineken.

"The first thing I want," Kerry said, "is to keep your guns from potential murderers.

"We talked about this in Washington. Federal law requires gun dealers to run background checks on buyers, so they're not selling to felons, wife-beaters, and others with a known propensity toward violence. But forty percent of guns sold are sold privately, without checks.

"Part of the problem is gun shows, where even an escapee from Bellevue can buy a Lexington semiautomatic." Pausing, Kerry sipped his beer and put it down again. "To start, I want Lexington to require gun shows to enforce background checks before it allows its dealers to sell any Lexington guns at the show. The same thing I proposed to Bresler's group."

"That's when we *were* a group." Callister took a larger swallow of his beer, gazing fixedly at Kerry. "To the SSA, your proposal infringes the right of private parties to sell guns without the government knowing who they are. If a buyer later kills someone, then *he* should be prosecuted to the full extent of existing law—including the death penalty."

"Will the SSA also resurrect the victim?" Kerry inquired mildly. "It strikes me that my brother is still dead."

For a moment, Callister was silent. "There's also my board of directors," he finally said. "They'll claim that agreeing to this would put us at a competitive disadvantage . . ."

"By not selling to mass murderers? That's just the clientele you need." Kerry's tone became incredulous. "Why in hell should anyone without a record care about a background check? And why sell guns to anyone who *does* care?

"You can't want Lexington handguns used in crimes—it's bad for business, and it leads to lawsuits. So unless you *do* want to market guns to criminals, a background check helps protect you."

Callister considered this. "Speaking personally," he said at length, "I don't have a problem with that. Neither do some of my fellow CEOs . . ."

"Good. Because I'll also want Lexington's help in lobbying Congress for background checks on every gun sold in America."

"In other words," Callister said with a fleeting smile, "suicide. Is that all you're proposing?"

Despite his skepticism, Kerry sensed, Callister was intrigued, waiting for the scope of Kerry's design to become clearer. "Not quite." Pausing, Kerry marshalled his resources of personality and persuasion. "No civilian needs a gun that fires forty rounds, or bullets designed to kill by shredding someone's insides. That's not about self-defense—unless you're a crack-cocaine dealer in Miami . . ."

"Some people," Callister interjected, "including the

SSA, think they need to defend themselves against their own government."

"Paranoia," Kerry retorted, "is not a basis for public policy. Or a license for mass murder . . ."

"*Other* people," Callister continued, "just enjoy owning high-capacity weapons. If I start saying some guns are 'bad,' I lose them . . ."

"Is nothing 'bad'? Are cop-killer bullets just a fun toy for hobbyists?" Kerry's voice turned cold. "Federal law limits the capacity of new magazines to ten rounds. But the old magazines hold forty, and Lexington's guns are designed to ensure that they still fit.

"That's not everyone else's fault, George. At some point, the weapons you sell become *your* moral choice. Make the wrong choices, and you deserve extinction."

Calmly, Callister finished his beer, placing the foam-streaked mug to one side. "What's the right choice, Mr. President?"

Kerry leaned forward. "Retrofit your guns—no magazines over ten rounds. At least make it a little harder for a mass murderer to slaughter twenty people. And stop selling bullets designed to eviscerate vital organs."

"Aside from the small matter of an SSA boycott," Callister objected, "you're asking me to change my product line overnight."

"High time. We lose over thirty thousand people each year to guns—a big chunk of those to suicides or accidents. Little kids shouldn't be able to kill themselves by accident; depressed teens shouldn't be able to commit suicide with a parent's gun; that woman you persuaded to buy a gun for self-defense shouldn't be murdered with her own weapon." Kerry paused for emphasis. "We need more than trigger locks. I want your commitment that in five years every Lexington gun will be programmed to respond only to the fingerprint of the owner. Anyone else, and the gun won't fire."

Callister nodded curtly. "You're talking about so-called smart guns," he observed in a more approving tone. "That's where I'd like to go. But they'd have to run on batteries, or computer chips, and withstand repeated firing. Have you ever put a computer chip in an oven? How many times does the battery in your watch die? If it does, are you worried that *you'll* die? But if you need a gun to fire, you *may* die if it doesn't. And if you *do* die, what are the chances your widow sues us for a product defect?

"These concerns are real, Mr. President. The SSA will tell you that your smart gun will never be safe, and that some bad guy with a good old-fashioned American weapon will blow you and your loved ones clean away. The technology just isn't there for us yet."

"You'll get there a lot quicker," Kerry responded evenly, "with a twenty-million-dollar research grant from my administration."

Callister raised his eyebrows. "*That's* part of the deal?"

"There's more. You're worried about a boycott. By law, I can't make promises. But I'm confident you'd be seriously considered to get a much larger share of military weapons purchases, as well as by the FBI, the ATF, and the Secret Service. For what it's worth, all thirteen cities have committed to arm their cops with a greater percentage of guns from whoever signs off first."

Callister emitted a long, silent breath. "You've been busy," he said slowly. "What else are you prepared to offer?"

"A complete settlement of all thirteen lawsuits, for ten million dollars in fees for the plaintiffs' lawyers." Briefly Kerry smiled. "For everyone but *your* lawyers, it's a bargain. You'd spend more on them in a year."

Callister's eyes held an answering amusement. "Any other incentives?"

"Several. While Lexington is transitioning to smart guns, its agreement to limit capacity, ban cop-killer bullets, and plug the gun-show loophole will all minimize future lawsuits. This administration won't sue you either. Between the thirteen settlements, and a whole new customer base, you'll become the envy of your peers." Kerry's tone became cool. "At some point, one or two of them will stop toeing the SSA line. And then we'll break those bastards for good and all. Before they take you with them."

Callister sat back. "In your brave new world, Mr. President, more people will wind up owning more Lexington guns. Is that really what you want?"

Kerry shrugged. "If they're not the wrong people, and their guns are safer, I can live with that."

For a good while, Callister was silent. "You seem to have answers for everything, Mr. President."

"Yes. I want this done."

Thoughtful, Callister adjusted his glasses. "It won't be easy. Even if I think it's worth it, I'd have to persuade our British parent *and* my own board of directors. For that I need total secrecy." He stood, restless. "If this gets out before we're ready, any deal's dead. The SSA would have no choice but to destroy us."

"Any leak on my side," Kerry answered softly, "and the leaker will envy Martin Bresler."

For an instant, Callister stared at him. "I believe you."

"Well, then?"

Silent, Callister gazed at the valley beneath them. There were voices, and then Lara and her family appeared on the trail to the patio, Marie running ahead.

Reaching the patio, she briefly glanced at Callister, then ran up to Kerry. "We're going swimming," she informed him. "Will *you* go?"

"Absolutely." He nodded toward Callister. "Marie, this is Mr. Callister."

Callister smiled. "Hello, Marie."

Managing a faint "hi," Marie sought refuge from her shyness by sitting in Kerry's lap. "Hello," Lara said from behind them.

As Callister turned, Kerry noticed—as he often did—the effect Lara's beauty and self-possession induced in others. When she extended her hand, he took it with a certain deference. "I'm George Callister," he said. "I think I'm supposed to say 'congratulations' to the President, but 'best wishes' to you."

"That sounds about right," Kerry observed. "Or maybe just 'good luck.' "

Lara smiled at Callister. "Thank you," she said and then, in turn, introduced Inez, Mary, and a somewhat subdued Joan Bowden.

Callister greeted them, then allowed that he was needed elsewhere, and that they should enjoy their afternoon. "We intend to," Inez told him. "This is quite an experience."

"For me, as well," Callister answered dryly.

With that, he said goodbye to Lara's family. Kerry walked him to his car, two Secret Service agents trailing at a distance.

"You have a nice family," Callister remarked. "Though I hope they forget they ever saw me here."

From his tone, Kerry inferred that "family" carried great weight with George Callister. "Do you have children?" he asked.

"Two. A boy, seventeen, and a girl, thirteen. And neither one much trouble." Stopping near his car, Callister added, "If it comes out that I was here, think you can get them police protection?"

Though this was offered with a smile, its undertone was

not as jocular. "From some maniac with a gun?" Kerry answered. "It's quite a world we live in, isn't it."

Callister considered this, and then extended his hand. "I'll see what I can do, Mr. President."

NINETEEN

SHORTLY AFTER FIVE on the next afternoon, Kit Pace asked to see the President.

It was a crowded day—a new tax bill; a meeting with civil rights leaders—and a long one: at nine that evening, the President and Lara would sit for a live interview on ABC. Though Kerry waved her to a chair, Kit elected to stand. "The other shoe's dropped," she said bluntly. "Carole Tisone from the *Chronicle* called.

"She's got the whole story—everything on Joan and Bowden, your various conversations with the D.A. . . ."

"Will she run it?" Kerry interrupted.

"Yes." Kit's face and voice betrayed her frustration. "I took her through it all, off the record—protecting Joan's privacy, giving her marriage a chance, letting Bowden work out his problems in peace. When none of that worked, I argued that you and Lara shouldn't be harried for looking out for her sister like any decent family would, especially on the eve of your wedding . . ."

"Oh," Kerry said, "*that* only makes the story more compelling."

"Apparently so—they're running this tomorrow, regardless of what we say. We've got only a few hours to respond. You and Lara will have to decide how and where."

"That's up to Joan, not us. But just for the hell of it, what do you suggest we do?"

"Get it over with, Mr. President." Pausing, Kit sat down. "I know how you feel. But if you say nothing, the story will keep going until we're forced to comment. Just as bad, the story is what the *Chronicle* says it is—intervention by a President in the criminal justice system—rather than what we know it is."

Chin propped on his hand, Kerry allowed himself a moment of depression, contemplating how unfair this was to Joan, and how it might affect her. "We'll talk to her," he said with quiet anger. "But first, get me the publisher of the *Chronicle*. Before they run this, he's going to have to tell me why."

Less than four hours later, Kerry and Lara sat with Taylor Yarborough of ABC in the Library, surrounded by cameras and sound equipment.

It was ten minutes before the interview. Taylor, Lara's friend and former colleague, chatted easily with Kerry and Lara about her children, mutual friends, the oddity of getting married in quite so public a fashion.

"I had my assistant run a search," Taylor told Lara with a smile. "He came up with several thousand articles, twice that many mentions on evening news shows, six television specials, and the covers of all four bridal magazines. There were more items on your mother, niece and sisters than on the conflict between Israel and Palestine, Mahmoud Al Anwar, and nuclear proliferation—combined."

Briefly, Lara gave Kerry a look tinged with worry, then turned back to Taylor. "About my family," she said quietly, "we have a favor to ask."

Drinking vodka and orange juice, John Bowden stared at the screen. He had not eaten, could no longer sleep. The continuous hits of alcohol seemed to surge through his veins, causing the picture to focus, then blur, as though suspended between reality and dream.

The telephone rang. Bowden did not answer. Nor did his machine: after seven messages from Carole Tisone—whoever she was and whatever she wanted—he had switched it off. The "urgent" message from his lawyer could wait; the only "urgent" matter was getting back his family. He stared at the screen, torn between numbness and rage, a sense of loss so deep he could feel it in the pit of his stomach, so profound that only death could relieve his pain.

On the screen, the son of a bitch Kilcannon smiled at Joan's ice queen of a sister, the television prima donna. Her sorority sister—the overpaid bottle blonde—kept up the cheerful patter. "How," she asked the ice queen, "has your family enjoyed getting to know the President?"

Lara took Kilcannon's hand. "They adore him," she said lightly. "But then, who wouldn't?"

Kilcannon smiled. "Should we start with the U.S. Senate?"

Bowden took another swallow of vodka. *Start with me, you little prick.*

The chirping from the screen enraged him now. He stood, staggering, and went to the refrigerator for more vodka. Returning, he stopped to snatch *The Defender* from his pile of gun magazines.

On the screen, no one was smiling.

"The *Chronicle* story is forcing us to talk about a very personal matter," Kilcannon said. "But I honestly don't know who it serves."

Lara touched his hand. "Joan's dealing with the challenges in her marriage," she told the blonde, "in large part thanks to Kerry. But not everyone has a former domestic violence prosecutor in the family to guide them through the legal system. All we can hope for now is that other victims of domestic violence, as well as their abusers, find the help they need . . ."

Bowden stopped, staring at Kerry Kilcannon. The glass trembled in his hand.

Afterward, Kerry and Lara retreated upstairs. "I'm exhausted," she told him. "But I'd better go find Joan."

Kerry unknotted his tie. "You should."

Lara began to remove an earring, then paused, gazing at Kerry. "Was that the best thing for her, I wonder? Because Mary says it's the worst."

"Just the only thing," Kerry said flatly. " 'Best' is to be left alone."

Lara was silent. Sitting on the edge of the bed, Kerry asked, "How did you feel about the rest of it?"

Pausing, she reflected. "I'd give us a B. Sometimes we were a little too Nick and Nora Charles."

"We're not that clever," Kerry assured her with a smile. "And we don't drink nearly enough Scotch."

Smiling, Lara kissed him. "I love you," she said softly. "I just can't wait to move in here. So that we can run away."

The telephone rang. Glancing at the caller ID, Kerry murmured, "Kit," then picked it up.

"What should I know," Kit asked him, "about you and Lexington Arms?"

TWENTY

AT SEVEN the next morning, workers were pitching an enormous canopied tent on the South Lawn. A few feet away, Francesca Thibault described the reception plans to the anchorwoman for *Good Morning America*. Clumps of early-rising tourists, the first wave of thousands, peered at them through the iron fence; Secret Service agents began staking out the perimeters intended to contain the crowds; beyond this, the networks erected platforms for their cameras and crews, vendors began hawking "commemorative" programs with photographs of Kerry and Lara, and the initial phalanx of SSA demonstrators, some wearing military decorations, carried signs protesting the President's supposed plot to confiscate all guns. More Secret Service agents checked into the fifteenth floor of the Hotel Madison, where Lara would spend the night; others completed background checks on hotel employees; still others prepared to occupy the surrounding rooftops. At Dulles Airport, crowded with more tourists drawn to the wedding, police arrested two Egyptians with suspected ties to Al Qaeda and Mahmoud Al Anwar. In the Oval Office—oblivious to all this—President Kerry Kilcannon surveyed the early editions of the *New York Times* and *Washington Post*, spread across his desk with excerpts from the Internet editions of the *San Francisco Chronicle* and other major dailies. Kit and Clayton stood beside him.

With one exception, the clips involved front-page stories regarding Joan and John Bowden, some with photographs of Joan and Marie arriving for the wedding.

The tone of the articles was sympathetic: an account of Joan's domestic troubles; Lara's pleas for her sister's privacy; quotes from Kerry, Jack Halloran and Marcia Harding confirming that the President had done no more than monitor the case, in order to ensure the safety of Joan and Marie. John Bowden had been unavailable for comment. "The stuff about Joan is as good as we could hope for," Kit said in a tentative voice. "And we've scrubbed today's media for Lara's family. Hopefully, it's a one-day story."

Kerry barely heard her. The article beneath the fold in the *Washington Post* read "President in Secret Talks with Gun Company."

The story was crisp and accurate—detailing that Kerry and George Callister had met three times at Camp David; the scope of Kerry's proposal; and Kerry's hopes of engaging other gun manufacturers in a comprehensive settlement. The reporter cited "sources familiar with the negotiation," and noted that both the White House and George Callister had declined to comment. The only quote for attribution was from the president of the SSA, Charles Dane: "We are concerned by reports that one of America's leading gun manufacturers is kowtowing to the most antigun President in our history. America's law-abiding gun owners have a right to know where Lexington stands."

Tight-lipped, Kerry asked, "Where did this come from?"

"Not us," Clayton answered. "No one but the two of us knew Lexington's identity."

"Are we still trying to track down Callister?"

"Yes. His assistant says that he's in conference."

Kerry sat, anger overwhelming his frustration. "Keep trying," he ordered.

*

Head throbbing, John Bowden listened to the saccharine voice of an airline reservationist. "I'm sorry, sir. But that credit card has been declined."

"Wait." Stomach raw, mouth tasting of bile, Bowden snatched his wallet from the nightstand, fumbling for his other credit card. "Try this one," he said, and gave the number.

"Thank you, sir."

He had not paid *this* bill, either. It lay scattered with the others, thrown at the wall in a hallucinatory rage. Sweat glistened on Bowden's forehead; waiting, he knew with a humiliating certainty that the reservationist had recognized his name.

"Thank you, sir," she said again. "Your reservation is confirmed."

"Who knew on your end?" Kerry demanded.

"Our British parent," Callister answered. "Our executive committee. Our general counsel. Until this morning, that was it."

Callister sounded depressed. "What happened this morning?" Kerry asked.

"We've called an emergency meeting of our board of directors, by telephone. It's still going on—I just asked for a five-minute break." Pausing, Callister sounded bemused. "When I got here, there were protesters outside. One old lady saw me, and burst into tears. The rest were so full of hate they could barely speak. Except for the guy who spat in my face.

"I've faced down some angry labor disputes, Mr. President. But I've never felt this level of hysteria and rage."

There was nothing to say; all too well, Kerry could remember confronting a crowd of gun fanatics, his certainty that some would gladly kill him. "Where does your board stand?" he asked.

"I don't know if we can stick, Mr. President. Right now they're focusing on damage control."

"Is there anything I can do?"

"Yes," Callister answered baldly. "Say nothing."

At the San Francisco airport, Bowden waited in the economy class line. He had not eaten; he was no longer drunk, but nauseated. His hand trembled slightly. The one suitcase he held contained his checkbook, a shaving kit, one change of clothes, and his stack of gun magazines.

The line snaked forward slowly, minute after minute, until staring at the neck of the old Chinese woman ahead of him made Bowden want to shoot her.

Kilcannon. Kilcannon and Joan's bitch of a sister had stolen his wife and daughter, cost him his job, his dignity, and any reason to live. And now they had degraded him on national television.

At the newsstand, his name had leapt out at him from the front page of the *Chronicle*: John Bowden, weakling. When at last he reached the desk, he could not look at the woman who asked for his ID.

She looked at his driver's license, then at him—for far too long.

"Thank you, sir," she said.

At four o'clock, after delivering a speech on health care, Kerry returned to the Oval Office and took a call from George Callister.

"This is a lousy wedding present," Callister said without preface. "But I can't go down this road with you, Mr. President."

Kerry slumped in his chair. "So the SSA," he said with muted anger, "is calling the shots for Lexington Arms."

Callister was silent. "It's a lot of things," he responded at length, "that I'm not free to talk about. Suffice it to say that we're putting out a statement, denying any intention to reach an agreement with your administration." Pausing, Callister sounded tired. "Before this, I had my hopes. But the board feels there's no way to deal with you, and assure peace for Lexington Arms."

For a moment, Kerry was silent. "There will be no peace, George. For any of us."

"Maybe so. But I don't expect they'll shoot me now, or drive us out of business. That seems the most we can hope for."

"It's not enough," Kerry said. "Not for me. Not even for you."

On the other end of the line, Callister drew a breath. "I'm sorry, Mr. President. And I enjoyed working with you. I think you're an honest man, and I credit your convictions."

More quietly, Kerry answered, "And I yours."

"Thank you. For whatever it's worth, best wishes for your wedding day, and for married life thereafter."

Kerry thanked him, and got off.

TWENTY-ONE

ON THE MORNING she was to be married, Lara's family came to her hotel suite.

As they arrived, the bearded White House photographer was photographing Lara with three of her bridesmaids—Anna Chen, a colleague from NBC, and her roommates from Stanford, Linda Mendez and Nakesha Hunt—who, collectively, had dubbed themselves "Lara's Rainbow Coalition." "Who'd have thought," Nakesha was saying to Lara, "that you'd be the first to get married?"

Lara smiled. "Not me. But then who'd have thought that I'd be unemployed?"

"Are you *complaining*?" Inez demanded.

Lara gazed up at her mother and saw, beneath the humor, a woman who still worried about her daughter's capacity for happiness. "No, Mom," she said gently, and then looked at the others—Joan, Mary, and Marie, her hair braided, as beautiful in her frilly pink dress as a six-year-old could possibly be. Lara felt her heart fill with love. "All of you look lovely," she told her family. "Before I go and change my life, can I have a few moments with you?"

"Of course," Inez told her. Together, the five Costello women retreated to Lara's bedroom.

Lara kissed Inez on the forehead, and then looked into her face. "I *am* happy," she assured her mother. "I know being married to a President won't be easy. But Kerry's the only man I've ever wanted."

Tears came to her mother's eyes. "I know your father

and I didn't show you much in the way of happiness. I've worried that you . . ."

Gently, Lara placed a finger to her mother's lips. "That was all so long ago, Mom. I have a man who's smart and sensitive and gentle—someone I can relax with, and love, and even lean on if I need to." Hearing herself, Lara, too, felt close to tears. "I'm fine, now. More than fine."

Turning, Lara looked first at Joan. As their eyes met, Lara felt their thoughts converge: on this day of Lara's happiness, Joan's own marriage was a shambles, made public because of the unrelenting light which focused on the man Lara had chosen to love. "I'm so sorry," Lara told her, "for everything we've brought down on you. But, for me, it's wonderful you're here."

For a brief moment, Joan hesitated, then came to Lara and hugged her. "I know you'll be happy," she said. "We'll all be happier, soon."

Lara clung to her for an extra moment, and then kissed Marie and, last, Mary. Silent, Mary gazed into her eyes, and then gave her a brief hug. "I love you," Lara told them, and then paused for the last moment before her very public day began, to take in the faces of those closest to her. "I'm so lucky to have all of you."

The other Costello women smiled at the First Lady–to-be. And then, protected by the Secret Service, they and Lara's friends went to the waiting limousine and drove slowly through the streets, bright with sunshine and thick with well-wishers, some with small children on their shoulders, others waving or calling out to her, on her journey to meet Kerry at St. Mathew's Church.

To John Bowden, Las Vegas was a neon whore, its convention center as soulless as an airplane hangar. An American flag hung from the rafters; beneath it were hundreds of laminated tables and makeshift booths, many with placards advertising weapons, or handmade signs with sentiments such as "Is your church licensed by the federal government?" offering souvenirs, T-shirts, SSA caps and coffee mugs, flak jackets, fishing gear, Nazi paraphernalia, hunting knives, and row upon row of rifles, handguns, ammunition, high-capacity magazines, silencers, flash suppressors, and kits to convert semiautomatic weapons to automatic fire. The floor was jammed with thousands of people—lone men, families, bikers in motorcycle gear—and so many guns that some sellers hawked their wares in the aisle or the lobby, swapping dull metal for wads of cash. Bowden had never been to a gun show before; he experienced the confusing tumult as an assault, a physical force which deflected him from his goal. Then, beside a spacious booth with a sign which said "The Gun Emporium," he spotted a life-size cardboard cutout of Kerry Kilcannon and Lara Costello, dressed for a wedding, with the concentric circles of a target on both their chests.

Bowden approached as if in a trance, his copy of the SSA *Defender* clutched in one hand. With a dissociated smile, he stared at the image of Kilcannon, oblivious to the cacophony surrounding him.

"Can I help you?" someone asked.

Turning, Bowden saw a slender man with slicked-back hair and glasses, palms resting on a table loaded with semiautomatic handguns. Bowden went to the table and, clearing a space for *The Defender*, opened the magazine to the page he had marked with a scrap of newspaper. "I'm looking to buy this."

The man looked at where Bowden's finger rested. "The Lexington Patriot-2. Yeah, we carry the P-2—lots of firepower."

"How much?"

"Good price. Four hundred dollars."

"Show me the gun."

The man reached behind the table and produced a black metal gun about ten inches long. "Concealable," he said. "You can squeeze off ten rounds in split seconds—however fast you can pull the trigger."

Bowden picked up the gun. In his hand, it felt heavy, lethal. His throat was dry; for a long moment, his eyes focused on Lara Costello, and then moved back to the face of Kerry Kilcannon.

You don't know what pain is, you fuck. But you will.

"Do you want it?" the man asked.

Stunned back to the present, Bowden reached for the wallet in the back pocket of his jeans, stuffed with bills from his visit to the check-cashing store which had gouged him for the money he needed. Silent, he peeled off four hundred-dollar bills and slapped them down beside the P-2.

"I'll need ID," the man said.

Bowden's neck twisted to look at him. "Why?"

The man frowned. "We're a federally licensed dealer. We have to certify you're a Nevada resident, and run a background check."

Bowden felt a flush at the back of his neck. "I can't wait that long," he said.

Dressed in a morning coat, Kerry rode with Clayton to St. Mathew's in the Presidential limousine. The streets overflowed with men and women who waved or carried signs expressing their best wishes, including one that said, "We wish you seven children."

"A little excessive," Kerry murmured with a smile. He studied the faces as he passed, warmed by the love and kindness he saw, reminded, again, of the responsibility he bore for the welfare of others, for making their lives better.

There was so much to do, and it was often so much harder than it should be. He had the will; he could only hope he had the wisdom to find a way, to leave the country he loved better for his Presidency.

But not today. Today, supported by his closest friend, Clayton, as well as by Chad Palmer and three old friends from Newark, he would begin his life with Lara.

"In about twenty-seven hours," he told Clayton, "I'll be on Martha's Vineyard. I'll let all this go for a while." Then he turned to the window again, smiling at a little girl who waved from her father's arms.

Clayton watched his friend: the ginger thatch of hair, the quick-flashing smile, the penetrant somewhat brooding eyes which made him such a wonderful photographer's subject, filled with contradictions—to those who loved him, the most charismatic figure since John F. Kennedy; for those who opposed him, or despised him, a ruthless and dangerous man. But the man Clayton knew was driven by compassion; Kerry's anger was reserved for those who, in his mind, kept him from acting on behalf of the people who most needed help. For all the ink spilled, the endless analyses of what drove him, too few people knew Kerry Kilcannon as the man he really was. Now his friend was marrying a woman who did, and for that, knowing how it would lighten Kerry's heart and ease his burden, Clayton Slade was today a happy man.

The man at the table had thick glasses, slicked-back hair, and distrustful eyes which moved constantly in an expressionless face, taking in all that surrounded him. The only items on his table were P-2s and their accessories.

"You a dealer?" Bowden asked.

Fixing on Bowden, the man's restless gaze became a stare. "A collector."

Bowden drew a breath. "How much for a P-2?"

"Five-fifty."

Bowden's hand froze on his wallet. "The Gun Emporium said four hundred."

One corner of the man's mouth moved, less a smile than an expression of contempt. "The Gun Emporium runs background checks."

Bowden felt himself tense. "I don't have time for a background check," he blurted.

The man's stare hardened. To Bowden, his scrutiny felt so intense that he wanted to step back. Then, in a flat voice, the man said, "Neither do I."

Slowly, Bowden counted out the money and laid it on the table. Then he reopened his copy of *The Defender.* "Got these?" Bowden asked.

The man turned the magazine to read it. Beside an advertisement for the gun show was one for Lexington Arms. A photo of the P-2 was captioned "Endangered Species—Banned in California." Below that was the picture of a bullet with grooves carved in its hollow tip, described as "the deadliest handgun bullet available—the ultimate in knockdown capability."

"Eagle's Claw bullets," the man said. "Cost you extra. They're made to rip your guts out."

Bowden flinched at the image of a bullet tearing through his flesh and bone and brain. In an ashen tone, he said, "Do I need those?"

"Only if you want to be sure."

Bowden was silent. And then, still mute, he slowly nodded.

The man glanced around him, eyes restless again. "What about a magazine?"

"What about it?"

Another flicker of the eyes. "I've got the old kind—holds forty rounds. Don't make them anymore."

Bowden picked up the P-2, cradling it in the palms of both hands.

"How much for the magazine?" he asked. His voice was almost a whisper.

At the moment they were married, Kerry gazed into Lara's face.

Her eyes met his, steady and sure. Kerry forgot the cameras, the countless millions who watched around the world. He thought only of this instant: Lara's family; their closest friends; the resonance of Father Joe Donegan's words, making this not just a partnership, but a marriage. There was a smile on Lara's mouth, a deep warmth in her eyes.

Yes, he silently told her. *We've earned this. The past is done.*

"I love you," she whispered.

On the screen, the little prick bent to kiss the ice queen.

Pen in hand, John Bowden watched in the crummy motel room. Next to him on the worn coverlet was a Lexington P-2, a forty-round magazine, and six cartons of Eagle's Claw bullets.

His hand began shaking. As the happy couple receded down the aisle, he picked up a spiral notebook.

He wrote in a fury, scratching out words, replacing them with more words as sharp as knives. By the end tears filled his eyes.

The letter was a commitment, a pact of love and hatred.

Folding the lined paper, he sealed it in the envelope he had already addressed. On the television, his brother-in-law and sister-in-law waved from the steps of the church. When his wife appeared, and then Marie, holding flowers, the cheers from the crowd became a shrieking in his brain.

In agony, Bowden switched off the picture.

Hastily packing his armaments, he left the hotel without paying and drove through the seedy streets until he saw a mailbox. Parking, he flipped open the lid and paused, letter suspended above the box in a final moment of irresolution. Then he dropped the letter into the iron maw and drove to the Las Vegas Airport.

TWENTY-TWO

FOR LARA COSTELLO KILCANNON her wedding day became a blur, beginning with a dash from St. Mathew's to form a receiving line in the East Room. But for Peter Lake the day was a series of freeze-frames, safety measures checked and rechecked. The concentric circles of security stretched as far as the Washington Monument; the area above the White House was a no-fly zone enforced by fixed-wing helicopters. The demonstrators were confined to a discrete area, their bitterness, expressed in slogans like "Mr. and Mrs. Baby-killer" and "Disarm the Secret Service," kept from view of the wedding party. Snipers on the nearby rooftops trained their sights on the South Lawn; others stared out from the roof of the White House at the area surrounding it. The guests showed identification before passing through magnetometers set up at the East Entrance. The White House itself was divided into five zones, each requiring a badge to enter; all five zones were monitored by a command center beneath the West Wing. Peter stood in the sculpture garden near the East Entrance, scanning his surroundings as he monitored security on a cell phone. Today the Kilcannons were as safe as he could make them, and their secrets were safe, as well.

The airport bristled with police and National Guardsmen in combat gear, standing guard against Al Qaeda and Mahmoud Al Anwar. Passing them, John Bowden showed his ticket to a security guard before entering the magnetometers.

Somewhere in the labyrinth conveying baggage was his suitcase filled with weaponry. He had filled out a form describing it precisely; on the way to his destiny, Bowden was in full compliance with the airline's regulations. It was astonishingly simple—now he need only pray that no one who saw the form would recognize his name.

The dignitaries and other guests filed through the reception line, a tableau which, for Kerry, melded moments of warmth and friendship with the more stilted greetings of obligatory invitees.

Nowhere was this more true than among the principals in the Masters nomination. With genuine pleasure, Kerry greeted Chief Justice Caroline Masters, whom he had not seen since her investiture: as regal in appearance as her wit was arid, Caroline allowed that life on the fractious but cloistered court was rather like "The Intifada confined to a monastery." Senator Charles Hampton, the scholarly but tough-minded leader of the Democratic minority, alluded to the corrosive battle, combining his felicitations with hope that the President's honeymoon extended to the Senate. But it was Senator Frank Fasano, the new Republican Majority Leader, who brought the fallout from Caroline's nomination most vividly to mind.

Barely forty, Fasano had ascended after Kerry had engineered the political destruction of his predecessor, Macdonald Gage, for Gage's apparent role in the ruin of Chad Palmer's daughter Kyle. While colleagues in the Senate, Kerry and Fasano had barely spoken: though they were superficially alike—young, ethnic Roman Catholics from a blue-collar background—the forces which backed Frank Fasano, and now hoped to make him President, despised Kerry with a vituperation rare in public life. Beneath his dark good looks and skilled media persona,

Fasano was as deeply conservative on social issues as Kerry was liberal: Fasano's genuine distaste for supporters of choice was, in the President's case, exacerbated by his belief that Kerry had betrayed Catholic teachings on the sanctity of unborn life. Shaking Fasano's hand, Kerry pondered an irony—that by eliminating Macdonald Gage, Kerry had moved up Fasano's timetable for the Presidency, making himself Fasano's target. "Congratulations, Mr. President," Fasano said. "We wish you all the joys of family. As well as the blessings."

The remark could have been a veiled, faintly ironic allusion to Kerry's failed marriage and annulment; or to Fasano's stay-at-home wife, pregnant yet again, and their five well-groomed children; or to Fasano's primacy as an exponent of the traditional family—anything, the President felt sure, save for a straightforward expression of sentiment. Pondering whether a sixth child in nine years might induce psychosis in Bernadette Fasano, tipping the scales toward infanticide, Kerry inquired dryly, "How many 'blessings' does the joy of family involve?"

Fasano flashed his teeth in a smile which managed to convey their differences. "As many as God wishes, Mr. President."

The President returned his smile. "I'll mention that to the First Lady," Kerry assured his putative successor.

John Bowden walked toward the gate without noticing the passengers around him. Somewhere beneath them, his suitcase moved toward its final destination. If they lost it, he could not fulfill his mission.

Stopping at the bar, he ordered one Scotch, then another.

Bowden counted on this now—the cauterizing glow which numbed his misery and narrowed his vision to the task ahead. He lapsed into a fugue state until he envisioned nothing but the agony on Kerry Kilcannon's face. He barely made his flight.

The tent was filled with flowers, food, and a corps of waiters bustling to keep glasses full. At the head table, Kerry watched his best friend rise to propose a toast.

"The *New York Times*," Clayton said with exaggerated self-importance, "once called me the most influential person in the White House." Smiling, he inclined his head to indicate the new First Lady. "Well, folks, welcome to the first day of the rest of my life."

There was an extended ripple of laughter. Joining in, Kerry nonetheless acknowledged the underlying truth—Clayton was still adjusting to the idea of someone as close to Kerry as only a much-loved spouse could be, let alone one as strong-minded as Lara. Beside her husband, Lara Costello Kilcannon gave Clayton her own cheerful smile of acknowledgment.

"When I first met the groom," Clayton continued, "he was a scrappy Irish kid who threw a mean elbow in touch football games—and in the courtroom. I wasn't sure what would come of him." He smiled at his wife, a slender bright-eyed woman, still handsome after twenty-two years of marriage. "But from the beginning, Carlie and I knew that *no one* could be a better friend.

"When you have a friend like Kerry Kilcannon, you wish the very best for him." Turning, he raised his glass to Lara. "Today, in Lara, our wish came true . . ."

The air inside the economy cabin felt unhealthy and chill.

John Bowden began to shiver. He could not ask for a

second Scotch. He knew that his voice would slur, and he did not want the flight attendant to notice him.

Folding his arms for warmth, he closed his eyes. But, as in the last six days, he could not fall asleep.

"In Kerry," Lara told the guests, "my mother and sisters acquired a wonderful source of love and support, and Marie a world-class uncle."

Pausing, her smile encompassed her family. "Of course, it was a little disconcerting to see them think, 'At last—a man so kind, so sensitive, so forebearing, that he can even live with Lara.' Their sense of relief was palpable." Turning to Kerry, she added, "And so was mine."

She paused, her eyes filling with emotion. "All my life I've wanted to succeed. And now I know what true success really is for me—to share my life with you . . ."

"Being engaged while being President," Kerry told the celebrants, "is like being on an extended date with two hundred eighty million chaperones. It's truly a test of love—and ingenuity."

Amidst the laughter, Kerry's expression grew serious. Softly, he said, "I've never thought I was born to be President—that was my brother, James. But thanks to my mother I always knew what love is. So that now I can recognize in Lara the woman I was born to love . . ."

The plane landed with a jolt.

Rising, Bowden forgot his seat belt. It pulled him back; embarrassed, he fumbled with its catch. When he stood, light-headed with alcohol and sleeplessness and days of meals gone uneaten, his self-belief was shriveled.

Like an automaton, he trudged off the plane, following the others to the baggage carousel.

Just before the dancing began in the East Room, the President found a quiet moment with Senator Chad Palmer. Even amidst the babel of celebration, the press of bodies anxious for a word with Kerry, the others left them alone.

"I saw you chatting with Frank Fasano," Chad said dryly. "Weddings bring out the best in us, don't they?"

Kerry smiled. "Frank and I," he said mildly, "try to visit every five years or so. But I expect it will be more often now that he's become your peerless leader. How are things over there?"

"Different," Chad said with a trace of the enduring bitterness he held toward Fasano's predecessor. "Mac Gage was Southern-boy cagey—Machiavelli beneath the smile. But you always knew better than to trust him. This guy's like a Jesuit with a business plan: totally focused, without a single unguarded moment, and much harder to read than Gage. I have no doubt that he deeply loves his wife and children. But to Frank, you and I are less people than corporate competitors, roadblocks to the business plan secreted in the recesses of his mind."

The remark was a reminder, if Kerry needed one, of the price Chad had paid for his own ambitions. "Screw Fasano," Kerry told him. "What I wanted to say is how grateful I am you're here."

Chad's smile of appreciation was tinged with sadness. "When you dance with Allie," he requested, "tell her that. Today was hard for her."

His mouth still sour with alcohol, Bowden waited for his luggage.

The carousel kept spinning. He stared at it as if hypnotized, feet rooted to the tile, fearful of being watched: as bags arrived, and others snatched them, the clump of people around him dwindled. Soon there were only three.

When at last his suitcase appeared, moving slowly toward him, Bowden was as alone as he was in life.

At eleven o'clock, Kerry and Lara Kilcannon began climbing the stairs to the residence.

With their guests gathered at the base, Lara glanced over her shoulder, and then tossed her bridal bouquet over her head.

Turning, she saw it still rising in the air, then, to her surprise, falling in a precipitous drop at the feet of her niece Marie.

As the celebrants laughed, Marie picked it up with the confused, delighted look of a child not quite sure what she has done, but certain that it must be notable. On the stairs, Lara covered her face, laughing; she had meant the bouquet for Mary, who regarded her niece with a fond bemusement which somehow conveyed "Always a bridesmaid . . ." To Marie's mother, Lara called out, "Put those flowers in trust, Joanie. In twenty years or so, Marie can take them out again."

Bowden lay in the motel room, shades drawn, the gun resting on his stomach. In the dark, he checked the time on his iridescent wristwatch.

He did not expect to see this time tomorrow.

In the dark, Kerry held her. Her breasts rested lightly against his chest.

"I feel like we've gotten away with murder," Kerry said.

Lara laughed. "That I get to stay over, you mean?"

"For openers. Doesn't this feel different to you?"

"Yes, actually. But maybe not the way you mean."

"How's that?"

As Lara kissed him, he could feel the smile on her lips. "I'm not worrying about birth control."

With that, the President and First Lady stopped talking altogether.

TWENTY-THREE

"I LIKED IT when you danced with me," Marie informed the President.

Together, Kerry and Lara laughed at an image from the evening before—Kerry in white tie and tails, scooping up a six-year-old in a frilly pink dress for a makeshift waltz. "We'll send you lots of pictures," the President promised.

He had come to see off Lara's family; the motorcade waited at the East Gate, their suitcases already in the trunk. Quickly, Kerry said goodbye to each in turn, Joan last. "Come back soon," he requested. "And, please, call me if there's anything you need. I don't think there's much more I can screw up, and we want to see you two through the rest of this."

Joan kissed him on the cheek, then gazed up at him, her face expressing gratitude, and more. "I still say Lara's lucky," she said, and then trundled Marie into the black limousine.

Saying goodbye to Mary, it struck Kerry that, once more, the youngest was the last in line. "You don't have to wait for the others," he told her. "Part of being single is that you can come see us anytime."

Smiling, Mary said she would, and then Lara squeezed her husband's hand. "Meet you at Andrews," she told him, and Kerry left for his national security briefing.

First, however, he placed a call to the head of the San Francisco security service recommended by Peter Lake. "Have your people meet them at the airport," he requested of Tom Burns. "With all of this publicity, I don't want them bothered."

"Mr. President," Burns answered, "it's as good as done."

Amidst flashing lights and shrieking sirens, the First Lady and her family headed for Dulles Airport.

Eyes narrowing in a mock wince, Inez murmured, "It gives me such a headache." But Marie could hardly contain herself—squirming in her seat belt one way, then the other, she watched the Metro police lead and follow on motorcycles, intersection by intersection, from the E Street Tunnel onto Interstate 66.

"Why do they do that?" Marie asked her aunt. "The sirens and everything."

"To protect us," Lara answered, and then, rather than explain the risks attendant to First Families, she resolved to focus on the intricacies of protection—the leapfrogging of motorcycles, the interplay of police and Secret Service, which kept Marie enthralled until the motorcade reached Dulles.

They proceeded to an empty building in General Aviation, home to private planes, which was easiest for the Secret Service to secure. The airport police were waiting—from here, Peter had explained, the police would escort Lara's family to their gate, putting them on their flight before the other passengers. They had four first-class tickets, a gift from Kerry and Lara.

Lara knelt in front of Marie. "I'm like Kerry," she told her niece. "I absolutely demand that you come back."

Marie looked at her solemnly, then gave her mother a tentative glance. "Do you think we can bring Daddy?" she asked Lara, then looked hastily away. "If he's good to Mommy, I mean. I don't want him to feel bad."

Lara and Joan shared a look of surprise; with a child's

sensitivity to forbidden subjects, Marie had not mentioned her father since arriving. And yet, Lara knew, a child's desire for the archetypal family, a mother and father who loved her and each other, was profound, and the slow death of such a dream created damage of its own. At six, Marie still nurtured the dream, an image of family where her father did not feel the pain *she* felt. Kneeling, Joan put her arms around her daughter. "We'll see," she told Marie. "I want Daddy to feel better, too."

Lara saw the ambiguity of Joan's answer reflected in the child's eyes. But there was little else to say. And so she kissed Marie's forehead and then, standing, hugged her sister. "I'm sorry," Lara told her. "Sometimes I'm a hard sister, I know. But I love you very much."

Joan looked at her steadily. "So do I," she answered, and kissed Lara on the cheek. Suddenly, Lara recalled them sleeping together as children, heads beneath the sheets, whispering so their mother would not hear, innocent of all that would come. Silent, she held her sister close.

But it was nearly time for them to go. Turning to Mary, Lara said, "I meant that bouquet for *you*."

Mary flashed an ironic smile. "You can't manage everything, sis. But Marie's promised I can be her Maid of Honor."

Lara kissed her mother last. *"Go,"* Inez said firmly. "You'll be late for your own honeymoon." But she fought the tears in her eyes.

Lara smiled at this. "I won't," she promised. "You have no idea what a good wife I'm about to be."

In spite of her emotions, this elicited from Inez a look of wry humor. "Oh, I believe you, Lara. You've never failed at anything you wanted."

Tentative, a policeman approached, waiting until Lara acknowledged him with a look. "Ready, Mrs. Kilcannon? We should get your family on the plane."

Lara glanced at her mother. "We're ready," she affirmed. And then her family was off, Inez turning to wave for a final time.

Lara watched them go; her sisters, whom she loved despite all of their differences; the child who would be the first of the next generation of Costello women; the mother who still cared for them all. And then she turned, escorted by two Secret Service agents, and hurried off to continue her life with Kerry Kilcannon.

Four hours later, a little before five, Lara and Kerry walked the beach on Dogfish Bar, trailed at a distance by a skeleton crew of reporters and photographers.

"A honeymoon," Kerry said dryly, "unlike most others."

In truth, Lara knew, it was a bastard compromise—the product of a four-sided dogfight between the First Couple, who wanted a measure of privacy; Peter Lake, who wanted to keep them safe; the media, who wanted images of the Kilcannons for their covers, front pages, and newscasts; and Kerry's political advisors, who considered the honeymoon spun gold, its choreographed "private moments" an invaluable piece of political property. The result was a limited schedule of photo opportunities, interspersed with much longer periods of media banishment, wherein the press scraped for news where there was none. This process had reached a premature apotheosis when CNN had asked Kit Pace for the First Couple's reading list. " 'Reading list,' " Kit had echoed, barely suppressing laughter. "Is that a serious question?"

"What *are* we reading?" Lara asked now.

Kerry took her hand. "I told Kit to say the *Kama Sutra*," he answered. "In all sixteen editions." Nodding toward the cameras, he added, "It helps to have a sense of the absurd."

It did. But Lara knew all too well the dark side of the

press pool watching every move. When Lara had covered Kerry's campaign in California, her peers had openly called it "the death watch"—even on a slow day there lurked, beneath the surface, the prospect that another madman would make history as one had done with Kerry's brother. And it was against this threat that Peter Lake had arrayed a security presence far more elaborate than the press would ever know.

Pausing, Lara surveyed the locus of Peter's challenge. The beach was a mile of white sand and half-buried rocks, stretching toward the final red clay promontory on which the Gay Head lighthouse stood, a deserted spike against the blue sky of early evening. To one side were the blue swells of the Atlantic, bathed in pale sun and tamed by a sandbar on which, at low tide, they could walk a quarter mile out; behind them was a gentle slope of sand and sea grass, at the top of which was the beach house where they stayed, all wood and glass and light. Starting with the house itself, Dogfish Bar was not what Peter would have chosen: there was a half mile of low vegetation beyond the house, and then a ridge of hills, looking down on them, dotted with homes and blanketed with trees which offered cover to intruders. Only the water was at all to Peter's liking: no one but a frogman could approach without being seen, and Peter had frogmen of his own.

They were among the more hidden aspects of Peter's plan. To ward off danger, he had chosen to advertise the area surrounding Dogfish Bar as an armed camp, with roadblocks, choppers, and Coast Guard cutters patrolling a half-mile perimeter. Close residents had been displaced—for exorbitant rents—by Secret Service agents, a medical staff, and the personnel essential to the continuing conduct of the Presidency or, should the worst occur, to confronting an emergency. Yet Peter had done all this, Lara appreciated, without depriving the Kilcannons of the sense that, the media aside, they existed in a cocoon of privacy.

Wearing jeans and cotton sweaters, they faced the ocean, a light breeze cooling their faces. In the distance, a patrol boat, barely audible, left a white skein in its wake. "Are you regretting all this?" Kerry asked.

"Not yet. How long until it's just us and the frogmen?"

"Six o'clock."

Lara glanced at the distant clump of photographers and cameramen, lenses glinting in the sun. Grinning, she said, "Then I suppose we should give them something," and, on tiptoes, kissed her husband for precisely seven seconds.

On the screen, the distant profile of the ice queen met that of the little prick. "The President and Mrs. Kilcannon," the anchorwoman said cheerfully, "have begun their honeymoon on Martha's Vineyard."

In the sterile motel room which he knew to be his final shelter, John Bowden drank from his last bottle of vodka and stared at his photo of Marie. His only food was a Snickers bar; his credit card was maxed out, his bank account overdrawn, and the twenty-one dollars in his wallet all that remained after prepaying for this pea-green nightmare. His life was done, his manhood stolen, his family pried from his grasp. Consciousness was agony, and yet he could not sleep. Not even alcohol could dull the pain which gripped him like a fever.

Only, he thought, the gun lying next to him.

The magazine of the Lexington P-2 held forty hollow-tipped Eagle's Claw bullets. For this he would need only one.

With a deliberation born of alcohol and despair, Bowden placed the P-2 to his temple.

Tears filled his eyes. The lightest pull of the trigger would end his suffering.

Slowly Bowden lowered his eyelids, still gripping the photograph of Marie.

There was a sharp rap on the metal door. Bowden's fingers twitched; quickly, he relaxed his grip on the gun.

"Who is it?" he called out in a trembling voice.

"Housekeeping," a woman's voice shouted.

"Go away."

There was silence. In the stillness, second upon second, Bowden thought of the only action which would make his death seem more than pitiful.

Slowly, he put down the gun, and found the airline schedule in the crevice of his wallet.

"Their plane is late," Lara told her husband. "A mechanical problem."

"Too bad. Whenever, there'll be someone waiting for them."

They sat cross-legged on a blanket tucked in a recess of the sand dune, watching an orange-red sun recede into the ocean. Lara had made them Caesar salad, and Kerry provided the lobster: while Lara had seen far more death than Kerry—though not of anyone close to her—she could not stand dropping lobsters into a boiling pot. Sipping chilled chardonnay, Kerry remarked contentedly, "This is like *The Thomas Crown Affair*."

It's like before, Lara thought. Of the many people surrounding them, only they knew that, four years earlier, Kerry and Lara had come to this house as lovers. It was during those few days, Lara guessed, that she had become pregnant with Kerry's child. But she had never said this to him, not even when he proposed returning. They were making new memories now.

"The version with Faye Dunaway?" Lara asked.

"Uh-huh. And Steve McQueen. They made love on the beach."

Lara smiled. Together, they watched the sun vanish beneath the ocean, leaving striations of orange-streaked clouds in a darkening cobalt sky.

When the Costellos landed at San Francisco International, Marie at last awakened.

As the others slowly gathered their belongings, Joan dabbed the sleep from her daughter's eyes with a moistened cloth. The little girl stretched. "Are we home?"

"Nearly home."

Together, the four Costellos left the plane, reentering a life without the privileges of proximity to Lara. Marie ran ahead on the moving rubber pathway, at times turning to glance back at her mother. Reaching the security gate, she paused, looking back again.

On the other side were cameramen and people with microphones. "Marie," someone called out. But before she could answer, two men in sport coats had swooped down, standing between her and the cameras, and then she felt her mother's hand on her shoulder.

"Marie," the man called again. But Marie had already learned to stare straight ahead. She hoped that his feelings weren't hurt.

Beneath a woolen blanket, Lara gazed at the star-streaked sky, brighter for the absence of city lights. "Do you know the constellations?" she asked.

"No."

"Neither do I. Maybe we can send someone for a book on stars."

That, Lara realized, had become her notion of a major project. Content, she listened to the deep spill of the ocean.

Abruptly, Kerry tensed, touching her arm in warning. Startled, she turned to see him staring ahead of them, quite still.

The skunk, its tail arched distinctively, sniffed at Kerry's feet.

Hostage to its impulses, the two humans watched the animal, afraid to move. At last, the skunk lowered its tail and ambled away.

"Where's Peter," Kerry inquired, "when we really need him?"

TWENTY-FOUR

WITH A PNEUMATIC HISS, the glass door opened for John Bowden.

His coordination was impaired by drink; as he walked, the rows of baggage carousels seemed to magnify, then recede. His mind oscillated between a foggy stupor and a fractured vision of what might come. In the crook of his arm was the box for a girl's pastel Lego set.

It was a little past six o'clock. The baggage area was crowded with passengers awaiting luggage; the digital sign above the carousel nearest Bowden listed three incoming flights. As he approached it, a middle-aged blonde woman saw the Lego set he carried, and smiled at him.

Ignoring her, Bowden read the sign. Boston, New York, Miami.

He moved on, more quickly now. He could feel anger pulsing in his temple, imagine the release of pain which would come with each pull of the trigger. Above carousel three the sign flashed "Flight 88–Washington/Dulles–IN."

Abruptly, Bowden stopped.

The first trickle of passengers began to gather at the empty carousel. To the side, Bowden began to pace.

The crowd thickened, surrounding the metal oval. A sheen of sweat dampened Bowden's forehead. He paced now in concentric circles, agitated, eyes darting as he scanned the new arrivals.

Still they did not come.

His skin felt clammy now. The heat of alcohol cooled into a numbness against which the compulsive pacing became his only weapon. His T-shirt was rancid with sweat; depression seeped through him like nightfall.

The carousel was still. At the edge of his consciousness, a woman's voice announced, "The baggage for Flight 88 from Washington-Dulles now will be arriving at carousel five . . ."

Bowden began moving.

Marie was glad her mommy had taken her to the bathroom.

The baggage was taking too long. Holding her grand-mother's hand, she waited for her bright-flowered suitcase, wondering how grown-ups could keep watching a rubber belt turning with nothing on it.

Amidst the crowd, her family formed a small group with the two security guards who had met them. This nearness to those she loved—her grandmother's hand, her head against her mother's waist, the sound of her mother talking quietly to Mary—made Marie feel warm and secure. Doll hugged to her chest, she peeked out at the men with cameras.

Her mother had refused to talk to them; her aunt and grandmother would not either. Although she did not know why, her mother seemed to fear these strangers. She looked away, and then peered out again.

Daddy.

He was carrying a box with pink ribbons wrapped around it. Startled, Marie glanced up at her mother.

Daddy had come to meet her with a present. But her mother did not see him.

Her daddy saw her now.

Tentative, she raised her arm, a tiny wave to say she saw him, too.

Bowden sank to his knees, eyes fixed on Marie. As her mouth formed words he could not hear, her mother turned toward him.

Fumbling, he opened the box.

As he slung it over his shoulder, the gun felt heavy, solid. The movement around him slowed, and then his eyes met Joan's.

First, she would watch the others die.

Gun at his hip, Bowden aimed at Inez Costello.

"No," his wife cried out.

Inez turned, startled at the anguish in her daughter's voice. Bowden pulled the trigger.

A red stain appeared from the shredded flesh of Inez Costello's throat.

Bowden froze, stunned at his power. Joan's screams filled the air; one of the guards reached inside his shirt. A gentle pull of the trigger launched him backward. In a split second Bowden sprayed three more bullets. A blonde girl slumped, then the second guard. Passengers dove to the floor.

There was no one in front of Joan.

An unearthly calm came over him. First she would watch her sister die, feel the weight of all she had done to him.

On her hands and knees, Mary scrambled onto the metal slope of the baggage carousel.

Shrieks of panic echoed behind her. As she crawled toward the mouth of the baggage tunnel, a bullet exploded the suitcase beside her.

Frenzied, she reached the opening, pushing aside the luggage it expelled. Another bullet smashed the rubber flaps across it, then two more. In a panic, Mary scrambled inside.

The belt kept carrying her backward. Twisting to face forward, she pushed against its momentum with the palms of both hands, the baggage piled behind her shoving at her feet. Through the swinging flaps she saw John Bowden aim the gun.

Alarms began shrieking. The sound made Bowden's finger twitch.

A bullet parted the rubber flap near Mary's face.

To both sides of the carousel people ran or fell flat on the tile, hands covering their faces or curled like fetuses. Now each movement was too fast for him.

Panicking, he turned to aim at Joan.

She clutched Marie, gaping in terror and disbelief. Her daughter's face pressed against her leg. At their feet her mother lay in a spreading pool of blood.

"John," she cried out, and then the bullet shattered her jaw.

Marie fell with her mother, looking into her ruined face. She turned away, eyes shut, doll clutched to her chest.

Her father stared at her, gun frozen. His eyes were still and wide.

"Stop!" a man's voice shouted.

Bowden flinched. In an involuntary reflex, the gun jerked in his hand.

"No . . . ," he cried out.

Marie's doll shattered in china pieces.

*

Desperate, Mary struggled to fight the moving belt. As her head cleared the rubber flaps she heard Bowden's wail of grief.

"Marie . . ."

Staring in horror at something Mary could not see, Bowden placed the gun to his temple.

There was a short, percussive pop, a spume of red. Bowden crumpled.

As Mary's arms went slack, the conveyor belt expelled her with the luggage. Turning facefirst on the carousel, she passed Marie.

Mary began sobbing.

With a shudder, the belt stopped moving. In the terrible silence, Mary slowly raised her head.

Around her, passengers wept, some prone, others rising to their knees. A woman, staggering past, chattered like a monkey. Police stood over Bowden's body. Near Marie a paramedic felt Inez's wrist. Beside them, Joan stared emptily at Mary. A burly man with a Minicam bent over them, filming.

Dropping Inez Costello's wrist, the paramedic turned to Marie.

The child lay on her back, chest stained with blood. The paramedic touched her wrist. "Bring a stretcher," she called out. "This one's still alive."

Entering the baggage area, Inspector Charles Monk passed a team of paramedics hurrying a dark-haired child to an ambulance.

It was rush hour. There was no heliport at SF General; the sheriff would have to block Highway 101, freezing traffic so that the ambulance could weave its way to the emergency room. Fifteen minutes, at least. Perhaps a lifetime.

Stopping, Monk surveyed the crime scene.

There were at least six dead—a slender woman of middle age; a plump woman of perhaps thirty; a blonde teenager sprawled backward on the carousel, arms akimbo; two clean-cut men in identical sport coats, one white, the other Hispanic; and, perhaps forty feet away, a skinny man in a T-shirt lying beside a spatter of his blood and brains.

Nearby was the empty box of a child's Lego set. A Lexington P-2 lay beneath his outflung arm.

Can't accomplish all this with a knife, Monk thought.

The scene was quieter now. The emergency response team had done its work: the baggage area was sealed; the media cordoned off; crime scene investigators sifted through the debris; the police were interviewing witnesses. A cop sat with a young woman, slumped in a chair near the entrance, eyes dull with shock.

Kneeling in front of her, Monk felt his weight, his age, the throb in his damaged knee. "What happened here?" he asked.

She could not form an answer. "This is the President's family," the cop said softly. "The shooter was his brother-in-law."

TWENTY-FIVE

DR. CALLIE HINES was staring at her office wall when the beeper went off.

She had just finished patching up a sixteen-year-old Asian kid with an abdominal knife wound—unusual in Callie's experience, which featured gunshot wounds at the rate of one a day. But this was the rhythm of an emergency room surgeon: crazy energy, stasis, then a beeper. She snatched it out of her pocket.

It was a nine hundred call; whoever they were bringing in was at risk of dying. Rising from her chair, Callie walked briskly to the elevator, a lean black woman with a model's figure, a smooth lineless face, and cool seen-it-all eyes. She had just reached the emergency room area when her cell phone rang.

This was the paramedic team. There had been a mass shooting at SFO; glancing at her watch, Callie envisioned Highway 101 at rush hour. In the background, she could hear the piercing whine of sirens. "Who's the patient?" Callie asked.

"A six-year-old girl." The woman's voice was taut. "It's a Room One case."

Inwardly, Callie winced. Gunshot wounds for teens were common, but not a child this small; Operating Room One was reserved for patients at death's door. "What kind of wound?" she asked.

"Abdominal. Her blood pressure's low—we intubated her, applied pressure to the wound, and started an IV."

"Is she conscious?"

"Yes." A slight pause. "This one's a VIP."

The remark was unusual—the ER was not a status-conscious place. "A VIP six-year-old?" Callie asked.

"It's Lara Kilcannon's niece. Her mother and one sister died at the scene."

Callie prided herself on nervelessness; now she drew a breath, calling on her reserves of calm. "I'll be waiting," she said.

"Mr. President."

Turning, Kerry saw a shadow walking quickly through the sea grass, backlit by the waxing moon above the sand dunes. "Mr. President," Peter Lake repeated, more softly now.

Something had happened, Kerry thought; perhaps they had found Al Anwar. He felt Lara's hand clasp his.

Peter knelt. In the darkness, Lara tensed: though he had called out to Kerry, Peter was looking at her.

"I have bad news." Peter's face was bleak, his voice hesitant and strained. "There's been a shooting at SFO. Your mother and Joan are dead."

"No . . ." For an instant Lara could not see; Kerry's grip tightened, as if to pull her back from some abyss.

"What about Mary?" she asked. "And Marie?"

Her voice sounded calm, as though someone else had posed the question. "Mary's all right," Peter answered, then glanced at Kerry. "But Marie was wounded. They're taking her to SF General."

Kerry pulled Lara close. Resistant, she twisted her face toward Peter. "Was it John?"

"Yes."

Lara felt her stomach knot, heard the thickness in Kerry's voice. "Get me the hospital," he demanded.

Callie Hines stood near the slick whiteboard, watching a resident enter the name of new patients in Magic Marker. In the last few minutes, she had seen a parade worthy of a Brueghel painting: two prisoners in manacles; a homeless black man with pneumonia; a twenty-year-old Hispanic woman with AIDS, overdosed on heroin; a bipolar white man, HIV positive, who had slashed his wrists; a cocaine addict pregnant with her fourth child, her left arm amputated.

This intake, though heavy, was lighter than in winter— with the chilly rains, the homeless would seek refuge in the waiting room or, in desperation, attempt to hide in the tunnels beneath the hospital. This was no place, Callie thought once more, for those who would close their eyes to pathology and poverty, hopelessness passed down from one generation to the next.

The ambulance bay burst open.

On the gurney lay a small dark-haired girl with tubes in her nose and throat. She was conscious: her eyes were wide with shock—not simply to her body, Callie thought, but to her spirit, her sense of what the world was.

Callie rushed with her to the trauma room.

Mary Costello could not think or feel. Her only focus was Marie.

Two cops in a squad car sped her to the hospital. At the door of the emergency ward one of them punched numbered buttons on a panel; the door swung open, and a plump black woman took her to a sterile room with a telephone and pastoral pictures on otherwise bare walls. Mary felt claustrophobic.

"I need to see her," Mary said.

The social worker took her hand. "She's already in the trauma room. The prognosis isn't good. They'll have to operate as soon as possible . . ."

"I *know* that. That's why I have to be there."

The woman appraised her. "Will you be okay?" she asked.

"Not if I stay here."

The woman nodded. "All right," she said, and led Mary to the trauma room.

Marie lay on a gurney. She was surrounded by men and women in purple scrubs or white jackets, all wearing masks and leaded aprons; two cylindrical lamps and an X-ray machine extended toward her from the ceiling; a screen monitored her heartbeat. A blonde woman doctor directed the activity; to the side, a handsome, somewhat imperious black woman watched with folded arms.

Marie's bloody clothes were in a paper bag beside the gurney. An anesthesiologist stood at her head, administering oxygen. Marie moaned softly. "I'll get the morphine," someone said.

Stunned, Mary tried to absorb this. A young doctor in glasses turned to her. "You the aunt?" he asked.

"Yes."

"Do you know who her doctor is, or whether she's taking any medication?"

Helpless, Mary shook her head.

"What about allergies?"

"I don't know."

He turned away. Beneath the calm, Mary felt the pulse

of urgency. "How much blood out?" the blonde doctor asked.

"About two in the tube, and two on the sheets. Maybe four hundred cc's—half the blood in her body."

A beeper went off. "Her pressure's dropping," someone said.

Marie's moaning ceased. An X ray appeared on the screen; to Mary, the white stain at its center looked like a starburst. The black woman studied it, eyes narrowing.

Turning, she ordered, "Get her to the OR—now."

Marie's eyes closed.

They hurried her to an elevator, the black doctor at her side. Mary and the social worker followed.

"She's crashing," someone said.

In the silence of the elevator, Mary looked into her niece's face, pale and still.

"Can I hold her hand?" Mary asked. When no one answered, she took the child's hand, cool to the touch.

The elevator rose two floors, then opened into a room with a long desk and steel doors marked "Room One." Slowly, Mary let Marie's fingers slip from hers.

The social worker took her arm. "I'm afraid this is as far as we can go."

Three nurses rushed the gurney inside the room, the black doctor following. Tears blurred Mary's vision. Blinking, she focused on the dark crown of Marie's head, and then the doors closed behind her.

In the dim-lit great room, Kerry gripped the telephone, watching Lara through the open door of the bedroom as she listened on another phone. Her face was pale, intent. To Kerry, the telephone was Lara's lifeline, Marie's struggle all that kept the grief and horror from crashing down on her.

"They're about to operate," the hospital director said. "All that I can tell you, Mr. President, is that Callie Hines is as good as they get."

In the bedroom, Lara's eyes closed, as if in a prayer. "As soon as you know," Kerry responded, "call us."

Struggling into her operating gown, Callie recalled the shooting of Kerry Kilcannon—cops surrounding the hospital; press jammed in the media room; the mayor of San Francisco hovering near Room One. It would happen again now. But Room One was empty and clean, a haven from chaos.

Marie lay on the table with her arms outflung. At her head three anesthesiologists administered a paralytic agent, a sedative, and a narcotic. A team of nurses ran blood to the OR. Another kept Marie's legs covered to fight the loss of body heat. The chief surgical resident, another resident and an intern watched Callie open an incision beneath the child's nipples. Perspiration began beading on her forehead—at Callie's orders, the temperature was cranked up to eighty, another measure against hypothermia. Their speech was clipped; their movements controlled. Soon they would sweat like athletes.

Callie's second cut went from the first incision to the pubis. As the head nurse inserted a retractor, dark blue blood of a hematoma erupted from Marie's abdomen.

"Clamp the aorta," Callie ordered.

The resident inserted a rib spreader, then cross-clamped the aorta to stop the flow of blood. Two others tried to staunch the bleeding with surgical packs so that Callie could do her work; a third began massaging the child's heart. Wearing double gloves, Callie searched for the bullet with a rubber tip extractor; the X ray had told her that to extract *this* bullet with her fingers might slash her tendons.

Callie found the bullet. Carefully, she removed it from amidst the roiling blood. Its tip had exploded into six metal shards, the pattern of a flower. Callie was tight-lipped with anger.

"Eagle's Claw," she said.

"What's that?" the intern asked.

"Quadruple the mortality rate." She had no time to explain that the shards ripped through vital organs like a buzz saw; that their jagged edges had ended surgical careers; that a shredded vena cava could be inoperable; that her chances of saving this child had slipped from probable to long; that the Eagle's Claw, in the words of her first mentor, was "God-awful," absolutely demoralizing to a surgeon; that the quiet which had descended at the name "Eagle's Claw" meant that only the young intern did not know this. "She's at 95 degrees," the head nurse said.

Racing against time, Callie searched for the wound.

On the telephone, Mary was sobbing. "I know," Lara said brokenly. "I know. But maybe they can save Marie."

She heard her sister struggle for control. "I'll adopt her . . ."

"I know you will. You'd be so good with her."

A ragged cry escaped. Grasping for hope, Lara said, "It's where they saved Kerry."

She felt his hand on her shoulder. Abruptly, her sister burst out. "You two made him so angry . . ."

The vena cava was shredded. Instead of a single clean rupture, there were three. Blood spurted from their ratty strands. The child's face was pale and still.

"No clotting," the chief resident said. "Temperature's at 94.5."

There was no time left to operate—Marie would die from hemorrhagic shock before Callie could suture the shredded vein. Sweat rolled down her face.

"Damage control," Callie snapped. Her last hope was to stop the bleeding, prop up the child's body temperature and hope the veins would begin to clot, so that tomorrow she could try to repair the wound. The head nurse pressed a plunger against the vena cava; two more nurses packed the shredded area with surgical pads; another placed a defibrillator on the child's heart, to shock it into action. Callie closed the flap of Marie's abdomen with towel clips. The child's lips fluttered.

"Ninety three degrees," the chief resident said urgently. "Her blood pressure's in free fall . . ."

Callie began to massage the child's heart. The only sound was the whirl of the ventilator.

Ten minutes later, leaving Room One, Callie Hines noticed the drops of blood on her shoes.

Cops ringed the OR. The hospital administrator and the mayor stood by the door. Callie stared at the mayor. "Get him out of here," she told her boss. "Then get me a telephone."

At eleven-oh-five, the telephone rang in Martha's Vineyard. In the living room, Kerry picked up first.

"Mr. President?" The voice was measured. "This is Callie Hines."

From the couch, Lara watched Kerry's face. "How is she?" Kerry asked.

"I'm very sorry," Hines answered softly. "But the wound

simply wasn't survivable. All that I can offer you is that she felt no pain."

A numbness passed through Kerry. Gazing at Lara, he slowly shook his head. She doubled over, hands covering her face, emitting a cry of agony which made him shudder.

"The bullet was an Eagle's Claw," Hines told him. "In a child that small . . ."

PART TWO

THE REFUSAL

Labor Day to mid-September

ONE

AT FIVE the next morning, Clayton was at the White House, preparing to move the Presidency to San Francisco. The C-130 had landed in Martha's Vineyard; Air Force One awaited at Logan Airport in Boston. The President and First Lady would stay at a private home in Pacific Heights, joined by the Secret Service, the White House physician, the military aide in charge of the codes for responding to a nuclear attack, and a small support staff headed by Clayton himself. Closer to the time of the funerals, Kit would arrive. The President's schedule would be limited to his daily national security briefing; to protect the First Family's private time, all other communications would go through Clayton.

Shortly after eight o'clock, Clayton stopped to watch CNN.

On a glistening day on Martha's Vineyard, Lara and Kerry walked across the tarmac toward their plane. Lara wore dark glasses. Exhausted, she leaned against Kerry who, to Clayton's eyes, looked weary and tormented. The clothes they wore—Kerry's windbreaker and polo shirt, Lara's summer dress—were a sad reminder that this once had been their honeymoon. Only Clayton had talked with them. Only Clayton knew of the President's haunting request—that all files of his dealings with Joan Bowden and her husband be shipped to San Francisco.

The President and First Lady, the anchorwoman said, *will fly to Andrews Air Force Base to commence the long, sad journey to California—where, thirteen years ago, Senator James Kilcannon was murdered by an assassin.*

President and Mrs. Kilcannon were first informed of the tragedy at around nine-thirty yesterday evening, and since then have been in seclusion. At seven this morning White House Press Secretary Kit Pace issued the following statement:

"The President and First Lady wish to express their heartfelt thanks for the thoughts and prayers of the American people at this time of deep anguish for their family, and for the three other families who lost loved ones in this senseless tragedy. In order to accompany the First Lady to San Francisco, the President has canceled his schedule for the next several days. He intends to remain in San Francisco with Mrs. Kilcannon and her surviving sister until after the interment of her mother, sister, and niece. No statement from the President or First Lady is forthcoming at this time."

On the screen, Kerry and Lara climbed the metal stairs to the C-130, Kerry's arm lightly resting on her waist. Even now, Clayton reflected, Kerry's instincts remained sound: this tableau of grief required no words from him. To the public that might seem a decision made by default, reflecting a President too shaken to express his emotions. This was partly true; speaking to Clayton, Kerry had seemed disjointed, his sentences trailing off into fragments. But then Clayton—because he must—had called to tell him that Mahmoud Al Anwar had just been killed in a cave in the Sudan. "At least they're ninety percent sure," Clayton explained. "The face is unrecognizable. But everything else, including height, says it's him."

There was a long silence. "Who knows?" Kerry had asked.

"A tight chain. Our people on the ground, General Webb, and the Secretary of Defense."

"Tell them to sit on it until after the funeral," the President had ordered coldly. "Any way you can. I don't want anyone thinking about anything but this."

As Clayton watched, Kerry and Lara vanished inside the plane. *In Washington,* the anchorwoman said, *sentiment is already growing that these shocking murders may change the terms of the gun control debate, feeding demands for the tougher gun laws which President Kilcannon has so urgently called for . . .*

"We need to put out a statement," Charles Dane began. "And then we need a strategy."

The president of the Sons of the Second Amendment sat in the conference room of the four-story glass building on K Street, one symbol of its power. To either side of him, the Legislative Director, Carla Fell, and the Communications Director, Bill Campton, drank coffee from SSA mugs. Fell was a petite strawberry blonde, Campton cherubic and sincere; part of their duties was to soften the SSA's public face, and Dane had never needed them more than now. The sheer volatility of the moment complicated the fixed imperatives of Dane's world—maintaining the SSA's daunting image of power; raising the money needed to fuel it; pleasing a board of true believers so alarmist that nothing put their minds at ease—and added a new one: ensuring that the murders changed nothing.

Putting down his mug, Campton began reading from a typed page with interlineations in red pen. " 'Our sympathy goes out to the victims of the massacre at SFO. The President and First Lady are in the prayers of all decent, law-abiding Americans, including the over four million responsible gun owners who constitute our membership . . .' "

"Cross out 'massacre.' " Lean, dark-haired and saturnine, Dane spoke in a resonant, commanding baritone which, even when muted, sounded as though it could fill a hall. "It sounds like melodrama from some bad military history—the kind of portentous pap liberals think we stay up nights to read."

With a sheepish smile, Campton inserted "tragedy" for "massacre," and then continued: " 'We hope this terrible loss of life will engender a common commitment from all spectrums of our society to reduce gun violence by enforcing existing law. What is needed is not more laws, but a new resolve to punish lawbreakers who misuse guns to commit a crime . . .' "

"The problem," Fell broke in, "is that *this* guy's already punished himself."

Dane turned to her. "Then the law should have punished him first. Bowden was a wife-beater—the Kilcannons said so on live TV. If they'd locked him up, no one would have died."

"Do we know where he got his gun?" Fell asked. "Or who made it?"

"Not yet. Pray that it's foreign-made, and that Bowden bought it on the street." Dane turned to Campton. "Look for some gun law on the books that Bowden violated. There's always something."

Nodding, Campton returned to his draft. " 'We must never diminish the constitutional right of all Americans to self-defense . . .' "

"Careful how you phrase that," Dane instructed. "We can't be heard as saying the First Lady's mother should have been better armed."

As Campton made corrections, Dane turned to Carla Fell. "What about Congress?" he inquired.

"The problems are worst in the Senate," Fell answered. "We've got four or five wobbly Republicans, like Palmer." Pausing, she took a last quick swallow of coffee. "If I know Kilcannon, he's already calculating how to use this. He's as cold-blooded a politician as ever passed through

Washington. His former colleagues may not all love him, but he scares the hell out of most of them."

"So do we," Dane answered. "We can't let them forget that."

The telephone rang. "Speaking of which," Fell informed the others, "that's our conference call with Frank Fasano."

Dane pushed the button for the speakerphone. "Charles?" Fasano began.

"Good morning, Frank," Dane said to the Senate Majority Leader. "If you can call it that under the circumstances. This is a tragedy, *and* a threat to gun rights."

"I'll be making a statement shortly, saying just that. Except the part about the threat." Fasano's voice was sober. "Imagine losing most of your family. I feel for them—her especially."

"Kilcannon will want more laws," Dane responded. "He'll use her to get them."

Fasano was silent. "He may well succeed," he said at length. "Before he does, we should consider whether there's something symbolic we can give him."

It was time, Dane decided, to be blunt. "We expect you to stand firm, Frank. We've spent a lot of time and money keeping you in the majority."

"I haven't forgotten," Fasano answered with equal directness. "But let me give *you* some advice—disappear. This is the President's moment: he can say whatever he wants, but *you* can't be seen as playing politics with the First Lady's misery. Lie low, Charles—your moment will come in time."

"How long?"

"Kilcannon can't move too fast—it would look unseemly, like he's exploiting his wife's dead relatives. I control the Senate agenda, so I can string this out. The more time passes, the more passions will cool."

"What about Chuck Hampton?" Carla Fell inquired.

"The Democrats have problems, too," Fasano answered crisply. "If some of Hampton's people never have to vote on a gun bill again, they'd bow and kiss his feet. Or mine."

Glancing at Fell, Dane slowly shook his head. "Kilcannon may not let them off the hook," he said. "The folks who say all liberals are wimps forget to account for *him*."

Over the speaker box, Fasano's laugh was low and humorless. "That's how I got my job—the last one to get in Kerry Kilcannon's way was Macdonald Gage. In twenty-four hours Mac went from the third most powerful man in America to a walking corpse. It took him almost that long to fathom he was already dead." Softly, Fasano finished, "Don't worry, Charles. My reflexes are sharper."

With that, Fasano got off.

In the kitchen of his Vermont farm, Senator Minority Leader Chuck Hampton ate bacon and eggs and monitored MSNBC. As he finished, the picture became a live shot of Kerry and Lara Kilcannon boarding Air Force One.

The President and First Lady are expected to arrive in California at twelve-seventeen, Pacific Daylight Time . . .

As always, Hampton reflected, Air Force One was an icon of speed and power, a symbol of Presidential authority. The White House Military Office planned each flight to the minute, and its arrival never failed to create a sense of occasion. But he could not easily imagine the nature of this flight. It triggered a series of memories which had begun when Hampton was twelve: the flight from Dallas, when Jacqueline Kennedy, her coat stained with blood, accompanied her husband's body; the terrible majesty, five years later, of the funeral train for Robert Kennedy; the day, one year after Hampton entered the Senate, when the Presidential campaign of James Kilcannon ended with a funeral watched by millions.

On this day, Chuck Hampton felt more depressed than at any time in his public life. And, perhaps, more worried. It was too soon to contact Kerry Kilcannon, either to convey his condolences or his concerns. But soon enough to call Senator Vic Coletti of Connecticut—as Kerry Kilcannon once remarked, for Vic Coletti, politics, like rust, never sleeps.

"What are you going to do?" Coletti asked.

Hampton gazed out the window at the green fields behind his farmhouse. "Express sympathy, of course. Just watching this has made me sick."

"What about substance?"

"A general statement—that we need to do more to stop gun violence. But I don't know exactly how this happened, and I can't get ahead of our members."

"I wouldn't," Coletti said soberly. "I've already talked to five. They feel terrible for the President and Lara, of course. But we've been making points on the stuff ordinary citizens care about most—health care, education, jobs. They don't want this shooting to swallow our agenda whole."

"And you?"

Coletti hesitated. "I don't mean to sound callous, Chuck. But, politically, I don't think we need this."

Listening, Hampton heard what Coletti did not say expressly: that Connecticut was the home of several gun companies—including Lexington Arms, vulnerable to SSA pressure after its meetings with Kerry Kilcannon. "What about your gun industry?" Hampton asked.

"I don't care about the guns. I care about the jobs. The people who hold them tend to vote." Coletti's tone became admonitory. "It's not just me—you'll hear this from our members in the South and Rocky Mountain states. The SSA's like the Communist Party—deviate from the party line, and they put you against the wall and shoot you."

"Our pro-gun control members," Hampton countered, "will want to strike while this is hot."

"Well, that's a problem, isn't it. Remember how you got your job-Carter Grace forgot he was from Tennessee, and came out in support of gun control and Kerry Kilcannon. The voters called him home."

Hampton frowned. "Tell me about it—whenever I want to discourage the President from charging ahead on this, I always mention Carter. But this could change things."

"He'll do *something*," Coletti mused.

"Well," Hampton agreed, "he pretty much has to now, whether he wants to or not. But the problem is he'll want to. The only question is what."

For a moment, Vic Coletti was quiet. "Depending on the answer," he warned his leader, "there'll be hell to pay in the Senate. And in both our lives."

TWO

SEALED INSIDE Air Force One, Kerry and Lara passed over the heartland of America.

In the first months of his Presidency, Kerry had taken pleasure in being master of this plane—taller than a five-story building and at least a city block long, with a conference room, commodious kitchen, and generous seating area—even as its operating room, arsenal of weapons, and antimissile devices reminded him of the grimmer aspects of his job. But now the quiet of his living quarters seemed eerie, its sleek modern decor sterile and depressing.

Lara slumped on the couch, arms clasped as if hugging herself, gazing emptily at nothing. Her eyes were bruised with sleeplessness, a night of sobbing so anguished and attenuated that, for now, she had no more left to give. "All that protection," she said quietly.

This, Kerry supposed, referred to the security ringing Andrews as they had departed, a terrible contrast to the meagerness of their provisions for her family. Kerry had no answer.

Someday you'll go too far, he had told John Bowden. *And then, trust me, you'll be the one who suffers most.*

His own demons had drawn him into Joan Bowden's life, perhaps driven her husband to the edge. If so, he had led her to her death, taking Inez and Marie with her. Perhaps it was a mercy that he would never know for sure.

He reached for Lara's hand—to give comfort or, he

acknowledged bleakly, to receive it. Her fingers were lifeless in his.

Lara barely felt his touch.

She had entrusted her family to-Kerry, and then lost
them to the Presidency, the merciless glare that had left
Joan's family with no private place to heal. They had been
hers to protect, and now Kerry's failure was hers.

"We sacrificed them," she said in a toneless voice. "To
the media, to the needs of the Presidency . . ."

Kerry turned to her, his expression miserable and imploring. "All we wanted was to have them at our wedding . . ."

"No," she interrupted softly. "It was never *our* wedding."

Even in his devastation, Kerry knew it was better to be
silent.

"Mary," Lara said at length. "However *I* feel . . ." Her
voice faded. "As soon as we get there, I want to see her.
Before anything else."

"I'll make sure of it," Kerry answered. And then he realized how ironic and how empty, coming from him, those
words must sound to her.

It was shortly before two p.m., Eastern Daylight Time,
when the first tapes of the murder appeared.

Clayton was about to leave the White House when Kit
came to his office, grim-faced. "Turn on Fox News," she
said simply.

He did that.

On the screen, Inez, Joan, Mary and Marie clustered
near the baggage carousels. *"Jesus,"* Clayton murmured.

There was one soft pop. Inez Costello fell, blood

spurting from her throat. Then there was chaos: the camera jerking; Mary crawling; a body spinning on the carousel; Joan's face; Marie's doll clutched to her chest, eyes frozen in fathomless horror.

"Stop . . ." someone yelled.

The doll shattered. The sheer force of the bullet knocked the child off her feet.

Marie . . . , a man's voice cried in anguish, and then the film went dark.

This remarkable footage, the anchorman said soberly, *was taken by a cameraman from our San Francisco affiliate. Only after a great deal of soul-searching did we conclude that it so illuminated the tragedy of domestic violence that the American public must see it for themselves . . .*

"Ghouls," Kit said tightly. "Now they're the king of cable news."

It would be the centerpiece of the frenzy, Clayton knew, played endlessly until the funeral. And it would follow Kerry and Lara to the end of their days. More than ever, Clayton felt in his bones the pitiless nature of the Presidency.

"They'll run it again," he told Kit. "Make me a copy."

Shortly after noon, in San Francisco, Air Force One landed at SFO.

The first to disembark was the Air Force colonel who carried the briefcase with the response codes for a nuclear attack. As he passed it to the Army counterpart who shadowed Kerry on the ground, Peter Lake emerged, then others from the Secret Service. All air traffic had stopped; a caravan of police and Secret Service agents again waited on the tarmac.

The President and First Lady were the last to disembark. Lara stopped at the foot of the stairs, as if searching for the place where her family had died. A young White House aide, dispatched the night before by Clayton, approached Kerry with a cell phone and the pained expression of a man who wished to be anywhere but this.

"Mr. President," he said. "The Chief of Staff is calling."

Clayton, Kerry guessed, was on a military aircraft headed for California. Taking the phone, he asked, "What is it?"

"There's a tape of the murders," Clayton said bluntly. "You'll want to make sure Lara doesn't watch TV."

Kerry's headache pounded from his temples to the back of his head. "Or read newspapers?"

Clayton's voice was soft. "Why would she want to, Kerry?"

The President glanced at his wife, looking warily about her as they unloaded his bulletproof black limousine from the cargo hold of Air Force One. "The tape," he said, "I hope you made a copy."

The motorcade took them to Pacific Heights.

Overlooking the bay, the imposing brick mansion was surrounded by more police and Secret Service, and the street blocked by police checkpoints two hundred feet in either direction. Mary Costello awaited in the sunroom.

Lara went to her. Awkwardly, Kerry stopped, several feet away.

Tentative, Lara took her sister's hands. "He just kept shooting," Mary said brokenly. "I tried to hide—I couldn't help them . . ."

Shivering, Mary began to weep.

Lara pulled her close, her cheek pressed against Mary's.

"Your wedding," Mary said in a ragged voice. "We never should have come . . ."

Over her shoulder, Lara stared through Kerry as if he were not there.

Clayton reached the mansion by four p.m., setting up his makeshift office in the library. But it was nightfall before the President came downstairs. Though they had not seen each other since the tragedy, Kerry said simply, "She's sedated."

Face ravaged, he seemed to exist in his own space, a man so different that Clayton did not know what to say. "I'm so sorry, Kerry. I'm just so sorry."

The President nodded. "Where's the tape?" he asked.

Clayton did not quarrel with him. Only when they stood in the commodious screening room did Clayton ask, "Are you sure?" Kerry's silence was his answer.

Clayton pushed the play button.

On the giant screen, Lara's family died in jerky images. "So fast," Kerry murmured. "It's just so fast."

His expression never changed. When it was done, the President asked Clayton to run the tape again.

THREE

To Inspector Charles Monk, the airport hotel room where John Bowden planned the shooting looked like the inside of a madman's brain. He had kicked the sheets off the bed, as though in his tormented sleep; strewn on the floor were the pastel pieces of a Lego set; an empty vodka bottle; a candy bar wrapper; and a copy of the SSA magazine, *The Defender*, its cover a grotesque caricature of Kerry Kilcannon as Adolf Hitler. But amidst the detritus was a clue to his final hours—an airline schedule with the flights from Dulles to SFO underscored in pencil. Perhaps Bowden had persuaded someone to tell him which flight the Costellos would take; perhaps he had guessed; perhaps he had met every flight. Monk might never know.

There was one more puzzlement—the stubs of boarding passes to and from Las Vegas. What, Monk wondered, had compelled a man so disturbed to make this trip in a single day?

Musing, he picked up *The Defender* and began to riffle its pages.

In the morning, Clayton found the President where he had left him, studying his file on John Bowden. His clothes were the same; his eyes slits. It was plain that he had not slept.

Fax in hand, Clayton approached him, feeling both dread and duty. "What is it?" Kerry asked shortly.

Standing by the wing chair where Kerry sat, Clayton

rested one hand on his friend's shoulder, and placed the fax before him.

It was a copy of a letter and the envelope which had contained it. The envelope was addressed to "Little Prick Killcannon"; its return address was "HELL." Pained, Clayton watched the President decipher the jagged handwriting:

Dear Brother-in-law,
   You only met me once. But that was enough for you.
   You took away my wife and daughter. She wouldn't have left except for you. Then you made sure the world hated me so much she'd never come back to me, no matter how much I begged her or tried to change.
   It must have felt good to have so much power. You took everything away from me. Except my gun. That's my power.
   By the time you get this you'll understand what you've done. You and your new wife will hurt much longer than me and my wife. Because I let you live.
   Read this to her, so you both can suffer like I did.
       Your friend,
       John Bowden

Kerry stared at the letter. Very quietly, he said, "Get me the police."

As she had wished, Lara had gone to the funeral home alone.

The room was cool and dim and quiet; as Lara requested, the caskets were open. She closed the wooden door behind her, leaving Peter Lake outside.

Slowly, Lara approached the caskets.

Her mother wore a high-necked black dress. Her features had the waxen cast of death; once more, Lara reflected how different a face was when bereft of its animating spirit.

Gently, her curled fingers grazed her mother's cheek. "I'm sorry," she whispered. "I didn't know."

After a time, she went to her sister.

Joan's jawline was distorted. Gazing into her face, Lara wondered at Mary's memories, and whether she could ever sleep in peace. "Please," she implored her sister, "forgive me, Joanie."

At last she stood over the smallest casket.

Marie's face was frozen in endless sleep. Lara touched her eyes.

In Kosovo, she had seen murdered women and children in scores, developed the psychic carapace she needed to survive. She had learned to accept the brutal compartmentalization of her trade—the face of a dead child one day; a dinner in Paris the next. But these three faces came with memories which formed the sinew of Lara's life. Gazing at Marie, Lara remembered the smell and feel of her as a newborn, less than a week old. Marie was not meant to die at six, scarred by terrible knowledge.

And now this murdered child would become the vortex of the worlds of media and politics, filled with calculation and ambition, swirling around her family as Lara mourned. Even in death she could not protect them; nor, as terrible as this moment was, could she leave them.

She stayed with them for an hour. Then, beginning with Marie, she kissed the cool foreheads of her niece, sister, and mother, saying goodbye, and closed their caskets forever.

When Lara returned, Kerry was waiting in their bedroom.

To Kerry, she seemed stripped to her essence—her eyes were open wounds, her last defense the steely calm of a journalist familiar with death. He could not ask about her visit.

"There's a letter from Bowden," he said gently. "It's

addressed to me. I wish you never had to read it. But it will be public—soon."

Briefly, Lara's eyes closed, and then she nodded. As she sat on the edge of the bed, Kerry placed the letter beside her. Without touching it, Lara read. When she had finished, she did not look up.

"Leave me," she requested with a fearful gentleness.

Heartsick, Kerry kept himself from touching her. Kneeling beside her, he still spoke softly. "There's more, I'm afraid. They're playing a video of the shooting. On Fox TV."

Her eyes did not move. "You've seen it."

"Yes." For a moment, Kerry hesitated. "So have the families of the other victims. While you were gone, I called them."

She spoke in a monotone. "And now you want us to see them."

"I should. If you can't, I'll do it alone."

"Oh, I'll go." Her mouth moved in a brief and bitter smile. "I'm the First Lady, after all." Her voice became soft again. "Just not today."

Briefly, he imagined her at the mortuary, alone with those she loved. "There's a police inspector coming, Lara. I want to find out how Bowden got the gun."

Still she did not look at him. "Does it matter?"

"It does to me." Pausing, Kerry studied her profile. "Do you want to see him?"

"Someone can tell me when he's here." When, at last, she looked at him, tears formed in her eyes. "But first I should see that film, shouldn't I."

Charles Monk took the bullet from its glassine bag and placed it on the coffee table.

The President stared at its serrated points. "This is Marie's?"

"Yes."

"On the film," Kerry said, "I heard twelve shots."

"That's right. The gun can take a forty-round magazine. This was the eleventh round. Bowden's was the twelfth."

Kerry fought back an anger so deep that it threatened his train of thought. "Did he mean to shoot her?"

Monk frowned. "We can't be sure. From the witnesses, we don't think so—seems like shouting startled him. According to the autopsy, he was legally intoxicated three times over. We don't think he was trained in gun use."

Silent, Kerry touched the sharp edges of the Eagle's Claw. "The points are made of copper," Monk explained. "Not alloy, which is softer.

"The tip is notched to split like that. Get hit in the extremities, and an Eagle's Claw will maim you. Get hit in the trunk, you're likely to die."

"And the gun?"

"A Lexington Patriot-2."

Slowly, Kerry looked up at Monk.

Though the man's face was impassive, his yellow-green eyes betrayed a deep compassion. "Tell me about the Patriot-2," Kerry demanded.

"It's not a sporting weapon." Pausing, Monk seemed to decide on candor. "You wouldn't use it for target practice unless the target's a refrigerator. What it does is what Bowden bought it for—spray a lot of bullets in split seconds."

"Where did he get it?"

It was Lara's voice, coming from behind them. Kerry looked up, startled. Awkwardly, Monk stood, straightening the creases of his pants. Lara did not extend her hand; watching her, Kerry was certain that she had viewed the film.

"Where?" she asked again.

Hesitant, Monk gazed at her in sympathy. "There's no evidence of a purchase," he answered. "Lexington claims they lost the record of whatever dealer they shipped it to, and we can't find any record of a background check. All we know right now is that he traveled to Las Vegas . . ."

"The inspector," Kerry cut in with muted anger, "found this in Bowden's room."

Lara walked over to the coffee table. Spread open was a copy of the SSA magazine; on the page, beside a notice for a gun show in Las Vegas, an advertisement described the features of the Lexington P-2. "Endangered Species," the bold print said. "Banned in California."

"Remember George Callister?" Kerry asked.

FOUR

THE NEXT MORNING, Kerry and Lara sat in the walled Italianate garden of the mansion. It was orderly and quiet—the flowers and bushes carefully pruned and tended, water spilling from a marble fountain the only sound—and would have seemed the perfect urban refuge save for the Secret Service agents on the rooftop. Lara picked at a plate of fruit.

"Kit sat down with me last night," Kerry said. "We talked about the funeral."

Lara looked up from her plate, her long, cool gaze more focused than at any time since the murders. "Mary and I have already decided," she answered. "We want the funeral to be as private as we can make it. I need you to be there as my husband, a member of our family."

But not as President, she was clearly saying. In the silence which followed, Kerry thought of his meeting with Kit Pace.

Kit had arrived the night before, after Lara had retreated upstairs. It was the first time they had spoken since the shootings: Kerry sensed that Kit, as others, had been waiting for clues about how and when to approach him. He had waved her to the chair across from him, accepted her condolences. A few awkward moments passed before Kit addressed what could no longer be avoided. "This is your tragedy," she said with unwonted hesitance. "But it's also the country's. My sense is that people need you to help them mourn, and to help them know how to feel."

Fruitlessly, Kerry wished for a respite from obligations.

"Compared to Lara," he answered, "it's not my tragedy at all."

Kit lapsed into contemplative silence. "Does Lara plan to speak?" she asked. "It might be enough for people to *see* her . . ."

"See her?"

"I know how you'll feel about this, but I think you should consider letting television do its work." To ward off a quick response, Kit had reached out to touch Kerry's wrist. "A funeral where you speak could be the best memorial. It would allow the nation to participate, and reflect on how the victims died, like in Columbine or Oklahoma City . . ."

Now, Lara put down her fork. "Kit wants to televise the service?" she repeated with an air of muted incredulity. "What a tribute to my family *that* would be. Perhaps we can read Bowden's letter, explaining how television pushed him to the edge."

Kerry could say nothing: to Lara, these deaths were so enmeshed with his decisions, the cost of being President, that he could not give voice to his own guilt, nor penetrate her sense of complicity. "I don't want to mourn them as symbols," Lara said more evenly, "but as three people I loved, who will always be a part of me. Even if I felt otherwise, I could never push Mary to bastardize the funeral. She's the one who saw them die, and she's all the family I have."

I'm your family, as well, Kerry thought. But all he ventured was, "If you want, Kit can help Connie Coulter with the media. Like it or not, they're out there."

Lara looked around her at the garden. "I'll ask Mary if she minds a press pool," she said with a faint sardonic undertone. "Perhaps in the rear of the church, as they did at our wedding."

I didn't kill them, Kerry wanted to say. *We didn't kill them.*

But he could not even persuade himself. "We're the President and First Lady," he said in measured tones. "We'll be that at the funeral, like it or not. We're also two people who've been married for five days, three of them so hellish that neither of us knows what to do. Once we leave here we'll need to begin to find our way." Reaching across the table, he took her lifeless hand. "You can start with the fact that I love you."

Silent, she gazed at their intertwined hands. "Then let me have my family back," she answered softly. "At least for the funeral."

An hour later, after Lara left to be with Mary, Kerry and Clayton watched CNN: in the unspoken protocol of Kerry's mourning, Clayton Slade was the only person—except as absolutely required—whom the President wished to see. The broadcast showed a collage of national mourning—cards and bouquets left at the base of the iron bars surrounding the White House; a deluge of letters to the President and Lara; impromptu memorial gatherings in scores of American cities, and several in Asia and Western Europe; interviews with women who wept for three victims they had never known; a commentator weighing the impact of these deaths against that of Princess Diana. Then Wolf Blitzer began reading a statement from George Callister:

"*All of us*," Blitzer began, "*are shocked and saddened that the murderer of seven innocent people used a gun and ammunition manufactured by Lexington Arms. On behalf of all the employees of Lexington, I've conveyed to the President and First Lady our profound sympathy and sorrow . . .*"

"He called," Clayton told the President, "while you were with Lara."

Kerry did not turn. "Callister? What did he say?"

"How sorry he was. I didn't want to interrupt you."

Kerry let a brief, harsh laugh escape through tightened lips. He did not respond in words.

On the screen, Blitzer continued reading. "*We must remember,*" Callister went on to say, "*that a gun in itself is neither good nor bad, and that millions of Americans use guns safely and responsibly, from hunting to sport-shooting to protecting their home and family from people like John Bowden. The essence of this tragedy lies not in the fact that Lexington makes guns, but in the recesses of this man's demented mind . . .*"

"Tell Callister," Kerry said quietly, "that he'll be hearing from me. In my own time and way."

That afternoon, the President materialized before a startled press pool, speaking briefly and without notice in the circular driveway. He took no questions; Lara was not with him. This was his first public statement since the murders.

He looked weary, but composed. "On behalf of the First Lady and her family," he began, "I would like to thank all Americans for their understanding and compassion in this very private time . . ." He did not mention Callister, or guns.

FIVE

THE FUNERAL MASS was held in a simple Roman Catholic church in the Sunset District, near the stucco home where the Costello family had lived since Lara was born. The mourners filling the church were parishioners and other friends. The sole public official besides Kerry was Vice President Ellen Penn, who had represented the district before advancing to the Senate; the press pool was limited to ten reporters, consigned to the rear and confined to pads and pencils. Kerry sat with Lara and Mary, Carlie and Clayton Slade beside him. A few times Carlie touched Kerry's hand, as if she knew that Kerry felt alone. He did not know what Lara would say, or how she would manage to say it.

The caskets holding Inez, Joan, and Marie were draped in cloth. When it was time, Lara walked toward them. Instead of pausing at the altar, she went to her mother's casket, gently resting a palm on the cloth. And then, softly, Lara spoke to Inez Costello.

"You always believed in me," Lara began. "You always believed, in the mystical way that mothers do, that I could meet whatever challenges awaited me.

"You didn't ask me to succeed for you. You didn't look at me, and see yourself, or see a surrogate for your own dreams. You just saw me." Lara paused, tears coming to her eyes. "And so, Mama, I saw myself as you did. Because I so believed in you."

Once more, Lara gathered herself; watching, Kerry could feel the depth of her loss.

"You gave that gift to all of us." Briefly, Lara smiled at her sister. "When I look at Mary, I remember all the stories you told me about her teaching, and about the children—sometimes troubled—whose lives she was making better. Because you just believed so deeply in all that she was doing . . ."

Minutes passed; the passage of emotion between Lara and those who listened, at first worried for her, settled into a calm communal sadness. As Lara finished speaking to Joan, the church was hushed.

"You saw our mother raise us alone. You saw how hard it was. But when it mattered—when you saw Marie at risk—you determined to protect her in every way you could." Fighting back tears, Lara said clearly, "And in every way you could, you did . . ."

Standing beside Marie, Lara spoke of watching her at Dulles Airport, walking away from Lara toward her future, as if now reminding the child of her past.

"You *were* our future," Lara said softly. "We imagined your graduations, your achievements, the life you might create. For us, one of the joys of growing older would be watching you become the person you were meant to be . . ."

Briefly Lara faltered; only the impossibility of doing so kept Kerry from reaching out to her. Then, once more, she regained her self-control. "Now," she told Marie, "too soon, you are at peace. And those of us who love you, and whom you have left behind, must find a way to give your life the meaning you would have given it by living . . ."

*

At last it was done. The black limousine bearing Kerry, Lara, and Mary led the funeral cortege from San Francisco to Colma, a suburb whose primary purpose was to serve as a final resting place for those who, because San Francisco had banned new cemeteries, could no longer be buried in the city. The featureless miles of grey monuments struck Kerry as Arlington without the grandeur, lending a bleak symbolism to what, the involuntary skeptic in Kerry feared, was an eternity of nothingness, the common indistinguishable fate of all who rested here. But all that had been left to him was to secure for the murdered women and child the rarest of Colma's blessings, a resting place beneath a tree, on a modest bluff some distance from the marble rows.

Her arm linked with Mary's, Lara stood beside her husband, watching the three caskets descend into a common grave. As the last dirt was scattered, it began to rain. Only then did Lara take Kerry's hand.

Their day was far from done. Before the funeral, Lara had called grieving parents in Illinois, whose nineteen-year-old daughter had flown to San Francisco to begin her sophomore year at Stanford; now they drove to the Richmond District, where one of the two security guards had lived with his family.

His widow was puffy-eyed with grief. "This is the President," Felice Serrano told her twelve-year-old son.

Manfully, he shook Kerry's hand as Felice expressed sadness for Lara's loss. "Tell me about Henry," Lara requested softly.

Felice glanced at her younger children, two dark-haired girls ages seven and four, as though to pluck a detail from memories too copious to summarize, emotions too complex to express. "Every night," she answered, "Henry read to the children. He wanted them all to go to college."

"Like my mother," Lara answered. "And so we did."

Felice nodded, less from conviction, Kerry thought, than from the hope of reviving her own shattered dreams. Then, as though concerned for him, she told her son, "Maybe you could show the President your father's wood shop."

"Could you?" Kerry asked the boy.

Self-consciously, George Serrano led Kerry to the garage, leaving the others behind.

The workbench was immaculate, the implements neatly put away, the signposts of a man who taught his son order, responsibility, and a respect for one's possessions. Their current project had been a bookshelf: to Kerry, there was something desolate about the shelfless frame, a symbol of a life which would never be completed.

"What part did you make?" Kerry asked.

The boy touched a wooden board, leaning against a wall, which would have become a shelf. "Everything," he answered. "This time, Dad let me use the saw."

"Show me," Kerry requested. "My father could never find the time."

For the next half hour, talking as needed, the President and George Serrano sawed and inserted the wooden shelves. When at last Felice and Lara came for them, conversing quietly between themselves, the bookshelf was complete except for varnish.

At the door, Lara clasped Felice's hands. "Thank you," Lara said. "This can't have been for nothing. None of us will let it be."

In the limousine, Kerry turned to Lara. Her face was etched with sadness.

"All day," he told her, "I've been watching you pay tribute to your family, comfort Mary, and give Felice Serrano at least a measure of peace. The word that comes to me is 'grace,' in all its meanings."

As if exhausted, she rested her shoulder against his. In quiet despair, she answered, "In the end, being with them helped me. But what do we do now?"

The next morning, Kit Pace announced that the President and First Lady would return to Martha's Vineyard, for several days of rest and seclusion. Among the staff, the decision was controversial, though none had a voice. But Kit was more than satisfied. Lara's eulogy, widely reprinted, had touched the vast public which wished to mourn with her, as had her calls and visits to the victims' families who, when asked, had remarked on her kindness and concern. As for their planned retreat to Martha's Vineyard, Americans would admire a man, even a President, who subordinates all else to supporting his wife in her time of loss. If the country waited a few more days, Kit believed, the Kilcannons' reentry into public life would be all the more compelling. She wondered if they understood this perfectly.

SIX

ON CNN, James Kilcannon lay on his back, a pool of blood beneath his head, dying as the crowd around him screamed its horror and grief. And then he vanished, replaced by a percussive pop as Inez Costello fell.

In the wake of the Costello murders, Bill Schneider reported, *support for stricter gun laws has swollen to over ninety percent . . .*

As Marie Bowden toppled backward, Kerry hit the remote.

In numb silence, he and Clayton gazed at the darkened screen. Lara had vanished upstairs: the two men sat alone. Quietly, Clayton asked, "Will Martha's Vineyard help, I wonder?"

"I don't know." Kerry's tone commingled irony and sorrow. "I have to comfort her—if I can—and be *seen* as comforting her. It feels like I'm trapped in a silent movie, as Lara's husband and as President."

Clayton narrowed his eyes in thought. "The husband part may be beyond me. But the politics of this won't keep."

Kerry turned to him. "I have to do something, Clayton. You know that."

"Because of Lara?"

"Because of me. Because it's time." Kerry stood, hands jammed in his pockets. "Standing up to the SSA is part of what I ran on. First I lost a brother. Now guns have decimated Lara's family. What's the point of becoming President if I don't use the office to accomplish what I've fought for ever since Jamie died."

"You have to do *something*," Clayton agreed. "The question is, what?" He puffed his cheeks, exhaling. "You can put in a bill to change the law, then push it symbolically, knowing you'll lose in Congress but gain an issue against the GOP when you run for reelection. Or you can go all out, split the Democratic Party, and put at risk the rest of your agenda . . ."

"An 'issue,' " Kerry replied with scorn and anger. "Is *that* what those three caskets were? An 'issue'?"

Clayton's voice was soft. "You hired me to be straight with you. I've watched you go over the Bowden file, obsessing about what more—or less—you could have done, as if the whole thing turned on *you*.

"You're not God, Kerry. *You* didn't abuse Joan Bowden. You didn't stalk her child. What choice did she have but to leave . . . ?"

"I convinced her to leave, dammit. I exposed Bowden on national TV . . ."

"Because the *Chronicle* was going to. So who killed Lara's family? The media? You? Maybe Bowden did . . ."

"Maybe Lexington did," Kerry said tightly. "Or maybe the SSA."

Clayton crossed his arms. "All I'm saying is to take your time. Politics isn't therapy."

Kerry's anger expressed itself in a mirthless smile, a voice muted with suppressed emotion. "Maybe I'm too self-involved for office. Maybe I hate the people who put this gun in Bowden's hands. Maybe I'm sublimating guilt through action. But I'm not a fool." Now Kerry's voice became quiet and cool. "If these murders are too much for me, just maybe, at last, they're too much for the country. You can take guilt and grief and anger and turn it into something better.

"For the past few days, I've been watching Lara, wondering what to do. And there's nothing." Kerry's tone was softer yet. "I'm sick of comforting victims when there is no comfort. I'm sick of the SSA. I'm sick of guns and death."

"Sick of guns," Clayton responded evenly. "Period. And everyone knows it. Which makes you less than the perfect Messiah." Clayton's face took on a stubborn cast. "I hope you know how little I enjoy this conversation. But we need to have it before you and Lara go to Martha's Vineyard. If you make this into Armageddon, people will be flooding gun shops, and the SSA will be shoveling money and votes at the GOP to take down every Democrat in Congress who stands a chance of losing . . ."

"That's supposed to stop me? Fear of losing?"

"Maybe it should," Clayton rejoined. "The SSA's the most powerful lobby in Washington—on this issue, far more powerful than you.

"Consider how the world looks to Chuck Hampton and the Democrats in the Senate. Last November, you barely won. You lost the South, the border states, and the interior West. Thanks to the Masters nomination—at least until these shootings—you were the first Democratic President in history to achieve a majority disapproval rating from Republicans two short months into your Presidency." Rising, Clayton stood face-to-face with Kerry. "Guns are even more polarizing than abortion. You'll have to be prepared to launch a second campaign—visiting every county sheriff in every border state, telling sentimental stories about your dad the cop until you want to throw up—and stake your Presidency on your success.

"Maybe Hampton's people wouldn't run from you like the plague. Maybe, Mr. President, *these* murders have changed everything. But you had better pray that's so."

Tense, Clayton looked into his best friend's cool blue eyes. "They *could* change everything," Kerry rejoined. "Now people know that a spousal abuser like John Bowden can go to a gun show and buy a Lexington P-2 and Eagle's Claw bullets. God help me, I couldn't have done better than Bowden if I'd invented him. Which, perhaps, I did."

"Which makes it personal," Clayton shot back. "The SSA will say that you're manipulative and obsessed, that you're excusing your failure to protect Lara's family by blaming it on them . . ."

"Fuck them," Kerry snapped. "I'll never get the Kilcannon haters, or the people who believe our government is out to get them. What I need is the majority of decent people—gun owners included—who think the life of a six-year-old girl outweighs the 'right' of a madman to buy any weapon he wants. Then maybe I can defeat the SSA in Congress, and save the next Marie." Pausing, Kerry's gaze became intense, almost implacable. "The SSA claims they've never lost. But there's a self-destructive quality about them, a tendency to go too far and say too much. They'll cannibalize the pro-gun movement if we can corner them . . ."

"Do that," Clayton admonished, "and they'll try to destroy you. They'll make the fight over the Masters nomination and late term abortion look like nothing."

"Maybe so," Kerry answered with a shrug. "But what divides people over abortion is an insoluble moral question: whether a fetus is an inviolate life from the moment of conception. The SSA has manufactured the division over gun rights out of paranoia and cultural distrust, and what's manufactured can be changed."

Perhaps, Clayton reflected, Kerry—despite his guilt and sadness—had thought this through. "I didn't ask for this," Kerry finished more quietly. "I'd give up this office in a heartbeat if I could give Lara back her mother, or her sister, or Marie. But that's not the hand fate dealt me. So now the only question besides healing Lara is how I use their deaths."

Once more, Clayton fell silent, debating whether to

speak. "Depending on what you do," he finally said, "trying to heal Lara could make this worse than you've imagined. If you put her out there with you, she'll become a target. Nothing will be off-limits." Clayton watched Kerry absorb his tacit reference to Lara's secret abortion. "Please," Clayton implored his friend, "don't let John Bowden overwhelm your Presidency. Or, if you can help it, your marriage."

Kerry did not respond. Walking to the window, he gazed into the darkened courtyard. "Let's talk about Al Anwar," Clayton said at length.

"Let's." Kerry did not turn. "How did you keep it quiet?"

"With difficulty. I put the fear of God into the Pentagon, and had them ship the body in secrecy to the air force base at Stuttgart. My excuse was that we needed a positive forensic identification, and that we'd all look incompetent, and worse, if we announced the death of a terrorist who then popped up on the Al Jazeera network. But there was never any real doubt it was Al Anwar, and now there's none at all. How CNN missed this I'll never know." Clayton's tone became imperative. "We can say you were only being responsible, Mr. President. But this lends itself to less charitable interpretations. You've sat on it as long as you dare."

For a moment, Kerry was silent. "Go find Ellen," he requested. "As soon as Lara and I are in the air, she can announce Al Anwar's death."

Kerry and his Vice President sat beside each other in wing chairs. When they had finished speaking of Al Anwar, Ellen Penn turned to guns, her dark brown eyes bespeaking her concern. "I know how hard this is for both of you," she began. "But either we change the gun laws in this country, or Lara's family becomes just another statistic. To paraphrase your inaugural address, 'If not now, when; if not us, who?' "

"Perhaps not me. People say I polarize. And I do."

Ellen considered this. "There's also Lara," she replied. "I watched her at the funeral, Mr. President. I saw what she can do."

Turning, Kerry looked at her, questioning. "The Costellos are victims," Ellen continued, "and Lara gives them voice. Like her, you're a survivor of gun violence; better than anyone, you know that the decision to turn a nightmare into a cause can be profound. But Lara can speak for women and children as no one else."

Ellen's tough and feisty surface, Kerry reflected, concealed a deep compassion. "The funeral," he told her, "was even harder on Lara than it looked. I don't know if she'll want to relive it, over and over."

"But what if she decides to?" Ellen countered. "Would you try to stop her? And if you could, where would that leave her? Let alone the two of you."

At this, Kerry felt an infinite weariness. "I have no idea," he answered.

SEVEN

THEIR FIRST NIGHT on Martha's Vineyard, Kerry awoke from a restless sleep.

Lara was gone. He pulled on blue jeans and a sweater and walked onto the deck. In the moonlight, Lara waded ankle deep into a chill ocean.

Watching, Kerry debated whether to go to her. Then Peter Lake said quietly, "She's all right, Mr. President."

Kerry turned. Standing beside the deck, Peter gazed at Lara.

She's not all right, Kerry wanted to say. *She barely sleeps. She drops things she's forgotten she's holding. At times she's angry and demanding, and then silence descends. She cries when she shouldn't, can't cry when she should. I don't know what to do.*

"Thank you," the President said simply.

At daybreak, Kerry found her sitting cross-legged on a windswept dune.

"Care to talk about it?" he asked.

Distractedly, Lara brushed the hair back from her face, still studying the water. She answered him with dispassion. "About hating myself? What is there to say? I abdicated my responsibilities in every possible way—assigning Joanie to you, helping the media to take her life over. Now they're all dead. So I sit here, hating the life we're supposed to lead."

Do you hate me? Kerry wanted to ask. But it was not the time to express his own anguish, or to ask for reassurance.

Or even, right now, fairness. He could not define what fairness was.

"You didn't fail them," he told her. "I did. Our system of politics did, and our laws. That's how Bowden got his gun."

Later they drank coffee on the deck. "Politics," Lara said.

This had become her recent pattern—talking in single words or phrases, at times connected to something said an hour before. When Kerry turned to her, she asked, "What will you do?"

"Break the power of the SSA, if I can. Pass a law that works. Try to keep this from happening to some other family—at least in the way it did."

Lara sipped her coffee. "Can you?"

"Perhaps. At a cost." Reflecting, Kerry studied the ocean, deep grey in a lingering mist. "People like Hampton will remind me about health care, or education—all the issues which affect more people than guns do—and worry that I'll cost us the next election.

"For my Presidency, this is a defining moment. I'm custodian of a lot of lives, a bunch of conflicting hopes, and the careers of a pack of senators and congressmen just trying to survive. Whatever I do will impact them."

Lara resumed her survey of the shoreline. "When I covered Congress," she said after a time, "I used to observe the pettiness and backstabbing, the sheer cowardice of politics, and pride myself on my worldliness. Now the whole thing makes me sick."

She tried to nap. When she emerged from the bedroom, hollow-eyed, Kerry placed two cups of clam chowder on the table.

Staring at the steaming cup, Lara picked up her soup spoon, put it down again. Tears welled in her eyes. "Do you know who I miss the most? My mother. She was the one who always cared for me.

"I know—she'd already lived her life. Joanie was breaking free, and Marie was so young. Mama would have gladly died to save them . . ." Voice catching, Lara bowed her head. "I feel so violated, Kerry. She was the first person I ever loved."

Kerry watched as tears ran down her face.

The night was deep and still—the faint whirring of crickets, sea grass rustling in the wind. Kerry and Lara sat on the deck, long moments passing in silence.

"A law." Her face and voice were affectless. "Can you promise me you'll pass it?"

This required no answer. Kerry offered none.

"If you're trying to protect me, don't." Her voice held a first trace of steel. "They were *my* family, not yours. This time I won't sit back and watch you."

They lay beside each other, sleepless in the dark. For an hour or more, neither had spoken.

"When I was little," Lara finally said, "my father owned a gun. Even then it scared me—like he did. Just passing a gun shop gave me the creeps.

"Then you were shot, and I nearly lost you." Her voice softened. "I made a pact with God—that if you lived I'd never leave you, no matter what sacrifices I'd have to make. And when you survived I believed that He had given you back to me, and now would never take you."

In the pause that followed, Kerry touched her hand. "He

gave me you," she finished. "And then He took them in exchange ..."

Heartsick, Kerry listened to the sound of muffled crying.

They walked the beach on a cool midmorning, hands in the pockets of their windbreakers. Out to sea, a Coast Guard cutter sliced along the perimeter mapped out by Peter Lake, beyond which two cabin cruisers carried photographers with telephoto lenses.

"Next week," Lara said, "there'll be a magazine cover of this moment, to remind me I'm First Lady. That's what I am now—a symbol. The only job I have."

"True. But there's much a First Lady can do."

Abruptly stopping, Lara turned to him. "Please, if I decide to do something about guns, support me."

In his worry and ambivalence, Kerry found no words. "Before this happened," she told him, "it might have been race and poverty—somewhere I could use my skills to make people *see* lives they choose to ignore, and actually give a damn. But I don't have a choice now. Now it's guns."

They ate more chowder by candlelight. "It's better the second day," Lara said.

Smiling faintly, Kerry watched her glass of wine kick in. At length he ventured, "There are some realities we should talk about."

"Such as?"

Aimlessly, Kerry stirred his chowder. "When it comes to First Ladies, Americans have problems with gender and lines of authority. They don't want the President's wife formulating policy, or running a task force. Marriage isn't enough—to push an agenda or propose new laws, you have to get elected to something."

"What about dead relatives," Lara answered coldly. "Is that too feeble a credential?"

"No. Not if your goal is to make people feel the tragedy of gun violence, the pain of lives lost for no good reason . . ."

"Because I'm a *victim*," Lara interrupted in anger and derision. "Do you know how much I hate being a victim? That's how too many people are most comfortable with women—as victims. 'Protect the mommies, save the children' . . ."

"There's more to worry about," Kerry warned. "If you get out front on this, people will say it's all about you—that if you'd become a paraplegic we'd be going full bore for stem cell research . . ."

"They say that about *you*," Lara snapped. "You need me, Kerry. You need women. You know it yourself—the only way to win this is by making women care even more than the gun fanatics do.

"I'm not going to tour the country with home movies of my mother, Marie and Joanie. They're dead, dammit—there's nothing I can do for them. But there are thousands of living people out there who've lost someone they love to guns.

"I know this can't be Lara Costello's traveling memorial service." Her tone was low and determined. "If I go out and do this, it will be with other men and women who are looking for a way to keep some other husband, wife or parent from suffering as they did. *I* can be that way."

At midnight, Kerry and Lara stood together, jeans rolled up, chill water nipping their feet and ankles. "There are risks to what you're proposing," Kerry said.

"Such as?"

"Getting shot, for one. We still get letters telling me how much better Jamie looked without the top of his head . . ."

"I'd have protection . . ."

"So did he. So did I."

Lara turned to him. "They killed my family, Kerry. When they killed Jamie, you didn't hide. You ran for Jamie's seat . . ."

"Dammit, Lara, to the kind of crazies who equate an AK-47 with their penis, you're a minority career woman with a high-toned education and a background in the liberal press, and now you want to take away their guns."

Lara shook her head, resistant. "I can't help it if people are crazy. Or that some frightened males see any assertive woman as emasculating."

Kerry watched a clump of seaweed swirl at his feet. "All right," he said wearily. "There's the abortion."

" 'The abortion,' " Lara repeated in mordant tones. "If that's to stop me, why didn't it stop you from wanting to get married?"

"Because I love you. I thought you knew that."

Silent, Lara gazed at him. Clasping her shoulders, Kerry spoke softly. "This is different. Like it or not, you're now a figure of sympathy for millions. It's a power you've never had before. Use that power, and the SSA will search for ways to destroy you.

"That would be enough for them. But it might not be enough for some fanatic with a gun. Guns and abortion is a combustible mixture—it's gotten too many people killed already. I don't want the next one to be you."

Lara studied him. "Is that *all* you're afraid of?" she demanded.

"What else do you think it's about?" he answered with real heat. "My visceral distaste for feminism? Or just politics?"

Lara's mouth formed a stubborn line. "If it isn't politics,

don't try to intimidate me. My life, my choice." Her voice became more level. "You nearly died, then got out of bed and kept on running for President. All I could do was pray. Don't ask me to turn my back on this so you don't have to worry."

Later, Kerry held her. But that was all. They had not made love since the murders. To Kerry, Lara's grief had left her hollow.

"I don't want a child," she murmured. "At least not now."

"Why?"

"What's the usual line—'I can't bring a life into a world as cruel as this'?"

Kerry stifled his dismay. "Is that really how you feel?"

Lara exhaled. "I don't know. In the last day or so, I've wondered if a child would help heal us—a new life, a new person to love after so much death . . ."

"I've thought that, too . . ."

"But it's not a reason. People should have children more for the child's sake than their own. Things are so unsettled now, even with us." Pausing, Lara spoke more quietly. "We need time to heal, Kerry. And I have something else to do."

Kerry fell silent.

"I worry about safety, too," Lara confessed. "All the people who'll hate me, and what could happen." In the darkness, she rested the crown of her head against his face. "I know what you want. But it's not the time to have a child."

After this Kerry could not sleep.

He lay thinking for what seemed like hours, waiting until Lara's stirring told him that she, too, was awake.

"If you do this," he told her, "use domestic violence as a wedge. Not even the SSA can advocate shooting women and children. If you keep the focus on the victims, instead of the gun lobby, there's less the SSA can say."

The next morning she asked to walk alone.

Kerry watched her become a small figure in an oversized sweater, perhaps a mile distant, gazing out to sea. It was an hour before she returned.

When she did, she took his hand. "At least *you're* here," she said. "If anything happened to you, I don't think I could bear it."

In candlelight Lara still looked wan. But at least, Kerry thought, she had begun to eat again.

"It's not just my family," she told him. "This is a once-in-a-generation chance to save thousands of innocent lives. What choice do I have?"

He could not quarrel with this. In his silence, Lara said quietly, "We've talked about everything but you."

"What has there been to say?"

"Quite a bit. We're caught in this cycle of guilt, me blaming myself, then blaming you. You've had nowhere to go."

Kerry could not speak. For the first time he fought back tears.

Lara watched his face. "John Bowden gave us a lot to live with. I'll try to do better, Kerry. For both our sakes."

When he reached out his hand, she took it, gazing at their fingers as they intertwined. "I'll never put this behind me," she said. "Whether I want to or not, my life will always be defined by this. The only question is what I do with it." Looking up at him, she finished softly, "I think I'm ready now."

The next morning, before they left, Kerry watched with Peter Lake as Lara took her last walk on the beach.

"Wherever she goes," Kerry said, "I want you to go with her."

EIGHT

ONE DAY after the President and First Lady returned to Washington, Senator Frank Fasano and his wife Bernadette paid them a condolence call.

The meeting was brief and awkward. To Fasano, Kerry Kilcannon looked subtly older, Lara's face hollowed by a loss of sleep and appetite. Though both were gracious, Fasano felt something beneath their cool façade which, while he could not define it, made him apprehensive.

Leaving, Fasano could not shed his disquiet. "What are you thinking?" Bernadette asked.

Perhaps, Fasano reflected, what he felt was the chill of death, a bone-deep grasp of the torment both Kilcannons must be suffering. But a single word leapt to mind, unbidden. *Lethal.*

"That this is trouble," he answered.

That night, the President invited Senate Minority Leader Chuck Hampton to dine with him alone.

They were seated in the Family Dining Room where, Hampton remembered reading, the Kilcannons had last dined with Lara's family. He could envision the Costellos admiring the Louis XVI mantel, the gold filigree, the silver centerpiece on the mahogany dining table. During Kilcannon's intermittent silences, Hampton could imagine him recalling the voices which had filled the room.

The President himself made Hampton edgy. They had never been close; for Hampton, beneath Kilcannon's quickness and charm lay a molten core which eluded Hampton's reckoning. The year before, he had supported then–Vice President Dick Mason for his party's nomination, and one thing he was sure of was that Kerry Kilcannon would never forget this. Himself lawyerly and cerebral, Hampton sensed that, in the wake of the Costello murders, Kilcannon would not rest. Even his quiet felt purposeful.

"Guns," the President said at last. "That's what we're here to talk about."

Watchful, Hampton dabbed his lips with a linen napkin. "We should make it an issue," he allowed.

"An issue?" the President echoed coolly. "I've heard that before, Chuck, including from you. But I'm less inclined to play the hollow man."

"You're hardly that, Mr. President." Hampton summoned a faint, ironic smile. "You gave us Caroline Masters, the gift that keeps on giving."

Kilcannon smiled as well, though his eyes did not. "And changed the Supreme Court for a generation. While preserving the right to choose."

"At a price," Hampton countered. "Abortion's divisive enough. If we push gun control too hard, we'll tear apart our party.

"You know your ex-colleagues, Mr. President. Close to an election year they're like feudal lords. They care most about their fiefdoms." Smoothly, Hampton adopted a mollifying tone. "Please don't misunderstand me. There's immense sympathy in the Senate for all that the First Lady and you have gone through. But our side is afraid of where that may take us."

"And where is that?"

Hampton sighed. "A political death spiral, Mr. President. Right now, the great majority of Americans say they favor 'stricter gun laws.' But no one's defined that for them. Once we propose a law, the SSA will attack it as confiscatory, and tell their people to vote against any legislator who stands with you." Pausing, Hampton ticked off states on the fingers of one hand. "Montana. New Mexico. Georgia. Nebraska. Missouri. In each state there's a Democratic senator up for reelection. In each state, ten months ago, you lost—lost rural votes, lost white males, lost by at least five percent. Our senators hold those seats by opposing gun control—that's the trade-off they have to make for favoring abortion rights. If you push this to the limit, you may well take them down."

Listening, the President's expression did not change. Quietly, he answered, "It's different now."

Slowly, Hampton shook his head. "Not to the SSA's core constituents. They're single-issue voters: 'protecting gun rights' is all they care about. There *are* no single-issue voters for gun control.

"Fasano knows that. He's praying for you to go all out and inflame the Republican base. First he beats our people in the Senate, and then he goes after you."

Once more, Kilcannon gave Hampton a thin smile. "Go on."

The President's calm, Hampton realized, unnerved him. "To survive," he continued flatly, "our people will have to abandon you. Being true to yourself may be the Kilcannon persona. But in Montana, being true to you is suicide. Remember the bumper stickers on all those pickup trucks, 'If Kilcannon wins, you lose'?

"You lost, Mr. President." Leaning forward, Hampton mustered all the conviction he possessed. "In the senate, we've got forty-six votes out of a hundred. I can't get forty for any gun law you could sign without gagging. That's the fact."

Gazing at Hampton across the table, the President

rested his chin against the curled fingers of one hand. "What else should I consider?"

"You *know* all this, Mr. President." Hampton stopped abruptly, stifling his aggravation, the strong sense that Kilcannon was toying with him. "There's also the union vote. At least forty percent of the rank and file has some sympathy for the SSA. In Michigan, they shut down auto plants on the first day of deer season.

"The AFL-CIO is *not* willing to sacrifice jobs or health care or better public schools to gun control. Their president told me just yesterday, 'more people get killed in car wrecks than with guns.' "

"Sweeney," Kerry said coldly, "can say a lot of things. But the AFL-CIO needs me to succeed. Without me, they're screwed."

Hampton sat back. In the rawest sense of power politics, this was true—the union leadership had nowhere else to go, and so must fight to save the president they had. "So let's talk about the SSA," Kilcannon continued calmly. "They're like the Wizard of Oz—as scary as you imagine them to be. After every election, they go around claiming victory—listen to them, and you'd think their candidates never lost a race. But last year they lost five of seven Senate seats they targeted. Then they proceeded to brag about their power, and lie about their losses.

"You keep mentioning the states I lost. How is it, I sometimes wonder, that I'm sitting here." Kilcannon's voice became sardonic. "Perhaps because of California and New Jersey, which I won partly *because* of gun control.

"Look at the map. This rural culture you keep worrying about is fading away, replaced by suburbanites who worry less about hunting season than keeping their local incarnation of Bowden away from school yards." Kilcannon's voice softened. "The SSA feeds on our own cowardice. Every day they hope we won't notice that they're more scared than we are. And have more to be scared about."

Hampton shook his head. "Fear works for them just fine, Mr. President. That's what they use *you* for—to scare their members into giving them votes and money so that they can keep their guns . . ."

"I've heard them," Kilcannon interjected with an ironic smile. "They're like tent show evangelists—'send us money, or Kerry Kilcannon will get you before the Devil does.' 'Confiscation was the first step to the Holocaust.' 'Without our guns, Kilcannon will set loose gays and blacks and lesbians, unleashing a new epidemic of AIDS and destroying the white male-dominated family which has made this country strong.' 'Once Kilcannon takes your gun, Al Qaeda terrorists will make house calls door-to-door.'" Pausing, Kilcannon added dryly, "After that, I'm planning to unleash the Internal Revenue Service."

Reluctantly, Hampton smiled. "My personal favorite," Kilcannon told him, "was the family of five slaughtered by a madman with a pitchfork because they'd locked away their guns. Too bad it's a total fabrication.

"There will always be a lunatic fringe, Chuck. But these people don't speak for most gun owners. Right now, no one does." Kilcannon leaned forward. "I'm not getting into a catfight with the SSA—that would make them too important. I intend to talk right past them, and let them get hysterical on their own."

"That won't be easy." Pausing, Hampton folded his hands. "I'm a duck hunter, Mr. President. But I can't bring that up at a dinner party in this town without some desiccated society woman thinking I'm a murderer.

"I was raised on a farm. When I was seven, my dad gave me a twenty-two and taught me to use it safely. I went to college on a sharpshooting scholarship, and I still collect guns. I've even got a shooting range behind my farmhouse.

"Vermont's full of people like me. We enjoy guns, period. I'm trying to make the Democratic Party a safe place for these folks. But every time you say 'gun control' what they hear is a city boy who views them with disdain." Hampton spoke more quietly. "Bowden should never have had a gun. As far as I'm concerned, the SSA has blood on their hands, including the First Lady's family's. But most gun owners out there believe that the SSA at least respects them, and that you don't.

"You could get us beaten. You could even lose the Presidency. Instead we'll have some blow-dried reactionary like Fasano who shafts minorities, women and the poor, doesn't give a damn about health care, *and* thinks the Second Amendment protects lunatics with rocket launchers."

Kilcannon's smile was faint. "Believe it or not," he answered, "I've thought a lot about white males, and all the states I lost. And about why I'm sitting here instead of the guy who won them.

"I *know* guns are symbolic. I still remember campaigning with a Southern congressman, counting the bullet holes in stop signs. A lot of them were his own, from when he was a kid." Abruptly, Kilcannon stood, hands braced against the back of his chair. "I can also read a map. The Republicans own gun territory, we own gun control territory. Because politics has turned into a culture war.

"Forty years later we're still fighting over the 1960s. If you believe that civil rights, the women's movement and protecting the environment were basically good things, then you're likely to be a Democrat. But if you think the sixties were the time when minorities got out of hand, women abandoned their duties, promiscuity ran rampant, movies became violent and rock lyrics obscene, and the only acceptable form of discrimination became shafting white males—in short, if you still feel threatened by the changes in our society, there's precious little chance you'll hear what I have to say. Even though I tend to agree about popular entertainment.

"That divide is strengthened by religion. I attend Mass every Sunday. But in the last election regular churchgoers voted against me three to two. The same proportion who voted *for* me if they didn't go to church.

"So where do guns fit in?" Kilcannon asked rhetorically. "For people who feel threatened they're emblematic— 'you've taken everything else away from me, but you can't take my gun.' Not my natural constituency."

"Nor," Hampton added, "representative of all white males."

"Precisely. But Fasano and his pals have conditioned a lot of them to vote for buzzwords—'prayer in school'; 'family values'—instead of programs. It's like all these white guys trapped in some right-wing lab experiment.

"What am *I* going to tell them in order to compete—that the Second Amendment embodies their most sacred right? I can't." Pausing, Kilcannon softened his voice. "The trick isn't to compete. The trick is to remind them that *we* protect their unions, their medical care and their retirement. And that the Frank Fasanos of the world will screw them in favor of their country club friends who bleat if they can't get a tax cut and a bigger second home.

"I can speak *that* language. But we can't obsess on white guys. Do their votes count more than the votes of women, or blacks, or Hispanics, or people who live in cities? Not unless we deny *those* voters a reason to come out for us. And that's what happens when Democrats are as gutless and whiny as we've become.

"We need to start chipping away women and Republican moderates who think their party has been hijacked by gun nuts, antiabortion extremists, and televangelists who believe that women's suffrage was our second bite of Eve's all-too-wormy apple. So for every Democratic senator worried about losing, there's a Republican like Chad Palmer who worries about where their party's going. If we create enough pressure, Fasano won't be able to hold them." Kilcannon's eyes bore into Hampton's. "Lara and I are going to make Fasano pay the price for kowtowing to the SSA. And it will be huge—if not next year, then soon enough.

"If I have to preside over a divided country, I'm going to divide it my way. And by the time I leave this office, you'll be in the majority."

For minutes, Hampton had watched and listened to Kerry Kilcannon with something like amazement. "Lara," he echoed now.

"Yes."

Hampton exhaled. "Mr. President," he said quietly, "I'm not sure you're the right messenger."

Kilcannon sat again, fixing Hampton with the same unblinking gaze. "Oh, I know. I made the mistake of having a brother who got shot, then getting shot myself, and then had the sheer bad taste to let my wife-of-one-day's mother, sister, and six-year-old niece get obliterated by someone who should never have had a gun. And never would have but for the avarice and cowardice of a gun company, and the callousness of a gun lobby that's bullied and bribed most Republicans in Congress—and not a few of our party colleagues.

"So once again I've lost my 'objectivity.' I'm disqualified from saving lives because too many people too close to me have already lost theirs." Pausing, the President spoke more softly. "Guns made me a senator, and then a President. I suppose I should be more grateful. But too much of my life has been determined by guns and now it's happened to Lara. I'll be damned if I'll sit by and watch it happen to others, day after day. And I'll be damned if I'll let *you* sit by, either."

Watching Kilcannon, Hampton no longer concealed his astonishment.

"There's one more thing," the President finished quietly. "You think I hold a grudge because you supported Dick Mason. I don't. Our only problem is how badly you've misjudged me.

"You never thought I'd be President. You're still amazed I *am* President. And now you may be wondering if my emotions have overwhelmed what little judgment I possess." A smile played at the corners of Kilcannon's mouth. "After this meeting, I can understand that. But perhaps, Chuck, you should start considering whether I know *exactly* what I'm doing. Pretty much all the time."

NINE

FRANCIS XAVIER FASANO did not lack for self-confidence. He was—and knew he was—attractive, articulate, media-savvy, and an extremely subtle tactician. These gifts had caused his peers to make Fasano the youngest Majority Leader in memory, in the hope that he could heal the damage caused by the downfall of Macdonald Gage, while matching Kerry Kilcannon in youth and determination. But Fasano did not underrate his difficulties. Among them was to propitiate the conservative forces which provided money and activists to the GOP, while ensuring that he neither was, nor appeared to be, under their control. With no group was this harder than the Sons of the Second Amendment—which was why, the morning after calling on the Kilcannons, Fasano sought Senator Gage's advice.

They met in the well-appointed suite which, one-half year ago, had belonged to Gage himself. To Fasano, his predecessor was a reminder of how unsparing Kilcannon could be. Amidst the fight over Caroline Masters, Mason Taylor—a lobbyist and key supporter of Mac Gage—had tried to eliminate Chad Palmer as Gage's rival by leaking Palmer's permission, despite his pro-life views, for his daughter to have an abortion. This had led to Kyle Palmer's tragic death; Kilcannon's use of the FBI to trace the leak to Taylor—and, by implication, Gage—had forced Gage's resignation as leader. While Fasano doubted Gage had gone so far as to authorize the leak, as opposed to merely failing to restrain Taylor, this was not a distinction which seemed to trouble Kerry Kilcannon.

For this, Fasano accorded Gage a deferential sympathy which had earned him Gage's appreciation and, at times, sound tactical advice. But Fasano had another reason for this meeting: Gage, Fasano was quite sure, maintained an intimate connection with Charles Dane, president of the SSA, though neither Gage nor Dane acknowledged this. Through what Gage said—or, perhaps, chose not to say—Fasano hoped to divine Dane's thinking.

"The SSA wants a meeting," Fasano began. "Very private."

Gage gave the smile which was no smile, the one in which his teeth did not show. Though he maintained the Southern charm and the amiable, shrewd persona of a prosperous provincial worthy, Fasano sensed a bitterness burrowing through Gage like a tapeworm, a wound, inflicted by Kilcannon, which soured his every day. "Well," Gage answered, "they're our friend—a friend in need of friends. Kilcannon's got all the sympathy." Sipping his coffee, he studied Fasano over the rim of his china cup. "What do you suppose they want?"

"On the surface? To ensure we're loyal. To remind me that I should be loyal. As a substantive matter, to strategize how to beat Kilcannon if he launches a crusade for tougher gun laws. If the SSA can whip him now, with Lara Kilcannon's family murdered, the Democrats will run from gun control like the plague."

"True enough." This time Gage's teeth showed. "Then maybe they'll replace Kilcannon with you—*if* you're as loyal as you should be. What more could they want?"

How, Fasano wondered, could a politician as practiced as Gage seem so nakedly duplicitous. "Perhaps something more immediate," he answered.

"Such as?"

"Remember Martin Bresler? He was working on a deal with Kilcannon. The same one Kilcannon later floated to the president of Lexington Arms."

Gage gazed at the chandelier, as if straining to remember. "As I recall, the gun companies decided Bresler was a bit of a loose cannon."

"That's one version. The other is that the SSA took Bresler down." Fasano finished his coffee. "Suppose you're Charles Dane. The SSA has adamantly opposed the President's proposed settlement of lawsuits against companies like Lexington in exchange for voluntary background checks at gun shows. Then this batterer gets a Lexington gun—maybe at a gun show—and executes three members of the First Lady's family. What, exactly, do you tell the gun companies *now?*"

Fasano watched Gage choose between maintaining a pose of ingenuousness and conceding inside knowledge. "That depends," Gage said at length. "To me, these lawsuits are a terrible abuse: suing gun companies for selling a legal product that some criminal later uses for his own evil purposes. That runs counter to the common sense of the American people."

Fasano suppressed a smile—never was Gage more disingenuous than when he spoke in pieties. "It does," he agreed. "Or did. Until the Costello murders."

Gage's eyes glinted. "You're thinking maybe that now Lara Kilcannon will sue Lexington for the wrongful deaths of her mother, sister, and niece, asking for enough in compensatory and punitive damages to drive Lexington into bankruptcy. An object lesson for anyone who kowtows to the SSA, courtesy of our President." Briefly Gage licked his lips, as though, Fasano imagined, tasting his own bile. "Kilcannon likes reminding us of what a prick he is—for him, that was the beauty of what he did to me. But using his wife is too unsubtle, using a First Lady too unseemly."

"Did Macbeth 'use' Lady Macbeth?" Fasano rejoined. "I saw them yesterday, Mac. As sorry as I was for her, it felt like visiting tempered steel. But you're right, of course—they're both too smart for that."

Gage studied him. "And so?"

"Go back and count sisters one more time." Pausing, Fasano spoke more quietly. "On the drive home, Bernadette asked what was troubling me. It took me a moment to remember the sister who survived."

Gage sat back with the ruminating air of a man discovering his own subconscious thoughts. "So the other surviving sister brings a lawsuit," he said slowly, "represented by some raging greed-head of a plaintiffs' lawyer who made millions suing tobacco companies. And you figure that's occurred to the SSA."

Fasano met his gaze. "I figure it's occurred to Kerry Kilcannon. And Charles Dane gives the President at least as much thought as I do."

Gage smiled like a teacher whose pupil has passed a tough exam. "Tort reform," he said flatly.

"Tort reform with a meat ax. The SSA will want us to pass a bill banning this kind of lawsuit." Fasano nodded toward his television, mutely flashing a picture of the First Lady in mourning, walking on the beach with her husband. "A tough sell at the moment. And we'd need a two-thirds vote to override Kilcannon's veto."

Turning, Gage watched the screen. "The principle's right," he answered. "It all depends on how we package it."

"Whatever the SSA might want," Fasano responded calmly, "I told them to wait for a meeting until we see what Kilcannon does. The President's got some real problems of his own, beginning with Chuck Hampton and the Democrats. At least five or six of them don't need a fight with the SSA."

Gage still eyed the screen. "If it's only *us* in Kilcannon's way, it's our problem. If it's Democrats, too, it's Kilcannon's problem. The SSA will see to that."

For a moment, Fasano also watched Lara Kilcannon's image on television, a slim figure in blue jeans and an over-sized sweater, leaning against her husband. The cynic in him wondered if, knowing the cameras watched, Lara had chosen to project her vulnerability. "Lara Kilcannon," he rejoined, "could change everything."

Gage turned to him, as if unmoved by what he had seen. "She'll get some short-term sympathy, I agree. But people may decide they're going overboard.

"She's from California; he's from New Jersey. The nearer you live to water, the more clueless you become. Good people with guns won't like being blamed for the actions of a wife-beater." Gage smiled grimly. "To millions of Americans, guns are a religion, like NASCAR. It's not economics which drives politics anymore—it's values. People in the heartland sense Kilcannon's not right with his God."

"On abortion," Fasano answered coolly, "he'll never be right with God. But our mistake is to believe that he's some sort of different species—a fanatic liberal running on emotion and intuition.

"I think he understands everything you just said, Mac, and has simply made a different calculation. Different, and huge—a cosmic gamble." Fasano's tone had lost all pretense of deference. "Kilcannon's game is nothing less than the realignment of American politics. He *wants* us to be the only place the SSA can go: he figures that issues like guns and abortion will drive women away in truckloads, along with moderates and suburbanites.

"The right wing can turn enough voters out in most Republican primaries that you just can't win against them. Then Kilcannon takes the SSA in states like California and jams them down our throat—in the states he needs to win, he figures, the right is strong enough to win our primary, and offensive enough to lose us the general election. *That's* his biggest reason for pursuing this."

Gage's expression was keen with interest. "Which makes him not only a prick, but a cold-blooded prick."

Fasano shrugged. "Have any quarrel with that?"

"None. Except that Kilcannon's wrong." Gage folded his hands in front of him. "Less than half the people in this country vote. We don't need a majority to win. We need a fully committed minority, one which votes the issues they care about first, last, and always. Our message on guns is simple: the Second Amendment is absolute; the government shouldn't interfere with gun rights; and existing laws are all we need. Ask yourself this: do folks want to ban stock car racing because Dale Earnhardt cracked up his car?"

"Tell that to our moderates," Fasano retorted. "New Englanders like Kate Jarman and Cassie Rollins. Not to mention Chad Palmer."

At this mention of Palmer, Gage stared fixedly at Fasano's Persian rug. "Palmer," he said quietly, "was what went wrong with Masters. Kilcannon got to him first. Don't let that happen here."

"I don't intend to. But Palmer will want something."

"Then find a way to give it to him. At least within reason." Gage sat back, his manner becoming more expansive. "Want my overall advice on how to beat Kilcannon on gun control?"

"That's what I was hoping for."

"Lie low. Let Kilcannon make all the noise, and let the SSA work below the radar screen. Control the calendar—slow things down until passions have cooled, so that the natural order of politics can reassert itself. Let other senators take the lead. Just remind folks of how much better it is when this great deliberative body is allowed to work its will, so that we get the right bill rather than a hasty one."

That, Fasano thought, was merely stating the obvious. Pointedly, he asked, "No nuances? After all, we're dealing with a President's murdered relatives."

Contentment crept into Gage's features, as if he had been waiting for this moment, certain enough of Fasano's purpose to know that it would come. "Just a story I heard," he answered smoothly. "Maybe it's worth passing on."

Gage paused, as if reluctant to impart unpleasant news. "Awhile ago you mentioned Martin Bresler, and whether it was the SSA that took him down for dealing with Kilcannon on safety locks. What I heard, Frank, is that Bresler brought this deal to *you* before he took it to Kilcannon."

Fasano felt his expression go blank, his reflex when cornered. "Go on."

"The story is that Bresler told you that this was our party's chance to moderate our image—embrace 'gun safety' and help the manufacturers find a way out of trouble. If it worked out right, the rumor has Bresler telling you, maybe our party could take some modest steps like background checks at gun shows."

Fasano mustered a smile. "And so?"

"So Kilcannon's argument is that Lexington could have stopped the murder of his wife's family." Pausing, Gage's voice softened. "His real argument, if he knew about this rumor, would be that *you* could have stopped it. But the only folks who know are all your friends. Or so the story goes."

Fasano shrugged. "In this town, Mac, you hear all sorts of things."

"I know." Glancing around his former office, Gage's

voice filled with sympathy and regret. "A false rumor cost me *your* job. But I felt honor-bound to pass this on."

And with it, Fasano guessed, a tacit message from the SSA. "Thanks, Mac," he answered blandly. "You've always been a friend."

TEN

TWO DAYS AFTER his return, Kerry met with Clayton Slade; Jack Sanders, his principal domestic policy advisor; and Alex Cole, his congressional liaison.

In those two days—despite the chorus of relief and praise stemming from the announcement of Mahmoud Al Anwar's death—the President had not appeared in public. Though the media was an echo chamber of speculation, in the tumult over Al Anwar there had been no leaks regarding his directive to Clayton, Sanders and Cole. This was as Kerry intended.

Before the others were settled, Clayton took Kerry aside. "Bob Lenihan called, Mr. President. He made his apologies for asking, but he desperately wants to see you."

This brought an ironic smile to Kerry's lips. "No matter how dire the national condition, or my own, I'll always have time for Bob." Turning, he spoke to Cole. "Run that tape for us, Alex. At the least it will focus our thinking."

Cole pressed the button on Kerry's VCR. On the screen, Paul Harshman of Idaho, a member of the SSA Board of Governors, stood in the well of the Senate. Gravely, he read from his copy of a letter sent to Kerry by George Callister, provided to Harshman by Lexington Arms.

"It's an interesting experience," the President said with muted sarcasm, "hearing your own mail read aloud. It almost sounds like I wasn't meant to read it."

"*It is with deep sorrow and regret,*" Harshman quoted, "*that we learned one of our handguns had been so terribly misused . . .*"

"Only handguns?" Kerry murmured. "Once again, Callister forgot the bullets."

On the tape, Harshman's gaunt visage assumed an expression of deep solemnity. "*To prevent such tragedies in the future, we propose the following:*

"*First, Lexington will pay for the cost of voluntary background checks at gun shows when any Lexington weapon is sold . . .*"

"No doubt Bowden would have volunteered," Clayton remarked.

"*Second,*" Harshman continued, "*we will join you, Mr. President, in urging Congress to fund a comprehensive drive to ensure that all criminal acts of domestic violence are entered into the database for background checks . . .*"

"No point in volunteering," Kerry observed, "unless you're certain you'll be caught."

"*In this manner,*" Harshman went on, "*we can better control all those prone to violence without abridging the rights of law-abiding gun owners . . .*"

"Insulting," Clayton murmured disgustedly. "Total eyewash, right from the SSA playbook, intended to make Lexington sound 'responsible' in the public mind. I'm surprised he remembered to send you a copy."

Kerry kept staring at the television. "Callister's playing games with me," he told the others softly. "In public. No one should try to do that with a President."

When the tape was over, Clayton spoke first. "No leaks," he ordered Cole and Sanders. "No speculation about the President's motives. I don't want to read some article in *Newsweek* or the *New York Times* about the anatomy of this decision."

Both men nodded. "Okay," Clayton said to Sanders. "Take us through the polling data."

"What we found," Sanders told the President, "is that

almost seventy percent of Americans think that the Constitution protects gun ownership for individuals. And well over half of those are concerned that you'll go too far in eroding gun rights. I'd save licensing and registration for another day . . ."

"We license drivers," Kerry objected. "We register cars."

"Seems right. But there's this libertarian mythology built around the Second Amendment. Where in the Bill of Rights does it say that a 'well-organized militia' has the right to drive a Ford?"

"What about the SSA mantra—'all we have to do is enforce existing gun laws'?"

Sanders glanced at the paper in his lap. "Fifty-four percent agree with the SSA. But that's misleading. Because almost no one knows what bullshit 'existing law' really is."

Silent, Kerry appraised him. Quietly, he said, "I take it your polling included questions about the murders."

For an instant, Sanders hesitated. "It did. A great majority believed that 'existing law' would have prevented Bowden from buying a handgun without a background check. When we explained that while 'existing law' made it 'illegal' for a batterer to buy a gun, there was no background check required to determine if Bowden was a batterer, most folks were amazed . . ."

" 'Existing law,' " Kerry interposed in mordant tones. "The honor code for criminals."

"Not a bad line," Clayton observed. "Better than when you called gun shows 'Tupperware parties for murderers.' Our rhetoric needs to distinguish between felons or spouse abusers, and the 'normal' folks who take their kids to gun shows instead of Disney World."

"That's fine," Kerry responded. "But our real challenge is to win. And that means saying clearly and succinctly exactly what we'll do to reduce gun violence, and then trying to enact it with all the weapons we possess.

"We Democrats have developed this sick attraction to losing, and an absolute fear of being tough—or even saying what we believe. That's why I beat Dick Mason in the primaries when nobody thought I would. Voters finally decided they didn't want a President with no idea of who he was from one week to the next.

"Oddly enough, Americans find an identity crisis unnerving in a leader. They expect me to be precisely who I am, and they've always known where I stand on guns. And why." Pausing, Kerry softened his tone. "I can make a clear distinction between responsible gun owners and people like John Bowden. But if this isn't the time for us to stop the cycle of violence, it never will be. The question is whether we're good enough to rally the country, and mean enough to beat the Republicans *and* the SSA."

Sober, the others seemed to ponder what this might involve. "How was your meeting with Chuck Hampton?" Cole asked.

"Chuck has his concerns," Kerry replied calmly. "Five or six senators who still think I'd screw up a two-car parade, if only out of recklessness."

"Maybe we can help him out," Cole suggested. "Throw in some stuff that'll never pass, like licensing and registration, then let Chuck's waverers strip them off the bill. That would allow them to stand up for the gun rights of ordinary citizens, and still vote for what we really want."

Kerry shook his head. "That builds in more delay, which is what *Fasano* wants. We need to propose the law we mean to see enacted and build pressure to pass it quickly."

Cole considered this. "Then the best way to do that, Mr. President, is to frame this as anticrime legislation. We're keeping bad guns and bad bullets away from bad people. Period."

Kerry smiled faintly. "Sounds simple, doesn't it. Accomplish that, and we'll deserve the Nobel Peace Prize." Turning to Sanders, he asked, "How *do* we manage that?"

"Universal background checks, to start. On every gun sold in America."

Kerry nodded. "At the least, a criminal shouldn't be able to break out of jail, walk across the street to a gun show, and buy a Lexington P-2. As I intend to tell a joint session of Congress, very soon."

"You're rolling this on national TV?" Sanders asked. "That raises the stakes, Mr. President."

"So did Bowden," Kerry answered softly. "With a little help from you guys, I think I can find the words."

The sense of consequence, and the pressure it placed on Kerry, seemed as sobering to the others as it felt to Kerry himself. "I can reemerge in public only once," he told them. "When I do, I'd better light up the switchboards. Or this is going nowhere."

The room was silent. "Lara will be with me," Kerry continued. "My speech to Congress should be the beginning of a national campaign—meetings with victims and cops, going to any state or district where the senator or congressman is susceptible to pressure. And if that doesn't work, we'll hold hostage whatever pet project they most want."

"Hardball," Cole cautioned the President, "could cost us down the road."

Kerry stood, restless. "We've got no choice, Alex. In the Senate we'll have to crack a filibuster—all Fasano and the SSA will need is forty senators to keep this law from coming to a vote. To pass it I have to impress—or buy—at least sixty-one senators. Failing that, we'll be forced to make our appeal somewhat more Darwinian."

Without pause, Kerry turned back to Sanders. "Just draft a law that works," he directed. "No guns for people like

Bowden. No guns that accept forty-round magazines. No Eagle's Claw bullets for anyone. I'll take it from there."

After the meeting, Kerry and Clayton sat alone.

"You'll need absolute self-control," Clayton told him. "Calculated fury—no public displays of anger, no mistakes of the heart. Just keep up the pressure until the SSA goes radioactive.

"This can't be about you, Kerry. Or even about Lara. You've already got all the sympathy you need, without asking."

Kerry stared at him. "Why do you suppose I had you sit on Al Anwar's death until after we buried Lara's family? For those four days we didn't need to ask."

For a moment, Clayton was silent. "What about Bob Lenihan?" he asked. "Do you want to see him?"

"Invite him back for my speech to Congress. It's occurred to me he could be useful."

Clayton studied him. "And Callister's letter?"

Turning, Kerry gazed out the window. "It can wait," he answered softly. "I'm saving Callister for last."

That evening, Kerry and Lara dined alone, by candlelight. Their conversation, as so often now, was desultory and muted.

"Has Mary talked about a lawsuit?" Kerry asked. "Or met with any lawyers?"

"Not that I know of." Across the table, Lara gave him a querying look. "She still blames me, Kerry, and she's still just trying to cope. What made you think of that?"

"A couple of things. Maybe you should ask her."

ELEVEN

At one side of the narrow hallway to the Democratic cloakroom, Minority Leader Chuck Hampton was seated in a phone booth reserved, with his nameplate, for his exclusive use. Enclosed in glass for privacy, Hampton spoke quietly to President Kilcannon.

"An address to a joint session of Congress," he repeated. "Tomorrow night. Unless you think it's a terrible idea."

And if I do? Hampton wondered to himself. "I suppose," he answered dryly, "that depends on what you're asking for."

"Merely a law that works," the President answered. "Universal background checks. More money to enforce them. No licensing or regulation, you'll be relieved to know. If it helps, you can tell your apprehensive friends you talked me out of it."

Hampton smiled. "How about beat some sense into you?"

The President laughed softly. "That, too. Assuming that they'll believe it." His voice became somber. "As for what I'm asking for, tell them that I mean to win, and expect their help in doing that. This isn't just an exercise."

By now, Hampton knew his man; roughly translated, "tell them . . . I expect their help" included, "and if I have to, I'll institute a reign of terror to get it." Despite his fear of the consequences, Hampton felt an odd exhilaration— as a matter of pure politics, the exercise of power and guile, Kilcannon's battle with Frank Fasano might well become a classic.

"I expect your people polled this, Mr. President. But my favorite technique's a little less scientific. Every weekend when I'm back home, I get in my pickup truck, drive to a country store, buy coffee and a paper, and talk to whoever's there. Then I get back in the truck, throw the paper in the back, and drive to the next store to buy coffee and a paper . . ."

Kilcannon laughed. "Do you ever actually read the paper?"

"No time. Too busy buying them to read them. Last Sunday I bought six or seven."

"And?"

"You're onto something. People find it disturbing that this guy could buy a gun. Oddly, the most pissed-off guy I talked to is a federally licensed gun dealer. He's sick of competing with folks who claim they're not in the business so they won't have to run background checks, then go around peddling their wares at gun shows or out of the trunk of their car to any deviant with money enough to buy them . . ."

"I'll take all the support I can get, Chuck, wherever I can find it. I won't quibble about motive."

Through the glass, Hampton saw Senator Vic Coletti pass by, flashing him a quick glance of curiosity. "Anyhow," he told the President, "I was a little bit encouraged. For once the SSA may have more trouble than it knows."

"If so," Kilcannon answered, "they'll start putting the screws to your list of suspect Democrats. Let me know whoever you think may need a call from me."

With grim humor, Hampton imagined the President's tender ministrations to the frightened souls whose votes would be in play. "What about the Republicans?" he asked.

"I only know what you do, Chuck. Five or six of them will wonder which way they should jump. We're going to need them all."

This corresponded with Hampton's calculations. "I guess you saw Paul Harshman's little show."

"Of course." The President's tone held the quiet calm Hampton knew to be deceptive. "Wouldn't have missed it for the world."

"That wasn't just the SSA, I'm sure. I'd guess it was Fasano. He's looking to give his people cover."

"Then he really should do better, shouldn't he."

"Oh, he will. If I were you, I'd hang up on me right now, and get Chad Palmer on the line."

Once more, Vic Coletti passed, quickly peering into Hampton's booth. "Palmer," the President answered, "is already on his way."

At seven o'clock, Chad Palmer entered the President's private office.

A student of history, Palmer briefly noted the early photograph of Lincoln, the cartoon caricatures of FDR and a laughing Teddy Roosevelt, the magnificent walnut table on which John F. Kennedy had signed the ratification of the nuclear test ban treaty and, more recently, the antagonists had signed the Israeli-Palestinian accord of 1993. Hand resting on the desk, Palmer mused aloud, "That seems like another time."

"It was. In far too many ways."

Palmer turned to him. "How is Lara, Mr. President?"

"Not great, as you can well imagine. But speaking out may give her something to hold on to." Waving him to a chair, Kilcannon asked, "And Allie?"

Stiffly, Palmer sat; two years of imprisonment and torture by Islamic extremists—which had ended his once-promising career as an Air Force pilot—still hampered the movement of his arms. "Some better," he answered.

"She's started doing volunteer work at a school here in the District. Like Lara, I suppose, she's needing to reach out."

At this, the President lapsed into a pensive quiet. "For Lara," he admitted softly, "that could be a lifeline. Perhaps for both of us."

For a moment, Palmer thought, the President seemed a very lonely man. Chad considered what to say, then spoke from his heart. "Perhaps more than you know, Mr. President, I feel for you. In a way, Kyle's death put me where you find yourself. Allie can't help blaming my career."

Silent, the President gazed off into some middle distance, as though at a painful and uncertain future. "All I can do," he said at length, "is get up every morning. And wait this out, however long it takes."

Palmer nodded his understanding. The President, he knew, revealed his private self to very few. But Chad could not know whether, tonight, to do so was a relief, or another burden for a man about to undertake a challenge which could make or break his Presidency. Perhaps, Palmer conceded with the unsparing self-scrutiny which was his nature, he himself wished to avoid the difficult subject at hand.

"You wanted to talk about this gun bill, Mr. President."

"Yes." Abruptly, Kilcannon refocused. "I need your help, if you can give it."

Frowning, Palmer chose his words. "Maybe in time," he said in a dubious tone. "Maybe. But I can't get out front on this."

That the President's expression betrayed such open disappointment told Palmer how deeply invested Kilcannon already was—as a practical politician, the President could not be surprised by Chad's reluctance. Quietly, Kilcannon said, "Walk me through that, if you don't mind."

There was no point in mincing words. "It's pretty straightforward, Mr. President. You're a pariah to the right.

Some of them have forgiven me for backing you on the Masters nomination—I suppose on the theory that losing a daughter unmoored me from sound principle. But they won't forgive me this.

"In my party, gun rights are a visceral issue. At the least I need to sound out sentiment within our caucus." Pausing, Palmer added, "And, of course, there's Frank Fasano."

"What about him?"

"He feels you coming, Mr. President. He already knows that you won't settle for a symbolic battle, or a tactical defeat."

Kilcannon cocked his head. "He's told you that?"

"In so many words. What he made quite explicit is that this is the first test of his leadership, and therefore an absolute test of party loyalty for the rest of us. If you crack us on guns, he argues, it's all downhill from there."

"Downhill for Republicans? Or merely for Fasano?"

"In Fasano's mind, they're the same. I may not give a damn about the SSA, but he does. In fact, he believes their support is essential to displacing you, and therefore to the benefit of all right-thinking Republicans." Briefly, Palmer smiled. "I'm a Republican, he reminded me. At least for now."

Kilcannon did not return his smile. "Whichever way you jump, Chad, you'll help the side you're on. A reputation for integrity will do that."

Palmer shrugged. "It's always amazed me," he answered dryly, "what getting yourself kidnapped and tortured will do for your career. Even if I wasn't a volunteer."

To Palmer, the President's smile was painfully fleeting. "Neither was I," he answered. "Like getting shot, this issue found me."

Once again, Palmer felt Kilcannon's solitude. "I'm truly sorry, Mr. President. All the way around."

TWELVE

IN HIS COMMODIOUS OFFICE at the SSA, Charles Dane watched CNN, waiting for Kerry Kilcannon to enter the House of Representatives.

With him were his legislative and communications directors, Carla Fell and Bill Campton. Silent, they watched as television cameras swept the chamber, crowded with congressmen and senators, members of the cabinet, the Supreme Court, and the Joint Chiefs of Staff. Even had he not known the circumstances, Dane would have sensed that this occasion was extraordinary. The chamber was unusually hushed, the assembled dignitaries forgoing the whispered asides and knowing smiles of those accustomed to pomp and power, instead choosing, on this night, to sit silent and somber. Briefly, the cameras caught Frank Fasano, his hooded gaze inscrutable, and then Lara Costello Kilcannon, sitting in the gallery with her sister, Mary, and the families of the other victims. Beside the First Lady was a black teenager whom Dane could not identify, but was grimly confident had lost a relative to gunfire.

Mr. Speaker, the Sergeant at Arms called out, *the President of the United States.*

The door of the chamber opened, and Kerry Kilcannon entered.

Save for his brief statement before the funeral, the President had not been seen in public. Almost none of those assembled had spoken to him since the wedding. Now they stood, the applause swelling and supportive. As he moved, unsmiling, down the aisle to the rostrum, Kilcannon paused to accept the condolences and good wishes of senators and congressmen, some of whom touched his arm or whispered their remarks. The aisle became crowded; Kilcannon stopped repeatedly, making no effort to hurry. The applause kept rising, mingled with cheers.

This, said Wolf Blitzer on CNN, *will no doubt be remembered as one of the more remarkable moments in the recent history of Presidential addresses to Congress.*

On the screen, Chad Palmer stepped forward, giving Kilcannon a firm handshake and a brisk word of support. Then the President continued on, turning one way, then the other, as legislators crowded around. The camera captured Kilcannon's perfunctory handshake and quick nod to Frank Fasano and then, just before he proceeded to the rostrum, a much longer moment with Senator Chuck Hampton. Bracing the President's shoulders, Hampton spoke softly; head lowered, Kilcannon listened, nodding, and then briefly grasped Hampton's arms, a display of warmth which seemed so genuine that Dane found it unsettling.

"The key," he told Carla Fell, "may be how hard Chuck Hampton works for him."

"Maybe so," she answered, "but in the end it'll all come down to Palmer and Fasano."

Kilcannon reached the rostrum, to be greeted by Speaker Thomas Jencks, a stocky, grey-haired Republican, and Vice President Ellen Penn. Silent, he handed each of them a copy of his message. For almost five minutes, the respectful applause continued unabated, with Kilcannon utterly still, eyes downcast in an attitude of deep reflection and humility. Only when, at last, the sound slowly receded did Thomas Jencks speak the ceremonial greeting.

Members of Congress, I have the high honor and distinct privilege of presenting to you the President of the United States . . .

Those attending rose as one.

From the rostrum, Kerry Kilcannon watched them, his chest tight with emotion. He recalled like yesterday the tumult as he accepted his party's nomination, the chill day of his inaugural address, but never a speech so fraught with moment. As the silence fell at last, he remembered Inez Costello, then Joan, and finally Marie, smiling with delight as he danced with her at the wedding. And then, stepping forward to the rostrum, he looked up at his wife.

On television, Lara Kilcannon's lips moved, as though in a silent encouragement only he could hear.

"They're certainly milking this one," Bill Campton said to Dane. And then Kilcannon began to speak.

Thirteen years ago, the President said in quiet tones, *my brother James Kilcannon died of a fatal gunshot wound. Thirteen days ago, three more members of our family were murdered with a gun . . .*

Dane stared at the screen in wonder. "This is a mistake. He's making it all about *them.*"

The chamber was hushed, as though muted by an opening so personal in nature. Taut, Lara watched, holding her sister's hand and that of Louis Morgan, knowing that Kerry had written these words himself.

"Because they were part of our family," he continued, "you know their names. As we have mourned, you have mourned with us. And no words of mine will ever match your grace and generosity . . ."

*

Pausing, Kilcannon seemed to gaze straight into Dane's office, and then his voice grew stronger.

But if this were solely a family tragedy, four senseless deaths separated by thirteen years, I would not have come here.

I am here because in those thirteen years, almost four hundred thousand other Americans have died from gunfire. Now Kilcannon looked up at the gallery, speaking slowly and respectfully. *When Lara's mother, niece and sister died, three more people died with them—Henry Serrano, a devoted husband and father of three; David Walsh, whose wedding would have taken place tomorrow; Laura Blanchard, one day from commencing her sophomore year at Stanford. And on that same day and hour, only a few short blocks from where we are gathered now, Mae Morgan was shot to death by* her *estranged husband.*

Their families are here with us tonight . . .

As Kerry recited their names, each survivor stood to more applause—Felice Serrano and her children; David Walsh's young fiancée; Laura Blanchard's parents, and, beside Lara, Mae Morgan's fourteen-year-old son, Louis. "I'll do my best," Kerry had promised them before the speech, and so he would.

"Mae Morgan," he went on, "died as eighty people die every day in this country—mourned by her family, invisible to the media, unknown to the rest of us." Pausing, Kerry's gaze swept the chamber. "Why is this? Because the carnage is so great that only the mass slaughter of schoolchildren, or the death of a public figure, ever gives us pause.

"All of us know that every assassination of an American President was committed with a gun. All of us then living remember our ineradicable grief when John F. Kennedy was murdered. But all too few of us know that since that awful day more Americans have died from gunshot wounds than died in all the wars of the twentieth century, the bloodiest hundred years in world history . . ."

Chuck Hampton could hear the passion in Kilcannon's voice, could feel the rapt attention of those who watched.

"Day after day," the President told them, "guns claim ten more children, three more women at the hands of a husband or intimate partner, eighty more people in all.

"Year after year, this terrible toll of death exceeds by at least ten times that of the next twenty-five industrialized nations combined." Kilcannon stood straighter, voice filled with anger. "Only in America, in *this* city, do surgeons prepare for combat duty by training at an urban hospital . . ."

"Did you know that?" Hampton whispered to Vic Coletti. Silent, Coletti shook his head.

"Only in America," Kilcannon said with sudden softness, "do we protect the right to sell bullets designed to tear apart the internal organs of their victim—in the case of our family, of Lara's six-year-old niece, Marie.

"What causes this? Are Americans less humane than the Japanese, or Australians, or the Swedes? Do we truly believe that the random slaughter of the innocent is part and parcel of the right to own a gun? Or that the death of a Mae Morgan is the price that we must pay?

"It is *not*." Now Kilcannon's voice resonated with moral urgency. "It is the price of our collective failure to pass laws to keep criminals and drug addicts and spousal abusers from taking the lives of women like Mae Morgan, or children like Marie . . ."

Led by Senator Chuck Hampton, the Democrats stood to applaud.

*

In Clayton's office, he and Kit watched instant polling, transmitted by closed circuit, appear beneath the President's face. Moment by moment, his approval numbers rose.

"Seventy-one percent," Kit murmured.

Watching, Lara's throat constricted. "What," Kerry called out, "do those companies who sell these weapons—and design these bullets—say to the death of Marie Bowden?

" 'We didn't know her father.

" 'We didn't ask him to slaughter his family.

" 'All that decency requires of us is to express our sympathy—yet again—and say that we should punish the perpetrators *after* they've misused a gun.' "

Once more, Kerry's voice grew quieter. "Well, John Bowden is not alive to punish. And even if he were, and then we took his life, it would not resurrect the six other lives he took.

"Our only chance to save those lives was to deny this man a gun which could murder seven people in less than seven seconds . . ."

Yes, Lara silently told her husband. *This is good.*

"Those who would keep things as they are," the President continued, "tell us we only need to 'enforce existing laws.' So let us consider that.

"Under 'existing law,' we took away John Bowden's gun at the time of his arrest.

"Under 'existing law,' we entered his name into a computer, so that he could not buy another gun from a federally licensed dealer." Once more, Kilcannon's voice was etched with irony. "And so—under 'existing law'—

John Bowden flew to Las Vegas and bought a gun and a magazine which could hold forty Eagle's Claw bullets.

"Under 'existing law,' 'private sellers' at gun shows don't have to run background checks before they sell a gun.

"Under 'existing law,' the provisions limiting gun magazines to ten bullets don't apply to those manufactured before the law was passed." Yet again, Kerry's voice softened. "Under 'existing law,' the eleventh bullet from her father's gun murdered Marie Bowden . . ."

At this, Fasano turned to Harshman. "You'd better have an answer," he said under his breath.

"How," Kilcannon asked, "did Bowden come to buy this gun? Because he read two advertisements in *The Defender* magazine.

"The first warned that the Lexington P-2 was an endangered species, 'banned in California.' " Briefly, Kilcannon shook his head in wonder. "And just in case John Bowden would not know where else to buy one, *The Defender* placed it next to an advertisement for a gun show in Las Vegas, featuring the Lexington P-2."

"They can't read a dead man's mind," Bill Campton said to Dane. "No one can prove where he bought that gun, or why."

"Kilcannon," Dane answered, "doesn't concern himself with fairness. Let alone the niceties of evidence."

Under "existing law," Kilcannon continued, *the maker of this deadly weapon placed it in John Bowden's hands . . .*

Listening, Chad Palmer glanced at his Republican colleague, Cassie Rollins. Her profile—the short blonde hair, the angular face of the athlete she had been—was still. Her attention was more than justified: in Maine, where Cassie would run for reelection, guns and hunting were ingrained.

"The essence of this tragedy," the President said in an incisive tone, "is that it makes no sense. Especially to the many millions of responsible gun owners who know these simple truths:

"That no 'sportsman' uses weapons that will kill twenty deer—or twenty people—in less than twenty seconds.

"That no 'marksman' uses bullets designed to tear human flesh to shreds.

"That no act of self-defense requires a gun designed for acts of war.

"That no license to hunt deer rests on the license to hunt down women and children.

"That no freedom in our Bill of Rights frees criminals and terrorists to turn those rights against us . . ."

All at once the gallery was standing, with the Democrats launching a wave of applause and cheers that seemed as though it would not stop. Awkwardly, the Republicans rose as well, most, like Fasano, applauding tepidly. Paul Harshman, Palmer observed, stood with folded arms.

"The SSA," Cassie murmured to Chad, "will have to go all out."

As the applause continued, Charles Dane went to his wet bar and poured himself a bourbon and water. "Universal background checks," he said to Fell and Campton. "That's where this is headed."

Fell shook her head. "Too big a stretch. He must know he'll never pass it."

Dane took his first sip of bourbon. "Do *you*?"

Under "existing law," Kilcannon called out through the applause, *criminals are prohibited from buying guns. But forty percent of gun purchases are made through private sellers—often at gun shows—whom "existing law" does not require to run background checks to see if the buyer is prohibited.*

"Existing law," in short, is an honor code for criminals . . .

Dane emitted a short laugh.

For too long, Kilcannon continued, *the debate about guns has been a matter of faith and fear, driven by a fanatic few who just can't sleep at night unless they feel that someone, somewhere is out to get them.* Kilcannon paused again, and then said in a clear, commanding voice, *No longer.*

No longer should this fanatic few be allowed to claim that commonsense laws to prevent criminals from buying weapons are the first step to confiscation by a tyrannical government of their imagining.

No longer should they be heard to say that our only defense against criminals is to buy more guns, until America is an armed camp of the lawless and the fearful, and the body count which follows dwarfs the carnage we know today . . .

His listeners rose yet again. "We need Democrats," Dane instructed Carla Fell. "That's the only way to ensure that no president, Republican or Democrat, feels free to make this kind of speech again."

As the applause died down, Kilcannon's voice became soft with scorn. *The same magazine that directed John Bowden to his Lexington P-2 told its readers that our only means of crime prevention is "meeting evil force with proven protection" through "armed self-defense for all peaceful Americans." If only Mae Morgan had been quicker on the draw, I suppose this means, her son Louis would not be, effectively, an orphan.*

On the screen, Louis Morgan appeared in close-up, listening with stolid grief. Beside him, Lara Kilcannon touched his arm.

"No shame," Bill Campton said.

All of us, Kilcannon called out, *owe Louis Morgan better.*

Once more, the listeners rose, applauding. "That's the fourteenth standing ovation," Carla Fell reported.

"Eighty-three percent," Kit Pace said in wonder.

With deep satisfaction, Clayton smiled. "A dinner at D C Coast says he hits eighty-five."

"You're on. For eighty-five, I'd gladly throw in a bottle of wine."

Some will say, the President said softly, *that this is personal to me.*

It is. It is also personal to the families of Henry Serrano, David Walsh, Laura Blanchard, Mae Morgan, and to the millions of other Americans who have lost a parent, a child, or husband; or who've been maimed or paralyzed, their dreams forever shattered; or who live in fear for themselves and those they love.

Kerry stood straighter, his voice determined. *There is only this difference: I* am *the President. And I* will *act . . .*

Kerry paused again, surveying the faces before him. He felt a kind of transcendence, a calm, unhurried resolve to convey at last the weight of all he knew and felt.

"And so I've come to the Congress," he continued, "in the name of humanity and common sense, to ask you to act with me.

"For their part, Americans ask little enough of their elected representatives. Decent health care. Schools that teach. A fair chance to use their talents. Safety from external threats. Protection from random violence . . ."

"A modest program," Dane said wryly.

We have all sorts of excuses, Kilcannon went on, *beginning with cost, as to why our schools are failing, our health care flawed,*

*our chances in life unequal, and the world unsafe. But we have no
excuse for the death of a Mae Morgan, when saving her life would
have cost us next to nothing . . .*

"Will it be 'Mae Morgan's Law,' " Bill Campton wondered aloud. "Or 'Marie's Law'?"

"Next to nothing," Kilcannon repeated softly. "Like John
Bowden, Mae Morgan's husband was a batterer. Unlike
John Bowden, he bought *his* gun from a licensed dealer
after passing a background check.

"How? Because under 'existing law,' Congress has failed
to allocate sufficient money to allow most jurisdictions to
enter domestic violence convictions into a computer—in
this case, the government of our nation's capital, where the
records of Samuel Morgan's spousal abuse languished in a
cardboard box . . ."

With a small smile, Hampton turned to Vic Coletti.
"Think we'll be hearing quite as much from Fasano about
the virtues of 'existing law'?"

Coletti looked uncomfortable. "The President's doing
what he needs to—reframe the debate. I just hope he
doesn't sink my constituents who work at Lexington
Arms."

On the podium, Kilcannon's voice was tinged with
scorn. "Where 'existing law' is not riddled with loopholes
and exceptions, those who argue for its enforcement have
done their best to make it unenforceable.

"In theory, 'existing law' prevents licensed dealers from
selling to those convicted of felonies or violent misdemeanors, spousal abuses, drug offenses, and the
adjudicated mentally ill.

"Under 'existing law,' half the states have entered less
than sixty percent of all criminal convictions into their
computer systems.

"Under 'existing law,' thirteen states have never recorded a single domestic violence restraining order.

"Under 'existing law,' almost *no* state has automated records of those incarcerated for mental illness.

"Under 'existing law,' illegal aliens—including Islamic terrorists—can and have bought weapons to use against us."

Kilcannon paused, and then finished pointedly. "And even though alcohol is a leading cause of gun homicides, under 'existing law' even those convicted of multiple DUIs are allowed to buy a weapon . . ."

"That was the alcohol lobby," Coletti murmured to Chuck Hampton. "One of their better efforts."

"And one of our more craven," Hampton replied.

" 'Existing law,' " Kilcannon said succinctly, "exists in defiance of common sense."

"I don't need this," Cassie Rollins whispered to Chad Palmer.

Palmer suppressed a smile. "Does Fasano?" he whispered back.

Above them, Kilcannon seemed to be leaning forward, as though propelled by his own momentum. "Common sense," he told the Congress, "requires a law which keeps guns away from those who pose a threat to innocent lives.

"This is what I propose:

"A background check on every transfer of every gun. It makes no sense to bar the dangerous and deranged from buying weapons, and then make sure that they can buy one.

"A federally funded system for computerized background checks, effective in all fifty states. It makes no sense to bar violent felons from buying weapons if we don't know who they are.

"A law requiring that we retain the records of all background checks. It makes no sense that law enforcement could trace the purchase of fertilizer to Timothy McVeigh, but not the purchase of a weapon."

Kilcannon's delivery was staccato now. Palmer watched his fellow legislators—jaded though many were—become caught up in the rhythm of his words.

"A ban on all high-capacity magazines and cop-killer bullets. It makes no sense to treat weapons suited to the mass slaughter of the innocent as a household tool of self-defense . . ."

The gallery stood, emitting a cry of approval, and suddenly the Democratic congressmen and senators were on their feet. Watching, the President briefly nodded.

"Look at the little demagogue," Harshman murmured to Fasano.

Fasano glanced at him sharply. "*You* look at him, Paul. When you chose to read that letter aloud, you teed this up for him."

He turned back to appraise the President. This time, Fasano noted, Kilcannon had let the roar subside, speaking softly into the silence. "More funding," the President continued, "to prosecute all those committing gun crimes. It makes no sense to say that we should enforce 'existing law,' and then ensure that we lack the resources to enforce it.

"Full funding for the Centers for Disease Control to conduct research regarding the impact of violence on public health. It makes no sense to do this for accidents involving cars and then cut every dime of funding—as Congress has—to suppress the truth about the causes and costs of deaths and injuries involving guns."

This time Fasano said nothing to Senator Harshman. He did not need to—it was Harshman who had stripped the CDC of funding at the behest of the SSA.

"Finally," the President concluded, "mandatory safety locks on every new gun sold, including combination locks which keep guns from being fired by someone other than the owner. It makes no sense to protect children from design flaws in toy guns and candy cigarettes, and do nothing to prevent them from killing themselves—or being killed—by real guns."

"Eighty-six percent." In her elation, Kit Pace grinned at Clayton. "You win."

Clayton nodded. In close-up, Kerry appeared relaxed now, more confident than Clayton had ever seen him.

Let me be clear, Kerry was saying in the gentle lilt that, to Clayton, held a trace of Irish poetry. *I do not accept that violence in America is caused by guns alone. I support the right of all law-abiding citizens to own a gun for any lawful purpose. And I believe that gun owners and non-gun owners can share a common dream: to someday make deaths like these so rare that our grandchildren will learn of them with disbelief and wonder.*

Together, we can do this. I call on you to join me. I implore the Congress to act. And, for my own part, I will do my best to reach across the senseless divisions of the past.

There is, I believe, a first step I should take . . .

"Here it comes," Clayton said to Kit.

Several days ago, I received a letter from George Callister, the president of Lexington Arms. Senator Harshman read it to the Senate. But in the difficulties of the moment, I could not find the words to respond.

I do so now.

To Mr. Callister, I say, I fully appreciate and understand the spirit of your letter. I invite you to meet with me, alone, to seek ways to end these needless deaths. With lives at stake, we must not fail.

"Callister," Clayton murmured with a smile, "will regret that letter more than he could ever know."

On the screen, the President gazed up at the gallery, and then at the members of Congress. *Before he was murdered by a man with a gun,* Kilcannon finished, *Robert Kennedy admonished us "to tame the savagery of man, and make gentle the life of the world."*

In the name of our common humanity, let us begin.

Beginning among the Democrats, a deep roar of approval issued from the well of the House, swelling as members applauded with both hands raised aloft for the President to see. Utterly still, Kilcannon made no move to leave. *And so President Kilcannon,* the commentator intoned, *has launched a personal crusade against gun violence in America . . .*

"Eighty-eight percent," Kit said. To her utter surprise, her eyes had welled with tears.

Dane turned from the screen. "We can't let him split off Lexington," he told the others. "The little bastard means to pressure George Callister."

"We stopped Callister before," Fell answered.

"It'll be harder now." Dane turned to Campton. "Get onto the Internet. Ask our members to e-mail Congress, especially Democrats. And tell them how to reach everyone on Lexington's board."

Campton nodded. "How do *we* respond?"

"With care. Fasano's right about that. The line should be that we sympathize with Kilcannon, but that he's drawn the wrong lesson—you should be able to pass down a gun to your eighteen-year-old son, or sell one to your next-door neighbor, without putting them through a background check. This isn't a police state, after all. At least not yet.

"As for safety locks, he's proposing the 'Criminal Protection Act.' Think some rapist will wait for his victim to fiddle with a safety lock?"

"Kilcannon's overreaching," Campton agreed. "But what's the right lesson?"

"Tougher law enforcement. John Bowden should never have been out on bail. We support better domestic violence records, and stiffer sentences. Period."

After five minutes, Wolf Blitzer was saying, *the applause for President Kilcannon continues unabated.* On the screen, Lara Kilcannon gazed down at her husband.

This is the crest, Dane promised them. Tomorrow begins the fall.

"As soon as you can," he ordered Fell, "set up that meeting with Fasano."

Hours later, having said goodbye to the families, Kerry and Lara lay in bed.

"You were right about Mary," she told him. "Bob Lenihan has approached her about suing Lexington Arms."

Kerry laughed softly. But he had begun to feel the residue of a sustained adrenaline rush—a vague depression, the first echoes of self-doubt. In a quiet tone, he told Lara, "I did the best I could."

"The best *anyone* could," she assured him. With that, knowing that he needed this as much as she, Lara slipped into his arms.

THIRTEEN

THE NEXT MORNING, after a lengthy telephone call with the Secretary General of the United Nations, Kerry greeted Bob Lenihan in the Oval Office. "Your speech was perfect," Lenihan assured the President. "As incisive as a final argument to a jury."

Why was it, Kerry wondered with some amusement, that even Bob Lenihan's compliments sounded like self-praise. "*This* jury," he answered wryly, "is considerably larger. And in the case of their elected representatives, a good deal meaner and more self-interested. I needed to make them wonder if voting against me might not be riskier than they thought."

Lenihan smiled. "Seems like you succeeded."

And so, this morning, it did. The editorial reaction across the country was uniformly favorable, and the media's overnight polls confirmed Clayton's instant soundings. Congress, Alex Cole reported, already had been inundated with phone calls, faxes, and e-mails, in which—for once—support for Kerry outnumbered the dire warnings of gun rights supporters. "For now," Kerry cautioned Lenihan. "But the Speaker and Frank Fasano have just started to dig in."

Lenihan sat back, as though soaking in the sunlight through the windows of the Oval Office. But even in repose, his imposing frame and visage—square jaw, restless blue eyes, determined pouter pigeon's mouth—reminded Kerry of a man bent on consuming everything around him. Others found this feral aspect close to frightening; Kerry

accepted Lenihan's boundless self-absorption as the necessary engine of a plaintiffs' lawyer's makeup, which—albeit
with caution—the President could usefully employ. "That's
what I wanted to talk about," Lenihan said at last. "The
long haul. Has Lara thought about suing Lexington Arms?"

Kerry summoned an expression of mild surprise. "A
wrongful death action? There's no way, Bob. It would make
last night's speech—in fact, everything we say or do—look
like we're bent on lining our own pockets."

Lenihan's blue gaze was shrewd and appraising. "I
understand, Mr. President. But it really is too bad. The part
of the speech I most enjoyed was when you summarized
Lexington's paltry response to the murders, and then set
up this guy Callister. By the time you're through with him,
I'd bet there'll hardly be a prospective juror in America
who won't be hell-bent on taking Lexington to the
cleaners."

Kilcannon smiled briefly. "Is *that* what I was doing last
night? Poisoning the jury pool?"

"In a word—yes." Lenihan's own smile was knowing.
"A fortuitous by-product of 'making gentle the life of the
world.' "

Lenihan was no fool, Kerry thought again, when it came
to hidden motives and complex calculations. No doubt
it came from Lenihan's clear understanding of his own.
"Even if that was what I intended," Kerry responded, "and
even if Lara *could* bring suit, what would it buy me except
for a distraction I don't need?"

"Leverage. And a public relations tool of incalculable
value." Lenihan made a quick chopping motion, as if cutting to the core of Kerry's challenge. "Right now you're
playing in two arenas—Congress, and the 'court of public
opinion.' To win in those two dimensions, and beat the
SSA, you need a third dimension: litigation.

"A lawsuit against Lexington for its role in bringing

about the wrongful death of Lara's mother, sister and niece will transform the gun debate. We can turn that fucking company inside out."

"Whereas I can't."

"How could you, Mr. President? By setting loose the Justice Department? Under what pretext? You'd look like the tyrant the SSA's always claimed you are." Lenihan's mouth framed a smile of anticipation. "I can expose Lexington's greed and calculation—how they marketed to criminals, the way they developed the Eagle's Claw, why they kowtow to the SSA—then feed it to the press. I'd take George Callister's deposition and pillory him for days. It might not even get that far.

"They're already scared of me," Lenihan finished with absolute certainty. "Arm me with *this* case, and they'll give you everything you want on gun control before they'd dare to face me in front of a jury."

"Lexington?" Kerry inquired softly. "Or the SSA?"

"Both. Do you think the SSA wants me to expose that *it* controls the American gun industry? Hell no." Lenihan's own voice softened and his smile became complicit. "I can hardly believe, Mr. President, that none of this has occurred to you."

Kerry shrugged. "Perhaps I had a mental block," he answered coolly. "I can't quite see what this scenario has to offer you. Not money, surely—Lexington's nowhere near as rich as Philip Morris."

"True," Lenihan rejoined, "but there's a certain moral equivalency.

"You nailed it last night—guns and tobacco are the only two products in America not regulated for consumer safety. We can't even get safety locks, which is why six-year-olds blow their playmates' brains out by accident, and sixteen-year-olds commit suicide with someone else's gun."

Lenihan's voice became stentorian. "I've got all the money I need, Mr. President. This is about morality.

"We both know these bloodsuckers market to criminals and crazies. We both know that they're perfectly aware that the fucking Lexington P-2 is a weapon of choice for drug lords.

"How much would it have cost them to retrofit the P-2 so it wouldn't take a forty-round magazine? And wouldn't *you* like to see how they tested the Eagle's Claw to make sure it could shred somebody's liver? Hell, I wouldn't put it past those bastards to prop up a cadaver . . ."

Kerry began to laugh. " 'Morality,' Bob? Is that all?"

"Okay." Lenihan opened his arms in amiable capitulation. "I'm an excitement junky, and this would be the Super Bowl of litigation. All these moving parts—Congress, the Presidency, the SSA, the media, the courtroom, human drama on a scale that would make the O. J. Simpson trial look like dinner theater in Dubuque."

And you, Kerry thought, *pulling all these strings—including mine.* Calmly, he said, "We're talking about Mary, of course."

This time Lenihan's smile, confined to one corner of his mouth, never reached his eyes. "Yes," he answered. "I was hoping you'd recommend me.

"I can take on the big boys, Mr. President. With a two-hundred-person firm, we've got the bodies. All we need is Mary Costello."

Silent, Kerry gazed at him. "I know Mary's talked with you," he answered. "As I understand from Lara—and I'm sure you understand—she's not yet prepared to embrace the rigors of a lawsuit.

"But that's up to her. If Mary asks my advice, Bob, you can count on me to tell her that there's simply no one like you."

After a moment, Lenihan nodded his satisfaction. "That's all I can ask for, Mr. President."

Kerry was careful not to smile.

Shortly before noon, Clayton interrupted Kerry as he prepared for a meeting on Social Security reform.

"We've lost three men in the Sudan," Clayton told him.

Three soldiers, Kerry thought. Not fifty thousand, as in Vietnam. But three more grieving families to console, three more lives lost as a consequence of his orders.

Kerry put down his briefing book. "Are they flying the bodies into Ramstein?" he asked.

"Yes. We're getting the contact information for the families and, as we can, any plans for funerals or memorial services. Kit's drafting a statement now."

"I'll want to deliver it myself. And get me everything you can about those soldiers. When I call, their survivors should almost feel as though I knew them. At least as much as possible." Looking up at Clayton, Kerry added quietly, "I'd be a lousy wartime President, Clayton. I hate death far too much."

Slowly, Clayton nodded. "Speaking of which," he asked after a moment, "how was your meeting with Lenihan?"

"Much as I expected. He congratulated me on loading the dice against Lexington in Mary's future wrongful death action. I felt like Dr. Frankenstein, sitting in the Oval Office with a monster of my own creation."

"A large and powerful monster," Clayton amended, "who's placed millions of dollars at the disposal of the Democratic Party, and whose trade association of trial lawyers is looking for a way to maintain their influence in the brave new world of campaign finance reform. A monster to be handled with care." He smiled slightly. "But a very useful monster, in his place. As you told me just two days ago."

" 'In his place,' " Kerry answered. "That's the key."

Clayton considered this. "Will Mary sue?" he asked.

"Lara thinks so, in the end. But this lawsuit is only as good for our purposes as our ability to influence the way it's run.

"Lenihan wants glory—and, no matter what he says, money. I want to transform our public policy regarding guns. I can't count on Bob to know his place."

Clayton sat down. "I telephoned the Kilcannon Center, as you asked. They've brought on Sarah Dash—the lawyer who represented Mary Ann Tierney in the abortion case— to handle any litigation against gun companies."

Kerry nodded. "I can't elbow Lenihan aside—too delicate, and he brings some real weapons to a lawsuit. But perhaps we could induce Mary to engage a cocounsel. The Kilcannon Center is extremely well funded, and, other than by surname, I have no connection to them whatsoever. But they'd no doubt be more sensitive than Lenihan to what we want . . ."

"Sensitive? Or malleable?"

"That, too. After all, the Center was founded by my brother's key supporters as a memorial to the causes he embraced." Pausing, Kerry added mordantly, "Many of those people still see me as a memorial with a pulse— certainly not Jamie, but all the DNA that's left. They'll go along."

Clayton reflected. "Before you ask them," he admonished, "you'd better figure out how. As well as how you intend to try to control this lawsuit."

"Not directly." Kerry's voice softened. "That's among the many lessons of my mishandling of John Bowden. Today's meeting with Lenihan is potential evidence. If I were to become a witness in Mary's lawsuit—which I very well might be—I could be cross-examined about it. So no more meetings with her prospective lawyers. I don't want my fingerprints on this one."

Gazing out the window, Clayton pondered this. "Lara?" he asked.

FOURTEEN

THE FOLLOWING Monday brought a fresh outburst of violence between Israel and the PLO and, for Kerry Kilcannon, a vexing reminder of the limits of his power. He considered the leader of the PLO to be treacherous and a liar; the Israeli Prime Minister to be obdurate and obtuse; and neither of them willing to urge upon their people the steps necessary to achieve peace, or even stop killing each other into the next generation. "Tell your people the truth," he snapped by telephone at the head of the PLO. "For once. They're not going back to Israel to reclaim their parents' ancestral homes. Either get them to accept that, or they'll fester for another fifty years in these squalid refugee camps terrorists use as training grounds. If you can't do that, what's the point of you?"

But the Israeli Prime Minister was little help. "We have to defend our settlements, Mr. President."

"Which you never should have put there," Kerry retorted. "They're an utter provocation.

"Let me explain something. We're morally committed to your survival as a nation. But the day is past when you can use that to define our Middle Eastern policy. You've got the next Saddam Hussein two countries over, developing nuclear and biological weapons, and we can't very easily take him out—even if we decide to—because our Arab 'friends' won't help us as long as you and the Palestinians keep slaughtering each other. I'm not waiting until his anthrax hits New York for you to get this right . . ."

"Mr. President," the Israeli interrupted, "I can't make

the concessions you want. To make the peace, I must keep my majority in Parliament . . ."

"Tell your friends in Parliament that the first nuclear missile will land on them, not us." Kerry softened his voice. "The Holocaust is one of history's nightmares. The humanitarian debt it created is Israel's precious moral capital. It's been fascinating to watch you do your damnedest to deplete it . . ."

When this conversation had ended, the skies outside were dark, and a fresh wind drove sheets of rain against the windows. Kerry glanced at his watch. He had kept George Callister waiting for forty minutes.

At least Callister had the decency, Kerry thought, to look pained. "I remember meeting your wife's family," he said in his direct midwestern way. "I was heartsick at what happened."

"I know. You wrote me about it."

Callister's frozen look hinted at his embarrassment. "I tried to call you, Mr. President. They wouldn't put me through."

"They'd been dead for two days," Kerry answered quietly. "Lara's mother, sister and niece, murdered with a gun and bullets Bowden purchased at a gun show. The very transaction you wouldn't agree to stop two days before they died." Pausing, the President slid a letter across his desk. "And so you sent me *this*."

Callister's mouth compressed. "We had to make a proposal, and respond to what had happened. It was the only way to communicate with you."

"I suppose that's why you chose Paul Harshman."

Briefly, Callister looked down. "I'm not naive, Mr. President. Given all that had happened, we couldn't count on you to say that we'd even tried."

"Tried what?" In a tone tinged with irony, Kerry quoted from Callister's letter. " 'Lexington will pay for the cost of voluntary background checks at gun shows when any Lexington weapon is sold.'

"Who was going to volunteer, George? Bowden, or who-ever sold it to him?" Kerry's voice was softer yet. "Reading the letter, I was embarrassed for you. Hearing Harshman read it, I was embarrassed for me."

This time Callister's gaze did not waver. "What is it you want, Mr. President?"

"It's very simple. I want you to endorse what I've pro-posed to Congress, and put it into practice at Lexington Arms. Support background checks on all your weapons sold at gun shows. Retrofit your guns so that they only take ten rounds. Stop making Eagle's Claw bullets. In short, I want you to take the actions which would have saved Lara's family."

Callister drew a breath. "I can't let that last part pass," he said slowly. "If Bowden hadn't found a P-2, he'd have bought someone else's gun. The result would have been the same."

"Maybe so. But then it wouldn't have been *your* gun, would it? Or your bullets. *Or* your responsibility. Don't hide behind the other guys. The law I'm asking you to endorse applies to everyone." Kerry's tone was clipped. "This is your chance to save lives, George. Don't tell me how sorry you are. Do something."

Callister's smile was faint and, to Kerry, melancholy. "For myself, I would. I think you know that. As president of Lexington, I'll work with you." Briefly Callister paused. "But I can't endorse your program. I'm certain you know why."

"The SSA."

Callister grimaced. "Their power is real, and it includes

the power to wipe out jobs. Lexington isn't just about its guns. It's about its people . . ."

"And you wouldn't want them to become an 'endangered species.' Like the Lexington P-2."

Callister folded his hands, choosing silence. "For the rest of my life," Kerry told him with lethal quiet, "there won't be a day I don't imagine the six-year-old girl I danced with at our wedding, lying on an operating table with her insides torn out by an Eagle's Claw bullet. I don't want my next thought to be about your refusal."

For an instant, Callister looked away. Then he shook his head and, with a composure equal to Kerry's, said, "I'm very sorry, Mr. President."

Kerry stared at him, the only sound the spattering of rain against glass. Then he pressed the button on his intercom. "Mr. Callister's leaving," he told his assistant. "Take him out the West Wing entrance. The press is waiting for him."

Callister studied him with rising comprehension. "So they can find out what you asked of me."

"No need," the President answered softly. "It's rather like your letter, George. They already know."

PART THREE

THE LAWSUIT

Mid-September to mid-October

ONE

THE NEXT EVENING, the President and First Lady dined on the Presidential yacht, which Lara had renamed the *Inez*.

The gesture was a fond one. As children, neither she nor Kerry had had the means to sail. But both liked the sensation of movement on water, and so, Lara discovered before the wedding, had Inez. Sitting on the deck, Lara imagined her mother's bemusement at having metamorphosed into the Presidential yacht, restored to the Presidency by its owner after thirty years in private hands.

Surrounded by a flotilla from the Secret Service, they cruised down the Potomac in the failing sunlight of early fall. Though unannounced, the expedition had worried Peter Lake; on the open deck, both Kilcannons were exposed. But Lara had insisted; their world, both physical and mental, had become far too claustrophobic. So they sat in deck chairs, sipping wine and doing some catch-up reading between snatches of conversation.

Kerry leafed through *Newsweek*. Its cover showed him addressing Congress; the lead article, headed "KFK?" compared him to John F. Kennedy, calling his speech "the most persuasive call to action since Kennedy's speech on civil rights . . . a quantum leap in his efforts to reach a broader spectrum of the public." The inside photograph showed a grim George Callister emerging from the White House.

" 'KFK,' " Kerry mused, "sounds like a bucket of fried chicken. Thus far, my speech has completely failed to move Fasano."

Nor would it. In his first public comments, Fasano had

counseled the Senate to "help craft prudent safety measures which don't infringe the legitimate rights of forty million American gun owners." This, Kerry knew, signalled a strategy of delay, in which Fasano hoped gradually to restore the Senate and the American public to their prior state of narcolepsy.

"As for Hampton," Kerry continued, "the messages he got yesterday were a lot more hostile.

"It's an SSA blitz, of course. Chuck owns *his* seat as long as he's still breathing. But there are a good half dozen Democrats who won't be so detached."

Quiet, Lara gazed at the wooden deck. Her weight had stabilized, and she looked more as she had before the murders. But there was a permanent sorrow in her eyes, reflecting a wound, Kerry feared, from which she would never quite recover. Part of her still could not accept, upon awakening each morning, that most of her family were dead, or that their murders had set in motion a brute exercise in power politics. And yet, coolly determined, she was directing secret negotiations for a prime-time interview which, as one of the contestants put it, would be "the first words America will hear Lara Kilcannon speak since the tragedy which changed her life forever." Or, in the caustic aside of Connie Coulter, "the biggest media 'get' this side of your own wedding."

In fact, the media had responded with an avidity which impressed even Lara. "I've received enough floral displays," she told Kerry, "to fill a funeral home, and enough baskets of fruit to feed America's homeless.

"And the *letters*." Plucking a letter from a thick manila folder, she read, " 'Only through our network can people truly know of your thoughts and feel your emotions. A prime-time interview on *Deadline* could transform you into the most inspiring—and important—woman in our history.' " Lara shook her head. "If only my mother could have lived to see *that*."

This last, Kerry thought, was said with irony, sadness, and a certain melancholy humor. "Imagine," Kerry remarked, "what you could have accomplished by throwing in some sex."

"Or by killing someone myself." Lara began riffling through her file. "In a particularly dark moment, I asked Connie to find a web site I remembered, filled with letters from the media importuning the Unabomber for an interview. Try this:

" 'The only way to truly understand someone is to see their eyes, hear their voice, their inflections, their passions . . .' "

"Rasputin," Kerry interjected, "died too soon . . ."

"Or this: 'I was born not far from where you live now.' " Lara laughed softly. "Which, as it happened, was a maximum security prison in Idaho.

"Of course, not all of it was quite so droll. When I got to the letter saying, 'To many, you are a hero and a pioneer,' I realized what a mercy it was that Joanie's husband killed himself. Or the two of us would be competing for prime time."

For a moment, Kerry was silent. "What are you going to do?"

Lara looked up, her hair blowing in a light breeze. "Go with NBC, I think. I trust Cathie Civitch—she didn't try to endear herself, or exploit our past relationship. And they offered me *Dateline* and *Today*, which would give me the largest potential audience."

Spoken like a professional, Kerry thought. "Live or tape?" he asked.

"They want me to do *Dateline* live—the more spontaneous the interview, the theory goes, the more powerful it will be. No doubt they think more people will watch to see if I break down." For a moment Lara paused, as though interrupted by sadness and disbelief. "The tape will only be aired once, on *Today*—no snippets on *Entertainment Tonight, Headliners and Legends,* or some special on First Ladies. No prime-time interviews with Charles Dane, or anyone from the SSA." Her voice softened. "No questions about that tape of the murders. No footage of my family dying in the promos."

Once again, Kerry's heart went out to her. But all he said was "Good."

After dinner, when night had fallen, they sat on the deck drinking brandy. "This lawsuit," Lara said, "do you really think it's that important?"

"I think it's a fact of life. Could you stop Mary if you wanted to?"

Lara gazed into the darkness. "Probably not," she answered. "To Mary, I have a wealth of avenues for acting out my grief. She has only this."

Quietly, Kerry gazed at the white dome of the Capitol, glowing in the distance. "Since 1938," he told her, "every serious gun safety proposal has enjoyed overwhelming public support. But Congress weakened or rejected them all. In 1968, when Martin Luther King and Robert Kennedy were shot, they couldn't even manage to ban bullets like the ones which killed Marie.

"For the SSA, this is Armageddon. They *can't* lose, especially not to me, or else the balance shifts. Once they're no longer invincible, they're a PR problem for the GOP and a lot less scary to Democrats. So they'll do anything to win, and they've put so much sweat and money into the Republicans that the Speaker and Fasano have no choice but to go along. As for Callister, they've got him by the balls."

"But a lawsuit could be your leverage."

"*Mary's* lawsuit," Kerry answered succinctly, "could destroy Lexington Arms. And that not even a President can do."

For a moment, Lara reflected. "And then you could break the SSA's stranglehold on the industry."

Kerry nodded. "In a lot of states, like Georgia, the SSA's been able to get laws passed immunizing gun companies from suits by public entities. The only kind of suit they haven't been able to wipe out is wrongful death actions by victims' families." He sipped more brandy. "The California legislature would never bar your sister from suing over the deaths of two women and a child millions of people came to know, and whose murders they witnessed on television. If I were George Callister, I'd be terrified of a jury."

As Lara listened, Kerry saw the pain of memory replaced by the cool scrutiny of the war correspondent she had once been. "Which would you prefer, Kerry? Destroying Lexington? Or forcing Callister to give you what you want?"

Kerry shrugged. "I'm indifferent. Either would show the gun industry that the SSA can't protect them."

Lara settled back, brandy snifter cradled in the palms of both hands. "There's just one problem," she said evenly. "This would be Mary's suit, not yours."

"We'd need to reach an understanding . . ."

Lara held up her hand. "Joan resented me to the end of her life. Now you want me to take over *Mary's* life."

Kerry touched her arm. "Once Mary sees what I'm after . . ."

"Just who," Lara broke in, "do you expect to *make* her see it? After all that's happened to us, I really can't believe you want me to do this. Have you completely forgotten how complex families are? And how little of mine is left?"

Kerry met her gaze. "So what do you do now, Lara? Do

you help me honor their memory? Or let Mary just cash in?"

Lara fixed him with a long look of appraisal. "I thought I knew you," she said softly. "Heart and soul. What surprises marriage brings."

Quiet, Kerry stifled the urge to reach for her. "I'm sorry," he answered. "But liberals too often whine, while conservatives do whatever it takes." He paused, then finished evenly, "With Mary's help, we can redress the balance. She should have that choice."

TWO

"THOMAS JEFFERSON DID IT," Avram Gold told the President. "To Aaron Burr, his own Vice President."

At Kerry's direction, Gold had entered through the East Gate, away from the press, and come directly to his private office. The fact of the meeting would be as private as its substance. Unlike the White House counsel, whose client was deemed to be the public at large, Avram Gold, a Harvard law professor and Kerry's unofficial advisor on legal policy, could counsel Kerry on personal legal matters covered by the attorney-client privilege. In Kerry's mind, he could hardly do better—Gold was brilliant, imaginative and committed to Kerry's agenda. If there was a way to execute the complex stratagem Kerry had in mind, Avi Gold would find it.

"Jefferson?" Kerry inquired. "How?"

"After Burr shot Alexander Hamilton, Jefferson secretly directed his prosecution for treason. He torpedoed his own Vice President."

Kerry smiled. "The good old days," he said with mock nostalgia, "when Presidents could exploit the justice system in private."

"It's different now," Gold agreed. "Especially in this scenario. If Mary brings a lawsuit, you and the First Lady are very likely to be witnesses. Were I Lexington, I'd argue that Joan died from the effects of inadequate law enforcement and bad advice—including yours. There's no way they won't press for depositions from both of you—on videotape, if the judge allows it."

Kerry shrugged. "I expect that. All I care about is whether we'd have to answer questions about our role in the lawsuit itself. The idea that I'm behind it would be absolutely fatal to what I have in mind."

Gold leaned forward, hands pressed together, the keenness of his gaze confirming his pleasure in the intellectual challenge Kerry had placed before him. "Okay," he said crisply, "let's start with what you can't do.

"First, you as President can never talk to whoever ends up being Mary's lawyer—and I do mean never. It's hard to find a rationale for keeping that confidential, and it's far better for you to be able to say—in absolute truth—that you never met or spoke with her attorney." Gold's bushy eyebrows raised in cautionary emphasis. "That especially means Bob Lenihan, no matter who else you may bring in. Your last chat wasn't privileged, and he's way too self-enchanted to conceal how completely you rely on his advice."

"I appreciate that," Kerry acknowledged. "But I'm afraid we may be stuck with him."

"Bob has his virtues," Gold answered in a sardonic tone. "Chief among them a total lack of shame. As his cocounsel, Sarah Dash would have her hands full.

"Back to the list of 'don'ts.' You and Lara can't pay Mary's legal expenses. While that might create a privilege, it would look like you're doing exactly what you intend to do: run this lawsuit from the White House. And, for exactly the same reason, Lara can't be a plaintiff. Also, it would erode the sympathy you're expecting from her interview on NBC."

"Just so."

"On the other hand," Gold said with cheerful anticipation, "if you and the First Lady can legitimately refuse to answer questions, and do so in a sympathetic way, you leave Lexington and the SSA with the unattractive option of accusing you of doing exactly what you're doing without any proof that you are, in fact, doing it. *That* could look insensitive."

"And would be," Kerry answered dryly.

"Finally, even if Lexington challenges your assertion of privilege in court, it's a rare judge who will want to rule against you and the First Lady—let alone charge a President with contempt." Gold spread his hands. "So the only problem, Mr. President, is constructing a chain of privilege which holds up. For that, as I suppose you know, the First Lady is indispensable."

Silent, Kerry faced anew his deep ambivalence about weaving this web of his own creation into the fabric of his marriage. "The spousal privilege," he said softly.

"That's the first part," Gold concurred, "and the easiest. The spousal privilege covers any communication between husband and wife, including those which begin with 'Tell your sister.' And the privilege lasts as long as the marriage does."

Eyes hooded in contemplation, Kerry gazed at his desk. "You should know, Avi, that I don't love this. I just can't think of any other way but using Lara."

Gold studied the President with dark perceptive eyes. "You don't need absolution from me, Mr. President, as long as you have it from Lara. I watched the film."

Kerry rested his chin on curled fingers. "What I tell Lara," he said at length, "is only the first link."

After a moment, Gold nodded. "So, let's address how Lara passes your suggestions on to Mary's lawyer. One way is for Lara to hire her own lawyer, and try to set up some joint privilege covering him and Mary's lawyer . . ."

"Too cumbersome," Kerry objected. "Too many people knowing too much."

"*Or,*" Gold continued with a smile, "she could claim to be seeking advice from Mary's lawyer about *her* lawsuit in the future. *Or* to be acting as Mary's agent, helping make decisions for a sister too traumatized to cope. *Or*, under California law, that talking to Mary's lawyer 'furthers the client's interests.' "

"Will any of that work?"

Gold nodded briskly. "All of it, I think. Especially in combination—none of these assertions is mutually exclusive."

Kerry found himself wondering, yet again, how his plans would affect Lara's relationship to Mary. "That leaves conversations between Lara and her sister," he replies. "The most delicate part of all."

" 'Delicate'?"

"Lara's not at all convinced that Mary will take kindly to our directions."

"It's also delicate as a matter of law," Gold cautioned. "But if Lara is a prospective plaintiff, that might create a joint privilege covering both her and Mary. In California, I *think* you can get by with that. Still, I'd keep those sisterly chats to a minimum."

Nodding, Kerry repressed his sense of foreboding. "We will," he assured his lawyer. "And unless Mary goes along with this, there won't be more than one."

When Kerry returned to the Oval Office, he called in Clayton Slade. "Did you check those military contracts?" the President asked.

"Yes. Lexington supplies sidearms to the Army. Chiefly for military police."

"Put a stop to it, as soon as possible. Our version of the SSA boycott, a modest attention-getter." Kerry sat back. "Also, I want a report on how long it would take for the Anniston Army Depot to start making M-16s. I'm not in the mood to keep subsidizing companies who think they owe their highest duty to the SSA."

"I'd watch it," Clayton admonished. "The gun folks will say you're abusing your power, and screwing around with national security."

"*That*," Kerry answered sharply, "depends on how well Anniston can make an M-16. As for abusing my power, I'm simply using it. When companies like Lexington stop making bullets like the Eagle's Claw, I'll use it some other way."

After a moment, Clayton shrugged. "At least we can look into it. Why was Avi Gold here, by the way?"

Kerry smiled fractionally. "To give me legal advice. Of a personal nature."

Clayton folded his arms. "Avi Gold," he said emphatically, "was *not* here to revise your will."

The President's smile vanished. "True. But if I told you what we talked about, it wouldn't be privileged, would it?"

Clayton studied him. "Have it your way, Kerry. But have a care. For your sake, and for Lara's."

THREE

SHORTLY BEFORE six o'clock in San Francisco, Sarah Dash glanced at her watch.

She was still at the office, and would be for several hours. Four months into her new job as a trial lawyer for the Kilcannon Center for Social Justice, Sarah found it as demanding as her past life at Kenyon and Walker, the city's premier corporate law firm, but far more compelling. Looking back at the last year, Sarah realized, this sea change in her career had been inevitable.

In January, Sarah—despite the resistance of the inner circle at Kenyon and Walker—had taken on the pro bono representation of Mary Ann Tierney. The pregnant teenager, fearful that giving birth to a hydrocephalic child would impair her ability to bear more children, had sought a late term abortion over the opposition of her militant pro-life parents. The televised trial which resulted, pitting parent against child, became a race against time, wherein Sarah sought to invalidate an act of Congress before Mary Ann was forced to deliver. But the trial court ruled against her; only in the United States Court of Appeals, by virtue of a landmark opinion written by Judge Caroline Masters, did Mary Ann prevail. This result, a stunning triumph for Sarah, had nearly caused the Senate to reject President Kilcannon's nomination of Judge Masters as Chief Justice. The fact that the aborted fetus proved to have no cerebral cortex did little to reduce the bitterness.

But for Sarah, the Tierney case proved that, at thirty, she was a gifted and resourceful lawyer. The other lesson came to her more slowly: having acted on her beliefs, she was no longer satisfied to spend her days meeting the needs of corporate clients. The Kilcannon Center was a perfect fit: its San Francisco office needed a lawyer to lead its lawsuits against the gun industry; Sarah believed that, given the SSA's influence over Congress, lawsuits were the only method which might force the industry to reform. From her first day, Sarah had felt emancipated.

And so she remained at her desk, a compact young woman with dark curly hair, liquid brown eyes and, she acknowledged, a social life which could use some work. Tomorrow, she promised herself, she would keep her dinner date. Tonight, she would make the legal brief she had drafted all it should be.

But first she had an hour of TV to watch. Like other women her age, she found Lara Costello Kilcannon—only two years older than Sarah herself—a compelling figure. And like almost everyone she knew, Sarah had seen the videotape of the murders. She felt sorrow for the Kilcannons, anger at the weapons used against Lara's family. That her own career had become a war against such weapons made watching Lara Kilcannon irresistible.

Promptly at six o'clock, Sarah switched on her office television.

In the library of the White House—where, three weeks ago, she and Kerry had disclosed Joan Bowden's problems—Lara faced Cathie Civitch.

With ten seconds until airtime, Cathie gave her a smile meant to be encouraging. But it did nothing to alleviate Lara's tension and betrayed Cathie's own. Despite all of her past success, Cathie no doubt knew that she would be best known for what transpired in this one hour.

In turn, Lara knew that Cathie would be well prepared,

and familiar with the viewpoint of the SSA—her questions would be respectful, but probing. Lara had steeped herself in the complex issues surrounding the gun debate, but had not tried to anticipate questions which were personal. Lara's life had been based on self-control and careful planning, but that would not work here. The audience expected self-revelation; the knowledge left her edgy, and a little sick inside.

Upstairs, in his office, Kerry watched. Lara had insisted on doing this alone.

This, Cathie Civitch said, *is the first time Americans have heard from you since the tragedy.*

Lara gave a small shrug of the shoulders. *I haven't been ready,* she said quietly. *I wasn't ready to lose my family.*

The abruptness of what happened was just so startling—three of the people I loved most were gone, and I hadn't said goodbye, or said the things one needs to say. And Marie . . . Briefly, Lara paused. *I just want to hold Marie. And I can't.*

Only someone who knew her as well as he, Kerry reflected, would know how much this cost her. And he could do nothing.

At six-eleven, Frank Fasano left the floor of the Senate and entered his office suite. Macdonald Gage was already there, watching Lara Kilcannon.

"How's she doing?" Fasano asked.

Gage's eyes did not move from the screen. "See for yourself."

Were it in my power, Lara told Cathie Civitch, *no one else would ever have to feel as I do.*

"Here it comes," Gage said. "This is going to be *her* cause."

But they do, Lara continued. *On the day my family died, eighty-seven more Americans died from gunshot wounds. We don't know their names; we don't see their families on television . . .* Abruptly, Lara seemed almost to snap, anger and emotion overtaking her. *Since then, how many families have lost a child, a father, a husband, or a wife? And how few of the survivors can even find an outlet for their grief?*

They feel helpless. We can try to fix the schools, but we can't educate children they've already lost. Every day we lose ten more. And that is not acceptable to me.

In close-up, Lara's eyes were filled with passion. Softly, Fasano said, "This is trouble, Mac. Life in the Senate will be that much harder."

Gage did not turn. "Has the SSA scheduled a meeting?"

"The day after tomorrow," Fasano answered. "I'd like a day to reflect on what we're seeing."

When Charles Dane glanced at his watch, it was nine twenty-seven.

"She's still got another half hour," he murmured to Bill Campton, "to finish poisoning the collective American mind. Imagine what *we* could do with Barbara Walters and four or five women who'd protected themselves with handguns."

In profile, Campton's smile was wan. "Dream on, Charles."

What, Cathie Civitch was asking, *do you think the answers are?*

I'll leave the specifics to the President, Lara said, *and to Congress. But the fundamental question is, How do we prevent these kinds of tragedies?*

Why do we have airport security, Cathie? To prevent armed terrorists from crashing a plane into a building. Because you can't punish a hijacker who's already dead, or save his victims once the plane blows up. Lara leaned forward, her voice forceful now. *We have to use our common sense. Do we just keep arming Americans with yet more handguns to protect themselves from other Americans with guns? And how do you know to shoot someone who's carrying a concealed weapon?*

Pausing, Lara spoke with remembered sadness. *I was a war correspondent, in Kosovo. In a war zone, you somehow manage to accept the murder of the innocent. But America shouldn't become a war zone. The way to protect ourselves in a civil society is to disarm the criminals, not arm ourselves. And if we buy guns out of fear, not choice, how many more accidents or teen suicides will we have, how many more domestic shootings where a gun turns a moment of anger or despair into an irreversible tragedy . . .*

"It's the same old line," Dane said. "Guns are the problem, so let's take them all away."

"At the moment she's on a pedestal," Campton opined. "We can't attack her directly—at least right now." For another moment, he studied her, and then looked up at Dane. "Ever wonder what their story is—her and Kilcannon, the way she tried to get to him after he was shot. Was that just dogged journalism? Their whole romance popped up real quick."

If I could bring my mother back, Lara was saying, *and the man who shot her, then I'd ask her to choose between punishing her own murderer, or saving other lives by changing the laws which allowed this man to buy this kind of weapon.*

I know what my mother would say: We can fill our jails and cemeteries, or we can try to stop the violence . . .

"*Too* quick," Dane answered simply.

Twenty-five minutes to go, Kerry thought. So far Lara had maintained her composure.

How, Cathie Civitch asked, *is the President coping with this tragedy?*

I think he's tried to concentrate on me, rather than himself. Lara's voice became regretful, quiet. *I haven't been much help to him, even though I know how terrible he feels.*

Civitch leaned forward, hands clasped together. *You have a new marriage, a terrible loss, John Bowden's letter blaming your husband for his actions. That would test the strongest marriage.*

Lara drew a breath. *There are certain things, Cathie, that I have to accept. One is that this man has forever redefined my life. But I will* not *let him redefine my relationship to the person I love most . . .*

Abruptly, Lara stopped, as if hearing herself. *You know,* she said softly, *I don't think I've ever told him that. But I've promised it to myself.*

Watching, Kerry felt more grateful for this moment than he ever could have imagined. Perhaps, he allowed himself to hope, Lara might begin rethinking her reservations about starting a family of their own.

Today, Cathie Civitch said, *is your mother's birthday.*

Tears welled in Lara's eyes. *Yes.*

Kerry had not known.

Silent, Chad and Allie Palmer sat in front of their television.

How, Civitch was asking Lara, *do you respond to those who say the cause of violence is not guns, but a culture which uses violence as entertainment?*

"For Middle America," Palmer observed, "this is the one she's got to answer. No matter what kind of shape she's in."

Pausing, Lara regained her footing. *I agree that guns are not the only cause of violence. What guns do is make violence lethal.*

If you compare us to Canada, Australia and New Zealand, you see many similarities. Our histories include the conquest of

*a frontier, and the violent displacement of indigenous people. Our
current rates of violent crime are comparable. But our murder
rate is exponentially higher, because our murderers use guns.
That's why in Japan, which hardly lacks for violent entertainment, a year can go by without anyone under eighteen dying from
gun violence.*

*Certainly, we need to tell the entertainment industry to stop
shoving violence down our throats in movies, television, video
games, and popular music. But we also need to concern ourselves
more deeply with what our children watch and hear, and to tell
them that violence is no answer . . .*

Allie turned to her husband, her expression pensive.
"Lara may be grieving. But she's certainly well prepared."

Briefly, Chad thought of his impassioned speech on the
Senate floor, a few days after Kyle's death, defending
Caroline Masters. "You can be both," he answered quietly.
"Some people may think it's calculating, or just plain cold.
The truth is that it keeps you from falling apart."

Silent, Allie took his hand.

For nearly an hour Sarah had never checked her watch.

Do you ever look back, Civitch asked Lara Kilcannon, *and
wonder how you might have changed things?*

All the time, Lara answered quietly. *But not just for Kerry
and me, or even for my family.*

*Well before these murders, Kerry went to the gun industry and
asked them to require background checks at gun shows. They
refused. Then he went to the president of Lexington Arms, and
implored him not to continue putting the wrong guns in the wrong
hands.* Lara paused, as though suppressing her emotions. *I
can't help but feel that if they'd listened, my mother, sister and niece
would still be living, and the families of three other victims would
not be wondering why bullets meant for my sister Mary murdered
the people they loved instead . . .*

Listening, Sarah could not easily imagine how Lara Kilcannon felt. Or, for that matter, the president of Lexington Arms.

"Brilliant," Charles Dane murmured. "Now they've *both* crucified George Callister on national TV. Lexington couldn't get a fair trial anywhere in America."

Campton looked up. "You still think they're setting up a lawsuit?"

"Of course. Except they'll use the sister."

In close-up, Cathie Civitch's face was filled with compassion. *As First Lady, you intend to make reducing gun violence your cause. What will you tell the American people?*

Lara seemed to gather her thoughts. *First, I will ask them to reflect on the over thirty thousand deaths we suffer every year. I will say to them, "Listen to your own heart, your own intellect, your own experience of life, and decide whether you think this is the way our country has to be." I will ask, "What kind of world do you want for your children, or your children's children . . ."*

And what, Civitch interjected, *would you say to the SSA itself?*

I would ask its members why we have this terrible division on guns.

They're being asked to fear us, and they have nothing to fear. I'll never forget watching Charles Dane hold up his hunting rifle at an SSA convention and say, "Kerry Kilcannon will have to pry this rifle out of my cold dead hands." Lara paused, her voice thickening with emotion. *I thought about that when I stood by my six-year-old niece's casket, looking into her face as I held her lifeless hand.*

Suddenly, she looked into the camera, saying softly, *I don't want your hunting rifle, Mr. Dane. Kerry doesn't want it.*

Americans just want a country where this never happens to another child . . .

Don't do this, Dane silently warned her. *It is such a grave mistake.*

Finishing, Lara imagined the faces of those who watched her.

"I hope that many more of you will join us. There is so much for us to do, so many lives to save. And the cost of failure is more than anyone should be asked to bear."

For a moment, Cathie Civitch was silent. Then she said simply, "Lara Costello Kilcannon, thank you."

Exhausted, Lara realized that the name still sounded strange to her. But that was who she was now. For her own sake, and Kerry's, she hoped she had done well.

In the silence, Kerry's phone rang.

It was Senator Chuck Hampton. "Tell the First Lady, Mr. President, that her interview was extraordinary, and deeply moving."

"Thanks, Chuck. I'll do that. And on your end?"

Hampton laughed softly. "If you mean my end of Pennsylvania Avenue, she's an asset. Frank Fasano can't be happy, and neither can the SSA."

Nor, Kerry realized, did he himself feel quite as happy as he could be. There was far too much to wonder about.

After the last hour, Sarah realized, it was hard to refocus on her brief. When her telephone rang, she almost welcomed the distraction.

"Is this Sarah Dash?" the woman asked.

The voice sounded so familiar that Sarah felt her skin tingle. "It is."

"This is Lara Kilcannon. Would it be possible to see you?"

FOUR

SARAH DASH and Lara Kilcannon met in the solarium.

Sarah had never visited the White House. But she understood that this area was the First Lady's domain; that, for reasons of politics, Lara could not conduct her business in the West Wing; that she did not wish Sarah to be seen at all. For Sarah's part, no one but the Director of the Kilcannon Center knew that she was here.

Briskly crossing the room, Lara took Sarah's hand. "For two weeks," she said with a smile, "I didn't miss a day of the Tierney trial. Though I imagine you could have done without the cameras."

At once Sarah felt at ease. "I hated them," she acknowledged. "And the media as a whole—the total invasion of privacy, this sudden interest in my personal life. I still can't pass through an airport without people coming up to me. Some of them are supportive. Others call me a baby-killer. All I want is to crawl into a hole."

This seemed to strike a chord. "Too late," Lara said with sympathy. "But everyone I know admires what you did. I know that Kerry was very glad to hear you'd joined the Kilcannon Center. He thought you were wasted in corporate law."

Kerry, Sarah thought. Already she felt the seductive power of the White House; on meeting, Lara Kilcannon referred to the President as though Sarah were an intimate. Though this flattered Sarah, it made her wary. The Tierney case, and its impact on the Masters confirmation, had taught her much about politics at the highest level—most of all that it was intoxicating, and that those who entered this world often pay too dearly.

The thought brought her up short, and back to the First Lady. Lara Kilcannon was quite beautiful, with pale skin, black hair and deep brown eyes more sensitive than television conveyed. In another context, Sarah might have given in to the fascination of meeting her. In this context, she must redouble her efforts to keep her wits about her, mindful of the crosscurrents between the Kilcannons' aspirations, and her own.

"Mrs. Kilcannon," Sarah ventured, "before we start . . ."

" 'Lara,' " the First Lady requested good-humoredly. "I know there's a place for protocol. But 'Mrs. Kilcannon' sounds like one of those sour oil paintings they've hung on the first floor."

"Lara," Sarah corrected with a smile, "you want this conversation to be confidential. Does that mean, in your mind, that it's covered by the attorney-client privilege?"

Lara's own smile reappeared, more faintly. "It does. For now, let's assume that I'm a potential plaintiff in a wrongful death action against Lexington Arms. As is my sister Mary."

"And you're considering asking the Kilcannon Center to represent her, or you. Or both of you."

The First Lady nodded. "The Kilcannon Center has been counsel in numerous suits against the gun industry. We think you can best represent our values."

Our values, Sarah thought. There was something more beneath the surface, beginning with Lara's pretense—which she clearly meant for Sarah to see through—that she herself was considering a lawsuit. Bluntly, Sarah asked, "Does Mary agree?"

A certain sadness, Sarah thought, surfaced in Lara's eyes. Watching, Sarah found her sense of caution tempered by a deeper feeling—that, for Lara, something still to be said occasioned genuine pain.

"I don't know," Lara answered simply. "I haven't talked to her yet."

Sarah Dash, it was already clear to Lara, had a grasp of the unspoken and an intuitive sense of people. There was no point in attempting to delude her, and Lara had no heart to try. "The painful truth," she continued softly, "is that, on a visceral level, Mary holds us both responsible for what John Bowden did. At least for now."

Speaking this aloud, Lara found, deepened her sense of sorrow. For a moment, she felt the impulse to express her misgivings about what she was about to ask, both of Sarah and of Mary. But though Sarah seemed to regard her with sympathy, this was not the reason that Lara had asked her here.

"The President," Lara told her, "has a personal interest in a lawsuit."

For a moment, Sarah was quiet. "In the lawsuit," she asked, "or in its conduct?"

"Both," Lara answered. "I think it was Clausewitz who said that war is diplomacy by other means. This lawsuit would be politics by other means."

"How so?"

"One of the harsher lessons Kerry's learned is that there are powers a President doesn't have, or can't exercise because the political price is far too high." Pausing, Lara heard the bitterness beneath the softness of her voice. "We couldn't protect Joan's privacy—the media wouldn't allow it. We couldn't use the Secret Service to protect her life— the law wouldn't allow it. We couldn't get background checks at gun shows—the SSA wouldn't allow it. And now Kerry can't be seen as using the legal system to advance a 'personal agenda.' That's what saving lives is called when a President's relatives are murdered."

Perhaps out of respect for Lara's feelings, Sarah paused before asking, "What does the President want from this?"

"The same things I want," Lara said firmly. "To expose the facts behind the development and marketing of the gun and bullets that killed my mother, sister and niece. To split Lexington off from the industry, and show that the SSA can't protect it any longer. To find out where the murderer got the gun. To keep building support for the law Kerry wants enacted. In short, to coordinate the legal and the political, without publicly acknowledging his role."

"And how would we accomplish that?"

Briefly, Lara hesitated. "Through me."

Sarah's gaze grew contemplative. "I admire you," she confessed. "You don't know how much. Part of me wants to help you in any way I can.

"But the more cautious part has to question my own motives. Am I so young—or ambitious—that I'd take direction from a President without knowing where it leads? Or so flexible that I'd put *his* interests ahead of my presumptive client's?"

The questions, Lara thought, reinforced her good opinion of Sarah Dash. "None of the above," she answered. "You simply care about this issue for its own sake."

"Same problem," Sarah rejoined. "Mary might wonder when *caring about the issue* takes precedence over her. She can find a host of able lawyers to represent her interests."

"*That's* the problem. One may have already found her. Robert Lenihan."

"Bob Lenihan?" Sarah said in surprise. "He's more than able. He's spent the last ten years extracting a fortune from my old firm's corporate clients."

Lara nodded. "Then you know that he also has his own

agenda—notoriety, political influence and money. Do you really think you'd have less concern for her than he might?"

Sarah gazed at her in open curiosity. "Just how," she inquired, "will you go about shouldering aside Bob Lenihan?"

Nothing but total candor, Lara realized, would satisfy Sarah Dash. "We won't. That's not in Kerry's political interests—he needs the plaintiffs' lawyers, and their money, as a counterweight to the SSA. What we envision is that you and Bob Lenihan will serve as Mary's cocounsel . . ."

"Wait," Sarah held up her hand, her tone combining humor with incredulity. "On top of everything else— including enough political and familial complications to challenge Machiavelli—you'd be throwing me in a scorpion pit with an egomaniac with twenty more years' experience, a talent for treachery and manipulation, and all the motive in the world to turn these gifts on me."

Lara found herself smiling. "I think that pretty well states it," she said wryly. "Or, perhaps, understates it."

Despite herself, Sarah began to laugh. "Please," she said, "don't try to oversell this. It's so attractive on its own."

Once more, Lara Kilcannon transformed before Sarah's eyes. While still pleasant, her expression became serious, her voice soft. "I know this is a lot to take in. All that I can tell you is that I'm not asking just for Kerry's sake. Or I could never ask Mary to consider how best to value the family we both lost."

Pensive, Sarah composed her answer. She had not fully gauged the pitfalls of the First Lady's proposal, most of all entering the world of Kerry and Lara Kilcannon. But that they had invited her was compelling. At heart, Sarah agreed with them—the case was far bigger than Mary Costello. It was the case of any lawyer's career: the chance to establish moral, if not legal, responsibility for the death of Lara's family and, by doing so, to transform America's relationship to guns. "*If* Mary wants to meet me," she said at last, "I'd explain that I'd be taking this on as a cause; that her lawsuit would be a political weapon; that whatever money she might recover is not my sole concern. After that, it's up to her."

For a moment, Sarah imagined the relief she saw on Lara's face warring with her deeper worries about Mary. "Thank you," the First Lady said simply.

FIVE

"SO NOW YOU WANT to pick my lawyer," Mary said.

On a bright fall afternoon, she and Lara walked along a path in Golden Gate Park. The cramped space of Mary's studio apartment, with its newly framed photographs of Inez, Joan, and Marie, had been too much for Lara. The park, with its spacious paths, the menthol scent from eucalyptus overhead, reminded her of the family picnics Inez would organize after Sunday Mass, evoking happier memories. But now her Secret Service detail led and followed. To Lara, the two surviving sisters composed an awkward picture—intense, unsmiling, walking slightly apart—belying the benign explanation that the First Lady had flown to San Francisco merely to spend time with Mary before commencing her travels as advocate.

"I can't pick your lawyer," Lara answered. "Only you can. But we wanted you to have the broadest range of advice. The Kilcannon Center sees these suits not simply as wrongful death actions, but as a way of saving lives. Isn't that what we want?"

" 'We'?" Mary's tone was pointed. "The other day, at school, a new teacher I barely know came up to me. I could see how hard it was for her to tell me how she felt.

"I was ready to say that I was okay, and that I was grateful for her thoughts." Mary's voice became quiet and bitter. "Do you know what she asked me, Lara? 'How is your sister doing?' She'd watched you with Cathie Civitch, and she was worried for you."

For a moment, Lara was speechless. For her, the

appearance on NBC had been an ordeal, intensified by the pressure of an audience which had proven to be the largest ever for a prime-time interview. But, for Mary, it was another chapter in the lifelong story of Lara eclipsing her sisters, served up with a sad new twist—Mary as the forgotten mourner. "I'm sorry," Lara said.

In profile, Mary's thin face, gazing straight ahead, conveyed her sense of distance. "I'm just trying to make you see this, Lara. You can go on television. You can give speeches, tell people what laws to pass." Abruptly, Mary stopped, standing with folded arms and tears filling her eyes. "I didn't decide how to 'protect' Joanie and Marie. No one even asked me. I had to hear about it two days before your wedding.

"Three days later they were *dead*. I was *there*, Lara—I saw them die. I went to the hospital and prayed for Marie. But all I've got is recurring nightmares and a lawsuit against the company who made the bullets that tore them apart. And you want to control that, too."

Despairing, Lara clutched her arm. "I don't *want* anything from this."

"As long as I let your lawyer run the case." Turning on her, Mary demanded, "Are you still my sister, Lara? Or are you just his wife?"

Lara's mouth felt dry. "I'm your sister. That makes us both Inez's daughters, Joanie's sisters, Marie's aunts. We both hurt. Why fight over them when they're dead?"

"Because they were my family," Mary retorted. "Not a prop at a wedding, or an unpaid political advertisement, or people whose problems I can talk about on television . . ."

"The *Chronicle* was about to print the story." Wounded, Lara stopped herself, feeling the depth of her own guilt. "I couldn't help what happened, Mary."

"You can help what you do," Mary said with muted anger. "Or expect me to do."

They had to stop this, Lara knew. She tried to step outside herself, to see two grieving sisters. "Tell me, Mary, what this lawsuit means to you."

"More than money," Mary answered with fierce possessiveness. "It's my way of remembering them, and honoring my mother."

"My *mother*," echoed in Lara's brain. "Then when you're alone," she implored her sister, "ask yourself how she would want us to be."

Silent, Mary gave her a wary, guarded look.

"Alone," she said at last. "Right now that's all I want."

Five hours later, Mary called Lara at her hotel, and said that she would meet with Sarah Dash. Only then did Lara cry.

SIX

TO SARAH'S SURPRISE, when Mary Costello appeared at the Kilcannon Center, Robert Lenihan was with her. As soon as Sarah had led them to her office, he said in a proprietary tone, "I gather that Mrs. Kilcannon wanted you to meet my client."

Casting a disdainful glance at Sarah's spartan office, he sat back, hands folded comfortably across his belly. His own office in Beverly Hills was as legendary as his ego: a former colleague of Sarah's had described its decor as "late Byzantine, accented by photographs of the Emperor Bob receiving tribute from Presidents and other lesser men." In contrast to Lenihan's arrogance, Mary's blue-green eyes conveyed the aftershock of a trauma so severe that it seemed to have overwhelmed her.

At once, Sarah decided to focus on Mary. "What I understand," she said gently, "is that you wanted to discuss a potential action for wrongful death."

Silent, Mary nodded. "What's *your* take?" Lenihan inquired of Sarah. "My message to the jury will be simple— that Lexington designed and marketed the P-2 as a weapon uniquely suited to killing human beings."

"That's fine," Sarah rejoined. "But you have to put the P-2 in its context." Pausing, she spoke to Mary. "Financially, the gun industry's in trouble. Guns don't wear out, and their traditional owners are slowly dying off.

"So the industry faced a choice. They could expand their customer base by making guns safer, or by persuading urban and suburbanites that they needed superguns

capable of firing more rounds more quickly, and of inflicting deadly wounds." Her voice softened. "You saw the
choice they made. Morally, it's analogous to big tobacco
deciding to put more nicotine in cigarettes . . ."

"The difference," Lenihan objected, "is that people
don't smoke in self-defense. As Lexington will drive home
to a jury."

Lenihan, Sarah thought with irritation, was positioning
himself as the voice of experience, uniquely capable of persuading twelve ordinary citizens to decide for Mary
Costello. "Self-defense," she said to Mary, "doesn't begin
to explain the record rate of gun violence in America.

"In nineteen sixty-three, there were a little over half a
million handguns in America. Today, there are over three
million. In 1963, only fourteen percent of handguns had a
magazine capacity of ten rounds or more. The next year,
the percentage of those guns tripled. And the P-2 is among
the worst. It's not designed for self-defense. It's simply not
accurate enough. All it's good for is spraying the most bullets in the least amount of time." Turning to Lenihan, she
finished, "That's your case. Because that's why Bowden
bought it."

Mary's gaze darted back to Sarah. "But why do ordinary
people *want* one?"

"Fear," Sarah answered. "Fear of minorities, or civil disorder, or the government, or violent crime. Fear sells guns
to homeowners, and single women." Before Lenihan could
interrupt, Sarah continued. "Fear even sells guns to cops.
The gun industry sold the first superguns to police, *then*
told them they were threatened by the even more lethal
guns they'd begun selling to civilians, *then* offered the cops
the newest superguns in exchange for their old ones, and
then resold *those* guns on the open market, double-dipping
while increasing the number of lethal weapons on the
streets. Which increased the risks to cops . . ."

"It's an arms race," Lenihan interposed, "as the President suggested. The message is that the world is a scary place, populated by people who are armed and dangerous, so you'd better be better armed than they are."

Sarah nodded. "That's how the SSA pushes these state laws creating an automatic right to carry a concealed handgun. The idea is that you need a hidden gun to defend yourself against someone else's hidden gun." Abruptly, she turned to Mary. "I'm sorry," she apologized. "Give two trial lawyers an audience, and we'll talk for hours. It occurs to me that you may actually have some questions."

Plainly nettled at being cut off, Lenihan, too, faced Mary. "There's one more aspect, Mary, that I think we should cover. I call it 'entertainment marketing.'

"Lexington creates video games where kids can fire a 'virtual' P-2. They also place their guns in movies and TV shows, often as the criminals' gun of choice. The idea is to create a whole new wave of techno-freaks—from kids to criminals to survivalists—who've just got to have the newest, lightest, fastest killing machine.

"That's what Bowden responded to. I'm confident that I can prove that the P-2 has *no* legitimate sporting use; that its sole function is to kill a lot of people quickly; that it contains features that are especially attractive to mass murderers and other criminals; that it's one of the weapons most frequently used in crimes; and that the Eagle's Claw is designed not to stop a would-be burglar or rapist, but to make death a near certainty." Now his own voice softened. "The deaths of your mother, sister and niece, for which Lexington should pay and pay and pay."

Mary glanced at Sarah, as though caught between competing forces. "How can we sue them," she asked, "if selling these guns is legal?"

"That's the crux of their argument," Sarah agreed. "But another argument is that the P-2 worked exactly the way it's supposed to. If it's not defective—unlike a faulty tire or an SUV that flips—how can they be sued?

"You can't sue them, Lexington will say, for murders that some demented stranger committed with a nondefective legal product. Even if Lexington knew to a certainty that someone *like* Bowden would choose a P-2 to commit murder." Sarah's tone became etched with disgust. "Which Lexington *did*, by the way. Remember the white supremacist who killed three kids at a Jewish day-care center in Los Angeles? He used a Lexington P-2."

"So what's your theory?" Lenihan asked sharply. "That Lexington could have imagined the illegal use of a legal product doesn't get Mary her verdict. Or else Ford would be liable if Bowden had killed them with your hypothetical SUV."

"Tell us *your* theory," Sarah countered. "If I have anything to add, I will."

Quickly refocusing on Mary, Lenihan spoke with the paternal air of a doctor prescribing medication. "Under California law, Mary, we need to prove that Lexington *caused* Bowden to act. In essence, that it persuaded him that the P-2 was the best available weapon for killing *all* of you . . ."

"How?" Mary asked in bewilderment. "John's dead."

"True. But we *do* know that he flew to Las Vegas on the day of the gun show. And after he died, the police found the SSA magazine in his hotel room, containing the ads the President mentioned in his speech—calling the P-2 an 'endangered species, banned in California.'" Lenihan permitted himself a smile. "There's an old saying that if you go to bed without snow on the ground, and the next morning awaken to snow, the inescapable conclusion is that it snowed."

"Snow aside," Sarah remarked, "it would be far better if

we could find the seller. Or, at least, someone Bowden talked to about buying the P-2.

"There's an unfortunate decision called *Merrill versus Navigar.* That case involved an office massacre in San Francisco where the murderer *also* killed himself. The survivors sued the gun manufacturer on much the same grounds—inflammatory advertising. But the California Supreme Court ruled for the gun company, saying it was protected by a peculiar state statute shielding gun companies from product liability lawsuits—partly because there was no direct evidence that the murderer ever saw the ads.

"The California legislature promptly repealed the statute. But Lexington still can argue that there are a thousand other places Bowden could have bought the gun—including the black market . . ."

"Of course," Lenihan told Mary, "if Lexington had required a background check at gun shows, Bowden *couldn't* have bought it there. Instead, they virtually invited him to Las Vegas—not only to acquire a P-2 but bullets designed, and I quote, to inflict a 'massive wound channel.' When we begin gathering documents and deposing Lexington witnesses, we'll explore what research they did to authenticate that claim. I intend to show the jury that they believed every word."

Silent, Mary stared bleakly at some middle distance of the mind—in remembered horror, Sarah supposed, perhaps combined with disbelief that Lexington would choose to profit in such a way. Turning to Sarah, Lenihan asked, "Speaking of juries, you tried the Tierney case before a federal judge. No disrespect intended, Sarah, but I have to ask how many jury cases you've tried."

Surprised, Sarah tried to appear unruffled. "Three."

"Any plaintiffs' cases?"

"None at all."

"Have you at least tried a personal injury case, or a wrongful death action?"

"I haven't. As *you* already know."

"That's just as well," Lenihan responded with an amiable smile. "God knows your mentors in your former law firm lost enough of them. To me."

Mary shifted in her chair. "If you're trying to embarrass me," Sarah said in even tones, "at least address the issues. To even get this to a jury, you'll have to prepare for the argument that any suit is barred by the Second Amendment."

Lenihan, Sarah sensed, was eyeing her with increased caution. "The Second Amendment defense has never flown," he parried. "Not in a civil case."

"Not in California," Sarah agreed. "At least not yet." Facing Mary, Sarah explained, "Until recently there's been an unbroken line of cases, including a Supreme Court case, which suggested that the Second Amendment does not protect an individual's right to own a gun—as opposed to a collective right which belongs to governmental bodies like the police department, or the National Guard."

Mary nodded. "That makes sense to me."

"And to me. But the SSA disagrees. They claim that the Constitution enshrined the right of armed insurrection by individuals against the government the men who drafted it created, replacing votes with bullets. They also claim that this right cannot be infringed for any reason—that leading the Western world in homicides is the price we pay for this precious 'freedom.'

"Until a few years ago, no one but gun fanatics took that seriously. Then the SSA began financing a wave of 'scholarship': one law review article after another which argued that Madison, Jefferson and the rest meant each of us to have the absolute right to own any weapon we want—including weapons that the Founding Fathers never dreamed of. Like the Lexington P-2 and Eagle's Claw bullets . . ."

"That's absolutely ridiculous." Mary's voice trembled in anger. "I *saw* that gun kill my family. I *saw* what that bullet did."

"It *is* ridiculous," Sarah echoed softly. "Even sick. But at the same time those articles started appearing, Republicans began appointing federal judges approved by the SSA—or, at least, who shared its views." Sarah slid some papers across the desk to Mary. "I've copied a Texas case which began in federal court. An abusive husband subject to a restraining order claimed that the Constitution created a right of individual gun ownership—one so absolute that it barred the government from taking his gun away. Even to protect his wife.

"Creating precedents cuts both ways. *This* judge, a Reagan appointee, found that the right exists. Whether it's absolute, permitting a spousal abuser to keep his guns no matter what, has yet to be decided. And a recent opinion from this circuit, *Silvera v. Lockyear*, the most thorough opinion written on the subject, says emphatically that the Second Amendment does *not* create an individual right to own a gun. But you can see where the SSA is going: if unregulated gun ownership causes so much violence that we all get sick of it, the SSA's only hope is to create an absolute right, embedded in the Constitution, which would bar us from passing new gun laws." To Lenihan, Sarah finished, "With the SSA's encouragement, I'd expect Lexington to argue that it can't be sued for an activity which enables citizens to exercise their sacred Second Amendment rights. Even in the face of the *Silvera* case, and even for citizens like Bowden."

Mary listened intently. Glancing at her, Lenihan told Sarah, "And even *I* read cases. In fact, I'm thoroughly familiar with the law surrounding guns. That's one of several reasons she's asked *me* to represent her."

"Which you'd like to do without me," Sarah answered calmly. "So let's stop playing games.

"I didn't call Mary—you did. I've never met with Mary alone. And after she leaves here, I'm not going to call her to explain why you shouldn't represent her, or *I* should." Sarah's voice became crisp. "On the other hand, I'm quite confident that as soon as *you* leave here, you'll give her any number of reasons why you should try this case without me. So why don't you tell us both?"

After an instant, Lenihan shrugged. "I'm sure you're an able lawyer, Sarah. At least you've read a lot about guns. That's because, for you, the client is the cause.

"To me, the client is Mary. My job is to bring thirty years of experience to a single cause—to simplify the case, to present the most attractive facts to the jury in the most persuasive possible way, and to win Mary the largest recovery possible." Pausing, Lenihan gave Mary Costello an encouraging smile. "And, not incidentally, inflicting so much pain on Lexington that an entire industry will shiver.

"I understand the First Lady's affinity for the Kilcannon Center. I'm sure, as an older sister, she means to look after you. But when it comes to the courtroom—as the President would say if he were here—there's no one better suited than I. You don't need me wasting time in needless quarrels over strategy."

Turning, he held up a placating hand to Sarah. "I, too, admire the Center. It's simply a question of whether you're the right lawyer for Mary's wrongful death action. You're not. Both because of inexperience and because public interest lawyers push the law to its limits. Even if that endangers the *client's* interests."

Smiling, Sarah spoke to Mary. "Bob's right," she

acknowledged. "I'd like you to advance this lawsuit in a way which protects others from suffering as you have.

"I'll never conceal that. I think you should *do* it. But I'll always tell you when the public interest diverges from your own." Sarah faced Lenihan. "Every lawyer has an agenda. Sometimes it's a cause, sometimes glory, sometimes money. Sometimes it's all three.

"I don't care about 'glory'—I had enough exposure in the *Tierney* case to despise it. I don't want any piece of the verdict. All I want is our expenses, and the chance to help Mary make this lawsuit matter."

Mary regarded her gravely. When Lenihan began to speak, she placed her hand on his wrist. "I want you both," she told him. "I'd just feel more confident if you could work together."

Lenihan's eyebrows flew up. "That's fine with me," Sarah answered promptly. "In fact, I'd be very grateful for the opportunity."

With a theatrical sigh, Lenihan sat back, regarding Sarah with a complex look of enmity, amusement, annoyance and calculation. "Then come along with me, Sarah. I imagine we'll *both* learn something."

SEVEN

"This is our biggest challenge," Charles Dane told Senator Frank Fasano. "At least since 1968."

He did not mention the murders of Martin Luther King and Robert Kennedy. He did not need to. That they met in Kelsey Landon's K Street office, not the SSA's or Fasano's, said enough about the volatility of the moment.

The SSA's choice of Kelsey Landon as its consultant spoke to this as well. A small, well-knit man with silver hair and a perpetual expression of shrewd but pleasant alertness, the former senator from Colorado's fund-raising prowess had secured him a unique influence among Senate Republicans, cementing his closeness to Frank Fasano: when Fasano had set out to succeed Macdonald Gage, Landon had quietly passed the word that major Republican donors and power brokers favored his aspirations. Now, deferring to Fasano, Landon merely responded to Dane's comment with a wry smile of acknowledgment—a cue, Fasano sensed, that he should remind Dane of how much the SSA needed them both.

"It's the worst I've seen," Fasano said bluntly. "Especially in the Senate. My moderates are worried—they've seen the numbers for Kilcannon and the First Lady. And Lexington's not warm and fuzzy."

Seated in an elegant wing chair, Dane wore a pin-striped Savile Row suit which accented his air of power and ease. "In the end," he told Fasano, "Americans will respect individual responsibility. Bowden pulled the trigger, not George Callister."

"That's not good enough," Fasano said. "At least right now." Pausing, he added softly, "Some would say that Martin Bresler had the right idea on trigger locks and gun shows. And that it's too bad someone crushed him."

From behind his desk, Fasano noticed, Landon followed the exchange with the air of a connoisseur of tennis watching two veteran players testing each other's game. "Bresler crushed himself," Dane admonished. "Sometimes you'd be better off, Frank, envisioning gun owners not as a 'special interest,' but as members of one of the great religions of the world. The core of our membership would give us everything they owned before they give Kilcannon an inch on guns."

"Sounds like religion," Fasano answered. "I know it isn't politics. The Kilcannons have hung Lexington with an image problem that'll be hard to overcome."

"That's the real problem," Landon told Fasano. "It's not just Kilcannon's gun bill—it's our old friend Robert Lenihan. He can't help bragging—seems like he's signed up Lara Kilcannon's sister for a wrongful death suit against Lexington. If Lenihan's doing this, Kilcannon's pulling his strings . . ."

"It's been like synchronized swimming," Dane interjected in sardonic tones. "First the tape of Bowden killing them, then Kilcannon's speech, then Callister turns him down, and then Mrs. Kilcannon gives her interview. At this rate Lexington will have to look for neutral jurors in caves."

"The gun manufacturers," Landon added smoothly, "are petrified. Lenihan can finance this with millions in tobacco money. If he delivers George Callister's head on a platter, the trial lawyers can write their own ticket in the Democratic Party. And the gun industry may well cave in to whatever Kilcannon wants."

So far, Fasano reflected, the meeting had gone as he had expected. The SSA, he suspected, had compelled the manufacturers to take a hard line, and now had to show that it had the power to protect them. And Dane needed results for special reasons of his own: he was both intimidator and beseecher, whose tenure as SSA president depended on pleasing a board of governors whose intransigence on gun rights was equalled only by its hatred of Kerry Kilcannon. Evenly, Fasano inquired, "What is it that *you* want, Charles?"

Dane folded his arms. "A bar on lawsuits by people like Mary Costello."

"Just 'people *like* Mary Costello'? Or do you want us to kill *her* lawsuit?"

"What we want," Dane said succinctly, "is a law barring all lawsuits against the manufacturers of guns for deaths and injuries caused by someone else's criminal misuse. That means suits by anyone."

Fasano found himself studying Landon's bust of an Indian warrior, the gift from a grateful tribe for whom he had secured exclusive gaming rights. "If you're right about Lenihan," he told Dane, "Mary Costello will file any day now. We'd have to cut her off in mid-lawsuit."

Dane frowned. "No choice, Frank. We've passed laws like this in other states, but we lack the wherewithal in California. So you're the only game in town."

Though Fasano was prepared for this, the pressure building in the room had begun to feel like a vise, tangible and sobering. "You don't want much," he told Dane. "Only that the United States Senate stomp all over Lara Kilcannon's sole surviving relative, with the bodies of the others barely cold."

"Not just the Senate," Dane responded coolly. "The House of Representatives. Speaker Jencks is ready to go."

"Well, good for Tom," Fasano said dismissively. "Even if *both* of us can pass this bill of yours, Kilcannon will veto it. To override a veto, you may recall, we need a two-thirds vote of the Senate.

"By my count, that means sixty-seven senators will have to spit in the President's eye. Or, as Kilcannon will have it, on the graves of the First Lady's family." Turning to Landon, Fasano continued, "You can do the math as well as I can, Kelsey. I've got fifty-four Republicans. I can count at least five who are up for reelection next year and don't want Kilcannon's very warm breath on the backs of their necks. They'd sell their souls not to cast this vote."

Kelsey Landon smiled. "You remind me of what my predecessor used to say: 'Half my friends are for it, half against, and I'm all for my friends.' Except that *your* friends are in this room, and we're all for you."

For Fasano, the soothing bromide eliminated all doubt— the SSA had engaged Kelsey Landon not just as an advisor, but to bring all the pressure at his command to bear on Frank Fasano. For a brief, intoxicating moment, Fasano imagined telling them both to go to hell. Then he weighed yet again the political impracticality of offending the SSA, the risks and rewards—both monumental—of waging this fight against Kerry Kilcannon.

"I don't like these lawsuits," he said to Dane and Landon. "And Kilcannon's fully capable of running *this* lawsuit from the White House. But you're asking me to put five seats at risk—which, as it happens, would lose us the majority."

"You wouldn't *have* a majority," Dane said bluntly, "without our help. In the last election cycle, the SSA gave the Republican Party over $2.5 million in soft money and spent millions more in support of pro-gun candidates. We turned out our people in nine close Senate races, and you won six."

By whose count? Fasano wondered. "Charles," Landon

told him in a soothing voice, "knows that you'll need protection. I believe he's prepared to give it."

"To begin," Dane said, "we'll put up more money than we did the last time—at least four million."

The bargaining, Fasano knew, had begun. "What else?"

"Anything that's legal." Dane's voice was cool and businesslike. "After all, this is the last election before Chad Palmer's misbegotten campaign reform bill takes effect. We'll form groups to run 'independent' ads to support any senator who votes our way. We'll run an onslaught of radio and TV ads at the grassroots level. We'll tell our members to send the most generous checks they can to senators of our selection, and to the Republican Senatorial Campaign Committee."

"The problem," Fasano told Dane, "is that it'll be the SSA versus the President, with Kilcannon calling us SSA stooges . . ."

"One more reason," Dane retorted, "for you to pass this now. The election's not for thirteen months. By that time, the Costello shootings will have cooled off—especially if there's no lawsuit. And we're much too smart to resurrect the issue in an election year.

"Most of our ads won't even be about guns. We'll hit the candidates who run against your people on crime, antiterrorism, prayer in school, lowering taxes—whatever works from state to state. The way the law is now, the Democrats won't know who ran them until six months after they've lost.

"Even *you* won't know, Frank. But you'll still have your majority, maybe bigger. And that will make you the preeminent leader of your party."

At this unmistakable allusion to his Presidential prospects, the room became silent. Kelsey Landon had stopped smiling.

"You know what Charles can do," Landon said at

length. "Not just with money, but by turning out his people.

"If Republican senators don't go along, he'll invest in Democrats who will—in Montana, the Dakotas, the South, or wherever gun companies are key employers. He'll engage the folks who work in the chain of distribution: dealers, distributors, employees. He can rally four million members, not to mention reaching the nearly forty million households which own guns . . ."

"Our message is simple," Dane interjected. "Today it's the P-2 and the Eagle's Claw, but tomorrow it's *your* gun. Right now, we could generate mail, calls, and faxes ten to one in our favor on any gun immunity bill we propose.

"I've made our own head count of shaky Republicans and persuadable Democrats. Do your damnedest, Frank, and we'll help get your sixty-seven votes. After that, Kerry Kilcannon won't be the most powerful man in Washington. It'll be *you*." As Dane leaned forward, his gaze, penetrant and unblinking, impelled attention. "As for us, if we can quash this lawsuit, and then defeat Kilcannon's gun bill, we'll bury gun control for a generation. Maybe for good and all."

Fasano stared at him. "Not if you bring a bill Kilcannon can claim is meant to 'quash' the memory of a murdered six-year-old. Then it *would* be about the Eagle's Claw. You'd be better off trying to put a cap on damages."

"That's not enough," Dane shot back. "The legal fees alone are bleeding the industry to death. And we don't want Kilcannon using Bob Lenihan to root around in Lexington's files, or interrogate its employees."

What, Fasano wondered, was the SSA afraid of? Quietly, he said, "Then you'd be better off with a law that never mentions guns. Something like 'No manufacturer, dealer or distributor will be liable for the use of a legal product in an illegal act by any person not under its direction or control.' "

Briefly, Landon smiled—an affirmation that, all along, Fasano had been one move ahead. In response, Dane's eyes, again fixed on Fasano, were keen.

"Tell us how to pass it," Dane said.

"By playing well with others," Fasano answered. "You need to tuck your language in a major tort reform bill backed by every lawyer-hating institution in America: the airlines, aircraft manufacturers, liquor and tobacco companies, auto makers, tire companies, employers with environmental problems, even the people who make farm implements.

"*Then* you reach out beyond the obvious—to fast-food businesses, for example, or accountants, or investment bankers. You immunize teachers against lawsuits, thereby neutralizing a union which always supports Democrats. You get HMOs to form 'Citizens for Better Medicine' and saturate the airwaves. You even limit punitive damages against charities like the American Cancer Society."

Pausing, Fasano looked from Landon to Dane. Both were silent, attentive, expressionless. "Most important," Fasano continued, "you rally all their employees to the cause.

"We need to bury the idea that we're pandering to the merchants of death. Our bill is a job protection measure, keeping greedy lawyers like Bob Lenihan from bankrupting companies and putting ordinary people out of work. It's also a *consumer* protection measure, insulating other ordinary people from outrageous verdicts which they wind up paying for in the form of higher consumer prices.

"That's the message we should keep on driving home: spurious lawsuits clog the courts and subvert our core belief in individual responsibility. Coffee is *supposed* to be hot—if Aunt Minnie spills it and burns her fingers, it's *her* fault, not McDonald's. Or *yours*." For the first time, Fasano smiled. "After that, we can depict Kilcannon and the Democrats as the wholly owned subsidiary of America's most loathed minority—the trial lawyers who buy corporate jets, two-hundred-foot yachts, and baseball teams which overcharge for hot dogs."

"The Chamber of Commerce," Dane reminded Fasano, "has tried to pass that bill for years. They never have."

"That's because they've never had the troops. You do. With your muscle and your money, placed at the disposal of a broad coalition, perhaps you can get this through . . ."

"And you," Dane interjected, "will have made your business constituency happier than it's ever been."

"Of course," Fasano said with a shrug. "Why stop with you?"

"I'm sure that's fine with the SSA," Landon put in. "But up to now the tort reform community has avoided the gun issue like the plague."

"And they've lost, haven't they? As Charles points out. By now, a lot of them will want the same provision which immunizes gun manufacturers.

"Let me give you an example. A couple of years ago our leading auto manufacturer was sued in San Francisco—where, I'm sure, Lenihan intends to bring this suit. The plaintiff was drunk, was speeding, and plowed into an embankment on his own. The gas tank in his car exploded, killing both of his children. But instead of blaming the driver, the jury focused on the fact that the company had done a cost-benefit analysis of the money required to make its gas tank one hundred percent safe, and decided that perfection wasn't worth it. So the jury awarded a *billion* dollars in punitives to a drunk who killed his kids." Pausing, Fasano said with irony, "Understandably, the company's chief lobbyist talks about it still. So I think you'll find him newly sympathetic to your goals."

"We need more than sympathy," Dane retorted. "A bill that broad will buy us a battle with Kilcannon and the trial lawyers tantamount to nuclear war . . ."

A quiet knock on Landon's door interrupted Dane as Landon's very pretty assistant entered with a silver tray—assorted sandwiches and small desserts, with a Diet Coke for Dane, a mineral water with lime for Fasano, and a bourbon on ice for Landon. Sipping it, Landon waited until she left.

"Frank's right," he told Dane. "And so are you. Frank would have to persuade your silent partners to share the cost of some pretty expensive fun." Sitting back, Landon tasted the bourbon on his lips. "The bill would come through the Commerce Committee—Chad Palmer's committee, unfortunately, since the shake-up when Frank replaced Gage as Majority Leader. You'll need a lobbyist to work each committee member. Also, you should make a donation to the state party of any of the members who are up for reelection."

Dane's smile held a trace of cynicism. "I assume you can help us direct all that."

Landon nodded. "If you like," he said amiably.

Fasano watched in silence. He had seen the process before—an interest group setting out to use its muscle finds itself muscled back by those it intends to use. Dane's needs were obvious and urgent. And by hiring Landon for his ties to Fasano, Dane had given both men leverage: for Fasano, to secure his dominance of the party; for Landon, to augment his wealth and influence. Finishing his bourbon, Landon leaned back in his chair, as though widening his field of vision. "If we're all agreed on our approach," he said in a conciliatory tone, "let's talk about what Frank can do for you. And how he best can do it.

"I don't know what Frank Fasano will decide his future holds. But to my mind, and I'm sure to yours, he has potential well beyond the Senate. It's in all of our interests to spare him needless controversy."

"In other words," Dane said with brusque impatience, "Frank can't take the lead. So who will?"

Dane cast an inquiring gaze toward Fasano. "Dave Ruckles, perhaps?"

This, Fasano thought, suited his own needs perfectly. As Majority Whip, Ruckles was already chafing under Fasano's leadership. Ruckles was nakedly ambitious—even if he saw the potential pitfalls, the temptation to ingratiate himself with such a wide array of interest groups would be too great to resist.

"That sounds right," Fasano concurred. "Dave should introduce the bill—Paul Harshman's image is too hard-line. You'll also want a woman to cosponsor, maybe Clare McIntyre. Or Cassie Rollins, assuming she's persuadable."

"In Maine she *should* be," Dane replied. "But she's up for reelection. In election years, the Yankees try to sit on the fence."

"The Yankees," Fasano knew, was Dane's pejorative for New England moderates Dane considered unreliable on gun rights—Kate Jarman of Vermont, Dick Stafford of Connecticut, John Smythe of Rhode Island, and Cassie Rollins of Maine. " 'The Yankees,' " Fasano replied, "are my department. As is my party as a whole."

Dane paused, appraising him. "How so?" he demanded.

It was time, Fasano decided, to spell out how things would be. "You want me to deliver," he said coolly. "So you play by my rules.

"*I* direct the money you give to our party. *I* allocate it to the national party, the Senate committee, and the individual senators *I* select. *I* pick the candidates you help, and *I* clear the Democrats you support. End of story."

Dane's eyes seemed to narrow. "*Your* story ends with

you as the most powerful senator in living memory. Using our money to do it."

Fasáno nodded. "True. But with the SSA more well positioned than ever. Because *I* am."

Now Kelsey Landon only watched. Coldly, Dane countered, "Then I want your commitment to go all out. No taking SSA money, then making some token effort and telling us it's all too bad."

Fasano's own expression was grim. "Fair enough. But I'm the Senate Majority Leader, not your hired hand. You screwed up with Martin Bresler's group, and then I let you get between us and Bresler. If Kilcannon or the media ever hears about *that* one, they'll say I'm holding the bag on three dead bodies.

"So I'm in charge of *this* one. I know how best to protect my party, and our majority. Respect *that*, and you won't have to live with a Senate controlled by Kerry Kilcannon."

For a long time, Dane stared at him. "Is that all?"

"Not quite. Kilcannon will use this lawsuit to drive a wedge between Lexington and the SSA, and Lexington and the rest of the industry. If Lexington caves, you've got no bill . . ."

"How long," Dane interrupted, "would Lexington last if our four million members stop buying its products. Or gun dealers refuse to stock them?"

"This involves much more than keeping Lexington quiet and in line," Fasano answered. "If you're *that* worried about what Lenihan might uncover in their files, Lexington can't let Mary Costello's lawsuit gain any traction whatsoever. That demands a scorched earth defense by the meanest lawyers they can find."

This induced a longer gaze from Charles Dane. "We've got the lawyers," he said at length. "They're not just mean, but establishment mean—as smooth as corporate lawyers come. We're confident that Lexington will agree to hire them." Abruptly, Dane's manner became commanding. "How long will it take you to pass a bill?"

"*This* bill? Three months at a minimum."

"Then you should find a way to speed it up."

"What clever trick would you recommend? Tacking it on some other bill? Kilcannon would veto the bill in a heartbeat, and pillory us in the bargain.

"We'll do this by the numbers," Fasano continued. "Introduce the bill; refer it to the Commerce Committee for a hearing; get it out of Palmer's clutches with a favorable committee vote; put it on the calendar; work out an amendment process with Hampton; kill his amendments gutting your provision; and pass it with sixty-seven votes. All of which takes time."

"Three months," Dane retorted, "is too much time. As soon as Kilcannon's people figure out what's in the bill for us—and they will—he'll try to rally support like he's been doing on his gun bill. The more time he has, the more our opposition hardens."

"Frank didn't say," Landon interposed, "that there was *nothing* you can do to make this easier. I think there is."

Dane turned to Landon. "Such as?"

"Start with the House of Representatives. Let Tom Jencks pass the tort reform bill without the gun immunity clause. Keep that language out of the Senate bill you send to Palmer. That way, there's nothing for Kilcannon's people to spot . . ."

"And we get nothing for our investment . . ."

"But then," Landon continued smoothly, "a few days before passage, someone like Paul Harshman inserts your gun immunity provision in the bill to be voted out of Palmer's committee. It's easily done. Suddenly the bill coming to the floor includes what you want, and, with luck, it will be a while before the President and Hampton notice that. Let alone rally support.

"With enough luck, they'll be too late. And once your bill passes the Senate, we go back to the House, wherein Tom Jencks swiftly inserts the gun immunity language."

Silent, Fasano watched Dane evaluate Landon's suggestion. At length, he turned to Fasano. "There's just one glaring problem. Palmer. Committee chairmen are dictators. And the last time I saw him he told me to go fuck myself."

Fasano smiled. "Sounds like Chad. I'll talk to him about you."

"Palmer," Dane objected, "is in the way . . ."

"I'll deal with Palmer," Fasano snapped. "You take care of Lexington."

"The *sine qua non* is to keep everyone together—Lexington, the SSA, and all the other entities in our great antilawyer, pro-job, pro-consumer coalition." Looking from Landon to Dane, Fasano paused for emphasis. "Our only chance of surviving Kilcannon's veto is to keep the gun provision in the final bill, forcing every senator to vote 'yes' or 'no' on the most sweeping reform of civil justice ever to pass the Senate."

Thoughtful, Dane seemed to withdraw from the conversation. "Is there any chance," he mused aloud, "that Kilcannon could be persuaded *not* to veto such a bill?"

For the first time since the meeting began, Fasano was surprised. "One that wipes out Mary Costello's lawsuit? That's a primal challenge to everything he holds dear."

At this, Dane looked up at him with eyes so placid that it took Fasano aback. "Still, Frank, your life would be much easier if you never had to get to sixty-seven."

EIGHT

THAT NIGHT, Frank and Bernadette Fasano attended a party at Cal Carlston's imposing home in Observatory Heights.

In her seventh month of pregnancy, Bernadette's feet were swollen, and the prospect of politically centered chitchat struck her as less entrancing than normal. But it was her firm belief that husband and wife should not lead separate lives, and a point of pride that—consistent with the demands of motherhood—she was there to support her husband whenever the occasion merited. This was one such evening: Carlston, a lobbyist whom the defense and pharmaceutical industries had made wealthy beyond Bernadette's imaginings, was throwing a dinner for Republican governors salted with conservative intellectuals, members of Congress, major donors, and other party luminaries—an event her man-who-would-be-President had felt it unwise to miss. So she had hastily fed the children, pulled her most soignee late-maternity dress from the closet, and sallied forth with Frank, a cheerful advertisement for their still-blossoming nuclear family.

On arrival, they idled in a line of cars waiting to be valet parked. Frank turned to her and promised, "We'll make it an early night."

Bernadette's smile mingled skepticism with fondness. "That was easier to believe when you were less important. I can always find someplace to sit."

Leaning over, Frank kissed her still-smiling lips. "I'm

incredibly important," he told her, "but you and our baby are precious."

Frank had meant it, of course. He felt so lucky in Bernadette that sometimes he pitied those politicians, like Kerry Kilcannon, whose spouses had their own agendas. But one of Frank's weaknesses was to count on the elasticity of his wife's good nature. And so, it was well past the time he had meant to leave—after hours of hearty hand-shakes, kisses on cheeks, confabs with governors whose support he deeply wanted, and calculated candor with columnists—when Senator Macdonald Gage pulled him aside.

Glancing around Cal Carlston's massive drawing room, Fasano saw Bernadette settled on the couch, listening in apparent fascination to the ever-courtly Kelsey Landon. Briefly, Fasano wondered whether Landon and Gage were functioning as a tag team, and then turned his full attention on Mac Gage.

"A grand coalition," Gage remarked. "That's what you sold the SSA?"

"Of course. It won't work any other way."

"Then this will surely be the lobbyists' Olympics." As he lowered his voice, Gage's smile turned shrewd. "Does the SSA understand you're using them to break the power of the trial lawyers?"

"Someone needs to," Fasano answered coolly. "Starting with the tobacco litigation, we've been watching the greatest transfer of wealth since they passed the federal income tax—this time from our corporate donor base into the pockets of the plaintiffs' lawyers like Bob Lenihan. Which means to the most liberal element of the Democratic party.

"The trial lawyers put more cash into Kilcannon's

campaign than anyone else. If we can cut down their recoveries against our corporate supporters, we can stop them from funding the Democrats—at least in such large amounts." Fasano glanced around them. "That'll make it easier to beat Kilcannon when he runs for reelection. Charles Dane can hardly object to *that*."

Gage's look of shrewdness deepened. "Leave it to you, Frank, to turn a problem into an opportunity. Still, the stakes are huge. It's a shame you can't put a little more time between this and the Costello shootings."

"Tell that to the SSA." With this, Fasano dropped all pretense that Gage would not be reporting back to Dane. "My next move is to recruit some high-tech companies who'll help me pick up swing Democrats. And techies don't want to be lumped with gun makers. If the SSA doesn't keep quiet and play by my rules, they'll screw this whole thing up."

Gage squared his shoulders. "Just be straight with Dane about what you're doing, and keep your coalition in line. Once he figures this out, Kilcannon will try to split the SSA from the others. You can't let that happen."

At the corner of his vision, Fasano caught a senator and two governors glancing at them surreptitiously. Moving closer, Fasano spoke in an undertone. "I don't intend to. That's why I'm making trial lawyers the issue.

"That'll help us get by with this. Look at Columbine— even with the liberal media pushing gun control, nothing happened. In the end, people will blame Bowden, not Lexington or the SSA. But only if we play it right."

As if to signal the room that he and Fasano remained in private conference, Gage bowed his head slightly in a pose of confidentiality, though his eyes remained fixed on Fasano. "Kilcannon thinks he can hang our activists— evangelicals, the pro-life folks, and the SSA—like a millstone around our neck. But in a time when under half of eligible Americans vote for President, and some of *those* for a third-party candidate, less than a quarter of the adult population can make you President. Which means the activists will count for a whole lot more.

"If all goes well, you'll have the conservative activists providing the troops for a Presidential campaign financed by the corporate interests who'll love you for tort reform. And the activists hate Kilcannon so much they'll let you soften your pitch a little, pick up some votes in the middle." Gage summoned his most amiable smile. "If you can pass tort reform, Frank, and stave off Kilcannon's gun control bill, you're halfway to becoming President."

Gage, Fasano knew, understood that he already had made precisely this calculation. But if the purpose of this make-believe was to convey messages to and from the SSA, it was now Fasano's turn.

"*If*," Fasano answered. "The sequence is important.

"We need to stall Kilcannon's gun bill. For that, the SSA's going to have to tolerate our alternative bill—something that seems to address how Bowden got his gun. Then we can say that *both* parties want to protect women and children, but that the Senate needs to work through how best to do it..."

"Which," Gage interrupted, "allows you to put the tort reform bill *ahead* of gun control on the Senate agenda."

Fasano nodded. "Of course. Except that the gun immunity provision won't even be *in* our bill, at least until it's voted out of Palmer's committee."

Gage's look of good humor evaporated. "Palmer," he said tersely, "is Palmer."

"Exactly. A war hero, a senator of unimpeachable integrity openly hated by the SSA, and—some would say— still a leading contender for the Republican nomination. If I can get Palmer behind gun immunity, we'll have the inside track on people like Kate Jarman and Cassie Rollins."

Gage's expression turned opaque. To Gage, Fasano guessed, the last remark was an implicit insult: Gage's failure to control Chad Palmer had cost him the job Fasano now held and, with it, his own aspirations to be President. "So," Gage said softly, "you can get Palmer, Kilcannon's great friend, to do all that for you."

Fasano did not waver. "Look around you," he said with equal quiet. "Chad isn't here. Since Kyle died, he's half of who he was. All he has left except Allie is his career. He needs for it to mean something."

This implied rebuke—expressing the father and husband in Fasano, not the politician—made Gage look briefly away. When he spoke again, his voice contained an edge. "And you think you can offer him that."

"Not exactly. But if the SSA gets out of the way, I can make Chad an offer he knows I intend to be meaningless, and let him try to outwit me."

Gage's eyes became narrow and tight. "And what would that be?"

Fasano's own stare was hard. "What you would never give him, Mac. The thing he wants most, besides for his daughter to be alive. Not just a law, but a place in American history. I know you'll want to help me."

NINE

ON THAT SAME EVENING, Chad and Allie Palmer were at the White House.

For their first effort to resume a social life, neither Kerry nor Lara felt up to a formal dinner. Instead, they invited a smallish group for a casual meal and an advance screening of a new romantic comedy with Kate Beckinsale and Hugh Grant—who, Lara had assured her husband, was a greatly inferior version of Kerry himself. Their guests were an eclectic collection of political and social friends—two of Lara's former colleagues from NBC; Clayton and Carlie Slade; Jimmy Laughlin, Kerry's former office mate from the D.A.'s office in Newark, now an official in the Justice Department; Kit Pace, his press secretary, and her partner Beth Wilson; and, after some thought on Kerry's part, the Palmers. Only at the last minute had he invited Chuck and Elise Hampton; though the Senate Minority Leader had never been an intimate, or even a supporter, Kerry concluded that now was the time to work on this. And so at dinner Kerry sat between Elise Hampton and Allie Palmer, and Lara next to Chuck.

This worked out better than either of the Kilcannons had hoped. Lara knew Chuck Hampton from covering the Hill. They had stories in common—the drama and comedy of clashing egos and the sometimes foolish behavior of self-serious men—and after a time Lara's laughter flowed as easily as Hampton's story of the buffoonish senator from North Dakota who, inebriated, had tried to exit a closed-door meeting and entered a closet instead. "We were speechless," Hampton concluded. "He just *stayed* in there—as though if he didn't come out, we wouldn't notice."

"What did the *rest* of you do?" Lara inquired.

Hampton grinned. "Waited him out, of course. The closet had no bathroom."

In the general laughter that followed, Kerry murmured to Allie Palmer, "The most remarkable thing about that story is that it's true. *I* was in the meeting."

Still smiling, Allie asked, "What did the poor man do when he *did* come out?"

"It was really quite astonishing. He sat down again, as though he'd just returned from the men's room, and launched into a monologue on farm subsidies. A true example of grace under pressure."

Envisioning the moment, Allie shook her head in amusement. After that, their own exchanges deepened. By the end of dinner, she had told him in detail about her volunteer work in an inner-city school, a conversation which Kerry sensed helped Allie put flesh on her new life. As for Elise Hampton, Kerry had always liked her. A Ph.D. in English, Elise had a jaundiced sense of humor and a perspective on politics which, Kerry sensed, had made her more sympathetic than her husband to Kerry's internecine battle with Dick Mason.

This proved to be true. As they walked from dinner to the screening room, Elise said wryly, "I have an admission to make. A convenient one."

Kerry smiled. "What's that?"

"I'm glad you're here, and not Dick Mason. Every time I tried to probe his smooth veneer, I discovered the veneer beneath." Serious now, she touched Kerry's arm. "I'm so sorry about all that's happened, to Lara and to you. But what you're doing needs to be done."

This was the only mention of guns until the evening—a

great success—was over, and the guests began slowly to peel off. Next to last were the Palmers. Leaving, Chad said with a smile, "What this country needs is more free movies," and went into the night, his arm around Allie's waist.

That left the Hamptons. Standing near the East Entrance with the President and First Lady, Hampton informed Kerry, "I've been counting votes on your bill, Mr. President. I think there's a fair chance that we can get to fifty-one.

"The problem is getting to sixty, and shutting down a filibuster. Also dealing with whatever sham bill Fasano puts together."

Kerry nodded. "Something else has occurred to me," he told the Hamptons. "Is there any sign that tort reform is on Fasano's agenda?"

Elise glanced at her husband, who raised his eyebrows—his curiosity seemingly aroused both by the question and by the fact that Kerry had asked it. "Not that I know about. If Fasano passes a bill with teeth, he has to know you'd veto it."

"True," Kerry allowed. "But do me a favor, if you will. If some Republican suddenly drops a tort reform bill, I want my legislative people to see it right away."

Hampton considered him. "Is this about the SSA? At the state level, they've been pushing bills to immunize gun manufacturers."

"The thought's occurred to me. But Fasano wouldn't be that blatant—not in this environment. That was what brought tort reform to mind."

Once the Hamptons were gone, Lara leaned against Kerry's shoulder. "How was tonight?" he asked.

"Good," she answered softly. "Sometimes, I almost forgot."

Gently, Kerry kissed her. In two days she would com-

mence a fifteen-city tour to meet with victims and survivors.

"Why do it this way?" Tony Calvo asked Frank Fasano.

The president of the Chamber of Commerce ate
breakfast with Fasano in a private corner of the senators'
dining room. Putting down his fork, Calvo added, "I
think these lawsuits against gun companies are abusive.
But the wake of the Costello murders is the absolute
worst place to start."

"It's also your only chance," Fasano answered.
"You've never passed a bill. The voters don't much care.
So my colleagues aren't scared or grateful enough to give
you the sixty-seven votes you need to survive Kilcannon's vetoes.

"The Chamber's been an equal opportunity donor to
both Democrats and Republicans. The SSA supports *us*—
period. I can't dump them just because you ask me to,
and you'd be foolish to ask. On the whole, our caucus
is far more scared of *them* than you."

Calvo glanced around the ornate room. At this early
hour, eight o'clock, senators dined with lobbyists, contri-
butors, or the occasional awed constituent—everyone but
each other, Calvo reflected. "The *Democrats*," Calvo
answered, "are scared of Kilcannon, and so are some
Republicans. They're right to be. Once he finds out what
you're doing, he'll make it all about guns."

"And we'll have all the money and votes that go with
them." Pausing, Fasano spoke softly. "How many votes
do you have, Tony? Do you think the average American
wakes up every morning hoping we'll immunize General
Motors? Putting down the trial lawyers is not a top-tier
issue for anyone but us. Guns are."

Calvo sipped his coffee, peering at Fasano over the rim. "What do you want from us, Frank?"

"What do *you* want?"

"Ideally?" Calvo's tone became clipped, businesslike. "Restrictions on class actions. Caps on punitive damages and attorneys' fees. A law allowing companies to require mandatory arbitration in place of jury trials. Ditto peer review in medical malpractice cases . . ."

"That's all?" Fasano inquired dryly.

"Nope. We want as many cases as possible shifted to federal court. On average, federal judges are more conservative. Also, a defendant shouldn't be liable for all damages in a lawsuit just because a codefendant is bankrupt, like Arthur Andersen after Enron tanked. And your bill should raise the burden of proof in personal injury cases."

"In your dreams," Fasano responded with a smile. "I can't get you all that, and still get enough Democrats to give us sixty-seven. But put together a coalition, Tony, and then send me a bill my staff can go to work on. Sooner rather than later."

Calvo studied his empty cup. At length, he asked, "Do you want language on gun immunity?"

Fasano suppressed any show of satisfaction. "No need," he assured Calvo. "We've got some language in mind."

With that, Fasano went to his meeting with the Speaker of the House.

"Why is it," Tom Jencks inquired with feigned disgust, "that the Senate is so candy-assed? My members would vote to immunize Lexington from lawsuits without breaking a sweat."

Fasano smiled. "The 'people's House,'" he countered,

"is so gerrymandered that maybe thirty-five out of four hundred thirty-five seats are even competitive. In the other four hundred, you could elect a tuna sandwich or a pedophile."

"Democracy," Jencks noted comfortably, "works better as a theory. I truly feel for your burdens, Frank."

"They are many," Fasano agreed. "And the biggest one is Palmer."

"Indeed. I've been wondering how you'd get Sir Galahad to play along with this game of smoke and mirrors."

"Hence this meeting," Fasano answered. "Give me a few minutes, Tom, to explain what you can do."

When Fasano had finished, Jencks looked at him gravely, his bulky frame settling farther into Fasano's overstuffed leather chair.

"I have to say, Frank, this one worries me. There's too much that can go wrong, too many moving parts—Mary Costello's supposed lawsuit, Kilcannon, Lenihan, controlling the SSA." Jencks spread his meaty hands in mock entreaty. "All that, and now you want *me* to fuck Chad Palmer for you."

Fasano shrugged. "The SSA's called in its due bill, Tom. All we can do is make this better, or worse."

"Better for *you*." Jencks's tone became tough and practical. "If you can pull *this* off, I suppose you deserve to be President."

"It's a time for greatness," Fasano answered calmly. "In exchange for his help on gun immunity, I give Palmer a vote on his dream campaign reform bill—the signature moment of his career. And then you kill it in the House, or pass a bill so incompatible with Palmer's that both bills die in conference without reaching

Kilcannon's desk. All I need to know is whether you've got the votes."

Narrow-eyed, Jencks studied his fingernails. "What does the SSA say?" he inquired. "They hated Palmer's *last* reform bill worse than I did."

Once more, Fasano smiled. "Dane's my very next call," he answered.

TEN

THAT EVENING, Frank Fasano came to Chad Palmer's office.

It was past eight o'clock. Chad felt tired. Since Kyle's death, his stamina had diminished; he was anxious to get home to Allie. But within moments of Fasano's arrival an adrenaline rush of sheer surprise cut through his fatigue.

"Let me get this straight," Chad said. "Once my committee takes up this tort reform bill, you want me to sneak in language wiping out any lawsuit brought by Lara Kilcannon's sister for the slaughter of their family."

Unfazed, Fasano nodded. "That's the first step. After that I want you to accelerate hearings, fight off any effort to strip that language from the bill, and get your committee to send it to the Senate floor with a positive vote. At warp speed."

"Because the SSA wants me to."

"Yes. Among other reasons."

"Now *there's* an incentive." Walking to his coffee table, Chad picked up the latest copy of *The Defender*. "I was flipping through this last night. Sandwiched between all the arguments that the Founding Fathers wanted everyone to own an Uzi are a few encomiums to me.

"As I recall, I'm an enemy of freedom, a friend to 'gun-grabbers,' a running dog of the left-wing media, and an advocate of thought control to muzzle patriotic Americans who defend the Second Amendment." Carelessly, Palmer tossed the magazine in Fasano's lap. "And what's my supposed sin? Trying to get special interest money out of politics, so that groups like the SSA can't bribe our party by giving us millions of dollars in so-called contributions . . ."

" 'Bribery' is nonsense," Fasano snapped. "Money follows ideology, not the other way around."

"Sure it does. We just happen to believe deeply in the Eagle's Claw bullet. If the SSA didn't line our pockets, we might actually vote our common sense now and then."

Fasano folded his arms. "The SSA has every right to back its beliefs with cash. Rosie O'Donnell can go on TV and pitch gun control for free. The only way the SSA can compete is to buy a seat at the table. You may not like it, but they're as entitled to a voice as anyone else."

"Maybe a voice, but not a veto." Pausing, Chad sat across from Fasano. "Our party is going the way of the dodo, Frank. We're far too dependent on gun nuts and mindless fundamentalists."

Fasano smiled. "Citizens, you mean. Who happen to vote."

Chad briefly shook his head. "You think you're using them. The truth is you're a hostage." Chad's blue eyes fixed Fasano with a penetrating gaze. "Wait until you run for President and discover you can't even admit that you believe in the theory of evolution. Which you damned well know you can't.

"When 'Darwin' is a dirty word, we're on the wrong side of history. We're pandering to the folks who brought us the Scopes monkey trial and the Costello murders. It's suicide in slow motion."

Smiling faintly, Fasano inquired, "Can I quote you?"

"Please do." Chad's tone was quiet but urgent. "I know this is heresy to most of our colleagues. But the President's right about background checks. The SSA's position is unconscionable—that's how Lara Kilcannon lost her family. By and large, the folks out there will get that.

"The last election was close, I grant you. But the states Kilcannon won are gaining population, while too many of *our* states are losing population. If you try to ride this tiger to the Presidency, Kerry Kilcannon will kick your ass from here to Tuesday."

Fasano assumed an expression of strained patience. "Let's stick to the here and now, Chad. On background checks, I mean to offer an alternative bill."

"Which'll be Swiss cheese," Palmer retorted, "drafted by the SSA."

Fasano shrugged. "Then I suppose I won't be asking you to vote for it."

"Why waste the breath? But you *are* asking me to help the SSA keep its power over the gun industry, while *enhancing* their power within our party—among other things, to better frustrate the next bill I'm pushing on campaign finance reform." Palmer cocked his head. "I'm honestly curious, Frank. Rather than sneak this dead and very smelly rat into your tort reform bill, why should't I oppose it?"

"For a host of reasons," Fasano said promptly. "At least some of which are principled. To begin, these lawsuits *are* an abuse—Eagle's Claw or no, you know in your gut that Lexington's not legally responsible for lunatics like Bowden.

"Then there's the trial lawyers. Care to talk about bribery? The Democrats are Bob Lenihan's wholly owned subsidiary . . ."

"Lenihan's pond scum," Chad interjected flatly, "and Kilcannon's too beholden to him. But you overrate the public disgust with trial lawyers.

"The President's too good, Frank. He'll find the votes to block this gun immunity thing, and make it stick."

Calmly, Fasano shook his head. "Not if I keep it in the overall bill. And not if you help me."

"Any why in the world would I do that?"

"Because you'll gain from it," Fasano answered in an even tone. "Your nominees to Republican seats on various commissions. That farm bill . . ."

"Kilcannon can give me that stuff," Chad scoffed. "You're not President yet. There's a limit to what you can offer me, and nothing I'd sell my soul for."

"Nothing?" Fasano responded quietly. "What about something Kilcannon dearly wants to give you, but can't? Unless I let him."

Watching the Majority Leader's expression, a study in opacity, Chad understood that this was where Fasano had been leading. With instinctive caution, he asked, "What might that be?"

"Let me answer you this way, Chad. Suppose you refuse to help me. What happens to your new campaign reform bill—this plan you have for public financing in all federal elections, driving corruption from our politics?"

Fasano's tone and phrasing, Chad knew, were intended to convey far more than irony. Chad kept his own voice matter-of-fact. "You'd rally votes against it. You'd try to keep it from the Senate floor—all you'd need is forty-one votes to sustain a filibuster . . ."

"Or," Fasano amended, "I'd tack it on as an amendment to the alternative gun bill you've just derided, and force Kilcannon to veto it."

No one had raised his voice, Chad reflected. But suddenly the space between them felt taut, almost stifling. Softly, Palmer said, "Forget it. I'd torpedo that abortion before it ever gets to Kerry."

Fasano shrugged. "You understand my point. I have a thousand ways of killing what you want. Turn me down, and that becomes a matter of principle. Or our caucus will think that you can roll me."

Chad stood, hands in his pockets. For a reason he did

not fully grasp, he walked to an end table near his couch, and reangled his photograph of Kyle. For a time, he found himself studying his daughter's face.

"What is it you're offering, Frank?"

"A straight up-and-down vote on your signature bill. I'll oppose it, of course. But all you need for passage is fifty-one votes." Gazing up at him, Fasano finished, "You're pretty close, Chad. I've counted the votes."

"So have I. Maybe I get to fifty-one, but no way I get to sixty. Every right-wing group in the party opposes my bill—the Christian Commitment, the right-to-lifers, and especially the SSA." Pausing, Chad spoke more quietly. "Your offer's meaningless. Somebody like Harshman will mount a filibuster, and those same groups will find forty senators to support it. My bill will never come to a vote."

"I promise you it will. Just keep Chuck Hampton on board, and peel off our moderates. I'll keep Harshman and the SSA in line." Pausing, Fasano smiled. "If you help me out with barring suits against gun companies, I'll have the capital to do that."

Palmer sat again. "You've already talked to the SSA, haven't you? And Harshman."

Fasano shrugged. "You think you can 'clean up' American politics. Personally, I think your solution is misguided. But this is the only chance you've got."

For a time, Chad stared at him in silence. "The path you've taken here," he said at length, "is truly mind-bending. You've married the business lobby to the gun nuts. You've gotten the opponents of my reform bill to promise not to filibuster. You've told the SSA you're going to cut a deal with me.

"It's a riverboat gamble by way of Machiavelli. Pull it off, and you'll be the unquestioned leader of our party. Unless, of course, the House passes my bill." Now Chad summoned a smile of his own. "By the way," he finished casually, "I hope you told Tom Jencks that shafting me in the House won't be quite as easy as he thinks."

Sitting back, Fasano laughed with what seemed to Chad a quite genuine amusement. "I'm glad to see," Chad remarked affably, "that your spirit of adventure remains intact. Because if Jencks screws up, the right-wing vultures will be dining on your corpse." Pausing, Chad spoke with sudden softness. "Why does this remind me of a dinner I once had with Kerry Kilcannon, where we made a deal on Caroline Masters? The time when one of us was too clever by half."

At once, Fasano became deeply sober. "About Kilcannon," he said at length. "No warnings. No co-operation. No notes thrown over the fence. The precondition of my deal is that you cut our President off." Fasano's gaze intensified. "Sell us out to Kilcannon, you'll be beyond my help. In our party, pariahs always are."

Palmer gazed at him, his tone remaining soft. "How many times, I wonder, did Mac Gage try to scare me. I've lost count. Just like I stopped counting all the other hacks who tried it before Gage.

"They looked at me, and saw themselves. They never understood that a pack of Arabs taught me an involuntary lesson: that there are far worse things in life than any politician can inflict." Pausing, he turned to Kyle's picture, and then back to Fasano. "At least now. Can you get your arms around that one, Frank?"

Fasano's eyes were somber. "Of course."

"Good. Because here's *my* precondition." Leaning forward, Chad's eyes locked Fasano's. "I'll put your language in the bill, and I'll support it. And then we'll tell the world exactly what we're doing. No tricks."

Fasano considered him, and then shrugged with

apparent resignation. "All right, Chad. Have it your way."

At that moment, the last piece of the puzzle became clear to Chad. Fasano had never intended to proceed by stealth—that was too fraught with risk. Chad had responded as Fasano had intended: Fasano could now inform the SSA that their enemy, Chad Palmer, had forced him to abandon a tactic he had never intended to pursue beyond Chad's committee. All Fasano wanted was a head start on Kilcannon.

"No," Chad corrected him. "It'll be your way, all along. At least until the end."

The following afternoon, with the floor of the Senate virtually empty, Majority Whip Dave Ruckles caused the filing of the "Civil Justice Reform Act."

Neither Ruckles nor Fasano was present, nor anyone else of note. In theory, Senator Ruckles should have stood up during morning business and announced his intention to introduce another sterling piece of legislation. Or, during some other hour when the Senate was in session, the senator might have asked unanimous consent to introduce a bill, a courtesy routinely granted.

From Ruckles's perspective, the problem with these standard processes was that they provided immediate public notice of a bill. For *this* bill no one spoke. Instead, Ruckles instructed the secretary for the majority, a veteran of such shortcuts, to hand the bill to the parliamentarian with the word "live" written on the upper-right-hand corner—code that the bill should be filed as if by a senator speaking.

Seated at his marble desk beneath that of the presiding officer, the parliamentarian received the bill with a figurative wink. It now became *his* job to refer the bill to the appropriate committee. But just to make sure, Ruckles's emissary had already arranged for the parliamentarian to dispatch the bill at once to the Commerce Committee, chaired by Senator Palmer.

ELEVEN

FOR KERRY, the last Tuesday in September was typically busy—appearances with police chiefs to promote his gun bill; a brief visit to a Head Start program; a meeting with the Israeli foreign minister; a luncheon speech on human rights; an interview with the *New York Times*; a telephone call with the chairman and the finance director of the Democratic National Committee. But, as always, Kerry insisted on exercise: he had just completed six miles on the treadmill when Chuck Hampton called from the Senate.

Sweat running down his face, Kerry took the cell phone from his assistant, his free hand clutching a chilled bottle of springwater. "The tort reform bill you were expecting dropped," Hampton told him. "Very quietly. They sent it straight to the Commerce Committee—the minority counsel was looking for it, and he's already read it through."

Kerry finished taking a deep swallow of water. "What's in it?"

"A corporate wish list—I'm sending a copy to your legislative people. But nothing which would immunize gun companies."

"What about language tailored to protect the industry?"

"Not that we can see. Still, a lot can happen between introduction and a final vote, a good bit of it in committee. Palmer's scheduled a hearing."

"Already?" Kerry said with real surprise. "When?"

"A week from now."

"Jesus." Wiping the sweat from his forehead, Kerry asked, "Can you stall it?"

"Not easy," Hampton replied in a dubious tone. "I can object to the hearing. But that's hardball, and invites retribution. There's nothing here to warrant all that."

"Not on the surface. But this is about guns, Chuck—trust me on that."

From Hampton there was the silence of reflection. "If it is," he said slowly, "then it seems like Palmer's playing ball with Ruckles. Or, more likely, Fasano."

Though Kerry did not care to think so, Hampton might well be right. "In that case, they'll likely slip something in before the committee sends it to the floor. Have our counsel keep an eye on it."

"I will. And you might want to give your friend a call."

"Oh," Kerry said softly, "I intend to. After I've given this some thought."

In late afternoon, Kerry and Clayton met on the fly with Jack Sanders and the Director of Legislative Affairs, Liz Curry.

Liz spread the pages of the Civil Justice Reform Act, annotated in red pen, across the President's coffee table. "It's like Chuck said," Liz told him. "A corporate wish list, a nightmare for plaintiffs' lawyers—limitations on class actions, caps on attorneys' fees and punitive damages, the works. You can hear their opening line: 'plaintiffs' lawyers are maggots.' "

"And defense lawyers never are?" Kerry asked sardonically. "You know what this is about, Liz? Social class, and privilege.

"It's easy to screw a lot of little people who don't have the money to fight back, and then hire a hoard of smug corporate defense lawyers who make five hundred bucks an hour—all to grind the victims to dust while whining about the fee awards lawyers like Lenihan get for representing them. What's an exploding tire or a little E. coli, after all? The truly important thing is that some sonofabitch of a CEO who's getting tens of millions for firing half his workforce doesn't get distracted by the annoyance of having to answer for some victim's misery."

"Oh, there's plenty of *that* here," Liz answered with a jaded smile. "Try this one, Mr. President. If this 'reform act' passes, no one can sue for a defect in an elevator over fifteen years old.

"Why? you might wonder. I happen to know. For a long time one of our leading elevator companies kept selling single line elevators—even though double cables were safer—because they had some in stock. Last year the single line in a seventeen-year-old elevator snapped, leaving a mother of three quadriplegic and without medical care. You can't have the poor elevator company paying for *that*."

Softly, Kerry said, "They just can't help themselves, can they?" Turning to Clayton, he said, "I want to pull together a supergroup to fight this bill—the Attorney General, a legislative team, our political director, someone to poll messages, a media consultant to look at advertising. I mean for us to sink this thing, any way we can." He paused, then finished, "And make sure we're primed on gun immunity."

Clayton nodded. Facing Liz again, the President asked, "What other stinkers are in here?"

"Any number. For one thing, it looks like this bill would bar wrongful death actions for victims of asbestosis."

The President cocked his head. "Besides Ruckles, who else is on the bill?"

Liz smiled. "Leo Weller, among others."

"Isn't asbestosis a problem in Montana?"

"A big one."

"Then it's a big problem for Leo—he's up for reelection

next year." To Clayton, the President said, "We might want to turn Leo Weller into an object lesson for Frank Fasano. Perhaps even a paid political advertisement."

Clayton smiled. "Leo," he said mildly, "was always mediagenic."

Smiling himself, Kerry thanked the group. But when he called Chad Palmer, the President's face was grim.

Bluntly, the President asked, "What's happening over there?"

Chad's voice was bland. "The usual—subsidies for agribusiness; a weapons system we don't need and the military doesn't want; a few million to expand our share of the world's mohair market . . ."

"Cut the shit, Chad. Ruckles files his stealth bill, and you set a new land-speed record for scheduling committee hearings. Can't you at least give asbestosis suits time for a decent burial?"

"Is *that* in there? I hadn't looked." A note of exasperation, perhaps defensiveness, crept into Chad's voice. "This isn't new. Asbestosis aside, we've been trying to pass tort reform for years . . ."

"Chad," the President cut in softly, "tort reform has never been your issue. Campaign finance reform *is*. Something's going on here, and I think we both know what it is—guns."

Chad was briefly silent. "There's nothing in this bill on guns," he said.

Kerry paused to reflect. Chad had not known about the asbestosis clause, but was very certain that the bill contained "nothing" on guns. His implicit addendum, Kerry realized, was "not yet."

Kerry thanked him, and got off.

*

A few days after the bill was introduced, Senator Harshman came to Chad Palmer's office.

This was rare; the two men detested each other. Gaunt and self-righteous, Harshman did not bother to sit. Instead he handed Chad a plain manila envelope.

"I believe you've been expecting this," Harshman told him. "I'm suggesting some additional safeguards for the Civil Justice Reform Act."

To Harshman's obvious annoyance, Chad opened the envelope and made a show of reading it quite carefully. " 'Safeguards,' " Palmer murmured. "After all these years, Paul, you're developing a gift for understatement."

Harshman scowled. "It's high time we choose between the Second Amendment and a bunch of corporate ambulance chasers."

"Oh, it's the patriotic thing, all right. I'm sure even Mary Costello would agree." Chad summoned his most pleasant smile. "You needn't linger, Senator. I'm sure you're busy, and it's time for me to take a shower."

Two hours later, Chuck Hampton called the President. "You were right," Hampton said. "There's a new clause. It doesn't immunize gun companies by name, but that's its effect. Chad's counsel gave us the language."

Still, Kerry reflected, he could not help but feel betrayed. He and Chad disagreed about many things, but *this* cut to the core. Quietly, he said, "With Lara's family four weeks dead. It's as direct a challenge as Fasano could make."

"More direct than you know, Mr. President. The provision wiping out gun lawsuits is retroactive. If it passes as part of the final bill, it will terminate lawsuits which have already been filed, even if they're ready for trial."

Including Mary's, Kerry thought. "Then Fasano's sold out to the SSA."

"True enough." Hampton's tone was grave. "And he's in a hurry, too. He already means to stall your gun safety legislation and try to pass this first."

"He can't pass it this way," Kerry answered. "The restrictions on plaintiffs' lawyers are way too extreme. He can't get enough Democrats to survive a veto."

"Agreed. But he's at least appearing to give an array of interests what they want. He's preparing for an all-out war, supported by a slew of business groups and the foot soldiers of the right. He clearly means to keep the gun provision in the final bill, and jam it through as a package."

Turning, Kerry gazed at the twilit garden outside the Oval Office. "It's no time for gentility," he said. "We need to split corporate interests from the gun lobby, any way we can. Or, at a minimum, to divide the gun manufacturers and the SSA."

"How do we accomplish *that*?"

"I'll reflect on it, Chuck."

But whether he liked it or not, Kerry already knew. His next call was to Lara.

TWELVE

Philadelphia. Frank Fasano's territory. Lara's sixth city in as many days. Exhausted, she sat in her hotel suite, reading the mail dropped off for her by strangers, and which she had demanded to see.

The last piece, a flat manila envelope, contained a photograph of skeletal corpses heaped in a pile at Auschwitz, a collage of decimated limbs and pale skin and vacant eyes. The note scrawled in one corner read, "This is what will happen once you disarm our country." The second photo in the envelope was taken from the videotape of the murders, with Lara's head superimposed on her mother's neck. In close-up the wound in Inez's throat was a jagged tear.

Carefully, Lara placed the photographs in the hate pile for Peter Lake.

She would be speaking soon, meeting with victims' families. That would help keep this bottomless hatred from driving her into a well of grief. Since her wedding, she had learned that grief must be managed.

Beside the pile for Peter was a service tray with the remnants of a tuna sandwich and a glass of iced tea. As with the meals she had eaten, her first seven days on the road were a blur—press conferences, speeches, interviews, meetings with victims, sessions with sympathetic Republicans, an hour on *Oprah Winfrey*, visits to women's shelters. Five days before, reminded of the AIDS quilt, she had proposed a web site dedicated to all those lost to guns in the last twenty years, with photographs and brief descriptions of their lives. Already thirty thousand photographs had joined Inez, Joan and Marie in a cyberspace memorial, growing hour by hour. Last night's town meeting in Pittsburgh had run past midnight; Lara had stayed to answer every question, to hear every story of pain and loss.

She was glad to be doing this. The cause was her mission, and forward motion was imperative. Every day took her farther from the moment of devastation until, she had to believe, a healing—perhaps so deep within her that at times she did not feel it—would bring her to *that* moment when, though forever changed, she would be herself again. She craved this as much for Kerry as for her.

Every night they talked, no matter the hour, before she fell asleep. She missed him then, desperately. It reminded her of Kosovo, when she had thought she might never see him. But now, absent some terrible event, she knew that she would.

Absent some terrible event.

From their first meeting, she had felt his bone-deep fatalism, his sense that happiness might be fleeting, contingent. Then she had attributed it to the murder of James Kilcannon. Now she understood it.

There was a brisk knock on the door. Briefly entering, Peter Lake glanced at the photographs, then Lara, without comment. She touched his sleeve, a mute thanks for his kindness.

"I'm ready," she said.

The hotel auditorium was jammed. This was good, Lara thought. Not only was Philadelphia Fasano's home, but the state's junior Republican senator, far weaker than Fasano, was up for reelection.

With other survivors seated behind her, Lara spoke in a

calm, clear voice. The audience listened with the taut stillness which now greeted her every appearance.

"None of us," she said, "wanted to believe that homicides or suicides or accidental deaths would take someone
we loved. But now they have.

"So what can *we* do? We can try to wall off our grief.
Or all of us, together, can give witness to these tragedies
and say that the violence *must* stop." Pausing, she felt her
listeners drawing closer, an emotional bond expressed in
a collective forward leaning of their bodies, an openness
in their expressions. "It's not enough," she continued, "to
share the comfort of good intentions.

"We must vote this issue—period—with no rationaliza-
tions or excuses. We must demand that our representatives,
and our parties, support an end to violence as the price of
our support. We must demand that they make protecting
victims a first priority of public service, not just a pious
wish. And when it's time, we must descend on Washington
and call for change until there *is* change."

Applause burst from the audience. Lara's voice cut
through the sound. "This commitment," she continued, "is
not easy. But it will be far harder to explain to the parents
and children of those who died, or their children's children, why so many deaths have followed . . ."

The audience lingered, wanting to share a word, or simply
touch her. Lara moved among them, Peter at her side.

Turning from the mother of a victim, Lara faced an
elderly man with a cane. His face was slick with perspiration, and his rough voice trembled. "I always wondered
what it would be like," he told her, "to look into the face
of evil."

Peter grabbed his arm. With an effort of will, Lara held

her composure. "Whose face do you see?" she asked. "My mother, or my sister? Or, perhaps, my six-year-old niece."

A second Secret Service agent moved the man away, still trembling with a rage which Lara would never fathom, his hands balled into fists.

"How was it," Kerry asked, "in the land of Frank Fasano?"

She had taken a bath and slipped between cool sheets before returning his call. "For a while I forgot about Fasano," she answered. "This is taking me somewhere different, Kerry. Journalists develop a shield. Now I'm learning not to protect myself." Pausing, she tried to put emotions to words. "I just feel it's good I'm here. Certainly for me."

"Then I'm glad you are." Now it was Kerry who paused. "Something's come up, Lara. Fasano's tort reform bill has mutated—it would wipe out Mary's lawsuit against Lexington, before Lenihan and Sarah Dash can even start."

In this moment, Lara felt herself being transported, against her will, back into the world of politics. "That's one way," she said after a time, "of suppressing evidence. I guess you want me to call Sarah."

"Yes. They need to file in a hurry, with maximum impact. And, if possible, to drive a wedge between Lexington and the SSA."

"How?" Lara asked.

Kerry answered with a question. "Do you recall Martin Bresler?"

THIRTEEN

"I'M NOT NAIVE," Martin Bresler told Sarah in an agitated voice. "If I cooperate with you, sooner or later my name will come out."

It was early morning, and Sarah's office was quiet. The night before, she had been revising the complaint against Lexington Arms, planning to file in two days' time, when Lara Kilcannon's call had turned these plans on their head. Calling Bresler in Washington, Sarah recited the facts as Lara related them: that Bresler had been working on a voluntary agreement to require background checks at gun shows; that Lexington had been amenable; and that, by destroying Bresler's association of gun manufacturers, the SSA had thwarted the deal and paved the way for the Costello murders. Even over the telephone, Sarah could hear the impact this blunt recitation was having on Martin Bresler.

"You've got two choices," Sarah replied. "You can cooperate with us in private, and we'll keep your name out of this as long as we can. Or we can take your deposition as soon as we file, under oath, with Lexington's lawyers in the room. Which effectively means the SSA."

"If I 'cooperate,'" Bresler retorted, "you may sue the SSA. Why would I touch *that*? I don't think you get it, Ms. Dash. I've got two kids in college, and my career's on life support. I'm just trying to land a job . . ."

"Exactly," Sarah said in a calm, implacable tone. "I'm offering you a chance to do the right thing in private, which gives you more time to regroup before the SSA finds out. But letting you off the hook is not an option."

Sarah waited out Bresler's silence. "I'll have to call you back," Bresler said in a defeated tone. Only then did Sarah permit herself to feel a certain pity.

With quiet fury, Kerry said, "This is the SSA's Trojan horse. Designed to humiliate me, politically and personally."

Alone with Kerry in the Oval Office, Chad Palmer remained calm. "Fasano," he answered, "would call that a 'leadership priority.' As for Trojan horses, I must say that you're taking a keen interest in Mary Costello's prospective lawsuit.

"We have a fundamental difference of opinion, Mr. President. You and people like Bob Lenihan think that lawsuits against gun companies will force them to give you what Congress won't. Others think they're an abuse of a legal system too open to abuse already . . ."

"Are you supporting this thing," Kerry interjected, "or just tolerating it?"

"Supporting it," Chad said baldly. "I mean to get it through committee and speak for it on the floor."

Kerry felt shaken. There was no need to remind Chad of the immensity of his decision, or of how much more difficult it would make the President's task. Softly, he said, "You despise the SSA almost as much as I do. What in the world did Fasano offer you?"

For an instant, Chad looked discomfited. Almost unique among politicians, in Kerry's mind, Palmer possessed a sense of shame which diminished his skill at functional insincerity. "I'm sorry this is personal to you," he said at length. "But, *this* time, I'm not carrying your water. Caroline Masters was enough."

Though spoken quietly, the last phrase reminded Kerry

that he would always be associated with the death of Chad's daughter and that Chad's bitterness, however well suppressed, would never entirely vanish. With equal quiet, Kerry answered, "Then I have a courtesy to ask. Not for me, but for Lara."

Chad hesitated. "What might that be, Mr. President?"

"You've scheduled hearings, including on this gun immunity clause. The witness list is up to you."

Chad stared at him. "You want me to call Lara."

"And Mary."

A grim comprehension stole into Chad's eyes. Personally and politically, he could not ban a First Lady and her sister, the survivors of a nationally televised slaughter, from confronting him on every cable news network in America. Now Chad would pay a price, and so would Frank Fasano. "Please tell the First Lady," Chad said with formal courtesy, "that I welcome them both."

FOURTEEN

TWO MORNINGS LATER, Martin Bresler met with Bob Lenihan and Sarah Dash.

To assure that no one saw them, Sarah rented a vacation home in Sea Ranch, a windswept compound along the rugged northern coast of Sonoma County, set amidst low vegetation and sheltering pines. The three sat drinking coffee on a wooden bench at the tip of a bluff overlooking the ocean, watching high waves slap against rocks and cliffs which turned blue water into a perpetual white spray. Seated between the lawyers, Bresler hunched in a defensive crouch.

"No affidavit," he stated flatly. "Nothing in writing."

He was a small man, with receding dark hair, liquid eyes and a mobile, expressive face. There was something diminished about him, Sarah thought, a natural volubility turned to suspicion. "We can't do that," Lenihan insisted. "What's to keep you from telling us any story you want, then walking away from it when crunch time comes?"

Remaining hunched, Bresler did not look at anyone. "And if crunch time never comes? What if your case settles or gets thrown out? I don't want some document sitting around with my name on it . . ."

"Are you *that* scared?" Sarah interjected.

"Are you *that* naive?" Bresler snapped. "Once you hear my story, you'll understand. Right now, let me ask how *you'd* enjoy this scenario—I can't get hired in the gun industry; Republicans treat me like a pariah; and I'm scouring Washington for a lobbyist job when the last one blew up in my face.

"I'm talking to you because it's the only way to avoid having to testify. But *if* I'm forced to, I don't want to have signed an affidavit so that Lexington's lawyers can use it as a fucking blueprint to grill me with." Pausing, he sipped coffee, still gazing at the sparkling blue water beneath an electric blue sky. "So do you want my help? Or do you want a deposition from someone who's suffering an enormous memory lapse?"

Sarah looked past him, at Lenihan. "Let's talk," she said.

Sarah and Lenihan stood at the edge of the bluff, out of hearing distance from Bresler. A high wind whistled past their ears. "Fuck him," Lenihan said. "Stick the little pissant in steerage and fly him back to Washington where he belongs. If we want his testimony, we take his deposition."

Sarah crossed her arms. "When the First Lady calls, she's calling for the President—as well as for herself and Mary, who's our client, after all. What do we lose by hearing this guy out?"

"Hearing him," Lenihan answered, "is probably just a waste of time. But *relying* on what he tells us is criminal stupidity." He turned toward Martin Bresler with an air of disdain. "That's treachery in human form."

Sarah shrugged. "He's also what we need."

Placing his mug on the burl redwood coffee table, Bresler settled back on the couch. "It started," he told the lawyers, "with me thinking I could find a middle ground between Kilcannon and the SSA. It ended with me as political roadkill, the First Lady's family slaughtered, and Lexington staring down the barrel of a lawsuit."

Still annoyed, Lenihan frowned at Bresler's portentousness. "We know how it ended," he said. "Just try your hardest to get us there. From the beginning."

Four months earlier, seated in his office, Frank Fasano had looked from Bresler to Jerry Kirk, Vice President of Bresler's association of gun manufacturers, the Gun Sports Coalition. As always, Kirk, with a placid face and sandy hair as thin as his glasses were thick, wore an expression of myopic amiability. "Marty's right," Kirk assured Fasano. "If *you* announce an agreement on trigger locks between our manufacturers and the Republicans in Congress, you steal the issue from Kilcannon and all of us look reasonable for a change. It's the classic win-win, which is why we're coming to *you* instead of *him*."

Bresler felt Kirk's enthusiasm feed his own. "Gun politics," he told Fasano, "is stuck in this endless loop: Kilcannon versus the SSA, with the rest of us—including your party—watching like we're hypnotized. We need movement, Frank."

Fasano nodded, seemingly interested but noncommittal. Bresler felt him calculate the political geometry. "Let me take some soundings," he said at length. "On *this* issue, I can't get ahead of my people."

For three days, Bresler hoped for a breakthrough. And then he encountered Paul Harshman in the corridor of the Russell Building. With a solicitous air, Harshman took him aside. "Watch yourself, Marty. You shouldn't ask us to abandon our friends."

That afternoon, without explanation, Fasano turned them down.

*

Bresler and Kirk met with Clayton Slade in a motel room at Dulles Airport.

"You've got three weeks," Clayton told them bluntly. "If we can't reach an agreement, the President's introducing legislation and taking on the industry. He's more than a little sick of begging you for safety locks."

Bresler glanced at Jerry Kirk. "All we can do," Jerry told Clayton, "is talk to our companies."

For an intensive week of meetings and phone calls, they did—at Bresler's insistence, in total secrecy. Gradually, reluctantly, the five CEOs agreed that a modest safety measure, even in partnership with Kerry Kilcannon, was better than more lawsuits and terrible public relations. Bresler called Clayton and set a date for an announcement.

This time, Paul Harshman did not wait for a chance meeting. "This is far worse than the last time," he told Bresler by telephone. "Now you're turning your back on *us*."

Bresler put the phone down and called Clayton Slade. "Who knows about our agreement?" he demanded.

"Jack Sanders. The President. That's all. So it's not coming from us." Clayton paused. "I want to move this up before the SSA unravels it."

"How far up?"

"Two days from now, at a Rose Garden ceremony for police chiefs."

"That's not enough time . . ."

"We can't afford more time. Call your CEOs, and let me know."

Bresler and Jerry Kirk began dialing.

"Kilcannon was terrific," Bresler told Lenihan and Sarah.

For a moment, his expression changed, remembering

a day when he was at the center of things and could imagine that gun politics was on the cusp of a tectonic shift. "He was easy and engaging," Bresler continued, "like a normal guy meeting other normal guys, one who honestly cared about saving lives. When he joked about putting us all in the witness protection program, everybody lightened up.

"That night we were all over the evening news—me, Kilcannon, and my CEOs, with a backdrop of police chiefs in blue uniforms. My CEOs loved it, Kilcannon loved it. The next day he called me personally, to thank me and say let's get to work on background checks at gun shows. Sure, I told him." Bresler emitted a harsh laugh, returning to reality. "Marty Bresler, the center of the known political universe. The honest broker, the media darling, impregnable as long as I succeeded for my members. With Kerry Kilcannon on *my* team, even the SSA would start returning my calls."

They didn't. Most Republicans barely did. An old friend, now at the SSA, told him in private that his photograph was taped inside the urinals at SSA headquarters. His only consolation was that his five member companies had suffered no public reprisal.

They never did. The day that everyone but George Callister withdrew their support and funding, one chagrined CEO told him, "I'll deny I ever said this. But once the SSA heard you were dealing with Kilcannon on gun shows, we had no choice."

"But how did they hear?" Bresler asked in a daze.

Heartsick, he broke the news to Jerry Kirk. Jerry took it better than Bresler had expected. Placing a collegial hand on Bresler's shoulder, he said, "Just worry about yourself, Marty. I'll be fine."

He was. The next week the SSA hired Jerry Kirk, and Bresler knew who had betrayed him, and why his career was over.

FIFTEEN

THAT NIGHT Lenihan and Sarah met in her office with Mary Costello. It was past nine o'clock. The two lawyers had just returned from Sea Ranch and, as Sarah had explained to Mary, the reason for haste was political—they needed to file before Mary and Lara faced Chad Palmer's committee. To Sarah, Mary looked overwhelmed, as if too many events, barely comprehended, were moving far too quickly.

Lenihan seemed to sense this as well and, Sarah suspected, hoped to use their client's unease to reassert control. "Maybe," he told Sarah, "*you'd* better explain to Mary why you want to add the Sons of the Second Amendment as a defendant in her lawsuit. Even after hearing Bresler's story, I'm having some difficulty articulating your rationale."

Ignoring him, Sarah faced Mary. "Two reasons," she said crisply. "The first is politics. As you know, the Senate is taking up a bill which would wipe out your lawsuit, and you're appearing within days before Palmer's committee. He, and the Republicans, will look *far* worse if what they're trying to do is immunize the SSA.

"Second, the SSA effectively controls Lexington Arms —both through intimidation and, I'm willing to bet, by funding its defense. We'll never get a settlement from Lexington unless we can divide them." Briefly, Sarah paused. "It's challenging, for sure. But as I understand it, the SSA snuffed Bresler, and then Callister told President Kilcannon that Lexington wouldn't voluntarily impose background checks at gun shows because the SSA wouldn't stand for it. If the SSA was in effective control of Lexington, then the SSA may be liable for the deaths of your mother, Joan and Marie."

As Sarah finished, Mary turned to Lenihan. With an elaborate show of gravity, he slowly shook his head. "It's a terrible idea, Mary—terrible. If this case becomes a holy war against the SSA, they'll launch the most vicious PR campaign you've ever witnessed, in or out of court.

"I can tell you what they'll say—'the President's behind this. He can't succeed in Congress, so he's using Mary Costello's lawsuit to smear and punish advocates of gun rights.' In the public mind, your case will go from a search for justice to an exercise in hardball politics."

This was clever, Sarah conceded. At once Lenihan touched a nerve—Mary's resentment of her sister and, perhaps, the President; her fear of being dragged into the morass of politics. He also spoke a truth: in and out of court, the SSA would be a well-funded and no doubt vicious opponent. "Bob's right," she told Mary. "As far as it goes. My point is different. The ultimate reason your family was murdered is not John Bowden or Lexington Arms. It's the SSA."

Listening, Mary Costello looked even slighter than Sarah recalled. "But is that a harder case?" she asked Sarah.

"Much harder," Lenihan interjected. "Legally, and even morally. Far worse, we'd be buying an opponent with fanatic zeal and tons of money, who'll use this lawsuit to raise still more. We'll be faced with hordes of lawyers, crushing expenses, and every delaying tactic they can dream of . . ."

"We'll get that anyway," Sarah said dismissively. "At least if you believe, as I do, that the SSA will pick and fund the lawyers for Lexington Arms. They've got a stranglehold on the industry and on Congress. The only way to break that is to expose them."

"*How?*" Lenihan's sharp tone combined exasperation with contempt for her inexperience. "This is a lawsuit to recover damages for Mary Costello, not a political crusade against the SSA.

"As citizens, Sarah, you and I may despise the SSA and all its works. But we're *lawyers*, for Godsakes. Tell me how the SSA has violated the law. Not by lobbying. The Kilcannon Center does that, just on the other side. Not by threatening boycotts. Martin Luther King boycotted segregated diners, and our entire country boycotted South Africa . . ."

"By violating the antitrust laws," Sarah shot back. "So hear me out, Bob. For our client's sake."

Cornered, Lenihan turned to Mary, eyebrows raised. "I don't understand any of this," Mary told Sarah. "What did the SSA do?"

"Given what happened to Martin Bresler," Sarah answered, "what I *think* they did is conspire against Lexington through the other manufacturers."

"In what way?" Lenihan asked with skepticism.

"By threatening the others; by coordinating resistance to the President; by promising the rest that—if the SSA put Lexington out of business for agreeing to background checks at gun shows—*they* could split up Lexington's market share." Turning to Mary, Sarah finished, "That violates the laws against unfair competition."

"It's also a fantasy," Lenihan rejoined. "Even Bresler couldn't tell us *that*. For that, we need the SSA to confess—if you can imagine it—or the other companies to rat them out. Or, at the least, testimony from George Callister more forthcoming than I can possibly imagine."

"True." Sarah still faced Mary. "So we'll go after the SSA's files—all contacts between the SSA and Lexington, and between the SSA and the other companies. We'll depose Charles Dane, all the CEOs. By far the best way of doing that is to sue the SSA itself."

"On what basis?" Lenihan persisted. "You're just guessing . . ."

"Not about the ad in the SSA magazine. So we can also bring a negligent marketing claim . . ."

"The SSA *ran* the ad, Sarah. They didn't write it. There's no precedent for suing them."

"Not directly. But I imagine you've read *Rice versus Paladin Enterprises?*"

Briefly, Lenihan hesitated. "Remind me of the facts."

"*Rice* imposed liability on a magazine for running an article describing how to commit a flawless execution . . ."

"I *might* recall that," Lenihan snapped, "if the case were relevant. I asked you to cite me a precedent."

"We can *make* the precedent," Sarah answered. "In my naïveté, I assumed that's what plaintiffs' lawyers do. Or are you suggesting that if Lexington wanted to place an ad saying that the P-2 was the best gun for batterers to use against their women, the SSA could run it with impunity?" Facing Mary, Sarah remained calm. "It's all a question of who's responsible," she said, "and why you've chosen to do this. To me, the SSA is morally responsible for thousands of needless deaths like these.

"Whether they're *legally* responsible is another matter. Proving that could be as hard as Bob says. But you should know what choices you have." Once more she turned to Lenihan. "Whatever we do, Bob, we need to accelerate discovery."

"Because Fasano's pushing the Civil Justice Reform Act?"

"Yes. The more we discover against Lexington and the SSA, the tougher it becomes to pass that law. If necessary, we'll take the depositions of people like Dane, and then leak them to the press."

For the first time, Lenihan smiled, his expression somewhere between agreement and amusement. "Every now and then, Sarah, you give me hope. But how do you persuade a judge to accelerate discovery? *Not* so you can leak sworn testimony at a quicker pace, the better to embarrass Senator Fasano."

"No," Sarah came back. "By asking for injunctive relief to prevent an ongoing threat to public safety."

Lenihan glanced at Mary. "An injunction?" he asked in a tone of muted wonder. "Against *what* ongoing threats? I don't mean to be insensitive, but Mary's family is already dead."

Silent, Mary stared at her folded hands. "And more *will* die," Sarah answered, "if this law passes, and then the President can't get *his* gun law through the Congress. This case is about far more than money, Bob. No amount of that will compensate Mary for what she's lost."

"That's politics, not law," Lenihan insisted. "On what basis do we get a judge to order discovery at maximum speed?"

"Lexington," Sarah retorted, "is committing a public nuisance. That means *any* unreasonable interference with a right common to all Californians. Including the right not to be murdered by guns banned in California, like the Lexington P-2.

"You've said it yourself, Bob. I think we can show that Lexington is flooding the state with guns sold just beyond the Nevada border. I also think we can show that an inordinate number of them are used to murder Californians—as with Mary's family. And we already know that Lexington and the SSA showed criminals and people like John Bowden where to buy it in Nevada without going through a background check." Looking from Lenihan to Mary,

Sarah finished, "It's not that hard a case. Your family's death is part of a pattern—a company selling bad guns to bad people in a number of rotten ways. A pattern that should be stopped by an injunction."

Mary sat straighter. "If that's what's going on," she said to Lenihan, "and we can stop it, I want to."

"And those are good intentions," Lenihan said respectfully. "But speeding up the discovery process so drastically exacerbates our problems. It allows the lawyers for the SSA to play more games—withholding documents so we question witnesses like Dane without having the facts we need, then forcing us into a trial we're not ready for. And adding the SSA will turn a fiasco into a nightmare.

"Sarah knows the drill as well as I do. We go in for a temporary restraining order, which we probably won't get. Then the judge will likely set a hearing on a preliminary injunction within *ten* days. Within sixty to ninety days, we'll have plowed through all of our discovery—getting jerked around at every turn, and be facing a trial we're not ready for."

"Bob," Sarah said, "you've sued IBM, AT&T, and half the Fortune 500. What does your firm have all these lawyers for, if not to use them?"

"So we can decide *when* to use them, and *where* using them makes sense."

"It's your money," Sarah answered. "No question. I can only hope that stopping the SSA, keeping more murders from happening, and helping President Kilcannon save lives will satisfy your sense of occasion."

To Sarah's surprise, Lenihan laughed aloud. "I should let you say that to my partners," he said with irony but less hostility. "I'm sure they'd be delighted to put their money and our firm at your disposal."

Sarah spread her hands. "That," she said with a smile, "is all I could ask. But let's put that aside. Assuming that we collectively decide to do all this, where and when do we file?"

Though far too clever not to know what she was doing, Lenihan's ego was such, Sarah judged, that she might mollify him by ceding center stage. And so it seemed; as he answered her, Lenihan's manner resumed its usual placid self-assurance. "When is simple—immediately. As for where, the same place I chose at the beginning: the Superior Court for the City and County of San Francisco.

"My firm has an office here, and we're close to most of the judges. If we file in state court, the TRO will go before Judge Fineman or Judge Rotelli." Lenihan smiled with satisfaction. "They're both friends of mine, and they're up for re-election. Along with every partner in our local office, I've contributed to their campaigns."

Which, Sarah thought, is the problem with electing judges. "And so," she said wryly, "you think they'll give us a fair hearing."

Lenihan shrugged. "Even if we *weren't* friends, who do you suppose an elected judge is going to favor—the First Lady's surviving sister, a native San Franciscan, or an out-of-state merchant of death?"

At this, Sarah noticed, Mary seemed to wince. Briefly, Sarah touched her arm. "What about the trial judge?" she asked Lenihan. "They're selected by lottery."

"Same reasoning," Lenihan answered comfortably. "But why leave things to chance. Presiding Judge Morrissey is another old friend, the last of the old-line liberals. We can go to him and say 'Your Honor, this is a complex case. We need a judge assigned specially, to take it from the preliminary through trial.' The local specialist in complex cases, Judge Weinstein, is also very progressive. I expect he's who Jack Morrissey would give us."

It was fascinating, Sarah thought, if a bit unsettling, to

listen to Lenihan game the system. "So you don't see any reason to take this to federal court?"

"God, no. There's no way of knowing who we'd get. And at least half of them are conservatives and they're appointed for life—the kind of judge who'd screw us without mercy. That's another problem with your theories, Sarah: they may try to gin up some argument to remove the case to federal court."

Sarah shook her head. "No grounds."

"So you say. Just remember who said it." He sat back, his self-satisfied gaze taking in both Sarah and Mary. "Whatever we end up filing, we go to state court with a complaint so colorful the newspapers and talking heads will quote it. Right after *that* we call a press conference. And then we use my public profile to launch an ongoing PR offensive."

Lenihan's "public profile," Sarah thought dryly, was somewhat less important than that of the President and First Lady—or, for that matter, the victims. And then it struck her that, once again, Mary Costello had been shunted to the margins. Turning to her, Sarah said, "You've been listening to *us*, Mary. Now it's your turn. Tell us what you want to do."

Mary looked from Lenihan to Sarah. "The same thing you do," she told Sarah. "I don't want more people dying. And if the SSA's responsible, it should pay."

To Sarah's surprise, Lenihan gave a shrug of fatalism. Perhaps he, too, was responding to the challenge.

"So when do we file?" Sarah asked him.

"The day after tomorrow," he said firmly. "In the morning."

SIXTEEN

AT NINE-FIFTEEN in the morning, having notified Lexington, the SSA, and the media, Lenihan and Sarah filed their complaint. Shortly after two p.m., they entered the wood-paneled courtroom of Judge Angelo Rotelli.

Jammed with media, the courtroom had the low expectant buzz of conversation which preceded a judge's appearance. Already seated at the defense table, John Nolan, the managing partner of Kenyon and Walker, Sarah's former firm, surveyed his adversaries with a barely concealed distaste. Beside him was Harrison Fancher, a senior litigator from another large corporate firm, Hartman & Miles, whose cadaverous appearance and relentless style of defense had earned him the sobriquet "Angel of Death." But while Fancher's presence signalled that the case would be as unpleasant as Lenihan had predicted, it was Nolan that Sarah feared more. In her experience, his utter ruthlessness, his adamantine belief that his clients' privileged status should be preserved by whatever means at hand, was concealed by a mandarin inscrutability and cloaked in an air of diplomacy which appealed to judges. As Sarah and Lenihan walked to the plaintiffs' table, Lenihan smiled broadly at Nolan and Fancher.

"John," he said, with a basso profundo which carried to the media. "And Harry, too. What a pleasure. Which one of you has the gun nuts, and which the merchants of death?"

Without standing, Nolan gave him a thin smile, though his eyes became slits in the broad plain of his face. In an undertone meant only for Lenihan, he said, "It's back to the sandbox, I see. Or the cat box." Turning toward Sarah, he added in a cool, patronizing manner, "Hello, Sarah. Are you here to learn at the feet of the master?"

This jibe, Sarah knew, was fresh proof how much Nolan detested her: she had forced Nolan to accept her *pro bono* representation of Mary Ann Tierney—wholly against his conservative instinct—only by fomenting a near rebellion among the firm's female partners. Though tense, Sarah managed to smile. "Which one of you would that be?" she asked, just before Angelo Rotelli entered his courtroom.

The buzz subsided. A stocky man with dark, curly hair, Rotelli nodded at the lawyers with a benign expression as he took his place behind the bench, pausing briefly to note the presence of the media contingent cramming his courtroom.

"All right," he began. "This is the case of *Costello versus Lexington Arms, et al.*, filed this morning. The matter before me is Mary Costello's request for a temporary restraining order, seeking to stop defendants' alleged activities endangering the lives of Californians. Who speaks for the plaintiff?"

As Lenihan rose, so did John Nolan. "Excuse me, Your Honor. John Nolan for defendant Lexington Arms. Before we proceed, I would like to bring the Court's attention to a matter which should prevent us from proceeding further."

Though seemingly surprised, Rotelli nodded briskly. "Yes, Mr. Nolan. I know who you are. What do you have for us?"

"A petition for removal to federal court." Advancing to the bench, Nolan handed up a sheaf of papers to Rotelli and then, turning with a glint of amusement the judge could not see, gave a duplicate to Lenihan.

"This is bogus," Lenihan protested to Rotelli. "In this

case, the standard for removal is that the lawsuit must raise issues which are uniquely matters of federal law. We assert no such issues. Clearly, the defense has filed a phony petition, solely for the purpose of delay."

This, Sarah knew, was utterly correct. But Nolan's reply was calm and unapologetic. "Despite Mr. Lenihan's uncharitable gloss, his complaint—if that's what you can call a document so rife with rhetoric and bereft of law—*does* raise important federal issues. Specifically, exotic antitrust and public nuisance theories which implicate the Commerce Clause of the United States Constitution *and* which, in our humble view, threaten rights guaranteed by the Second Amendment of the Bill of Rights . . ."

At once, Sarah realized that she had baited her own trap: though Nolan's argument was clearly erroneous, the theories she had urged on Lenihan gave it whatever plausibility it possessed. "In any event," Nolan continued, "a removal petition is automatic. Once a defendant files it in federal court, as we have, the federal court must rule on it. As of now, this court has no jurisdiction and, therefore, no power to proceed."

On *this* point, Sarah thought with dismay, Nolan was correct. "This is a bad-faith motion," Lenihan objected. "Deserving of sanctions . . ."

Rotelli raised a hand, cutting Lenihan off. Brow furrowed, he riffled the pages Nolan had provided him, seemingly nettled by the motion and his imminent loss of an audience. Looking up from the papers to Nolan, he said, "Without adopting Mr. Lenihan's characterization, I must say, Mr. Nolan, that my first impression of this is that it's *very* thin. But you're correct that I have no discretion." Glancing at Lenihan, he spoke past the lawyers to the media. "If this case again comes before this court, as I believe it should, a federal judge will have to send it here."

With that, Rotelli stood, nodded to both sides and

vanished from the bench. Flushed with anger, Lenihan murmured to Sarah, "That's only the down payment on suing the SSA. From here on out, we'll be paying on the installment plan."

But at their press conference, Lenihan was the picture of confidence.

He sat at a table between Sarah and Mary Costello, fondling the microphone in front of him as if it were a lover. Watching on CNN, Kerry remarked to Lara, "For Bob, meeting the press is an erotic experience."

This, Lenihan stated, *is the beginning of the end of gun violence in America.*

"I wish it were that easy," Lara murmured. Kerry nodded: Lexington's opening salvo, the removal petition, had sobered them both, as did Mary's wan expression on the screen.

Pausing, Lenihan placed a paternal hand on Mary's arm. *The defendants* know *that,* he continued. *That's why they've induced their congressional protectors—including Senator Fasano and Speaker Jencks—to put forward a shameful piece of legislation solely designed to strip Mary Costello, and all those like her, of their right to pursue justice.*

This, Kerry acknowledged, was the beginning that he had hoped for. But its end was as unpredictable as its impact on Lara and her sister. Silent, he rested his hand on Lara's shoulder.

Shortly after seven p.m., Eastern Daylight Time, the SSA countered with a press conference of its own. Standing behind a podium, Dane's saturnine mien was solemn and stern. He spoke with a slow and measured indignation which was more impressive than Frank Fasano could have hoped—a reminder of the magnetism Dane exerted on his supporters.

Drinking bourbon with Macdonald Gage, Fasano turned up the volume on his remote. *This lawsuit,* Dane began, *is a moral outrage.*

This was murder. The murderer is to blame. If there is more *blame to assign, it belongs to the legal system and* . . . a brief pause . . . and *the victims' powerful relatives, both of whom failed in their duty to protect them from John Bowden.*

Sitting beside Fasano, Gage laughed softly. It struck Fasano that anything Dane would say or do to torment Kerry Kilcannon was satisfying to Mac Gage. But Fasano himself was not so sanguine.

But who do they blame? Dane went on. *The SSA and Lexington Arms—one of America's time-honored purveyors of guns to freedom-loving citizens* . . .

"A little florid," Fasano observed. "This isn't the Fourth of July."

The SSA, Dane continued, *is not a monolith. It's four* million *individual Americans, lawfully exercising rights granted them by our Founding Fathers. Our members didn't know John Bowden. They didn't control his actions. They played no role in Lexington's legal marketing of a completely legal product.*

Pausing, Dane jabbed his finger at the camera. *Make no mistake, America—the monolith in this case is the federal government, deployed by a President who is using this case to destroy the very companies who make your rights a reality,* and *the one organization which can protect those rights from harm.*

Kerry Kilcannon's weapon is not a gun. It is a cabal of plaintiffs' lawyers, in league with the left-wing group which bears his family name, exploiting a tragedy to which, sadly, his own personal derelictions were a primary contributor . . .

"He's on the edge," Fasano remarked. "Let's hope he doesn't say that Kilcannon has blood on his hands."

"Doesn't he?" Gage said with quiet bitterness. "He certainly has mine."

Defending this abuse, Dane continued, *may well cost us millions. But we will never settle. We will fight this case to the bitter end—if necessary, in the Supreme Court itself—in defense of that fundamental freedom which makes all other freedoms possible: the right to keep and bear arms.*

We call on our members to support us. We call on the American people to rise up as one in protest. Staring into the camera, Dane finished solemnly. *We call on the leaders of Congress to put this outrage to an end . . .*

He was stuck, Fasano realized, and so was Kerry Kilcannon. What Kilcannon had set in motion—a race between a lawsuit and the Senate; a clash between Kilcannon and the SSA—might spin out of control, with consequences worse than anyone could imagine. Only Macdonald Gage, turning to Fasano, could feel happy.

"Ready, Frank?" he asked.

SEVENTEEN

THE FOLLOWING MORNING, as the result of random selection by computer, Sarah and Lenihan found themselves in the chambers of United States District Judge Gardner W. Bond.

Lenihan's grim demeanor reflected the harsh truth: out of fourteen judges they could have drawn, Gardner Bond was the worst for Mary Costello. That Bond had always disdained Robert Lenihan—sabotaging his cases to the extent he could—was the least of it. Bond was an idealogue in bow ties, a passionate conservative who, as a lawyer, had made his name by litigating *pro bono* against gay scoutmasters and in defense of demonstrators who harassed abortion clinics.

This was among the reasons that so many had opposed Bond's appointment to the bench. To Sarah, Bond seemed temperamentally unable, either in his professional or personal lives, to tolerate anyone who did not believe as he did. Another reason was his membership in two old-line private clubs which proudly excluded women. And still another was his active involvement in the Federalist Society, a group of right-wing lawyers dedicated, among other things, to their own ironic form of judicial activism— stacking the federal courts with conservatives dedicated to combating what they perceived to be the excesses of liberalism.

Completing this grim picture was the fact that, in the monochromatic world of Gardner Bond and his allies, Kerry Kilcannon was the leading *bête noire*, an illegitimate President who must, at all costs, be driven from power.

That Kilcannon then would be succeeded by a Republican, like Frank Fasano, would serve Bond's interests as well. Only a Republican President could elevate Bond to the Court of Appeals and, with great good fortune, to the Supreme Court itself.

In his mind's eye, Sarah thought, Gardner Bond was halfway there. Dressed in a blue pin-striped suit, Bond sat stiffly at the end of his conference table, looking—with his gold-rimmed glasses, closely trimmed greying hair and mustache, and white breast pocket handkerchief—like an oil portrait of himself. To Bond's right, sitting with Harrison Fancher, John Nolan appeared comfortably self-satisfied. Bond and Nolan were members of the same political party and the same private clubs, and for Nolan the moment must be redolent of wing chairs and cigars, black waiters in white jackets gliding with silver drink trays amidst cosseted white males. Lenihan and Sarah did not belong.

Still, Sarah thought, Nolan's removal petition was, transparently, nothing more than a legal prank. She and an associate from Lenihan's firm had spent all night researching the law and drafting a reply. If anything, the purported grounds for Gardner Bond to retain the case were even more frivolous than they first appeared. Bond, in Sarah's hopeful estimate, was too smart not to know this, too prideful to abet John Nolan in quite so transparent a way.

After perfunctory nods around the table, Bond said abruptly, "I've read the defendants' brief, and plaintiff's opposition thereto. Unless any of you have something particularly compelling to add, I'm prepared to rule."

This was plainly an invitation to silence. The three men—Nolan with a blank expression; Fancher with sharp, expectant eyes; Lenihan with folded arms—said nothing. As for Sarah, she chose to interpret the judge's brusqueness in a hopeful light: Gardner Bond had resolved to make short work of John Nolan's legal nonsense.

"According to the petition," Bond continued in his polished baritone, "the plaintiff's antitrust and public nuisance theories present unique issues under the Commerce Clause, including the fact that plaintiffs are asking a state court in California to control Lexington's alleged behavior in *another* state, Nevada. The petition also asserts rights under the Second Amendment to the United States Constitution.

"For these reasons, I agree that this court is the proper forum."

Sarah felt jarred, as though feeling the first tremors of an earthquake, unprepared to believe what was transpiring. "Your Honor . . ."

Bond turned to her with a closed expression. "As I recall, Ms. Dash, I asked if you had anything to say."

"I didn't," Sarah persisted in desperation. "But, with all respect, I need to address your premise." Pausing, she steadied herself. "State courts have concurrent jurisdiction over antitrust cases. State courts routinely deal with claims under the Bill of Rights. State courts are empowered to protect their citizens from actions which imperil their welfare, even if taken in another state. And the claims at the heart of this case—wrongful death and public nuisance—are uniquely matters of state law.

"We've researched this issue up, down and sideways. There's no precedent whatsoever for removal. Mr. Nolan's petition cites none."

Behind his glasses, Bond's eyes were hard. Stiffly, he said, "Then you have the right to appeal, don't you?"

Sarah's despair deepened. "A very limited one, Your Honor. But I'm asking the Court to reconsider its ruling. If Miss Costello is forced to appeal, that could build in months of delay . . ."

"Well that's *your* problem, isn't it? You decided to include the claims cited by Mr. Nolan—apparently for the purpose of casting a net broad enough to reel in the SSA." Bond seemed to catch himself, pausing to moderate his language. "That this case emanates from a tragedy no one doubts. Whether this suit is the proper remedy is an entirely separate question. But *if* it's meritorious—and I emphasize *if*—the nature of the forum should not matter."

The clever cynicism of this sentiment stymied Sarah. Bond was turning their tactic around on them: the judge understood full well that she and Lenihan had chosen state court for a reason, and had determined to frustrate them—precisely because, given Bond's own biases, the "nature of the forum" might indeed determine the outcome. "In any event," Bond concluded, "I'm denying your motion to remand to state court. Unless the Court of Appeals decides otherwise, this case stays with me."

Bond turned to Nolan and Fancher. "That being the case, I'm denying plaintiff's motion for a temporary restraining order. Plaintiff's complaint raises issues too complex for such a peremptory remedy, and I find her claim of imminent harm insufficiently persuasive."

Sitting back, Bond looked from one side to the other. "I'm setting plaintiff's motion for a preliminary injunction down for hearing in ten days, and accelerating any motions to dismiss to be heard at the same time. In the meanwhile, plaintiff may conduct *no* discovery whatsoever. Until we determine what claims survive, if any, Miss Costello's lawyers should not consume defendants' time pursuing them.

"Is there anything else?"

"Yes, Your Honor." Abruptly, Lenihan had found his voice. "The new rules allow television in the courtroom. Because of the public interest in this matter, we ask that the hearing be televised . . ."

"Denied," Bond snapped. "Your wrongful death claims, if either survives, will be heard by a jury. Television can only taint the jury pool—which, in my estimation, has been tainted already by the true combatants in this case, both here and in Washington. This is a lawsuit, not politics by other means."

Nolan, Sarah realized, had not needed to say a word.

In the courthouse cafeteria, over coffee, Sarah murmured, "We're stuck."

"Stuck? We're fucked." Lenihan glowered at his coffee. "That reactionary sonofabitch will use your injunctive relief claim to screw up our discovery.

" 'Want this fast-tracked?' he'll say. 'I'll fast-track it up your ass.' It's a license for Nolan and Fancher to jerk us around—withholding evidence, forcing us to take depositions without documents. And *that's* only if Bond doesn't decide to throw us out of court ten days from now."

Glumly, Sarah nodded. "We've got no way to get rid of him. Bond's well aware that we can't appeal until after trial. Unless we file an extraordinary writ, or we ask *him* to certify it for appeal himself . . ."

"Forget it. Bond's prick enough to *do* that, then put the case on hold until the appeal is decided. Which would take months." Lenihan's voice became a monotone. "He knows damn well that Fasano's fast-tracked the Civil Justice Reform Act. And that Fasano's got a better chance of passing it if Bond keeps us under wraps."

This sounded right. Effectively, Gardner Bond had hijacked the case, correctly assuming that, in the need for haste brought on by Fasano's political maneuvers, there was nothing Sarah and Lenihan could do.

"Going forward," Sarah said at last, "we can only hope that Bond won't feel free to be as bad as he was today. A high-profile case can make or break a judge, and Mary Costello's sympathetic . . ."

"Not to *him*," Lenihan said with quiet fury. "If Bond wants the next Republican President to promote him, he has to tilt to the SSA. Without their support, he's over with."

"True," Sarah allowed. "But he has to screw us without looking like he's gone in the tank."

"Subtlety, Sarah, is not Bond's problem. He's as diabolical as Nolan." Lenihan seemed to brace himself. "I've dealt with fascists before. Like it or not, we've gotten a hearing in ten days' time, and this particular fascist is our judge. I just can't wait to see what he does next."

EIGHTEEN

Amidst the ornate trappings of the Old Senate Caucus Room, Lara Costello Kilcannon faced the Senate Commerce Committee.

Seated to her right was Mary Costello, looking over-whelmed and yet, Lara suspected, feeling resentful at her renewed dependence on her older sister. To her left sat Henry Serrano's widow, Felice. Behind them were Felice's son and daughters, the parents of Laura Blanchard, and Kara Johnson—the slight young woman who, by now, would have been the wife of David Walsh. The room was bright; angled toward them were the cameras which broad-cast Lara's testimony on CNN, MSNBC and Fox. From a raised platform, seventeen senators peered down at them, aides hovering at their shoulders. As Chairman, Chad Palmer sat in the middle, with eight Republican senators to his right, eight Democrats to his left. Though she was tense, to Lara nothing was unfamiliar—not the hearings, any number of which she had covered for the *New York Times*; nor the necessity of speaking live and under pres-sure, a staple of her life in television news. The only new element was the outrage she felt.

For his part, Senator Palmer looked as though he wished to be elsewhere. He listened to her statement with grave courtesy, deferring to the senior Democrat, Frank Ayala of New Mexico. Senator Ayala's questions—pre-scripted with the White House—were designed to elicit sympathy with-out contention. Only when Senator Paul Harshman commenced asking questions did the atmosphere change.

Even now, Lara thought, it was difficult for Harshman to conceal how deeply he despised both Kilcannons. For the hard right wing, which Harshman embodied, they were a nontraditional marriage in a permissive society that had discarded the roles, and the rules, which had once made life in America so decent and predictable. After a perfunctory expression of sympathy, Harshman said, "As I recall, Mrs. Kilcannon, you're not a lawyer. So you're not claiming firsthand knowledge of the many excesses which the Civil Justice Reform Act seeks to correct."

Taking her time, Lara fixed Harshman's gaunt face and bald pate with a gaze as level as she forced her voice to be. "No, Senator. The 'excess' of which I have firsthand knowledge is this new language in the bill, which I understand you support, the effect of which is to destroy—retroactively—the right of those whose loved ones have been killed by guns to their day in court, a jury of their peers, and whatever protections state law now affords them . . ."

Harshman leaned forward. In a condescending tone, he interrupted, "As an attorney and a legislator, I cannot agree with your interpretation of this law . . ."

"Surely," Lara cut in, "you're not suggesting to Mrs. Serrano that your 'reform' doesn't eradicate her right to seek recovery from Lexington Arms. You're not saying *that*, are you, Senator Harshman? Unless you are, please let me finish . . ."

Watching CNN in his office, Fasano said to Gage, "I told Paul to let her go."

"That's the problem," Gage answered sardonically, "with having deeply held beliefs. But the real problem's Palmer."

Fasano shook his head. "What could he do? Stiff the First Lady of the United States? Or cross-examine her? We all know that the Kilcannons must be mixed up in Mary Costello's lawsuit. But all of us—even Paul, I hope—know that there'll be a better time and place to raise that."

Felice Serrano, Lara Costello continued, *has a twelve-year-old son, two daughters aged seven and four, and the modest insurance policy which was all that she and her late husband could afford.*

The grief they feel at Henry Serrano's death is terrible enough. But the loss of a husband and father blights their future in yet another respect—their financial security died with him. Now, Senator, you propose legislation which would kill their sole remaining hope of replacing the only thing which can *be replaced: enough money to keep their home and secure the college education Henry Serrano never had, but was determined to provide them ...*

Some would say, Senator Harshman interjected, *that* John Bowden *killed it when he killed their father.*

That will surely be true, Senator, if you pass this legislation. Lara's gaze swept the other senators, and then returned to Harshman. *You question my qualifications to speak to this issue. In one sense, my qualifications are no different than those of Felice Serrano, my sister Mary, the Blanchard family or Kara Johnson. None of us are lawyers. Our expertise is in grief and loss ...*

"Why does Harshman bother?" Fasano murmured. "Has he totally forgotten who she is?"

But I do have one other credential, Lara continued. *In my former life as a reporter, I covered the Congress. And so, rather early in my career, I immersed myself in the phenomenon known as "special interest legislation."*

This provision, to be plain, is a particularly squalid piece of special interest legislation, which revictimizes victims and insults the memory of those they loved.

"What you've just witnessed," Fasano told Macdonald

Gage, "is the sound bite which heads the evening news. Paul Harshman's finest hour."

"In fairness to Palmer," Clayton told the President, "he handed her this moment. He could have tried to sneak this through without you knowing."

On the screen, Lara continued, *If this Committee cares about their loss, and shares their grief, it will protect them from this injustice.*

Kerry shrugged. "Chad chose to do Fasano's bidding, then tried to maintain his 'honor.' So now he's about to pay for both."

Propelled by her sense of outrage, Lara turned to Palmer.

"Accordingly, Senator Palmer, we request that before this committee votes on whether to send the bill to the full Senate, you hold a separate vote on whether it should immunize gun manufacturers from victims seeking justice.

"If you do, I cannot help but believe that this shameful provision will never reach the Senate floor."

From the platform, Palmer held her gaze. A month ago he had been in her wedding party. Now, in her imaginings, he felt too much shame to look away.

Beneath the table, Mary, who had danced with Chad at the wedding, touched her sister's hand.

"It's so tangled," Lara said to Kerry.

The time was close to midnight. Lara had stayed up late, listening to Mary's fears about the lawsuit, trying to ease the strain beneath the surface of their truce. Now Lara could not sleep.

"You and Mary?" Kerry asked.

"That. All of it, really. Facing Chad today, wondering why he's doing this, and how he could. Speaking for Felice Serrano, when I'm also speaking for you in a power struggle with Fasano. It's like our family was murdered, and somehow Mary and I—and you and I—got sucked down the rabbit hole."

Lying beside her in the dark, Kerry pondered what to say. "A rabbit hole," he answered softly, "where we make up the rules as we go, and real becomes unreal. Until no one knows what's real anymore."

Lara was quiet. "Are *we* real?" she asked.

Kerry drew her closer. "I want to be. Again."

After a moment, to his surprise, she kissed him. The surprise was not in the kiss itself, but the nature of it, and what this told him without words.

Gently, for the first time since the murders, Kerry and Lara made love.

NINETEEN

On the morning of the hearing before Judge Gardner Bond, Sarah and Lenihan were greeted by reporters, satellite trucks, and angry demonstrators on both sides, yelling at each other across a pathway to the federal building maintained by two lines of uniformed police. United States Marshals guarded the door to Bond's courtroom, and the wooden benches overflowed with more reporters and partisans. But at least the starkly modern courtroom was quieter, its sounds muted by decorum and dissipated by the majestic ceilings which distinguished the Federal District Court. Perhaps, Sarah reflected, justice, like mercy, was best hoped for in airy spaces.

But her own hopes diminished within moments of Judge Bond's appearance on the bench. After curtly noting Lenihan and Sarah's presence, and that of John Nolan and Harrison Fancher, Bond said, "The Court will begin by denying plaintiff's motion for a preliminary injunction."

No discussion, Sarah thought bitterly. In a clipped, relentless cadence, Bond continued, "The next matter before the Court is defendants' motions to dismiss plaintiff's wrongful death, antitrust and public nuisance claims. We will take them each in turn, by defendant." Facing Nolan, he concluded, "Mr. Nolan, you have ten minutes to argue for the dismissal of Mary Costello's cause of action against Lexington Arms for the alleged wrongful deaths of her mother, sister and niece."

With that, Nolan stepped briskly to the podium. "Let

me begin," he told Judge Bond, "by acknowledging two principles.

"First, on a motion to dismiss, this Court must assume that the facts alleged by Mary Costello are true. Second, if the facts alleged—even if *true*—do not state a cause of action under California law, which this Court must still apply, it must dismiss Miss Costello's claims for wrongful death."

Hands flat on the podium, Nolan paused, his voice resonant, his gaze up at Bond respectful but serene. "This case," he continued, "began with a monstrous rampage in which John Bowden wounded the survivors beyond all hope of recompense. In our hearts, we hope for some way of healing what so many of us found very close to unbearable. But the law acknowledges what reason tells us—that the terrible scene at San Francisco International was the work of a single demented mind."

It was an elegant beginning, Sarah thought, Nolan at his most statesmanlike. Stone-faced, Lenihan began scribbling notes for his refutation.

"Reason," Nolan said abruptly, "also tells us a harsher truth: that this lawsuit is nothing more than a publicity stunt—brought contrary to settled law—in the service of power politics . . ."

"Mr. Nolan," Bond admonished in his patrician manner, "leave the 'power politics' to politicians. It's the 'contrary to settled law' which is the business of this Court."

"Of course, Your Honor." Unfazed, Nolan continued as though the mild rebuke had been instructive, even agreeable. "Plaintiff asks this Court to hold the maker of a legal firearm liable for its criminal misuse by a murderer it never heard of, and whose actions were beyond its control. *That*, we submit, is not—and cannot be—the law.

"On this point, Congress has spoken. Guns are a legal

product. The sale of a Patriot-2 and Eagle's Claw bullets in Nevada—*if* that's what happened here—is perfectly legal. And even if John Bowden purchased his P-2 at a gun show—a guess which we must, for the moment, accept as truth—not even plaintiff's highly creative counsel can allege that Lexington had anything to do with that.

"Your Honor, we don't punish the maker of Ferraris because some driver breaks the speed limit. We don't sue the distiller of a single-malt Scotch because the driver was inebriated. California law recognizes that responsibility resides in the individual: in the reckless driver, the alcoholic—and in John Bowden, the murderer . . ."

"And your authority?" Bond inquired.

The hearing had begun to resemble a minuet, Sarah observed, in which both partners, Bond and Nolan, executed their steps with precision. *"Richards versus Stanley,"* Nolan responded promptly, "held that the owner of a stolen car is not liable for the reckless driving of a car thief, even though he carelessly left the keys in the ignition. That core principle is still the case."

Bond held up a hand. "The difference, Mr. Nolan, is this so-called 'inflammatory advertising.' According to plaintiff's complaint, Lexington's ad in the SSA magazine was a positive incentive to purchase and misuse by the demented."

"Damn right," Lenihan murmured. At the podium, Nolan gathered himself. "All that we *really* know, Your Honor, is that Bowden had the SSA magazine. We don't know—and I expect will *never* know—why or where or even when he bought it, who sold it to him or even what he was doing in Las Vegas. Without such proof, plaintiff has no case."

"That may well prove right," Bond interrupted. "And plaintiff's complaint may well be based on speculation . . ."

"Sure," Lenihan whispered to Sarah, "Bowden picked up *The Defender*, then flew off to play the slot machines . . ."

"But," Bond continued, after a brief, sharp glance at Lenihan, "at this point, as you conceded, this Court must accept plaintiff's allegations that the advertisement led to Mr. Bowden's purchase. Given that, couldn't Lexington foresee that its ad copy might enhance the prospects of criminal misuse?"

Nolan spread his arms in an elegant shrug. "Certainly," he said in the same placid tone, "it may be possible for a manufacturer to foresee—or at least imagine—that at an unknown place, at an unknown time, some unknown person may perpetrate a tragedy. But foreseeability is merely one element of an action for wrongful death. The most essential element is causation—that Lexington caused *this* man to kill *these* victims.

"Lexington did not *tell* him, let alone *cause* him, to murder Mary Costello's family—any more than it caused him to abuse his wife or hate the President and First Lady for their apparent, though insufficient, acts of intervention on his wife's behalf."

This, Sarah thought, was artful: the first suggestion, stated as an afterthought, that Mary Costello's lawsuit was designed to expiate the Kilcannons for their own neglect. "This lawsuit," Nolan continued, "is legislation by litigation. Because the plaintiff dislikes the gun laws as written by the Congress, she asks this Court to invent some. But it is the role of this Court to interpret existing laws, not make up new ones. That job belongs to the House and Senate . . ."

And Fasano and the SSA, Sarah thought, *were working overtime on* that. But Bond appeared content. With a brisk nod, he told Nolan, "I understand your argument, Mr. Nolan," and then turned to Lenihan and Sarah. "Who will speak for the plaintiff?"

*

"A Ferrari," Robert Lenihan opened bluntly, "is not a killing machine. Nor is a bottle of Scotch. But load up a Lexington P-2 with forty Eagle's Claw bullets, and that's exactly what you have—a weapon whose only use is to shoot a lot of people quickly, at very short range, with the maximum assurance that all of them will die."

In style, Sarah thought, Lenihan could not be more different than John Nolan—staccato, impassioned, contemptuous of legal niceties. Immediately, Bond shot back, "Mr. Nolan's point is that under California law, Lexington Arms—like the makers of a Ferrari or Glenfiddich Scotch—cannot be liable if their product is not defective."

"On that point," Lenihan said with scorn, "I can't agree more with Mr. Nolan. John Bowden's P-2 was certainly *not* defective. It worked exactly as advertised.

"What else is the P-2 good for but killing humans? Not for hunting deer, unless the deer approaches you—after which there wouldn't be enough left of him to hang up on the wall. And the Eagle's Claw bullet? That was good for only one thing: ensuring that Marie Bowden did not outlive her family.

"That's why it was designed to become the six deadly knife points which shredded Marie's vena cava. That's why the P-2 was designed to accommodate forty such bullets. And *that*, Your Honor, is the manner in which Lexington chose to market them."

Already, Sarah understood why Robert Lenihan excelled with juries. But it was far from clear that Gardner Bond would let this case reach a jury. In contrast to his demeanor with Nolan, Bond scrutinized Lenihan with the clinical disdain of a pathologist examining a cancer through a microscope. "Not foreseeable?" Lenihan asked rhetorically. "What Lexington's defense comes down to is this: 'We may be marketing to murderers and criminals, but we didn't cause *these* murders because we didn't know *this* murderer by name . . .' "

"What about the *Richards* case?" Bond snapped.

"Irrelevant. There's no profit in leaving keys in an unlocked car. Lexington profited by marketing death to people like John Bowden . . ."

"You're not claiming," Bond persisted, "that these ads are in any way misleading?"

"Far from it," Lenihan answered sardonically. "That's my point."

Bond leaned forward. "Then aren't they—however objectionable you may find them—commercial speech protected by the First Amendment?"

"No, Your Honor—for two reasons. First, commercial speech is less protected than pure political speech. Second, freedom of speech is not absolute, as Justice Holmes recognized in saying, 'There is no right to shout "fire" in a crowded theatre.' Freedom of speech must be balanced against the *harm* of speech such as this . . ."

"And yet," Bond retorted, "one *can* shout 'fire' if it's true. If selling the P-2 should not be legal, isn't that a matter for Congress? And isn't this lawsuit, as Mr. Nolan suggests, an effort to usurp the role of Congress?"

"Not at all," Lenihan countered. "As our brief details, this lawsuit is grounded in the California law of torts . . ."

"I've read your brief," Bond interrupted brusquely, "and comprehend your argument. It's time to hear from the SSA regarding the claims against it. Such as they may be."

Disheartened, Sarah picked up her pen.

Everything that Lenihan was, Sarah thought, Harrison Fancher was not. His voice was thin but harsh, and his demeanor suggested a man who preferred dark corners, the nooks and crannies of concealed strategy, to the messiness of dealing with humanity at large. His skills were those of a tactician gifted with a first-class mind, a monomaniacal persistence and an inexhaustible sourness of spirit. In the law, Sarah had noticed, such persons tended to go far.

"This," Fancher told Gardner Bond with an air of spite, "is a spite suit. Let me be clear: the Kilcannon Center and its political allies have failed to achieve their goal of discrediting the advocates of gun rights. So now they would use this court to deny the SSA its First Amendment rights to defend the Second Amendment rights of all Americans."

"Then clear *this* up," Bond interjected. "If Lexington were liable for its advertisement, would the SSA be liable for printing it?"

"Not at all." Fancher folded his hands in front of him, body hunched in a defensive crouch. "No question—the claims against Lexington are phantasmagorical. But to rope in the SSA is an outrage.

"Mary Costello's lawyers make two claims. First, that the SSA ran a truthful ad, written by Lexington, that they imagine John Bowden saw." Fancher's voice filled with sarcasm. "So if the *San Francisco Chronicle* accepts an ad by a maker of pesticides, and a disaffected wife puts it in her husband's soup, the *Chronicle* is liable to his children?

"What nonsense. In desperation, these lawyers have concocted worse nonsense: a 'conspiracy' in which the *SSA* forces *Lexington* to sell the P-2 and Eagle's Claw bullets at gun shows—the first 'conspiracy' in history, at least under the antitrust laws, where the alleged pernicious purpose is to compel a wholly legal act . . ."

"Plaintiff's broader claim," Bond corrected him, "is that the SSA directed Lexington in the acts leading to the so-called wrongful death of Ms. Costello's relatives."

"But on what basis?" Fancher asked. "That the SSA aggressively advocates gun rights, in the Congress and out?

That's our right as citizens. Just as our members have the right not to buy a company's products because they no longer like what it stands for." Pausing, he turned to Sarah. "A choice, when exercised against so-called villains like 'big tobacco,' which is advocated by the Kilcannon Center itself."

With a studied lack of expression, Sarah scribbled on her notepad, "Economic gain." As if on cue, the judge told Fancher, "Plaintiff also alleges that the SSA encouraged other gun makers to isolate Lexington in the event of a boycott, encouraging them to divide Lexington's market share should it reach an agreement with the President regarding gun shows. Might not that violate the antitrust laws?"

Fancher grimaced. "It's a pity," he said with reedy contempt, "that, on motions to dismiss, the presumption of truth is given to the scrupulous and unscrupulous alike. At this juncture, this Court is required to credit such fantasies. But plaintiff's counsel is required to have a reasonable basis for *believing* them. At *some* juncture, I hope the Court will inquire as to whether counsel has defrauded it."

"You can be sure," Bond countered stiffly, "that this Court will never permit a fraud to go to trial. But, as of now, all it can do is wonder." Abruptly turning to Lenihan and Sarah, Bond demanded, "Which one of you cares to respond to *that*?"

Reaching the podium, Sarah paused to steady herself, drawing one deep breath. Bond's judicial stare bore into her.

"Your Honor," she began, "if the *Chronicle* ran ads for rat poison headed 'lethal to husbands in sixty seconds,' then the *Chronicle* would answer for it . . ."

"Is *that* what the SSA did, Ms. Dash? I don't recall that the ad incited murder."

"Effectively, it did. The ad touted the lethal capacity of the Lexington P-2. It reminded criminals and batterers that the P-2 was banned in California. And then—in a companion ad for the gun show itself—the SSA magazine told them where to acquire one without a background check."

"So now," Bond interrupted, "the SSA is responsible for *two* ads—one by Lexington, and one by the promoters of the gun show."

"Which were placed side by side." Sarah felt anger overcome her nervousness. "Don't the editors read their own magazine? They had no obligation to run these ads at all. Instead, they did so in a manner designed to maximize the chance that what *did* happen *would* happen—that John Bowden would set out for Las Vegas . . ."

"According to your complaint."

"Which I stand by, Your Honor." Sarah hesitated, and then reached the most delicate point. "As I do our allegation that the SSA helped other manufacturers conspire to take Lexington's share of the market, should the SSA commence a boycott . . ."

"Mr. Fancher," Bond cut in, "claims that you have no basis for alleging that. *I* have no basis for knowing. But *you* know—as we speak—whether or not you do.

"You're an officer of the court, Ms. Dash. Under Rule 11, each claim in your complaint must have a good faith basis. If *this* claim does not, you may be liable for defendant's legal fees and expenses. Or even, in the most extreme of cases, subject to disbarment."

Sarah could not protest. Unrestrained by the presence of a jury, Bond could castigate her as he liked, and be as peremptory as he wished. And his barely veiled threat, Sarah realized, reflected Lenihan's own reservations. Steeling herself, she answered, "Rule 11 does not require us to prove our case before we've had a *chance* to prove it. That is what discovery exists for. At this stage, we must have a good faith basis for believing—should this Court let the case proceed—that we *can* prove it." Pausing, she finished firmly, "I would not be standing here, Your Honor, were that not the case."

From the bench, Bond scowled at her. "At this point, Ms. Dash, we'll take a fifteen-minute recess. Then I'll wish to hear about another point I question—this public nuisance theory, and the haste you seek in pursuing it. And, specifically, whether it's a pretext to accelerate discovery."

"Palmer," Chuck Hampton told the President, "is playing hardball."

Alone in the Oval Office, they reviewed the increasingly tense partisan politics surrounding Palmer's hearing. "I can't believe," Kerry said, "that Chad's scheduled the committee vote for three o'clock."

"And with as little notice as possible," Hampton replied. "He won't even tell Frank Ayala whether he'll hold a separate vote on gun immunity."

Despite his thirteen years in politics, Kerry found Chad's opposition difficult to accept—not the fact, but the manner of it. "Less than three weeks ago, Chuck, Chad was here for dinner, when you were. Now he's fronting for Fasano as if he were Paul Harshman. The vote Lara requested is utterly routine."

"Maybe not on *this* bill," Hampton responded. "A chairman can do pretty much whatever he wants. In Fasano's place, I wouldn't want my Republican colleagues on Palmer's committee sticking their necks out on barring Mary's lawsuit. I'd want to give them the cover of voting 'yes' or 'no' on the entire bill."

"Will any of the Republicans break ranks?"

"At this point, Ayala thinks not. I agree."

For a moment, the President reflected. "However this goes down," he said emphatically, "I need a party line vote against the bill—all eight Democrats. If Democrats peel off in committee, there may be more defections on the floor. This is our first test of strength, and I don't want to signal weakness."

Hampton nodded. "Then you'd better call Vic Coletti, Mr. President. I can't quite nail him down."

TWENTY

"PLAINTIFF'S PUBLIC nuisance theory," Nolan told Judge Bond, "has two purposes—both of them abusive.

"First, by asking for a permanent injunction against this so-called threat to Californians—the legal sale of a legal product in another state—plaintiff seeks to create an air of crisis where there is none . . ."

"For what purpose, counsel?"

The seemingly straightforward question, Sarah knew, presented Nolan with a challenge. If he accused plaintiff of attempting to push toward a trial before the passage of the Civil Justice Reform Act, he must acknowledge defendant's interest in delay. "To further inflame the media," Nolan said at length. "To make their political points, plaintiff's counsel must be able to feed their supposed evidence to the press, sooner rather than later. Pushing through depositions to an early trial will enable them to do that."

"Not in this Court," Bond said sternly. "What's your second point?"

"That by recasting a wrongful death action as an ongoing public nuisance, plaintiff's counsel have created a monster which would swallow the entire law of wrongful death." Nolan hesitated, his manner suggesting a reluctance to speak harsh but necessary truths. "To be plain, Mary Costello's family is already dead. Enjoining Lexington Arms from selling weapons in Nevada cannot change that . . ."

"What plaintiff alleges," Bond interjected in a dubious tone, "is some form of continuing danger."

"That's entirely speculative," Nolan said dismissively. "And there is no precedent whatsoever for enjoining so-called excessive sales in another state as a public nuisance in California.

"Even accepting plaintiff's allegations, she cannot assert that Lexington controls sales at gun shows in Nevada, or anywhere else, an allegation required under the law of public nuisance. Which, as our brief points out, exists to protect property, not people . . ."

"Very well," Bond cut in. "Does counsel for the SSA have anything to add?"

At the defense table, Harrison Fancher stood. "This isn't even our gun, Your Honor. A public nuisance claim against the SSA is more than innovation—it's a mutation. If anything, the case shows why there's a pressing need for legislation to protect legitimate organizations from legalized blackmail by plaintiffs' lawyers. Where the only restraint on such suits is the conscience of the lawyers who bring them, our only protection is this Court."

Bond smiled faintly. "Which of plaintiff's counsel," he inquired, "wishes to respond?"

Walking to the podium, Sarah felt edgy, angry and sharp. "Plaintiff's argument is this: the people of California can protect their homes, but not their lives.

"That's not the law. In *City of Boston versus Smith & Wesson* . . ."

"Boston," Bond said sharply, "is in Massachusetts. The murders occurred here, and therefore California law applies. What about the California case of *Gallo versus Acuna*?"

"*Gallo* supports us, Your Honor. There the Court enjoined gang members from selling drugs. . . ."

"In a specific neighborhood, Ms. Dash. Because the

illegal activities involved made the neighbors virtual prisoners in their own homes. *This* case involves a legal sale in another state . . ."

"Of a gun banned in California," Sarah retorted, "but which Lexington advertised in California, through the SSA, providing a virtual blueprint for how criminals and batterers could buy one without a background check.

"It's illegal to sell a P-2 in California. In *California*, it's illegal to sell *any* weapon at a gun show without a background check. Lexington lured John Bowden to Nevada . . ."

"Bowden's dead," Bond came back. "As Mr. Nolan points out, so are Mary Costello's relatives. What's the 'ongoing harm' here?"

"Last year," Sarah answered promptly, "over two thousand Californians were murdered with a gun. And nearly one-third of all guns used in crimes against Californians were sold outside California—principally in Nevada and Arizona . . ."

"Crimes," Bond retorted, "are committed by criminals . . ."

"Whom Lexington need not control." Sarah was in a rhythm now, and any awe of Gardner Bond had vanished. "All that the law requires is a substantial threat to public safety, and Lexington's failure to minimize it. '*Minimize*'?" Sarah repeated with undisguised contempt. "We allege that the P-2 is a top ten crime gun—and that Lexington knows it.

"We allege that a disproportionate number of P-2s sold in Nevada are used to murder Californians—and that Lexington knows *that*. They know all that, and profit from it. Assisted by—if not controlled by—the SSA itself." Pausing, Sarah spoke more slowly. "Mary Costello is not confined to seeking damages for her terrible loss. She is entitled, under the law of California, to protect the many others who may die—who surely *will* die—because of defendants' willful conduct . . ."

"So what do you propose I do?"

"Permit us to go to trial. After which we'll ask you to enjoin Lexington from flooding California with P-2s; from advertising P-2s within the state; and from selling a P-2 in *any* state without a background check."

Frowning, Bond rejoined, "That's a drastic remedy, counsel. One might even say draconian."

"Enough is enough," Sarah answered. "For far too long, we've lived by bromides like 'guns don't kill people, people do.' If *that* were true, why not just ship people off to war without the guns?

"Mr. Fancher has made free with the word 'nonsense.' The real nonsense is defendants' argument, which amounts to one extended plea: 'Keep the plaintiff's lawyers from picking on us.'

"Consider *that*, and then consider the Lexington P-2, good only for killing.

"Consider Lexington's ad, which is all *about* killing.

"Consider Mary Costello, whose family was killed.

"Consider all the Californians who *will* be killed." Sarah softened her voice. "And then ask yourself, Your Honor, who it is that needs this Court's protection."

Silent, Bond regarded her with narrowed eyes. "Defendants," Sarah continued, "are right about one important thing. Because of the power and money of the SSA, 'existing' federal law did not protect Mary Costello's family from defendants' conduct in marketing this deadly weapon to John Bowden. It does not protect any of us now. The only protection for future victims is this Court's resolve to apply the law of public nuisance.

"If under that law, there's a line a gun maker shouldn't cross, and yet Lexington didn't cross it *here*, where on earth is the line?" Briefly, Sarah inclined her head toward Nolan and Fancher. "These defendants," she concluded, "have asked this Court for immunity from suit. This Court should turn them down, and let Mary Costello go forward."

Turning, she walked slowly back to the table. As she sat, Lenihan's eyes held the hint of a smile.

"At this time," Bond said abruptly, "the Court will announce its rulings."

At this time, Senator Frank Ayala said, *it seems appropriate to call a vote on the gun immunity provision. As requested by Mrs. Kilcannon.*

Kerry and Clayton watched CNN. In the Chairman's seat, Senator Palmer seemed to steel himself. *I deeply respect the First Lady*, he responded. *But if we proceed in a piecemeal manner, we open the door to deconstructing this entire bill, voting on every clause which concerns any member of this committee . . .*

Senator, Ayala said with rising indignation, *this is not a matter of nitpicking every line. Among other things, this language would federalize the law of wrongful death to protect companies like Lexington Arms—by erasing whatever remedies are presently provided by state law . . .*

Now wait. Paul Harshman's voice cracked with anger. *That kind of accusation has no place in the United States Senate. If you wish to amend this bill, the place for that is the floor of the Senate itself. Let all one hundred senators consider this question, not merely the seventeen of us . . .*

Watching, Kerry felt fresh anger of his own. "It's choreographed," he told Clayton. "Chad's trying to jam this through."

On the screen, Senator Palmer banged his gavel. *The manner of voting*, he said curtly, *is the chair's prerogative. We will vote once, now, on the entire Civil Justice Reform Act as revised by this committee.*

TWENTY-ONE

ADJUSTING HIS GLASSES, Gardner Bond coughed. To Sarah, nervous herself, these tics suggested that the judge also felt the tension of the moment. Across the courtroom, Nolan and Fancher were stiff, attentive.

"The Court," Bond gravely pronounced, "wishes to add its own expression of sorrow regarding the events which have brought us to this day. That we must view them through the prism of law should not be taken, in any way, as an effort to minimize this tragedy.

"But this *is* a court of law. The task before us is limited to deciding a legal issue: whether the facts alleged in plaintiff's complaint constitute, under the laws of California, claims which the Court must allow to go forward."

Apprehensive, Sarah glanced at Lenihan. His stillness suggested that he, like Sarah, sensed that Bond's self-exculpatory statement was his prelude to dismissal.

"To be plain," Bond continued, "plaintiff's accusations against *these* defendants exist at the margins of the law, and rest on 'facts' which will be extremely difficult to prove.

"At the least, Ms. Costello must prove that *Lexington's* actions caused *John Bowden* to act.

"That Lexington's actions in Nevada are a public nuisance in California.

"That the *SSA* controlled these actions in a manner which violates the law of antitrust, or is otherwise cognizable as law.

"And that this Court should—or even can—issue an injunction of almost unprecedented breadth . . ."

Where, Sarah wondered, *is Bond going?* Her fingers gripped the edges of her chair.

On the bench, Bond sat upright. "That said," he continued, "what the Court cannot say—at least prior to discovery—is that, under the law, there is no conceivable set of facts through which plaintiff can support these claims."

Lenihan drew a breath. Eyes closed, Sarah heard Bond conclude, "For these reasons, the Court must deny defendants' motion to dismiss . . ."

With Senator Ayala scowling beside him, Senator Chad Palmer asked the Senate Commerce Committee to vote on the Civil Justice Reform Act. Watching the proceedings on CNN, Kerry murmured to Clayton, "Vic Coletti's the one who's still shaky. And now I can't reach him."

"Then he doesn't want you to. With Lexington's headquarters in his home state, plus all those insurance companies, he must be feeling the pressure."

One by one, the vote proceeded; one senator after another, including the Republican moderates, voted with their party—"yes" for the Republicans; "no" for the Democrats—on a bill which would wipe out Mary Costello's lawsuit. Kerry's tension focused on Coletti.

Senator Coletti?

Sitting amidst his Democratic colleagues, Vic Coletti fidgeted. But he cast his vote in a flat, businesslike voice that, to Kerry, hinted at defiance.

Yes.

"I hope," Clayton murmured, "that Vic's not expecting any favors."

The President did not answer. He was already thinking ahead, weighing the motives of one hundred men and women.

By a vote of ten to seven, Chad Palmer announced, *this committee recommends that the Civil Justice Reform Act be considered by the Senate.*

"The next business," Bond told Lenihan and Sarah, "is to shape discovery. How will plaintiff attempt to prove her case?"

Seemingly heartened, Lenihan stood. "Our proposed discovery is quite straightforward. We need any and all documents and witnesses relating to the design and marketing of the Patriot-2 and Eagle's Claw bullets; to the sales of the P-2 in states adjacent to California; to the use of the P-2 in crimes; and to Lexington's negotiations with the Kilcannon administration . . ."

"What about discovery from the SSA?"

"Among other things," Lenihan answered carefully, "all communications by the SSA regarding the contacts between Lexington and President Kilcannon—or between the President and the gun industry . . ."

"Which," Bond objected, "might well be an intrusion on legitimate political activities—such as lobbying and advocacy—protected by the First Amendment."

"Not necessarily," Lenihan responded. "And it's the only way we can prove that the SSA was at the hub of a conspiracy."

"I expect that defendants may have another view. In the meanwhile, whom do you plan to depose?"

"Representatives of the other manufacturers. The decision-makers at the SSA—in particular, Charles Dane. The key personnel at Lexington—including in design and marketing. Certainly George Callister, its CEO."

Bond turned to the defense table. "And whom might *you* depose, Mr. Nolan?"

Nolan stood at once. "To start, all witnesses plaintiff

intends to call at trial. We request that the Court order counsel to submit a witness list, in sufficient time for us to schedule depositions."

This, Sarah knew, implicated Martin Bresler; as his exposure neared, Bresler might become even more anxious. "That's only reasonable," Bond said to Nolan. "What other depositions do you want?"

"The obvious ones—Mary Costello; the police inspector, Charles Monk; Dr. Callie Hines, who operated on Marie Costello." After a pause, Nolan added, "Also, anyone involved in the relationship between Joan Bowden and her estranged husband. Including the President and First Lady."

Stunned, Sarah absorbed this. Despite Nolan's protestations that she and Lenihan were abusing the lawsuit for political purposes, questioning both Kilcannons under oath was an intensely political act, and a unique opportunity for the SSA. But this seemed to leave Gardner Bond unfazed. "As to the President and Mrs. Kilcannon," he answered, "they may wish to be heard. At least regarding the time and manner of deposition."

"Of course," Nolan agreed. "Indeed, *all* discovery—including depositions—should be subject to stringent rules set out by this Court. For example, we ask the Court to bar discovery regarding lobbying, political strategy, or other activities protected by the First Amendment—including communications between Lexington and the SSA."

"That," Bond remarked with veiled irony, "seems to be the lynchpin of plaintiff's alleged conspiracy."

Nolan spread his hands. "Would the Kilcannon Center want Lexington or the SSA to probe *its* lobbying, *its* political strategy, *its* contacts with politicians? Plaintiff's supposed discovery is nothing more than political espionage."

"What do you propose, counsel?"

"The appointment of a Special Discovery Master. Before we give plaintiff any document which implicates legitimate political activities—whether they relate to plaintiff's highly suspect antitrust claim, *or* to the industry's response to President Kilcannon—the Special Master should determine their relevance to an 'unlawful activity.' "

"Your Honor," Lenihan called out in protest. "A discovery master should not be able to decide what documents or witnesses are relevant to our case . . ."

"And *you*," Bond said abruptly, "should not use this complaint as a hunting license." Turning to Nolan, Bond said, "I'm granting your request. Is there anything else?"

"There is. Specifically, we believe that the purpose of this case is political, not legal—to develop 'evidence' of so-called wrongdoing which plaintiff's counsel can siphon to the media." With an accusatory glance at Lenihan, Nolan finished, "We therefore ask this Court to ban the parties from sharing the fruits of discovery with any outside person other than expert witnesses, and to order that any documents or depositions filed with the Court will be sealed until trial."

"So ordered," Bond said promptly.

With one stroke, Sarah realized, the judge had just walled off discovery from public view. In protest, Lenihan rose again. "Plaintiff's counsel," Nolan continued calmly, "mentioned deposing Mr. Callister, Lexington's Chief Executive Officer. We believe any such deposition is an effort to take up valuable executive time, when the plaintiff can get the exact same information from other witnesses . . ."

"The plaintiff," Lenihan objected, "is entitled to question *all* relevant witnesses."

"But who determines relevance?" Nolan inquired in his most reasonable tone. "We request that the Court bar Mr. Callister's deposition until plaintiff has examined all *other* prospective witnesses, and only if counsel then can demonstrate that Mr. Callister has information unavailable from any other source."

In anger, Sarah stood. "May *I* be heard, Your Honor?"

Turning, Bond gave her a perfunctory nod. "Go ahead, counsel."

"It's preposterous that Mr. Nolan proposes to take up the time of the President of the United States, but claims that the president of *Lexington Arms* is too important for us to bother . . ."

"President Kilcannon," Bond interrupted, "can speak for himself. But Mr. Nolan speaks for Mr. Callister."

"Mr. *Callister*," Sarah shot back, "*dealt* with President Kilcannon. Any pressure by the SSA or Lexington would have been on Mr. Callister."

"Pardon me," Nolan broke in. "Are you saying, Ms. Dash, that Mr. Callister conspired with *himself*, or *pressured* himself? Under your own conspiracy theory, Mr. Callister's uniqueness as a witness is conceptually impossible."

"Indeed," Bond said emphatically. "So I'm granting your request." Facing Sarah, the judge spoke in his most astringent tone. "Whatever this case turns out to be, counsel, it will *not* be a tool of harassment, a pipeline to the media, or fodder for national politicians.

"Let me be clear. Mr. Nolan's requests are now the order of this Court. Any party or attorney who violates our order will be subject to contempt and, should the Court deem it appropriate, referred to the State Bar for disciplinary proceedings."

Speechless, Sarah sat down. "Now let's discuss scheduling," the judge told her. "According to your complaint, defendants are perpetrating a continuing public nuisance which threatens every citizen of this state. If, indeed, this case is a matter of life and death, this Court feels compelled to expedite its resolution." Bond's voice became peremptory. "Therefore you will complete discovery—on both the injunctive relief to be decided by this Court, and the remaining claims to be decided by a jury— on the following timetable:

"Within seven days, the parties will serve all requests for documents.

"Within fourteen days from that, all documents will be produced.

"Within sixty days—not one day more—the parties will conclude all depositions . . ."

"Your Honor," Sarah objected, "for meaningful depositions we need defendants' documents. This schedule is a license for defendants to withhold them . . ."

"That," Bond snapped, "assumes bad faith. I don't. If there's a problem, you can file a motion with the Court."

Lenihan's face, Sarah saw, was stained with anger. "Even assuming *good* faith," she answered with precarious calm, "there will be many thousands of documents. An inspection by the Special Master will further limit our time to review any number of them. We can't take meaningful depositions on the schedule you've outlined, let alone prepare for trial . . ."

"You requested an injunction, Ms. Dash. I'm giving you the benefit of your request—accelerated discovery." Folding his arms, Bond leaned forward. "Not only will I rule on your proposed injuction within two weeks after discovery, I'll rule on defendants' summary judgment motions—if any. If plaintiff lacks sufficient facts to support her claims, there will *be* no trial.

"In short, the facts had better be there. Or this Court will not further waste judicial time and resources." Head snapping, Bond nodded to Nolan and Fancher and then, more curtly, to Lenihan and Sarah. "That's it. Tomorrow morning the Court will issue its written order."

"All rise," the courtroom clerk called out, and the hearing was over.

The elevator doors closed. As it glided downward to the main floor, Sarah and Lenihan were alone.

Stunned, she leaned against the metal wall. Lenihan stared at the floor. "Throwing us out," he said, "wasn't good enough for Bond. Dismissing the case might have looked arbitrary. He might even have been reversed. But *this* is truly elegant: he's burnished his credentials for promotion—Gardner Bond, a man so fair that he gave us the rope to hang ourselves. By fucking us with your goddammed public nuisance theory." His voice echoed in the stifling space. "Even *you* can see what's coming, Sarah. On this schedule, Nolan and Fancher will shaft us under the cover of a media blackout.

"We'll never be able to prove our case, in the press *or* in the courts. And then Bond will grant their motions for summary judgment. Assuming, of course, that Fasano hasn't rushed the Civil Justice Reform Act past Kilcannon."

Before Sarah could answer, the elevator shuddered to a stop.

A fresh herd of reporters awaited them. "Ms. Dash," a woman called out, "the Senate Commerce Committee has just voted out the Civil Justice Reform Act, and President Kilcannon has denounced its action as a 'speed record for injustice.' What is your reaction?"

"We'll complete discovery in sixty days," Sarah answered. "If the Congress tries to pass this law before the public sees our evidence, we're looking at a cover-up."

The contest of law and politics, Sarah knew, had begun.

PART FOUR

THE BETRAYAL

Mid-October to early November

ONE

As a courtesy, Frank Fasano, though Majority Leader, came to visit Chuck Hampton in the Minority Leader's office.

For a time, amidst the ornate trappings of Hampton's office suite, they chatted about personal things—Fasano's burgeoning family, Hampton's twenty-four-year-old daughter's first job as a reporter, the amusing vagaries of Fasano's adjustment to becoming leader and, as such, a manager of towering egos with conflicting ambitions. To Hampton, it was reminiscent of the more decorous and genteel time he knew only through Senate lore, when politics was more leisurely and less lethal, the veneer of professional respect a balm for partisan rancor. But no amount of civility could change what both men now would face. The murder of Lara Kilcannon's family, and the future of this President, would be resolved on the Senate floor. At length, Fasano said, "We have some business to do."

Though instantly on guard, Hampton smiled faintly. "Scheduling a vote on the President's gun bill?"

Fasano maintained a bland expression. "You'll have it, Chuck. Or, at least, a debate on various proposals. All in good time."

This somewhat delphic response, Hampton knew, conveyed three things: a threat to filibuster Kilcannon's bill; a reminder that Fasano controlled the schedule on which the bill would be considered; and the reality that, through artful stalling, the Judiciary Committee had not yet reported out *any* gun bill to the Senate, and might well gin up an alternative. "If you delay this," Hampton answered, "the President won't sit idly by. Nor will I."

Fasano studied him, as though to appraise the depth of his resolve. "Tort reform comes first," he answered bluntly. "You and I can get it done, or we can go to war."

" 'War'?" Hampton said dryly. "Over tort reform? This wouldn't be about the Costello lawsuit, would it?"

Fasano hesitated, and then discarded all pretense. "By suing the SSA, Mary Costello's lawyers have made things ten times worse—for both of us. If any vulnerable Democrat votes against our bill, Dane's going after him."

This time Hampton's smile was quizzical. "So what do you suggest?"

"That we both look after the Senate, and our own." Elbows resting on his knees, Fasano leaned forward with an air of candor. "Kilcannon *likes* wars, Chuck—it's in his nature. And, to be fair, what happened to his wife's family might cause a less combative man to go for broke. It may even be true that his appetite for combat helped him get elected. But it's also the reason your colleagues would never have made him leader . . ."

"*And* the reason," Hampton interposed, "despite my exquisitely calibrated judgment—which I'm sure you're about to compliment—that I may never become President. The President's genius wasn't made for the stately rhythms of this body—he lacked the patience for it. *His* gifts are Presidential."

"*This* President," Fasano said emphatically, "doesn't give a damn about your colleagues. If swing state Democrats support Kilcannon's gun bill, or oppose this gun immunity provision, the SSA will unload on them. And now the business community will, as well.

"With your help, maybe Kilcannon can bludgeon them into supporting him. But it'll be like handing some of them a glass of Kool-Aid laced with hemlock. Suicide in Georgia or Louisiana."

"Then shouldn't you be encouraging me to try?" Once more, Hampton smiled. "I thought you *wanted* our people to lose. Can it be that *you* don't like this, either?"

Fasano permitted himself a brief smile of his own. "There are those," he conceded, "who don't find immunizing the Eagle's Claw their most attractive option . . ."

"Like Cassie Rollins," Hampton interrupted. "So before you worry about my people, spare a tear or two for Cassie.

"Maine's a hard-core gun state, especially among Republicans. If Cassie votes against the SSA, they'll fund a primary challenge against her, maybe cost her the nomination. But if she votes *with* the SSA, it'll cost her votes in the middle, and maybe reelection. A painful dilemma, except for her opponent in the general election."

Fasano shrugged. "We *both* have problems," he acknowledged. "But how bad they are depends on how big an issue *you* choose to make it." Fasano's words took on a quiet urgency. "Discovery in the Costello case has been sealed. There won't be any more dramatic revelations—the President and First Lady will have to carry this one on their backs.

"People forget, and memories fade. Three months from now, if CNN is still airing that tape of the murders, the two or three people watching will just be numb. Even now, most people instinctively know that suing Lexington isn't right—let alone suing the SSA. But the SSA will *never* forget a senator who opposed it." Fasano spread his hands in a gesture of entreaty. "I'm here to offer you a way out on this. On this issue, a Senate which is unpredictable is bound to be unpleasant."

This was right, Hampton knew. Already there was a stirring within his caucus, an apprehensive restiveness among those who felt endangered; Vic Coletti, he feared, was the harbinger of things to come. With genuine curiosity, Hampton asked, "What 'way out' do you have in mind?"

"For you to lie back," Fasano answered briskly. "On tort reform, your only means of raising the stakes on gun immunity—making life hard for both of us—is to offer an amendment stripping immunity out of the bill, and force senators to vote on that alone. But you'll never get enough votes to pass it, and any swing Democrat who votes with you may well go down in flames.

"Tell Kilcannon that. Then let the entire Civil Justice Reform Act come up for a vote, and pass—which it will. If Kilcannon wants to veto it, he can. Then he can try to get the thirty-four votes necessary to uphold a veto, and you can decide whether to help him."

"You've clearly thought this through," Hampton answered with a smile. "So doubtless you've considered that, with a mere forty-one votes, I can mount a filibuster and keep the entire bill from ever coming to a vote."

"You *could*," Fasano retorted. "But you won't. Because you'll lose. Despite the no doubt considerable pressure from the lobby for the plaintiff's lawyers, not enough of your people will want to oppose the most sweeping reform of abusive lawsuits passed in a generation—even if it contains a gun immunity provision. And *none* of mine will. Including Cassie Rollins."

"Which," Hampton replied, "is why you want me to help you send Kilcannon a tort reform bill with gun immunity still in it. You think you can hold your people, and peel off enough of mine to override the President's veto."

Fasano gave an affirming nod. "Kilcannon loses, I win— and more of your vulnerable Democrats survive. Giving *you* a fighting chance to take my place if the Democrats pick up seats in the next election. But if you choose to go with Kilcannon—at least in my humble opinion—you've got no chance at all."

Listening, Hampton better understood the skill and guile with which Fasano had taken the SSA's incendiary demands, cobbled together a tort reform coalition and, somehow, managed to co-opt Chad Palmer: his proposal encapsulated Hampton's worst fears and fondest hopes, and suggested a path which, in prudence, Hampton could not fault. Except that, in prudence, Hampton need not yet choose.

"You've given me food for thought," he answered. "Now let me give you some. Because if I were you, and Kerry Kilcannon were coming after me, I'd be a whole lot more worried than you pretend to be." Pausing, Hampton adopted his most affable tone. "How vividly I remember the day when Mac Gage, your sainted predecessor, invited me to his office and urged me not to help the President confirm Caroline Masters. With great reluctance, I turned him down. The next thing I knew Masters was Chief Justice and Mac wasn't leader anymore. And here you are, giving me more good reasons not to help the President with this one.

"Kilcannon looks at the same electoral map you do, and sees the same demographics. But he figures that you can't win—at least in the long run—by pandering to fundamentalists and gun nuts, any more than the Catholic Church could hold back Galileo." Hampton summoned an ironic smile. "The President may be grieving. But I also think he's sitting there in the White House, thinking, 'Please, Frank—please don't stop now.

" 'Please stamp out my sister-in-law's right to sue.

" 'Please spit on a six-year-old girl's grave.

" 'Please set me up for the next slaughter on a playground, or in a classroom, or at a day-care center. Please, Frank, do whatever the SSA wants you to.' " Hampton's tone became crisp. "So ask yourself, Frank, which one of you is right.

"But you *have* asked yourself, of course. And you're not sure at all. All you know for sure is that you're stuck with the SSA because they've got your party by the balls."

Throughout this sardonic monologue, Hampton observed, Fasano listened with admirable calm and an expression of mild interest. Only a slight edge in his voice betrayed any tension. "Am I to take it, Chuck, that you're keeping your options open?"

Hampton nodded. "For both our sakes," he answered. "There may come a time when you want me to get you out of this."

TWO

THREE WEEKS LATER, Sarah Dash stood in a cavernous warehouse outside Hartford, Connecticut, watching a team of paralegals comb through reams of paper crammed inside rows of metal filing cabinets.

They would have to read through every document. Sarah was certain that Lexington had provided the documents because their contents were as innocuous as their volume was oppressive. But it was always possible that Lexington had tucked amidst the dross that single, damning memo which would prove Mary's case against it and, perhaps, against the SSA as well. And so, at great expense, this work went on, running down the clock on plaintiff's discovery.

These last three weeks, Sarah acknowledged, had proved to be the nightmare which Lenihan envisioned. John Nolan had deployed an array of tactics to bring plaintiff's discovery to a standstill: producing "document bricks," hundreds of cardboard boxes so crammed with irrelevant papers that the paralegals had been forced to purchase box cutters in order to remove them; scheduling meaningless depositions, which Lenihan's associates were required to attend; serving hundreds of pages of written questions for which still more associates were required to draft responses. All of this, Sarah knew, served two obvious goals: first, to make the suit so costly and so fruitless that Lenihan's firm might prefer to settle than pursue it; second, to assure that the case went nowhere—let alone to trial—before Senator Fasano and Speaker Jencks had passed a law to extinguish it. A third goal was more subtle: to make every day sheer misery for Lenihan and Sarah.

This day, spent in the squalor of an ill-lit warehouse, was Nolan's ultimate revenge.

Sarah's trip had been prefigured five days earlier, in a discovery hearing before Judge Gardner Bond.

Solemnly, Bond read aloud from the first report by the Special Discovery Master, Professor Ian Blaisdell of the Stanford Law School: " 'The Special Master,' " Bond intoned, " 'has reviewed documents produced by Lexington and the SSA regarding their communications with each other, and with other manufacturers.

" 'At this time, there are no documents which suggest that the SSA conspired to keep Lexington from reaching an agreement with the Kilcannon administration; that the SSA exercised control over Lexington or any other manufacturers; or that it played a role in directing Lexington's affairs. Therefore the Special Master has not provided plaintiff's counsel with any of the documents reviewed.' "

Robert Lenihan stood. "Our problem, Your Honor, is not with the Special Master. But defense counsel are the sole arbiters of what documents he sees."

Bond stiffened. "Are you suggesting that Mr. Nolan *or* Mr. Fancher are acting in bad faith?"

"What I'm suggesting," Lenihan answered, "is a systematic effort to bring this case to a grinding halt."

Swiftly, Sarah glanced at the benches, filled with reporters; with discovery sealed, Lenihan's only chance to score points in the media was to document defense obstruction. "Our motion to compel," Lenihan continued, "is a litany of abuses: delaying production; forcing us to depose witnesses without the relevant documents; scheduling irrelevant depositions to consume our time;

continuing to insist that Mr. *Callister's* time is more valuable than that of the President and First Lady . . ."

"Your Honor," Nolan interposed in his most conciliatory manner, "might I make a proposal?

"If it would help dampen this controversy, we would be happy to give plaintiff's counsel direct access to all our files, without the delay caused by our current practice of culling and copying them for counsels' inspection. In short, we'll simply open up our records."

With an indignation born of deep frustration, Lenihan retorted, "That's even more fraudulent than what they're doing now. They'll drown us in garbage, with no conceivable relationship to our case . . ."

"You and Ms. Dash," Bond snapped, "were the ones in such a hurry. It was you who asked for an injunction. It was you who expanded the case to include the esoteric antitrust and public nuisance theories. It was you who served massive document demands, imposing massive burdens on the defendants to produce them. And now you're casting aspersions on their manner of production, no matter what it is." Bond lowered his voice. "Nothing they do seems to please you, counsel. It's time for you to live with the choices you made—without complaint."

Which was how Sarah found herself in a warehouse, as another day slipped away from them like sand in an hourglass.

The next morning, she flew to San Francisco to meet with Lenihan.

They settled on lunch at Farallon. Lenihan ate in a cold fury, part of it directed at her insistence on accelerating discovery and naming the SSA. She could not blame him. Nolan's form of Chinese water torture, obstructing discovery while consuming the resources of Lenihan's firm, was driving them further apart.

"It's not over," Sarah said at last.

In obvious disgust, Lenihan put down his fork. "That's what I'm afraid of. You don't have to be a prophet to see that we'll never get to trial before they pass that fucking law. And even if they don't pass it, we'll never get the evidence we need to prove our case." With an accusatory stare, he finished in a tone as acidic as Judge Bond's, "Assuming, as to *your* case, that the evidence exists."

Unflinching, Sarah took her time to answer. "You've made your point, Bob. A hundred times. And the only winner is John Nolan.

"We can sit here and whine. Or we can suck it up, and try to figure out how to get what we need . . ."

"What we need," Lenihan retorted, "is a fucking miracle. Or, at the least, a whistleblower. Someone inside Lexington or the SSA who despises what they're doing."

Sarah nodded. "That's why I asked them for a list of former employees—I was hoping to find a malcontent, or someone who left in a dispute. You already know what happened: Nolan and Fancher refused to comply, and Bond refused to make them."

Lenihan stared at the remnants of his seared ahi tuna. "Fuck Bond," he said at length. "We'll set up a web site asking for information about Lexington and the SSA, and publicize it in Washington and Hartford. To find ex-employees, we'll hire an investigator.

"The formal discovery process is all that Bond controls. Anything we get outside it, we can feed to the press."

Sarah pondered this. "If anything's traced back to us," she cautioned, "Bond will take it out on us."

"As long as we didn't violate his order, how could things be worse?" Lenihan's jaw set. "We need a mole, and we need publicity. Simple as that."

Sarah toyed with her soup spoon. "Look at Bresler, though. It's hard to imagine what the SSA would do to an employee who betrayed it. Or even what Lexington would do."

Lenihan gave a somewhat melancholy smile. "How many times," he observed, "have I seen a whistleblower who thinks he understands the risks.

"They never do. They never imagine how bad it will be— divorce, bankruptcy, all the friends who turn their backs on them, the ruin of a whole career. The last whistleblower *I* had killed himself in the driveway of his ex-wife's home."

And yet, Sarah thought, Lenihan was prepared to ferret out another one. With a shrug, he finished, "But what can we do? By tomorrow, we'll have our invitation on the net."

THREE

ON THE SAME DAY, also for the third consecutive week, Senator Chuck Hampton took the floor of the Senate during morning business, and eulogized a victim of gun violence who had died in the week before.

He had begun this ritual on the morning after his meeting with Frank Fasano. Hampton's calculus was simple—the best way to corner the Republicans, including on gun immunity, was to remind the press and public that Fasano had not yet scheduled a vote on the President's gun bill. And his choice of victims from Lara Kilcannon's web site was artful: invariably they were mothers, fathers, or children; in each case the murderer—as with John Bowden—had acquired the gun without a background check; each murderer, because of a criminal conviction or record of domestic violence, would have failed the universal background check required by the President's bill. At the end of his statement, Hampton totalled the number of people killed with guns since the moment Lara's family was murdered. On this morning, after fifty-one days, the toll of death stood at four thousand one hundred and twenty nine—personified by a four-year-old boy killed by his abusive father in a murder-suicide which had also claimed his mother and two sisters.

"If the President's bill were law," Hampton concluded, "Scotty Morris would be dressing for preschool as we speak. How, I would ask, can any of us even look his *picture* in the eye?"

With that, Hampton yielded the floor, glancing at Frank

Fasano. As in the last three weeks, the Majority Leader was impassive in the face of Hampton's daily torment. For the moment, Fasano had little choice: Hampton had stalled the Civil Justice Reform Act by threatening to introduce poison pill amendments—deleting the gun immunity provision, or adding the entirety of Kilcannon's gun bill—which a handful of moderate Republicans like Cassie Rollins, fearing the effects of the First Lady's tour and her confrontation with the Commerce Committee, had no current appetite to vote on. But centrist Democrats, as Hampton well understood, were similarly beset—some fearful of the SSA; others sympathetic to tort reform; still others waiting to gauge the longer-term effects of the Costello murders on the public temper. And so, beneath the surface, a core group of senators waited and watched, as did Fasano, waiting for his moment, and Hampton, watching Fasano.

By tomorrow, Hampton knew, another eighty or so Americans would have died.

"My people need cover," Fasano told Charles Dane that afternoon. "Especially the moderates. As I've been telling you for weeks."

Once more they met in Kelsey Landon's office. A benign and calming presence, Landon sat in an antique wing chair, Dane and Fasano in matching chairs of polished mahogany. "Whatever you propose," Dane answered, "should be consistent with our message—that the problem isn't guns, it's the violence and permissiveness in our popular culture."

"Scotty Morris," Fasano countered sardonically, "wasn't murdered with a VCR. I don't know about *your* culture, Charles. But in *mine* Chuck Hampton's scoring points."

"So take the moral offensive, for Godsakes. Even Lara

Kilcannon admits that our movies, TV and pop music are rotten to the core. You should treat yourself to a few gangster rap lyrics about beating women and killing cops . . ."

"I despise that trash," Fasano cut in. "Bernadette and I won't let our kids get near it. So now that we agree on *that*, let's talk about the U.S. Senate."

Brightly, Landon interjected, "I believe that Charles has a proposal, Frank."

"A law," Dane said promptly. "Establishing a commission to study the effect of violence on American youth; requiring V-chips in all TVs so parents can control what children are watching; and setting up a rating system for TV programs, compact discs, music videos, and movie rentals for children below eighteen. How can our society glamorize violence, Frank—even use it to thrill our young people until it's second nature—and then blame America's gun companies for the sickness in our society?"

At this, Fasano began to laugh. "Maybe because some of the gun companies market their own videos showing kids how to use their guns." Turning to Landon, he said, "Skip the fact that this is eyewash, Kelsey. Tell Charles about the entertainment and communications lobby, and why the Senate's collective piety will never be enacted into law."

As well-paid go-between, Landon was too discreet to share Fasano's amusement. "What is it you need, Frank?"

"Something—at a minimum—that addresses the so-called gun-show loophole."

For a brief moment, Dane seemed to reflect. "Then let me suggest this," he answered, and Fasano knew at once that his opening proposal was a ploy.

" 'Gun show,' " Dane continued, "is an elastic term. We can redefine it to exclude outdoors shows, hunting and fishing shows, and other shows where guns just happen to be sold . . ."

"A loophole within a loophole," Fasano interjected dryly.

Impervious, Dane went on. "Gun shows occur on a weekend. Applying a seventy-two-hour background check would unfairly impede their business. Instead, we'll require that any background check at gun shows be completed within minutes . . ."

"That's impossible," Fasano interrupted. "We don't have the database, or the technology. But I suppose that's the point."

Dane chose not to answer. "*Our* bill," he continued, "would only become applicable to gun shows when ninety-nine percent of all records regarding felonies, violent misdemeanors, and domestic violence are entered into the system."

Fasano glanced at Landon, who listened without expression, and then back at Dane. "You recall Kilcannon's speech, I suppose. He pointed out that the records are nowhere near that, and proposed to allocate millions to fixing it. How much do you propose to allocate?"

"Zero," Dane answered calmly. "That's for the states to fund."

Fasano paused, reining in his irritation. "In the Senate," he observed, "we hold cynicism to a certain standard. In its higher forms it's not quite so transparent."

Dane folded his arms. "Your moderates and Yankees can vote for this, and not be punished. We'll even help you by objecting to it. If your goal is to help us, and keep your Cassie Rollinses in line, that should be enough for you."

"What's enough for me," Fasano snapped, "is something more than transcendent bullshit.

"Give me your proposal, Charles. And I'll tell our staffers to add some things you actually don't like, such as some money to fund this instant background check of guns. Then you can oppose it with more sincerity."

"If you pass it," Dane objected, "it could look like we're losing power."

Turning to Landon, Fasano said in his weariest tone, "I imagine, Kelsey, that *you've* followed my train of thought."

"I believe so," Landon answered, and then faced Dane again. "You want Frank to push through tort reform, immunizing Lexington *and* you, while he stalls Kilcannon's gun bill until public sentiment cools off. What Frank's saying to *you*, Charles, is that Kilcannon and Hampton are making that more difficult. So he needs another element . . ."

"Specifically," Fasano interjected, "a gun safety law of our own. Something plausible enough for our moderates to vote for, but which doesn't give Kilcannon anything close to what he wants.

"If we come up with a suitable bill, I'll schedule it ahead of the vote on tort reform. That will give our moderates some real cover, and make gun immunity an easier vote. And once Kilcannon vetoes it, we can claim he's an extremist."

To Fasano, Dane looked both dubious and intrigued. "And if he doesn't?"

"He will," Fasano answered. "I know the man, and I'll make sure he does."

FOUR

TRAPPED IN A conference room on the twenty-seventh floor of Embarcadero Three, one of five floors inhabited by her former firm, Sarah watched John Nolan interrogate Homicide Inspector Charles Monk.

To Sarah, the deposition process was familiar: a court reporter swore in the witness and then, sitting at the end of the conference table, recorded the questions and answers on a stenotype machine, providing a transcript which could be used for cross-examination of the witness at trial. But even more important, a deposition nailed down the witness to a story. Sarah had seen cases won or lost in a single deposition and, plainly, that was Nolan's purpose here.

He had chosen—quite deliberately, Sarah knew—to sit with his back to the distractions offered Monk and Sarah through the tall glass windows of the conference room: a sweeping panorama of the San Francisco Bay on a sparkling day in late October, complete with a view of Alcatraz, a small flotilla of sailboats, and, at the moment, a Maersk freighter cruising slowly toward the Oakland harbor. But Sarah's focus was on Nolan. His deceptive air of calm could seduce a witness into carelessness, and his questions were unconstrained by the rules of evidence—hearsay, for example—which applied at trial. In a deposition there was no judge; only the witness's lawyer—if present—could direct him not to answer a question. Without judicial supervision, the rules were roughly those of a knife fight—

anything goes. In such a forum John Nolan was particularly lethal.

This witness had no lawyer. A black man of intimidating height and bulk, Monk leaned over the table with his hands folded in front of him, his face impassive and, to Sarah, unimpressed. She had only a sketchy notion of what he might say: in San Francisco a homicide inspector was a busy man, and Monk had been too overworked to talk to Sarah and, she could only hope, to Nolan. In silence, she watched as Nolan began boring in.

"Did the President," he asked, "ever request police protection for Joan Bowden or her family?"

Briefly, Monk searched his memory. "Not to my knowledge, no."

"What is your impression of the private security firm that the President selected to protect them?"

" 'Impression,' " Sarah echoed. "As to what? Their table manners?"

Nolan did not condescend to look at her. "What is your impression," Nolan asked Monk, "of the firm's ability to adequately protect Joan Bowden from harm?"

"Objection," Sarah said. "Lack of foundation. There's nothing in the record to suggest that the witness has a basis in knowledge for answering the question."

Still Nolan did not turn to her. Calmly, he told the witness, "You may answer."

Monk gave a lazy shrug. "Rent-a-cops are all over the map. From my investigation of the background of the two men killed at the airport, they had no experience in law enforcement or the military. Just the kind of perfunctory training they need to get a license."

"Would *you* have entrusted your family to these two men?"

"Me?" Monk answered with a flicker of irony. "I'd have

done the job myself. But then the President doesn't have that luxury, does he."

Nolan's face, an expressionless mask, betrayed no irritation. "Would you have selected these two men to protect your wife and children?"

Monk frowned, plainly reluctant to answer. "No," he said at length. "I would not have."

For the first time, the hint of a smile appeared in Nolan's eyes. "In the course of your inquiry into the murders, Inspector Monk, did you inquire into Bowden's background?"

"To some extent. Understand, we knew he was the murderer, and he was way too dead to prosecute. So our principal worry was ensuring that he didn't have accomplices. We found no evidence of that."

"Did you determine motive?"

"We couldn't interview him, obviously." Pausing, Monk added with some reluctance, "The President did provide us with a letter."

Nolan reached into a manila folder, and withdrew a copy of a page torn from a spiral notebook. Even at a distance, a glimpse of Bowden's jagged scrawl made Sarah's skin crawl.

In the same phlegmatic voice, Nolan told the court reporter, "I have a one-page document, which I wish you to mark as 'Lexington Exhibit Three,' " and then slid copies across the marble conference table to Sarah and Fancher's associate. Though she had read the text before, Sarah found herself transfixed.

"Is this a copy of that letter?" Nolan inquired of Monk. "Yes."

"And did you determine that Mr. Bowden's motive for the killings was his hatred of the President and First Lady and, specifically, their exposure of him as a spousal abuser on national television?"

Sarah looked up. "Objection," she said at once. "The letter speaks for itself, and Inspector Monk never spoke to Mr. Bowden."

"That's correct," Monk said promptly, and placed one large finger on the letter. "All I know is what's in here. To our knowledge, Bowden never told anyone what he was planning, or why."

"But you're not aware of any other motive."

" 'Other'?" Sarah inquired with mild derision, "than that his wife left him, kept him from seeing his child, and twice brought charges relating to spousal abuse? Or do you mean other than that Bowden had an obvious propensity for violence?"

For the first time, Nolan faced her. In a tone of cold politeness, he said, "In your inexperience, Ms. Dash, you may have overlooked that what you just favored us with was a speech, not an objection—the effect of which was to coach the witness. It's my prerogative to ask the question I wish to ask."

This was a test, Sarah knew, Nolan's initial effort at intimidation. But it also told her that she had succeeded in angering him, and in disrupting the rhythm he had hoped to establish with Monk. "I apologize," she answered with a smile. "In my inexperience, I expected your questions to make sense."

Nolan stared at her across the table. Stirring with apparent impatience, Monk told him, "I don't know *why* the man did what he did. But there's a lot of reasons he could have."

Silent, Nolan gazed down at the outline of his examination—to mask his irritation, Sarah suspected. She found it a pleasant moment.

At length, Nolan looked up. "In your investigation," he asked, "did you determine whether Bowden had any connection to Lexington Arms?"

" 'Determine'?" Sarah inquired. "Or even *attempt* to determine?"

This time Nolan ignored her. In a chill voice, he instructed the witness, "You may answer."

"That wasn't something we focused on," Monk responded.

Sarah suppressed a smile. "Did you find a connection?" Nolan persisted.

"No."

"Was Lexington involved, in any way, in the sale of the P-2 to Mr. Nolan?"

" 'In any way'?" Sarah repeated in a quizzical tone. "They *made* the gun. They *advertised* the gun. I don't understand the question."

"I *could* try to explain it," Nolan retorted caustically. "But only God can grant understanding." To Monk, he said in a testy tone, "You can answer the question, Inspector. Without reference, if possible, to Ms. Dash's repeated intercessions."

"If what you mean," Monk answered, "is did Lexington sell the gun to Bowden, I don't know *who* sold it to him."

Sarah's sense of satisfaction vanished. Monk's amendment went to the heart of the problem with Mary's case, as Nolan would be quick to see. Leaning back, Nolan placed one finger to his lips. "Is it correct, Inspector Monk, that Mr. Bowden took a round-trip to Las Vegas and back one day before the murders?"

"It is."

"What, if you know, was the purpose of his trip?"

Monk glanced at Sarah—a hint, she believed, as to where his sympathies lay. Carefully, he answered, "We believe to attend a gun show."

"On what do you base that belief?"

"Several things." Briefly, Monk stopped to organize his thoughts. "First, before he left for Las Vegas, police had searched his house in response to his wife's complaint, and found no guns. Second, there was a gun show in Las Vegas at which P-2s were sold. Third, among his personal effects was a copy of the SSA *Defender* magazine, with an advertisement for the P-2 next to one for the gun show."

"Do you have any *other* basis," Nolan persisted, "for assuming that the purpose of Bowden's trip was to attend a gun show?"

Awaiting the answer, Sarah tensed. Monk hesitated, and then said flatly, "No."

"Do you have any information, Inspector, as to Mr. Bowden's movements in Las Vegas?"

"We do not."

Almost imperceptibly, Nolan leaned forward, closing the distance between lawyer and witness. "Did you discover any evidence that, in fact, Mr. Bowden attended the show?"

"We did not."

"What efforts, if any, did you make to determine whether he was there?"

Monk pondered his answer. "They were limited, I'd have to say. One problem is that gun shows don't seem to keep records of who attends, and a lot of guns are bought for cash. The point seems to be to conceal the identity of anyone who doesn't want to purchase a weapon through a licensed dealer."

Exactly, Sarah thought. But the reason Bowden had gone to the show—as he so obviously had—was the reason that this would be difficult to prove under the rigorous evidentiary standards of a trial. And if she and Lenihan could not prove it, their case was at an end—as Nolan, his air of calm restored, well knew. "Did you," Nolan asked, "inquire of anyone connected with the gun show?"

Monk nodded. "The promoter, and the employees who actually collected money from the people going in. We showed them a picture of Bowden, and asked if they'd seen him. Nobody remembered."

Or wanted to remember, Sarah was certain. The last thing the promoter needed was John Bowden as a customer. "Our focus," Monk added, "wasn't on the gun show, but whether Bowden had acted alone. So we didn't take it any further, and I'm not even sure we'd have known where to start. There were thousands of people at the show, and hundreds of sellers—most of them unlicensed."

With this, Monk had encapsulated plaintiff's dilemma. That Lexington claimed—to Sarah's utter disbelief—to have had no record of where they had originally shipped the murder weapon made this even worse; the journey of the P-2 into Bowden's hands was, from beginning to end, a mystery. "In short," Nolan said, "Bowden could have bought the gun on the street, in California."

Monk shrugged. "We can't rule that out."

"Or even through a dealer who decided not to run a background check."

Sitting straighter, Monk stared at him, as though Nolan had pushed him a little too far. "The P-2," he answered, "is banned in California. So you're talking about a licensed dealer breaking at least two laws.

"I can't cite statistics, Mr. Nolan. But I can tell you that a fair number of P-2s are used in homicides in San Francisco—drug dealers seem to like them. And the point of origin for most of them are sales in Arizona or Nevada."

Silently, Sarah gave Monk a word of thanks. Nolan sat back, stung. "But you don't have figures, you say. So your 'evidence' for that last statement is anecdotal."

"Yes."

"Have you ever discussed that 'evidence' with anyone from Lexington?"

"No."

"So as far as you know, even if there *is* a problem, Lexington's unaware of it."

Monk paused, choosing his words with care. "Mr. Nolan," he answered, "they *claim* to have lost the record of who they shipped the gun to. I don't know *what* those people know, or if they care. Do you?"

"Know?" Sarah inquired with a smile. "Or care?"

Briefly, Nolan turned to her. *"Très amusant,"* he murmured with disdain, and then fixed his stare on Monk. "In sum, Inspector, you can't tell me how this murderer got *this* gun."

"No."

"Yet in plaintiff's complaint, counsel asserts that the two ads you mentioned *caused* Mr. Bowden to buy the gun. Given that you can't tell where he got the gun, or from whom, are you aware of any facts which support that allegation?"

"As I said, we found the SSA publication among his effects, and he went to Las Vegas. There's nothing to tell us that he had any other reason than buying the P-2."

"Really?" Nolan paused with raised eyebrows. "Did you check out any of the casinos?"

"No."

"Then let's stick to the facts at hand. You mention *The Defender* magazine. Did you find other gun-related magazines in Bowden's room?"

"Yes."

"How many?"

Monk paused to consider this. "Maybe twenty. I didn't count them."

"Did any advertise this gun show in Las Vegas?"

"One did, I recall. It had a listing of gun shows in September."

"All right," Nolan said in a more comfortable tone.

"You mentioned *The Defender* magazine. Was Bowden a subscriber?"

"No."

"Or a member of the SSA?"

"No."

"Do you know where he got the magazine?"

"No."

"Do you, in fact, even know whether he read it?"

Monk stared at him across the table. "Only by inference. The advertisements as much as said that the P-2 is good for killing people, and that's what Bowden did. That gun sure isn't good for anything else."

"Do you," Nolan repeated tightly, "know whether or not John Bowden read *The Defender* magazine you found?"

Monk gazed at Nolan with a dispassion which somehow conveyed dislike. "No," he answered softly. "Not for a fact."

"So you don't know—because you *can't* know—whether he saw that ad."

Monk sat back. "Under the rules of common sense, Mr. Nolan, I *do* know. Like *you* know. Just not under the rules of evidence."

Silent, Nolan considered him, and then, smiling faintly, turned to Sarah. "Your witness, Ms. Dash. I think that's all I need."

FIVE

WHEN KERRY had first fallen in love with Lara Costello, there were moments when he had felt consumed by the wonder of being with her—her quick grin, the way she turned her head to look at him, and, a rarity in his life, the sense of understanding and of being understood, of being seen for who he was. After a time, there was no thought he feared to express, no emotion he feared to share with her. Seeing her after several days spent apart, he would feel a fresh jolt of excitement, and then the gentler, deeper sensation of being whole. Kerry had been a lonely boy, who gave his trust to few; his trust, once given, was deep, his loyalty complete. But the harsh world of politics had reinforced his instinct that trust, like love, could be painful and fraught with risk. So that Lara became at once a refuge and so central to his life that it began to scare him.

He had been married then, to Meg. That had cost him a child with Lara. Then two years followed without seeing her, during which he used his uphill, insurgent race for the Presidency as an antidote, until it had consumed him. When Lara at last returned, Kerry, since divorced, discovered that he wanted two things equally—the Presidency, and a life with her.

Now he had them both, and Lara and he had paid an incalculable price. Often he wished that he could return to the days before the abortion; he would divorce Meg and marry Lara, so that they could live their life as a family, never feeling as they both did now. Then he would have seen her once-familiar smile of amusement—clean and white and sharp—instead of the sorrow he now read in her eyes, a reminder of her constant grief, the obligation she felt to Kerry's drive against gun violence, the only fit memorial they could offer.

One night Kerry told her all of that.

He had not planned to. She had been in their bathroom, brushing her hair before bed. Kerry had been preoccupied. Still in jeans and a sweater, he had stretched out on the bedroom couch, contemplating the complex calculus of the Senate, the thorny and uniquely vicious politics of guns. And then he looked up, and saw her reflection in the mirror.

The change he felt was surprising, almost chemical. For a time, he simply watched the graceful curve of her neck, the dark eyes, filled with thought, indifferent to her image in the glass. Then he went to her.

When his face appeared behind hers, she looked surprised, and then her reflection smiled faintly at the sight of his. When he kissed her neck, she leaned back against him.

"What is it?" she asked.

He told her.

Her eyes in the mirror were soft, intent. Only after he was done did she turn to him, resting her forehead against his chin. "I know," she murmured. "But that's not how it is for us."

Kerry held her. And then he felt her hands slip beneath his sweater to trace the line of his back. As she arched back, looking up at him, he untied the sash at her waist. With a whisper, her silk robe slipped to the floor.

"Yes," she said softly. "Yes."

Afterward they lay awake in the dark, the fingers of one hand curled in the other's, and talked about the past—not with regret, but remembering the signs, trivial and deep, that they were falling in love without yet being lovers. "When something happened," she recalled, "good or bad, you were the person I wanted to call. Or an issue would pop up, and I wanted to know what you thought.

"It was ridiculous, of course. You were married, a senator, perhaps even a future President. I was the highly objective professional who viewed you with the utmost skepticism. And suddenly I stopped." Her voice filled with remembered warmth. "It was a rotten trick, transforming yourself from a subject into a person."

"No choice," he said casually. "It was the only way I had of sleeping with you."

"Really? When did you start flattering yourself that *that* would happen?"

"About a minute before it did." His tone was serious now. "I never felt entitled, just lucky. I still do."

"Looking back, Kerry, you were inevitable. The night it happened, from the moment I kissed you, I wanted you so much I couldn't think straight." Pausing, she added quietly, "Sometimes I felt like we were the same person. What you needed from me, I did from you."

Kerry hesitated. "And now?"

"I still do." Her voice was quieter yet. "More than ever."

His fingers tightened around hers. For several minutes they were silent.

"Lying on the couch," she inquired, "what were you thinking? You were so still that it was like you were somewhere else."

"You were *watching* me?"

"Oh, I do that sometimes. Typically when you're too preoccupied to notice. Which describes a fair chunk of your day."

"Have I become that bad?"

"You were always like that—here, and then gone. I never minded." Another moment passed. "So what was it?"

"Other than you?"

"Yes."

Carefully, he explained his calculation.

After he finished, she was silent for some time. But in the relaxation of her grasp, Kerry could feel her keen political mind focusing wholly on his problem. "The key," she finally said, "is Lenihan. Handle *him* and the SSA's in trouble."

The next morning Kerry took Air Force One to Chicago for a speech on stem cell research and therapeutic cloning. The subject was delicate. In tone and content, his message—that "respect for life requires using medicine to save the living"—would further inflame the religious right and its allies in the House and Senate. But, in conscience, Kerry felt he had no choice. To him, the plight of those afflicted with Alzheimer's, Parkinson's, paralysis and the like far outweighed the presumptive plight of a frozen embryo already slated for destruction. Carefully, he read and reread his speech, changing words and phrases. Satisfied, he put it aside, gazing out the window.

Below, the woods and fields of Ohio, Chad Palmer's state, were burnished with the last colors of late fall, its farms and villages dots on the tinted landscape. As he often did, Kerry found himself imagining the lives represented by the dots. Never more than in Air Force One, crossing the American continent, did he feel the depth of his responsibility for the country he loved, the people he was sworn to serve. He brooded on this awhile longer, and then called Robert Lenihan.

"The House will pass tort reform this week," he told Lenihan. "In the Senate there's still a logjam, mostly over gun immunity. But it could break any day—if it breaks against us, it might pass fairly quickly."

"It never has before," Lenihan answered.

His tone was weary but resistant, that of someone too preoccupied to accept bad news and, perhaps, resentful of Lara's—and, inferentially the President's—intercession with Mary on behalf of Sarah Dash. "This year's different," Kerry said. "Fasano's managed to unite the SSA and the business interests. We need to re-divide them."

"What do you suggest?"

Steeling himself for a burst of outrage, Kerry answered calmly, "That we offer the business interests a watered-down version of tort reform . . ."

"*Any* tort reform," Lenihan said with indignation, "is a sellout to the big boys. What in hell do Democrats stand for if not for the average American?"

"That's not a lecture I need, Bob. But, in *this* case, I plan on making Frank Fasano the 'average American's' new best friend."

"How is that?"

"Because I'm putting him to a choice between the business interests and the SSA. And I already know which one he'll choose." The President's voice was no less commanding for its softness. "I won't let you be my SSA. That's the difference between me and Frank Fasano."

"Lenihan signed on?" Chuck Hampton asked the President.

Even in the motorcade shrieking toward the Blackstone, Kerry could hear the astonishment in Hampton's voice. Dryly, he answered, "With some reluctance."

"I can imagine. Did you tell him what you have in mind?"

"Most of it, including that your Democratic colleagues could use some cover on tort reform. But not quite all."

Pensive, Kerry gazed out the tinted window at the streets of Chicago. "Unless I've misjudged both Fasano and Charles Dane, it won't matter. All I really need is to put the business coalition in motion."

It was the first time since Kerry's election that Tony Calvo of the Chamber of Commerce had been invited to the White House. That he found himself in the Oval Office, meeting privately with the President, seemed to deepen his astonishment.

Slowly, Calvo repeated, "You're proposing, Mr. President, to limit contingency fees for plaintiffs' lawyers. And to cap punitive damages."

The President smiled. "I hope I haven't upset you," he said wryly. "All these years, when you were complaining about punitives and greedy trial lawyers, I thought you really meant it. This is your chance." Abruptly, the President's voice became cool. "The bill Fasano's pushing is a wish list—I'd have to veto it even if it *weren't* a Trojan horse for gun companies. Your last, best hope to pass anything is to work with me, or wait three years for the voters to run me out of office. And seven if they don't."

Calvo gazed past him out the window, as though imagining the futility stretching before him. "The trial lawyers have actually signed off on this?"

"Yes. Specifically, Bob Lenihan and his group. All I need is you, Tony, and we can pass it."

Soberly, Calvo faced him. "I assume that there's a price."

"Only one," Kerry answered succinctly. "I'm replacing the gun immunity provision in the current bill with language providing that *none* of its protections apply to lawsuits involving guns. I'll expect you to support that."

Dismay crept into Calvo's eyes. "There's the SSA, Mr. President."

Kerry shrugged. "The SSA got greedy, and piggybacked on your bill. That's intolerable to me."

Somber, Calvo weighed his choices. At length, he responded. "I can't give you an answer on my own. Not about this."

"Of course not. So talk to your allies. And then go to Frank Fasano." Kerry's voice softened. "Ask Fasano if he wants to do something for *you*, or just wants chits with the SSA. I hope you don't find out that I'm your only friend in town."

SIX

In the SSA's main conference room, replete with a wall display of historic handguns and rifles, Sarah Dash interrogated Charles Dane across a lacquered table.

Hawk-faced, Harrison Fancher sat next to Dane, tautly vigilant to any traps concealed in Sarah's questions. Her strategy, as risky as her task was delicate, rested on a single fact: in one week, plaintiff would have to list its prospective witnesses at trial—among them Martin Bresler. By deposing Dane before this deadline—despite the absence of a concrete foundation for her cross-examination—she hoped to lure him into sworn testimony which Bresler would then refute. This would have two virtues: discrediting Dane as a witness—including with respect to his dealings with Callister—and, thereby, buttressing Sarah's claim that deposing Callister was essential. But this required a considerable deftness; her questions must be pointed, yet general enough to conceal Bresler's cooperation. Ten minutes into the deposition, Sarah remained on edge.

At the far end of the table sat John Nolan, relegated to the role of onlooker; at the other was a natty court reporter in horn-rimmed glasses and bow tie. Glancing at the copy of *The Defender* magazine which Sarah slid across the table, Dane answered her pending question in a tone of boredom, "Of course I've seen this, Ms. Dash. Including the advertisements."

"Did anyone from the SSA review these ads for content?"

Tall and lean, Dane conveyed an impression of ease and power, and his expression combined indifference with the contempt of an important man inconvenienced by a lower species. "I wouldn't know."

"What is *your* understanding, Mr. Dane, as to *The Defender*'s obligation to review the contents of advertisements such as these?"

"I have no understanding."

Sarah kept her face expressionless, her manner unruffled. "In your view, is an advertisement calling the P-2 'lethal in split seconds' acceptable?"

"Yes."

"Or one which calls it the 'deadliest military-style weapon on the market'?"

For the first time, Dane seemed amused. "Are you saying that's not true?"

"Are *you* saying that the SSA's sole obligation was to determine whether Lexington's description of the P-2's killing capacity is accurate?"

"We *had* no obligation." Dane's tone resumed its tightly reined impatience. "Not unless we knew for a fact that this language was deceptive."

Sarah pointed at the magazine. "So claiming that the Eagle's Claw 'opens a massive wound channel' is also fine with you."

Dane shrugged. "As far as I know, the Eagle's Claw 'opens a massive wound channel.' If it doesn't, then Lexington's to blame."

To Sarah's annoyance, Nolan smiled faintly. "What," Sarah asked, "is your magazine's obligation with respect to Lexington's statement that the gun is an 'endangered species,' 'banned in California'?"

A smile appeared at one corner of Dane's mouth. "It's true, isn't it?"

"So an ad inducing Bowden to come to Nevada, in

order to buy a gun banned in California, is acceptable to the SSA's *Defender*?"

"Ms. Dash," Dane responded with a hint of righteous anger, "selling the P-2 in Nevada is protected by federal law. You're suggesting that we should assist you in your goal of disarming America . . ."

"I'm just trying to determine your standards—if any. Are you saying that Lexington's description of the killing capacity of the P-2 and Eagle's Claw creates no duty unless the SSA considered it *less* deadly?"

"Without the sarcasm—yes." Dane leaned forward. "The information in this ad is protected by the First Amendment. Americans have the right to know it. Just as they have the Second Amendment right to buy *this* gun and *these* bullets . . ."

"Prior to the murders," Sarah said abruptly, "did you ever discuss with George Callister whether Lexington would continue to sell the P-2 and Eagle's Claw?"

Seemingly surprised, Dane hesitated. "Objection," Fancher said sharply. "Your question is outside the scope of your own complaint."

Sarah kept looking at Dane. "In a deposition," she answered, "a question need only be 'reasonably calculated to lead to the discovery of admissible evidence.' If the SSA influenced whether—or under what conditions—Lexington would continue selling these deadly products, that goes to the heart of our claim . . ."

Fancher grasped Dane's wrist. "I'm directing the witness not to answer," he snapped. "You can take your fishing expedition to Judge Bond, and find out if *he* thinks it relevant."

Sarah turned to Dane. "Did you," she persisted, "ever discuss with Mr. Callister whether he would enter into an agreement with President Kilcannon regarding sales at gun shows?"

"Same instruction," Fancher said in a monotone. "The right of political association is granted by the First Amendment. We don't have to reveal our discussions regarding gun rights."

This assertion, Sarah knew, was thin—except, perhaps, in the courtroom of Judge Gardner Bond. And, without a judge, no one present could force Dane to answer now. Facing Nolan, Sarah said politely, "It seems that *you* have an interest here, John. Are you willing to let Mr. Callister answer the questions Mr. Dane declines to answer?"

Surprised, Nolan glanced at Fancher. "We are not."

"And so both of you are withholding any and all testimony regarding whether Mr. Dane and Mr. Callister discussed the President's proposal?"

With plain annoyance, Nolan answered, "The record speaks for itself."

"Just checking." To Dane, she said, "Let's see how far this goes. Did you threaten Mr. Callister with a boycott if Lexington cooperated with the President?"

"Boycotts are legal," Dane answered smoothly. "If our members are displeased with a company or its products, it's their privilege to buy elsewhere. We don't have to threaten anyone."

Sarah cocked her head toward Nolan. "Mind if we check *that* out with Callister?"

Nolan scowled. "You already know our position."

Sarah turned to Dane. "Did you discuss with any other gun manufacturer the prospect that a boycott might put Lexington out of business?"

"We refuse to answer," Fancher interjected. "Your question implicates perfectly legal conversations protected by the First Amendment."

"Then let's try this," Sarah said to Dane. "Did you discuss with other manufacturers whether they might profit from a boycott of Lexington Arms?"

"Same instructions," Fancher snapped. "There's nothing illegal about discussing what might happen within an industry."

Smiling, Sarah turned to Nolan. "Surely *Lexington* must want an answer? Under *my* theory, you've got a lawsuit against the SSA."

Nolan's own smile failed to neutralize the hardness of his eyes. "Thank you for your advice, Sarah. Which our firm no longer has to pay you for."

"Speaking of which," she inquired mildly, "who's paying *your* fees in this matter—Lexington or the SSA?"

Nolan stared at her with genuine anger. "That question is wholly out of bounds."

"But understandable. Because it's been so hard to tell." Sarah propped her chin on the cupped palm of her hand. "Mind if I ask *that* of Mr. Callister?"

The record she was making—the multiple reasons for Bond to order Callister deposed—seemed to give Nolan pause. Tonelessly, he said, "Waste the Court's time, if you like. But let's stop wasting Mr. Dane's time."

"He's been so quiet," Sarah answered, "that I hardly think we're wearing him out." Abruptly she demanded of Dane, "Did you discuss with other manufacturers the prospect of dividing up Lexington's market share in the event of an SSA boycott?"

Once more, Dane glanced at Fancher, and then answered as though carefully reciting prepackaged lines. "If you mean did I recommend—or attempt to compel—such an agreement, the answer is 'no.' "

At once, Sarah was certain that there had been such conversations. But whether she had the time to pursue this depended, in great measure, on whether the President—or Senator Fasano—prevailed on gun immunity. Adjusting her manner, she adopted a tone of indifference. "Am I correct, Mr. Dane, that at some point you became aware that

George Callister had met with President Kilcannon regarding sales at gun shows?"

Dane hesitated. "It was in the newspapers."

"Is that the *only* source of information you had regarding the meetings?"

Dane shifted slightly in his chair. "No."

"Was *Callister* among your sources?"

"Same instruction," Fancher interrupted. "Press on, Ms. Dash. You've asked the same question nineteen different ways."

She had made her record regarding Callister, Sarah knew. Now it was time to set up Dane for Martin Bresler. "Did the SSA," she asked Dane, "have a view on whether the gun industry—or any of its members—should reach an agreement on gun shows with President Kilcannon?"

"Yes." Dane answered firmly. "We were unalterably opposed."

"Did that opposition predate your awareness of Callister's discussions with the President?"

This seemed to give Dane pause. "I don't recall."

"Then let me try and help. Did you become aware that, prior to his meetings with Mr. Callister, the President was negotiating with a trade association of gun manufacturers headed by a Martin Bresler?"

Dane sat back. "I remember an agreement," he answered, "but that was with respect to safety locks."

"What was the SSA's position on *that*?"

"We were opposed," Dane snapped. "*You* try to fool with one while a rapist is banging down your bedroom door. You may not care, Ms. Dash. But it's our First Amendment right to protect the Second Amendment—the one right which makes all the others possible. Whether it's the right to resist a tyrannical government or an intruder preying on defenseless women."

"Thank you," Sarah said pleasantly. "Did you threaten

Mr. Bresler with the loss of his job should his trigger lock proposal be adopted?"

"To feel 'threatened,'" Dane countered, "Mr. Bresler would have to be very sensitive. How can I threaten a man who doesn't work for me?"

For a split second, she was tempted to question Dane about threatening Senator Fasano, but she resisted; too obviously, it would betray Martin Bresler's cooperation. "Did there come a time," she asked, "that you became aware that Mr. Bresler was discussing *gun shows* with the President?"

Again Dane's hesitance was marked. "I'm not sure," he finally answered. "There came a time when Mr. Bresler ceased to be a factor in gun politics."

"At what point was that?"

"The point when his members decided he was a divisive force, bent on his own self-aggrandizement, and disbanded the group."

"Did *you* discuss disbanding the group with any of its members?"

"Instruct not to answer," Fancher interrupted. "On First Amendment grounds."

"Our motion to compel answers," Sarah rejoined, "will be thicker than the phone book." Of Dane, she asked, "Do you know a man named Jerry Kirk?"

Dane shrugged. "Jerry works for us."

"Directly before that, who employed Mr. Kirk?"

"The Gun Sports Coalition, I believe. Bresler's group."

Sarah sat straighter. "During his employment by the Gun Sports Coalition, did Mr. Kirk tell you that Mr. Bresler was negotiating with the President regarding background checks at gun shows?"

"Ms. Dash," Dane answered wearily, "I have all sorts of discussions with all sorts of people. However much you might wish it, I can't recall them all . . ."

"Let me get this right," Sarah interrupted. "You loathe President Kilcannon. You hate his policies on guns. You're vehemently opposed to background checks at gun shows. But you can't recall whether Kirk told you that the President was discussing background checks with Martin Bresler."

"No, I can't."

"Tell me, Mr. Dane, did *you* consider Mr. Bresler's group a 'divisive' force?"

"Yes. Beyond that, I'd consider *him* a traitor to the Second Amendment."

Sarah smiled. "And yet you offered *Mr. Kirk* a job."

"Yes."

"Before or after Mr. Bresler's group disbanded?"

"What's the relevance of this?" Fancher broke in. "I see none."

Sarah's gaze at Dane did not waver. "You can answer, Mr. Dane."

Fancher clutched Dane's arm. "Not before *you* explain the relevance."

"All right," Sarah answered. "I want to know whether Mr. Dane persuaded Kirk to spy on Martin Bresler in return for the promise of a job." Pausing, Sarah spoke more slowly. "If you want a further explanation, Mr. Fancher, I believe that the SSA controls the American gun industry—including Lexington, a former member of Bresler's trade association group. I believe the SSA blackballed Bresler. I believe the SSA threatened Callister. I believe the SSA seduced and bludgeoned other manufacturers to keep them from following Callister's lead.

"I believe, in short, that Mr. Dane and the SSA are ultimately responsible for the murder of Mary Costello's family." Turning to Dane, Sarah said softly. "As part of the process which led to these three murders, Mr. Dane, I think you engaged Mr. Kirk to help you keep gun companies from freely making their own political and economic decisions—including imposing background checks which might well have prevented a tragedy. So I'm asking the reporter to read back the question, and then I'm asking you to answer it."

At once, Fancher stood, nodding toward Dane. "This is harassment," Fancher said in a tone of outrage. "Mr. Dane's deposition is over. If you want him back, go to the judge."

With that, Fancher and Dane—the latter expressionless—left the room. Turning to Nolan, Sarah said, "I guess that leaves George Callister."

SEVEN

FROM THE START, Frank Fasano had known that the meeting was trouble.

The three other chairs around his office table were occupied by Tony Calvo of the Chamber of Commerce, Mary Bryant of the National Association of Manufacturers and, perhaps more worrisome, John Metrillo of the National Federation of Independent Businesses—the insurance brokers, shoemakers, pizza restaurant owners, and other individually owned enterprises whom the Republicans claimed to represent.

Dark-haired, burly, and intense, Metrillo spoke in a rapid-fire staccato. "We've wanted tort reform for years," he told Fasano. "Now Kilcannon's offering us something real. Until he's gone—whenever *that* is—it may be the best we can do."

There was no point ducking the issue. "Not for the SSA," Fasano answered. "Dane's the one who got this bill up and running in the first place. But for that, Kilcannon wouldn't have offered you what little he has."

Clasping his hands, Metrillo leaned forward, intent on Fasano. "Look, Frank—we'll support gun immunity, which we never have before. You can tell Dane that. It just has to be in a separate bill . . ."

"Which Kilcannon will veto with impunity."

"Not our problem," Metrillo answered with a shrug. "For years our members have been asking if we'll ever accomplish anything. Whatever his motives, the President's offered us a lock . . ."

"More like a poisoned chalice," Fasano answered in mordant tones. "You damned well *know* why he's doing it—to split the business community from the SSA by using you as pawns."

"Spare us, Frank." Metrillo's tone was brusque. "I'm not ashamed of winning, and I don't give a damn how."

Fasano looked to Calvo and Bryant, broadening the dialogue. "Then let's define 'winning.' For me, it's passing a bill that gives you what you really want."

"Over Kilcannon's veto," Calvo countered. "All he needs is thirty-four senators to uphold it, and we get zip . . ."

"Kilcannon," Mary Bryant interrupted, "is delivering the trial lawyers. We want *you* to deliver the SSA."

Though angry, Fasano took his time. "Ever since I reached the Senate," he told them, "your organizations have played both sides. On a national level, the SSA gives only to Republicans. So now I'm supposed to shaft Dane at your convenience."

"Before you 'shaft' him," Metrillo answered, "you might want to *talk* to him. We're hoping he'll see the point of having us as his allies."

Mirthlessly, Fasano laughed. "I'll urge that on him, John. Unfortunately, Charles Dane is steeped in American history. From Benedict Arnold forward."

With a slow, theatrical turn of the head, Charles Dane looked at the grandfather clock in one corner of his office. "At this time yesterday," he told Fasano, "Sarah Dash was trying to nail me to the cross. Now you want me to provide the nails, and the time she needs to use them."

"That's a little melodramatic," Fasano answered with a sardonic smile. "I hope the first Easter after your death won't prove to be too big a disappointment."

Dane studied him coldly. "You weren't there," he answered. "I was. And you're extremely lucky that Dash doesn't know to ask about you and Marty Bresler. Unless, that is, she was sandbagging me."

This sobered Fasano. "All the questions about Bresler," he ventured. "Where's *that* coming from?"

Dane's shrug resembled a twitch, suggesting anger suppressed. "We'll see," he murmured, and then spoke with renewed authority. "*You* brought these people in, Frank. And now you want them to cut ahead of us in line. It's *us* who came to you, and now it's *us* who's been sued. Spineless country clubbers like Calvo and Metrillo couldn't deliver their own mothers at the polls, let alone help you maintain control of the Senate. Only *we* can do that."

Beneath Dane's show of confidence, Fasano knew, he was worried. Only Fasano, by delivering gun immunity, could preserve Dane's power, both inside and outside the SSA. Fasano picked up a silver letter opener on Dane's coffee table, studying its ornate handle. In a neutral tone, he said, "Metrillo promises to support a separate bill."

"Fuck Metrillo. And fuck you, Frank, for wasting my time with drivel."

Fasano placed down the opener. Softly, he said, "Watch yourself, Charles."

"You watch *yourself*." Pausing, Dane adopted a cooler tone. "You and I both know these people have nowhere else to go. If you tell them that the only tort reform bill you're supporting protects the gun industry—*and* gets them what they want instead of this sop that Kilcannon's throwing them—they'll fall back into line, and try their damnedest to override his veto . . ."

"He's setting us up," Fasano interrupted. "Kilcannon expects all of us to do exactly what we're doing. Once we do, he'll make us pay."

"No choice, Frank. We just ride it out."

"Before we do, consider this. In return for Kilcannon's acceptance of gun immunity, we offer to make guns subject to the consumer protection laws. Kilcannon's always whining that there are no safety standards for guns . . ."

"No," Dane snapped. "Period. Putting the industry at the mercy of the consumer gestapo is the first step toward ending gun rights in America."

"Everything," Fasano retorted, "is the first step." His voice crackled with impatience. "By your logic, the income tax is the first step to confiscating our money, and the death penalty the first step to Nazi crematoriums. Has it ever dawned on you that society stands on a continuum, not poised on a slippery slope?"

Dane settled back in his chair, his face and voice emotionless. "You know our price—*this* bill. If Kilcannon wants to veto, he'll be digging his own grave."

Fasano studied him. "Electorally, you mean."

"In ways he hasn't contemplated," Dane answered. "And won't until it's far too late."

"The SSA," Fasano told Tony Calvo, "accuses you of selling them out to Kerry Kilcannon. Somehow, Dane finds it incongruous for me to broker the deal."

Over the telephone, the only clue to Calvo's feeling was his silence. "Did you try the consumer protection angle?"

"Yes. Are you familiar with the phrase 'dead on arrival'?"

"You can *pass* this bill," Calvo said in desperation. "Kilcannon will sign it . . ."

"Kilcannon," Fasano interrupted, "won't see it. Because *I* won't bring it to the floor. As of now, this bastard compromise of yours is roadkill."

Calvo's voice rose, the last vestige of resistance. "If so, I'll have to inform the President. And tell him why."

Fasano gave himself a moment. "You do that, Tony. Why surprise him? It's exactly what he expects from you.

"So run off and see 'the President.' And after that, I sincerely suggest you get behind my bill."

On the next afternoon, to the surprise of the White House press corps, Kit Pace announced that the President would hold a press conference.

Fasano and Gage watched on CNN. As usual, the press room was jammed; as usual, the President appeared confident and relaxed.

The Republican leadership in Congress, said David Bloom of NBC, *supports a ban on so-called therapeutic cloning. What is your opinion of its prospects?*

Kilcannon smiled at this. *About the same as my opinion of its merits,* he answered. *Considerably lower than my opinion of the good sense and goodwill of the American people.*

The distinction between cloning human beings—which all of us oppose—and using science to combat spinal cord injuries, or diabetes, may have eluded the sponsors of this bill. But I doubt that it eludes the average American. Let alone the millions to whom this new science may offer relief from suffering.

"Kilcannon," Gage complained, "always makes things sound so simple."

"No," Fasano answered. "He always makes *us* sound so simple."

On the screen, Kilcannon pointed toward John King of CNN.

Rumor has it, Mr. President, that you offered the business community a compromise on the Civil Justice Reform Act. Is that true and, if so, could you describe the status of negotiations?

"It's a setup," Gage murmured. "The White House must have fed King the question . . ."

"It's all a setup," Fasano corrected. "He didn't just wake up this morning, and decide it was a swell day for a press conference . . ."

Dead, Kilcannon was answering. *And it's a shame. The proposal I offered—cutting legal fees, and capping punitive damages—would have afforded real protections to the hundreds of thousands of Americans who run small businesses, and the millions they employ . . .*

"This whole thing," Fasano observed, "has been like being under hypnosis. I knew the President was going to push me off a cliff, and still I couldn't move . . ."

Every major representative of American business, Kilcannon continued, *was in favor of this compromise. There was just one problem: it no longer wipes out the existing right of victims of gun violence to seek justice from the gun industry and the SSA. So the SSA—Senator Fasano's constituency of one—instructed him to keep the bill from ever coming to a vote. And Senator Fasano, mindful of the millions of dollars the SSA gives to his own party, has complied . . .*

Gage stood, as though propelled by rage. "What about the trial lawyers, you little hypocrite . . ."

Those who own small businesses, Kilcannon said, *have learned a bitter truth: that the party who claims to speak for them is a wholly owned subsidiary of the Sons of the Second Amendment. And that the senator's seeming haste to protect their interests is a cover for the* one *interest that really matters . . .*

The moment, Fasano found, was no less unpleasant—indeed, perhaps more so—for its complete predictability. "The SSA," he said, "is getting all they asked for. And more."

For my part, the President concluded, *I will veto any so-called tort reform which is a smoke screen for the SSA. I urge the*

Republican leadership to put an end to this unseemly race, and to join us in the slow and patient effort to lift the burdens of litigation from America's honest businesspeople . . .

Fasano laughed aloud.

Back in the Oval Office, Clayton remarked to his friend, "What an embarrassment for poor old Frank. How much time do you think you cost him?"

"Days," the President answered with a smile. "Maybe weeks. Vic Coletti will be lonely for a while."

EIGHT

TEN MINUTES INTO John Nolan's questioning, Dr. Callie Hines's expression remained as impassive as her tone was flat. To Nolan, Sarah guessed, it must feel like Hines was looking through him.

For her own part, Sarah found the trauma surgeon a fascinating study. Interviewing Hines before the deposition, Sarah was greeted with an imperviousness which could be taken for hauteur: the process of socialization which drives most people on first meeting to attempt to be engaging or, out of shyness, to appear uncomfortable, seemed never to have touched this angular and handsome woman. She did not smile, and evinced no particular emotion—let alone any desire to ingratiate; only Sarah's instincts, or perhaps imagination, led her to sense that another Callie Hines assessed her from behind the mask. As they spoke, Sarah found herself conjuring the layers of experience—as a black confronting prejudice; a woman in a profession still dominated by males; a virtuoso in a specialty which required nervelessness and self-control—which made Hines seem so utterly indifferent to the trivial niceties of human interchange.

Then, toward the end of their meeting, Hines had done something which Sarah found quite astonishing—searching her office for a file with her back turned to Sarah, Hines had begun singing snatches of blues lyrics in a clear and resonant voice. Hines found the file: handing it to Sarah, she had resumed their laconic conversation as though nothing at all had happened. Sarah realized that she had never before liked a person so much who made so little effort to be liked.

This, plainly, was a reaction John Nolan did not share. Nolan had the frustrated manner of someone who had been trying to charm a wall. After a few moments, he had dropped any effort to establish a rapport, and begun to ask questions in a rapid-fire rhythm. Sarah wondered if the timing of Hines's responses—a few seconds would pass before she uttered her first word—was intended to unsettle him.

"What is your experience," Nolan asked now, "with injuries caused by guns?"

Pausing once again, Hines took no note of the others present—Sarah, Fancher, or the court reporter. "Extensive," she answered in the same flat voice. "In San Francisco, gun violence is the second leading cause of death by trauma."

"Can you estimate the number of times you've treated gunshot wounds?"

"Once a day, on average, every workday for the past six years. Roughly fifteen hundred surgeries."

Nolan raised his eyebrows. "In the course of all this experience, have you become familiar with particular types of guns?"

"Handguns."

"For what reason?"

"They're responsible for ninety-five percent of the deaths or injuries I see. The majority of those involve semi-automatics like the Lexington P-2."

Nolan's tone became faintly hostile. "On what do you base *that*, Doctor?"

"Fifteen hundred surgeries." Though her tone did not change, something in Hines's manner suggested her impatience with belaboring the obvious. "Semiautomatics can fire more rounds. That causes more deaths and injuries."

"Are you *personally* familiar with the Lexington P-2?"

"Not at firsthand." This time the pause came in mid-answer. "Only the bullets."

Nolan's gaze hardened. "And what is your experience with the Eagle's Claw?"

"Removing them."

Nolan shifted in his chair. Tense, Sarah awaited the first mention of Marie. Among Nolan's purposes in discovery—as Sarah well knew—was to ferret out bad news. Of the prospective witnesses, Callie Hines was potentially the most dangerous to Lexington.

"In how many cases?" Nolan inquired.

"Roughly twenty-five to thirty."

"In these twenty-five or thirty cases, what were your surgical observations regarding the Eagle's Claw?"

"That it teaches one humility."

The answer was so surprising that Nolan groped for a follow-up. At length, he said, "Please explain that."

This was greeted with the same unnerving silence. "The Eagle's Claw," Hines finally answered, "is designed to tear up human flesh. The effect is that of a buzz saw—maximum tissue damage, more bleeding, greater trauma to internal organs and wounds which are harder to repair.

"For a trauma surgeon, these difficulties are enhanced by the jagged edges of the bullet, which can cut the surgeon's tendons and end his or her career. As it did to one of our residents."

The flatness of her tone, Sarah realized, made her answer seem more lethal. In response, Nolan, too, became expressionless. "Could you," he asked evenly, "describe Marie Bowden's injuries?"

For the first time, Hines seemed drawn into a very specific memory. "The patient," she said at length, "had a wound to her lower abdomen. On opening the cavity I encountered a grape-sized hematoma—a collection of blood. It immediately burst, complicating our efforts to remove the bullet and locate the wound." Hines paused and then continued with the same dispassion. "The wound, when I found it, was severe. An ordinary bullet would create a hole. This bullet shredded the vena cava."

Nolan cocked his head. "Describe what you mean by 'shredded.'"

"Torn apart," Hines answered tersely. "On impact, the point of the Eagle's Claw becomes six razor edges. They ripped apart the vein in three different places. The ends of each wound were ratty."

The description seemed to give Nolan pause. "As a surgeon, what was your response?"

"Limited. The patient's blood pressure was crashing, her temperature was falling quickly and her blood had lost the capacity to clot." Once more Hines's pause came in mid-answer. "I determined to pack the wound and close her up as best I could. The hope was to raise her temperature, stabilize her, and operate in twenty-four hours. There wasn't time."

In Sarah's mind, this clipped account conveyed a purposeful frenzy, swift improvisation, and almost superhuman self-control. But Nolan seemed not to hear it. "Why didn't you attempt to repair the wound?"

At once, Hines refocused on the man in front of her. "Because," Hines answered succinctly, "she was dying.

"With an ordinary bullet wound, I could have operated right away. An adult would have had a ninety percent chance of surviving, and a six-year-old girl more than half. But the Eagle's Claw had functioned as intended."

The final sentence—with its intimation of Callie Hines's true feelings—caused Nolan to sit upright. "Do you have a personal antipathy toward Lexington Arms?"

For the first time there *was* no pause. "I'm a doctor," Hines answered in even tones. "I described the cause of death exactly as it occurred. Therefore—as a doctor—I consider your client an accessory to murder. There's nothing personal about that."

Nolan stared at her. "It's nearly ten o'clock," he said at last. "Let's take a fifteen-minute break." Only then did Hines, standing, favor Sarah with a glance, the hint of a bitter, complicit smile in her deep brown eyes.

NINE

AFTER A QUICK stop at a fund-raiser for Paul Harshman, Senator Cassie Rollins of Maine dined at the Cosmos Club with her predecessor, Warren Colby.

In a blue pin-striped suit, wing-collared shirt, and his trademark gold cuff links, Colby—as always—looked fit, trim and impeccably tailored, and his clear blue eyes and still-black hair lent him an aura of youth. At once suave, principled, and unusually literate, Colby was a particularly urbane model of the Washington insider, whose reputation for integrity and balanced judgment had led to his appointment, though a Republican, as Attorney General under the prior Democratic administration. This selfless record of service, Colby had wryly observed, might help him achieve his ultimate ambition—Commissioner of Baseball. In the meanwhile, he had to content himself with frequent mention as a possible Supreme Court justice; the income of a named partner in a prestigious Washington law firm; and a second marriage to a beautiful and savvy woman who ran the city's premier public relations group. His life, as he remarked to Cassie, was truly a bitter pill.

Their dinner, a monthly ritual, had begun when Cassie had become a senator. Before that, she had been an aide in Colby's office, then his Chief of Staff. Blonde and freckled, with an open face and a wholesome outdoorsy appeal, Cassie had proven a quick learner. When Colby had determined not to seek reelection, Cassie, with his support, had literally started running: a former tennis star and marathoner, she had campaigned by jogging from town to town, crisscrossing the state, until she had run through every county. Though victorious, her margin had been thin. Since then, she had walked a fine line between the moderation of Maine voters and the demands of the Senate leadership, far more conservative, and now she faced the next election with apprehension.

It was after dinner, as Colby swirled Courvoisier in a snifter, that he broached what proved to be his own concern. "You have a secret admirer," he said.

"And who might that be?"

"Chuck Hampton. We had a meeting the other day, regarding the government of Lithuania's heady aspirations to join NATO. Afterward, he mentioned you with fondness." Skipping a beat, Colby added dryly, "And worry."

Cassie smiled. "Over guns?"

"Indeed. He hears that Fasano's positioning you to vote with the SSA and wondered aloud if that would damage you in Maine." Reflective, Colby studied the dim-lit dining room, the clusters of members, principally older men, engaged in quiet but amiable discourse. "It was all very artful. Chuck is going to war."

This made Cassie smile again. "This one," she told him, "is shaping up to make a reunion of the Borgias look like pin-the-tail-on-the-donkey. As for Hampton, to my surprise, it looks like he's going to the barricades with the newly minted 'KFK.' That's not good news."

" 'KFK,' " Colby mused aloud. "When he first came to the Senate, who'd have thought it?

"In any event, this could be a classic. I've always thought of Fasano as fusing the best of Lyndon Johnson and the KGB: pragmatic, shrewd, hard as nails and a master of indirection. Whereas Kilcannon's essentially a romantic, which—combined with a considerable inventiveness and what the generous might call his strength of will—makes him the most dangerous man in Washington. Because he'll cut your throat in the service of a higher cause." Colby sipped his brandy. "I hear he plans to visit every state where a senator is on the fence. It seems that may implicate you."

Cassie nodded. "The threats and blandishments have begun to fly from all sides. Dane's demanding a meeting— with scant courtesy, I might add."

"I can imagine. It feels wonderful, I must admit, to have graduated to statesman." Pausing, Colby adopted an encouraging tone. "You should be all right, Cassie. Granted, I don't think you've ever shot anything, but you're foursquare for hunting and that recent photo of you trout-fishing was inspired. The last time I looked, your approval rating was well over half, and there wasn't any talk—serious talk, at any rate—of a primary challenge. Which, as of now, leaves you with only one problem: Abel Randolph. Assuming he decides to run against you in the general."

"Oh, he'll run," Cassie said with certainty. "He's a popular incumbent governor, term-limited, with nowhere else to go and approval ratings at least as high as mine."

Thoughtful, Colby gazed past her. "There *are* certain constants," he said at length. "You'll win the conservative areas upstate, and Abel will carry Portland and most of the other cities.

"The fulcrum will be the suburbs. They're largely populated by moderates—plus the new people moving up from Massachusetts, which is not the *best* thing in the world for you. But you're positioned to do well enough to win: conservative on taxes and defense, moderate to liberal on social issues like abortion. And being a woman helps you there." Pausing, Colby looked at her directly. "Aside from prescription drug costs, the one joker in the deck—the one that loses you our seat, if anything does—is guns."

Cassie placed her napkin on the table. "The SSA has tolerated me," she said. "But they don't love me, and Maine's got the second highest gun ownership per capita. There's no way that Charles Dane is giving me a pass on these two bills."

Colby finished his brandy. "The SSA," he acknowledged, "accounts for some of my most shameful votes in the Senate. The price of survival, I told myself."

"I only wish," Cassie said tartly, "that selling out *this* time was so easy. I don't even know which *way* to sell out.

"The last election showed how fenced in I could be. A week before the primary, I was leading Bill Poole by thirty percent. Then in the final debate he pushed me into saying something favorable about the assault weapons ban. The SSA sent out one hundred thousand orange postcards headed 'voter alert,' pointing out my left-wing deviation to everyone on their mailing list." Cassie gave a sardonic smile. "My polls went into free fall, and I won by six percent. Another week and I might have lost."

"Maybe. But then you won the general election."

"By the grace of the SSA," Cassie retorted. "When the Democrats put up Sam Towle, they overlooked his sins. Not only did he vote for the assault weapons ban in Congress, but he'd sponsored a bill advocating safety locks, and banning cop-killer bullets like the Eagle's Claw. This time the hundred thousand orange SSA postcards identified Sam as the author of the 'Burglar Protection Act.'

"By this time I'd learned my lesson—I kept quiet about the Eagle's Claw, and loved the Second Amendment like the child I never had." Pausing, Cassie added quietly, "When I think about Lara's family, I remember that. But I beat Sam Towle by four percent, and the SSA may well have made the difference."

Colby's face was sober. "Sam," he remarked, "is a good man. He's also finished in Maine politics."

"I know. But Hampton's right this time—either way, I've got a problem."

Colby pondered this. "Not that, on gun issues, I'm any model. But if the only factor you were to consider is what's right, where would you come out here?"

Cassie touched her finger to her lip, her blue eyes clouded by doubt. "I'm not sure," she finally said. "I've always been for tort reform—to me, the Lenihans of the world are parasites. I also worry that this Costello lawsuit is more about politics than law, and that antigun lawsuits in general stretch the law way too far.

"But then why should *anyone* need an Eagle's Claw?" She shook her head. "There, my judgment is complicated by emotion—I've liked Lara ever since she covered the Hill. I like *him*, too: whenever I saw him in the Senate, I had the strange desire to hug him . . ."

"Must be a gender thing," Colby interjected wryly. "I never had that problem. But then I've never kissed a cactus."

Cassie gave him a knowing smile. "I never said, Warren, that Kerry Kilcannon wasn't as ruthless as he needs to be. But there's also this feeling of vulnerability, and of seeing other people as something more than chess pieces on the political landscape.

"When I first came to the Senate, I found a place full of 'real guys' who were exactly who you expect them to be—ambitious, self-involved, and as introspective as a rock. But with Kilcannon, you always had the sense that whatever he'd been through had caused him to feel more, not less, and made him more interested in other people than most. For several years he was the only male senator who asked about my life in more than a superficial way, and the only one besides Chad Palmer I'd trust with anything personal." Cassie sipped her brandy. "They were two of a unique kind, at least in the Senate. Neither talked about himself very much. They didn't want to, and didn't need to. Especially Kilcannon."

"Perhaps so, Cassie. But it changes nothing."

"Oh, I know." Her voice was level, fatalistic. "If I oppose the President, there'll be consequences. If campaigning in Maine will help Abel Randolph, Kilcannon will come. If staying away and raising money for Abel is what's best, he'll do that. And on the other side I've got Dane and the SSA."

"So what *is* right?" Colby persisted.

Cassie summoned a look of deep contemplation. "There *is* this place," she mused, "called Siberia. Maybe they need a senator."

Colby smiled faintly. "Keep me posted."

TEN

As MARTIN BRESLER began to testify, Sarah felt edgy.

This was natural: Bresler was central to Mary Costello's case against the SSA—that it effectively controlled the gun industry, including Lexington, and had prevented an agreement between Lexington and the President which could have kept John Bowden from buying a P-2. But there were smaller, nagging worries. Since being listed as a witness, Bresler had obtained a lawyer, Evan Pritchard—a lanky, sharp-eyed Southerner with a soft voice and cool manner—who had explained to Sarah, without apology, that further contact between her and Bresler would compromise Bresler's credibility. So Sarah watched, barred from talking with her own key witness.

And Bresler's manner had changed. At Sea Ranch, Sarah had noted his expressive eyes, the fluttery hands which seemed to punctuate each phrase with some new gesture. But now, in the conference room of Nolan's firm, he was almost as still as the lawyers who watched him. Sitting beside her, Robert Lenihan studied Bresler with skepticism.

Carefully, Nolan posed a series of neutral questions, and then broached the subject of Bresler's contacts with President Kilcannon.

"Prior to your meeting with the President," he inquired, "did you discuss a possible agreement regarding trigger locks with any representatives of the Republicans in Congress?"

The inquiry startled Sarah. But she knew the answer well enough: Frank Fasano and Paul Harshman.

To her surprise, the question induced in Bresler a silent stare at the table which, Sarah suddenly thought, seemed intended to avoid her gaze. "I'm not sure," Bresler answered in a monotone. "Right now I don't recall any."

Sarah tensed. Beside her, Lenihan expelled a breath, audible to Sarah. The only people in the room who seemed contained were Nolan, Fancher and Evan Pritchard. Calmly, Nolan said, "Then you also don't recall discussing with any Republicans in Congress the SSA's attitude toward such an agreement."

Still Bresler gazed at the table. "No."

"Bullshit," Lenihan muttered with quiet fury.

No one but Sarah looked at him. "Or," Nolan continued, "discussing your approach to the Republicans with any manufacturers?"

Briefly, Bresler shook his head. "I'm sorry," Nolan prodded. "For the sake of the reporter, your answer must be audible."

Bresler cleared his throat. "The answer is no."

With a tap of her fingers, the reporter added Bresler's denial to the record of his sworn testimony, and the knowledge of what was happening demolished the last vestige of Sarah's disbelief.

"Did you," Nolan was asking, "discuss your approach to President Kilcannon with anyone from the SSA?"

"Yes," Bresler said more firmly. "With Charles Dane. Just before we went to the White House."

"Could you describe that conversation?"

"Charles expressed his disappointment in no uncertain terms. In his view, compromising with Kilcannon would embolden him to further attack gun rights."

"Did you agree?"

For the first time, Bresler looked up. "Obviously not."

Perhaps, Sarah allowed herself to hope, Bresler had decided not to alienate the Republicans, but would tell the truth about the SSA. Silently, she urged him to resist John Nolan.

"During this conversation," Nolan asked quietly, "did Mr. Dane threaten you in any way?"

Bresler folded his arms. "He did not."

"Or any members of your group, such as Lexington Arms?"

"No."

"How would you describe the conversation?"

Nolan, Sarah recognized, was phrasing his questions as though he already knew the answers. Bresler resumed staring at the table. In a voice so soft that it was barely audible, he said, "Very professional. Charles's tone was 'more in sorrow than in anger.' I appreciated that."

Shaking his head in disgust, Lenihan stared at Bresler. Evan Pritchard turned to him. "Let the record reflect, Mr. Lenihan, that you're engaging in a series of muttered asides and discourteous gestures toward the witness. I have to ask you to behave professionally."

"Define 'professional,'" Lenihan said with genuine anger. "Does that mean suborning perjury, as you and Mr. Nolan are doing now? Or does being professional consist of watching you do it?"

Bresler, Sarah noticed, briefly closed his eyes. "I hope," Pritchard answered coldly, "that you're prepared to take these charges to the bar association. If not, I'm prepared to advise Judge Bond that you made them without grounds, and let him determine the appropriate sanction."

Sarah placed a hand on Lenihan's arm. "Let it go," she whispered. "You're making things worse."

Lenihan turned to her, flushed. "How could I?" he whispered back in an accusing tone. "You based an entire complaint on the word of this fucking weasel."

Expressionless, Nolan sat there as if nothing had happened. After a silence consumed by Pritchard's continuing stare at Lenihan, Pritchard turned to Nolan, and nodded.

"Did there come a time," Nolan asked Bresler, "that you discussed with President Kilcannon a possible agreement regarding voluntary background checks at gun shows?"

"Yes."

"Did you discuss *that* proposal with anyone from the SSA?"

Bresler shook his head. "I had no need. I knew Charles was opposed."

As Nolan sat back, placing a pen to his lips, Harrison Fancher trained a fixed gaze on the witness. Still Bresler did not look up.

"For what reason," Nolan asked, "did you and the President fail to reach agreement regarding gun shows?"

Bresler bit his lip. "My trade association disbanded."

"For what reason?"

"I lost the support of my members." Bresler's tone was soft, almost rote. "I got carried away with myself, and tried to move too fast. The companies I represented weren't comfortable with that."

"How do you know that?"

"Three CEOs called me—a majority. They felt I was splitting the gun movement, being too high profile. In retrospect, they were right."

It was perjury as recantation, Sarah thought, a confession of error worthy of a Stalinist show trial, delivered in the manner of a beaten man. And she could only watch.

"Did *any* of these CEOs," Nolan asked, "attribute their attitudes to the SSA?"

"No."

"Do you have *any* basis for believing that the SSA did anything to disband your organization?"

Bresler shook his head, a vague, disheartened gesture. "No."

"Did you ever discuss the SSA with Mr. Callister?"

"I did not."

Nolan leaned forward. "In short, Mr. Bresler, are you aware of *any* basis in plaintiff's complaint for the allegation that the SSA controls Lexington Arms?"

With an expectant glance, Pritchard turned to Bresler. Hunching farther in his chair, Bresler responded, "None whatsoever."

Savagely, Lenihan whispered, "Except for you, you little fuck."

This time Pritchard ignored him. "Indeed," Nolan continued, "didn't the SSA hire your top aide, Jerry Kirk?"

Bresler's nod was almost as imperceptible as his voice was hushed. "Yes."

"And how did that happen?"

There was a brief pause. "Charles Dane hired Jerry," Bresler answered, "as a favor to me. I was worried about Jerry's family."

Stunned, Sarah stared at him. But Bresler had yet to look at her. "And so," Nolan concluded, "as far as you know, Charles Dane's only action in connection with the disbanding of your group was the benign one of hiring Jerry Kirk."

"Yes."

With this, Sarah thought, Bresler's subjugation was complete. "Did there come a time," Nolan asked, "when you met with plaintiff's counsel—Mr. Lenihan and Ms. Dash?"

Though Bresler raised his eyes at last, his tone and manner remained robotic. "At Sea Ranch. Shortly before they filed their complaint."

"At whose initiative did it occur?"

"Ms. Dash called me."

Nolan's expression became a barely perceptible smile. "And who paid your expenses?"

"Plaintiff's counsel."

"What was the purpose of the meeting?"

Bresler's arms, still crossed in front of his chest, seemed to tighten around himself. "As I understood it, they wanted to make a case against the SSA."

"On what did you base that understanding?"

Bresler's shoulders twitched. "Pretty much all they asked me about was the SSA."

"And what did you tell them?"

It was strange, Sarah thought: now Bresler's gaze was trained on Nolan, as though steeling himself to complete his lie. "Exactly what I just told you."

"In *all* respects?" Nolan persisted.

Another brief pause. "Yes."

"Did you discuss with plaintiff's counsel whether you'd execute an affidavit?"

Silent, Lenihan scowled. "Before we talked about what I'd say," Bresler answered, "Mr. Lenihan said that they might like one. Afterward they never mentioned it."

"And were you willing to give them an affidavit, saying what you've just said here?"

"Yes."

Outraged, Lenihan half stood. Sarah, frozen, was filled with impotent fury at the extent of Bresler's betrayal. With a last brief smile, Nolan said, "Thank you, Mr. Bresler."

Standing outside the conference room, Lenihan and Sarah whispered furiously.

"No affidavit," Lenihan said in a savage undertone. "From the moment Bresler said that, we should have sent him packing. Instead you've given us a case without a basis."

"There *is* a basis. Bresler's lying."

"What a surprise." Lenihan's tone dripped with venom.

"In my experience, the American justice system is one long and noble search for truth . . ."

"They blackmailed him," Sarah said. "Or offered him something. Maybe a job if he recanted."

"Think so? My *goodness*, that might mean that Evan Pritchard is part of it. Imagine that kind of conduct from an officer of the court."

Sarah drew a breath. "I'll cross-examine . . ."

"No," Lenihan cut in. "They're mine. *All* of them."

Arms resting on the table, Lenihan leaned toward Bresler. Though Bresler's face was round, it seemed pinched, his expression miserable. "Prior to today," Lenihan began, "have you discussed this case with anyone from the SSA?"

Evan Pritchard raised a hand, signalling his client not to answer. "Other than attorneys?" he said to Lenihan.

Lenihan gave him a cynical smile. "Let's start there, Mr. Bresler."

Bresler hesitated. "No."

This, Sarah was certain, could not be true. As if reading her thoughts, Lenihan asked, "How did you select Mr. Pritchard to represent you?"

Bresler glanced at Pritchard. Quietly, he said, "I knew of him by reputation."

"You'd never met him?"

"No. Not before this case."

"How did you hear of Mr. Pritchard?"

"I don't recall."

Lenihan's face set. "Isn't it true that the SSA recommended that you hire Mr. Pritchard?"

"No."

"Then who's paying your legal fees?"

"Objection," Pritchard interjected. "Direct not to answer . . ."

"On what basis?" Lenihan snapped.

"Because," Pritchard said in a laconic drawl, "it's outside the scope of discovery. And protected by the attorney-client privilege . . ."

"Outside the scope of discovery?" Lenihan repeated incredulously. "Not if the SSA's paying your fees."

"Same objection," Pritchard said. "Same instruction. Move on."

"Move on to the judge, you mean."

"Fine. Have anything else, Mr. Lenihan, or are we through here?"

Lenihan sat straighter. "Have you," he asked Bresler, "discussed this case with Mr. Fancher or Mr. Nolan?"

Bresler glanced at Pritchard. After a moment, Pritchard nodded. "Yes," Bresler answered tersely.

Lenihan's expression was grim. "With whom, precisely?"

"With both."

"Where, and when?"

"Yesterday. In this room."

"And who paid your expenses to get here?"

"Objection," Pritchard said. "Outside the scope of discovery."

"We didn't object when *you* asked."

"That's your privilege, counsel. Or your lapse. You can take *that* to the judge, as well."

Lenihan paused a moment, reining in his temper, and then turned back to Bresler. "What did you discuss with Mr. Nolan and Mr. Fancher?"

In Bresler's liquid eyes, Sarah imagined, there was a look of shame. "My testimony."

"And what did Mr. Fancher and Mr. Nolan say about your testimony?"

"Objection," Nolan interjected. "The substance of our conversation may reflect the legal strategy of counsel and, therefore, is protected from disclosure by the work-product doctrine . . ."

"That's not absolute," Lenihan interjected.

"True. But before you get an answer, the information must be unavailable by any other means." Nolan's faint, annoying smile returned. "My questions today have already elicited the relevant information. You're simply unhappy with the answers—as, apparently, you were upon meeting Mr. Bresler at Sea Ranch. To me, the one enduring mystery is why you listed him as a witness."

Pritchard nodded his agreement. "In light of that," he told Lenihan, "I'm bound to honor Mr. Nolan's request. I'm directing the witness not to answer any substantive questions about his discussions with defense counsel." Abruptly turning to Bresler, he said, "Let's put this to rest, Martin. Did anyone in that meeting ask you to lie, or to change your story?"

"No." Bresler stared at the table. "All Mr. Nolan said was to tell the truth."

There had been several ways, Sarah thought dejectedly, for someone to arrange Bresler's subornation. Nolan and Fancher could have been an active part of it. More likely, even now they only suspected what Sarah thought had happened after she had listed Bresler as a witness: that Dane had suborned Bresler directly, to avoid the exposure of his own perjury, and then directed Bresler to Pritchard—who had arranged to choreograph this recantation with Harrison Fancher and John Nolan.

"The witness's meeting with defense counsel," Lenihan reiterated, "goes to the heart of our case: whether the SSA controlled—and continues to control—the American gun industry and, specifically, Lexington Arms."

Silent until now, Harry Fancher turned a spiteful stare on Lenihan. *"You,"* he spat out, "have brought a complaint against the SSA without any basis in fact. If you didn't know that before now—which I doubt—Mr. Bresler has just explained it to you.

"You can either drop my client from the case, or we'll ask Judge Bond to order your firm and the Kilcannon Center to pay every dime of our expenses. And to refer you and Ms. Dash to the State Bar for your professional misconduct."

With that, Sarah knew, the SSA's trap had shut.

ELEVEN

It HAD BEEN startling to be called by the First Lady. Calling her felt presumptuous. But Sarah and Lara Costello Kilcannon had formed a partnership, however tentative. And Sarah was desperate.

"Today was a disaster," Sarah reported baldly. "Martin Bresler took back everything he had told us."

"Everything?"

"Yes." Restless, Sarah stood, and walked to her office window. "As of now, we've got nothing on the SSA." She hesitated, and then asked, "Can the President use the antitrust division to investigate them?"

"No." Lara's voice was quiet. "I'm sorry, Sarah. Politically, Kerry just can't do it."

You *led me to Bresler*, Sarah wanted to retort. But she could not, in fairness, blame Lara for whatever the SSA had done to Martin Bresler. "We're in trouble," Sarah confessed. "Not just our case against the SSA, but against Lexington. Charles Monk couldn't place Bowden at the gun show. Neither can we.

"Lexington claims not to have the records of where they shipped the gun. Under the law, the first sale of any gun has to be made through a licensed dealer—who may well have sold the gun to whoever resold it to John Bowden. We need to find that person, and we're absolutely stymied."

Lara was silent. At length, she asked, "And you think Kerry can help?"

"I don't know," Sarah acknowledged. "But I was hoping

the Bureau of Alcohol, Tobacco and Firearms might be able to find out something. At least we have a serial number, and tracing crime guns is part of what they do." Pausing, she gazed out at the scattered lights of the South of Market area, the bare streets and low-rise buildings surrounding the Kilcannon Center. "If we can't prove that Bowden bought the P-2 at a gun show," she finished, "we also can't prove—to a legal certainty—that Lexington and the SSA caused the murder of your family."

This time, Lara's silence stretched far longer. "Thank you," she said at last. "For telling me, and for everything you've done. I'll do the best I can to help you."

"Tell me about Leo Weller," Kerry asked.

Clayton smiled grimly. "It's even worse than we thought. For Leo, that is. And for quite a few of his constituents.

"The problem is a vermiculite mine in Libby, Montana. Vermiculite is a material used to make pottery . . ."

"Then what's this about asbestosis?"

"Vermiculite," Clayton answered, "turns out to be a form of asbestos. But the company, Montana Mines, assured the workers it wasn't harmful. So they were bringing it home on their clothes, also exposing their wives and children. Essentially, the entire town was infected with asbestosis. The death toll's over fifty, with a lot more folks on respirators, fixing to breathe their last."

Angry, Kerry shook his head. "Stories like this give the lie to *laissez-faire*. Some poor guy shows up at work, thinking to support his family, and what he's really doing is killing himself. And maybe them, as well." He paused, reverting to the practical. "So what's Leo done about it?"

"Worse than nothing. When a victims' group from Libby asked to see him, he sent an aide. Now he's put a clause in Fasano's tort reform bill, immunizing Montana Mines from liability." Clayton's tone became sardonic. "To my complete surprise, the CEO is one of Leo's chief supporters—and fund-raisers."

"I always knew," Kerry said disgustedly, "that Weller was one of the dumbest men in the Senate. But to be so callous, and such an obvious whore, suggests that Leo still has room for growth."

Clayton nodded. "As you say, Leo's a prime subject for TV spots."

"No one," Kerry agreed, "can say he's not deserving. I wonder how Bob Lenihan's group of trial lawyers might react to Leo's blunder."

Clayton studied him. "Who would tell them? If our fingerprints are on the ads, you'd be accused of coordinating your own political operation with outside groups. Which, as you'll recall, may well violate the law."

Kerry smiled. "Do you really think that our man Robert can't get there on his own? If so, I'll have to pray that he's telepathic."

There was a buzz on Kerry's intercom. "The First Lady's calling," his assistant said.

Clayton chose to leave. Picking up the telephone, Kerry said, "I just heard something you need to know."

"So did I," Lara replied. "But you go first."

"Bowden's gun was stolen?" Kerry repeated the next morning.

Clayton nodded. "After the murders, Lexington told the ATF it had no record of shipment. But within forty-eight hours of a theft, the law requires licensed dealers to report it to the ATF—complete with the serial number of any and all guns taken. When the ATF went back and pushed the right button, Bowden's P-2 came up. It turns out the gun was part of a batch of fifty or so P-2s stolen from a major gun dealer in Phoenix, Arizona."

"When?"

"About six months ago. With fifty more stolen P-2s out there, it's a fair bet that some of them have already popped up in crimes—or soon will. If so, it may be possible to trace one back to the seller of Bowden's gun."

"Then push the ATF on that," Kerry ordered. "Whoever sold to Bowden may be trafficking in stolen guns. Where better than a gun show?"

Clayton folded his arms. Quietly, he said, "I assume this is for the lawsuit. So I can only hope you're being careful."

Silent, Kerry felt the painful memory of the murders flooding back to him, as fresh in his mind and heart as the faces of Inez and Joan, the moment of dancing with Marie. Now he might know who put the gun in Bowden's hands—and where.

"Just get the ATF to do it," he directed. "I'll worry about the rest."

"It's a start," Lara told Sarah Dash. "If I find out any more, I'll call."

Grateful, Sarah thanked her, and got off.

Elbow propped on her desk, Sarah rested her forehead against tented fingertips. The migraine had intensified, throbbing from the cords of her neck to her eyes, turning her stomach to a persistent pit of nausea. But through the pounding in her head she tried to focus on what Lara Kilcannon had just told her: that, for good or ill, they might finally know the truth of Bowden's trip to Las Vegas.

Her telephone rang again. Sarah reached for it, trying to summon a veneer of crisp professionalism. "Sarah Dash."

There was silence. "Is this a secure line?" her caller finally asked.

It was a man's voice—high, and almost screechy. But it was the oddity of his inquiry that caused Sarah to sit up. "Yes," she answered. "Who is this?"

"I visited your web site." The caller paused, and then the timbre of his voice fell. "I work at Lexington Arms. I know things."

Tense, Sarah tried to ignore the throbbing in her temples. "What things?"

There was another pause. "Information damaging to the company," the man answered. "Covered up by my supervisors."

"By Callister?"

The man's voice remained tight. "If I tell you, I may lose my job. Or worse."

Sarah tried to think swiftly, searching for what was best to say. Some whistleblowers are paranoid, Lenihan had told her, some are on a mission from God, some see wrongdoing where there is none. But some—the ones you pray for—can turn a case upside down.

"I can offer you absolute security," Sarah assured her caller. "Unless you authorize it, I won't use whatever you tell me."

The man hesitated. "How can I be sure of that?"

"I'm a lawyer. If you're coming to me for legal advice, even if you don't retain me, the state ethics rules require me to keep this in strict confidence. I could lose my license if I don't."

"Because if I come to you," the man persisted, "I don't want you outing me. Now what about my job?"

Involuntarily, Sarah thought of Bresler, her own fear of having yet another witness flip. "There's a risk," she acknowledged. "Did Lexington make you sign a confidentiality agreement, promising to protect internal corporate information unless you're under oath?"

"Yes." The man's voice fell off. "Everyone had to sign."

Skull pounding, Sarah rubbed her eyes. "That only goes so far. Lexington can threaten you with a lawsuit. But under Connecticut law, you can bring a wrongful termination action if Lexington fired you for reasons which violate public policy. If you tell me what you know, I can advise you."

Her last statement, Sarah realized, had the desperate tone of a plea. Perhaps in response, her caller fell silent. "Can you at least tell me your name?" she urged. "Or a number where I can reach you?"

"Not yet," the man said softly. "I have to think."

Before Sarah could answer, the line went dead.

PART FIVE

THE VOTE

EARLY NOVEMBER TO EARLY DECEMBER

ONE

THERE WERE DAYS, rare ones, when Senator Chuck Hampton approached his work as Minority Leader with a fierce combativeness so pure that it was akin to joy.

This was such a day. As a rule, Hampton's pride of leadership was tempered by the complexity of dealing with the forty-six egos—including his own—who comprised the Democratic caucus; the soul-grinding paranoia of dueling with a shrewd and relentless foe, Frank Fasano, who as Majority Leader held the upper hand; the knowledge that Kerry Kilcannon placed his own priorities as President above Chuck Hampton's more parochial concerns, such as ensuring the survival of Hampton's flock and thus Hampton's survival as leader. There were even days when Chuck Hampton half wanted to tell the several Democrats who aspired to replace him that any of them could have the fucking job, which he clung to out of the primal, Darwinian knowledge that giving it up would feel even worse than keeping it. But today he spoke during morning business with a deeply satisfying sense of power, purpose, and outrage.

"Three days ago," he told the scattering of assembled senators, "as the majority party stalled, the five thousandth American was killed with a gun since the day that the First Lady's family was slaughtered."

Turning, he pointed at the picture of a young African-American boy with cropped hair and a bright aspect which shone through the compulsory smile of a school photograph. "Antonio Harris was twelve. He lived in

Philadelphia with his mother, and two older sisters who adored him. He was murdered in a drive-by shooting by a sixteen-year-old who mistook him for the younger brother of a member of a rival gang. The shooter bought the murder weapon from another gang member who had stolen it from his uncle—a spousal abuser who was able to buy it because the record of his conviction was never entered into the system."

Turning from the boy's photograph, Hampton continued with genuine anger. "If the President's proposals were law, Antonio might not have died. Now it is too late for him. But the clock is running on other Antonios, day by day and hour by hour, whose lives are in our hands, and whose deaths will haunt our consciences." Facing Frank Fasano, he added, "Or, at least, the conscience of some of us."

Fasano seemed to freeze. Hampton, too, paused, just long enough to note the still attentiveness of Cassie Rollins, a principal target of his remarks. "But what has the majority offered us? Nothing. Until yesterday, when Senator Fasano and the leadership offered us a bill which is worse than nothing." An edge of scorn crept into his tone. "And what does it contain? A 'commission' to 'study' the causes of violence among our young people. Were he alive, I'm quite certain that Antonio would have been fascinated by its findings—assuming, hypothetically, that we'll receive them during what *would* have been Antonio's normal life span."

At the periphery of his vision, Hampton saw Chad Palmer's brief, grim smile. "But never let it be said," Hampton went on, "that Senator Fasano's bill leaves the gun-show loophole unaddressed. To the contrary, it promises an instant background check once *ninety-nine percent* of records of felonies, violent misdemeanors, and adjudicated domestic violence are entered into the national computer system.

"And how will we fund this extraordinary feat? Unlike the President's bill—which would allocate the millions necessary to do so—the money Senator Fasano proffers might be sufficient to overhaul the records in, say, Rhode Island, or even, perhaps, my own state of Vermont. But not, regrettably, Senator Fasano's home state of Pennsylvania. Where Antonio Harris was murdered."

Fasano, Hampton noted, listened with the inward, impenetrable expression that Hampton was learning to associate with concern and, perhaps, anger. "But there are much cheaper ways," Hampton continued, "to prevent such a death. Combination safety locks on guns, for example, to prevent people who steal guns from using them. About which the senator's bill says not one word."

Now Hampton faced Frank Fasano directly. "Perhaps I am doing my friend from Pennsylvania a disservice. Perhaps—despite the suspicions of some cynics in my caucus—he does not intend his bill as cover for the opponents of meaningful laws to reduce gun violence. Perhaps, after all, he does not plan to bring this up for a vote prior to the President's bill, to provide further cover for his drive to pass a bill extinguishing Mary Costello's lawsuit. Perhaps this bill is as innocent of hidden motives as it is ill written and ill considered."

Hampton's expression became wry, his tone etched with an astringent humor. "But just to be sure, I intend to offer an amendment to the senator's bill to ensure full funding for his ambitious goal of near-total compliance for background checks, and to bar tort immunity for gun manufacturers. I may even offer the President's bill as an amendment to the senator's own." Abruptly, his speech became slow and very serious. "And if the senator attempts to bar us from debating these amendments, the 'cynics' in our caucus will keep his bill from coming to a vote—*unless* he permits the President's bill to be considered simultaneously."

Briefly, but to Hampton's satisfaction, Fasano looked skeptical and surprised, as though he doubted Hampton had the forty votes necessary to sustain a filibuster. Hampton rested one hand on the Styrofoam board which framed Antonio's picture. "This," he said, "is not done simply out of the respect that this body owes President Kilcannon. It reflects the decent regard we owe to the memory of Antonio Harris. Anything less should embarrass us all."

With this, Chuck Hampton sat down.

When morning business had ended, Hampton crossed the aisle to speak to Frank Fasano.

Fasano had long since retrieved his air of imperviousness; only the glint in his eye betrayed his annoyance. "That was quite a performance," Fasano said. "Almost worthy of KFK himself."

Feeling his sense of satisfaction deepen, Hampton paused a moment before indulging it fully. "I'm beginning to take that as a genuine compliment, Frank—especially after the beating he gave you on his tort reform proposal. My colleagues noticed it, too. So I'm delivering a message from all forty-six of us—even those whom the President's bill makes nervous."

"And what might that be, Chuck?"

Hampton smiled. "Deal straight up with KFK's bill," he answered in his most amiable tone. "Or we'll screw you like I just promised we would."

Arrested by Hampton's speech, Cassie Rollins returned to her office preoccupied. Which was not the proper state of mind for a Republican senator up for reelection and fifteen minutes late for a meeting with Charles Dane.

She found him watching C-SPAN in her reception area, and ushered him to her office with a graceful apology. "This was one morning," she concluded, "when I thought it best to hear out Chuck's body count to the unusually bitter end. He seems to have been eating his Wheaties."

"I saw." Dane's manner was respectful but direct. "So there's no need for either of us to mince words. This is *the* vote, Cassie."

Cassie rested a curled finger to her lips, eyes narrowing in an expression which was good-humored yet pointed. "Exactly which vote," she asked, "is 'the vote'? The one against Kilcannon's gun control bill? Or in favor of your tort immunity bill?"

Dane's already intent look deepened. "Both," he answered flatly. "They're the same vote—the acid test of who our friends are, and who cares to remain our friend. Where do you stand, Senator?"

The abrupt switch to her formal title, Cassie knew, was meant to signal Dane's willingness to consider her an adversary. Though this put her on edge, Cassie kept her voice even and, to her satisfaction, seemingly unruffled.

"Tort immunity," she observed, "is one thing. But the President's bill is largely focused on keeping guns out of the hands of criminals and wife-beaters, not law-abiding gun owners."

Dane leaned forward, his posture suggesting suppressed impatience. "Why should 'law-abiding gun owners' be subjected to intrusive background checks, whether at gun shows or elsewhere? It's the first step toward keeping ordinary people from owning guns—confiscation by harassment and inconvenience, where neighbor can't sell a gun to neighbor, or a father give one to his son."

Crossing her legs, Cassie sat back in her wing chair, her

chin resting on clasped hands. "Before I accept that, Charles, I'm going to ask you to persuade me that it's so. From the sound of Hampton's speech, you'll have the time.

"As for immunity, I think these lawsuits are pretty flimsy, and you know my strong position in favor of tort reform. But the one lawsuit everyone knows about is Mary Costello's. Effectively, you're asking us to vote against Lara Kilcannon, her surviving sister, their three murdered relatives, and three other families whose loved ones Bowden slaughtered by accident. Why make your 'friends' cast that vote if your lawyers can get this judge to throw Mary Costello out of court, which is what the best legal minds I've talked to think he'll do. *If* we can restrain ourselves from trampling on the First Lady before he gets the chance."

Dane paused before responding, seeming to measure his words. "She's not only the First Lady," he said quietly. "She's the wife of our foremost enemy. Her sister, their pawn, has sued the SSA itself. You can't give them aid and comfort and be our friend."

Despite the softness of his tone, Cassie felt that this response—simplistic, with a whiff of melodrama—betrayed a desperation at variance with Dane's accustomed self-assurance. For the first time, she sensed this was not simply about ideology, or power: for whatever reason, Cassie guessed, the lawsuit worried him. "I'm always your friend," she assured Dane in a placating tone. "Whenever gun rights come up, I have a bias in your favor . . ."

"Not on the assault weapons ban," Dane interrupted pointedly. "That nearly cost you your party's nomination."

This *was* going to be unpleasant, Cassie realized. She mustered a smile. "You have a long memory, Charles, and so do I. That was five years—and many a pro-gun vote—ago." Her voice assumed the faintest tinge of defiance. "I'm entitled to the occasional show of independence. But I understand that this is fundamental to you. I take you, and that, very seriously—and will before I vote. In the meanwhile, my door is always open to you and to your members."

Dane frowned, rested his arms on his knees with—Cassie noted wryly—his index fingers pressed together, pointing toward her like the barrel of a revolver. "I don't like to do this," he said bluntly. "But you've earned fair notice. If you vote against us on *either* bill we're prepared to run George Bolt against you in the primary."

Cassie was genuinely startled. George Bolt was a crusty former governor, moderate on many issues but adamant in support of gun rights—a far more serious opponent than some right-wing stooge. "George Bolt," she answered coolly, "is savvy enough to know that a man of seventy-one, who hasn't run statewide in a decade, is past it. He's got no organization left. Why embarrass himself?"

Dane gave her a brief smile, a chilly play of the lips. "To save Maine from the embarrassment of a senator who's betrayed the Second Amendment. As for organization, we'd fill the gaps nicely."

And so they would. Was George Bolt's law practice flagging so badly, Cassie wondered, that he needed the renewed attention? And then she wondered, with a piercing onset of real fear, why she—or her mentor Warren Colby—hadn't seen or heard this coming. "George can't beat me," she repeated. "And if he does, he'll lose to Abel Randolph in the general. Precipitating a primary fight against me is all it will take to persuade Randolph to make the race. Either way, you'll enhance your chances of trading me for Abel."

"That's right," Dane answered calmly. "And your colleagues will remember that when you're gone. So will you—even if you manage to scrape by." Dane paused, finishing with an air of regret. "This isn't personal, Cassie, and we don't want to do it. But you need to know before it happens, in the hope that it never will."

For a long time Cassie gazed at him. "I hope so, too," she said simply.

TWO

"BEFORE YOUR SISTER left John Bowden," Nolan asked Mary Costello, "did you do anything to help her?"

Near the head of the conference table, Harrison Fancher fixed Mary with the vulpine gaze of a bird of prey, while an innocuous male reporter awaited her answer. But ten minutes into the deposition, Sarah's world had narrowed to the tense, three-sided relationship between Nolan, her somewhat fragile client, and herself. Sitting beside Mary in Nolan's conference room, Sarah saw hostility and self-doubt flicker in her eyes, resolving themselves in a stiff, stubborn posture—rigid back, compressed lips, gaze fixed on the table. "Until Lara saw Joan's bruises," Mary answered in a defensive tone, "we didn't know anything was wrong."

Nolan raised his eyebrows. "*You'd* never seen any injuries?"

"No." Mary looked away. "She'd stopped doing much with us. But we just thought she must be busy with her family."

"You 'thought,' " Nolan echoed with muted incredulity. "Did you ever ask her?"

"No."

Tense, Sarah prepared to intervene. Nolan's first line of attack was becoming clear: Joan's family of origin had failed to protect her and now, by suing Lexington and the SSA, Mary was seeking to deflect her guilt while profiting from her own indifference. "So," Nolan pressed, "John Bowden was keeping your sister and Marie virtual prisoners, and it never occurred to you to inquire as to whether they were okay?"

"Objection," Sarah cut in. "That's not a question—it's harassment."

Fortified by Sarah's defense, Mary raised her eyes, fixing Nolan with a gaze of rebuke. As though noting this, Nolan chose a milder tone. "In your heart, Ms. Costello, didn't you know that something terrible was happening in your sister's home?"

This seemed to strike a chord of self-doubt, causing Mary to hesitate before insisting in a thinner voice, "You don't know how charming John could be. We just didn't know."

" 'We'? Did you ever discuss with your mother whether Joan's husband might be mistreating her—or, at the least, isolating your niece and sister from their own blood relatives?"

Once more, Mary looked away, confirming, by her silence, what Sarah believed to be the truth: that neither Mary nor Inez could bring themselves to verbalize their fears. At length, Mary said, "We both thought it was sad that we barely saw them. But we didn't know the reason until Lara told us. After that, we knew that Lara and Kerry were talking to her, and that Kerry could give Joan good advice."

"But you were in San Francisco." Nolan's tone was mild yet argumentative. "Did you or your mother offer Joan and Marie a home—some shelter from the abuse you belatedly discovered?"

In vain, Sarah searched for an objection. But Nolan's legal point, however offensive, was clear enough: that Mary's neglect had helped enable Bowden to slaughter three members of her family. Briefly, Mary closed her eyes. "Not in those words. But Joanie knew she could always come to us. She was depending on Lara and Kerry."

The last phrase, Sarah thought, held the faintest tinge of an emotion somewhere between resentment and regret. From his newly keen expression, John Nolan had heard it, too. "You've referred to the President and First Lady several times now. Prior to the interview where they exposed John Bowden as an abuser, did you know they were going to do that?"

"Yes."

"Did you approve?"

Mary paused, as though to parse the question. "Lara told us what would be happening, and that the *Chronicle* already had the story. It seemed like everyone was stuck."

"Didn't you ask yourself whether shaming Bowden on national TV might inflame him?"

"I worried about it." Now Mary sounded tired, as though envisioning the tragedy which followed. "But Kerry and Lara knew that world. I didn't. So I decided to trust them."

Nolan propped his chin in the palm of his hand. Softly, he asked, "How do you feel about that now?"

This, Sarah knew, was the second prong of Nolan's strategy: to divide Mary and Lara by exploiting the younger sister's shame and envy. But he risked being too obvious, turning Mary's resentment back against him. Sarah decided to help this process along. "Bad taste, Mr. Nolan, truly knows no bounds. The witness lost most of her family. She watched Marie slowly dying from the hideous internal damage *your client* designed the Eagle's Claw to inflict. Why not just ask her if the President and First Lady caused her six-year-old niece's vena cava to shred."

Nolan's eyes glinted with the resentment of an advocate thwarted in his mission—exacerbated, Sarah was certain, by the fact that his opponent was young, a woman, and a former underling now wholly lacking in deference. She herself, Sarah concluded, was Nolan's Achilles' heel. "Your comments," he shot back, "are improper and grossly unprofessional. If you persist, I'll be forced to bring them to the attention of Judge Bond."

Over drinks at one of your boys' clubs? Sarah was tempted to ask. In her most indifferent tone, she answered, "Your outrage is duly noted. Please move on."

Momentum broken, Nolan paused before turning to Mary. "Did your sister Lara mention that the Kilcannons' exposure of John Bowden was intended to spare the President political embarrassment?"

" 'Mention,' " Sarah repeated. "I certainly object to *that*. It implies that slander contained in your question is a matter of established fact."

"A slander on whom?" Nolan shot back. "The Kilcannons? I thought you were here to represent Mary Costello."

Sarah flushed: Nolan's thrust was calculated to exploit Mary's fear of being controlled by Lara, which complicated Sarah's own relationship to Lara's surviving sister. "I'm here," Sarah answered with tenuous calm, "to point out when your questions lack foundation in fact."

Nolan smiled faintly. "As to what? The President's motives for the interview? Or your own allegiances?" Turning to Mary, he asked, "Did your sister discuss with you whether exposing your sister's abusive marriage served some interest of the President?"

Pensive, Mary gazed at the table. "What I remember is that the *Chronicle* would be printing that already, because he *was* the President, and because Kerry was involved with Joan's case. This was more about the best way to deal with that."

"But how did exposing Bowden serve *Joan's* interests?"

Mary hesitated. "Just by getting it over with, I guess."

Nolan paused, as though seeking a way to probe the answer. Then, abruptly, he switched topics. "You attended the University of San Francisco, a private school. Who paid your tuition and expenses?"

Though she could not acknowledge the lethal psychology of such a question, Sarah knew at once that she must object. With an air of faux mystification, she asked, "What is the possible relevance of that?"

This time, Nolan appeared unruffled. "Humor me, Ms. Dash. Or are you directing your client not to answer?"

To do so, Sarah knew, would risk reopening Mary's deposition at a later time, giving Nolan a second chance to do what he dared not do before a jury—interrogate Mary without regard to the niceties due the survivor of a tragedy. Cornered, Sarah answered, "I'll indulge you, counsel—to a point. But a deposition is not a license to rummage through Ms. Costello's life at random."

With a fleeting smile of satisfaction, Nolan faced Mary. "I paid part of it," she answered in a prideful voice.

"Who paid the rest?"

Mary frowned, glancing at Sarah. "My sister," she said at length. "Lara."

"And did she help you after college?"

Slowly, Mary nodded. "To buy furniture for my apartment. And pay my deposit and first month's rent."

"Did she send you money on other occasions?"

Once more, Mary folded her arms. "She paid for all our plane tickets to the wedding."

Nolan was silent, allowing the irony implicit in the answer to linger. "And you're grateful to the First Lady for her help?"

"Yes," Mary answered tersely. "Of course."

"Would you say that Lara Kilcannon is wealthy?"

"What," Sarah snapped, "does the First Lady's net worth have to do with anything?"

This time Nolan ignored her, daring Sarah to keep her client from responding. "You may answer," he told Mary.

"Yes." Mary replied flatly. "Lara's done well."

"And are you included in her will?"

Mary looked surprised. "I believe so, yes."

"And you're grateful for *that*, I assume."

At this, Mary sat upright. "I was included in my mother's will, Mr. Nolan. It's never occurred to me to be grateful that she's dead."

The retort so disconcerted Nolan that, for a moment, he was silent. "All I meant," he said at length, "is that your sister continues to look out for you financially. Is that why Mrs. Kilcannon is not a plaintiff in this lawsuit?"

Tense, Sarah leaned forward. "I instruct the witness not to answer."

Nolan spun on her. "On what grounds, counsel?"

"As you point out, Mrs. Kilcannon is a potential plaintiff in this action—or her own action against your client. That creates a joint litigation privilege between the surviving sisters as to all communications regarding this suit. With or without a lawyer."

This, Sarah knew, was the weakest of her privilege claims—which Nolan surely knew, as well. With an air of disbelief, he asked Mary, "Are you following your counsel's instruction?"

Briefly, Mary glanced at Sarah. "Yes."

"But you do acknowledge that, as of now, you alone will benefit from any recovery or settlement."

"Yes."

"Except for your lawyers," Nolan amended in an acid tone. "Speaking of which, how did you come to select Mr. Lenihan?"

Once more, Sarah considered objecting. But she had made too big a point of probing Martin Bresler's 'selection' of Evan Pritchard as his lawyer to stage-manage his retraction—as, she realized now, Nolan must have appreciated at the time. Quietly, Mary answered, "Mr. Lenihan offered his services."

"What a surprise. And how did you locate Ms. Dash?"

Mary folded her arms. Tersely, she responded, "My sister."

"Did your sister also offer not to share in the recovery if you accepted Ms. Dash as cocounsel?"

To her chagrin, Sarah saw that she was trapped—to permit an answer, however exculpatory, might permit Nolan to claim that she had waived Mary's claim of privilege. "Same instruction," she snapped. "You can ask my client if she and the First Lady conspired to join a terrorist cell, and my instruction would be the same."

"Really. Let me test that." Turning to Mary, Nolan asked, "Did Mrs. Kilcannon tell you that Ms. Dash would help carry out her and the President's directives as to how to conduct this lawsuit?"

Mary shifted in her chair—caught, Sarah thought, between her resentment of Lara; the question which inflamed it; and Sarah's directions to maintain silence. "Same instruction," Sarah said firmly.

"Or," Nolan persisted, "does Lara 'instruct' you directly?"

"Same instruction . . ."

"Lara," Mary burst out, "doesn't tell me what to do."

"Then you won't mind," Nolan responded smoothly, "ignoring your counsel's instruction, and telling me what she does say. Or would you prefer that I go before Judge Bond?"

With this, Sarah saw that the core of Nolan's strategy of division was more psychological than legal—to estrange Mary from Lara, and from Sarah herself, until she fired her lawyers or dropped the suit. But she could not know how clearly Nolan grasped the full potential of this strategy, all the intricacies—the jealousies, old wounds, and fresh resentments—hidden by the successes of Inez Costello's now-blighted family. "Same instruction," Sarah repeated.

Nolan's keen gaze remained focused on Mary. "Are you following your counsel's orders, Ms. Costello?"

Taut, Sarah could only watch. Answering, her client spoke without inflection, looking at no one. "Yes."

For a moment Nolan studied her, and then shrugged his dismissal. "Then I suppose I'll have to ask your sister."

THREE

Entering the Republican cloakroom after morning business, Frank Fasano had hoped to test his colleagues' reaction to Senator Hampton's uncharacteristically lacerating critique. Instead, he found Chad Palmer and Leo Weller absorbed in watching Kerry Kilcannon on CNN. Joining them, he perceived at once that Hampton's speech was part of a broader attack orchestrated by Kilcannon himself.

The President had ventured into opposition territory, choosing to address a Chamber of Commerce convention in Atlantic City, part of a one-day media blitz devoted wholly to guns. Faced with a potentially hostile reception, Kilcannon seemed more cheerful—in a sardonic way—than Fasano had seen him since the murders. Palmer, too, seemed amused, watching Kilcannon with the detached appreciation of one warrior for another—enhanced, the Majority Leader suspected, by Palmer's distaste for his own alliance with Fasano.

"For Kerry," Palmer observed, "a little antagonism is the spice of life." Watching the screen, Leo Weller chuckled.

Frivolous lawsuits, Kilcannon was telling his listeners, *ought not be encouraged. But some of the antilawyer rhetoric used to promote tort reform is based on calculated disinformation. To be blunt, it's more attractive to attack "greedy trial lawyers" than a ten-year-old quadriplegic facing life in a wheelchair because of a defective tire . . .*

"To be blunt," Fasano repeated with a smile. But he was gaining a fresh appreciation of how deadly such directness could be.

I understand the temptation, Kilcannon went on. *A lot of people hate every lawyer except the one they need. It's rather like politicians. In fact, as a class, we're both so widely despised that it's easy for our detractors to claim that lawyers buy politicians on the open market.* Kilcannon smiled, skipping a beat. *In fact, one of your previous speakers implied that about* me, *just yesterday.*

The speaker, Fasano knew, had been Paul Harshman. Kilcannon continued in the same ironic tone. *Seven times, in fact, he employed the words "Kilcannon" and "trial lawyers" in the same unflattering sentence. Never once did he utter the word "victim." But that's what you get from a defective tire; or an exploding gas tank; or a plane which blows up in midair.*

Lawyers don't create victims. But all too often, victims need lawyers. Because without legal representation, ordinary people are all too often powerless to gain recourse from the institutions whose carelessness or callousness has blighted their lives forever . . .

"Cheap populism," Leo Weller snorted. "You'd think we're a nation of victims."

Fasano glanced at him. "Best not to say that in public, Leo. At least until the 'ordinary people' of Montana have voted you a second term."

And so, Kilcannon suggested to his captive audience, *let's address some other questions Senator Harshman failed to ask.*

Time and again, he complained that the cost of "needless litigation" is passed on to the consumer.

But is litigation "needless" when it secures the constant care our ten-year-old quadriplegic will require for the rest of his very difficult life?

Didn't "needless litigation" compel the auto industry to improve the safety of its cars?

And why are plaintiffs' lawyers more blameworthy than the defense lawyers for the tobacco and asbestos industries—some from the most prosperous firms in America—who earn five hundred dollars an hour bludgeoning plaintiffs who are dying of cancer or emphysema?

Palmer laughed softly. "Where's Paul?" he asked. "*I'm* dying to hear his answer."

Senator Harshman, Kilcannon continued, *emphasized time and again that you represent the men and women of Main Street. Many of you own small businesses. But who does he suppose supports your companies and stores? For the most part, ordinary people. After all is said and done, we all should be together in this.*

This leads to yet another hard truth the senator failed to mention—that a knee-jerk condemnation of lawsuits too often favors the rich and powerful at the expense of the injured and the powerless—including, perhaps, your own family and friends.

He bitterly condemned class actions. Would he argue that it's all right for a crooked corporation to destroy the pensions or investments of ordinary people who, as individuals, no longer have the means to sue?

He attacked contingent fees for plaintiffs' lawyers. Would he deprive ordinary people of lawyers because they lack the wherewithal to pay one to oppose the array of lawyers a massive corporation can use to grind them down?

He deplored politicians who accept the support of plaintiffs' lawyers. Is he suggesting that those who accept donations from defense lawyers and their corporate clients somehow are immune from his criticisms?

Leo Weller, Fasano observed, was now glued to the screen, all scorn or jollity vanished. There was a political problem, Fasano faintly remembered, in Montana— something about mines and asbestosis. On the screen, Kilcannon raised his head with an air of challenge.

My political opponents, he said in a calm clear voice, *will accuse me of class rhetoric and facile populism. But their anti-lawyer rhetoric too often masks a defense of privilege against the rights of ordinary Americans.* Pausing, the President gazed out at his listeners. *Too often, this simplistic lawyer-bashing helps them to manipulate the legislative process to protect their corporate patrons, and to bar the ordinary people their patrons injure from seeking justice.*

If this sounds too harsh, ponder why we have consumer protection laws which protect children from defects in toy guns and candy cigarettes, but exempt the real thing . . .

"No mystery," Palmer answered. "It's because the folks who made the real thing have bought us. That's what campaign finance reform is all about." Under his breath, Leo Weller issued a grumble of dissent.

In those *cases,* Kilcannon was saying, *litigation is not simply the last resort of ordinary people—it's the only protection they've got.*

Abruptly, his tone became softer and more conciliatory. *The question is not whether some lawyers are unscrupulous—they are.*

The question is not whether some lawsuits are frivolous—they are.

The question is not whether litigation burdens your businesses— it does.

The ultimate question, simply, is whether ordinary people who are injured deserve their day in court.

And that, regrettably, is the most basic question Senator Harshman—and his leader, Senator Fasano—have failed to address.

Watching, Fasano tried to detach himself as Palmer had, to study his opponent as one professional appraising another. Kilcannon's gift for confrontation and edgy rhetoric, Fasano believed, was a distinctly two-edged sword, creating both fervent admirers and dedicated detractors by the minute. But Kilcannon was skilled at turning on a dime from confrontation to conciliation, with a persuasive power which might beguile many of those listening. And he had another strength, just as disconcerting. Unlike some politicians, whom television tends to flatten to a single dimension, Kilcannon was as vivid on the screen as he was in person. All of which made Fasano's knowledge of what was coming even more unpleasant.

Although Senator Harshman also failed to mention this, Kilcannon continued, *I'm quite sympathetic to your concerns. But we have to find a balance. That's why I proposed tort reform legislation which would cap attorneys' fees, and limit the punitive damage awards which can be so catastrophic to your businesses.*

Your own leaders favored such a compromise. But Senator Fasano refused to support it . . .

"I imagine," Palmer observed wryly, "that he's about to tell us why."

Fasano smiled. "I'm sure he'll be at least as kind to me as Paul was to him."

The reason is simple, Kilcannon went on. *Buried at the heart of the Civil Justice Reform Act supported by Senator Fasano is a provision immunizing gun companies from lawsuits.*

I asked that it be stricken. Your officers agreed. Senator Fasano refused. So you may want to consider whether the Republican leadership's priorities are your priorities. And then, perhaps, you might ask Senator Fasano why the gun lobby's wish list takes precedence over your much broader core concerns.

" 'Because,' " Palmer answered dryly for Fasano, " 'the right of patriotic Americans to bear arms should be sacred to you all.' "

It's a curious thing, Kilcannon was saying with a glimmer of amusement. *Senator Fasano and his colleagues are fervent defenders of states' rights and local control. Yet they propose to rewrite the laws of* all *fifty states, to wipe out* all *future lawsuits against gun manufacturers by the victims or survivors of gun violence.* Gaze sweeping the hall, Kilcannon added in a soft, ironic tone, *They even propose to wipe out suits which have already been filed, whoever the plaintiff and wherever the lawsuit may be found . . .*

"I wonder," Fasano remarked, "if he has any particular plaintiff in mind."

"Why not?" Palmer answered. "The SSA does."

Many of you may not believe that such victims or their families should recover damages. Fine. If they're not entitled to do so under existing state law, then they won't. But the Republican leadership should not sacrifice the many interests of your members simply to ensure that the survivors of those who are killed with guns never receive a dime . . .

"Ever hear of life insurance?" Leo Weller retorted.

"Jesus," Chad Palmer jibed good-naturedly. "I hope you don't try that one on the stump. Your opponent will kick your ass without ever leaving home."

"The people of Montana," Leo rejoined, "don't like gun-grabbers or plaintiffs' lawyers. Or East Coast liberals like your pal Kilcannon." With a disgusted wave of the hand toward the President's image, Weller left.

I will veto this bill, Kilcannon concluded. *I cannot, in good conscience, accept what is unconscionable. But the compromise I've offered you still stands. Just tell Senator Fasano to call me, day or night . . .*

"Still with me?" Fasano asked Palmer in a muted, mocking tone. "Or should we call KFK together?"

Palmer shoved his hands in his pockets. "We're not whores like Leo," he answered. "We gave each other our word, and now we're both going to keep it."

Returning from his meeting with Cassie Rollins, Dane switched on CNN, intending to glance at it while returning his messages.

From Atlantic City, Kilcannon had traveled to his hometown of Newark—on the television, with the word "LIVE" emblazoned beneath their images, the President and First Lady were visiting an elementary school in Vailsburg, Kilcannon's old neighborhood. Beside them, looking discomfited, was Democratic Senator James Torchio of

New Jersey, a swing vote on tort reform. As they sat in a circle with a mixture of black, white, and Hispanic schoolkids, a boy of roughly seven described the killing of his sister by a playmate with a loaded gun.

Finishing, the boy turned to Lara. Baldly, he said, *They shot your sister, too. I saw it on TV—she was bloody and everything.*

For an instant, the First Lady seemed stricken. The boy looked confused, as though wondering if he had said something wrong. Then Lara crossed the circle, taking him in her arms. *Then you know how I feel,* she told him gently. *And I know how you feel.*

Dane stabbed the remote button, and the screen went dark.

FOUR

Trying to suspend her disbelief, Sarah watched the President of the United States face John Nolan across a conference table in the Washington office of Nolan's firm.

Sitting beside the President was his personal lawyer, Professor Avram Gold of Harvard Law School. Sarah had known—because Lara Kilcannon had told her—that Kerry Kilcannon would not resist Nolan's demand for a deposition. To comply, Sarah had agreed, would provide a telling contrast with Lexington's resistance to producing George Callister. But Nolan's barely reined-in aggressiveness was palpable. From her tenure as Nolan's associate, she knew that he regarded Kilcannon with the bone-deep loathing—irrational to Sarah—that the Republican right reserved for this particular President. Drawn by this admixture of history and emotion, the other principal combatants surrounded the conference table: both Lenihan and Sarah; Harrison Fancher and his chief associate; the lead associate for Nolan. To commemorate the occasion, and to ensure that any flashes of Presidential temper or embarrassment were captured on film, Nolan had obtained an order from his fellow ideologue Gardner Bond that the proceedings be videotaped. From a corner, a cameraman aimed his lens directly at Kilcannon.

Briskly entering the room, the President had seemed a magnetic figure, regarding its occupants with an air of detachment which, Sarah sensed, concealed his distaste at being there and his antagonism toward those representing Lexington and the SSA. But, given his own stake in the proceeding, Sarah was certain the President was intimately familiar with the issues and thoroughly prepared for Nolan's attack. Meeting him, Sarah felt a current of energy and hyperalertness. He paused, looking directly into her eyes as though to convey a sense of complicity and warmth complemented by the lilting quiet of his voice. "I watched you in the Tierney case," he said with a smile. "If you weren't already taken, my friend Professor Gold would be holding your coat. As it is, I suppose I'll have to reserve you for impeachment."

The remark—with its wry acknowledgment of how hell-bent the right was to be rid of him—made Sarah's nervousness at meeting him dissipate. Then she felt a second, more embarrassing, reaction: that the always-present possibility of her attraction to a man had focused—for a brief, intense moment—on Kerry Kilcannon. Covering this thought with a smile of her own, she answered, "Thank you, Mr. President. If I have any pointers, I'll pass them on through your interim counsel."

But—at least in the initial stages—it was clear that Kerry Kilcannon needed no coaching. Ignoring the camera, he kept his responses calm and concise while Nolan led him into the legal and psychological minefield of the events leading to the murders.

"You were aware, were you not, that Joan Bowden was relying on you for advice on how to deal with her husband's abuse?"

Kilcannon nodded. "Acutely aware."

"And did you advise her to leave the marriage?"

"Yes."

Pausing, Nolan fixed the President with a contemplative gaze. "As a former domestic violence prosecutor, would you agree that the point at which a battered spouse breaks off her relationship marks the moment at which her life is in the greatest danger?"

Kilcannon changed expression, a slight narrowing of the eyes. "Not necessarily, Mr. Nolan. The point of greatest danger *could* be when the abuser beats her to death before she decides to leave."

The response made Nolan hesitate. "Nonetheless," he persisted, "you were aware from your own experience that batterers often react to a loss of control by escalating the violence from battery to murder."

" 'Often'? I don't know that I'd agree. But it can happen that way."

Nolan leaned slightly forward. "In fact, didn't your first domestic violence prosecution end in the murder of the victim by her estranged husband?"

Kilcannon folded his hands. "I believe that's a matter of public record."

"Did you happen to mention that to Joan?"

The President hesitated. Softly, he answered, "I don't believe I did."

"Because you were afraid she wouldn't leave?"

Betraying no anger or antagonism, the President seemed to consider this. "Her husband had been beating her for years, and it was affecting her six-year-old daughter. The night before she left, Bowden held a gun to her head and threatened to kill her. I didn't think she needed to be told she was at risk, either way. She was as in touch with that fact as she was with the gun at her temple. What Joan—and Marie—needed was to be free from Bowden before it was too late."

"But *you* knew from hard experience that, by leaving, she might enrage John Bowden enough to kill her."

"I considered that, yes."

"But you didn't see fit to warn her."

Next to Sarah, Lenihan whispered, "This is unbeliev-able."

"Try odious," she whispered back. She had never despised John Nolan more, both for the nature of his questions and the utter lack of deference with which he posed them.

But Kilcannon gave no sign of noticing. In an even tone, he answered, "Joan and Marie were living under monstrous conditions. I didn't 'see fit' to frighten her into staying."

Nolan gave him a quizzical look. "So you decided to assume the risk for her?"

With a long, deliberate silence, Kilcannon studied him. Softly, he answered, "I didn't think there was any risk to me, Mr. Nolan. If there were, and Marie and Joanie would have been safer, I'd gladly have assumed it. Or have I misconceived your question?"

If anything, Sarah thought, the quiet of Kilcannon's voice enhanced the tension in the room. The others around the table seemed as rapt as she.

"Isn't it true, Mr. President, that Bowden's threats against his wife escalated after she went to the police—pursuant to *your* encouragement?"

"Yes. Predictably. I couldn't stop that."

"So what *did* you do?"

Before answering, the President seemed to inhale, sug-gesting to Sarah a patient man whose patience was being tried. "I called the District Attorney, made sure the police took away Bowden's guns, and monitored the issuance of a restraining order. When his threats persisted, I saw to it that the police searched his apartment yet again, and hired private security people to protect both Joan and Marie." Briefly, the President paused. "For my pains, the *Chronicle* contacted my press secretary, demanding to know whether I was using 'special influence' on their behalf."

"And that's why you and the First Lady chose to expose Bowden as a batterer on ABC?"

"Chose?" Kilcannon considered Nolan with muted disdain. "You can't be expected to appreciate this, Mr. Nolan. But in dealing with the media, a President's choices are often limited. Faced with the prospect that the *Chronicle* would string this out, we decided the better course was to get it over with."

"Whose interest did *that* serve?"

The President stared at him. "Joan's, I thought. Unless we got this out, the media would have hounded her for days. As well as Bowden."

Nolan tilted his head in an attitude of skepticism. "With respect, Mr. President, wasn't one of your concerns to put your role in this matter in its most appealing light?"

A faint smile did nothing to diminish the new hardness in Kilcannon's clear blue eyes. "With respect, Mr. Nolan, that question is beneath contempt."

Nolan sat back. After a moment, he said, "Whatever your emotions, sir, I'd appreciate an answer."

The smile lingered. "What about my previous answer—did you fail to understand?"

Lenihan emitted a short, sardonic laugh. Hearing this, Nolan froze, but did not look toward Lenihan. Sitting beside the President, Avram Gold—clearly under instructions not to intervene—raised his eyebrows at Nolan as if to ask what he'd expected. Unable to resist, he inquired, "Would you like the reporter to read the answer back?"

Scowling, Nolan checked his watch, as though to indicate that any attenuation of the deposition was

Kilcannon's own doing. Then, wisely, he gave up on the question altogether.

"In giving the interview, Mr. President, didn't you consider that you might inflame Mr. Bowden to violence?"

"To the ultimate violence? I couldn't know. I was certain he'd not only be inflamed, but humiliated. But no more than he would have been by a story in a hometown paper with a circulation of a million, which then would have been picked up by every national and local media outlet in America . . ."

"Given that, did you take additional measures to protect Joan and Marie?"

"They were with *us* at the time, under the protection of the Secret Service. What I did do was make sure that the private security firm which we'd hired to watch Joan's home also met them at the airport." The President paused, and his voice became soft with regret. "What I failed to consider was that your client's advertisement would induce Bowden to travel to a gun show in Las Vegas, where a convicted spousal abuser could acquire a Lexington P-2 and Eagle's Claw bullets. And that those at risk included Lara's mother."

This stopped Nolan. For a moment, he seemed undecided as to his course. Then, from a folder to his right, he slid a copy of a document with the jagged scrawl Sarah knew at once to be John Bowden's.

As she watched, appalled, Nolan asked the reporter to mark the paper as "Kilcannon Exhibit One," and then slid it in front of the President. "Can you identify this document?"

Gazing at Bowden's words on paper, Kilcannon seemed to pale. "It's a letter from John Bowden. The contents speak for themselves."

"In that John Bowden blames you for the murder he intends to commit?"

"Yes."

"Given this, would you still have exposed him before an audience of roughly forty million people?"

The President drew a breath, still gazing at the fateful words. "There isn't any aspect of what I did," he answered softly, "that I don't question every day. And will, every day for the rest of my life. But I truly believe I did everything I could to protect Lara's family—including disarm John Bowden." Pausing, the President looked up at last. "But there was no way, Mr. Nolan, to completely protect them from your client."

Briefly, Nolan seemed taken aback. Then, with a rising undertone of anger, he asked, "Isn't it true, Mr. President, that you're attempting to blame Lexington Arms for your own decision to provoke a man who *you* knew was prone to violence?"

The words "Mr. President," Sarah noted, were spoken with a slighting emphasis which suggested that Kerry Kilcannon did not deserve the office. "No," Kilcannon answered in a cold but even tone. "I'm blaming Lexington for *its* own decision to market uniquely lethal weapons to criminals and wife-beaters. I blame Lexington for its failure—even after this tragedy took three members of Lara's family and three members of other families—to lift a finger to keep still more deaths from happening. Or do anything at all, it seems, except to hire you to deflect *their* blame onto what remains of a family still grieving for our losses.

"That's why you've brought me here—despite the fact, which you occasionally seem to recognize, that I *am* the President and, as such, somewhat busy. Perhaps even busier than the President of Lexington Arms. Nonetheless, I'm answering your questions. So where, I have to wonder, is Mr. Callister?

"I haven't heard from him. He hasn't been seen. In fact, Professor Gold tells me that you're refusing to produce him for a deposition. What are you afraid of, Mr. Nolan? That the experience will be insufficiently congenial for him? Please assure him for me that he'll be treated with respect."

Watching, Sarah felt a deep surge of satisfaction, both because the President had, at last, retaliated and because he had so pointedly contrasted his own availability with Callister's. Were she John Nolan, Sarah thought, she would burn the videotape before anyone could see it.

This seemed to have occurred to him. Staring at the President, Nolan shed the last veneer of courtesy. "Isn't it true," he asked in a hectoring tone, "that Mr. Callister refused your demands to change Lexington's marketing practices?"

"No, it isn't true," Kilcannon answered calmly. "But he did decline my request in that regard. Both before and after the murders."

"And it's also true, is it not, that you blame the SSA for Congress's failure to enact the kind of gun laws *you* think should exist?"

"In some measure, yes. I also blame myself for failing to get them enacted. I'm trying to rectify that."

"In fact," Nolan pressed, "isn't this lawsuit part of an effort to do that?"

"Whose effort? I'm not a party. And if anything tarnishes your client, it will be the facts you seem to be trying to suppress . . ."

"Isn't," Nolan snapped, "Mary Costello conducting this lawsuit at your direction?"

"Mary," Kilcannon answered, "has never talked with me about this lawsuit."

Nolan scowled in disbelief. "Have you discussed it with Ms. Dash?"

Briefly, the President glanced in Sarah's direction. "I admire Ms. Dash's work. But I've never spoken to her before this morning."

"But you do know Mr. Lenihan. And have for some time."

"True."

"In fact, he's your leading supporter."

"I try to encourage a little competition for that title. But he's certainly been supportive."

"And have you discussed this lawsuit with Mr. Lenihan?"

"Once. Shortly after the murders, he asked me if Mary might require representation. I replied that, if she did, I couldn't think of anyone better. Nothing more was said. Sometime thereafter, I learned that Mary had engaged Mr. Lenihan as cocounsel."

"Do you know how Mary Costello came to engage Ms. Dash?"

The President shrugged. "I think Lara may have suggested it. What did Mary say?"

Frustrated, Nolan renewed his attack. "Did you discuss Ms. Dash's engagement with the First Lady?"

The President sat straighter, looking straight at Nolan. "Lara's my wife, Mr. Nolan. Three of her family members were slaughtered. You can fairly surmise that, from time to time, the subject comes up—even, on occasion, Mary's lawsuit. In fact, we may even discuss this deposition over dinner. But that's not for you to know."

"Are you refusing to answer?"

At this, Avram Gold began to speak. Gently, the President placed a hand on his wrist. "Lara and I may be public figures," he told Nolan. "But we have the same privilege of privacy between us as any other couple . . ."

"Are you," Nolan cut in, "directing this lawsuit through Mrs. Kilcannon?"

" 'Directing'? No. That's the job of the lawyers, I would have thought."

"Then you can clear all this up, Mr. President, by telling me whether you're using your wife as a conduit for your instructions to Mary Costello and her attorneys . . ."

"There's about to be some 'directing' done," Avram Gold interjected. "By me. By asking your last question you're trying to get the President to waive the marital privilege, now and in the future. I'm directing the President not to answer *any* questions about his private marital communications with the First Lady. That's the law, and it's also a matter of simple decency. It's a shame that I have to remind you of either."

"Are you," Nolan demanded of Kilcannon, "refusing to answer my question?"

"Yes." The President's faint smile returned. "Out of respect for Professor Gold. And, of course, my wife."

Nolan drew himself up. "I must advise you, sir, that we may be forced to bring a motion to reopen your deposition. And that the necessity of doing so may delay your sister-in-law's case from coming to trial."

"We're both lawyers," the President answered. "So we both know that such a motion would be groundless—*your* effort to manufacture yet more delay, not mine.

"You have, I understand, managed to conceal all discovery from public view. I can certainly see why. But you'd have to bring this motion you're threatening in open court, before the press and public, urging that Lexington has the right to insinuate itself into our lives even more than it already has. I'd welcome the chance to respond. So, I think, would Lara."

For once, Nolan seemed without words. His motion, Sarah felt confident, would never see the light of day.

Next to her, Lenihan inquired lazily, "Are we through here, John? Some of us have things to do."

That night, as Lara slept, Kerry went to the Oval Office.

In the top drawer of his desk was a file of notes written in his own hand—conversations with Joan, the telephone number of the District Attorney's office and, later, the security firm. The final document was his own copy of John Bowden's letter.

He had not dared to look at it in weeks. Now he could not stop reading it. All that served to distract him from the words was his even more indelible memory of the murders themselves.

FIVE

THE NEXT MORNING, when Kerry returned to the Oval Office, he brought with him a copy of the SSA *Defender* magazine.

The cover featured a caricature of President Kerry Kilcannon sipping champagne in white tie and tails, captioned in bold letters, "Has this man ever been to a gun show?" The article inside praised gun shows as a place for "American families to enjoy the sporting traditions central to our way of life." Kerry flipped to a page he had marked with a paper clip, a calendar of gun-related events.

Underlined in red was a gun show in Las Vegas. He placed it next to a typed itinerary for the next two days, built around a speech in San Francisco. Then he picked up the telephone and called Kit Pace. "I want to change tomorrow's schedule," he told her.

Bernadette Fasano was one week from her due date and her husband—who despised cell phones, but was committed to being present for the delivery of each of their children—had stuffed a phone in his pocket before he left home. It was still there when, at noon, he ate a sandwich with Charles Dane in the SSA's conference room.

Dane pressed the start button on a VCR. "What you're about to see," he said in an orotund impression of a television reporter, "is just one of the many important *pro bono* services of America's trial lawyers."

On the screen appeared photographs of Henry Serrano, David Walsh, and Laura Blanchard, the other victims in the Costello shootings. Scrolling beneath them were the words of Lexington's advertisement in the SSA magazine. Their faces faded to black, and a quiet voice asked, "*Just who is the 'endangered species'?*"

"Is this from Lenihan's group?" Fasano inquired.

"Yup. They've started running ads in major media markets. We're compiling their greatest hits."

The next spot focused on Felice Serrano, holding a photograph of her late husband playing a board game with their children. *I pray that every member of Congress will remember George before they vote against gun safety . . .*

"Shameless," Dane remarked. "She may be mouthing the words, but I can hear Robert Lenihan speaking to a San Francisco jury."

Abruptly, Felice was succeeded by the faces of several children under ten, appearing with their ages above the words "killed by classmates." *These,* the voice-over explained, *are some of the eighty children killed every week by guns. But Senator Fasano thinks that safety locks to save their lives threaten our freedom. What's more important than the freedom to grow up?*

Despite his hard-earned thickness of skin, Fasano realized that he felt defensive. When Dane gratuitously observed, "They're making you the target," Fasano considered responding, *And it's you who put the bull's-eye on my forehead.*

He was restrained by the images of a former press secretary and his wife, who had become gun safety activists after the husband's wounding by a would-be assassin. The husband had suffered a grave cerebral injury; in clear but halting speech, he said, *I'm all for hunting and sport shooting. All I want is to make our country safer.* Nodding, his wife looked into the camera, *That's why we were so offended when Senator Paul Harshman told the SSA convention that "next to Kerry Kilcannon," my husband was the "leading enemy" of gun owners in America.*

"Do me a favor," Fasano remarked. "Quit inviting Paul to speak. It's like giving gasoline and matches to a pyromaniac . . ."

He was cut off by a metallic beep—his cell phone. "Bernadette," he murmured. As Dane hit the stop button, Fasano turned away. "Sweetheart?" he answered softly.

"I'm sorry," Bernadette's voice was wan but wry, "but if I'm any judge of these things, our newest product in development is about to go on-line."

Through his anxiety, Fasano felt himself smile: their sixth child in nine years qualified Bernadette as an expert. "Will he or she hang on until I get there?"

"I'll tell 'her' to," Bernadette said, hoping aloud for a daughter. "But this one time I want your promise to 'be home soon' to be more than aspirational."

"Promise," Fasano said, and hung up.

"Another Fasano on the way?" Dane inquired amiably.

"My wife's never wrong. Got to run."

Dane nodded toward the screen. "Too bad. You're missing the best one—a knife in Leo Weller's back."

Fasano reached for his briefcase. "Why am I not surprised? But I'm afraid it'll have to keep."

"Don't let all this worry you," Dane told him. "We're ready to respond to this garbage. We promised to protect you and your people, and we will—big-time."

He was supposed to feel grateful and beholden, Fasano knew. Nodding, he headed for the glass door.

"Good luck," Dane said. "I guess you don't know what flavor this one is?"

"We never ask." Briefly, Fasano paused in the doorway.

"When you're in my business, Charles, you treasure the few surprises which are nice ones."

A day later, after the President's noontime speech on corporate responsibility to the Commonwealth Club in San Francisco, Kit Pace surprised the traveling media contingent by announcing an unscheduled three-hour stopover in Las Vegas. She explained this only as "personal time"; to repeated inquiries, she intimated that Kerry would be meeting with unspecified supporters. "I doubt he'll be playing the slots," she observed, "but I'm sure the press pool will catch him if he does." All of which, Kerry was certain, would suggest to the ever-alert White House press corps that something surprising was up—the precise reaction he had hoped for.

On the flight from San Francisco, Kerry placed a congratulatory call to the Majority Leader on the birth of his fifth son. "Come up with a name?" Kerry asked.

"Francis Xavier Fasano, Junior." Kerry heard the smile in Fasano's voice. "After five boys, Bernadette's a broken woman, and we'd about run out of names. So I was able to sneak 'Frank Junior' by her."

It would be a nice anecdote for the media and home-state audiences; to Kerry's trained ear, it already had a certain practiced sound. But beneath this he heard Fasano's joy and pride—even in an obligatory conversation with an adversary who, Kerry well knew, Fasano personally disliked. Feeling a moment's envy, Kerry rued the absence of children in his life, and then, sadly, thought of Marie. "Lara has a will of steel," he told Fasano, "and I'm sure we'll stop well short of six. I doubt the world will ever see Kerry junior."

"For some of us," Fasano said dryly, "Kerry senior is more than enough to handle." But this was the closest they got to politics. Kerry passed over his own family concerns, including today's source of anxiety and anger—Lara's deposition. Hanging up, he wondered how it was going.

In search of distraction, Kerry went to his private quarters with Kit, to review the television ads prepared by the Trial Lawyers for Justice.

Of the first five, his favorite showed a retired Army general—a veteran of Vietnam—dressed in hunting gear and holding a Lexington P-2. *When I was in Vietnam,* the general said brusquely, *I needed this kind of gun. But I sure don't need it for hunting deer. All it's good for is hunting people . . .*

"Who don't have a sporting chance," Kerry added softly. "We have to separate the hunters from the crazies. This one does."

"That's not bad," Kit agreed. "But check out the next one."

Abruptly, the war hero was replaced by pictures of a picturesque frontier town. *This,* the narrator began, *is Libby, Montana.*

It's a place where folks work hard, and don't ask for anything more than a fair shake. But now many of its people are dying from asbestosis, and their families are facing an uphill battle against asbestos companies who are using big donations, deceptive ads, and high-priced lobbyists to persuade our elected representatives in Washington to protect them . . .

"Didn't take Lenihan long," Kerry remarked.

The bucolic scene was replaced by somber faces. First, a gentle, grey-haired woman said, *They killed my husband, and now my four boys are dying, too.* Then came a man with sad eyes and hollow cheeks, *They lied to us,* he explained. *We knew it was dusty, but we didn't know it was deadly.*

To Kerry, the testament of real people packed a raw power no artifice could match. *Three members of my family died,* a pretty young woman told the camera. *My brother*

Hank, my Uncle Lee, and my cousin Alex. We'd *be held account-able if it was us who did this . . .*

"Not," Kit interrupted, "if you've given Leo Weller a hundred thousand or so."

As if on cue, Weller's face appeared. *Now Senator Leo Weller,* the young woman's voice continued, *is sponsoring legislation to keep us from holding the company responsible.*

With a jarring abruptness, Weller was replaced by a dying man breathing through a respirator. *I'd like an apology from Leo Weller,* he said in a labored wheeze. *But he wouldn't even meet with us. I want to know before I die what makes an asbestos company's profits more important than my life . . .*

"Seems fair enough," observed Kit. "Wonder what Weller would tell him."

The first woman reappeared, her words more piercing for the plainspoken flatness of her speech. *The asbestos industry is spending millions of dollars pushing legislation they wrote, sponsored by Senator Weller, to protect them from the people they poisoned.* They *call it the Civil Justice Reform Act. We hope you'll call Senator Weller and ask him why he won't stand up for us.*

Against a black background, the telephone number of Weller's Washington office appeared in white. Softly, the woman finished, *Please help us,* and then the screen went dark.

It was a moment before Kerry spoke. "Know what the media buy is?"

"Two million," Kit answered. "In Montana, that's enough to run it every night, on every station, for the next three weeks. Lenihan's people have already taken this to CNN and *Nightline,* and they're both looking at doing stories."

Kerry looked up at her. "A couple of weeks of this and Leo may be a tad more flexible on tort reform." He briefly shook his head. "It's exactly what I wanted them to do—

put their money on the screen. It's also what Chad Palmer and I spent half our careers complaining about—except now the trial lawyers are almost as powerful as the corporations, and they're *both* at least as powerful as the parties they're trying to buy. All that's changed is that we've all become a little worse, and the system a little worse off."

Kit did not answer. Kerry realized that the plane had slowed; glancing out the window, he saw the mirage which was Las Vegas.

"Do you really want to do this?" Kit asked. "You've got no idea in the world what will happen."

Kerry smiled faintly. "Just stand back from me a little. With any luck, they'll miss you."

SIX

AT TWO O'CLOCK in the afternoon, Lara and Avram Gold entered the conference room of Nolan's firm.

Though it felt awkward, Lara greeted Sarah with polite formality. The others—Lenihan and the defense lawyers, Nolan, Fancher, and their associates—shook her hand with deference, a receiving line of litigators. This false decorum made her edgy. Despite all of her experience as a public person, the risks she had run as a war correspondent, she had not been able to eat since breakfast. There was a knot in the pit of her stomach.

She sat across from Nolan. Somewhat theatrically, Avram Gold looked about the room. "What," he inquired with a mocking edge, "no video camera?"

To Lara, a trace of cynicism showed beneath Nolan's mandarin air of calm. "For Mrs. Kilcannon," he answered smoothly, "we didn't feel it necessary."

Lara studied him. His face was broad and flat, his forehead high, and he wore a double-breasted blue pinstripe like an armor of wealth and privilege. Lara detested the fact that this stranger—the representative of so much she disliked—could make her relive the worst moments of her life, or account for her relationship to those whom she had lost. She determined to give him nothing—no emotion, no pretense of cordiality, only a cool façade. They would see who would be the first to crack.

"Please state your name for the record," Nolan said to Lara.

"Lara Costello Kilcannon," she replied, and the deposition began.

In the first few moments, Nolan established that she once had had a living mother, Inez; a sister, Joan; and a six-year-old niece, Marie. To Lara, the familiarity with which he spoke their names was an affront.

"When," Nolan inquired, "did you first realize that John was abusing your sister?"

"During a trip to San Francisco with my husband, shortly after the President was elected." She paused briefly. "When I went to see Joan she had bruises on her face."

"How long had this abuse been going on?"

"I don't know, exactly. But I gather for some time."

Nolan raised his eyebrows. "Why is it that you didn't know?"

It was starting, Lara knew—the implication, slowly planted, that Joan's negligent family, by failing to help or intervene, had sown the seeds of its own tragedy. Part of her tensed with anger; another part wished to cry out in grief and protest, pleading for exculpation. But this deposition was not a human process, and Nolan far from her confessor. "I'm afraid," she responded coolly, "that only Joan can answer that."

Though expressionless himself, Nolan paused. "Then why do you believe that it had been happening for some time?"

"Joan indicated that to my husband."

"In your presence?"

"No."

Facing Nolan, Gold leaned forward between Lara and her interrogator, palm raised to interrupt the questioning. "To the extent that the question asks the witness to divulge confidential conversations between husband and wife, that is covered by the marital privilege, which exists to protect the sanctity of that relationship. As to those, the witness will not answer."

Coldly, Nolan asked Lara, "Is it your position, Mrs. Kilcannon, that you will refuse to provide any information about your sister's abuse—*or* the circumstances leading to her murder—if you discussed them with your husband?"

Lara paused, gripped by disbelief that this obtrusive stranger could keep her in this stifling room, forcing her to parse his twistings of a tragedy which had seared her soul forever, and about which he cared nothing. "No," she answered. "Mr. Gold stated my position. Why don't you have the reporter read it back."

Lara felt the others watching, tense and quiet. Nolan seemed to gauge her, weighing his choices.

"Did you ever," he demanded of Lara, "discuss with Joan, *your sister*, her history of abuse?"

"Not my *sister*, Joan. Was there some other Joan you were curious about?"

Across the table, she saw Nolan assimilate the dimensions of their contest: Lara felt under no compunction to cater to him, and was determined not to indulge the human impulse to justify her actions or inactions. She would reserve any display of her humanity—with its more elaborate answers—for the jury.

"Were there," Nolan persisted, "strains in your relationship with Joan?"

"Not on my part. My deepest regret is that I was so far away, in Washington or overseas . . ."

"What about on Joan's part?"

"Joan always knew I loved her. I'm only sorry that she's not here to reassure you of that herself."

Nolan leaned forward. "For what reason, then, did you never discuss with her what must have been a nightmare of abuse?"

Lara folded her hands in front of her. "Because it *was* a nightmare, and I knew she was ashamed. Kerry was also family, and a former domestic violence prosecutor—the best possible person for Joan to talk with. It seemed cruel to make her repeat the painful facts to me in person, just out of some warped sense I was entitled to that as her sister. Helping Joan was about what was best for her, not me."

Once more, she watched Nolan calculate how to find the iceberg of dysfunction he seemed certain lurked beneath her answers. Abruptly, he asked, "Precisely how did *you* help her, Mrs. Kilcannon?"

"Through my husband."

Faced with the same cul-de-sac, Nolan shifted ground. "Did *you* refer her to a counselor?"

"No."

"Did *you* call the police on her behalf?"

"No."

"Or the District Attorney?"

"No."

"What about her protection? Did you play any role in that?"

"Outside of conversations with my husband? Not directly."

"Did you think her protection was adequate?"

In a spasm of memory, Lara saw the Eagle's Claw bullet ripping through Joan's jaw. Softly, she answered, "At the time. What your client did was beyond our imaginings. As my husband may have mentioned."

Nolan placed his palms on the table. "To be clear, Mrs. Kilcannon, what do you believe my client did?"

"Specifically? Lure a spousal abuser to a gun show in Las Vegas, where he could buy its deadly weapons without a background check, the better to kill my mother, niece and the sister for whom you're showing such concern." Swiftly, Lara thought of Kerry's plans. "As far as I know, Lexington is *still* doing that, and still more people will die as a result. Or have they at last started protecting people like Joan?"

Nolan stared at her. "Did you . . ."

"Are *you*," Lara cut in, "going to answer *my* question?"

Nolan managed a brief smile. "I'm sorry, Mrs. Kilcannon. But as Professor Gold may have informed you, depositions are a one way street. I'm only a lawyer here . . ."

"With no moral responsibility as to whether your client *still* makes its guns available to prospective murderers, and sells them bullets to help ensure that they succeed. Will you at least have the decency to be embarrassed if you find out that they do?"

Nolan's smile vanished. "Did you," he persisted, "transfer *your* obligation to help your sister to your husband?"

"No, Mr. Nolan. My husband acted on our behalf."

"And on behalf of his own political interests?"

Lara paused, marshalling anew her air of calm. "I'm sorry, Mr. Nolan. I don't understand your question."

"Then let me approach it another way. Was the decision to expose John Bowden's abusive nature on television driven by politics?"

"No . . ."

"Specifically, Mrs. Kilcannon, to eliminate a major distraction from your televised wedding, and the political boost it was intended to give the President."

"Oh, come off it," Lenihan interjected in a tone of disgust. Beside her, Avram Gold leaned forward. "That's not merely out of bounds, Mr. Nolan. It's offensive, insulting and outrageous."

"Even worse," Lara said with a tenuous smile, "it's wrong."

Nolan turned from Gold to Lara. "Didn't your husband decide to expose Bowden to eliminate a family embarrassment and fight off charges of undue influence in a domestic violence prosecution?"

Lara gazed at the ceiling, as though pondering the

question. "It doesn't *sound* like Kerry," she replied. "Did you ask him?"

"I'm asking you."

Lara's eyes turned cold. "Then ask me something that's not absurd."

"Why absurd, Mrs. Kilcannon? Did *you* play any role in that decision?"

"The person who decided," Lara answered promptly, "was Joan."

"Did you discuss it with her?"

"Not directly, no."

"So you didn't know, of your personal knowledge, *who* decided to expose John Bowden, or what your husband and sister may have discussed?"

"I wasn't there."

"After the murders, did you discuss it with your husband?"

"*Care to talk about it?*" Kerry had asked.

"*About hating myself?*" she had answered. "*What is there to say? I abdicated my responsibilities in every possible way— assigning Joanie to you, helping the media to take her life over. Now they're all dead.*"

"All such conversations," Avram Gold admonished, "are subject to the marital privilege."

With a satisfied expression, Nolan said to Lara, "Is that *your* position, Mrs. Kilcannon?"

"My position," Lara answered, "is that Kerry and I are entitled to whatever peace we have left."

"Are you at least willing to discuss your conversations with Ms. Dash?"

"Any such conversations," Gold responded for Lara, "are covered by the attorney-client privilege. As I understand Ms. Dash explained during Mary Costello's deposition, as a prospective plaintiff, Mrs. Kilcannon also has the right to Ms. Dash's confidential counsel."

"Is that *your* position, Mrs. Kilcannon?"

"Yes."

"It is true, is it not, that you suggested to your sister Mary that Ms. Dash represent her?"

"Mr. Nolan," Gold interrupted with an air of weariness, "that's been explained to you, as well. As they are both parties in interest, Mrs. Kilcannon's conversation with her surviving sister—at least concerning this lawsuit—are privileged."

"Including any inducements for Mary to employ Ms. Dash?"

"Yes," Gold answered. "If any."

Nolan spun on Lara. "Is *that* your position, as well?"

"It is."

"Are you also unwilling to tell me whether it was your husband who suggested Ms. Dash in the first place?"

At last, Lara felt the trap shut, could feel the full impact of the warning beneath Nolan's line of questioning. At trial, she would become the callous and indifferent sister who left Joan's problems to her calculating husband, and then helped manipulate her surviving sister, Mary, for Kerry's political gain. Nolan meant to create two soulless ciphers and then pillory them in public, destroying Lara's relationship with Mary in the bargain.

Lara raised her head. "I'm unwilling to tell you anything about what my husband and I may say to each other—ever. Or even whether something was said. The same is true with Mary." She paused, adding quietly, "Our family's much smaller now. What's left of it is too precious to share with someone like you."

That evening, Lara wept alone.

She had not cracked; at last, Nolan had run out of questions. But he had made his point and, worse, ripped open wounds which had barely begun to heal. Now she wondered if they ever would, and what would happen if she and Kerry stayed on this collision course with their enemies on the right.

Through a film of tears, Lara saw their bedside clock.

She had, perhaps, another ten minutes to grieve. Then she must repair herself and once again become First Lady. In Kerry's absence, she was hosting a dinner for the winners of the Special Olympics and their coaches, and this was a cause dear to Lara's heart.

SEVEN

LANDING, KERRY was struck by the jagged brown rocks of the mountain range beyond the city, outlined against a thin blue desert sky. The vista had a shimmering quality, enhancing Kerry's sense that Las Vegas was surreal, perhaps dropped from the moon by some impresario of excess, Walt Disney on acid. Kerry's motorcade streamed down the strip, past a sequence of enormous hotels which, together, comprised a time-bending theme park: an ersatz Paris, Venice, New York City, the Rome of the Caesars, Luxor, and Camelot, punctuated by a space needle. Kerry felt a bemused admiration for the ambition and inventiveness of man, unconstrained by the limits of either money or good taste. The unusual number of billboards advertising tort lawyers reminded Kerry of Robert Lenihan.

Turning from the window, he steeled himself for the task ahead.

Two hours before, an advance team, unannounced and unobtrusive, had circulated through the gun show, reporting back on what they had seen. Only then did Kerry make his final decision. Kit had not alerted the press until they landed. Avid, they followed in two buses, although Kit had designated only one pool camera and three reporters to accompany the President inside the convention hall. As his limousine pulled up to the glass doors of the sprawling tan complex, Kerry's Secret Service detail spread out amidst the startled, loitering smokers.

For a last moment, Kerry remained inside, frozen by the risk and volatility of what he was about to do. Exiting the car, he imagined John Bowden's arrival at another show just weeks ago and, despite the searing heat, felt chill.

A phalanx of Secret Service agents surrounded him. Startled, a beefy smoker wearing a T-shirt with an Iron Cross above the slogan "NO FEAR" uttered a one-word obscenity as Kerry and his protectors pushed inside.

The cavernous hall had a steel web of lights and catwalks high above hundreds of tables marked by placards offering armaments of every kind. The people crowding the tables remained unaware of Kerry's arrival. At first glance, they were white, most of them male, and their appearance evoked an urban liberal's overheated fantasy of a gun show—caps, T-shirts, beards, ponytails, tattoos and sloping bellies—reminding him of the bitter cultural divisions in the country which he governed. He would find few Kilcannon voters here.

"This way, Mr. President," Peter Lake directed.

With the Secret Service detail as outriders, the alien cluster headed for Kerry's objective. Beneath a sign proclaiming "No SSA, No Gun Shows," two grim-faced men and a petite, pretty woman glared at him in anger and surprise.

"Gun-grabber," one of the men called out. Tempted to confront them, Kerry hewed to the mission he had come for.

The stir of people noticing him rose to a din of protest. Moving down a corridor between two rows of tables, Kerry looked from side to side, feeling tension pass through him like a current from the hate-filled faces, the weaponry all around them—sniper rifles, handguns, swords, knives, bayonets, plastic guns designed to slip through magneto-meters. One booth sold hand grenades; another hawked "pre-banned AK-47s" and forty-round magazines; another offered freeze-dried survival rations and gas masks beneath the warning, "You Can't Fight If You Can't Breathe." A plethora of American flag decals competed with bumper stickers, one of which portrayed a black man anally penetrating another. "Save Our Military" it admonished, "Just Say No."

"Patriotic," Kit observed.

A crowd had massed around them. Behind a woman with two kids in a stroller, her mouth spitting venom he could not quite hear, Kerry spotted his objective in the dead center of the hall: a sign proclaiming "Eagle's Claw Ammo."

Imagining Bowden drawn by the words, Kerry felt his nerves twitch.

As the press of bodies slowly parted for the wedge of his security detail, Kerry moved forward. A bearded man stood behind a table displaying armor-piercing bullets; high-capacity magazines; and a row of black metal guns labeled, "Lexington P-2–The Patriot's Weapon of Choice." Beside him was a life-size cardboard image of Kerry and Lara with concentric circles imprinted on their chests.

Secret Service agents encircled the table. The Minicam followed Kerry toward its proprietor and his wares. "Go back to Washington," someone shouted, his rasp audible in the growing silence.

Stopping at the table, the President examined a forty-round clip; boxes of Eagle's Claw bullets; bumper stickers which read, "Kilcannon–American Traitor," and "Lara–Traitor Bitch"; a tape on a portable television demonstrating how to convert the P-2 to automatic fire. As Kerry watched, the converted handgun vaporized a pile of watermelons into a spew of pink juice. *Get it while you can,* the narrator urged, and a grainy photograph of Kerry replaced the slaughtered melons.

At last, Kerry turned to the seller.

The rictus of a smile twitched on the man's face—agitated, hostile and sickly. Silent, Kerry scooped up a box of Eagle's Claw bullets in the palm of his hand.

He waited until the man's gaze was drawn to the box. With a soft underhand flip, Kerry tossed it in his face.

Startled, the man caught the box inches from his eyes. "Lucky," Kerry told him. "You had time."

The man's eyes flickered toward the camera. Kerry took a Lexington P-2 and pressed it into his other hand. "Three hours ago you sold a friend of mine two boxes of Eagle's Claw bullets, a forty-round clip, and a Lexington P-2— exactly what John Bowden bought. And you never asked his name, or anything about him."

The man would not—or could not—respond. Stepping behind the table, Kit Pace lifted the cutout of the President and First Lady and laid it across the pile of bullets. "But it seems you know who I am," Kerry said. "How much do you want for us?"

Still the man did not speak. Reaching into his pocket, Kerry pulled out his wallet and placed some twenties on the table. "Tell me if you think it's not enough."

Mute, the seller stared at the green bills. Then Kerry tucked the cardboard cutout under his arm, and turned away.

At home, Frank Fasano watched the last few minutes, telephone propped to his ear. "Guerrilla theater," Dane was saying. "Most people will see this stunt for what it is—a President and his thugs, bullying Americans who believe in the Second Amendment for cheap political gain."

But the SSA president sounded unsettled. On CNN, Kilcannon departed through the rows of weaponry, Lara's cardboard face still visible beneath his arm. Fasano had the sense of a conflict slipping out of control.

"What most people will remember," he answered, "is a man standing up for his wife and her murdered family. What's the antidote to that?"

Dane was silent. "Trust me," he answered with a renewed calm that Fasano found unnerving. "There is one."

In the limousine, Kerry gazed out the window. Softly, he said, "He could have been the seller."

The ATF would question him, of course. But Kerry might never know.

"You did enough," Kit answered. "At least for one day."

EIGHT

FOR FRANK FASANO, the first harbinger of change was Senator Betsy Shapiro.

A somewhat imperious moderate Democrat from California, Betsy had been caught between her advocacy of gun control and her ties to the high-tech overlords of Silicon Valley, an important base of financial support, for whom tort reform was fundamental protection from shareholder suits. Fasano had expected her to split the difference by supporting both Kilcannon's gun bill and Fasano's tort reform measure. But the film clip of Kilcannon confronting the seller dominated the morning news in a seemingly endless loop. When Fasano looked up from the color photo of Kilcannon at the gun show on the front page of the *New York Times*, the clip had been succeeded by a live interview with Senator Shapiro.

As usual, Betsy looked buttoned-down, her dark brown coif as disciplined and controlled as she was. *In good conscience,* she was saying, *I have to question whether giving legal immunity to the Eagle's Claw bullet can really be called "reform."*

Across from him at the breakfast table, a weary Bernadette held Frank Junior, his small head with its sparse black hair resting at her breast. "I'm not sure what I think about the politics," she told her husband. "Or the law. But that target of the Kilcannons was disgusting."

That, Fasano thought, captured neatly what Betsy Shapiro was reacting to; with a stroke of intuition, Kilcannon had reduced gun immunity from the abstract to the personal. "Anyone who makes or sells that kind of stuff is crazy," he agreed. "But that's got nothing to do with tort reform." Excusing himself, he went to his den and called Lance Jarrett.

It was only six o'clock in California, but—as Fasano had known he would be—the president of the world's largest chipmaker was up and running. "Is this about Betsy?" Jarrett asked gruffly.

"Yup. She seems to have forgotten you."

"Betsy Shapiro hates guns," Jarrett said. "So do a lot of Californians. All your pro-gun, pro-life crap doesn't sell too well out here."

Fasano laughed softly. "As opposed to all your pro-business, anti-tree-hugger stuff? We appreciate your financial support, Lance. But if we want to control Congress, we need to turn out votes in states you fly over on the way to St. Moritz—like Kansas or Maine or Arkansas—where pro-gun and conservative Christian voters make a difference. As for California, you've tried to play it safe by backing Democrats like Betsy. It's time to see if your strategy pays off."

"In other words," Jarrett rejoined, "you want me to lean on our senior senator."

"You're one of her leading fund-raisers. She might appreciate knowing how you feel, and hearing from your mutual friends in the Valley."

Jarrett was quiet. "Kilcannon really hurt you," he said at length. "Maybe you can't get past it."

Fasano felt his jaw tighten. "You'd better hope you're wrong. Unless you're willing to take that feeble compromise Kilcannon was hawking to the Chamber of Commerce."

"Of course not," Jarrett answered scornfully. "I just don't understand why your bill turned into the Gun Protection Act."

"Because that's the price," Fasano snapped. "I don't tell you how to make chips, so don't tell me how to get you protected from specious lawsuits for the rest of recorded history. All I need is for you to help me realize your dream. As for Betsy, your dream should be her dream—the high-tech community is too important to ignore. Your fellow CEOs, venture capitalists, and investment bankers should be calling her day and night."

For a few seconds, Fasano waited for a reaction. "All right." For a man accustomed to command, Jarrett's tone became unusually respectful. "I'll get to work this morning."

That afternoon, with great reluctance, Fasano left Bernadette and the baby to meet with his Majority Whip, Dave Ruckles.

They counted votes over soft drinks in Fasano's office. "What's the damage?" Fasano asked.

Lean and alert, Ruckles was the perfect operative: a fierce conservative, an indefatigable fund-raiser, a gimlet-eyed counter of votes—and, in Fasano's estimate, neither bright nor supple enough to displace Fasano himself. But he also knew that, in Ruckles's mind, this was a not-too-distant dream, and one which Fasano hoped Ruckles would think was best served by helping the Majority Leader replace a President they both disliked. "I don't know yet," Ruckles admitted. "I think what Kilcannon's done on tort reform is keep the critical votes in play—some of our people, and swing Democrats like Shapiro, Torchio, Coletti and Slezak."

"It's a problem in two parts," Fasano reminded him. "We want to pass tort reform with the sixty-seven votes we'll need to overrule Kilcannon's veto, and this gun immunity provision's got us stuck around sixty. But first we have to keep Hampton from getting the fifty-one votes he needs to pass an amendment stripping gun immunity out of the final bill."

Ruckles squinted at his Diet Coke. "Right now that's too close to call—a few votes one way or the other."

Fasano agreed. With a sigh of resignation, he said, "Let's start from the beginning—who's still in play; who needs campaign money; who wants a new committee assignment; who's vulnerable to the SSA; or anyone we can get to."

Ruckles considered him. "That's all well and good, Frank. But you have to make this vote a test of your leadership. If our people know that crossing you is a personal affront, it'll be hard for them to say no. They have to succeed in this place, and that pretty much depends on you.

"What *Kilcannon's* depending on is emotion. But we've both heard our colleagues give speeches which would bring tears to your eyes and didn't change a vote. Survival cuts deeper than sympathy."

Fasano smiled at this, though perhaps for different reasons than Ruckles imagined. To make this vote a test of leadership would raise the stakes immensely. Losing it might leave Fasano more vulnerable to a challenge from Ruckles. Winning would strengthen Fasano among the party's most fervent financial and ideological backers, strengthen his claim to the Presidency, and clear a path for Ruckles in a congenially bloodless way. As to that, their interests were the same.

"Dave," Fasano answered, "I think it's a test of us both."

This made Ruckles smile as well. There was a certain cynical comfort, Fasano supposed, in such a seamless mutual understanding. "If we can make this an up-and-down vote on a final bill," Fasano continued, "with gun immunity still in it, we'll probably win. Getting the votes to beat Hampton's amendment is where the fight will be. On our side, that comes down to a handful of undecideds—Dick Stafford, Kate Jarman, John Smythe, Cassie Rollins."

"Smythe is gone," Ruckles opined. "He's the price we pay for electing a Republican from Rhode Island. But Stafford's a probable, and Kate Jarman won't go off the reservation again—not after voting for Caroline Masters . . ."

"This time Palmer's on our side. He gives the moderates cover."

Ruckles nodded. "That brings us to Cassie. This morning I only caught her briefly. But I don't think yesterday helped."

Fasano sipped his Coke. "She's taking too long," he said at length. "The longer she's in play, the more danger there is of losing her—like we did on Masters. It's time to make this one a matter of her survival."

NINE

IN THE CHILL of early evening, the President walked alone on the South Lawn of the White House, hoping to stretch his legs and breathe fresh air after too much time on Air Force One, and in hotel suites or indoor meetings and events. He and Lara needed an escape, Kerry concluded, a weekend away before the drabness of an eastern winter closed around them—somewhere with books and quiet and fewer of the artifacts of man. He paused in the descending dusk, hands in the pocket of his suit, smelling a faint, pungent odor which reminded him of burning leaves. Then he spotted the familiar form coming from the White House with a brisk, purposeful stride, and knew that his reverie was over.

"I'm closed for business," he said in mock complaint. "Whatever it is, take care of it."

Clayton's smile was perfunctory. "Even if the ATF may be closing in on the seller?"

Surprised, Kerry asked, "That maggot I confronted?"

"They don't think so. But two weeks ago, some guy on parole robbed a convenience store in Oklahoma City with a P-2 from the same stolen batch as Bowden's."

Kerry felt his weariness drop away, replaced by a new keenness of mind. "Do we know where he got the gun?"

"At a gun show in Phoenix." Clayton's voice had the suppressed excitement of a prosecutor on the verge of a potential breakthrough. "Last week there was another show in Phoenix. When the ATF took our perpetrator there, he identified the guy who sold it to him.

"Just to make sure, an ATF agent bought another P-2 from this same guy. Its serial number matched still another gun stolen with Bowden's. So the ATF got a warrant, searched the guy's truck, and found nine more stolen P-2s. That was when they busted him."

"Who is he?"

"A man named George Johnson. He's a member of something called the Liberty Force—a pack of white supremacists located in rural Idaho. The ATF's theory is that they were financing their activities by selling stolen P-2s at a premium to people who don't pass a background check—sort of like Tim McVeigh and his friends did . . ."

"Is Johnson talking?"

"Only through his public defender. As of now, he admits stealing the batch of P-2s but says that he's never been to Las Vegas. There's no evidence he ever was."

Impatient, Kerry shook his head. "Even if that's true, he's got to be the source of Bowden's gun. Either Johnson *knows* who put it in Bowden's hands, or—at the least—he sold to the guy who did."

Clayton folded his arms. "You know the problem. There's no record of the sale, or who had booths at the Las Vegas gun show, or even of who went there. So the evidence that Bowden bought it there is circumstantial. We're at the mercy of a racist who hates the U.S. government and, I'm sure, you."

"He doesn't have to like me," Kerry answered softly. "He just has to be afraid of spending some very long years in jail, making a few very special friends from among the more diverse elements of our populace. A grim prospect for a white supremacist from Idaho."

"There's always that." Clayton's eyes contained a fleeting, cold amusement. "Which is why, I suppose, Johnson's lawyer implies his man didn't steal these P-2s by himself."

Silent, Kerry imagined Johnson's calculations: that the

ATF's questions about John Bowden meant that he might hold the key to the Costello murders and, if so, had all the leverage on the President that implied. Then, tracing the likely path of Bowden's gun, he much more viscerally envisioned the racist underbelly of America spawning the murder of Lara's family in a hothouse protected by the SSA and advertised by Lexington Arms. "What an irony," he murmured in a bitter tone. "Seven deaths, and Lexington made no money from them."

Clayton said nothing. Kerry turned from him, gazing up at a full, ascending moon in the twilight gathering around them. "I need the seller," Kerry said at length. "I don't care how."

"I think you should. For a lot of reasons . . ."

"Clayton," the President interjected coldly, "the seller connects John Bowden to the gun show, and to Lexington's ad. A *paramilitary* seller means that the worst forces in our society cashed in on Lexington's ads in order to sell stolen P-2s, without the background check which Lexington refused to require of gun-show promoters.

"It reinforces the case for my gun bill. It gives Dash and Lenihan the evidence they need to prove that Lexington's ad drew Bowden to Las Vegas. It even makes me wonder whether Lexington has known for months that this batch of stolen guns could lead us to the seller, and decided not to reveal that fact to Mary's lawyers or to me."

"All true," Clayton answered. "But first consider the cost of finding out. Johnson's already committed three violent felonies. That means that under the federal sentencing guidelines, he's due to get a minimum of fifteen years in a maximum security prison for theft, possession of stolen guns, and trafficking.

"That doesn't leave much leeway for a deal short of throwing out his case . . ."

"That's a lot to ask."

"There's more," Clayton continued in the same impervious tone. "Johnson's lawyer implies that the guy who sold to Bowden may be a fellow member of the Liberty Force. You may think that helps you. But I think Johnson's pitch will be that helping you puts his life in danger, in or out of prison."

Kerry turned to face him. "You mean he'll ask for a Presidential commutation. And a place in the witness protection program once he's done with testifying."

"It smells like that." His friend's stocky form seemed rooted to the ground in stubborn warning. "Think about the implications of *that*—legally, morally and politically. What President, you'd have to ask, would kick a man like Johnson loose."

"Maybe this one," Kerry answered. "But only if he gives me what I need."

Sarah had a date—rare since the Costello suit had propelled her around the country—and anticipation of dinner with Jeff Weitz, a longtime friend who seemed intent on becoming more had, for once, left her eager to leave the office. And so when the telephone rang she hesitated, glancing at the caller ID panel before deciding to answer.

"Private," it said. Sarah recalled her resolve to miss no calls, and the reason for it. As if the thought itself would be a jinx—as it had been for two weeks now—she answered with little hope that this call would be different.

"Is this Sarah Dash?" her caller asked.

Though she had heard it only once before, the man's high, reedy voice gave Sarah goose bumps. "Yes."

"We talked earlier." Whether from an accurate sense of his importance, or the belief of an unstable mind that his reality was central to the world's, her caller seemed to know how intently Sarah had been waiting for this moment. "I saw that film of the President at the gun show, and felt we have a bond. There are things I need to tell you."

She would be late for her date with Jeff.

TEN

"CASSIE ROLLINS hasn't budged," Dane told Fasano over breakfast at the Metropolitan Club. "When was the last time you talked to her?"

"Ruckles did. I'm prepared to make this a loyalty test, but I thought I'd save myself until you'd done your worst. What *is* your worst, by the way?"

Dane held the pepper shaker above his eggs, frowning as only a few black specks broke loose despite a vigorous flicking of his wrist. "A mass mailing, to start—every person in Maine who bought a hunting license, went to a gun store, bought a concealed carry permit, or is registered as owning a pickup truck . . ."

Fasano laughed aloud. "That would work in my state. Especially the trucks."

"The mailer should start hitting tomorrow," Dane continued in a satisfied tone. "Then comes a half-million dollars in spots. We put Cassie's face on the screen, tell everyone about the threat to gun rights and ask if she's standing up for Maine values . . ."

" 'Call Cassie Rollins,' " Fasano intoned.

"Exactly. We'll put her office number on the screen and ask her constituents to let her have it."

Fasano spread marmalade across his English muffin. "We want to scare Cassie—but not kill her. I'm not willing to lose a senator because you want tort immunity."

Shrugging, Dane contemplated the scattered flecks of pepper. "When are you scheduling a vote?"

"I'm going to have to deal with Hampton, who seems

to have cast his lot with Kilcannon. But what I'm thinking now is that tort reform comes first—maybe in two weeks."

"That'll give us time." Looking up from his plate, Dane added pointedly, "And give you time with Cassie."

Three days later, Air Force One swooped down into Portland, Maine. Kerry traveled from the airport followed by a horde of local media, commencing a day of public exposure no amount of money could buy and only a President could command. His first public meeting was with a victims' rights group; his second with members of a police union who supported gun control; his third with the widows of three former officers who had been killed by felons with guns. "My dad was a beat cop," he reminded each audience. "There were nights I stayed awake until he came home, worrying about what might happen." He did not mention that the fear he felt was for his mother, not his father, or that, in the guilty recesses of his soul, he had wished that his father would never come home again.

His last stop was for dinner with local hunters. They met in a rustic restaurant outside town, with long, family-style tables and a deer head on the wall. In a work shirt and jeans, Kerry sat amongst them, working on pot roast, potatoes and a Budweiser. Leery of the cameras, the hunters were quiet and unanimated. After a few edgy moments, Kerry cut to the core.

"Here you are," he said pleasantly, "stuck with the President of the United States, trying to be polite. Even though pretty much all of you voted against me."

A few of the men looked sheepish; one shifted in his chair. In front of Kerry, a large, gentle-looking man with a seamed face repressed a nervous smile. "It's not that hard to figure out," Kerry continued amiably. "It was because of guns, right? The gun lobby kept saying I'd take your guns away."

As did others, the man across from him avoided his gaze. "That's okay," Kerry assured his listeners. "That's why I'm here. I don't even take it personally.

"Why should I? Six years ago, you turned down a good man who wanted to be your senator—Sam Towle—who had the guts to vote for the assault weapons ban. And I bet a lot of you remember hearing that Sam and the assault weapons ban would take your guns away."

Eyes still averted, the man across from Kerry permitted himself a more reflective smile. When Kerry glanced around the room, more faces seemed to have opened to him.

"So let me ask you this," Kerry went on. "Since Sam Towle helped pass the assault weapons ban, how many of you have missed a day of hunting season because of it?"

There was silence, a few more smiles, expressions newly alert and engaged. "Because if you did," the President told them, "you should keep on voting against folks like Sam and me every time you get the chance. But if you didn't— if all you've missed is giving Sam Towle a fair shake—then you've got to figure the SSA lied to you to get him."

Pausing, Kerry jabbed at the table with his index finger. "Well, they did. They lied about Sam, and then they lied about me. And now they're clogging your mailboxes and flooding the airwaves with more lies about these gun bills, trying to scare Senator Rollins with what they did to Sam.

"I won't try to speak for Senator Rollins. But their latest lie involves asking you to defend the right of a criminal or a wife-beater to walk out of prison, cross the street, buy a weapon *you'd* never think of using and kill whoever suits him.

"If that's got anything to do with hunting deer, it's escaped me." Pausing, Kerry permitted himself a smile.

"I know one thing—when people keep on lying to me, I do my damnedest to get back at them. Maybe you've heard that's how I am."

There were quiet chuckles around the room. "We've heard rumors," someone said.

Sitting back, Kerry spread his arms. "So ask me anything, and tell me what's on your mind. Because I don't want to leave here until we've gotten straight with each other."

Three hours later, Kerry was still there, drinking beer and talking. No one else had left.

ELEVEN

IN A STARK MOTEL room just off a highway interchange outside of Hartford, Sarah waited for her caller.

His rules were strict and unbending. Sarah must come alone. She must take a room in this motel. She must wait until he came. She could not know his name, or anything about him.

Apprehensive, she looked about the depressing rectangle—cheap pastoral art; a spindly fake brass lamp; an aqua bedspread; one dirty window with a view of the parking lot. Her caller had insisted that she take a smoking room, and the bedcover reeked of cigarettes. She wondered whether he would need a smoke after slitting her throat and raping her. Instead of a gun there was pepper spray in her purse.

When the telephone rang, she started.

"Are you alone?" the reedy voice inquired.

"Yes."

"I'm in the lobby. But they won't give me your room number."

Sarah felt her flesh crawl. "Two-oh-three."

There was a click as he hung up.

It would be all too easy, Sarah thought. A predator prowling the Internet had found their web site and, drawn to Sarah by the Tierney case, decided to lure her by posing as a tipster. His rules—designed to suggest excessive caution—were a cover for sexual pathology, or perhaps an antiabortion fanatic. She had never felt so vulnerable.

When the quiet knock came at last, Sarah put the pepper

spray in the pocket of her suit coat. Slowly, she cracked open the door.

He was perhaps fifty—slight and fairly short, his red thinning hair streaked with silver. The skin drawn tight over his face had a shiny, scalded look and his blue eyes were sharp and wary. "Are you alone?" he asked again.

Wordless, Sarah backed inside.

He was carrying a battered briefcase. In a flash of black humor, Sarah wondered if that was where he kept the Lexington P-2.

"Why all the secrecy?" she demanded.

Softly, he closed the door behind them. She barely heard the latch.

With a mute gesture, Sarah directed him to the Swedish modern chair she had moved to the corner farthest from the door. He hesitated, resistant, before perching on its edge. Only then did Sarah sit at the end of the bed, saying, "You didn't answer my question."

To her alarm, his lips formed a dissociated smile which did not display his teeth. "Long ago, Sarah, I learned that people can't be trusted. That includes my superiors at Lexington."

"You know who *I* am," Sarah persisted. "I've done exactly what you asked—however foolish that may be."

Comprehension entered his piercing eyes. "You think maybe I'm some sort of pervert."

"No. Maybe a particular sort of pervert."

This elicited a harsh, disturbing laugh. "Look," Sarah said with the force of apprehension, "I promise to play it straight with you. But I'm not staying another minute without knowing who you are."

The mirthless smile returned. Softly, he answered, "I'm Norman Conn."

His tone carried an assertion of his significance. Searching her memory, Sarah struggled to recall whether she had seen the name. Then the numbing hours spent sifting through worthless files in Lexington's warehouse yielded their first useful scrap of knowledge.

"You're in quality control."

"The manager," Conn amended. "My department also processes trace requests for crime guns."

This was real, Sarah knew at once. She felt herself release a breath. "Why did you call me?"

He gave her a withering look of amusement. "You don't remember Vietnam, do you? Do you even know anyone who served?"

Whatever this question signified, Sarah sensed that he expected candor. "Not well," she acknowledged. "Somehow my father got out of the draft. He doesn't talk about that much."

This time the smile held a sour hint of bitterness and moral superiority. "Neither do I, Sarah. But I've had thirty-five years to think about it."

His repetition of her name made Sarah uneasy. And yet it hinted at a certain intimacy; were she patient, he would deign to tell his story. She was suddenly sure that this was indispensable to their transaction. "The war?" she asked.

"The deaths."

There was nothing to say. Silent, Sarah tried to convey an empathic patience for what surely must be difficult to express.

"I was in the infantry," Conn said abruptly. "One morning I was walking point. In twelve days I was going home, and they still had me rooting for land mines." The smile twitched. "I missed one.

"Three men were mangled beyond help. But it took Boynton—the black guy—two hours to die." A film moistened his eyes, and his smile betrayed an effort of will. "In the movies, he always told me, the black guy dies first."

For Sarah, this last detail invested the banal sparseness

of Conn's account with the echo of a long-ago psychic explosion. But the glimmer of empathy did little to ease her fear that he might be unstable, or that his view of reality was skewed by guilt, the distrust of authority bred by having become flotsam in a senseless war.

"If what you know can help us," she admonished, "we'll have to list you as a trial witness. Not only would your employers know, but they'd take your deposition. Secrecy's not an option."

Conn's gaze was implacable, almost contemptuous. "I was nineteen," he said. "Ever since, I've wished I could go back and save three lives. Now I've got a second chance, even if I never know how many lives, or whose."

For the first time, Sarah acknowledged the briefcase at his feet. "What's in there?" she inquired.

Reaching for the cigarettes in his shirt pocket, Conn's eyes bored into hers. "The documents they told me to destroy."

Alone in the motel room, Sarah called Lara Kilcannon on her private line. She felt exhausted. The brown briefcase lay beside her on the bed.

"I'm glad you called," Lara said without preface. "I've got something to tell you. We need to find the person who sold John Bowden the P-2, correct?"

Lara seemed so intent that Sarah decided to defer her discovery, however important. "To start," she answered. "Ultimately, we need to prove that Bowden bought it because of Lexington's ad."

Lara was briefly silent. "There may be more to it than that. Let me tell you where to look."

TWELVE

ON THE CRISP Sunday morning before Thanksgiving, Kerry and Lara kayaked across Chilmark Pond.

Martha's Vineyard was sunny, fortuitous for their weekend away. The rambling home on the pond, new to them, was quiet and filled with books. They did not stay on Dogfish Bar, or even visit. On Saturday, they had read and talked and enjoyed each other, renewing themselves. On Sunday, more ambitious, they packed bagels and a thermos of coffee and set out in two kayaks for the beach. They moved steadily across the water toward the dune concealing the ocean, Lara rotating her paddle with a graceful, almost mathematical precision, Kerry making up in vigor what he lacked in form. A breeze rippled the pond, bright with sunlight, stirring the sea grass at its edge. The only sound was the soft thudding of outboard motors powering the rubber rafts driven by the Secret Service; the only other humans visible were two more agents atop the dune.

Beaching their kayaks, Lara and Kerry climbed the wooden catwalk which traversed the dune, pausing at its top to gaze out at the blue sweep of the Atlantic, curling outward on their right to the Gay Head cliffs. In late fall, the water seemed a chalkier blue, and the confluence of sand and surf and distant cliffs had a stark severe beauty marred only by the figures of more agents stationed along the shoreline. Taking the catwalk to the beach, Kerry and Lara spread out a woolen blanket and poured steaming black coffee into two mugs, warm in their cupped hands.

"I almost hate to bring this up," Lara said. "But where do we stand on gun immunity?"

It was the first reference since their arrival to politics or, more obliquely, to the loss of Lara's family. Kerry chose to address the question as asked. "In the House," he answered, "the SSA will jam it through. But it's close in the Senate and the final push begins tomorrow.

"Chuck Hampton thinks we've got roughly two weeks. It's time for me to start personally leaning on the Democratic swing votes—promising to campaign or swapping dam projects and jobs for relatives; pressing Chuck to withhold money from the Senate Campaign Committee for senators who vote with Fasano."

"Will he do that?"

Kerry sipped his coffee, its warmth as bracing as the cool breeze in his face. "Maybe," he replied. "As with Fasano, Chuck's leadership is on the line. The carrot is that we've done some polling, to show people like Torchio and Coletti how they can sell a vote against the SSA." Kerry put down his mug. "I'll do whatever I need to do. Losing this would feel like death to me."

Lara turned to him. "How can I help?"

Her words reminded Kerry—despite all that had happened—of the ways in which the tragedy united them. Not only did they share a common goal, but Lara understood what a President must do and accepted it without judgment.

"Joe Spivey," Kerry answered, "wants you to campaign for him. He thinks that could help him clean up his problems with pro-choice women—especially his vote against Caroline Masters."

As Lara smiled at this, Kerry saw the irony of an ex-reporter who once had covered the senator from Missouri—with all the disillusion bred by that experience—and who recognized that, as First Lady, she now had the power to help him perpetuate his mediocrity for yet another term. "Tell Senator Spivey," she authorized her husband, "that I've got no more shame than he does. But only if he gets it right this time."

Monday morning, the President began calling, or summoning senators for breakfast or lunch or cocktails in the residence or Oval Office.

On the telephone with James Torchio, he promised a personal call to Torchio's principal fund-raiser. Over breakfast with Ben Jasper of Iowa, he politely inquired if the SSA could help the senator with flood relief, or whether that was something which might require a President. In the Oval Office, he more pointedly asked Jason Christy of Maryland—who badly wanted to succeed him when Kerry's term was over—whether he thought he could win their party's nomination over the opposition of the incumbent. All of this involved the usual trafficking in favors, a knowledge of each senator's motivations reinforced by their clear understanding of Kerry's; hence none of it surprised him. The exception was Hank Westerly of Nebraska.

They sat in Kerry's private quarters in the White House, sipping Scotch from crystal glasses. Westerly seemed so tormented by his dilemma that Kerry felt something close to pity. "I often thought," he told his former peer, "that being a senator would be terrific if we never had to vote."

But Westerly seemed beyond the salve of humor. He blinked at Kerry behind thick glasses, his genial midwestern face a portrait of uncharacteristic misery. "I'm afraid of these people," he blurted out.

"The SSA?"

"Yes." His tone became confessional. "I mean, physically."

This was one fear for which Kerry was not prepared. Reading the President's face, Westerly seemed to wince, recoiling from this admission to a man who had not only lost his brother and the greater portion of Lara's family to guns, but had also been shot himself. Softly, Kerry answered, "Unlike the pro-life fanatics, the pro-gunners don't seem to shoot their adversaries. Although I suppose there's always a first time. But if my experience is any guide, it probably won't be you."

The senator made no attempt to answer. With the same quiet, Kerry said, "I need your help, Hank."

Sipping Scotch, Westerly pursed his lips, his wrinkled face a blueprint of unhappiness. "I'd like to, Mr. President. Believe me. But I just don't know that I can."

Kerry felt all compunction vanish. "Then let's consider your life this side of heaven. If you want anything—a dam, a road, or that federal building with your name on it—I can make it happen, or not. If you want me to campaign for you, or just raise money, I will—or I won't.

"I plan to be here for another seven years. That's a long time to spend in purgatory. Assuming, of course, that you make it to the end." The quiet of Kerry's voice held no hint of mercy. "Life is choices, Hank. You get to choose what scares you most."

But the most unpleasant meeting in this sequence was made so by its absence of humanity.

In Kerry's informed estimate, Jack Slezak of Michigan was crude and amoral, a politician whose sole interest was to amass power, and to eliminate all rivals by whatever means at hand. Kerry disliked him on instinct and on principle. As part of Slezak's complex calculus of survival, he had become an advocate of gun rights, judging that this could help him with a core of voters who usually voted Republican without offending his blue-collar base, many of whom owned guns. A similar calculus had led him to support Vice President Dick Mason over Kerry in the Michigan primary and, Kerry was certain, had inspired a scurrilous last-minute round of phone-banking—casting Kerry as irreligious and antiunion—which had contributed to his narrow defeat. Though it was early evening when Slezak came to the Oval Office, Kerry did not offer him a drink.

"I need your vote against gun immunity," Kerry said. "Simple as that."

Beneath Slezak's swept-back reddish hair, his shrewd green eyes peered back at Kerry from a broad Tartar face, all planes and angles, which, Kerry had always suspected, originated when Genghis Khan and his hordes had swept across some vulnerable part of Eastern Europe, pausing to rape the village females. "Not so simple," Slezak said without deference. "I'm up for reelection next year. What do I gain by crossing the SSA?"

The answer, Kerry knew, was the President's help in raising campaign money from sources to whom Jack Slezak was anathema. But for Kerry the knowledge that this was what Slezak expected, despite his efforts to deny Kerry the office they now sat in, demanded a different response. "My forbearance," Kerry said. "You think I'm only concerned with the next election. In the last election, *I* lost your primary –thanks in large measure to you. Now you're facing a primary against Jeannie Griswold, and if you lose, you're gone for good. *This* election, it's pretty much up to me."

Slezak's face took on an adamantine cast of someone who would not be moved. "Michigan's my state, not yours. I thought we settled that the last time."

Kerry shook his head. "No," he answered. "All we settled the last time is that I want you gone. And if you screw me on this, some other folks are going to share my vision. One thing is sure—the response will be a lot more elegant, and far better deserved, than a round of sleazy phone-banking."

Slezak folded his arms. "Like what?"

"Any number of things. But I'll give you a clue to one—keep an eye on Leo Weller."

Slezak's eyes hardened. "Those asbestos ads."

Kerry smiled. "You've already heard. But, of course, you don't have asbestos mines in Michigan. So let me explain what this is about for you.

"A twelve-year-old boy in Detroit was shooting baskets on a playground when a teenage neighbor shot him in the spine. Now the boy's a quadriplegic for however long he lives.

"The shooter bought his gun from a dirty dealer who didn't bother with background checks, despite the fact that the guns he sold kept popping up in crimes. The dealer's chief supplier, a gun company in Southern California, kept shipping him guns even *after* they knew that. One of their guns left this boy paralyzed.

"His mother sued. This bill you're thinking about supporting would wipe out her lawsuit and immunize that same company *and* the crooked leader." Pausing, Kerry leaned forward. "Vote for it, Jack, and I'll make you a promise.

"Two weeks before your primary against Jeannie Griswold, the trial lawyers are going to put that boy and his mother all over the airwaves. I won't have a thing to do with it. But what I will do is raise millions of dollars for Jeannie, and then campaign against you wherever it hurts the most.

"You'll lose, and I'll get Jeannie Griswold in your place." Kerry's voice was cool, indifferent. "*My* only problem is that I don't much care what you decide."

THIRTEEN

BECAUSE OF what she knew, the deposition of Dr. Larry Walters held a tension that Sarah alone could feel.

John Nolan sat across from her, set to cross-examine. But not until he finished would Sarah hand him a revised witness list which now included Norman Conn, and a notice of deposition for a federal prisoner named George Johnson. For the next several hours, Nolan would question her expert witness without knowing that his answers were the foundation for the lethal damage which—she fervently hoped—Conn and Johnson would visit on Nolan's defense.

As unaware of this as Nolan, Walters exuded a calm precision. His wire-rimmed glasses and careful speech suggested the academic he had become, a Ph.D. in criminology who published extensively on the phenomenon of gun violence in America. But in a past career he had been a firearms expert who had served as a senior administrator for the Bureau of Alcohol, Tobacco and Firearms. This was enough to induce caution in John Nolan but not, to Sarah's satisfaction, the deep wariness he would feel had he known of her surprises. For the moment, knowing what Walters *would* say was more than enough to give her pleasure.

"The Lexington Patriot-2," Walters told Nolan, "is a weapon of war."

Combined with his tone, the simple statement caused Harrison Fancher to lean closer, Nolan to hunch in a defensive yet determined posture. "On what do you base that statement?"

Referring to the document before him, Walters marshalled his thoughts, presenting them without inflection or emotion. "Begin with how Lexington describes the P-2 in its manual. It describes a weapon with a 'militaristic combat sling' which facilitates 'spray firing.' It depicts the P-2 being used in 'hip-fire mode at shortest range.' It represents that its design facilitates 'rapid sustained fire impossible with most handguns' . . ."

"Why," Nolan interrupted, "might not a gun fancier enjoy the P-2 simply for its advanced design?"

Walters looked up from the manual with raised eyebrows. " 'Advanced design'? Its sights are crude, it weighs too much, and it's unwieldy to shoot. In short, this gun is not designed for any serious recreational purpose. Nor am I aware of any instance when the P-2 has been used for household self-defense. What it *is* good for—as this manual suggests—is shooting multiple human targets during rapid sustained fire." Pausing, Walters finished, " 'Advanced' is in the eye of the beholder. But as a matter of 'design,' Mr. Bowden applied the Patriot-2 to its only useful purpose."

"On what do you base *that* opinion?"

"Among other things, I reviewed the tape of the murders." Glancing toward a video screen at the head of the conference table, Walters said mildly, "Unless you'd prefer otherwise, I'm prepared to walk you through it."

With reluctance, Nolan's eyes followed Walters's to the screen. Picking up a remote control, Walters pressed a button.

On the screen, John Bowden knelt near a baggage carousel, facing his unwitting victims. He pulled the P-2 from the Lego box, slinging it over his shoulder, his eyes vacant.

As a bullet tore through Inez Costello's throat, Walters froze the picture.

"That's the First Lady's mother, of course. In terms of the gun's 'design,' a lucky shot. What follows, as you will see, hews more closely to the P-2's design function."

Once more, the picture came to life.

"No," Joan Bowden screamed.

As Sarah flinched, she heard five rapid percussive pops. Henry Serrano fell; then the young blonde student from Stanford, Laura Blanchard; then the second guard, David Walsh. Nolan's eyes became slits. "All five shots," Walters explained, "were meant for his wife. Instead, Bowden killed three strangers."

Frozen, the picture captured Mary Costello, scrambling on the carousel. "That," Walters continued, "was when he turned his attention to the plaintiff."

Mary Costello jerked into motion, crawling inside the mouth of the baggage tunnel as more bullets struck metal. Sarah's mouth felt dry. "Fifteen feet," Walters observed dispassionately. "Three shots. And still he couldn't hit her.

"And so he turned to his wife again."

Joan Bowden appeared, and then a bullet destroyed her lower face. This time Walters's click of the remote made Sarah wince. "Note," he said, "the damage done by the Eagle's Claw. Note further that Bowden now has fired ten of them, and that the score stands at two intended victims, three random deaths, and five outright misses.

Sarah looked away. The film and Walters's eerie commentary had reduced the others to silence. "The next death," he opined, "is where the design of the gun, its forty-bullet magazine, and the design of the bullet itself meet in deadly confluence."

With a click of the remote, Marie Costello stared in horror at her mother's ruined face. Then she turned away, eyes shut, doll clutched to her chest.

"With a ten-bullet magazine," Walters observed, "this little girl lives."

The picture cut to Bowden. "Stop," a man cried out.

The gun jerked in Bowden's hand. "In my opinion," Walters said blandly, "he didn't mean to shoot. But the trigger of the P-2 can pull at the slightest twitch. As designed."

Marie lay amidst the shattered china pieces of her doll. Gaping in horror, Bowden put the gun to his head.

Walters stopped the tape. "This is the twelfth shot," he concluded. "A not uncommon end to a domestic violence murder. Except that four people died at random, and one intended victim escaped. The plaintiff."

On the screen, blood and cerebral matter spewed from Bowden's head. "Let's take ten minutes," Nolan said. Perhaps, Sarah thought with a certain bleak amusement, he felt the worst was over.

"Picking up your inquiry on design," Walters said when the break was done, "Bowden got close because the gun was concealable. The sling enabled him to fire rapidly but randomly, resulting in accidental victims. The magazine gave him an eleventh bullet, and the hair trigger caused him to fire it at Marie. Who died because the Eagle's Claw is designed to kill.

"Another gun, another bullet, and a ten-clip magazine—or any one of those things—and that murdered child would still be with us." Pausing, he gave the slightest shrug. "As for the others, Mr. Nolan, you're free to argue that three of them died at random. But in my opinion, they *all* died by design."

"By Bowden's design," Nolan corrected tartly. "Wouldn't you agree that the design of a gun is neutral in itself, and that the responsibility for a murder rests with the murderer, and not the manufacturer?"

"Agree?" Once more Walters arched his eyebrows. "No. Not even if you don't impute responsibility for designing a weapon of death."

"On what do you base *that* assertion?"

"Lexington markets to criminals. You're aware of the SSA magazine which was found in Bowden's possession?"

Nolan held up a hand. "Is any part of your opinion, Dr. Walters, based on your belief that Mr. Bowden relied on that advertising in acquiring the P-2? Or even, to a certainty, that he read it?"

Walters hesitated. "No," he answered. "Not at this time. Though it's certainly reasonable to *infer* that Bowden saw it."

"Perhaps to you," Nolan said dismissively.

"Perhaps to me," Walters answered agreeably. "Certainly to Lexington. That's why they've worked so hard to place the P-2 in movies and TV crime shows, often in the hands of criminals. Which is appropriate—police don't use this gun."

Sarah suppressed a smile. But Nolan was doing what he must—getting Walters to detail the opinions he would render at a trial, however harmful. "What other evidence," Nolan persisted, "do you have which suggests that Lexington 'markets to criminals'?"

"The same evidence Lexington does. Start with the fact that the increase of gun violence in America coincides with the rise of the handgun. Rarely do hunting rifles show up in crimes, and even the shotgun is statistically insignificant . . ."

"Every manufacturer in America," Nolan interjected, "makes handguns. Does that mean they're marketing to criminals?"

Walters's eyes grew cold. "If they are, Mr. Nolan, they're nowhere near as successful as your client.

"According to the ATF, the P-2 is the number one semiautomatic handgun used in crimes. So criminals have gotten the message, and so has Lexington. Which accounts for the nature of the ad you imply that Bowden never saw.

"That brings me to a second fact: because California has background checks, thirty percent of guns used in crimes in California come from out of state. Again, the P-2 is the number one semiautomatic crime gun in California. A disproportionate number of those guns originate with sales in Arizona and Nevada. As Lexington surely knows, it sells more guns in Nevada than the local traffic will bear—the so-called flooding phenomenon.

"If Lexington doesn't believe some of those guns get passed to secondary buyers at gun shows in Nevada, it's because it doesn't want to. But, again, their ad suggests that they know this very well."

Having a good expert, Sarah reflected, is akin to driving a Rolls Royce; you can just sit back and enjoy the ride. "And then," Walters went on, "there's the question of stolen guns.

"It's an epidemic—roughly five hundred thousand thefts a year. The most prominent thieves are gun traffickers and survivalists: selling a stolen gun jacks up their profit margin to one hundred percent. And according to the ATF, the most popular stolen semiautomatic handgun is the Lexington P-2.

"The best place for thieves and survivalists to sell weapons is at gun shows. There are potentially thousands of customers, unrestricted by any fear of background checks. In this case, Lexington chose to promote the sale of P-2s at gun shows, ostensibly by licensed dealers." Pausing, Walters gazed keenly at John Nolan. "But Lexington also knows, because it *has* to know, that gun shows are an important secondary market which keeps its product moving."

Nolan stared at him. "Are you aware of any evidence,"

he demanded, "that John Bowden's gun is linked to traffickers or survivalists?"

"No," the expert answered. "But that makes my point about Lexington's refusal to require background checks of gun-show promoters. Because we may never know.

"But there's one thing we do know. If Bowden went to that gun show and the promoter had required a background check, he couldn't have bought that gun."

Nolan hesitated. Then, to Sarah's silent satisfaction, he asked a question rooted in his ignorance of the ambush which awaited him. "But that's all speculation, isn't it? Survivalists, traffickers, stolen guns, whether Bowden saw this ad, even what Lexington actually *knows* about the purported use of its guns in crimes—none of it, in this case, has been established as fact."

"Not at this time," Walters answered calmly. Even Nolan's coffee, Sarah reflected, was tasting unusually good.

After lunch, Fancher commenced his questioning on behalf of the SSA.

"Why," Fancher asked aggressively, "did you leave the ATF?"

Walters folded his hands. "Because your client gutted its effectiveness."

"Explain that, if you will."

"Gladly. Through its allies in Congress, the SSA confined unannounced inspections of gun dealers to one a year—even for dealers the ATF believes are failing to run background checks. They reduced most violations to misdemeanors. They reduced the number of inspectors. They made sure that all records of background checks are destroyed within a day. They threatened to have their allies further reduce our budget if we fought this systemic war on our enforcement.

"Even that wasn't enough. Unlike tobacco, guns can be made safer. But the SSA opposed laws requiring safety locks, or even safe gun storage, and other steps to prevent thousands of suicides and accidental deaths. All to further the Second Amendment."

Fancher's tone became cutting. "Are you suggesting, Dr. Walters, that the SSA has no right to advocate gun ownership for law-abiding Americans, unfettered by the intrusiveness of the federal government?"

"Then the SSA should be prouder of its best work." Walters's tone held the first hint of emotion. "For several years, the Centers for Disease Control kept figures on the frequency, costs and causes of gun violence in America. Then, again acting through its allies in Congress, the SSA cut off all funding for gun-related research. It's catch-22: your client blocks the development of empirical evidence to support laws like President Kilcannon's proposal, and then argues that no evidence exists."

Walters paused, as though to retrieve his aura of calm. "As part of that effort, Senator Paul Harshman asked the head of the CDC if it was 'sending money to a Dr. Lawrence Walters.' I've never met Senator Harshman. But your client made sure that the senator had heard of me, and that the CDC knew to stay away."

Walters sat back. "The SSA," he finished, "promotes fear and enforces ignorance. Imagine if we'd done that regarding polio or smallpox. The result would have been what the SSA has accomplished here: hundreds of thousands of crippled lives and needless deaths."

When the questioning was over, Sarah slipped the witness list and deposition notice into Nolan's hands. "Not great for you," she said blithely. "At least in my opinion. But that's all speculation."

FOURTEEN

WHEN CASSIE ROLLINS arrived on the Hill from a long weekend visiting her constituents in Maine, she remained, as she had told them, undecided on both tort reform and the gun bill. She was listening to their voices, she had assured them. In truth, the voices were a cacophony, and she felt buffeted by the SSA and Kilcannon's visit to her backyard. She did not look forward to her meeting with Fasano.

Glancing at the Capitol, Cassie stopped.

Customarily, she took a private entrance. Today, drawn by a crowd of demonstrators, she walked up the marble steps of the Senate side.

What gave her pause were the shoes.

They were carefully arranged on the steps—the empty shoes of women or children, row upon row. The demonstrators, mostly women, held signs saying "Help Our President Save Lives," and "No Immunity for Murder."

One, a pleasant, round-faced woman with grey hair, stood beside a pair of black pumps and a smaller pair of tennis shoes. Gazing at the endless rows of shoes, Cassie gently asked her, "Whose shoes are these?"

"Women and children murdered by abusers." Pausing, she glanced down at the shoes beside her. "Those were my daughter's and grandson's."

Nodding, Cassie touched the woman's arm, and then went on her way. But as she entered the Majority Leader's suite of offices, the empty shoes stayed with her.

*

"I saw them," Fasano acknowledged.

"Did you also see the coverage of Kilcannon with those hunters? He's getting pretty good at this."

Fasano did not respond to her directly. "The week after next," he said at length, "I'm planning to bring up tort reform. I need you to be with me."

Cassie pursed her lips in thought. "I'd like to be, Frank. But I'll admit that this one bothers me—personally, and politically."

Fasano gave her a shrewd, pragmatic look. "Is there something I can give you?"

"Yes," Cassie answered promptly. "A compromise with Kilcannon on his gun bill. A real one."

Fasano slowly shook his head. "I've gone as far as I can go. You already know that."

"I know all about the SSA," she said tiredly. "But have a care, Frank, about who's using whom. You could wind up like the boy who chose to ride the back of the tiger. Maybe you won't get eaten, but the tiger will decide where you should go."

Once more, Fasano was silent. At length, he said, "Only one of us will get eaten, Cassie. And that's you.

"I accept the deal you had with Mac Gage when *he* was leader. Three out of ten votes you'll cross me to please some part of your electorate. Some of those votes will be on abortion and even, on occasion, guns. In turn, I get seven votes out of ten, and a Republican senator who helps keep us in the majority, and me as leader.

"I'm not into jihads. You understand that, I hope."

"I do," Cassie said with a nod of deference. "And I appreciate it."

"Then this is where you show me." Though any movement was imperceptible, Fasano suddenly seemed closer to her, and his voice became flat and cold. "I expect both your vote on gun immunity *and* against Kilcannon's bill. Our party has to deliver and those votes are too damned close. If you oppose me, I can't control the SSA. I won't try. And by next November you won't be here anymore. So you'll be spared the consequences of having to deal with *me*."

She had run out of room, Cassie realized. In the same tone of civil deference, she thanked Fasano for his candor and promised him every consideration. But not, as of yet, her vote.

Unlike his Democratic colleagues, Leo Weller preferred, at this sensitive juncture, to keep his distance from a President who so inflamed his right-wing base. So to spare him further embarrassment, Kerry contacted the senator by phone.

"I just saw some polling data," he observed with mock solicitousness. "I've never seen an incumbent senator drop nineteen points in fourteen days. Your approval rating's in free fall, Leo."

"It's temporary," Weller said stubbornly.

"Temporary? You're dying from asbestosis. And Beltway tunnel vision." Kerry's tone maintained the same ironic sympathy. "Believe me, I understand how this can happen. You're playing golf with the president of an asbestos company, who starts complaining about how all these bogus lawsuits will drag his company under. You, too, hate bogus lawsuits, *and* plaintiffs' lawyers, and your golf buddy is so committed to your common principles that he's already raised three hundred thousand for your next campaign.

"So you're glad to stick an immunity provision in Fasano's tort reform bill, and sign on as its cosponsor. The problem is that you've got constituents who are dying off from asbestosis—but not quite fast enough to keep them from voting against you." Kerry's voice became crisp. "And now they've started dying off on television. Airtime in Montana is cheap, and the victims are plentiful. They'll be dying on you from now until next November. Then it's your turn."

This, as Kerry expected, induced silence. "What do you want?" Weller asked.

"They're not my ads, Leo. Only the trial lawyers can help you. But I can suggest what a sensible man in your position would do.

"I wouldn't vote in favor of my gun bill—too risky. But before another day passes, I'd take my name off that tort reform bill and promise to vote against it." Kerry's voice hardened. "The *whole* bill. Then the trial lawyers will have to find some other way of getting rid of you."

Weller responded with more silence. The man might be a fool, Kerry knew, but he had his pride. He disliked being made an object lesson in such a public way—the helpless symbol of Kerry's resolve—and the humiliation which would follow such a public change in the balance of the Senate. "I'll consider it," Weller said in grudging tones.

"You do that, Leo," the President replied. "Personally, I find those ads truly painful to watch."

FIFTEEN

IN A CRAMPED windowless room in the Federal Detention Facility in Phoenix, Sarah cross-examined George Johnson.

On the long flight to Arizona, Sarah's imagination had summoned a Hells Angels prototype—bearded, fleshy, tattooed. But though the person across from her had committed three violent felonies and had spearheaded the robbery of the Lexington P-2 used to slaughter Lara's family, Johnson was slight and pale, distinguished only by close-cropped hair, darting eyes, and a twitching restlessness which kept some part of him constantly in motion. The contrast with his voice—flat, emotionless, distant—made his tics more unnerving.

Watching the prisoner, Nolan, too, looked uncomfortable. For all of his authority and arrogance, Nolan had little experience with the underside of America, and Sarah had left him to guess why she had noticed the deposition of a federal prisoner. "Why are you in custody?" Sarah asked Johnson.

Briefly, he glanced at his lawyer, a federal public defender with spiked hair, a severe face, and incongruous turquoise earrings. When the woman nodded, Sarah realized that Lara Kilcannon had been right—this man was prepared to admit his guilt. With a shrug of the shoulders, so quick that it resembled a spasm, Johnson answered, "I stole a truckload of Lexington P-2s from a gun store in Phoenix."

Nolan's eyes met Harrison Fancher's. "For what purpose?" Sarah asked.

A contemptuous smile played at the edges of Johnson's mouth. "Selling them."

"Why did you need the money?"

"For the Liberty Force. To finance our resistance."

His tone betrayed something beyond anger—a rigid adherence to an ordered view of his surroundings, peopled by his enemies. "Resistance to what?"

"Jews." His eyes bored into Sarah's, and the word held a distinct contempt. "The cabal that uses our so-called democratic government and drug and entertainment culture—all the blacks and queers and dykes and race traitors—to control our economy, castrate male authority and pollute the white Christian race. Their master plan is to force us into their polyglot world order."

And take away our tree forts, Sarah thought. But Johnson's tone of certainty chilled her—it bespoke the kind of conviction needed to blow up buildings. "Where were you arrested?"

"At a gun show, in Phoenix. The ATF busted a buyer and he turned on me."

By now Nolan's taut attention was palpable. "Why did you sell at a gun show?" Sarah asked.

Again, Johnson twitched his shoulders. "The shows get listed in that SSA magazine, and people are willing to pay a premium. Arizona and Nevada are the best. Lots of buyers, no questions."

Briefly, Sarah hesitated. "Was there a particular reason you stole P-2s?"

With an oddly fastidious gesture, Johnson examined his fingernails, so pristine and closely trimmed that she wondered where he had obtained the manicure. "The P-2's popular at gun shows, and you can't buy them in California." Pausing, he added with quiet irony. "It's not accurate enough for the resistance. But customers like its features."

"What about the customer who turned you in?"

"Don't know." His flat voice hinted at disdain for the pettiness of his customer's ambitions. "All I know is they caught him robbing a 7-Eleven."

Slowly, Sarah slid a photograph across the table. "Have you ever seen this man before?"

Gazing down, Johnson emitted a harsh laugh. "John Bowden. Some call him an American patriot."

The poison in his answer stunned Sarah into momentary silence. She rested a finger on one edge of the photograph. "Do you know where Bowden got his gun?"

Silent, Johnson glanced at his lawyer. Turning to Sarah, his eyes were veiled, and his body stiff with tension, as though fighting against his deepest instincts. In a reluctant tone between mumble and whisper, he said, "You'd have to ask Ben Gehringer. He stole the guns with me."

Sarah, too, felt tense. "To sell at gun shows?"

"Yes." Staring at Bowden's picture, Johnson seemed to contemplate the imponderable workings of fate. "I took Arizona, and he got Nevada."

By the time Nolan began his interrogation, the room felt hot and stifling, and Sarah had begun imagining the smell emanating from Johnson's body as the sour stench of fanaticism.

"You do realize," Nolan said pointedly, "that you spent this morning incriminating yourself."

"Who defines the 'crime'?" Johnson answered with disdain. "Our 'government,' this handmaiden of Jews and mongrels? I refuse to acknowledge its authority."

This seemed to spur in Nolan an answering contempt. "Have you made any arrangement with the government —however you might despise it—in exchange for your testimony today?"

"No."

Nolan stared at him. "Or discussed such an arrangement with anyone at all?"

"When you answer that," the lawyer admonished Johnson, "exclude any conversations with counsel."

The frustration seemed to issue from Nolan like heat. She could feel his suspicion harden to certainty—that a deal contrived by Kilcannon himself was eroding his client's defense. "No," Johnson answered in an undertone of defiance. "No one from the government. Only my lawyer."

But he did not look at Nolan. To Sarah, George Johnson's distaste for his turncoat customer had doubled back on himself. Faced with growing old in prison, he had turned Judas, become another nail in the coffin of the white Anglo-Saxon race. Had he led them to Gehringer? Sarah saw Nolan wonder. Then she watched Nolan realize, swiftly, that Sarah had not asked this, and thus must already know.

"Where," Nolan asked in a low voice, "is Mr. Gehringer now?"

Johnson sucked in his hollow cheeks. "I hear the government's got him," he said tonelessly, and, for Nolan, the realization of what had happened was complete.

SIXTEEN

FROM THE START of his meeting with Chuck Hampton, Frank Fasano was caught between opposing forces.

The first, captured on the front pages of this morning's *Post* and *Times*, was Leo Weller's defection, creating the perception—which could well become reality—that Kerry Kilcannon might seize the balance of power. The second, known only to Fasano, was new pressure from the SSA to hold an early vote on tort reform.

On the telephone, Dane had sounded edgy. "When's the vote?" he had demanded to know.

"I was planning on the week after next," Fasano answered. "But Cassie's still not on board, and Leo's left us at least two votes short on gun immunity. Why bring it to the floor when you don't know if you'll win?"

"Because Kilcannon's scoring points. Back off now and it's an admission of weakness."

In tone and substance, Fasano thought, Dane sounded too simplistic, too demanding, too forgetful of the deference due Fasano himself. "There's no deadline," he answered coolly. "At least not in the Senate. Is there some problem in the lawsuit?"

The sudden thrust induced silence, confirming its accuracy. For the first time, Fasano found himself wishing that he had access to the depositions in the Costello suit. But the judge had ordered them sealed, and Dane seemed unwilling to pass on whatever the lawyers were telling him. "Look," Fasano persisted, "if there's some disaster lurking in that case, I need to know before I put our party at risk to kill it."

"If you kill it," Dane retorted, "there *is* no risk. If you can't get to Rollins, we will. The rest is up to you."

As a courtesy, Hampton came to Fasano's office. "It's time for a vote," Fasano told him.

With the trace of a smile, Hampton inquired, "On the President's gun bill? It's surely time to stop the killing."

The ease in Hampton's manner induced the opposite effect in Fasano—a wary suspicion that Hampton, as well as Dane, knew something Fasano did not. "To bring up tort reform," Hampton added, "you need the unanimous consent of all senators. Right now you don't even have mine."

"Quit playing games," Fasano answered testily. "You can force me to file a motion to proceed with the tort bill, and then debate the motion. But you'll lose the vote, and what will you gain in the meanwhile? A delay of maybe three days, four at most."

Hampton sipped his coffee. "Which you seem desperate to avoid. What's the problem, Frank—hearing the President's footsteps? Or is it the SSA?" Abruptly Hampton's amiable tone was replaced by one of tough practicality, all the more impressive for its quiet. "Every week brings a fresh harvest of children dead from guns. Until we vote on the President's bill, all I can do is bring their *pictures* to the floor. A poor substitute for action.

"Give us a vote on Kilcannon's bill. If we don't get it, I mean to propose every piece of it that the SSA doesn't like as a separate amendment to your tort reform bill, along with a few ideas of my own: universal background checks; a ban on making or selling Eagle's Claw bullets; mandatory safety locks; and a provision to close the gun-show loophole." His smile flickered. "You did see the news clips of that gun show in Las Vegas, right? They were selling AK-47s.

"I'm going to force you to cast vote after vote, and let people like Cassie Rollins decide between the SSA and commonsense measures the public wants. After ten votes or so, your caucus will look like whores for the gun lobby—at least the people who stick with you. And if you're still up for a fight, I'll throw in some more amendments which will make terrific issues in the next campaign: a raise in the minimum wage, prescription drug benefits for seniors, maybe a patient's bill of rights . . ."

"Do that," Fasano cut in, "and the Senate will be a bloodbath, with relations across the aisle so poisoned the public will end up hating us all. What about this President makes him worth all that?"

"It's not just Kilcannon," Hampton answered easily. "You've been trying to roll us. I'll blow this place up before I'll let that happen. Your choice is this—compromise with me or start defending the Eagle's Claw, and prepare your people to pay their debts to Charles Dane with some of the worst votes they've ever cast."

Fasano fought back his disbelief. Either he had missed the steel in Chuck Hampton, or events were turning this scholarly pragmatist into someone harder and far less predictable. "Compromise?" Fasano repeated.

"A straight-up vote on the tort reform bill—no filibuster from us. But only after a vote on my amendment stripping gun immunity out of the final bill."

To Fasano, this was no surprise. The one way that Hampton—and the President—could beat back gun immunity was to force a vote on that alone. "The only way I'll ever consider that," Fasano answered, "is if we vote on tort reform *before* Kilcannon's gun bill."

"How long before?" Hampton parried. "I want a date certain."

"If we can bring up tort reform the Tuesday after next, we'll bring up the President's gun bill two weeks after that. But only after we vote on *our* gun bill."

"A poor thing," Hampton observed with a smile, "but all the SSA allows." After a moment, he stood, extending his hand. "Deal."

"Deal," Fasano answered, and the two men shook hands.

SEVENTEEN

To SARAH, much of Ben Gehringer's appearance had the otherworldly aspect of a high school nerd—thick glasses with flesh-colored frames; thinning, slicked-back brown hair; the posture of a comma on a frame so thin it looked unhealthy; pale skin with strawberry blotches on his cheeks, seemingly untouched by sunlight. But any innocence had been cauterized by fanaticism and distrust; behind the glasses, his blue eyes had the feral keenness of a bird of prey. Knowing she was poised at the edge of a breakthrough, Sarah felt tense.

The setting, a stark room in a federal prison in Idaho, resembled that for the deposition of George Johnson, and the cast of characters was much the same: John Nolan, Harrison Fancher, a court reporter, and a federal public defender, this one a stout, fortyish man in a shapeless grey suit. But this time her adversaries were prepared.

"For the record," Sarah asked the witness, "when were you arrested?"

"A week ago."

"And the charges?"

"Trafficking." His answers were terse and grudging, as though every word were a precious coin. "Stealing a crate-load of Lexington P-2s."

"Where did you steal them," Sarah prodded, "and with whom?"

"Phoenix. With George Johnson."

He spoke the name with the contempt of someone spitting on the sidewalk. Nolan placed a pen to his lips, staring at the witness. "Where did you sell them?" Sarah asked.

The witness hesitated—unwilling, Sarah guessed, to confess to more than he needed. "At a gun show in Vegas."

"When?"

Impatient, Gehringer shifted in his chair. "Around Labor Day."

Sarah placed a photograph in front of the witness. The silence became so complete that it felt eerie. Except for the reporter, the others were still.

"I show you a photograph marked 'Gehringer Exhibit One.' Can you identify this man?"

A brief glint appeared in the pale blue eyes. "Yes."

"Where did you first see him?"

"At the gun show."

His terseness had begun taxing Sarah's tenuous patience. More sharply, she asked, "Did you speak to him?"

"Yes."

"About what?"

"Buying a P-2."

Sarah's skin felt clammy. "Did you sell him one?"

Silent, the witness clasped his wrist with a clawlike movement of his right hand. However detached from normal sensibilities, Gehringer clearly grasped the enormity of the question—the answer could have him placing a P-2 in the hands of the man who had used it to slaughter the mother, niece and sister of the First Lady of the United States. Then an unpleasant smile crossed Gehringer's face—whether in satisfaction at the fact of this, or at what the answer might gain him, Sarah could not tell.

"Yes."

The cold monosyllable seemed to echo in the room. More calmly, Sarah asked, "Did he tell you why he wanted a P-2?"

"Not exactly."

Damn you for your indifference, Sarah thought. "Did he indicate to you—in words or substance—the reason he was buying a Lexington P-2?"

Gehringer's eyes still rested on Bowden's face. "He showed me an ad."

Nolan's expression became a studied blank. Opening a manila folder, Sarah said, "I have here a copy of *The Defender* magazine, premarked as 'Gehringer Exhibit Two.' Was the ad he showed you in this magazine?"

"Yes."

"Had you seen the magazine before?"

Gehringer flipped its pages. With the same detachment, he said, "I subscribe to it."

"Is there a particular reason?"

"It has a calendar of gun shows. That's how I knew about the show in Vegas."

To Sarah's left, Fancher scribbled a note. Taking the magazine from Gehringer's hand, she turned to a page marked with a paper clip. "I show you page fifty-five. Is this the advertisement?"

"Yes."

"The one for Lexington Arms?"

"Yes."

"And next to it is an ad for a gun show."

"Yes." The witness paused. "That was another reason I came to the show. I knew I'd have some customers."

All at once, Nolan's causation defense—that Sarah could not prove Lexington's ad had drawn Bowden to Las Vegas—was gone. Feeling the invisible hand of Kerry Kilcannon, she wondered how he had brought this moment about, and what it might cost him.

"When did you learn Bowden's name?" Sarah asked.

Gehringer's mouth twitched. "After he was dead. From television."

"Not at the gun show?"

Gehringer studied the page before him. "I'm not a licensed dealer," he said with faint derision. "Under the law, I don't have to run a background check."

"Did you discuss this with Bowden?"

"Yes. He didn't want a background check. Said he didn't have time."

Sarah pushed *The Defender* to one side, gaze fixed on Gehringer. "How much did you charge him?"

"Five fifty."

"Did he bargain?"

"No." An edge of disdain entered his voice. "He *complained*. He said the Gun Emporium was selling them for less."

"Did he say why he was paying you a premium?"

The unsettling smile reappeared. "The Gun Emporium ran background checks."

Nolan pressed his palms together. It struck Sarah that, outside this room, no one—save for George Johnson, a few federal prosecutors, or those in the chain of information leading to the President—knew the damning facts which the reporter, stone-faced, was recording in black and white. But its public impact could be devastating. Like Bowden and his victims, Ben Gehringer put a face—in Gehringer's case, an inhuman one—on the need for Kilcannon's gun bill. Once again, she chafed at the order through which Gardner Bond had entombed the facts until Congress could entomb this case.

"Did you," Sarah inquired, "discuss with Bowden the features of the Lexington P-2?"

"Yes."

"For what reason did he buy one?"

"The same reason that we stole them." For the first time, Gehringer chose to elaborate, speaking in the clipped tone of an expert. "More firepower, adaptable to a higher-capacity magazine."

"Did you discuss *that* feature with Bowden?"

"Yes. He figured ten bullets weren't enough."

An image shot through Sarah's brain—Marie Costello, blood oozing from her shredded abdomen. "Did you also discuss the bullets?"

"Yes."

"And what was that discussion?"

Next to Gehringer, his lawyer gazed soberly at the SSA's *Defender*. "If he needed to shoot someone," the witness answered in a matter-of-fact tone, "he wanted to be sure he killed them."

"Why are you testifying?" Nolan asked with feigned incredulity.

The breakthrough, Sarah realized, had only hardened her dislike for Nolan and his methods. "Objection," she interposed. "The question is vague and overbroad. Why does anybody testify?"

Nettled, Nolan turned to the reporter. "Please read back the question."

"Why?" Sarah snapped. "It won't get any better."

"Yes," the public defender agreed. "I'd like you to rephrase the question."

Nolan stared at the witness. "Do you," he asked in an accusatory tone, "have an agreement with plaintiff's counsel regarding your testimony here today?"

"You mean like yours with Martin Bresler?" Sarah asked. "Let me clear that up for you. We've never met with Mr. Gehringer. Except for scheduling matters, we've never spoken to his counsel. We have no deal with either one.

"What about you, John? Did you meet with Martin Bresler? Did you help choose his lawyers? Did you and Bresler's lawyer work out some arrangement? Or did Mr. Fancher do all that?"

Nolan turned from her in icy disdain. "Why don't you answer the question?" Sarah persisted. "I answered yours."

Nolan remained silent, plainly reining in his temper. Then he asked the witness, "Do you have any arrangement with the United States government which includes your testimony in this lawsuit?"

As Gehringer stared at nothing, his lawyer intervened. "Any answer," he said, "is governed by the attorney-client privilege . . ."

"Nonsense," Nolan interrupted. "Any *deal* goes to this witness's credibility."

"There is no deal," the lawyer answered firmly. "That's all I'm privileged to tell you."

Abruptly, Harrison Fancher jabbed a bony finger at Sarah. "*You* know what's happening here. Kilcannon fed you this witness. He's abused the power of the federal government to resuscitate a worthless case."

"That kind of abuse," Sarah retorted mockingly, "cries out for exposure. Why don't you two go to Gardner Bond and ask him to unseal this deposition. Then you can call a press conference and give copies to the media. I'm sure they'll share your moral outrage."

Fancher's mouth worked. Raising his head, Nolan allowed himself only an angry smile. Sarah wished that this brief moment of pleasure could salve her hatred and frustration.

EIGHTEEN

ON THE TELEVISION in her office in Portland, Maine, Cassie Rollins watched an obese actor caricaturing a trial lawyer rip the stars off an American flag.

Tell Cassie Rollins, the voice-over intoned, *that it's time to stop greedy plaintiffs' lawyers from raising prices and wiping out our jobs.* The white print at the bottom of the screen gave the telephone number of Cassie's Washington office and the name of the ad's supposed sponsor "Citizens for Consumer Rights."

"Tell the SSA," Cassie remarked wryly, "that it's un-American to use an alias." She turned to her Chief of Staff. "How many calls have we had on this?"

"About four hundred," Leslie Shoop responded. "But the ad has only been running three days."

Cassie had a new appreciation of the term "punch-drunk." A full-page ad called "The Case for Tort Reform" was running in Maine's daily papers; political writers were reporting rumors of a primary challenge by the SSA's pet candidate; her office was receiving a rising tide of phone messages, letters, faxes and e-mails; groups she had never heard of—such as "Maine Women for Self-Defense"—were calling to demand a meeting.

"It's like an avalanche," Cassie had murmured to Kate Jarman of Vermont as they left the Senate floor. "I'm spending every weekend back home, and my approval rating's five points down."

Chuck Hampton's junior colleague gave her friend a shrewd but sympathetic look. "It's not an avalanche," she had answered. "It's Frank. The SSA wants this, so he can't afford to lose. He's given them a hunting license—as it were."

Cassie nodded. "He as good as told me that. Never doubt him."

"I never did." Kate kept her voice low. "Frank wants to be President, and he knows who's got the money, and the votes. Maybe Chuck can get by with supporting Kilcannon—their party's different. But I'm not bucking Frank on this one. A lot of my gun owners are figuratively up in arms, and they're not nearly as fervent as yours."

To Cassie, this warning was more disheartening for its source, a fellow moderate whose judgment she respected. "In other words, I'm being dumb."

Kate looked at her askance. "Never dumb, Cassie. I'm not up for reelection, and you could get nailed either way. But the safe play may be to cave in to Fasano."

Perhaps so, Cassie mused as she watched the screen. But she did not like the influence of gun owners and fundamentalists within her party's base, the increasingly shopworn claim of her fellow moderates—even as the right wing marginalized them in the Senate—that they were working for change from within. On her television, Governor Abel Randolph appeared, brandishing a gun.

"This is the newest one," Leslie Shoop advised her.

The setting was a press conference held to dramatize Randolph's support for safety locks. As he fumbled with the device, failing to unlock it, his audience began to snicker. The camera caught the state's lieutenant governor, a woman, vainly trying to suppress a smile.

If this were a rape, the narrator said, *not a press conference, how much time would* you *have to protect yourself? Call Cassie Rollins and tell her you're not laughing.* This time the white print read, "Maine Women for Self-Defense."

"At least this clears up who they are," Cassie said. "Charles Dane in drag."

"True. But they sure make Abel look dumb." Leslie hit the remote. "It's both an invitation, and a warning. The warning is obvious—'look at what we're doing to you.' The invitation is 'look what we'll do to Abel Randolph *for* you if you give us what we want.' "

For a moment, Cassie gazed at the blank screen. Then they left for a Kiwanis meeting, the start of a busy weekend.

Four days later, on the floor of the United States Senate, Senator Charles Hampton of Vermont moved to strike the gun immunity provision from the Civil Justice Reform Act.

Afterward Hampton crossed the aisle and, smiling, placed a hand on the shoulder of his friend Chad Palmer. "I only did it to get you time on C-SPAN," Hampton assured the senior senator from Ohio. "After all, this sterling piece of legislation came out of your committee."

Hampton saw a flash of irritation, perhaps embarrassment, and then a more equable expression returned to his colleague's handsome face and, with it, the look—belied by the harshness of Chad's life—of the all-American boy, one of life's winners. "My finest hour," Palmer answered with a shrug.

Hampton's own gaze turned sober. "I'm glad it's someone's," he said. "This is going to be a bloodbath."

In her office on the first floor of the Hart Building, the junior senator from Maine took a call from her erstwhile colleague. Dryly, she inquired, "Is this the artist currently known as 'KFK'?"

"Yes," the President answered with a laugh. " 'Kentucky Fried Kilcannon.' Or so your leader hopes."

"My leader," Cassie rejoined, "is a serious man."

"So am I, Cassie. I've been trying to figure out what to threaten you with. I can't think of anything nearly as good as the SSA, except to help Abel Randolph."

"To do what, Mr. President? Operate a safety lock?"

This time the President's laugh was rueful. "It's a lesson to us all. I've been practicing at night."

His candor and capacity for humor in adversity reminded Cassie of why, as peers, she had been so fond of him. But since he had been President, and particularly since the murders, he had seemed far graver, much less inclined to laughter. "It's certainly a lesson to *me*," she admitted. "Up in Maine, these people are playing for keeps. And they've got access to more cash than me *or* Abel."

"I know," the President answered with droll resignation. "So I'm forced to ask you to vote with me because it's right."

Alone in her office, Cassie smiled. "Really, Mr. President, have you no respect? I was hoping you'd deem me worthy of what you dished out to Leo Weller and, rumor has it, Slezak."

She heard his quiet laughter. "That's the problem." Kilcannon's tone was serious now. "I do respect you."

This was true, Cassie was quite certain. "How many times," she inquired, "are you hoping I'll do what's right? Once, or twice?"

"Twice. Hampton's amendment on gun immunity, and then my gun bill."

Cassie sat back in her chair, gazing out at the failing sunlight half-concealed by her blinds. "Twice is a lot," she answered. "*Once* is a lot. They probably weren't the rage in Newark, but have you ever been to a hunters' breakfast?"

"No. What's that?"

"It's a Maine tradition, passed down from father to son.

On the opening day of hunting season, in town after town, men meet for a hearty breakfast at some local spot before heading off for the woods with their hunting rifles.

"It's more than a tradition. For a lot of them it's ritual, part of the Maine mystique. Some believe that our culture may have gone to hell, but they still can hang on to their way of life as long as they've got their guns." Pausing, Cassie tried to convey this depth of feeling. "It's not ideological so much as it's psychological, almost mythological. Even people who don't have guns view them as woven into the fabric of who we are."

The President's sigh was audible as was, now, his weariness. "I met with them, too," he answered. "I don't think they're a lost cause. In the end, they can't believe their way of life is about the bullet that killed Marie."

His tone was etched with wonder and despair. In the end, Cassie thought, politics was a very human process and—as ruthless as he could be—Kilcannon hoped to appeal to the better angels of human nature. "I'll think on what you've said," she promised. "All of it."

NINETEEN

THE VICE PRESIDENT of marketing, Mike Reiner, had worked at Lexington for twenty-one years. Now he sat across from Lenihan and Sarah in the conference room of a Hartford law firm, a barrel-chested man with a pompadour of steel grey hair, a seamed face and bright blue eyes which glinted with dislike for Mary Costello's lawyers. Even his paunch seemed aggressive.

But beneath Reiner's pose of arrogance Sarah sensed a tension similar to her own. Her attempts to reach Norman Conn had not succeeded; she feared that Conn, like Martin Bresler, had been intimidated into silence. But what Conn knew could be devastating to Lexington and to Reiner, his superior. The choice for Reiner was clear: admit facts damaging to Lexington, or lie, hoping that Conn had not—and would not—betray him. As for Nolan, he must know at the least that he was defending a problem witness. But unless Lexington had broken Conn completely, only Lenihan and Sarah knew the depth of Reiner's problems.

"For what reason," Lenihan asked the witness, "does Lexington include the P-2 in its product line?"

Sitting beside Reiner, Nolan was impassive; only his gaze, moving between Lenihan and Reiner, betrayed the importance of this witness. But Reiner's exaggerated squint seemed meant to convey the rank stupidity of the question. Bluffly, he answered, "To expand our customer base."

"By what means?"

The squint gave way to a show of white, obviously capped, front teeth. "By making a semiautomatic handgun with features people want."

"What features?"

Reiner rested both arms on the table, expanding his personal territory. "Things like a barrel shroud. To enable you to touch the gun even when the barrel overheats."

"Will ten shots cause the barrel to heat?"

Nolan's glance darted to Reiner. "No," the witness answered. "It takes more than ten."

Lenihan leaned toward Reiner. To Sarah, they seemed mirror images of self-assertion and self-regard, save that Lenihan—with his curly hair, soft chin, and more gradually sloping belly—looked far less tough than his antagonist. "Why is that a problem," Lenihan inquired, "when it's illegal to manufacture magazines which hold more than ten rounds?"

"We can't *make* them," Reiner retorted, "but it's legal for anyone to *buy* them. Just as long as they were made before the ban."

"Why would 'anyone' need more than ten bullets?"

Reiner shrugged. "Why not?"

The casual answer caused Lenihan to lower his voice. "Aren't you concerned someone might 'need' more than ten bullets to slaughter a lot of people quickly?"

" 'A lot of people,' " Reiner rejoined, "are gun fanciers or collectors. I don't question their motives, any more than I ask why someone would want a vintage Ferrari capable of hitting a hundred eighty miles an hour."

"Why not retrofit the gun to only accept ten-bullet magazines?"

"Why take on the expense? We'd have to eat it."

"How expensive would *that* be?"

Another shrug. "Don't know. Not my department."

To Sarah, the gleam in Lenihan's eye suggested a poker player sitting on an ace-high straight. "Then I'll try to stick with what you *do* know. Are you aware that automatic weapons are illegal?"

Reiner's expression conveyed both amusement and contempt. "Yes."

"Would you agree that automatic weapons can be used to kill 'a lot of people' even quicker than the Lexington P-2, because they can fire multiple rounds with one pull of the trigger?"

"Sure."

"Isn't the P-2 designed to be easily convertible to automatic fire?"

Reiner covered one wrist with the meaty fingers of his other hand. "I know some people do it."

Pulling out a videotape and crudely printed pamphlet, Lenihan asked the reporter to mark them as Reiner Exhibits One and Two. "In fact, aren't this manual and tape—showing how to convert the P-2 to automatic fire—commonly sold at gun shows?"

The squint returned to Reiner's face, but without its former amusement. "I wouldn't know."

"Have you seen this manual before, Mr. Reiner?"

"I don't recall."

"Did you," Lenihan snapped, "help the author write this manual?"

Nolan turned to the witness. Trained on Lenihan, Reiner's bright blue eyes were chill. "I talk to hundreds of gun enthusiasts every year, in person or on the phone. I can't remember them all, or what I may have told them."

It was the only answer he could give, Sarah knew—except the truth. "Let's take ten minutes," Nolan said abruptly.

Lenihan shrugged. "Fine. But once a client starts to lie, it's awfully hard to stop him."

*

Recommencing, Lenihan inquired without preface, "Did you help design the Eagle's Claw bullet?"

As though to relieve an aching joint, the witness squeezed his wrist. "I only gave advice. From a marketing perspective."

"From a marketing perspective, what's the purpose of the Eagle's Claw?"

"To have more stopping power." Assertiveness returning, Reiner combined his squint with another show of teeth. "If you're faced with bad guys, you want to eliminate the threat."

"By killing them?"

"By stopping them." Reiner's rough eastern-accented voice thickened with disgust. "If you have to defend your family, you're not worried about making these fine distinctions."

Nolan placed a pen to his lips. Pausing, Lenihan smiled with a pleasure which struck Sarah as close to sensual. "Are you aware, Mr. Reiner, of a single successful use of the P-2 against a rapist or an intruder?"

Reiner frowned. "I don't collect that kind of information."

"No?" Lenihan said with incredulity. "I'd think 'that kind of information' would really help your marketing."

Reiner shrugged. "Maybe it would."

"Would it also help if a police department bought Lexington P-2s?"

"Maybe."

"Isn't *that* 'the kind of information' the Vice President of Marketing might want? Or does your driving lack of curiosity extend to the police?"

"Objection," Nolan cut in. "Stop harassing the witness."

"Forgive me," Lenihan answered with exquisite politeness, and trained his eyes on the witness. "Does any police force in America use the Lexington P-2?"

"I don't know."

"What about military forces, whether at home or abroad."

Reiner hesitated. "The South African security forces did . . ."

Lenihan smiled. "Before apartheid ended?"

"Yes."

"Little wonder. Who uses it now?"

"We have a contract to sell P-2s to the government of Myanmar."

"The dictatorship of Myanmar, you mean. For what is euphemistically described as 'crowd control.' "

Reiner's fingers tightened on his wrist. "I'm just a workingman. I don't do foreign policy."

"Or foreign slaughter? Like the recent killing of twenty protesters against the 'government' of Myanmar."

"I don't know what they used."

"Why not? I'd think *that* would be one hell of a tool for marketing . . ."

"Skip the editorial comments," Nolan snapped. "You can conduct this deposition with courtesy, or we can leave."

Smiling, Lenihan answered, "We'll give Mr. Reiner every courtesy, John. Because we'd just hate for him to leave." Turning back to Reiner, he asked, "Isn't it true that American police or military forces don't buy the P-2 because it's not accurate enough?"

The armpits of Reiner's dress shirt, Sarah noticed, were stained with damp circles of sweat. "It's designed for rapid fire, Mr. Lenihan. If you fire enough, you get the job done."

Lenihan laughed aloud. "That's why we're here."

*

By eleven a.m., after the witness's second break, the room had begun to feel stifling. Only Lenihan seemed cheerful.

"Isn't it true, Mr. Reiner, that the design of the Lexington P-2 is based on a prior model, the P-1?"

"Basically."

"Why do you no longer make the P-1?"

"Because it was outlawed by the assault weapons ban."

Lenihan's eyebrows flew upward. "So how is the P-2 different from the P-1?"

Reiner gave a brief, scornful laugh. "We eliminated the perforated barrel which helped prevent jamming, and the threaded barrel, which allowed the user to screw on a silencer. All we needed to comply with that stupid law was to make our prototype inferior."

"*Federal* law," Lenihan pointed out. "After the P-2 replaced the P-1, didn't California ban it?"

"But Congress didn't," Reiner shot back. "So we can sell in other states . . ."

"In fact, didn't you use the ban in California to market the P-2 in Nevada?"

Flushed, Reiner unknotted his tie. "We didn't have to use it. Prohibition created a pent-up demand."

Sarah noted Nolan's frown, a tightening of lips. *Press Reiner on that,* she silently implored her cocounsel. Lenihan airily let it pass—or, she feared, was too fixated on his own design to notice. Pointing to the SSA magazine lying open in front of Reiner, he said. "But you did write this ad, calling the P-2 an 'endangered species, banned in California'?"

Reiner gazed at the printed words. "Yes. Because it's true. California banned the gun, and then Kilcannon was elected President. Buyers should know they had an opportunity they might not have later."

"Including buyers in California?" Lenihan asked pleasantly, and Sarah realized that her co-counsel had missed nothing.

"I wouldn't know," Reiner answered, and glanced at the gold Rolex dangling loosely around his wrist. "If it's not time for lunch, I need to use the powder room."

Lenihan hesitated, a predator interrupted. Glancing at Nolan, Sarah wondered again if he knew what Conn had told her, and how much trouble his witness faced.

"Sure," Lenihan answered, his amiability restored. "Just don't forget to use soap."

When the questions resumed, Lenihan—to Sarah's surprise—abruptly changed the subject. "Concerning this advertisement, did you contribute the language saying that the Eagle's Claw 'opens a massive wound channel'?"

"Yes, because it's true."

"And that the P-2 is designed to deliver 'a high volume of firepower'?"

"Yes," Reiner repeated with a defiant edge, "because it's true."

"Who were you trying to appeal to? Skeet shooters?"

Reiner folded his arms. "Gun collectors. It's not my business to judge their reasons."

"But you already *know* what their reasons are. For example, did you also write that the P-2 'can be used to initiate combat in offensive-type situations'?"

"Yes."

"Who were you appealing to *there*? The government of Myanmar?"

Once more, Reiner rested his forearms on the table, but, it seemed, more heavily. "Guns," he said, "have a variety of uses . . ."

"Weren't you trying to appeal to someone with plans for—or fantasies about—a military-style assault?"

Reiner shrugged. "There's nothing wrong with fantasies."

"Or plans, I suppose. Are you aware of any shooting competitions which feature the P-2?"

"Not to my knowledge."

Lenihan smiled. "What about competitions between drug dealers? Are you aware of any drug dealers who use the Lexington P-2?"

"I don't hang out with drug dealers."

"Do drug dealers," Lenihan persisted, "use the P-2?"

"I don't know *what* drug dealers use."

"Isn't it true, Mr. Reiner, that Lexington paid the producer of the ABC series *Strike Force* to feature the Lexington P-2?"

Reiner eyed him with disdain. "Everybody does product placement."

"In the case of this particular product," Lenihan asked pleasantly, "who was portrayed using the P-2?"

Reiner held his gaze. "The drug lord."

"And did you approve the script?"

"I don't specifically recall."

Lenihan smiled. "Really? Why don't you reflect on that one over lunch?"

Lenihan sipped iced tea. "I'm saving that for dessert," he said in response to Sarah's question. "I want to squeeze him dry before he knows how bad things are."

That made sense. "Unless he already does. Does Nolan know, I wonder?"

Lenihan's smile was grim. "Unless they've flipped Norman Conn, neither of them knows. But we've already got enough to do some real damage."

Though this was true, Sarah found it more dispiriting than hopeful. "You know what sucks, Bob? Unless the President can kill gun immunity, none of it will matter."

*

Before continuing, Lenihan hung his suit coat loosely over a chair. Reiner's tie remained loosened, and he had rolled up his sleeves. Even Harry Fancher was in shirtsleeves; only Nolan remained buttoned up.

Again, Lenihan leaned forward. "Are you aware," he asked the witness, "of any states besides California which ban the P-2?"

"No."

"But you are aware that the P-2 is commonly used in crimes in California?"

"Commonly? How would I know?"

"But you *were* aware—even before the Costello shootings—of at least *one* crime where a P-2 *was* used in California."

Reiner frowned. "Yeah—the day-care center in Oakland. The media called us for comment."

"How many kids died in *that* particular incident?"

"Four."

"Where did the shooter get *that* gun?"

"I don't remember knowing. *We* didn't sell it to him."

Lenihan stared at him. "Aren't you at least curious? After all, don't you commonly receive tracing requests concerning guns used in crimes?"

"We get some."

"Specifically, don't the legal authorities involved provide the make and serial number of the gun, and ask you to identify the dealer or distributor you shipped it to."

Reiner emitted a sigh of boredom and weariness. "Yes. But I'm not involved. There's no legal requirement that we retain trace requests."

"No? Didn't the ATF specifically, in writing, ask you to retain them?"

If Reiner was unaware of Conn's betrayal, Sarah knew, this was his first hint that something had gone badly wrong. Nolan glanced at his client with new keenness, his expression suggesting that he sensed, rather than knew, that there was trouble. "It's our policy," Reiner answered in a monotone, "to discard nonessential records. But I have no specific memory of that kind of letter."

"Or ordering it destroyed?"

Once more, Reiner squeezed his wrist. "No."

"What about tracing requests from California? Did you order *them* destroyed?"

"I have no specific memory," Reiner repeated, "of ordering documents destroyed."

Lenihan regarded him with a skeptical smile. "Do you have a more specific memory of learning that the ATF lists the P-2 as the leading semiautomatic handgun used in crimes?"

Almost imperceptibly, Reiner seemed to relax. At least, Sarah sensed him thinking, this question was based on public information. "I pay no attention," he answered. "We sell a lot of P-2s, so some of them show up in crimes. Not our fault."

"Even if those same figures show that many of those crimes occur in California?"

The witness hunched his shoulders. "Not our fault."

"Even if you suggested to the promoter of the Las Vegas gun show—the show where Bowden bought his gun—that he place *his* ad next to yours?"

"If I did that, I don't remember it."

Lenihan considered him. "When," he inquired, "did you first become aware that the gun John Bowden used to kill six innocent people was part of a shipment stolen by a paramilitary group called the Liberty Force?"

Reiner's eyes widened slightly, and then Nolan touched his client's arm. "We've been going for an hour," he told Lenihan. "Before the witness answers, I'd like a ten-minute break."

As they left the room, Sarah whispered to Lenihan, "Nolan doesn't know."

After their return, Reiner seemed to lean away from Nolan. "Before this lawsuit," he answered the pending question, "I have no memory of connecting the stolen guns to any group or person."

Lenihan gave him a smile of incredulity. "No memory," he repeated. "Not even in connection with the slaughter of Ms. Kilcannon's family."

"That's right."

Lenihan's smile vanished. "Did you," he asked softly, "destroy the record of a communication suggesting that the Liberty Force was reselling those guns at gun shows?"

The witness gave an elaborate shrug. "Why would I?"

"The why is obvious," Lenihan snapped. "Did you destroy such a record, or *order* it destroyed?"

Reiner stared at the table. "I have no specific recollection of this thing you're asking about."

"Then let's get back to the Eagle's Claw. During its development, did Lexington run tests of its effectiveness?"

"I believe so."

"Were those tests documented?"

"Again, I believe so."

"Did you order *those* documents destroyed?"

The witness reached for the pitcher of water with exaggerated care. It was as though, Sarah thought, he feared that his hand would tremble. "No," he answered.

Touching Lenihan on the shoulder, Sarah bent her head to him. "Callister," she whispered. "It's time."

Abruptly, Lenihan pointed to the SSA magazine. "Did you review this ad with Mr. Callister?"

"No." Though Reiner's tone remained gruff, he sounded

spent. "The ads are my department. Mr. Callister had only been there for six months."

"Did Callister see the ad before the murders?"

"I don't know."

"Did he discuss with you his meeting with President Kilcannon?"

"No."

"Or his opinion regarding the President's request for background checks at gun shows?"

"No."

"Or whether the SSA threatened him with reprisals if he entered such an agreement?"

Watching, Harrison Fancher scowled. "I have no knowledge of that," the witness answered.

"Nor even of what *you* did, it seems." Lenihan turned to Nolan. "These questions are critical to our case. It's now utterly apparent that Mr. Callister alone can answer them. Either you produce him for deposition, or we'll renew our motion before Judge Bond."

"Based on what?" Nolan's tone was scornful. "The witness's failure to read George Callister's mind, and come up with thoughts which fit your theory? But then abusing the legal process is what this lawsuit's for."

"What it's for," Lenihan rejoined, "is obtaining the occasional truthful answer. However difficult." Turning to Reiner, he asked, "Did you inform Mr. Callister about the documents you destroyed? Or did he ask you to destroy them?"

Reiner stood. "I'm not answering that kind of bullshit question."

Turning to Nolan, Lenihan inclined his head toward Reiner. "Charming guy. He'll do well for you at trial." Smiling, he added mildly, "I don't know about you, John. But were I Mr. Callister, I'd want to clear that up."

TWENTY

THAT EVENING, on the Mall, two opposing forces, each numbered in the thousands, gathered to raise their voices for, or against, the President of the United States.

By far the quieter demonstration was a somber candlelight vigil which enveloped the Lincoln Memorial. Flanked by Secret Service agents, Kerry addressed them from the head of the marble steps. Thousands of candles surrounded the deep black pool of the Mall, casting shadows on the demonstrators huddled in the chill of night, or, more haunting, on five thousand life-size cardboard figures of men, women and children murdered with guns. From Kerry's vantage point, the difference was that the cutouts were utterly still.

"In the next hour," Kerry told them, "and *every* hour until we change our gun laws, four more of us will die."

Pausing, Kerry listened to his words echo through the sound system, carrying to the edges of the pro-gun demonstrators surrounding the Washington Monument, white marble against black sky. "At the other end of the Mall," he said, "the SSA is calling for our defeat. But how do they honor the memory of those who have already died—these silent witnesses to violence whom you commemorate tonight—or the eighty Americans who will die tomorrow, and the day after that, and every day in a toll of death as inexorable as it is unnecessary.

"They offer only this: 'kill someone with a gun, and we'll throw the book at you—up to, and including, the death penalty.' "

In the attentive silence of his listeners, Kerry heard a primal roar issue from the demonstrators centered on the obelisk. "But," he said with quiet force, "we know, all too well, precisely what that means. That *two* deaths are better than none."

Kerry gazed out at the far end of the Mall where, he knew, Charles Dane was speaking. In a clear voice, he finished softly. "We can do better in this country. And with your help, we will."

"The President's goal," Charles Dane told his legions, "is to use a coalition of trial lawyers and liberal authoritarians to disarm each and every one of you.

"And how does he plan to do it?" In a show of anger, Dane crashed his fist down on the podium. "By promoting a climate of hate in which *you* are less than human, a collection of four *million* twisted souls who love your guns more than your own children . . ."

Protest issued from a thousand throats. "Tell him," Dane called out, "that you love your children enough to defend them. Tell this man that you are the SSA, the defenders of *freedom*, the largest civil rights group this country has ever seen, the largest gathering of freedom fighters in the history of the planet.

"Our Constitution is the product of the Founding Fathers' steel-gut, iron-jawed, unflinching devotion to a freedom bought with their own blood. And *you* are their heirs, with the honor and duty of saving that freedom from the tyranny of this illegitimate President, King George in a pin-striped suit . . ."

The outcries commingled anger and derision. Gazing at the shadowy figures, Dane felt a surge of hope that he could defeat his enemy. "Like King George," he called out, "Kerry Kilcannon is waging war on you. But his war is a culture war—a latter-day McCarthyism which denigrates you and everything you hold dear. If you believe that white pride is equal to black pride; that gays are not *more* equal than straights; and that singling out gun owners is like singling out Jews, then—in the world of our new McCarthy—you're 'politically incorrect.' " Bathed in light, Dane flashed a smile of defiance and disdain. "But true Americans know a simple truth—the Founding Fathers of political incorrectness were the American heroes who signed the Declaration of Independence in defiance of a tyrant.

"You must not be silenced. You, not Kilcannon, are the true voice of America." Dane's own voice became a shout. "And with our voices raised, we must tell America the truth—that this self-styled 'KFK' is the worst threat to our freedoms since we rid the world of Communism, and that we will *never* be safe until we're rid of *him* forever . . ."

With the deep roar of the crowd Dane felt transported by his power. He stood, fists upraised, suffused by the seemingly endless sound of their devotion. He remained silent, still, until, like an actor, the drama of his stillness drew them back at last.

"There are only two sides," he told them, "his, and ours. The Senate must choose between us."

In her efficiency apartment on Capitol Hill, Cassie Rollins watched Dane achieve near rapture on CNN. Yes, she thought, the Senate must choose. She did not look forward to that moment.

TWENTY-ONE

If the purpose of deposing an expert witness was to help him hang himself, Sarah meant to be as helpful as possible to Dr. Frederick Glass.

"Dr. Fred," as he cheerfully called himself, was as chipper as he was conservative, having risen from academic obscurity to prominence as a prolific contrarian who boldly challenged what he labeled "fatuous liberal orthodoxy." With the unflappable good nature of someone well pleased at the attention this had garnered, he proffered his research on topics ranging from the fallacy of affirmative action to the role of the entertainment industry as a purveyor of violence. His view of gun rights was summarized by the title of his seminal book *More Guns, Less Death*.

"In my opinion," Glass told her emphatically, "the Lexington P-2 has an affirmative social utility."

Dr. Fred, Sarah thought, was a bit too pleased with himself. "And what might that be?"

"It's small enough to be potentially concealable, at least in someone's briefcase. The laws licensing civilians to carry concealed weapons make all of us a whole lot safer."

Contemplating the witness, Sarah was aware of the quiet in Nolan's conference room, the attentiveness on the faces of Nolan and Harry Fancher. "Are you implying, Dr. Glass, that Inez Costello should have been carrying a Lexington P-2? Or that Joan Bowden should have had one in her handbag?"

The expression on Glass's round, cherubic face was unfazed, almost beatific. "That would have been up to them. But, in California, the right to carry concealed weapons is severely restricted. If they weren't, Bowden might have believed that someone—if not his intended victims—would take out a gun and shoot him. In which case, the First Lady's family might well be alive."

Sarah raised her eyebrows. "Because Bowden would have been afraid to fire a weapon? Or because some armed civilian might have drilled him once he did?"

"Either," Glass answered with a shrug. "Or both. Doesn't matter to me—any more, I imagine, than it would have mattered to the victims. If you'll permit me, Ms. Dash, you're caught up in the syndrome of blaming guns for crime." He paused, his manner combining patience with a certain evangelical fervor. "The real blame falls on the entertainment industry—many of whom, ironically enough, are President Kilcannon's principal supporters.

"Until children are six or seven, when they start to distinguish fantasy from reality, TV is very real, and killing is a normal and essential skill in a brutal and frightening world. That's why the *Journal of American Medicine* concluded that the introduction of television in the 1950s caused a doubling in the homicide rate when those children reached adulthood, and that long-term childhood exposure to TV is a causal factor behind roughly half the homicides committed in America . . ."

"Most of them with guns," Sarah interjected. "Isn't it true that the same rise in homicide rates coincided with a steep increase in handgun ownership?"

Glass shook his head in dismissal. "Have you ever heard of operant conditioning?"

For Sarah, it had become easy to imagine Glass taking over a courtroom. "You're the expert," she answered in an even tone. "Why don't you explain it."

"All right. In the army, we teach new soldiers to fire repetitively at man-shaped silhouettes which pop up again, over and over. Video games which simulate murder have much the same effect. If anything, the AMA has concluded, video games are worse than movies. Which," Glass added with obvious relish, "brings me to John Bowden.

"I've interviewed his parents. As a child, Bowden had unfettered access to television; as a teenager, he repetitively played video games, often well past midnight, which required him to kill his video opponents.

"His parents thought the only harm was to his grades. In my opinion, the ultimate harm was to the six people he murdered."

This opinion, and the implacable certainty with which Dr. Glass delivered it, convinced Sarah of how dangerous he was and, in her mind, how completely irresponsible. "In your opinion, Dr. Glass, were Bowden's repetitious beatings of Joan Bowden also attributable to video games?"

"Violence of any kind is a learned response. It's time for our society to control the purveyance of violent imagery to children, just as we control access to guns, pornography, tobacco, sex, and cars. A failure amplified, in Bowden's case, by society's decision not to jail him even though he was a clear and present danger to his wife. With this litany of failures, why in the world are you sitting here trying to blame a law-abiding manufacturer who didn't even know him?"

With this, Sarah resolved to abandon any pretense of politeness. "Then let's turn to your academic career, and, specifically, to your connection with the subject of guns. How many universities have employed you as a professor?"

As though prepared for this line of inquiry, Glass answered equably, "Five."

"And how many offered you tenure?"

"None. But I was only eligible for tenure at the University of Connecticut."

"Because the others let you go too quickly?"

The witness's smile resembled a grimace. "I'd classify the decision as mutual—their lack of real academic freedom, and my resistance to the prevailing liberal ideology."

Whatever, Sarah thought. Crisply, she asked, "For what reason did Connecticut deny you tenure?"

Glass steepled his fingers. "Their stated reason was that my academic research was 'insufficiently rigorous.' The actual reason was that I voiced forbidden thoughts."

"Such as your suggestion that women's suffrage has led to an increase in crime?"

The witness shrugged. "It's easy, Ms. Dash, to mock a statement isolated from the research which supports it. But it's a demonstrable fact that, since 1920, women's more permissive attitudes toward crime—as reflected in their voting patterns—has relegated crime prevention to a low priority compared to what I call 'the nurturing issues,' matters like education and health care. This has led to greater laxity among our elected officials and, as more women have ascended the bench, our judiciary."

"Then you'll be relieved to know, Dr. Glass, that I'm unlikely to become a judge. But I'm haunted by the concern that Mary Costello's family might have lived if only I'd refrained from voting."

"Don't worry," Glass responded airily. "Under your theory of shared responsibility, there's lots of blame to go around. Including an academic world which refuses to think forbidden thoughts."

"I gather that the Sons of the Second Amendment is more hospitable to forbidden thoughts. Since leaving the University of Connecticut, hasn't the principal financing for your research come from the SSA?"

"Yes. They believe, as I do, that financing is indispensable to competing in the marketplace of ideas. So they've placed me on retainer."

"For how much?"

"Five hundred thousand a year, for the next five years."

"That kind of money," Sarah remarked amiably, "will finance a lot of forbidden thoughts. Let's turn to one of them—your thesis that the more guns Americans own, the less crime we'll have.

"In *More Guns, Less Death,* you claim that concealed carry laws cause a drop in rape and murder, diverting criminals into property crimes like burglary. Has it ever occurred to you, Doctor, that a serial rapist won't consider stealing a transistor radio to be a fair exchange?"

Glass briskly put down the pencil, a first show of impatience. "What's your point?"

"That the pathology of a rapist is distinct from that of a burglar. Or did your courses in criminology skip that part?"

Glass mustered a renewed aura of dignified scholarship. "All of my education and experience suggests that criminals, by definition, are criminals—people unable to live within the laws. Depending on circumstance and motive, the particular crime may vary."

For the first time, Sarah gave John Nolan a long look of incredulity. Nolan remained impassive. Turning to the witness, Sarah said, "Let's discuss your methodology. On what basis did you conclude that, last year, there were roughly 2.5 million instances where Americans used guns in self-defense?"

"On the basis of a random—and therefore utterly objective—sampling: a telephone survey of five thousand heads of households."

Sarah cocked her head. "In other words, rather than relying on police reports, you relied on total strangers who reported their own behavior."

"Yes." Briefly, Glass ran his fingers through the stubble of his crew cut. "As experts in the field know, many acts of self-defense go unreported to authorities."

"In your survey, how many respondents reported acts of self-defense?"

"Fifty-one."

"In other words, slightly over one percent of your respondents. How did you extrapolate 2.5 million acts of self-defense?"

"By applying the one percent of affirmative responses to our total adult population."

Pausing, Sarah smiled. "Do you happen to know how much of 'our total adult population' is considered mentally ill?"

"No."

"Try *three* percent. Did it dawn on you that a considerable number of the people who reported acts of self-defense might, instead, be crazy?"

Reaching for the water pitcher, Glass reminded her of Reiner. After a leisurely swallow of water, he said, "I have no reason to believe that."

"Or disbelieve it. So let's turn to the broader problem of self-reported acts of self-defense." Briefly, Sarah checked her notes. "For example, are you aware of a 1994 Harvard survey concerning acts of self-defense in a five-year period, where fifty of those responding reported *thirty-five* acts of self-defense, comprising *seventy percent* of the incidents reported?"

Carefully, Glass placed down the water. "No."

"Then I'd suggest you read it." Briefly Sarah paused. "What about the *Washington Post* survey of fifteen hundred Americans as to whether they'd seen an alien spacecraft in the preceding year."

Glass mustered a wan smile. "I don't follow aliens, Ms. Dash."

"You might find it interesting. Accordingly to the *Post*, one hundred fifty-one of these respondents reported having seen an alien spacecraft—an affirmative response of ten percent."

Nolan turned to his witness. "As I said," Glass responded in a stubborn tone, "I'm not aware of that."

"So you're also unaware that sixteen people of those responding—approximately one percent—reported actual contact with an alien."

"Yes. Again."

Sarah's mouth twisted slightly, a smile suppressed. "Isn't it possible that *your* one percent was the same as the *Post*'s one percent, and that what you came up with is the incidence of defensive uses of a gun against alien invaders?"

"Enough," Nolan cut in bitingly. "If you have a serious question, ask it."

"Silly answers," Sarah retorted, "tend to provoke silly questions. As does fuzzy math." Turning to Glass, Sarah asked coldly, "Are you at least aware that the *New England Journal of Medicine* reported that for every gun in the home, it is three times more likely that a family member will be killed than if the gun weren't there?"

"No."

"Or that such families showed roughly five homicides of family members for every act of self-defense?"

"Enough, counsel," Nolan interrupted. "He said no. Move on."

Sarah sat back with a smile. "Actually, John, I'm almost through. I've just identified a Martian, and I'm dying to report him."

TWENTY-TWO

AFTER DINNER in the residence—pepperoni pizza, because they felt like it—Kerry rubbed Lara's shoulders as she described the funeral of a woman killed in Maryland by a random sniper, at which the family had implored her to speak. "I felt so ambivalent," Lara told Kerry. "I didn't know the victim, and by coming to her funeral I'd drawn a crowd of demonstrators. *Demonstrators*, Kerry, at a funeral.

"But there they were. So I felt I owed the husband whatever comfort I could give him. Like me, he'd had no time to say goodbye." Leaning back, she rested the crown of her head against Kerry's cheek. "And unlike me, he had no one to lean on."

"And the demonstrators?"

"Were the crazy ones." Kerry felt, rather than heard, her sigh of resignation. "I know they don't represent most people who own guns. But they reminded me of why this debate is so intractable—the complete absence of any empathy or imagination. In their minds, the widower and I should put aside what happened, and realize that guns are a sacred right and our families merely collateral damage—the price of America's Second Amendment freedoms.

"In its own way, it's almost as dissociated from humanity as what I saw in Kosovo. And when I think of John Bowden, it scares me just as much."

This was as much as she had said, Kerry realized, since their retreat to Martha's Vineyard. "It's good to talk," he told her. "We've spent so much time in motion, trying to make it all mean something. Especially you."

"Me?" Lara gave a quiet laugh. "It's been like 'don't look back, grief might be gaining on you.' Or fear."

"That something may happen to you?"

"Not really. About that, I worry much more for you."

Kerry did not tell her that at moments, as at the Lincoln Memorial the night before, he was struck by the fear of a sudden death—more piercing because of his love for her, for whom he feared much more. "These days," he told her, "I'm the safest man in America—Peter sees to that. So what is it *you're* afraid of?"

"Of failing. That we'll do everything we can, but that we'll fail in the end. That people will keep on dying for nothing, like the woman we buried today. And that all this will turn to ashes."

This, Kerry acknowledged, was his own deepest fear—to live with failure as he was already forced to live with guilt, for the rest of his life, for the deaths that Lara suffered from even more than he. He kissed her, and returned to the West Wing.

Looking up from his desk, Clayton was surprised to see the President.

"Go home," Kerry told him.

Clayton smiled. "Easy for you to say. You *are* home— I've got a couple of hours yet."

"Two too many. When was the last time you had a normal dinner with Carlie?"

Clayton laughed. "Four days ago. Who are you, Dr. Ruth? I thought you were King George."

"That was then. This is now." Kerry sat, looking like a man prepared to stay. "Between the residence and here, I had two minutes to reflect. I try to do that now and then."

"Bad for you, Mr. President. You should be beating up senators."

"Oh, I intend to. But it occurred to me to waste a little time with you beforehand." Kerry, his friend realized, looked unusually thoughtful and self-questioning—not for the man Clayton had known long ago, but for the harder man which circumstances, and ambition, had wrought from a lonely Irish boy, his family's less favored son. "Politicians," Kerry continued, "are users. Presidents are the worst. All that matters is our success, and what others do to ensure it. 'Friend' becomes an elastic term."

"That's fine. I accept that. But not for you and me." Kerry's tone was quiet. "Before I ever went into this business, you were my closest friend. As Chief of Staff, you've made me a better President." Briefly, Kerry smiled. "Give or take the occasional screwup. But as a friend, there's only one of you. Go home."

Touched, Clayton did that, his gift to Kerry Kilcannon as much as to his own wife.

"So," the President asked abruptly when Senator Hampton answered his phone. "Where are we on gun immunity?"

"Rollins, Coletti, Slezak," the Minority Leader answered crisply. "My count says we need all three."

"I've done all I can with Cassie—an appeal to conscience."

Briefly, Hampton laughed. "Desperate measures for desperate men. The SSA is doing more."

"No help for that. What about Slezak and Coletti? Did the Silent Witness demonstration make any kind of impression?"

"Nope. To those two guys it was all sound and fury—signifying, as usual, nothing. Slezak and Coletti are both pro-choice; they figure they've already got all the women they're going to get. So their concerns are more local—and practical.

"Coletti's got Lexington right in his backyard. He's been hearing from employees who are scared about their jobs. And he's got all those insurance companies in Hartford who feel no love for guys like Lenihan . . ."

"And Slezak?"

"Is just a prick. Besides that, he figures he's got elbow room on the left, but that the SSA can help him on the right. It doesn't help *you* that a lot of blue-collar guys in Michigan own guns."

"Even though I threatened him with a primary fight?"

"I expect that worries him, Mr. President. But Michigan's a funny state. Even with you against him, he's got some careful calculations to make."

Depressingly, this matched Kerry's assessment. "What else is left to offer them?"

"Nothing. Except the chance *not* to piss you off."

"I'll remind them of that," the President answered.

Ten minutes later, the White House switchboard tracked down Vic Coletti.

The senior senator from Connecticut was at the bar of the Caucus Room, having drinks with his finance chairman and two well-heeled backers. Against the backdrop of talk and laughter, Coletti spoke softly into his cell phone.

"It's a tough vote, Mr. President, is all I can say at the moment." Briefly, Coletti paused. "On *your* gun bill, I'm with you. But this lawsuit thing? Frankly, what looks like a defendant to your sister-in-law is a major constituent to me. I hate to say so, but that's the truth of it."

"A 'major constituent,' " Kerry repeated with mild scorn. "I understand about the insurance companies. But how many of Lexington's employees voted for you in the first place?"

"Less than half," Coletti acknowledged promptly. "But

they've got families—wives and kids and parents—a lot of whom vote, too." He lowered his voice still further. "In Connecticut, Lexington's not a villain—it's a home state employer. Maybe if there were bad stuff coming out of this lawsuit, like in the tobacco litigation, I'd have a public relations counterweight. But there's nothing."

Kerry considered his response. "There's *something*. And for Lexington, it's going from bad to worse. Keep the lawsuit alive, and it'll all come out at trial."

Coletti pondered this. "What if I vote against gun immunity," he asked, "and Fasano jams it through anyhow? Then the lawsuit's dead, and I've got no cover. And for what? By my calculation, unless Rollins and Slezak both vote with you, my vote doesn't matter."

It was a reminder, if Kerry needed one, of Vic Coletti's shrewdness. "Vic," he said quietly, "I mean to be here for the long haul. And over the long haul, you succeed or fail with me. I can accept a vote on tort reform. But if I lose a vote involving guns—after all of this—the balance of power will shift to Frank Fasano. If you're any part of that, I'll use whatever's left of my diminished power to ensure you pay for it."

In the silence, Kerry heard more laughter issuing from the bar. "I'll think on it," Coletti promised soberly. "Very hard."

The last manhunt conducted by the switchboard, for Senator Jack Slezak, ended at eleven p.m.

The senator was sleeping, Kerry was told, and could not be disturbed. Putting down the telephone, Kerry wondered what had made the senator from Michigan so arrogant—or so secure—that he refused to accept a call from a President who could ruin him.

*

Three thousand miles away, in Beverly Hills, the telephone rang in Robert Lenihan's den.

He was reviewing his calendar for the next three months, a tangle of conflicting demands which included a complex but potentially lucrative trial—perhaps deferred, much to the discontent of his partners, by the possible hearing in Mary Costello's lawsuit. Preoccupied, Lenihan hesitated before deciding to answer.

"Is this Bob Lenihan?" the deep voice inquired.

The question was asked with a tone of portent which, combined with the strange familiarity of the voice itself, made Lenihan instantly alert. "It is."

"This is Charles Dane."

Is this a joke? Lenihan almost asked. And then, reviewing the tone of voice and the logic of events, he was certain that it wasn't. "Are you calling to surrender?" Lenihan inquired. "Clients usually do that through their lawyers."

Dane's voice held no answering humor. "Our lawyers don't know I'm contacting you. Nor does anyone else. Unless it stays between us, this call goes no further."

Lenihan paused, parsing the permutations of such a request. "All right," he answered in a businesslike tone. "What's on your mind, Mr. Dane?"

"That you're going to lose."

More from a sense of challenge than conviction, Lenihan laughed. "Have you read Mike Reiner's deposition? I hear Fred Glass wasn't too great, either. I promise there's more to come."

"We know all about that," Dane said with cold assurance. "It doesn't matter. None of it does."

"And why is that?"

"Because the House just voted to bar your lawsuit. By this time next week, the Senate will have done the same."

"The Senate's still in play," Lenihan answered calmly. "Thanks to Leo Weller. And if the Senate passes the Civil

Justice Reform Act with a gun immunity provision, the President will veto it before you can open the champagne."

"If he does," Dane answered in tones so somber that the word *sepulchral* popped into Lenihan's mind, "Kilcannon is finished. The least of which is that the Senate will override his vote."

Now Lenihan laughed aloud. "This conversation is happening in the Twilight Zone. No wonder you don't want me to repeat it."

Dane laughed as well, but softly. "I don't want you repeating it, because you don't know what it means. Or nearly enough about your President.

"You're an amateur, Robert. You think castrating Leo Weller is the ultimate in realpolitik. That's why you're going to lose."

Lenihan's amusement vanished: the thought that Dane was overdoing it was superseded by the disturbing realization that the man who had called him was a far different proposition than the indignant populist patriot who had spoken on the Mall. "And so you want me to be emotionally prepared? Nonsense. You're worried about this lawsuit, and you damned well should be."

"Worried? No. I'm allowing you to make a choice. One choice is to be the trial lawyer who not only had the Costello case snatched out from under him but, by bringing it, helped bring about the passage of the most comprehensive tort reform in our history. As matters stand, you teeter on self-parody. *That* would make you a buffoon."

Stung, Lenihan fought back the instinct to respond in kind. Dane's laser focus on his fears—public humiliation, the loss of political power and legal reputation was far too telling. "And the second choice?" he inquired coldly.

"Settle the case. Before our allies in the Senate pass gun immunity, then override Kilcannon's veto."

Though he had known this must be coming, Lenihan felt the residue of surprise. "Merits or politics aside," he answered, "I can't settle this case alone. I've got cocounsel to consult, and our client is the ultimate decision-maker."

"We've been wondering who your client is. But not much."

"Mary Costello," Lenihan snapped.

Dane emitted the same quiet laugh. "Assuming that's true," he answered, "then you've got no need whatever to consult with Sarah Dash."

Lenihan paused. More softly, he asked, "What are you suggesting?"

"That Mary Costello can continue on as her sister's puppet—the plaintiff in an aborted case—or ten million dollars richer. Minus the three-million-plus dollars which go to your firm."

Lenihan's own laugh was a startled reflex. "You *are* scared."

"Talk to your client," Dane retorted calmly. "Or by next week your lawsuit will be worth its weight in Tsarist Russian bonds."

TWENTY-THREE

ON THE MORNING that John Nolan cross-examined Dr. David Roper, the atmosphere in the sterile interior conference room of the Kilcannon Center was quiet, the cluster of lawyers sober and silent.

Roper was Sarah's final expert, a professor at Columbia with a doctorate in public health, whose work focused on refuting the assertion that increased gun ownership makes Americans safer. In manner, Roper was the opposite of Dr. Glass: clipped and precise, a scholar who conveyed his passion through a seriousness of speech and attitude. As an expert witness, Roper was allowed under Bond's order to review all depositions, and he had done so with great care. "What Fred Glass practices," he told Nolan flatly, "is theology, not science. The myth of self-defense is as essential to the SSA as the biblical theory of Creation is to fundamentalism: without it, their belief system—their whole rationale for being—crumbles."

Nolan studied him. "Why," he inquired, "do you call the belief in armed self-defense a myth?"

Dark and lean, Roper returned the intensity of Nolan's gaze. "Because it ignores what social scientists call 'opportunity theory': the more of something there is, the more that something is likely to be used. And misused.

"In particular, Dr. Glass overlooks how firearms enhance the opportunity to kill." Roper counted his points on the fingers of his left hand. "First, you can kill at a far greater distance. Second, you can kill at far greater safety to yourself. Third, you can kill with far more certainty.

Fourth, the decision to kill becomes irrevocable far more quickly—unlike a knife, you can't pull back a bullet." Glancing at Harrison Fancher, he finished, "Using 'scientists' like Dr. Glass, the gun lobby not only perpetuates its myth of self-defense, it actually strips us of the means of genuine self-defense. Because it has the political power to convert quack science into tragedy."

"When you say 'quack science,'" Nolan asked with some asperity, "do you include Dr. Glass's testimony?"

The witness nodded briskly. "Fred Glass is the gun lobby's equivalent of the scientists the tobacco companies employed to 'disprove' that smoking causes lung cancer. Glass starts with the result he wants, then finds the 'facts' to support it."

Nolan's scrutiny of Roper became at once clinical, wary, and determined, as though he was resolved to learn the worst that faced him. "What has *your* research suggested regarding the correlation between public safety and gun ownership?"

"That gun ownership diminishes the public safety." Roper leaned on his elbows, hands clasped in front of him, intently watching his interrogator. "There are an estimated sixty-five million handguns in America. This is reflected in the high firearms death rate among our citizens, nearly fourteen per one hundred thousand people—as opposed to Canada's roughly four, Australia's three, and England's less than one.

"Compare Seattle with Vancouver, Canada. They are remarkably similar in about every respect save one: handguns are easy to obtain in Seattle, and tightly restricted in Vancouver. Their rates of crime and violence are also similar; indeed the rates of burglary, robbery, and assault are virtually identical. The only difference is that Seattle's homicide rate is sixty-three percent higher. Why? Because the rate of homicides with handguns is five times higher in Seattle . . ."

"What pertinence—if any—does the homicide rate in Seattle have to Mary Costello's claim against Lexington Arms?"

This time, Roper cupped his palms; the frequent movements of his hands, Sarah realized, bespoke a passion repressed. "There are several correlations. Last year, handguns like the Lexington P-2 were used to murder slightly over twelve hundred women. Fifty-six percent of those women were killed by husbands, live-in partners, or current or ex-boyfriends. And, like Bowden, one-third of those who murdered killed themselves.

"John Bowden was an adjudicated spousal abuser—that's a matter of public record. According to Ms. Costello's complaint, President Kilcannon asked the president of Lexington Arms, George Callister, to impose background checks at gun shows before its dealers could sell Lexington products. Callister declined. According to Ben Gehringer's deposition, Gehringer then sold the P-2 to John Bowden without a background check—Bowden having been drawn to the gun show by Lexington's ad." Roper's left hand clenched. "It's more than arguable that, *without* the ad, or *with* the background check, the seven people Bowden killed—including himself—might still be alive."

Nolan mustered a look of skepticism. "Is that the entirety of your opinion?"

"Not quite." Once more, Roper glanced at Harrison Fancher. "The SSA would have you believe that most homicides occur in the commission of a felony. Not true. Most homicides result from arguments between people who know each other, and the number of women shot to death by intimate partners is over four times greater than those killed by strangers." Pausing, Roper spoke more quietly. "As I said, that comes to over *twelve hundred* murdered women. Compared to *twelve* women who used guns to kill in self-defense.

"That's one hundred murdered women for every act of self-defense. But enough of numbers, Mr. Nolan. These are people we're talking about. The sixteen-year-old Japanese exchange student killed while looking for a Halloween party because he rang the wrong doorbell. The fourteen-year-old who her father mistook for an intruder and who died saying 'I love you, Daddy.' The twenty-year-old mother who thought she heard gravel crunching in the driveway, pulled out a gun without a safety lock, and killed her eight-month-old by accident. The countless times when 'self-defense' turns out to be what happens when you arm drunkenness and anger with a gun.

"Triggers don't pull themselves, Mr. Nolan. But we're at far greater risk in the presence of a gun. That's why the most well armed country in the world is also the most deadly."

Listening, Sarah could only hope that Senator Fasano failed, and that Mary Costello's day in court would come. Then she felt a tap on her shoulder. Turning, she saw her assistant hovering with a look which combined urgency with hesitance at interrupting.

"Pardon us," she said to Nolan. Turning from his annoyed expression to Janet's worried one, she knew immediately what had happened.

"It's the phone call you were waiting for," Janet whispered.

Though they had not spoken since their meeting, Norman Conn blurted without preface, "I refused to meet with their lawyer—a man named Nolan."

The reedy tautness in his voice confirmed Conn's stress. Sarah glanced at the closed door of her office. "Who asked you?"

"Our general counsel. If I don't meet with them, they're going to depose me." His voice rose, quickening. "They say if I stole records or gave away corporate secrets, they can sue me and take the house I've had for twenty years."

To Sarah, the telephone felt like a copper wire, a conductor of Conn's tension. "I left you a message," she said, "referring you to a lawyer in Hartford who specializes in protecting the rights of whistleblowers . . ."

"I was going to see him." His voice broke. "Now I don't know."

Sarah paused, suspended between pity and desperation. Bent on his own redemption, Conn had disdained to fear the loss of something as trivial as a job. But one could fear things as simple, and as profound, as the loss of the familiar. A house.

"I'm sorry," she said quietly. "But if they notice your deposition, you'll be required to testify under oath."

"What if you tell them I'm not going to be a witness?"

At once, Sarah was reminded of Martin Bresler. "I could do that. But I won't." Her voice was softer yet. "I'm sorry, Mr. Conn. But I have a duty to my client. I suggest you ask the lawyer I mentioned about how to protect your rights. Because I'll use those documents you gave me to make sure that you don't lie."

This was an empty threat, Sarah knew—a self-discredited witness was useless at trial. In Conn's silence, she wondered if he knew this.

"I understand," he answered with a croak which, nonetheless, had a measure of dignity. The line went dead before Sarah could say more.

TWENTY-FOUR

RIVEN BY DOUBTS, Chad Palmer prepared to commence the debate on gun immunity.

Senator Palmer had always thought of himself as conservative—a believer in free markets, military preparedness, and individual accountability and initiative. With others of his Senate colleagues—Cassie Rollins among them—he had watched in rising dismay as men like Paul Harshman equated "conservative" with the unfettered gun rights and a militant social agenda fueled by fundamentalism and financed by those for whom, too often, a truly free market meant freedom from the constraints of law.

The latter forces, Palmer knew, bought influence in either party. But while their Democratic beneficiaries adopted what Palmer thought of as a simpering hypocrisy—claiming to take large donations in self-defense—the Republicans of Harshman's stripe cast their voracity for special interest funding as a constitutional right. Thus, Chad's battle against money in politics had earned him the bitter enmity of those within his party for whom guns and money and religion were a recipe for power.

This was why he had struck his Faustian bargain with Frank Fasano, trading gun immunity for a clear shot at campaign finance reform which Kerry Kilcannon wanted almost as much as he. But Kilcannon was President. For the senior senator from Ohio, seemingly blocked by Fasano and his supporters, reform might be his only recompense for a career paid for with his daughter's life. And so Chad went to the floor of the Senate, supported by his most ardent enemies, to oppose a friend whose own wounds Palmer felt more keenly than his allies of convenience ever could.

It was best, Chad knew, to stick with what he truly believed.

He stood at his lacquered desk, notes in front of him. The Senate was full. At its front were Frank Fasano and Chuck Hampton, separated by the narrow aisle which divided the two parties.

"This pestilence of lawsuits," he told his colleagues, "is both symptom and disease. For many small and honest businesses, it is terminal. But for all of us it symptomizes a breakdown in our social fiber where law replaces morals, mischance becomes opportunity, and the courtroom converts neighbors into predators.

"The Civil Justice Reform Act is an effort to restore the time when lawsuits were not a form of social insurance; when lawyers were advocates instead of opportunists; and legislators—not judges—made our laws."

The Senate was still, attentive. Unlike some of their colleagues, Frank Fasano reflected, Chad Palmer was most effective when he spoke from core belief—he was too free of self-delusion to be facile at dissembling. To Fasano, equally free of delusion but far more inclined to pragmatism, it was what made his Republican rival both admirable and dangerous. To be allied with him, however briefly, was a luxury to be enjoyed, and to have turned Palmer on Kilcannon a genuine work of political art.

"We are told," Palmer continued, "that class actions are the last redoubt of the small investor against financial fraud. If only that were so. But most investors are lucky to recover a dime on a dollar, and only *after* their wealthy lawyers have pocketed a multimillion-dollar fee." Palmer permitted himself a smile. "For one such lawyer, the definition of a 'small investor' is the pet client who has purchased one share of stock in every company listed in the Fortune 500. Enabling his legal champion—as of yesterday—to bring twenty-six class actions in his name.

"Let there be no doubt who ultimately pays this lawyer's fees. *We* do—in higher prices, lost jobs, and the erosion of the principle that the purpose of a lawsuit is to gain genuine redress for an authentic wrong."

Palmer paused, gaze sweeping the chamber. "But I have another concern," he said firmly. "That lawsuits have become a tool of our own corruption, funnelling money from litigation into our political system so that trial lawyers can wield unprecedented—and in my mind—unprincipled power."

Fasano glanced at Senator Hampton, who remained inscrutable. "This debate," Palmer continued, "is about more than the corrosion of our justice system. At its heart, it is about the corrosion of our politics through money, and whether we have the courage to stop it."

At this, Hampton acknowledged Fasano with an ironic lift of his eyebrows. *What about* your *special interests?* Hampton seemed to say. But perhaps he was conveying more—his admiration of the neatness with which Palmer had moved the debate to grounds more congenial to him than to Fasano.

Smiling with his eyes, Fasano shrugged in answer. The truth, though Hampton might not know it, was that Fasano had expected nothing less. Whatever its momentary discomforts, a Chad Palmer in character enhanced Fasano's chances of capturing Cassie Rollins. Toward the rear of the chamber, the junior senator from Maine watched Palmer with unwavering attention, heedless of the packed gallery of press and public gazing down on all of them.

In the Oval Office, the President watched C-SPAN with Kit Pace and Clayton Slade. Kerry did not speak, nor did the others; among the one hundred senators, only Chad Palmer's opposition was too personal for comment.

Let us turn, Palmer said, *to the most vexing and contentious question presented by this bill: whether to protect gun companies from lawsuits based on the violent acts of others.*

That gun violence is a tragedy is beyond debate. And, to me as to the President, it is long past time for us to hold human life more precious than blandishments of a gun lobby whose power outstrips its decency.

Silent, Kerry shook his head: this was the kind of bluntness, rare in politics, which endeared Chad Palmer more to average citizens than to his colleagues—except, perhaps, to Kerry himself. To see it placed in the service of Frank Fasano—and thus, perversely, the SSA—was difficult to watch.

But, Palmer continued, *as legislators we should discharge our responsibility directly—not delegate it to the courts. Let alone to trial lawyers who seek to shift our own responsibility to where it least belongs: on those who* make *the trigger, rather than those who pull it . . .*

"Read the depositions," Kerry murmured to himself. But, of course, Palmer could not. No one could.

In a just society, Palmer said, *personal responsibility means just that. When parents fail to lock up loaded guns,* they *bear responsibility—however painful—when their child kills himself or someone else.* Palmer's voice softened. *Whether by accident, or by design. For, in the end, every suicide is the act of an individual, and every murder the act of a murderer.*

The quiet statement, with its echoes of his daughter's

death, reechoed in Kerry's mind. As much as the President had imagined it, this speech—this moment—was worse than he had feared. He could only wonder how it felt to Palmer.

And so did Cassie Rollins.

"How," Palmer asked the Senate, "can we allow sales at gun shows without a background check and then punish the gun company for the act of whoever buys it? *That* is an act of cowardice."

This, to Cassie, clearly staked out the course Chad was commending to her: to oppose the President on gun immunity, and then support Kilcannon's gun bill. But Chad's motives remained obscure, a matter of conjecture.

"But there is a more subtle form of moral cowardice," he continued with the same quietness of tone, "and that is to degrade the justice system through our desire—however human—to find a remedy for sorrows which have none." Palmer stood straighter, pausing to meet the gazes of his colleagues. "I ask you to pass the Civil Justice Reform Act as it stands."

In the hush that followed, Cassie glanced across the aisle toward Vic Coletti, head bent in contemplation. Among their undecided colleagues, only Jack Slezak, two rows behind Coletti, appeared indifferent to the moment.

Sitting, Chad Palmer felt wearier for the knowledge that had opened the way for the senator he most despised.

"In at least one respect," Paul Harshman told the Senate, "I must part company with my friend and colleague from Ohio, to whom I listened with unstinting admiration. For these lawsuits are more than just misguided, nor are they merely the work of lawyers. They are the invention of instinctive totalitarians—the most deadly weapon in the arsenal arrayed by the most powerful enemies of the Second Amendment rights established by our Founding Fathers."

Chad closed his eyes. Washington, Jefferson—Harshman. To Paul, it must have a certain ring. But then only a fool could be so pompous; only a moral midget could envision Thomas Jefferson as the father of the Lexington P-2. "Their aim," Harshman continued, "is the destruction of a legal industry, and, with it, the most basic right of all—the right to defend ourselves, our families, and our freedoms.

"We should not mince words. In the hands of a woman living alone, a semiautomatic handgun—and yes, an Eagle's Claw bullet—can deliver her from death or degradation. To paraphrase Senator Palmer, it is not the job of lawyers to calibrate her means of self-protection, approving only those guns, or those projectiles, *least* likely to ensure her safety."

He had made a deal, Chad told himself. But it did not involve listening to this. As soon as he decently could, Paul Harshman's "friend and colleague" left the Senate chamber.

TWENTY-FIVE

JET-LAGGED FROM taking the red-eye from San Francisco to New York, but even more tense than tired, Sarah watched Nolan interrogate Norman Conn.

They were crammed in the small conference room of a two-person firm in Hartford, of which Conn's lawyer, Joseph Schwab, was the principal partner. Schwab was a large man, firm but gentle in manner, and his presence seemed to have a soothing effect on Conn. But this did not extend to Sarah. Schwab had deflected all of her inquiries, asserting that his client's only interest was the truth—which all the parties could hear at once. Sarah's version of the truth, though suggested by Conn's documents, was near-worthless without his help. And now the man would barely look at her.

His own tension, though subdued, expressed itself in a certain twitchiness, a darting glance which probed his surroundings without coming to rest. For his part, Nolan seemed tentative, as though handling a bottle of nitroglycerin. His tone was quiet, his demeanor cautious, his questions phrased with care.

"Prior to this morning," Nolan asked, "have you spoken with, or met with, any of the lawyers in this room?"

Conn touched his temples, fingers grazing his thin red hair. "Both," he answered.

Nolan looked puzzled. "Both?"

A glint of malicious amusement passed through Conn's eyes. "Met with. And spoken with."

Quickly, Nolan repressed his annoyance. "With whom?"

"Sarah Dash."

Though speaking her name, Conn refused to make eye contact. It was as though Sarah was not there.

"And where did that meeting take place?"

This induced the briefest of smiles. "A motel room."

"For what purpose?"

Conn glanced at Schwab. The lawyer inclined his forehead, as though granting permission to proceed. Reaching beneath his chair, Conn placed a battered leather briefcase on the table, and removed a two-inch stack of documents.

"To give her these," he answered.

Nolan eyed them grimly. "What are they?"

"The documents Mike Reiner ordered me to destroy."

His quiet words were poisoned by an undertone of resentment. Still gazing at the documents, Nolan considered his choices, weighing how best to proceed.

"In your mind," he inquired at length, "what is their significance?"

"That varies." The malicious smile returned. "The common denominator is that they implicate Mr. Reiner in misconduct."

With mounting disquiet, Sarah realized how deeply Conn despised his superior—an emotion which, once established, would make him easier for Nolan to discredit. A slightly patronizing tone crept into Nolan's voice. "Then why don't we go through them, from first to last."

For the next fifteen minutes, Nolan directed the court reporter to mark documents as exhibits. Sarah and Harry Fancher watched in silence, more tense for the suspension of the questioning. At last Nolan asked, "What is the significance of Conn Exhibit One?"

In response, Conn spread a sheaf of documents in front of him, regarding them with the scholarly satisfaction of a paleontologist sorting prehistoric bones. "Exhibits One through Twenty-seven are trace requests received by Lexington Arms from the Bureau of Alcohol, Tobacco and Firearms."

"And what do they show?"

"In each case, the ATF gave us the serial number of a Lexington P-2 used to commit a crime, and asked us to identify the distributor or dealer we shipped it to." Conn's smile contained a palpable spite. "These documents cover a six-month period. Taken together, they indicate that the P-2 was commonly used by criminals and that Lexington—at least Mike Reiner—knew it."

"On what do you base that?"

Conn's gaze flickered across each document. "After the First Lady's family was murdered, Mike asked me to destroy them."

"Where were you," Nolan asked with quiet acidity, "during this supposed conversation?"

"Mike's office."

Nolan permitted himself a faint smile of disbelief. "Just the two of you?"

"Yes."

"Did you consider yourself a confidant of Mr. Reiner?"

"No."

The one-word answer, delivered in the flattest of tones, hinted at more. But Nolan—for strategic reasons, Sarah was certain—chose not to pursue it. "Do you have any explanation as to why Reiner chose to rely on you, rather than destroy these documents himself?"

"Yes. He didn't know where to look. I did."

To Sarah, the answer was mundane, and yet so unexpected, that it had the ring of truth. But Nolan raised his eyebrows. "While he was enlisting your assistance, did Mr. Reiner explain his motives?"

"That he remembered seeing the documents, and didn't want Lexington to get in trouble."

"Why were Exhibits One through Twenty-seven 'trouble'?"

Conn looked annoyed at his questioner's opacity. "Because the P-2 is a crime gun," he answered stubbornly.

"That's it?"

"Not all of it." Trembling slightly, Conn's right hand flittered across the documents. "The P-2 is banned in California. But twenty-four of these guns were sold in Arizona and Nevada, mostly close to the California border." Conn's reedy tone became accusatory. "Obviously Reiner's marketing plan was to flood Nevada with guns Californians would buy. These documents proved that it worked—that Bowden's buying this gun was no surprise to Mike."

"Are you suggesting," Nolan snapped, "that Mr. Reiner knew where and how Bowden acquired a Lexington P-2?"

The question was a stratagem, Sarah knew. Its obvious answer—"no"—was intended to keep Conn from over-reaching, and, at least tacitly, to expose his bias against Mike Reiner. Conn knew it, too. With a smile of superiority, he fixed his gaze on Nolan, and uttered a soft, surprising, "Yes."

Sarah suppressed a shudder of relief. However well or badly he fared, Conn was now committed. "Where in any of these documents," Nolan asked harshly, "does it show—or even suggest—that Mr. Reiner could have known where John Bowden got his gun?"

"None of them."

"Then what's your basis for that aspersion?"

The smile vanished. "I told him."

Nolan scrutinized him with disbelief. "And how did *you* know?"

"Two reasons." Sorting through the documents, Conn

rested his finger on Exhibit Twenty-eight. "This document
is a report listing the serial numbers of a shipment of P-2s
stolen from a dealer in Phoenix, Arizona. The dealer didn't
want to pay us, and Reiner was pressing them. After the
murders, we got a trace request, and realized that the serial
number of the murder weapon matched one of the stolen
guns. Mike asked me to destroy it."

"What would his motive for *that* be?"

Conn glanced at Schwab, a benign presence at his side.
From the equanimity of his lawyer, Sarah could divine how
carefully the two men had prepared. "About two months
before," Conn said in an ashen tone, "I received a telephone complaint from the owner of a Lexington P-2.

"He told me the gun kept jamming. When I asked if
he'd bought it from a dealer, he said no—at a gun show in
Las Vegas. So I asked him if he knew the seller, and maybe
could swap guns." Once more, Conn's gaze darted toward
his lawyer. "The guy just laughed."

The answer stopped abruptly, as though its final sentence explained all. "Did he respond in words?" Nolan
inquired caustically. "Or did he just keep laughing?"

Conn did not seem to register the sarcasm. Softly, he
answered, "The caller knew the guy from Idaho, he said,
but that he wasn't easy to find, or the kind to worry about
customer relations. Then the caller asked me if I'd heard of
an organization called 'the Liberty Force.' "

Sitting across from Sarah, Harrison Fancher stopped
scribbling notes, staring at the witness with his pen suspended in midair. With an air of renewed caution, Nolan
asked, "How did you respond?"

"That I hadn't. So he told me that Liberty Force was a
group of white supremacists, and that this guy was more
likely to blow his head off than give him another gun."

"What did you do then?"

"I asked him for the serial number. When I checked our

files, it matched with one of the stolen guns." Briefly, Conn's mouth pursed. "I went to Reiner and said it looked like some paramilitaries were peddling them, and asked if we should call the ATF."

Nolan grimaced. "How did Mr. Reiner respond?"

"He said no—that he didn't like the aroma it gave us." The bitterness seeped back into Conn's voice. "I didn't 'like the aroma,' either. Only the stench was coming from Reiner. So I wrote him a memo confirming what I told him." Pausing, Conn added with lethal quiet, "After the Costello murders, I reminded him of that."

Nolan shot him a cynical glance. "For what reason?"

"At first, I thought maybe the shooter was a member of Liberty Force. Whatever, it was pretty clear to me that the murder weapon had passed through the hands of these paramilitaries, and that we ought to tell the ATF."

"You said that to Reiner?"

"Yes." Conn's speech slowed, underscoring his contempt and condemnation. "Instead he ordered me to take these documents from our files, and bring them to his office."

"Did you?"

"Yes. But only after making copies."

Nolan waved at the exhibits. "But not, apparently, of your alleged memo about the Liberty Force."

"I couldn't find it," Conn answered quietly. "When I asked Reiner where it was, he told me not to worry."

Nolan studied him. "Is there any corporate policy requiring you to retain the documents Reiner supposedly asked you to destroy?"

"No."

"Is there any *law* which mandates their retention?"

"Not to my knowledge, no." Hastily, Conn riffled the documents. "Only Exhibit Thirty-eight."

Nolan frowned. "For the record, what is Exhibit Thirty-eight?"

"A letter from the ATF, asking us to retain all trace requests for P-2s used in crimes. After the murders, Reiner asked me to destroy it."

"Remarkably thorough, wasn't he," Nolan observed in caustic tones. "Did you report all this malfeasance to anyone at Lexington?"

Gazing down, Conn flexed the fingers of his hands; perhaps, Sarah thought, to repress their renewed tremor. "No."

"Not even Mr. Callister?"

"No."

"And yet you were *appalled* by Mr. Reiner's supposed orders. Didn't you owe it to the company who'd employed you for twenty years to let them in on your little secret?"

Almost imperceptibly, Conn leaned closer to his lawyer. "At first, I was worried about my job. After the murders, when I knew how bad it was, I didn't know where to turn."

"And so you chose Ms. Dash, a total stranger."

It was this implausibility, Sarah recognized, that suggested hidden motives. Conn stiffened in his chair, defensive, heightening her fear that Nolan already knew what those motives were. "For one hundred fifty years," he answered in a rising voice, "Lexington was a proud part of our nation's history. We armed Americans in two World Wars, and in Korea and Vietnam. Our standards were exacting, our guns impeccable, and our customers people who deserved the best—soldiers, cops, or law-abiding sportsmen . . ."

However deeply felt, Sarah thought, the speech was worrisome in its irrelevance, offering a hint of instability. But now the lid was off what seemed to be a cauldron of emotions. "The P-2," Conn went on with palpable loathing, "is cheaply made, an effort to compete with the sleazy companies in Southern California who make junk guns for criminals. It's what Mike Reiner would be if God had made him a handgun . . ." As if hearing himself, Conn paused abruptly, lowering his voice. "The P-2 was Mike's idea, and it's where we sold our soul. Because we knew who we were selling it to—people like John Bowden." With a trembling hand, Conn snatched a multipage document from among the others. "That's why Reiner asked me to destroy this."

Nolan summoned a look of wariness and pity. "And what is that?"

"Conn Exhibit Thirty-five," Conn answered with a defiant pride. "The testing data for the Eagle's Claw bullet. We filled life-size plastic dummies with gelatin, and then blew them full of holes. It was a proud moment, Mr. Nolan. We proved that our holes were bigger than for any other organ-shredding projectile on the market. More than good enough to slaughter a six-year-old.

"You asked me why I went to Ms. Dash. Because *Mike Reiner* had turned Lexington Arms from the paragon of our industry into the arms-maker of choice for a cold-blooded killer."

To Sarah's relief, Schwab looked at his watch, his mask of serenity suggesting that nothing remarkable had happened. "We've been going for some time now," he said to Nolan. "Why don't we take ten minutes?"

Please, Sarah thought. But Conn reached for a glass of water. "I'm not tired," he insisted. "I want to finish this."

The degree to which he personalized the deposition unsettled Sarah, summoning a disturbing vision of how Conn might bear up at trial. But it seemed she might find out right away—for Sarah to plead for a break, however plausible her excuse, might add to Conn's agitation.

"When," Nolan asked abruptly, "were you last promoted?"

Crossing his legs, the witness shifted his weight. "Twelve years ago."

"Since then, have you sought promotion within Lexington?"

"Yes."

"How often?"

To Sarah, Conn's smile of resentment embodied his psychic scars. "Several times."

"And each time, you were refused."

"Yes."

"By whom?"

"Mike Reiner."

"Isn't it also true that you complained about Reiner to Mr. Callister's predecessor?"

Conn hesitated. "Yes."

This time it was Nolan who smiled. "Regarding what? His disregard for quality? His neglect of Lexington's proud history? His penchant for destroying documents? Or was it something else?"

"I told Mr. Cross that Reiner was prejudiced against me."

"On what basis, if I might ask. The denial of promotions?"

"The *repeated* denial of promotions."

"Perhaps—repeatedly—Mr. Reiner thought you less than qualified."

"I do my job," the witness answered stubbornly. "I take pride in my work and cut no corners."

Nolan looked at him askance. "Was one of Mr. Reiner's complaints that you refuse to follow instructions?"

"He claims that."

"And that you have a problem with authority?"

Conn raised his chin, eyes narrowing in dislike. In that moment, Sarah felt certain that Nolan had hit his mark. "I have a problem with stupidity," he answered.

Inwardly, Sarah winced. But Nolan's expression was one of condescending kindness. "While at Lexington, have you ever taken disability leave?"

Abruptly, Conn hunched in his chair, seeming to deflate in front of Sarah's eyes. "Yes."

"For what?"

"Post-traumatic stress disorder. From Vietnam."

"And how did that affect you?"

"It affected my concentration."

"And your emotional equilibrium?"

"How do you mean?"

"Did you," Nolan asked more harshly, "have outbursts of temper?"

Conn folded his arms. "That was ten years ago," he said in muted protest. "Not since."

"Were there outbursts of temper directed at Mr. Reiner?"

"We had words."

"But instead of firing you," Nolan said softly, "Lexington and Mr. Reiner allowed you to take disability leave."

Incongruously, Conn shook his head. "It was only for two months. I was in Vietnam for thirteen months, and it's stayed with me for thirty-five years. Two months isn't much to ask."

"But you asked," Nolan continued in the same quiet tone, "and Reiner gave them to you. And this is his reward."

The statement required no answer. Sarah could imagine easily Nolan's version of Norman Conn: a difficult employee, kept on out of charity, his perceptions so skewed that they perverted this gratuitous kindness into a denial of his worth. "Isn't what happened," Nolan asked, "that you saw Ms. Dash's web site, pleading for informants, and decided that this was your opportunity to destroy Mike Reiner?"

"No."

"No? Specifically, Mr. Conn, didn't you copy these documents, destroy the originals, and then concoct a story blaming Reiner for their disappearance?"

Conn folded his arms. "I did not."

"No again? Isn't the reason there's no memo of your conversation tying the Liberty Force to Bowden's gun that no such conversation occurred?"

Briefly, the witness shut his eyes. "It happened. Believe me, it happened. I didn't make it up."

In Nolan's place, Sarah might have left it there: given Conn's apparent instability, his enmity for Reiner, and the absence of corroboration, Nolan's story line was, at least, plausible. But Nolan went for the kill. "You did," he said flatly. "Because you first heard about the Liberty Force from Sarah Dash. Isn't that why there are no witnesses?"

Sarah stifled her indignation. "No," Conn answered.

"Yet again. Isn't the reason you didn't go to Lexington because your employers know you all too well?"

Suddenly, Conn sat upright again, his face and body animated with a tensile alertness. His finger jabbed a document. "Are you saying that this trace report is a fake? Or this one, showing that they made the Eagle's Claw to tear your guts out? Or these, proving that Reiner was marketing to criminals?"

Nolan's eyes went hard. "I'm not here to answer questions."

"Well you can *read*, can't you? So now you know what they knew." Conn's voice rose in anger. "You can't say I made *these* up. So you try to divert attention by saying I made up a story to go with them. Because you're just like Reiner. You don't give a damn what you do or say as long as you get paid for it."

The two men stared across the table. Startled by Conn's comeback, Sarah awaited Nolan's counterthrust, not knowing whether to be heartened or distressed. "That break I mentioned," Conn's lawyer interposed. "It might be good for several of us."

Sarah released a breath.

TWENTY-SIX

ON THE MORNING of the day that the Senate would vote on gun immunity, Chuck Hampton rose to deliver the final speech in opposition.

The White House had done all it could to help him. The headline in the morning's *New York Times* was "Bowden Gun Traced to White Supremacists." The article reported the indictment of one Ben Gehringer who, as part of a plea bargain, acknowledged selling the Lexington P-2 to Bowden at a gun show in Las Vegas. With its unsavory mix of racism, trafficking and gun shows with the slaughter of Lara's family, the announcement by the United States Attorney for Idaho was a boon for Kerry Kilcannon, ratcheting up the pressure on the last three undecided senators—Rollins, Coletti, and Slezak—without violating Gardner Bond's gag order regarding information emanating from Mary Costello's lawsuit. Hampton could only wonder at the nature of the President's involvement—the no doubt indirect conveyance of his wishes and directives—which had led to this exquisitely timed announcement. As to Kilcannon, the media reported nothing.

But the Senate could feel his presence, personified by Vice President Ellen Penn presiding, prepared to cast a tie-breaking vote should the Senate deadlock fifty–fifty. All one hundred senators were in attendance. Their demeanor, reinforced by the morning's headlines, was unusually grim. By the end of the day they would vote on gun immunity and then, with or without it, the Civil Justice Reform Act as a whole. Even had not the vote been so personal to

Kilcannon—but more so because it was—each senator knew that this battle was a defining moment for this President and, by implication, for Frank Fasano's ambition to succeed him. At best, Kilcannon hoped to strip gun immunity from the bill. Failing that, he must garner the thirty-four votes against the final bill which—assuming they held—he would need to sustain his expected veto. As to both, Hampton felt far more uncertainty than he liked.

And so, it appeared, did Fasano. Across the aisle, his expression—though opaque and self-contained—hinted at an intensity which excluded irony or humor. When, before commencing his speech, Hampton accorded the Majority Leader the briefest of nods, Fasano seemed to stare right through him.

"In the last few days," Hampton told his colleagues with a fleeting smile, "we've heard much about trial lawyers, and guns. As it happens, I used to be a trial lawyer, and I own twenty or so guns. Astonishing as it may seem, I happen to be proud of both.

"Let's take the trial lawyer first. There's been much complaint from my Republican friends about lawyers who accept contingent fees or make 'excessive' requests for punitive damages. I know about these from personal experience, because my biggest case involved both.

"It began with a couple who, until her death, had been the parents of a five-year-old girl—their only child. They had lost her in the most senseless, the most unanticipated, of ways: she had sat on the drain of a public wading pool, and had her intestines suctioned out."

His colleagues, Hampton noted to his satisfaction, were hushed. "Her parents," he told them, "had no money. As much as anything, they came to me looking for an explanation for a tragedy which, to them, seemed inexplicable.

"I conducted some discovery." Pausing, Hampton permitted himself to recall his anger. "The explanation turned out to be simple; the pool company had refused to spend money on a fifty-cent part which would have prevented this child's death. But perhaps the little girl was lucky. It turned out that another victim in another state—a six-year-old boy—would require tube feeding, twelve hours a day, for however long that he might live. All for the lack of a four-bit drain part.

"When I told the parents about all this, they ordered me to turn down any settlement offer—even the last one, for five million dollars. Their charge to me was simple: expose this company, and make sure—*very* sure—that they never did this to another child.

"They never did," Hampton added softly. "Because the jury awarded my clients twenty-five million in punitive damages.

"My esteemed colleague, Senator Palmer, tells us that not all of life's misfortunes have a remedy. To this extent, I agree: my clients would have happily traded their new-found wealth for the child they adored, or even for the surcease of heartache. But they had the satisfaction of knowing that no one else would *ever* know that feeling."

Pausing again, he sought out Palmer, who studied his desk with hooded eyes. "As for me," Hampton added in a throwaway tone, "I stand guilty of taking the case on a contingent fee. I profited from that. Perhaps that makes me less noble than the defense lawyers for the pool drain company and its insurer, who profited by the hour, no matter the outcome for their clients.

"So let's turn to the matter of *gun* companies, whose lawyers must also surely be tribunes of virtue, and whom Senator Harshman has implored us to protect from predators like me."

The sardonic comment, so personal in nature, so

surprising from a senator whose previous image—at least until the Costello murders—had been one of lawyerly temperance, seemed to startle some of his colleagues. But Jack Slezak, Hampton noted, regarded him with an unimpressed half smile which tempered his own satisfaction.

"And what," he continued, "is the nature of this protection? Not merely to limit punitive damages—which, I would note, chiefly benefit nonworking women and children who, because they can't project their future earnings, would otherwise get short shrift. Nor even to limit contingent fees, which serve to prevent plaintiffs of modest means from being reduced to penury by lawyers for the giant corporations who are paid by the proponents' chief patrons, hour by hour, to make suing their clients too expensive to bear. For *gun* companies, even this kind of legislative class warfare against the not-so-privileged is not protection enough. Because unique among *all* companies, they deserve nothing less than total immunity from suit."

Hampton's voice filled with indignation. "The Eagle's Claw bullet, it seems, is more sacred than tires which blow up, gas tanks which explode, diet pills that kill—or a pool drain which sucks the life out of a five-year-old girl. Because like the Lexington P-2, it kills not by accident, but by design. No wonder the proponents' only hope is to ban all lawsuits.

"So much remains for them to do. They've merely gutted the ATF. They've only exempted guns from the laws protecting consumers. They've simply opposed gun laws designed to make us safer." Hampton shook his head in wonder. "The Second Amendment, it seems, is truly a harsh mistress."

Watching C-SPAN, Kerry laughed softly. Lara took his hand.

At least, Hampton went on, *these labors have their compensations. Last year, the Sons of the Second Amendment were the second largest donor to the party of the majority—a fitting reward for such idealism. But merely a down payment, I am sure, on the money which would follow the success of their mission here today.*

"He's going for broke," Kerry murmured to his wife. "No one could ask for more."

Feeling the sting of Hampton's words, Fasano lost all hope that the bitterness of this debate, or the subject of his alliance with the SSA, could in any way be muted. Maintaining his air of calm, he added a note to the text of his response.

Hampton continued, "It is *we* who let Lexington sell this gun—and those bullets—without a background check. That is our disgrace. Why add to it now?"

Pausing, Hampton glanced at Cassie Rollins, prim and composed at her desk near the back of the chamber, and then, closer, Vic Coletti. "And yet," Hampton told them, "the worst disgrace of all is near at hand. For this bill would not merely end all future suits, but wipe out all *current* ones, no matter how close to trial.

"None of us here are innocents. We know precisely what—and whom—this very special interest provision is aimed at. And we can only marvel at the hypocrisy of its proponents."

Cassie Rollins, Hampton saw, had fixed him with an unwavering, but unhappy, gaze. Perhaps he would not change her vote—or any vote. But he would know that he had done all he could. "More than unfair," Hampton continued, "it is unconstitutional. And worse."

*

Watching, Kerry was moved.

On the screen, the senior senator from Vermont stood straighter, eyes sweeping his silent colleagues. *Like millions of Americans,* he told them, *I value guns designed for sportsmanship, not slaughter. But America has become the world's shooting gallery. God help us if we pour gasoline on the fire of gun violence.*

This body is supposed to save lives. But in the area of guns, we have contributed our bit to the taking of lives. Pausing for a final time, Hampton finished quietly, *Truly, there is blood on our hands. It is long past time that we begin to wipe it off.*

Lara felt a constriction in her throat. "It's probably just a phase," she managed to tell her husband. "But I think I'm in love with Chuck."

"When I call him with our thanks," Kerry answered, "I'll mention that."

As Hampton sat, the gallery burst into applause. Grimly smiling, the Vice President took her time before gaveling it down, and then Frank Fasano rose to answer.

"The Chair," Ellen Penn declared, "recognizes the senior senator from Pennsylvania."

Though outwardly unfazed, Fasano paused to calm his nerves and collect his thoughts. His role in this drama was difficult: to tamp down the emotion aroused by the Minority Leader, and to provide his colleagues with a rationale—principled and reasoned—which would make them other than instruments of the SSA.

After a brief obeisance to Vice President Penn, the usual flurry of courtesies, Fasano promptly set about his task. "My distinguished friend, the senior senator from Vermont, need not have told us that he once was a trial lawyer. For he has gifts which would stir a jury, and must surely impress us all. Including a rare ability to infuse his point of view with passion and conviction.

"But it is, after all, *only* that—a point of view. There are others. So let us begin by rejecting the easy notion that one point of view is uniquely good, and that another is a matter of cynical self-interest. Because, in candor, it requires great courage for members of this body to oppose with simple reason the tsunami of emotion unleashed by my gifted colleague.

"But we *must*."

With this sudden, emphatic statement, Fasano saw, he had seized the close attention of his colleagues—most particularly Cassie Rollins. "We must," he repeated more quietly. "Because ensuring the quality of our justice system requires more from us than a blind deference to the passions of the moment—however heartfelt those passions may be."

Watching, Kerry tried to detach himself. "He's doing what he has to do," he observed to Lara. "He always does. What I've honestly never known is whether Fasano has a soul." "If he did," Lara remarked with quiet bitterness, "wouldn't you know by now?"

"We should first dispel," the Majority Leader continued, "any notion that circumscribing existing lawsuits is any way unusual—let alone unconstitutional."

Fasano, Hampton thought, was like a watchmaker, meticulously constructing his argument piece by piece. And "circumscribe" was a particularly artful synonym for "erase."

"Changes in the law," Fasano continued in this tutorial manner, "always affect existing rights. The courts acknowledge that. Thus when the state of Louisiana passed an immunity provision very similar to this, the United States Supreme Court declined to entertain a constitutional challenge.

"If there is any 'retroactive' abuse of law, it is the effort to impose a hitherto nonexistent liability on the manufacturers of a legal product—guns—for their criminal misuse by unknown third parties whose actions they do not control." Fasano spread his hands. "Multiply that effort by fifty states, and what you have is chaos—a legal minefield where the question of liability is a crazy quilt of conflicting outcomes, the iron whims of a thousand courts. All of it the random result of whether a gun is fired in, say, Illinois as opposed to Indiana."

Watching, Hampton acknowledged Fasano's talents, on this day employed more subtly than his own. Unable to divine the thoughts of Rollins, Coletti or Slezak, Hampton could only wonder whether anything said today—or some other, more hidden, influence—would cause one of them to tip the balance.

Lara was finding it hard to watch. *The purpose of the law,* Fasano urged his colleagues, *is not simply to decide each case as it comes, but to assure a uniformity—and predictability—of outcomes.*

"Nothing," Lara observed tartly, "could be more uniform—or more predictable—than locking the door of every courtroom in America." But, to her, it was far more visceral than that: she could never again see Senator Fasano without hating him.

Well satisfied with the beginning of his argument, Fasano cut to its core. "*This,*" he said firmly, "is *not* about a faulty

tire or an exploding gas tank. It involves a nondefective—
and wholly lawful—product. And as terrible as were the
murders ascribed to O. J. Simpson, no one thought to sue
the maker of the knife."

With this, Fasano set about walking the tightrope
between a clinical dissection of the law and the tacit implication that Kerry Kilcannon, by distorting it, sought to
enhance his own unwarranted power. Fasano trusted that
this would serve to keep his votes in place and, perhaps,
gain him just one more.

TWENTY-SEVEN

SARAH FERVENTLY wished that she could watch the Senate vote on gun immunity. But instead, she and Lenihan went before Gardner Bond to demand the right to interrogate George Callister.

Sarah had hoped this hearing would be public, an opportunity to cite before the press from the depositions of Ben Gehringer, Mike Reiner, and Norman Conn—the better, even at this late hour, to influence the Senate's debate. But Nolan had argued that a public hearing would undermine the judge's order sealing all depositions. To the distress of Lenihan and Sarah, Bond had agreed. And so they gathered around a conference table in Bond's chambers—Bond, Nolan, Fancher, Lenihan, Sarah, and the court's stenographer—to resolve the matter of George Callister.

As always, Bond was impeccably tailored—a handmade suit, gold cuff links, crisp white breast pocket handkerchief—precise, and imperious. At the moment he was also angry, though they had yet to discuss George Callister.

"What," he inquired sternly of Nolan, "is the basis for your assertion that plaintiff's counsel are leaking information to the press?"

"It's not merely an assertion." Nolan shot a look at Lenihan and Sarah. "Last night CNN called me at home. They had received documents from Lexington files produced by a hostile employee, Norman Conn. The documents purport—according to the very unstable Mr. Conn—to contain information damaging to Lexington. We believe they show nothing of the kind. But CNN intends to divulge them to the public, perhaps as early as today."

Startled, Sarah glanced at Lenihan, whose expression did not change. "I can assure the Court," Nolan concluded with asperity, "that we did not provide them to the media. Nor did the SSA. That leaves Ms. Costello and her lawyers."

Lenihan appeared unruffled. "I'll try not to take offense at counsel's accusation," he responded. "I'll simply note that it betrays a rather glaring failure of imagination.

"Neither we *nor* Lexington control these documents." Briefly, Lenihan smiled. "Until Mr. Conn provided them, Lexington never owned up to their existence—whatever *that* suggests. As a result, these particular documents are not even subject to the Court's ban regarding those produced in response to a discovery demand. Anyone may have leaked them, and anyone can read them. Including CNN."

Sarah's amazement became a flash of amusement, followed by several certainties which made her anxious: that Lenihan had leaked the documents; that he had hoped to influence the Senate debate and enhance the settlement value of Mary's case; that he had attempted to skirt Bond's order on the barest of technicalities; and that he would admit to none of this. She could only admire his nerve, even as she feared its consequences—to both of them, and to Mary.

"Your Honor," Nolan said in a tone hard with indignation, "that statement lends new meaning to the phrase 'contempt of court.' The intent of this Court's order was very clear: to prevent the parties, through selective leaks, to try this case through the media. Yet this morning's *New York Times* reflects information from the deposition of a witness, Ben Gehringer. And now this."

"This morning's *New York Times*," Lenihan snapped, "reflects the federal indictment of the white supremacist who now admits selling the murder weapon to John Bowden at the gun show which, in defiance of all logic, Mr. Nolan intimated that Bowden might not have attended. No doubt that's damaging—if not devastating—to Lexington's defense. It may even be unhelpful to Lexington's efforts to wring immunity out of the United States Senate. But it's beyond the pale to suggest that Ms. Dash or I is responsible for the actions of the U.S. Attorney for the District of Idaho, or that those actions are anything but praiseworthy."

Disdainfully turning from Lenihan, Nolan fixed his gaze on Bond. "Your Honor," he said more quietly, "everyone knows the identity of the U.S. Attorney's ultimate superior—Ms. Costello's brother-in-law, the President of the United States. A man who, whatever his dignity of rank, is also a witness in this case, and subject to this Court's order.

"What appears to be at work here is a conspiracy, involving plaintiff's counsel and the White House, to evade that order. The leaking of these documents to CNN serves that end. Palpably, *they* have nothing to do with the U.S. Attorney in Idaho, and everything to do with seizing legal and political advantage by any means at hand."

Listening, Sarah wondered if the President had known of the disclosure of Conn's documents. Then she realized that Bond was addressing her in biting tones. "What do *you* know about this, Ms. Dash?"

"Nothing," Sarah said, and was very glad that this was so. "As the Court knows, I disagree with this particular order. But it's not my right to flout it—even when I think that might serve a valid public purpose."

The last remark was, perhaps, more than she should have said. But it served as a reminder that some of Lexington's problems were now in the public domain, and that an ambitious judge like Bond must be wary of the appearance—however accurate—that he was seeking to protect it. The judge paused, seemingly more reflective, before Nolan said, "Your Honor, I request the right to depose plaintiff's counsel in order to determine who may have leaked these documents to CNN."

"What about 'nothing,'" Sarah demanded of Nolan, "escapes you? Or were you not listening when I answered Judge Bond's question?"

"Enough," Bond cut in, gazing at Lenihan with severity. "Mr. Lenihan?"

Lenihan spread his palms. "Your Honor, my answer is Ms. Dash's answer. Nothing."

It was not—heard literally—a denial, and Bond was too observant not to know that. For a long moment he stared at Robert Lenihan with obvious distrust. "That aside," he said in caustic tones, "you seem to have grasped an unfortunate fact: that the documents voluntarily provided you by Mr. Conn fall outside the letter—if not the spirit—of this Court's order." Pausing, the judge expanded his gaze to take in Sarah. "At this time, and for the moment, I'll deny Mr. Nolan the chance to depose opposing counsel. But if anyone, ever, leaks information which is clearly subject to my order, I'll conduct the inquiry myself. And if the person responsible turns out to be any one of you, I'll bring you before the State Bar of California, and ask for your disbarment. You're now on notice."

In the silence, Nolan nodded grimly. To Sarah, the judge's threat—which he plainly meant—went to any lawyer's deepest fear: to be denied the right to practice his or her profession, and to carry that stain for life. Part of her cursed Lenihan's audacity.

"All right," the judge continued acidly, "let's take up the nominal subject of this proceeding—the deposition of Mr. Callister. Which of plaintiff's counsel cares to enlighten me on why this is such a pressing need?"

In the judge's current mood, Sarah thought, she wished this task had fallen to Lenihan. But that might have made the situation worse—as matters stood, the outcome looked unpromising enough. "For a host of reasons," Sarah answered. "To begin, there's the question of what Callister knew—whether from Reiner or someone else. Did he know that Reiner had undertaken to destroy key documents? Did he know that Lexington was flooding adjacent states with the P-2? Did he know that white supremacists were using gun shows to traffic a cache of stolen guns, which included the gun later sold to Mr. Bowden . . ."

"According to Mr. Reiner," Nolan interjected, "Mr. Callister knew *none* of that . . ."

"Counsel," Bond admonished Nolan, "wait your turn. This Court's not through with plaintiff's counsel yet."

Though glad to see Nolan stifled, Sarah did not care for the sound of this. "For Mr. Nolan to ask this Court to accept the credibility of a witness as slippery as Reiner, while dismissing that of plaintiff's counsel, turns logic on its head.

"Finally there is the question of a conspiracy between Lexington and the SSA . . ."

Bond eyed her with skepticism. "What evidence do you have that such a conspiracy existed?"

"That's the problem, Your Honor. Without Mr. Callister, we'll never know."

Bond's brow knit. "The problem, Ms. Dash, is that your argument literally makes something out of nothing: your total absence of proof. Mr. Nolan?"

"Your Honor is precisely right," Nolan answered with an air of confidence. "Under persistent questioning by Ms. Dash, Charles Dane—Mr. Callister's counterpart at the SSA—vehemently denied the existence of any such conspiracy. If plaintiff's counsel have such damning facts, let them try their case. With no proof to warrant it, why take up the time of someone as busy as Mr. Callister? Who, in any case, is on an extensive trip to Europe on business vital to the company."

This, too, was a surprise, confirming for Sarah how averse Nolan was to any questioning of Callister. Then it struck Sarah that fear of Callister's testimony might not be Nolan's principal motive: by interposing yet another delay, he created the possibility that the Senate might pass an immunity bill, and then override the President's veto, before more damning facts could surface—or, even more critical from Nolan's perspective, before the public trial of Mary's case began.

"In the annals of delaying tactics," Sarah responded crisply, "this is one of the more arrogant. Mr. Callister is too 'busy' to participate in discovery? What of the President or the First Lady, both of whom Mr. Nolan deposed? What of the three murdered family members who are the subject of this action? Is Mr. Callister's time more precious than all of that? This tactic is absurd, and the Court should put an end to it."

"Mr. Callister," Nolan responded with composure, "should not be asked to interrupt his travels. Let plaintiffs finish up their discovery, and then come back to the Court if they still insist on deposing him."

"How long," Bond inquired, "might those travels take?"

Nolan shrugged. "Roughly three more weeks. Give or take a day."

Whatever Nolan's other purposes, Sarah grasped that this would delay the case well beyond the ten-day deadline for a Presidential veto, and perhaps, the time Fasano needed to override it. "Three *weeks*," she protested, "is entirely unreasonable. Mr. Callister's supposed activities, whatever they are, don't rise to the importance of President Kilcannon's. Who managed to make time on the first date

Mr. Nolan asked for. This Court can order Callister to do the same."

"Indeed." With a thin smile, the judge turned to Nolan. "Were this an action in state court, Mr. Nolan, an out-of-state witness like Mr. Callister might be able to seek protection in the courts of his home state of Connecticut. But we're in federal court. At your insistence, I distinctly recall.

"So it seems you're at my mercy. You've got two weeks from today to produce Mr. Callister for deposition."

Surprised, Sarah felt a split second of elation at her unexpected victory, and then, seeing the glance pass between Nolan and Harrison Fancher, realized that two weeks might be sufficient time to satisfy their purposes. "Your Honor," she said respectfully, "might I request that your deadline be shortened to a week?"

"You can. And the answer's no." Bond seemed prepared to leave it there, and then to think better of it. "I'm not willing to put a businessman traveling in Europe on quite so short a tether."

Bond, Sarah suspected, might also believe that a two-week delay was enough for Frank Fasano, yet one which made Bond's own sympathies less obvious—particularly as compared to barring Callister's deposition altogether. But there was nothing she could do. "I have a final request, Your Honor. That, as Mr. Nolan did for the President's deposition, plaintiff's counsel be allowed to videotape our deposition of Mr. Callister."

Swiftly, Nolan turned to Bond. "That's wholly unnecessary."

Bond gave him an inquiring look. "Isn't, as Ms. Dash suggested, the president of Lexington no more privileged than the President of the United States?"

"President Kilcannon didn't object," Nolan answered. "We do."

"On what grounds?"

"That his sworn testimony in transcribed form is more than sufficient for plaintiff's purposes."

"Not true," Sarah asserted. "Mr. Nolan's obvious purpose in videotaping President Kilcannon was the hope of creating an embarrassing video moment, or some dramatic piece of tape which showed the President dissembling. That it never happened doesn't detract from the prospect that, in the case of Mr. Callister, it might.

"Mr. Nolan's aversion to a deposition of the *only* person at Lexington who dealt with Kerry Kilcannon makes me wonder what Lexington has to hide. To videotape both principals seems only fair."

Bond steepled his hands in front of him, the edge of his forefingers touching his lips. Sarah sensed that he was reluctant to concur but, weighing the public perception, felt stuck. "Very well," he said at last. "You may videotape Mr. Callister."

"Your Honor," Nolan said through tightened lips, "given today's leak of documents, and the importance plaintiff's counsel assign to this additional discovery—as well as their insistence on videotaping Mr. Callister—it may be necessary to remind them of their obligations under this Court's order."

Reminded of his own displeasure, Bond faced Lenihan and Sarah. "*Need* I remind you?" he inquired softly.

If Bond's purpose was to frighten her, Sarah thought, he had succeeded yet again. "No, Your Honor," she said promptly. As did Lenihan, a second later.

TWENTY-EIGHT

IN THEORY, the vote on gun immunity should have been conducted by roll call of senators stationed at their desks, declaring their votes in alphabetical order. But *this* vote was deemed too dicey, especially for the holdouts—Coletti, Slezak, and Rollins—each of whom wanted the others to make the first move. And so the vote was accomplished through a far less formal procedure. When the clerk conducted the initial roll call, most senators would not respond. Then, for a fifteen-minute period, while the senators milled about the floor in a disorderly scrum, each senator could cast his or her vote at the desk of the Senate clerk. The clerk would then repeat the vote, allowing those who kept a tally to know where the voting stood.

But for the stakes, this process would have held a certain edgy comedy: Rollins, Slezak and Coletti each eyeing the other as their colleagues eyed them, all waiting for one of the three to approach the clerk. A single vote would give Fasano the fifty-one he needed. If any of the three voted in favor of gun immunity, it freed the others to avoid casting the deciding vote, instead acting as their political interests dictated. As Cassie waited at the rear of the chamber, one senator after another ventured forward.

"Fourteen minutes to go," Chad murmured in her ear. "Do me a favor, and hold out. I just bet Hampton a steak dinner at the Palm that Coletti cracks first."

"Who did Chuck get?"

"The field. You and Slezak." Chad lowered his voice. "So here's the deal, Cassie. Hold out until Vic votes, and

I'll come to Maine and campaign for you. Whether in the primary, or in the general."

She studied him, surprised. Chad was no longer smiling. He knew how difficult this was for her: out of friendship and generosity, and despite his support of Fasano, Chad was telling her to vote as she liked, even if it meant helping her buck the SSA in a primary fight.

She touched his sleeve. "Thank you, Chad."

He shook his head in demurral, as though his offer was nothing of note. "Life's too short," he told her. "And this is way too serious."

In the Oval Office, Kerry watched on CNN. Superimposed on its image of the milling senators was a vote tally—eleven to ten in favor of gun immunity—and a second-by-second count of the remaining time: 12:43. When Clayton entered, the President asked, "Does Hampton have the transcript?"

"His Chief of Staff does. It's only a matter of minutes."

Peering at the screen, Kerry tried to pick out Vic Coletti.

On the floor of the Senate, Palmer and Cassie Rollins watched the minority leader take Vic Coletti by the elbow, gently but firmly pulling him aside, and hand him what appeared to be a one-page document.

"What's that about?" Cassie wondered aloud.

Chad, too, felt curious. "Can it be?" he murmured. "The White House finally found that compromising photograph of Vic with a sheep?"

"*A* sheep," Cassie inquired dryly. "Only one?"

"Yeah. But *he* was underage."

Whatever it was, the document had Coletti's close attention.

*

"You've been worried about Lexington," Hampton told Vic Coletti. "This is a transcript from Wolf Blitzer's newscast. CNN's got documents which Lexington concealed in the Costello lawsuit, showing that Lexington knew that the P-2 was being widely used by criminals in California. They also include the ballistics tests on the Eagle's Claw."

Coletti finished reading, then looked slowly up at Hampton. "Not pretty," he said in grudging tones. "But it doesn't say they knew the P-2 was being sold by white supremacists."

At the corner of his vision, Hampton noticed Jack Slezak observing them. "Or by Adolf Hitler," Hampton answered tersely. "You told the President you needed cover. Obstruction of justice should be cover enough. Do you really want to reward *that* with immunity?"

Coletti mustered a flinty smile which tightened the corner of his eyes. "The President doesn't mean to lose, does he."

"Surprise," Hampton said with a laugh as soft as it was brief. Then he put one hand on Coletti's shoulder. "The President would appreciate your help, Vic. So would I."

To both sides, senators kept stepping forward toward the clerk. With a curt nod, Coletti folded the paper and tucked it into the inside pocket of his suit coat. "Does Slezak know?" he asked.

Hampton smiled. "He will."

With four minutes left, Cassie saw Vic Coletti approach the clerk of the Senate with all the animation of a death row prisoner taking his final walk.

"Congratulations," Cassie said to Chad. "Looks like Hampton's buying."

Chad shrugged. "Just another scene from *Profiles in Courage*. I think I'll wander down there for you, find out how Vic voted."

This was another kindness, sparing Cassie the discomfort of looking. "Please don't wander," she said. "Sprint."

But Fasano found her before Chad returned. "Coletti?" she asked.

"Kilcannon flipped him. Time to choose, Cassie."

Senator Rollins inhaled. "It will be—in about three minutes. Where's Slezak?"

Fasano's eyes bored into her. "No clue. Whoever he's promised his vote to, it isn't me." His voice reverted to its cool, clipped tenor. "Slezak's not on my team. You are. Don't embarrass me any further."

Around them the edgy buzz of conversation rose, both the senators and the gallery anticipating the end game. "Then don't embarrass *me*," she said softly. "There are people watching."

"No need," Fasano answered. "I've said all I should ever need to say." Abruptly turning, he walked away.

On the screen the count stood at forty-eight to forty-eight, with one certain vote for each side yet to come. The clock read 2:14.

"Come on, Cassie," the President murmured. Something kept him from speaking Slezak's name.

"*That* looked chummy," Chad said on his return. His voice was conversational, as if reporting something of mild interest. "You and Slezak still have a couple of minutes. Care to know what turned Coletti?"

Contemplating yet again the potential consequences of defying the Majority Leader, Cassie remained shaken. "Sure."

With a smile, Chad told her.

After a moment, Cassie shook her head. "You know, I really despise these people."

"Lexington?"

"The SSA."

Chad gave a querying look. "And so?"

Somewhat belatedly, it struck Cassie that, all kindnesses aside, Chad would not mind at all if Fasano lost. "Tell me something," she replied. "What inspired you to sign on as Frank's point man?"

Chad glanced about them. "We cut a deal," he told her in an undertone. "*This* thing for a straight up-and-down vote on campaign finance reform."

After a moment, Cassie nodded. "I thought it must be something better than what Frank offered me—an end to my career. Or the President."

"What did Kerry offer you?"

"A chance to do the right thing. I just hate it when that happens."

Chad, she saw, was looking over her shoulder. "Slezak isn't moving," he reported. "You've got about a minute."

Cassie glanced at her watch. "Fuck it, Chad. This is becoming *way* too undignified."

With that, she walked briskly toward the clerk.

"There goes Cassie," Clayton said.

At the corner of the screen, the countdown showed 1:14. As Cassie spoke to the clerk, Kerry heard the door to the Oval Office ease open, and turned to see Lara slipping through. Softly, she told her husband, "I couldn't stand watching up there alone."

Kerry's whole being felt taut. "You're in time for the final curtain. Cassie's about to vote."

Aware of the drama of the moment, the clerk peered at the junior senator from Maine through glasses so thick that they magnified his eyes—which, at the moment, resembled those of a startled bug. Smiling, she said, "Doing a brisk business, I see. Where does the vote stand?"

"Fifty 'no,' " he answered. "Forty-eight 'yes.' "

"Close. What do *you* think I should do?"

Mute, he looked up at her, unwilling to venture a response. Cassie felt her colleagues crowding in behind her, straining to hear whether her vote would be "yes" with the President and Hampton, or "no" with the Majority Leader and her party. "Oh, well," she told the clerk. "Record my vote as 'yes.' "

Behind her she heard a stir. Glancing up at the Vice President, Cassie gave Ellen Penn a smile. After all, there were so few times a Vice President got to seize the limelight, and one of those was voting to break a tie.

"It's all on Slezak," Kerry told his wife.

Standing behind him, Lara gripped the top of his chair. Her fingers were white, she noticed. For a moment, remembering the murders, the tortured dealings with her younger sister which had led to the filing of the lawsuit, she had been unaware of herself.

"Please, God," she murmured, an utterance which was half prayer, half superstition. Reaching back, Kerry touched her hand.

*

On the floor of the Senate, the gazes of her colleagues—some direct, some more circumspect—moved to the junior senator from Michigan.

Slowly, Slezak walked forward. "He can't bolt now," Chad whispered from behind her. "He'd be cutting Kerry's balls off."

That was probably right, Cassie thought. Odds were that Slezak had been holding back his vote to find out, through Cassie, whether the vote would make a difference to the leader of his party. But when she glanced at Senator Hampton, he was standing stock-still, watching Slezak's progress with the same raptness as the others. With Paul Harshman at his shoulder, Senator Fasano pressed close to the clerk's desk.

As Slezak reached the clerk, head butting forward, Fasano edged aside. Briefly, Slezak glanced at him, and nodded.

On the screen, the tally hung suspended, fifty to forty-nine. Kerry and Lara knew only that Slezak had cast his vote.

A white numeral changed, a "zero" became a "one."

The President stood in disbelief. "We lost," Clayton said tersely. "Slezak fucked us."

Standing, Kerry turned to Lara, heedless of anyone else, and took her in his arms. "It's not over," he promised. "All I need is thirty-four votes against the final bill."

She would know this, of course, just as she knew that the struggle to hold those votes could be even more vicious than what had gone before, political trench warfare waged senator to senator. It was just that he felt the need to speak. In answer, Lara held him close.

*

Shortly after eight o'clock that evening, by a vote of sixty-six to thirty-four, the Senate passed the Civil Justice Reform Act. Senators Rollins and Coletti voted with the majority.

PART SIX

BALANCE OF POWER

EARLY DECEMBER TO CHRISTMAS WEEK

ONE

EARLY THE NEXT morning, the President responded.

His first call was to Jeannie Griswold, the Attorney General of Michigan, promising as much support, funding, and campaign assistance as she needed to unseat Jack Slezak in the primary. After thank-you calls to Vic Coletti and Cassie Rollins, he gathered Clayton and his congressional relations team to determine the best course for sustaining his intended veto of the Civil Justice Reform Act.

Once vetoed, the bill would return to the House of Representatives and, should it override the President, to the Senate. The House was hopeless, all concurred; the bill had passed by a margin well in excess of two-thirds. The battle would be in the Senate, where, at the moment, Frank Fasano was one vote shy of the two-thirds needed to overcome Kerry's veto. All effort would go there.

The next subject was timing. Kerry had ten days to sign a veto message. The question was whether he was served by waiting, or by sending the bill back to Congress quickly, decisively and dramatically. The conferees read the morning's headlines like tea leaves. The most prominent of these, the Senate's vote, warred with the disclosure of documents adverse to Lexington and Judge Bond's order—public only in its bottom line—that George Callister be deposed.

Jack Sanders, Kerry's Chief Domestic Policy Advisor, and Alex Cole, his Congressional Liaison, reached opposite conclusions. Sanders favored rapid action to underscore

Kerry's resolve. Cole believed that the momentum of events—the arrest of Ben Gehringer; the leak of Lexington's documents—meant that Kerry could use the full ten days to build support and solidify Senate Democrats. Kerry dismissed the meeting with the tentative decision that he would wait before returning the bill to Congress.

Only Clayton lingered. When the two men were alone, he pointed out, "You can control *your* timing, Mr. President, but not Fasano's. He can wait to schedule an override vote until this Congress ends—up to a year, by my reckoning, choosing whatever time you're weakest. That argues for throwing the bill back in his face tomorrow and daring him to act."

Briefly, Kerry looked out the window at the bleakest of days, the steady drizzle spattering the glass. "I've considered that. But no matter what I do, Fasano won't wait, even if he has to keep the Senate in session up to Christmas Eve." Turning back to Clayton, the President added, "He can't."

A fleeting smile crossed Clayton's face. "Mary's lawsuit."

"Yup. Fasano's patrons can't let it go to trial or even risk more leaks. So Fasano's stuck in a vise between me and the SSA."

Clayton considered him. "And you," he said pointedly, "want to give the lawsuit time to blow up in public before Fasano can hold a vote. Maybe some tidbit from George Callister's deposition."

"It's only an idle wish," Kerry answered with a shrug. "No point in sharing it with Jack and Alex."

Clayton chuckled softly. With no change of expression, but in a cooler tone, Kerry asked, "Did you confirm our information about Lexington?"

"Yes. Its British parent, Shawcross Holdings, has a major interest in North Sea Oil Leasing and, not-socoincidentally, is an ardent supporter of the Prime Minister. Who has a considerable say about the future of North Sea drilling."

"As between guns and oil, what does Shawcross care about most?"

"Oil. There's way more money in it."

The President thanked him. Leaving the Oval Office, Clayton marveled at the intricacy of Kerry's four-sided chess game with the SSA, Fasano, and Bob Lenihan and Sarah Dash, so subtle and complex that no reporter would ever divine it.

Alone, the President placed his scheduled call to the Prime Minister.

The two men, telegenic leaders of a similar age, liked each other. So the exchange of pleasantries was genuine, as was the respect with which they exchanged views on their painstaking war against the Al Qaeda successors of Mahmoud Al Anwar. Only toward the end did Kerry observe, "I took a bit of a black eye yesterday."

"Yes," the Prime Minister said with sympathy. "I saw. Fortunately, under your system they don't run you out for losing one vote in the legislature."

"Not yet. But I certainly wouldn't care to lose again." Briefly, Kerry paused. "On a tangent to that, I have a favor to ask—assuming you feel free to grant it."

"If I can, Kerry. As long as you're duly grateful."

"Always," Kerry answered. "A man named George Callister seems to have washed up on your shores. His ultimate employer is Shawcross Holdings. It's dawned on me that a word from you might hasten his return."

"It might," his ally answered pleasantly. "What do I need to know?"

*

"Twelve million dollars," Sarah said, gazing coldly at Lenihan. "When—if Mary hadn't—did you intend to tell me?"

Lenihan crossed his arms. "Nolan and Fancher still don't know. There was no point in telling you unless Mary had an interest."

"In what?" Sarah snapped. "Telling me? Don't bullshit me, Bob. You and Dane were trying to settle this case around me. And might have if Mary hadn't fulfilled *your* obligations."

Their client sat between them in the interior conference room of the Kilcannon Center, an unhappy wraith at the meeting Sarah herself had demanded. Glancing at their client, Lenihan folded his arms. "Don't accuse me of being some sort of fifth column for those Nazis at the SSA. Or is how CNN got those documents still a mystery to you?"

The boldness of this statement gave Sarah pause. "That's another thing," she said more slowly. "Bond could have hung us both, and with it Mary's case. But I suppose it's all worthwhile to you if it made Dane up his offer."

"Of course it did. Don't be naive."

"I'm hardly that," Sarah rejoined. "If Mary settles, that would remove the biggest obstacle between Fasano and a veto override.

"Dane's stated condition is that the settlement amount never be disclosed, and that the files remain nonpublic. Why? Because without disclosure the public will think we're acknowledging that the case has no merit." Turning to Mary, Sarah added softly, "You get eight million, and Bob's firm gets four million as its contingent fee. And no one will be able to sue a gun company or the SSA, ever again. Because you'll have helped cause the President to lose."

Now Lenihan spoke to Mary. "The President," he countered, "may well lose anyway. Then you'll end up with nothing."

Mary looked sallow, thinner, so diminished by their conflict that Sarah, feeling both empathy and alarm, turned her focus back on Lenihan. "I'm all for Mary being compensated. But isn't this lawsuit also about saving lives?"

"Of course . . ."

"Of *course*," Sarah said with the edge of disdain. "So shouldn't this settlement require Lexington to discontinue making the bullet which ensured Marie would die? Or the gun Bowden used to kill her, Inez, and Joan? And wouldn't a *public* disclosure of settlement terms *help* the President and encourage *other* gun companies to alter their behavior?"

Lenihan slammed down his coffee mug. "And requiring George Callister to commit public hari-kari would send an even stronger signal. But the SSA won't agree to any of that, and they're the ones who'll put up most of the money." Facing Mary, he said more quietly, "It's not just that the *President* may lose. Even if he doesn't, *we* may— because of Gardner Bond. It's not a betrayal of anyone to make a prudent assessment of the risks, and where you may wind up in the end."

"They're scared," Sarah retorted. "Far more scared than we are. In the last three weeks we've been killing them, and now Callister's coming up. If the President hangs on in the Senate—unless Bond throws us out before trial, which I don't think he can now—we're going to try this case in front of God and everyone." Urgently, Sarah turned to Mary. "That's why Dane went to Bob. Unless you stiff the President, this case will be worth a whole lot more than twelve million dollars. *And* you'll have the power to change how the American gun industry does business.

"Bob's partners made an investment. They're worried

they won't get it back. But that's the risk they took, and this isn't about *their* mother or sister or niece." Sarah's voice softened. "It's about yours. Before you take eight million dollars of hush money, *please* search your soul. Because it's also blood money. Once you take it, you can never give it back."

Mary's face betrayed a silent agony. Once more, Sarah felt the depth of her dilemma, paralyzed by her complex relationship with Lara and the President; her duty to her murdered relatives; her obligation to future victims; an offer of more money than she had ever imagined; and the diametrically opposed reactions of her lawyers. With palpable strain, she asked, "How long do I have to decide?"

"Seven days," Lenihan answered. "After that, Dane's taking all twelve million dollars off the table."

Mary touched her eyes. "Seven days," she repeated dully.

TWO

IN THE OVAL OFFICE, the President and the Majority Leader met alone.

Fasano had requested the meeting. Kerry did not need to ask why; gun immunity hung in the balance of power between the President and the senator who intended to displace him. Though there were nine days left for the President to act, Kerry could veto the Civil Justice Reform Act at any moment. Then there would be no time for second thoughts, no brake on their collision course. The final reckoning was at hand.

As to Fasano, the President's habits of mind had long since formed: Kerry assumed a cold, undeviating self-interest which made thinking of Fasano in human terms a waste of time. The President did not trust him; did not try to charm him; and thought the small amenities they must observe as hollow as a dumb show. He supposed, without caring, that Fasano felt much the same about him. In his most philosophical moments, Kerry might ponder the psychic costs of such learned indifference. But he had come far since Newark, and the harshness of his enemies had taught him that such reflections were a luxury.

And there was Lara. Fasano might have a wife and children. Perhaps he even loved them. But Fasano the would-be President meant to seal Lara's tragedy to propitiate the SSA. Facing him now, Kerry felt far more than coldness.

"Well," he said. "What is it?"

Perhaps surprised by Kerry's dismissal of even superficial pleasantries, Fasano erased all expression from his face. His dark eyes met Kerry's without flinching. "I think you're going to lose, Mr. President."

Kerry stared at him. Forced to elaborate, Fasano said evenly, "Tort reform trumps guns. You're asking thirty-four senators to sink it merely because you want them to. All I need is one of them."

With a chill smile, Kerry glanced at his watch. "Then don't waste time on me, Frank. You'd best get to it before someone else gets shot."

The laconic brutality of this response induced silence. The President watched Fasano weigh his words. "This isn't personal to me."

Kerry shrugged at the implied rebuke. "What is?"

To Kerry's surprise, Fasano summoned a look which approximated compassion. "I understand your feelings, Mr. President. I've got no wish to humiliate you, and it wouldn't serve my interests. Let's try to discuss this in that spirit."

Fasano's unblinking composure was, to Kerry, as annoying and impressive as his hubris. "That's why we're meeting," Kerry said with tenuous patience. "So what *are* we discussing?"

Fasano settled back on the President's couch. "A deal."

"That's hard to imagine. Your interests are irreconcilable with mine."

"Substantively, yes." Fasano's expression became one of deep sincerity, his tone quieter. "But a train wreck would damage both of us, and our parties. Unless both of us choose to stop it."

The President considered him. "Frank," he said crisply, "this isn't just a meeting between us two statesmen, moving to a higher plane. The SSA knows you're here. They authorized your call to me. So explain to me the statesmanship which can accomodate all three of us."

Fasano smiled without humor. "I've consulted them, yes. We all have our Robert Lenihans."

Do we *not*, the President thought. He wondered if Fasano knew of Dane's back-channel offer, but could find no way to probe this. "Please go ahead," the President answered. "I can always call Bob later."

"All right. The first part of my solution's simple: you don't veto tort reform."

The President smiled. "Of course. That way you don't run the risk of trying, but failing, to immunize Lexington—after which it's exposed at trial as a bloodsucker effectively run by the SSA, your bankers. So what's the rest?"

Fasano seemed unfazed. "The rest is equally simple. I promise you a straight up-and-down vote on your gun bill—no amendments, no tricks, no filibuster. If you can get your fifty votes, you pass it. If not, you get to run on it."

That Fasano's air was so matter-of-fact, Kerry thought, made the context of his offer almost breathtaking. Behind Sarah's back, Dane had used Lenihan to ask Mary Costello to sell out both her sister and Kerry's political interests. Now, to Kerry's face, albeit through Fasano, Dane was asking the President to sell out Mary, Lenihan, Sarah—and Kerry's own wife. The only rein on Kerry's anger was his fascination with Fasano himself; if Fasano knew of Dane's offer to Mary Costello, his self-possession was truly superhuman.

Another thought gave Kerry pause. On the level of cold-blooded abstraction—of sheer calculation—the offer had its merits: the swap of a veto he might lose for a clean shot at passing a bill which would certainly save lives. And, if Kerry failed, the chance to use it in the open against Fasano and the SSA.

For a moment the President could say nothing. Clayton had been right from the beginning—Kerry was now caught in a web of his own design, the personal and political so hopelessly intertwined that he could never disentangle them, or even parse his own motives. And for that moment, he envied Senator Fasano his detachment.

But, in the end, there was only one answer.

"No," he told Fasano.

Lara gripped the telephone. "Mary," she said quietly, "if we take the money on *those* terms, our settlement will seem like an apology. Or worse."

"Worse?"

"A sellout. In either case, the votes to uphold Kerry's veto will begin to melt away."

Speaking from her efficiency apartment in San Francisco, Mary sounded wan. "Did I hear you say 'we,' Lara?"

At once, Lara realized her blunder. "I'm sorry," she said. "I was thinking of our family."

"That's good," Mary answered. "Because it's different for me than you. It seems like from the moment I was born you were already this great success."

The myths of families, Lara thought sadly. "I was in second grade, Mary—a seven-year-old who was scared to death of our own father. Now I'm a woman who, like you, has lost the rest of her family but for a sister."

"A woman," Mary repeated in a tone Lara heard as both stubborn and defensive, "who's also married to the President and made millions with NBC. Coming from you, 'we' sounds false."

Stop, Lara thought. "Do you think the SSA's *eight* million dollars," she shot back, "will make you a 'success'? It's like selling our own mother to these people." Abruptly, Lara heard herself. "I apologize, Mary—really. Like you, I'm frayed. I understand that I've been lucky, that our lives are nothing alike. But this offer's just appalling."

On the other end, Mary was silent, perhaps stunned by the harshness of their conflict. "Lara," she said in a trembling voice, "I'm not selling our mother—or Joanie and Marie. If I were, I wouldn't have called Sarah. That's as good as calling you."

Not only was that true, Lara saw, but Mary's thrust was a fresh reminder of her intrusion into Mary's suit. "I apologize," Lara said in a mollifying tone. "I understand the difference between having money or not . . ."

"Well, I *don't* understand the difference, Lara. I've never had the chance."

Once again, Lara heard the justice in her sister's words, felt the yawning gulf in their perceptions. With an anxiety close to desperation, she promised, "I can help you, Mary. If it still matters, I can even help get you a contract for that book on our family you mentioned. Whatever I can do."

"What if I take this settlement?"

Lara paused to speak deliberately. "It would be hard to imagine a book, Mary, with *that* as its ending."

Her sister began to cry.

As soon as Clayton entered the office, Kerry knew from his friend's expression that he was troubled.

"What's up, pal?" the President inquired. "It's been a long day."

"Slezak wants a meeting."

"And here I thought there were no surprises left. He must have heard about Jeannie Griswold."

"He already knew you'd do that," Clayton demurred, and sat wearily in front of Kerry's desk. "He says it's a private matter—'extremely sensitive'—which can't wait another day. And that no one should know he's coming."

Abruptly, Kerry felt the pulse of Clayton's instinct, the

first glimmer that Slezak's insolence made a certain awful sense. With a fair show of calm, he answered, "Doesn't sound like an apology, does it? You'd better tell him to come tonight."

THREE

WITH DEEP FOREBODING, Kerry received Jack Slezak in the President's private office.

Slezak hunched in a wing chair, ankles crossed, hands clasped, his thick body held slightly forward. But for the brightness in his light green eyes, betraying a hint of superiority, he had the somber look of a worshiper at Mass, bent before the imponderable will of God. Even his voice was hushed.

"I'm sorry, Mr. President. I had no choice but to come in person."

Briefly, Slezak averted his gaze in what Kerry saw as feigned embarrassment. Increasingly certain of Slezak's purpose, the President spoke in a voice drained of welcome or encouragement. "Concerning what?"

Though still bent forward, Slezak gave the President a swift, keen glance which lifted the red eyebrows beneath the broad plane of his forehead. "I received a call. The man told the receptionist he was the president of the AFL-CIO. That's a call I've got to take." As he watched Kerry from behind his mask of reluctance, his voice became harsher. "Turned out it was a man I didn't know, saying he had a message for you.

"I was so pissed I nearly hung up on him. Then I thought"—here Slezak interrupted himself with a helpless shrug—"you know, that it might involve some threat against your life."

The tacit reference to Jamie's murder, and Kerry's own near death, made Slezak's pretense of humanity more offensive. With a faint cold smile, Kerry said softly, "But, of course, it wasn't."

The disbelief implicit in Kerry's remark caused Slezak to look at him sharply. "No. It was about the First Lady."

To Kerry, his own smile felt as though it could crack glass. "Only Lara?"

"No." Slezak studied his clasped hands. "He said that the two of you were involved when you were still married to your former wife."

Though prepared for this, a thickness in his throat forced Kerry to pause before mustering a tone of irony. " 'Involved'? Was your caller all that delicate?"

Plainly annoyed, Slezak looked straight at Kerry. "He said you'd made her pregnant, and that she'd gotten an abortion."

With veiled contempt, Kerry murmured, "At last."

Slezak stared at him. In their silence, the pale light of two standing lamps, Kerry began absorbing the calamity, long deferred, which now would fall on Lara and on him, pervading every corner—public and private—of their lives. Then Slezak added bluntly, "There's more."

"I thought there would be."

Without the pretense of any encouragement from the President, Slezak finished in a toneless voice. "He said they have the counselor's notes from the abortion clinic your wife went to, and that the notes confirm you were the father."

Despite Slezak's presence, Kerry was helpless to fight the current of memory—the emotional wreckage which Lara had become, his own pleas to have their child. "An interesting story," Kerry observed coldly. "Rich in detail. Did your source explain why he was sharing it with you?"

Slezak's eyes narrowed in shrewd appraisal. "Not exactly. Only that you'd know that it was true. And that once I told you, so would I."

The tacit statement of Slezak's leverage triggered, in Kerry, a mute fury at his own impotence. Standing, he said dismissively, "So now you know whatever you assume to know."

Slezak stood as well, seemingly propelled from his chair by a banked antagonism of his own. "That's not the end," he said curtly. "The guy said if you veto the Civil Justice Reform Act, all of America will know."

And Charles Dane already knew. To Kerry, the pattern was now crystalline. The SSA had the memo, and had promised Slezak cover if he defied the President. Slezak felt impervious: his charade was Dane's message to Kerry, the final piece of a three-pronged effort—preceded by Dane's settlement offer to Lenihan and Fasano's offer to Kerry—to assure the President's quiescence. Perhaps Fasano knew; perhaps he, too, was a pawn. But of one thing Kerry was quite certain: though he could not prove it, Jack Slezak was a liar, a knowing party to blackmail.

"Why do you suppose," Kerry asked quietly, "that they picked you?"

Left unspecified was who "they" were. In the same flat tone, Slezak answered, "Because they knew I would deliver the message."

"No doubt," Kerry told him, nodding toward the door. "So now you can leave. Lara and I don't get much time, and I don't like being late for dinner."

They sat on their bed as Kerry told her.

Her reaction was more devastating than he could have imagined. Nothing but the tears on her stricken face.

Kerry took her hands. "I'm sorry," he said softly. "Sorry that my becoming President has brought so much harm to us."

Her eyes were black pools of horror and grief. "They're

using '*us*,' " she said with quiet wonder, "to erase the public memory of my family." She grazed her cheekbones with the fingertips of one hand, as though to wipe them clean of dampness. "And you, Kerry. Nothing about what I did was ever fair to you."

Quiet, Kerry sorted through the tangle of his thoughts: that Lara did not deserve this; that those who had believed in him—indeed the country—did not deserve it either; that his ambition to be President had outrun his reason; that he *was* President, and could not let love, or even fear for their future, obscure the iron fact of his political dilemma, the harsh choices he must make. It was pointless to wish that they had never faced this moment.

"I love you," he said.

With a shiver of emotion, she rested her forehead against the hollow of his neck. "You would have loved our child."

Kerry simply held her. At length, she murmured wearily, "We've got no time for this."

The pitiless accuracy of this statement moved her husband to protest. "We've got time."

"Not now." Leaning back from him, she said, "You *are* President. And I've got Mary to think of."

To his own shame, Kerry realized that he had not considered Mary. Even if he did not yield to blackmail, a President crippled by scandal might not be able to sustain a veto which, even now, rested on a one-vote margin. Whatever their decision, Mary would have to know. "I suppose that's the good part," Lara added softly. "Never again will Mary envy me my perfection."

Silent, Kerry considered the toxic consequences he had thrust on Lara, the fruits of his decision to wound the SSA through Mary's lawsuit. From first to last, he had been poison to Lara's family.

I'll do whatever you want, he almost said, and then realized he could not promise even that. "We both know the playbook of our times," she told him with quiet bitterness. "I do the media calvary, the stations of the cross, dragging my sins from network to network. A few days of *that* will transform disgust to pity."

Kerry imagined her enduring this ritual of self-flagellation, the humiliating mix of theater with a remorse too personal to dramatize. Equally embittering was his regret that Lara must be so clear-eyed.

"I'd resign," he said simply, "before I'd watch that happen."

Her lips parted, as if to argue, and then she absorbed how literally he meant that. "And I won't watch you protect me at any cost. To you, or to me."

Feeling their impasse, the conflict of love and politics, Kerry absorbed anew the consequences of whatever they chose to do, their inability—now—to consider only the personal costs of dealing with a long-ago private act.

"We'll need advice," he said at last. "We can't decide this on our own."

Once more, tears filled Lara's eyes. "I know," she answered.

FOUR

PENSIVE, CLAYTON stared at the carpet.

It was a little past one a.m. Even in an administration staffed by driven and dedicated people, the West Wing was silent, allowing Clayton to slip into the Oval Office unnoticed. At length Clayton said softly, "They'll use it."

Kerry was quiet. "When I called," he inquired at length, "what did Carlie say?"

"That you keep strange hours." Still leaning forward, Clayton peered up at him, the wisp of a smile vanishing in an instant. "She still doesn't know about you and Lara. In twenty-seven years, it's the only secret I've ever kept from her."

For eighteen of those years, Clayton had been his closest friend. Gazing at Clayton's round, familiar face, Kerry thought again that he could not have hoped for a better one. He knew how deeply—almost superstitiously—averse Clayton was to keeping anything from his wife. "Does anyone else know?"

"Only Kit."

Clayton nodded. During the campaign, when a national magazine had been close to uncovering the story, they had agreed that it was necessary to prepare Kit for the worst. "But not about Slezak?"

"Not yet." Kerry stood, hands thrust in his pockets. "I want Kit's advice on this."

Clayton puffed his cheeks, silently expelling air. "I can already tell you, Kerry. She'll say that you have to get this story out yourself."

"Maybe. But I need another point of view. I'm not going to kick this one around with our political people—let alone convene a group of wise men to cogitate on Lara's abortion as if it were the Cuban Missile Crisis. Even if I could imagine that, which I can't, can you imagine the stories if it leaked?" Kerry paused. "A few weeks ago, I might have talked to Chad. But not now."

Clayton gazed at him as though absorbing the dimensions of Kerry's solitude. "Do you want me to bring Kit in now?"

"Please. This one won't wait."

At a little past two a.m., Lara waited with Kerry in his private office, their chairs pulled close together—Lara dressed in a blouse and blue jeans, Kerry in khakis and a pullover sweater. When Kit and Clayton entered, Clayton rested a hand on Lara's shoulder. Without looking up, she covered Clayton's hand with hers. Then he joined Kit on a sofa facing the President and First Lady.

Kit's round features had assumed a sober professionalism which could not mask her worry. "Slezak's story is bullshit."

Kerry nodded. "We're all agreed on that."

"If you could implicate the SSA," Kit continued, "you'd have all sorts of choices—including moral outrage. With no one to blame, your options narrow."

"I'm afraid that's where we are. Short of tearing out Slezak's fingernails until he implicates Charles Dane."

Kit glanced at Lara, and then spoke to Kerry again. "Maybe we're so used to being afraid of this that we've forgotten what all of us know. Millions of women face this choice. To them, for *you* to be blackmailed over it would be grotesque, something from the *Jerry Springer*

Show. There's more sympathy out there than the SSA may think. And potentially a lot more anger."

"Sympathy?" Lara cut in. "Not from the media. I'm imagining *The O'Reilly Factor* amplified by a thousand right-wing talk shows. Unless I tell the truth—that Kerry never wanted an abortion—we'll be portrayed as a ruthless and ambitious couple who'd do anything to claw our way to power." Briefly, her eyes clouded. "They'll say that we've exploited the murder of my own family for cheap sympathy, but didn't hesitate to murder our own child. That we lied our way into office. That we're morally unfit to stay here. That no child in America can see us as fit role models for private conduct or public integrity."

"Even," Kit ventured quietly, "if you *did* tell the truth about Kerry?"

Lara glanced at her husband. "I'm more than willing to do that. But perhaps Kerry's right that they'd accuse me of trying to pin a rose on an adulterer by lying for him. And accuse *him* of using me to hide behind.

"But you're right about the anger. The country will become an endless echo chamber of attacks and recriminations, until Kerry and I can never go anywhere without everyone else's thought bubble being about abortion." Her voice grew husky. "*I* know that his marriage failed because Meg didn't want children, and that he'd have given all this up to have our child. But public life is not a place to look for sympathy. The hard-line social conservatives will be demanding that people like Fasano prove their devotion to family values by making Kerry a moral object lesson. They'll use me to ruin his Presidency, any way they can."

Lara felt depressed, exhausted by the weight of her own guilt. Both Kit and Clayton gazed at their laps. At length, Kit said, "I grant you that abortion's an incendiary topic. Coupled with the gun issue, the right will use it to rip open the whole culture gap—'the Kilcannons don't share our values.' But it only gets as bad as you've imagined if we let the SSA control the means and timing of disclosure."

"What 'means of disclosure,' " Kerry asked, "do you suggest? Because Lara and I are *not* going on Barbara Walters."

"Put this in the hands of the *New York Times*," Kit urged him. "Or, better, the *Post*: given that Lara covered you for the *Times* when you first became involved, they might be a little touchy about her ethics. We could grant the *Post* an exclusive interview with strict ground rules—no asking Pat Robertson for his reaction; print the entire transcript verbatim . . ."

"What reason do we give for this confessional? 'We just thought that you should know'? If that were true, we'd have said so during the campaign."

"And cost yourself the election? Or the Masters nomination? You didn't owe *anyone* that." Kit spoke slowly, balancing entreaty with firmness. "The two of you are married now, and you've both suffered too much already. The American public is far more compassionate—and sensible—than the extremists on either side would have them be. They'll understand if someone is trying to blackmail you and that you have to divulge on principle that which, in principle, you believe too private to disclose." Pausing, Kit finished flatly, "That's the other thing, Mr. President. If you *don't* expose this, you're arguably complicit in your own blackmail."

"If I veto gun immunity," Kerry shot back, "I'm not giving into blackmail, am I?"

"You're not being candid, either. You need to speak to the American people without a filter. The *Washington Post* aside, Barbara Walters is *not* such a terrible idea. If you can tell the public what you've gone through, with the appropriate references to human infallibility and your own belief in God, they'll hear you . . ."

Clayton turned to her. "The media age," he interjected, "is so permeated with bad taste that we're forgetting what good taste is. No matter how they say it, how do the President and First Lady keep their audience from cringing? How do *they* keep from cringing?

"We'd need an identifiable enemy to redirect the focus. An interview might work if we had enough evidence to blame the SSA. But without proof we'd only be making the SSA look like the victim of two maudlin demagogues slandering American patriots—in this case, to cover their own immorality." He turned to Kerry. "Then consider the Senate. You know how hard this fight over guns has been on swing-state Democrats. For the people who've stuck with you against their better judgment, it may not be enough to criticize your morals. They may feel the need to override your veto."

"And so?"

"A lot of people hate the media. They won't like whoever puts this out. Once they do, we answer with a brief and dignified statement, then hope the story starves for lack of oxygen."

"They won't let it die," Kit demurred. "The right wing *or* the media."

"Then let them wallow in their own shit until the American people turn away in boredom and disgust. What else is there to do once the President acknowledges the truth, and regrets the environment in which such a private matter is fodder for the press." Facing the Kilcannons, Clayton spoke softly. "I'm truly sorry for what you'll have to go through. I know it's easier for us to tell you what to do than for you to do it. But Lara is one of the most admired First Ladies in recent history, and you're both objects of great sympathy. You'll receive more sympathy for handling this with grace, and for drawing the line." Clayton paused, eyes glinting. "I think this story will damn whoever touches it. If *I* were President, I'd consider leaking the story to Fasano, then blaming him when it comes out."

"There's a certain appeal in that," Kerry answered with the flicker of a smile. "But when does it ever end?"

Clayton shrugged. "I suppose," Kit ventured gamely, "that the announcement of a pregnancy is way too much to hope for."

No one answered. Kit hesitated, and then faced Kerry again. "There's one more option," she said bluntly, "and someone has to raise it.

"I agree with Clayton: guns are a hard issue, even with all that's happened. Gun immunity's an even harder issue, especially when it's mixed with tort reform—a lot of people don't like lawsuits, and Democrats pay the price." Pausing, Kit appeared to steel herself once more. "As of now, you've got a single vote in the Senate standing between you and a veto override. We need to ask: is this the issue, and the time, that we want to risk a scandal in exchange for a 'victory' against tort reform that a lot of Democratic senators never wanted in the first place?"

"In other words," Kerry said, "give in to blackmail for the good of the party. Not to mention my own."

"I understand, Mr. President," Kit responded evenly. "But you *are* President, with a responsibility to look beyond your own feelings, to facts. The facts are different than they were this morning."

The room fell silent. Taking Lara's hand, Kerry asked her, "Do we have anything else to add?"

His wife gazed at him, weary but unwavering. "Only

that if you decide to give in to blackmail, there'll *be* no end to this."

The President turned to Kit and Clayton. "Thank you," he said. "We'll let you know what we decide."

FIVE

AFTER A FEW HOURS of fitful sleep, Lara called her sister.

It was five-thirty in San Fráncisco. "What's wrong?" Mary asked in a voice slurry with sleepiness and anxiety.

With as much dispassion as she could muster, Lara told her.

Finishing, she awaited a response. "You had an abortion?" Mary said in obvious wonder. "I didn't know."

To Lara, this statement of perplexity carried the faintest hint of being slighted—that, as always, Lara had held herself aloof, as the distant, superior sister who offered help, or direction, but needed nothing from her family. "No one knew," she answered. "This wasn't just about me, but about Kerry. I couldn't tell anyone."

"Except a stranger," Mary gently amended.

This allusion to the abortion counselor who had betrayed her reopened the wound anew, threatening Lara's precarious calm. "Mary," she said in a strained voice, "my world was coming apart. I'd fallen in love with a married senator I was covering as a reporter, and suddenly I was pregnant. I did what I thought was best—for Kerry even more than me. But I was sure it was the end for us, and had to be. That was why I took the NBC job overseas. If I'd thought that you, or anyone, could fix all that . . ."

Her voice trailed off in a memory of hopelessness. "You could have come to us," Mary insisted. "We were your family."

"Maybe," Lara conceded, "I could have come to you. But knowing about my abortion would have broken our mother's heart." Hearing herself, Lara heard emptiness and evasion. The stark truth was that she had never considered leaning on her sisters, or believed that they would understand. Perhaps, she thought sadly, pride of place had become her habit, the duty of perfection a form of spiritual imprisonment. And then another thought struck her, so glaring now that she wondered at her failure to see it as clearly as she needed to when it would have mattered most. Just as Kerry's life had been defined by being James's younger brother, Lara, to the detriment of them all, had been her sisters' James Kilcannon. "Mary," she began again, "having me for a sister has cost you too much already. I don't want you to pay for this as well. That's why I'm telling you now."

"Because you're not sure Kerry can protect my lawsuit."

The quiet statement, with its echoes—perhaps intended, perhaps not—of his inability to protect their family made Lara pause again. "If you take this money," she answered, "I don't think Kerry can hold the Senate. But if you turn it down, and this comes out, you both may lose. That's not something I could keep from you."

"What if he doesn't veto it? That's what they want him to do."

The question drove home how unwilling Lara was to imagine this. "Then we all lose," she said simply. "But I won't let him do it on my account. For me, I'd rather face whatever happens."

For a moment, her sister said nothing. Then, still quietly, she asked, "If you were *me*, Lara, what would you do?"

Replaying the question, Lara searched her sister's tone for irony, and could detect none. "I'm not you," she answered. "I can't begin to know. All that I can promise is to love you, and never to judge whatever you decide."

Pausing, Lara suddenly realized how much she needed this to be true, and fought against the tremor in her voice.

"We're all that's left of Mama, Joanie, and Marie. I don't care what you do about the lawsuit. What I need from you is love and understanding and forgiveness for what my marriage has brought upon our family."

In Mary's silence, Lara sensed that hearing this surprised her as much as, seconds before, saying it had surprised Lara. "Are you going to be okay?" Mary asked with a curious timidity. "You and Kerry, I mean."

Lara realized that, in all of her imaginings, she had shrunk from imagining that which was most personal, and most important. "I don't know," she answered softly. "It's so hard to know how all this will turn out for us."

"I'm sorry," Mary said with equal softness—whether in condolence, or in apology for what she was about to do, Lara could not tell.

Sequestered in the residence to ponder his decision, his cover a spurious sore throat which required Ellen Penn to stand in at a breakfast sponsored by the Council on Foreign Relations, Kerry felt himself diminishing moment by moment.

"How did Mary take it?" he asked Lara.

"She was kind." Lara sat beside him on the couch. "I realize I'm so used to listening for an undercurrent of blame or resentment I may supply one where there is none. But I've got no idea what she'll decide, and I told her it was up to her. I guess that just leaves us."

Kerry studied her face, the bruises of sleeplessness which reminded him, with an intensity so piercing that he still flinched from it, of the days and nights which had followed the murders. "What do you think?" he inquired.

"That what would help me the most is winning. The next best thing is doing all we can."

The flicker of harsh memory lingered in Kerry's mind.

"That's what I thought I was doing for Joanie—all I could. Even when we decided to go public about Bowden. And look what's come of it."

Lara touched his face. "There's something about deconstructing your own guilt," she told him, "that puts other people's in perspective. Consider all the trouble you'd have saved yourself by deciding not to marry me."

Kerry managed to smile. "Oh, I knew better. I just couldn't help myself."

"Neither could I." Lara paused. "You took a chance because you loved me. So did I, because I was too selfish not to love you back. I even thought that, once we had a child, we could put the hurt of my abortion behind us."

This was something she had never put into words. It touched him more than he could tell her, even as he reflected on the sad, retrospective innocence of her wish to heal damage which was dwarfed by that which followed. "Instead, we're here," he answered. "So what do I do now?"

"What you always intended to do—veto the Civil Justice Reform Act. The only questions are when you do that, and how—or whether—you tell the world about us."

Braced by her dispassion, Kerry knit together his thoughts. "The 'when' part is simple—I wait out the eight days I've got left before I veto the bill, and pray that we can somehow pin this on the SSA."

Lara's expression betrayed that she felt little hope of this. "And the rest?"

Kerry took both of her hands in his. "First, I want you to believe me about something—that the reason I don't want you crawling across ground glass on national television involves more than male pride, or even love for you. It's about who we are, or should be. Once you allow someone to violate your own best sense of that, you're no one. That's fatal in a person—or a President.

"Clayton knows me far better than Kit. What he was

doing, though he'd never say it, was speaking to who I am, and who I need to be." Kerry looked at her intently. "I think he was speaking for you, as well. If we don't draw the line for ourselves, how will we feel later? And what validation will we be giving to whoever decides to victimize the next First Family, or the next? What public act of contrition will they have to perform in order to top ours? However we leave this place, I don't want that to be our legacy."

"Then it won't be," Lara answered. "Whatever else."

SIX

AT NINE THE NEXT morning, Sarah sat next to Lenihan at Bond's red mahogany conference table. Glancing at Nolan and Fancher, she pondered the twelve-million-dollar offer from Charles Dane which neither knew of. Mary Costello's dilemma was as complex, and as delicate, as any Sarah could imagine.

"The first order of business," Bond said, "is to set some dates. First, for hearing defendants' summary judgment motions. And then, should the Court deny them, for a trial."

Silent, Sarah shot an untrusting glance at Lenihan. Since his effort to settle the case around her, they had struck a wary truce, agreeing that Mary's interests—whether in going to trial or further enhancing the settlement offer—were best served by stepping up the pressure on Lexington and the SSA. Part of this strategy was to appear unfazed by politics. After all, as Sarah's hasty reading of this morning's *Times* had confirmed, with three days left for a veto message no senators seemed inclined to switch their votes. If that held—and Sarah could not see why it wouldn't—the Senate would sustain Kilcannon's veto.

"Give us George Callister," Lenihan said on cue, "and we're ready to move swiftly. His deposition's all we need to oppose the defendants' motions, or prepare for an early trial. Frankly, I wish we were deposing him tomorrow. If Lexington hadn't held him out so long, we'd be in trial right now. As matters stand, and subject to your convenience, we're prepared to respond to any motions within five days of his appearance, and to go to trial two weeks later."

"This case is too complex for that," Nolan began in protest.

"Really?" Bond interjected tartly. "You've given me the impression that it was simple. The words 'frivolous' and 'groundless' leap to mind."

"If aggregated in sufficient bulk," Nolan rejoined, "even frivolous arguments and groundless assertions demand a detailed rebuttal. Preparing our motions will require more time than Mr. Lenihan proposes."

"Which brings us back to Mr. Callister," the judge replied. "Five days ago I gave you two weeks to produce him, and plaintiff's counsel complains that they still don't have a date—let alone a mutually convenient venue." Bond's tone combined patience with a trace of judicial testiness. "I've given you all of the discovery you've asked for, whenever you asked for it—often at considerable inconvenience to Mr. Lenihan and Ms. Dash. So where do things sit with Callister?"

Sarah expected Nolan to commence a mournful litany of difficult logistics, the intricacies of Callister's extended business travels, and then ask for another week—giving the Senate sufficient time, should Senator Fasano muster the votes, to override the President's veto. Bond knew this very well: in Sarah's estimate, the judge's show of huffing and puffing was only that. In the end, Nolan would innocently wonder aloud what possible difference one more week could make to Mary Costello, and Bond would give him the sternest of warnings that *this* was his last delay. Merely another piece of theater, a moment from Gilbert and Sullivan.

"Mr. Callister," Nolan responded calmly, "is willing to interrupt his travels to assuage the Court's concerns."

Turning to Lenihan and Sarah, he asked, "Would five business days from now, in San Francisco, meet your needs?"

Three days past the veto deadline. Astonished, Sarah briefly thought to press for an even earlier date, but could find no basis for complaining. Nor, it seemed, could Lenihan.

"Cat got your tongue?" Bond asked him. "Or do you want to hold the deposition in your living room?"

Lenihan glanced at Sarah. "No, Your Honor. Our San Francisco office will do just fine."

"Good, Mr. Lenihan. Then let's thrash out the remaining dates."

Moments later, leaving the judge's chamber, Sarah glanced over her shoulder. "What was *that* about?" she whispered. "I expected to depose Jimmy Hoffa before we saw George Callister. Why so amenable at the eleventh hour?"

Lenihan grimaced. Pointedly, he answered, "Maybe somebody from Nolan's firm reviewed all of our discovery with Callister, and reassured themselves that he's a complete dry hole. Which bears on our next appointment, doesn't it?"

Both fell silent. Their next appointment was with Mary Costello, and it overshadowed the conundrum of George Callister. Once more, Sarah and Lenihan would be adversaries; today was the deadline for responding to Dane's offer.

They met in Sarah's office. Even by the standards of her prior behavior—quiet, confused, often overwhelmed—Mary Costello seemed unusually subdued. But then, Sarah supposed, not many women had been offered eight million dollars in exchange for their murdered relatives.

"This is it," Lenihan told her. "Not just the deadline, but

defendants' moment of maximum uncertainty, and your moment of maximum leverage. The President's poised to veto the bill; Callister's set for deposition; the trial date's set in stone. That may be good for a couple of million more."

"If the President can hold his veto," Sarah retorted, "your leverage will mushroom exponentially. Lexington and the SSA do *not* want a public trial, with our evidence trumpeted in the media, and neither does Fasano. Even if you decide to settle—and I hope you won't—don't do it now. Do it on the eve of trial."

Mary gazed at her so steadily that it seemed artificial, an effort of will. Sarah had a curious memory: that she herself had used this expression as a teenager, when she'd tried concealing something from her mother. To her dismay, Sarah wondered if Lenihan and Mary had reached some private understanding, and that this meeting was yet another charade that only Sarah could not comprehend.

"Mary," Lenihan countered with quiet insistence, "the leverage Sarah imagines will exist only if the President wins. If he loses, and he still may, this *lawsuit* ceases to exist. There'll be no money, no trial, no justice for your family . . ."

"Is a sealed settlement 'justice for her family'?" Sarah asked. "A secret payment in return for a dismissal, perhaps dooming the President's chances of sustaining a veto? Instead of trying to save lives, Mary would be helping the SSA to keep anyone else from suing the gun industry, ever. So why don't we call this what it is, Bob—blood money."

A flush crept across Lenihan's neck. "At least the SSA will have paid for what happened. They'll know it, and Mary will know it. There are a thousand ways to dedicate some of this money to the memory of Inez, Joan, and Marie, ways that would have touched them."

How many ways, Sarah wanted to ask, can you say

'venal'? She felt the clutch of her stomach, and then, glancing at Mary, decided that silence was more eloquent than speech.

Head lowered, Mary was rubbing her eyes. Even Lenihan knew enough to join Sarah in her quiet.

They both watched Mary for some moments. Then, squaring her shoulders, Mary looked up at Lenihan, her voice quiet but clear. "I just can't do it," she told him. "No matter what."

Sarah felt a brief spurt of elation. But there was no defiance in Mary's words, no hope of a public triumph. Only a curious resignation, a note of weary fatalism. Perhaps the torment of this decision had exhausted her but, if only for her own sake, Sarah selfishly wished for a greater show of spirit.

Lenihan saw this at once. "Exactly what are you saying, Mary?"

"That it's wrong to take money from these people." A hint of steel crept into Mary's voice. "Tell them that for *me*."

For the two days after Lenihan's call, Charles Dane worked the phones, pressuring Fasano, cajoling senators to switch their votes. The surface of Washington—including what Dane alone felt as an eerie silence from the White House—remained unchanged.

On the final day, Kerry Kilcannon appeared in the White House press room. "This morning," he began, "I have vetoed the Civil Justice Reform Act . . ."

SEVEN

ONE DAY AFTER the veto, at a time which assured that it would consume the newspapers and airwaves for the next twenty-four hours, the story struck.

Shortly after eight o'clock in the morning, a wan Kit Pace appeared in the President's office and handed him copy from a right-wing Internet columnist. Its narrative was devastating: that Kerry was married when his relationship with Lara began; that they had commenced a "two-year clandestine affair" while Lara had covered Capitol Hill for the *New York Times;* that Lara had become pregnant; that she had "aborted Senator Kilcannon's unborn child"; that she had exiled herself by taking an overseas assignment to preserve his political future; that after Kerry's subsequent divorce, "having laundered their secret, Kilcannon and Costello presented themselves as newly involved, concealing the truth so that they could seek election as America's sweethearts"; and, finally, that "their presence as First Couple is the result of cold-blooded infanticide and a coolheaded deception designed not only to disguise their moral unfitness but to endear themselves to an unsuspecting electorate." The story was accompanied by a verbatim transcript of the counselor's notes from her postabortion interview with Lara, still dazed from anesthesia, her torrent of emotion recorded under the veil of supposed confidence.

Kerry had never seen the notes. The devastation he found there evoked the visceral memory of his own desperation—making call after call which went unanswered;

pleading with Lara through her voice mail to save their child; rushing to her apartment to find her gone; her final call to him, once it was done, to say that they had loved each other, that neither had intended harm, that their relationship was finished, that Lara was going away. "I have to start over," had been her final words. "Please, if you still love me, the one gift you can give me is not to make it harder . . ." Then her voice had broken off, just before the click of her telephone preceded a dial tone.

Looking up, Kerry knew at once that Kit had read it all. Within hours, the embarrassment and pain he could see on her face would be reflected, often with less charity, in the hearts and minds of every American within the reach of a television, or radio, or computer, or telephone, or newspaper, or of any friend, neighbor, coworker or stranger at a grocery store who had heard the story first. All that his adversaries had needed to do they had done: the Internet column was a pebble dropped in an electronic pond, and its ripples would swiftly reach the water's edge.

"I've already prepared copies of our statement," she told him. "If we don't get it out now, the Bob Woodward game will start—a media free-for-all, with thousands of reporters competing for new details. At least this way the story will lead with what you have to say."

Gazing at the counselor's notes, Kerry shook his head. "I don't think our statement covers this. It's not enough now."

When Kit had gone, Kerry called Lara and, a few difficult moments later, Minority Leader Chuck Hampton. Then he picked up a legal pad and swiftly scrawled some notes.

At nine-fifteen, the President appeared in the White House press room. A stunned Frank Fasano watched his office television with Senator Paul Harshman; Fasano had known of the story for less than twenty minutes and he was still absorbing, with no little sense of dread, the pattern and meaning of the events which now enveloped Kerry Kilcannon.

Kilcannon looked somber but composed. *I have a brief statement to make,* he began. *I will not be taking questions.*

"My God," Fasano said, "it's true."

"Of course it's true," Harshman answered with grim asperity. "The only value he's ever held is accumulating power."

The caustic remark, Fasano found, induced a brief reflexive sympathy for the President he opposed—even in the face of personal conduct which appalled him. On television, the slightest edge of disdain entered Kilcannon's voice. *Ten days ago,* the President continued, *Senator Jack Slezak came to the White House. He said that he'd received a warning—anonymous, he assured me—that if I vetoed the Civil Justice Reform Act certain facts regarding my life before becoming President would be made public.*

Dane, Fasano thought. Only this could explain the confidence with which Dane had assured him that Kilcannon would be beaten. Glancing at Harshman, Fasano surmised that he did not know. Through deliberate hints, Dane had wanted Fasano to discern—at the same time as Kerry Kilcannon—the secret behind Kilcannon's ruin and, to that extent, for Fasano to be complicit in the SSA's hidden exercise of power. Never again would Fasano doubt the risks of defying Charles Dane.

Yesterday, Kilcannon said, *I vetoed that bill. This morning an Internet columnist printed a story regarding my relationship to Lara prior to our engagement. In all factual respects—as opposed to its characterization of our motives or emotions—that story is true.*

"Even the abortion," Fasano murmured. In his soul, he

believed that abortion was the taking of human life; in the most graphic way, this illustrated the gulf between Fasano and a man he often thought to be devoid of spiritual values—a Catholic who passed himself as personally devoted to the teachings of their Church; a President who "reluctantly" distinguished between his religious beliefs and what government could dictate in the realm of private conduct; an adulterer who—in the hidden recesses of his life—cared nothing for the life of his own child. With unsparing self-knowledge, Fasano realized that his disgust over Kilcannon's acts soon would distance him from his visceral horror at Dane's use of them, enabling him to coldly assess their impact in the public sphere.

"It's over with," he murmured. "Certainly this veto, and maybe even his Presidency."

"If we don't take the lead," Harshman answered, "we don't deserve to be senators." Weighing Harshman's words, Fasano reflected on how difficult it would be to walk the public line between disapproval and savagery in a way which served his goals. Once more, he focused on the President.

But there is a deeper truth, Kilcannon said firmly. *Personal lives are as complex as the reasons that people are happy, or sad. I'm lucky to have met the woman I was meant to be with. I don't think I need explain the hows or the whys, or that Lara need discuss with anyone a decision which—in simple decency—other women are allowed to make in private.*

" 'In simple decency,' " Harshman repeated with scorn. But the background buzz of astonishment from the press corps had yielded to silence.

In any life, the President continued, *there are decisions which keep us up at night, long after they are made. There are decisions which others would make differently. But I do not think a public burning should be the price of a public career. I trust the American people to judge us on how we fulfill the public responsibilities they have given us.* Pausing, Kilcannon looked unflinchingly into the camera. *For our part, we will do our best. But as to this deeply private matter, we have nothing more to say.*

With this, he turned, heading for the exit. *Mr. President,* a woman's voice called out, *does this mean that Mrs. Kilcannon will cease to be a spokesperson regarding the gun issue?*

The President kept walking. Then, abruptly, he turned, fixing his inquisitor with a long cold stare. *I really did mean nothing,* he said. *To you or anyone. You'll have to do without us.*

With that, Kilcannon left the room.

"Well?" Harshman inquired.

"No one said he lacks for nerve." Pausing, Fasano made his tone imperative. "I want the leadership in my office—now. We need to be disciplined, and let other people do whatever damage there's left to do. I don't want our senators on CNN before we've assessed the public mood."

"Don't you think," Harshman objected, "that we should lead the public mood?"

Fasano appraised him. "Have you stopped to wonder just where this story came from? I'll bet Kilcannon has. You may remember my predecessor, the once-powerful Macdonald Gage." He slowed his speech to underscore each word. "Suppose Kilcannon finds whoever planted the story. If that happens, you won't want to be their Siamese twin. So do me—and yourself—a favor, Paul. Shut up."

Before Harshman could respond, Fasano's intercom buzzed. "You'd better drop whatever you're doing," his Chief of Staff said tersely. "Hampton's taking the floor."

In the minute or so it took Fasano to lope from his office to the Senate's swinging door, Chuck Hampton had begun.

"I can't speak to the President's and First Lady's personal life," he told the Senate, "except to say that it's their business, not mine. The President was typically candid and direct, and the line he has drawn is one that we can all respect. Because of this, I fully trust that today's events will not affect his relationship to the members of this body."

You have every right to hope, was Fasano's mordant thought—he could hear the strain of the moment in Hampton's voice, detect the shock his counterpart must be feeling. This moment was pivotal to Hampton's leadership. In Fasano's wake, a steady stream of senators was repopulating the chamber—now Vic Coletti and Cassie Rollins—creating the crackle of crisis and drama.

"Blackmail," Hampton said in a rising voice, "is deplorable, and whoever did this is despicable. Whoever did this must *not* know Kerry Kilcannon.

"No gutter tactics can cause this President to back down. No blackmailer too cowardly to show his face in public can change the merits—or the *de*merits—of the Civil Justice Reform Act."

Hampton, Fasano realized, was making a credible effort to cauterize the damage and keep his troops in line. Next to Fasano, Macdonald Gage had appeared, appraising Hampton with a cool eye which did nothing to conceal Gage's pleasure at the harsh recompense now visited on the President who had tarnished him so effectively.

"We can only hope," Hampton told the Senate, "that this act of viciousness will not drain further public life of all decency or compassion. For if compassion attached itself only to perfection, there would be little mercy for any of us."

"How true," Gage said with quiet bitterness. "And how convenient for Hampton to remember that now." But Fasano heard a moral different from that which Gage intended: Gage had stood too close to the man who had destroyed Chad Palmer's daughter, and Kilcannon had made him pay for it. Fasano had no intention of joining his predecessor in the ranks of the walking dead.

Hampton's eyes scanned the chamber, almost full now. "The current Hobbesian state of nature which pervades our political life—the survival not of the fittest, but the most vicious; the use of scandal through the media by groups or individuals bent on destroying their ideological opponents—threatens to drive the higher decencies from public life. It has, and will, cost us the services of good men and women of exemplary public character. And it causes, like the slow, repeated dripping of water on a stone, the erosion of all forgiveness, all ability to value others for the whole of who they are. Martin Luther King was an adulterer, and he taught a nation to be far better than we were . . ."

"Martin Luther King," Gage scoffed under his breath. "Why not Jesus Christ himself? If Chuck's desperate enough to exhume old Martin's tired sins, Kilcannon's beyond saving . . ."

But Fasano was not yet—not quite—sure.

Leaving the Senate after Hampton's speech, Palmer took the Senate subway through the grey subterranean corridors which traversed the bowels of Congress. His fellow senators and their aides were as grim as cave dwellers uncertain of the environment in the greater world beyond.

Cassie Rollins sat beside him in the open car. "What did you think?"

Chad turned to her. Very softly, he said, "That I hoped never to see anything like this again."

Nodding, Cassie touched his arm. Their quiet lasted until the subway reached its destination.

Entering the elevator, Chad asked, "Care to watch some cable news?"

"Thanks. It might be good to get an initial reading on the echo chamber."

The corridor near Chad's office was jammed with reporters, Minicams, microphones. "What did you think of the President's statement?" someone asked the two senators.

Cassie shook her head. Sweeping by the swarm of media, Chad snapped brusquely, "Chuck Hampton said it for me. You can run clips of him in my place."

As they reached the inner sanctum of his office, Cassie murmured, "Frank won't like that."

"Fuck Fasano. All he bought was my crummy vote, not the right to turn me into a prick like Harshman." Palmer grabbed the remote and materialized CNN.

A half hour of CNN reassured Fasano that, as he had fervently hoped, the SSA was remaining silent. It was left to the Reverend Bob Christy, avuncular head of the Christian Commitment, to set the tone for the right-wing drumbeat that would consume every minute between the President's announcement and the last moment of *Nightline* and, in the endless frontiers of cyberspace, beyond.

Christy addressed the interviewer from his office in Charlotte, North Carolina. *Paula,* he admonished, *this is not a private matter. It goes to the heart of the immoral policies advocated by this President and this First Lady.*

How much better, now, do we understand the nomination of the pro-abortionist Caroline Masters to lead our highest court?

How much more clearly do we discern the true depth—in every sense of the word—of our President's all-too-personal commitment to the taking of unborn life?

How much more naked, now, is the contradiction between our First Lady's concern for "saving lives" when the murderer has a gun, and the taking of an innocent life which God himself had placed into her hands . . .

There was no turning back, Fasano knew. Not when even a sanctimonious blowhard like Bob Christy could touch the viscera of Fasano's own deepest convictions. Dane had played this brilliantly: the armies of the cultural right—the fundamentalists, the antiabortionists, the avatars of traditional values—were as essential to his party as the SSA and, in their fresh revulsion for Kilcannon, would demand no less than his emasculation. It was now Fasano's unavoidable task to accomplish this while maintaining the aura of a statesman.

The appalling truth, the Reverend Christy was saying, *is that Lara Kilcannon used her own family to promote a cynical, secular, antilife, pro-government agenda, asking us to mourn for her six-year-old niece after killing her own unborn child . . .*

Fasano turned him off.

EIGHT

AT ONE O'CLOCK that afternoon, Fasano took a call from Charles Dane.

The media was in full cry, although not, thanks to Fasano's crisp directions, with the help of a single Republican senator. Nor, as of yet, had any Democrats save Hampton leapt to the President's defense. On CNN, a pro-life woman sparred with the president of a leading pro-choice group, personifying the war of ideologies which, Fasano thought, would inevitably diminish the Kilcannons by virtue of its subject matter.

"It appears," Dane said blandly, "that God has smiled on us."

The irony held a pointed subtext—the deliberate intimation, in Fasano's view, of their mutual complicity. "Have you and God been in touch?" Fasano could not resist asking.

"No need, Frank. He speaks to me through the Reverend Christy. The Christian Commitment is going national with ads calling the Kilcannons morally unfit to lead us. Your political base hasn't been so galvanized since Kilcannon crammed Caroline Masters down their throats." Dane's tone became imperative. "They understand that overriding Kilcannon's veto is their first chance to strike while this is hot. Gun rights is now the issue which will break the little bastard for good and all."

Beneath this conversation, Fasano thought, was another: that Dane had set Kilcannon's downfall in motion; that Fasano's tacit knowledge made Dane the new proprietor of a corner of his soul; that—at least for this political moment—Fasano must carry out the SSA's directives. "My obligation is to win," Fasano parried, "not to schedule the quickest possible vote to override.

"On the final vote for passage, I carried our entire caucus except for Leo Weller. Kilcannon only had thirty-four votes—all Democrats. The votes you need may have to come from there. Before I schedule an override vote, I want to know that the votes are there."

"*Vote,*" Dane snapped. "Singular. Weller's ripe for the picking—this scandal gives him cover for turning on Kilcannon, a distraction from his screwup on asbestos. Schedule the override and we'll make sure you win. All *you* need to do is keep Palmer and your fucking moderates in line, and get this done. Then the very next order of business will be defeating Kilcannon's gun bill."

Dane's insistence on haste made Fasano wonder again whether something about the Costello lawsuit concerned him or, now, whether Dane worried that this morning's scandal might in time be laid at his door. But there was objective sense in his demand. In the aftershock of Kilcannon's exposure, the political leverage belonged to Fasano, not Kilcannon, increasing the pressure on Fasano to deliver for the forces whose support he needed to become President himself. Dane had devised the perfect trap, pitting him against Kilcannon like two scorpions in a bottle.

"Deliver me Leo," Fasano told him, "and you'll get your instant vote."

It was nearly six before Cassie Rollins arrived at Fasano's office. Winter darkness had fallen, and the black rectangle of Fasano's window framed a distant, spotlit view of the Mall. Somehow Cassie knew that it was cold outside.

"Well?" Fasano inquired.

The monosyllable carried the reminder of her betrayal on gun immunity, an intimation that she must earn her way back into her leader's good graces or face banishment to some senatorial Siberia—or worse, the humiliation of a primary loss, the end to her career in politics.

"How are you going to play this?" was Cassie's blunt response. "We can't keep quiet forever."

Fasano shook his head. "My staff's preparing a statement. You can read it if you like."

"Give me the Cliff Notes."

"The A-words—adultery and abortion—never cross my lips. This problem is a lack of candor, and its real victim is the American people, including the next generation, who are losing trust in those who seek to lead them. As for me, I don't want to dwell on the President's personal life. I'm simply 'as disappointed as I expect the rest of the country is.' "

It was shrewd, Cassie thought. "No freelancing," Fasano continued, "from Paul or anyone. I'll expect all of you to 'echo the sentiments expressed by the Majority Leader' and then soberly proceed to override Kilcannon's veto, and send his gun bill to defeat. That should about do it for his Presidency."

Balling a fist, Cassie rested it beneath her chin. "Where do you suppose this story came from?"

Fasano shrugged. "The important thing is that nobody think that we played any part in it. That's why we all need to be as sober as an undertaker."

"That won't be hard for me," Cassie answered quietly. "I feel sorry for the Kilcannons—both of them. From what I can see, every conservative so-called journalist is swarming to Fox News to complain about Lara's ethics. But in my experience with her as a reporter she always played it completely straight. No one's ever claimed that she cut Kerry any breaks."

Fasano gave her a wintry smile. "Or Kilcannon's former wife."

"Believe me, Frank, I'm not going to be out defending their affair. But if a lifetime of marital fidelity were the test of fitness to serve in the Senate, there'd be only you and me left to turn out the lights. And that's only because I've never been married."

Fasano's smile compressed. "I don't love this, either. But we didn't make Kilcannon do it, and this is business. Where do *you* stand on his veto?"

"Where I stood before. I don't like gun immunity, but on balance I favor the final bill. So you've got my vote to override." Cassie gazed at him intently. "As for what's happening to the President, I don't like the feel of it. Not just because of the blackmail and whose interests it serves—a thought which, by the way, does *not* lead me to the Chamber of Commerce or their friends in the business community. It's that there are too many moving parts here, too much I don't know."

"And never will, I suspect. Nor will I."

Eyes narrowing, Cassie studied her nails. "There's something else," she said. "Lara exercised a right I happen to believe in, and now the President's being pilloried for it. My reading was that most of his statements in favor of choice were shot through with ambivalence." She looked up at Fasano. "Now I think I know why. If I had to guess, I'd say that Lara did it on her own, and that Kilcannon's refusing to say so."

"What?" Fasano said with incredulity. "You're suggesting that he wanted her to have a child and ruin his career? But that *now* he's too noble to say so? How many death wishes can someone that ambitious entertain?"

"You and I," Cassie responded, "have always disagreed

about the nature of Kerry Kilcannon. I contend he has a soul—unlike many of our colleagues, I might add. That's why he and Chad always got along." Having delivered this veiled barb, Cassie changed subjects. "His motives aside, the President was clever about one thing. He got the story over with quickly—the press won't be trying to prove what he's already admitted. By tomorrow they'll be fixated on the identity of the blackmailer. Dollars to doughnuts it's someone who's a 'friend' of ours." She smiled briefly. "And Slezak's, Kilcannon seemed to imply. That would narrow the field a bit."

At once, Cassie saw this thrust strike home: Fasano's face became a mask, and his eyes froze on her face. He *knows*, she thought for a split second, and the instinct for self-preservation gripped her, the fear of standing too close to Fasano too soon. Then Fasano conjured a belated smile. "Why not just say what you mean, and get this off your chest."

It was a reminder that the subject was radioactive, and that a careless word, conveyed to the wrong person, could cost her a great deal. "I've said what I had to say," she answered.

Fasano's voice and manner changed abruptly. "Eleven days ago you crossed me on a leadership vote. The next one is on Kilcannon's gun bill. For you, I'd call it sudden death."

Cassie met his gaze. "Because the SSA will mount their primary challenge?" she inquired coolly. "So either they'll beat me there, or weaken me for a race against Abel Randolph. And you won't raise a finger, or a dime, to stop them."

"That's how it is."

"Not quite." Sitting back, Cassie drew a breath. "Believe me, Frank, I'm respectful of your position. But I'm less enamored of mine than I was when I woke up this morning. Tiptoeing through sewage does that to me.

"So you can tell the SSA to give me a little space. If you don't feel free to do that, then let them do their worst. Even if they disinter George Bolt and pump him full of embalming fluid, he won't beat me in a primary. And if *that* miracle occurs, there's no way on earth he'll defeat Abel Randolph in the general." Pausing, Cassie kept her voice more dispassionate than she felt. "That gives you two alternatives—a new Democratic senator who may threaten your majority, or one very disaffected female incumbent." Cassie smiled. "The last time our leadership fucked around with a Republican from New England, he left the party to become an independent. He seemed a whole lot happier than I feel right now."

Quiet, Fasano paused to appraise her sincerity. "Some people like being pariahs, Cassie. I don't sense that in you."

"Then give me a fit home, Frank. And the next time you want my vote, or anything from me, speak for yourself instead of for Charles Dane."

NINE

THE FOLLOWING MORNING, an overnight poll showed that fifty-three percent of respondents felt the President's effectiveness was impaired, and that twenty-seven percent favored resignation. But with no denial to fuel the story, speculation began to center on its origin. Jack Slezak had given a carefully orchestrated interview stressing that his purpose was not to promote blackmail by his unknown caller, but to allow the President "time to do the right thing in a difficult personal situation." Republicans had confined themselves to muted statements of disappointment and disapproval, leaving the calls for impeachment to the more fervid of the talking heads. Democrats, still finding their way, ventured the tepid defense that the President's preelection personal life should be separate from his Presidency. On the Senate floor, as morning business opened, Fasano called for a speedy vote to overturn the President's veto.

As Kerry watched on C-SPAN, Hampton responded. *Why this unseemly haste,* he asked the Senate, *where there is no deadline for an override except the end to this Congress itself, over a year from now? Are the proponents of gun immunity so desperate to extinguish Mary Costello's lawsuit? Are they so afraid that if the courtroom doesn't go dark until mid-trial it will be too late to conceal who bears the blame for the murder of six people? Why not wait for the judge and jury to decide?*

It was the best Hampton could do, Kerry thought— attempt to shift the spotlight from Lara to her sister, from abortion to the victims of gun violence. And it was a sad reminder of how much damage the President had sustained.

Speaking to the President by telephone, Hampton sounded worried but determined. "This could happen to you, I keep telling our people. If we don't step up, we'll all be hostage to whatever has happened in our personal lives for the rest of our public lives."

"How is that going down?"

"They understand. But they're worried about being associated with your so-called moral lapses. They're living in the here and now. What might happen to *them* will happen down the road."

"What about the override? Can we hold our votes?"

"I don't know. No one's told me they're jumping yet— they don't have an answer when I ask what this story has to do with gun immunity. But I'm getting foreplay from a couple of them, like Torchio and Spivey, softening me up for a potential fucking. More than a few are looking around, wondering who will be the first to flip." Hampton's tone admitted to his frustration. "The real problem's Weller—I imagine Fasano and the SSA are doing everything but plant a severed horse's head on his pillow. If he switches sides, there may be a deluge."

Kerry felt his own discouragement deepen. "Is there anything I can do?"

"Other than locating the blackmailer?" Hampton paused, as though groping for an answer. "You can make some private calls to senators. In your current position, public arm-twisting could blow up in your face."

Restless, Kerry stood. "I know that. But if we lose Weller, we need to pick up a vote somewhere."

Hampton hesitated. "Is there any way to force Slezak to tell the truth? After all, if someone saying he was the president of the AFL-CIO had really called Slezak's office, wouldn't his receptionist remember?"

"I've thought of that," the President answered. "But imagine the reaction if I turn the FBI loose on Slezak's office? The most his receptionist will say is that he or she doesn't remember a call from one of the most important figures in the country. Implausible to you and me, but an absolute dead end. Slezak's told the perfect lie—a phone call which never happened, which no one can disprove.

"Maybe the press will get this counselor to say who she gave her notes to. Maybe in *that* sphere I could even get the FBI involved, and try to trace this story to its source. But whoever *is* involved will lie as well, and the columnist who printed it will never reveal his source. In the meanwhile, I'd be accused of unleashing the Gestapo to distract attention from my sins. As a matter of practical politics, I have to save the FBI for later." Kerry began to pace. "Even if we let them loose, I doubt the FBI could trace the story before the vote to override my veto. Or even the vote on my gun bill." Pausing, Kerry finished, "That's happening next, I suppose."

"We think so." Hampton's tone was sardonic. "Fasano may be deeply saddened by what's happened to you, but he's adjusted rather quickly to its uses."

Kerry was quiet. What had saved him from dwelling on his own personal humiliation, and Lara's, was to focus on its political aspect, the fight to regain his standing in time to save his veto. Now his feelings overwhelmed him. "You know," he said, "I could have never imagined how this would be for Lara, or for me. Or how it would feel to have it define my Presidency."

Hampton was silent. Kerry guessed at his thoughts: that, burdened by this secret, Kerry should not have run for President; that Hampton had gone out on a limb for him, not knowing what could happen; that Hampton's life as

Minority Leader would be brutal, arrayed with a wavering caucus of Democratic senators against an implacable Frank Fasano and a now more compliant group of Republicans, and supported only by a President perhaps too wounded to survive. "Mr. President," Hampton said evenly, "I don't blame you for where we are. Frankly, you've been a better President than I thought you'd be—better, I'm now convinced, than Dick Mason would have been. You've given us more reason to be proud of our party than we've had in a good while."

For twelve years in the Senate, Kerry reflected, he and Hampton had been colleagues, but not friends. Now Kerry wondered why he had underrated Hampton's mettle, and undervalued his decency. "When you were my leader," Kerry told him, "I should have been a better soldier."

Softly, Hampton laughed. "Good soldiers," he said, "don't always make good Presidents. Chad Palmer used to tell me that before he mislaid his soul."

At this mention of his friend and rival, Kerry faced again the dimensions of his problem. "We needed Chad on this," he said. "It would have helped."

"So it would have."

They both had spoken in the past tense, Kerry realized. He thanked the Minority Leader, and got off.

When her private line rang, Cassie Rollins picked up the phone herself. "Cassie," her caller said quietly, "it's Lara."

Startled, Cassie blurted, "I'm so sorry about what's happened."

"So am I," Lara replied. "I've been sorry for years, and now I'm even more sorry for Kerry than I was. He didn't want it to begin with."

At this revelation, so personal and painful, Cassie suppressed a sigh—the meaning of "it" was unmistakable.

"I'd guessed as much," Cassie said. "Not that it matters to me."

"That's why I called you. Better than most people, I understand the pressures you're under. I can't make them disappear, or even help. But what's happening is wrong, and we both know it."

"We do," Cassie agreed. "But it's also the world we seem to live in, I'm afraid."

"But should it be?" The First Lady stopped abruptly, taming the note of protest in her voice. "He doesn't know I'm calling, Cassie. I'm not even sure what I'm asking you to do. But it makes no sense to vote down Kerry's gun bill, or wipe out Mary's lawsuit over this."

"I understand," was all Cassie could say, except to wish the President and First Lady well. And so she did.

When, Fasano wondered, had Leo Weller begun shrinking? Perhaps the process had started with the trial lawyers and asbestosis, but a half hour with Charles Dane had left his colleague so stripped of his usual bluster that he seemed, quite literally, smaller. Even the residual shrewdness in his eyes reminded Fasano less of a crafty politician than a woods animal cornered by a predator.

Although he knew the answer, Fasano asked, "How was your talk with Dane?"

" 'With,' " Weller answered with wounded dignity. "You make it sound like a conversation. He reminded me they've got more money than the trial lawyers, and that there's no way I win a primary if they don't want me to. The kindest name he called me was 'capon.' I'm a United States Senator, Frank, not his fucking employee. I won't be treated like that."

Fasano mustered a look which combined sympathy and detachment. "That's what happens when you turn out to be *the* vote we need to override Kilcannon's veto. It's the perfect storm of political screwups, Leo. You've alienated the trial lawyers, your supporters in the asbestos industry, the SSA, and your own leadership in the Senate. Now you're standing on the precipice, staring into the abyss of a career even deader than Kerry Kilcannon's. It's not a spectacle I've enjoyed watching."

Sinking farther into Fasano's couch, Weller folded his arms. "It doesn't have to be like this."

"But it is like this," Fasano said, not unkindly. "You're not suggesting that you've never beaten someone senseless with their own mistake—real, or imagined? As I remember, you got here by accusing your opponent of 'flirting with the gay agenda' because he'd agreed to meet with somebody from the Human Rights Campaign—and only because his son, who *is* gay, asked him to hear them out. There's no one here who hasn't, at some time, been as tough as they needed. So why complain when the SSA feels aggrieved enough to do the same to you."

Unable to answer, Weller gave a shrug—part protest, part acknowledgment. "This is worse."

"Agreed," Fasano said, his tone a mixture of commiseration and curiosity. "Just how do you get out of it?"

Weller grimaced. "That's what I'm asking, Frank. The asbestos companies are pissed at me. If I vote against the SSA it's suicide. But if I vote *with* the SSA, then the trial lawyers come after me, and put all my dying constituents right back up on television."

And you want me to save you, Fasano thought. *The neatest trick since Lazarus was summoned back to life.*

"I can't grant you absolution," Fasano said. "Not from the SSA. But if you get out front, and switch your vote, you could precipitate the avalanche which buries Kerry Kilcannon. That could purchase a fair amount of amnesia from Charles Dane."

Slowly, Weller nodded. "But that leaves the asbestosis," he ventured.

Fasano feigned reflection. "That's where I can help, I think. Suppose you vote for the Civil Justice Reform Act, and then introduce a bill establishing a special fund for asbestosis victims and their families."

Weller cocked his head. "How would it work?"

"We'd have to think through the details. But once we get up a bill, Hampton can't oppose it and Kilcannon can't veto it. Because without lawsuits, your bill would be the families' best shot at a real recovery." Fasano smiled. "I can imagine that our Senatorial Campaign Committee might have an interest in running ads that show you meeting with grateful families. Who knows, the SSA might even finance a few of those itself."

That a cynic like Weller could look so genuinely grateful told Fasano how frightened he was. "Frank," he said in a voice filled with emotion, "I think that could really help."

"It just might," Fasano assured him comfortably. "I really would hate to lose you."

TEN

In the Oval Office, Kerry reviewed his phone messages. The last one, but the first the President answered, was from Senator Chad Palmer.

They had not spoken for weeks. "Weller's switching on tort reform," Chad said bluntly. "Fasano worked up some legislation to get him out from under asbestosis and the SSA. Fasano wants it secret until Leo meets the press tomorrow morning. But I thought you might care to know."

The magnitude of this understatement was exceeded only by the dire implications for Kerry's veto. In the House, where Speaker Jencks had set a vote for tomorrow, an override was certain, and now Fasano held a one-vote margin unless Kerry somehow found a way to steal one back. But as bad as this news was, the President was grateful to know it—what Fasano would define as Palmer's betrayal was, to Kerry, an act of grace.

"Thanks for calling," Kerry said simply. Chad did not put into words, and thus compel a response from Kerry, how sorry he was for what had happened to Kerry and Lara, or what seemed about to happen in the Senate.

"The Senate's close to terminal," Kerry told Lara. "I don't know how I can get that vote back."

This assessment was preface to what she was about to see—a TV spot hastily prepared by Lenihan's group, the Trial Lawyers for Justice. "Run it," she told him quietly.

Kerry pushed the remote button.

On the screen, the blurry faces of a man and a woman were slowly splattered with mud, each addition marked by a soft thud. And then, as slowly, the mud slid down the photograph, revealing Kerry and Lara.

This is what they've tried to do, the voice-over said, *to make you forget.*

"I can't believe this," Lara murmured.

As they watched, their own faces gradually morphed into a photograph from the wedding, Inez and Joan holding hands with Marie. The picture zoomed in on Marie in her frilly dress, bright-eyed with delight. Then, accompanied by the soft, repeated clicks of a camera, her face became that of David Walsh, then George Serrano, then Laura Blanchard. The picture froze on Laura, fresh-faced and blonde, a basketball trophy pressed to her cheek.

This is Laura Blanchard, the voice-over said. *One more life too important to forget.*

The *"Civil Justice Reform Act,"* the voice concluded with disdain. *It's not reform, and it sure as shooting isn't justice. Tell your senator to help uphold the President's veto.*

Lara folded her arms, gazing at the carpet. "Where do they want to run it?"

"Any state where we have a fighting chance to flip a senator, with the telephone number for each. I'm not sure I could stop Lenihan's people if I wanted to."

With this admission of his helplessness, Kerry faced how much he was diminished—the forces of money and power on the left were overtaking him as surely as the vast resources of the SSA had overtaken Fasano. "We're approaching the time," he told Lara, "where politicians are bit players, and Presidents reduced to props."

"Like my family is, you mean." She looked over at her husband. "Do you suppose Lenihan's still angling for a settlement?"

The quietly caustic inquiry captured her own despair. After a moment, Kerry asked, "What do you want to do about this?"

"Tell them to run it. We're well beyond worrying about our dignity, don't you think?" Her tone became hard. "I won't accept that my family died for nothing. We need to keep our votes in place, then pray for something better."

At seven that evening, the telephone in Sarah's office rang.

She was still preparing for Callister's deposition, scribbling notes into her typed outline. By mutual consent, though Lenihan's was somewhat condescending, they had agreed that Sarah would stand a better chance of lulling Lexington's president into some misstep than a notorious trial lawyer who would set George Callister's teeth on edge. Immersed in the intricacies of her design, she put down her ballpoint with reluctance.

"Sarah?" the now familiar voice said. "It's Lara Kilcannon."

Sarah hesitated, looking for a way to express her sympathy. "How are you?"

The First Lady laughed softly. "Lousy," she answered. "Angry. Heartsick. Embarrassed. Feeling guilty about Mary and terrible for Kerry. Scared to death that I'll wind up being part of the reason our society keeps on killing people. All the emotions that make life worth living."

Sarah was surprised—Lara's expression of her torment in black comedic terms made her seem at once more human, and more despairing, than the grieving but collected woman Sarah had first encountered. "I've been pretty worried myself," Sarah answered frankly. "For you, and about what could happen to this case."

"You should be. Back here, things are slipping."

"The Senate?"

"Yes. The vote's set in three days, and as of now we're going to lose."

"I've been so afraid of that." Sarah paused, sorting through her emotions. "Not just because of how hard we've tried, or even because of how Mary hung in with me when I didn't think she would. But because I know about the evidence.

"We have depositions sealed in a lead-lined vault that would keep the Senate from overriding the President's veto. But I can't make them public because of Bond's order. In the guise of keeping us from indulging in selective leaks, Bond and the defense lawyers are perpetrating a cover-up."

Lara was silent. "Can you take the depositions to the judge," she inquired at length, "and ask him to change his order?"

"Even if he were inclined to change it—which he never will—it's too late. I'd have to file a motion, allow time for the defendants to respond, and then go before the judge. There's just no way to do that in three days." Sarah felt the frustration of explaining to a nonlawyer how indifferent a court could be to the ends of justice. "Besides, what can I say—that I want Bond to release the depositions in order to tilt the Senate? He knows all about the Senate and what it means. That's why he's hiding the files beneath the pious pose that the law should be above such things."

"So there's nothing you can do," Lara persisted.

At once, it struck Sarah that Lara's query involved more than a desperate hope, and that her openness with Sarah involved far more than venting. Bluntly, Sarah said, "No matter how I feel, I can't release the files. Unless my law license goes, as well."

"I understand," Lara said simply.

This was offered with such promptness that Sarah wondered whether her answer had assumed more than the First

Lady had asked. "George Callister's tomorrow," Sarah told her with resignation. "All I can do is put my blinders on, and cross-examine him like it matters. What happens in the Senate is out of my control."

ELEVEN

AT NINE O'CLOCK the next morning, Sarah faced George Callister.

It was the last desultory moment before the deposition would commence. To one side of Callister was John Nolan and, separated by an empty chair, Harrison Fancher on behalf of the SSA. To Sarah's left, Robert Lenihan sipped water. Between the combatants was a silver carafe of coffee and Nolan's copy of the *New York Times*, displaying an article above the fold headed "Weller Expected to Switch on Tort Reform." The court reporter, young and strawberry blonde, hunched over her stenotype machine at the end of the table. Standing behind Sarah, a ponytailed technician in blue jeans and a T-shirt adjusted his video cam to focus on the witness.

Arranging her papers in front of her, Sarah surreptitiously studied the witness and his lawyer. With a casual air, Nolan chatted with Callister about the Super Bowl prospects of the New England Patriots, Callister's team of choice. As always, Nolan projected confidence, the entitlement of those accustomed to authority.

But Callister was different. For weeks, Sarah had imagined this elusive figure as a corporate version of Charles Dane, scornful of the process she was seeking to inflict on him. But the real man projected the practical aura of a midwesterner who would as happily tinker with an engine as populate a boardroom. He had a naturally gruff voice with the intonation of the Great Plains, a greying flattop to match, a nondescript blue suit, and freckled, thick-fingered hands which clasped the Styrofoam cup of coffee he brought in from the street. His grey eyes were level and his range of expressions did not lend themselves to social exaggeration. His responses to Nolan bespoke polite interest, his smile was measured, and he seemed to regard his lawyer with the detached but not unpleasant appraisal he had trained on Sarah at first meeting. He did not strike her as a man who was easily fooled, or rendered implausible in the eyes of a jury.

"Ready, gentlemen?" Sarah asked.

Callister glanced at his lawyer. "We are," Nolan answered, and the deposition began.

For the first ten minutes, Sarah established the preliminaries: that Callister was an engineer by training; that he had spent most of the adult portion of his fifty-six years in the American gun industry; that, less than a year ago, Lexington's British parent had hired him as CEO with a mandate to make the company both profitable and stable; that he had carefully reviewed the company's revenues and product line in order to chart his course. Then Sarah turned to the subject of the Lexington P-2.

"In your view," she asked, "what was the market for the P-2?"

"People who wanted firepower."

"Including criminals?"

Nolan placed a hand on Callister's sleeve. "Objection," he interjected. "Calls for speculation."

Sarah kept her eyes on the witness. "You may answer, Mr. Callister."

Callister smiled slightly. With the air of the good soldier, he responded, "You're asking me to speculate."

This would not be easy, Sarah thought—men of Callister's generation had not climbed the corporate ladder by disobeying orders, and this man knew very well the risks presented by this lawsuit. She settled in for hours of trench warfare.

"Are you aware," she said, "that tracing records compiled by the ATF indicate that—in the last two years—the P-2 has been used in more crimes than any other semi-automatic handgun?"

"I've seen those numbers," the witness answered calmly. "But you have to put them in perspective. Arguably, the P-2 outsells all of its competitors. If you sell more guns, more of them are likely to be misused."

Nolan, Sarah noticed, looked serene. Not only was Callister buttressing their defense, but he did so with a practical and nondefensive air which lent his answers credibility. "Did you," she continued, "also review Lexington's internal records of trace requests to assess the frequency of the P-2's use in crimes?"

"I did not."

"For what reason?"

Callister placed down his cup, contemplating his hands as he rubbed them together lightly. "Understand something, Ms. Dash. I've wanted to discontinue the P-2 almost since the moment I arrived. I didn't need to go rooting through our files."

Though direct and more than a little surprising, Callister's response, Sarah sensed, hinted at something unsaid. The answer—closely analyzed—was really no answer at all. Though her instincts were aroused, Sarah deferred until later the line of questioning this suggested. Instead, she asked, "Why did you want to stop making the P-2?"

"Two reasons." Callister's tone was impersonal but pointed. "It was drawing bad publicity, and attracting lawsuits like yours. Our industry's profit margins are too thin as it stands. The P-2 was becoming more of a problem than a solution to our problems."

There was nothing wrong with the gun, Sarah heard him saying—just with an ecology populated by gun controllers and trial lawyers. Little wonder that Nolan had chosen to produce him.

Sarah's coffee had become lukewarm. Nonetheless she sipped it, taking the moment to appraise the man in front of her while she searched for the question. Then she put down her mug, gazing at him closely.

"You just testified that you never examined trace requests received by Lexington regarding the use of the P-2 in crimes, is that right?"

"Yes."

"Did you ever *attempt* to do so?"

The ghost of a smile moved one corner of Callister's mouth, so quickly that Sarah wondered if she had imagined it. "Yes."

For the first time, Sarah felt her nerve ends stir. "And when was that?"

Any trace of humor vanished from Callister's face, and his level grey eyes turned cold. "After the First Lady's brother-in-law killed three members of her family and three other people who were in his way."

As Nolan watched the witness intently, Sarah asked, "Did you ask anyone to look for those records?"

"Mike Reiner."

"And what was the result?"

Folding his hands in front of him, Callister looked straight at Sarah. "Reiner told me that we had no policy about retaining trace requests."

"And therefore had none in your files?"

"That's what he reported."

"Did you believe him?"

Callister's eyes seemed chillier yet. "I believed that we had no policy. And that the records were gone."

Sarah felt Lenihan lean toward her, preparing to whisper

advice. "When you say 'gone,'" Sarah asked, "do you mean destroyed?"

"Yes."

"*Before* or *after* John Bowden killed six people?"

"I had no way of knowing." Pausing, Callister spoke in measured tones. "It's important to remember, Ms. Dash, that this occurred before you filed this lawsuit and served us with a demand for the records we're discussing."

In other words, as Sarah understood the answer, no one had obstructed justice. "Nonetheless," she inquired, "did you believe that Mr. Reiner himself had destroyed the records you asked for?"

Callister's eyes narrowed. "Before or after I requested them?"

Surprised, Sarah hesitated for an instant. "After."

"Again, Ms. Dash, I had no way of knowing."

Sarah placed both arms on the arms of her chair, leaning slightly forward. "Did you suspect that?"

Briefly, Callister hesitated. "Yes."

"For what reason?"

Nolan, she saw, looked hyperalert now, but lacked the grounds, or perhaps the inclination, to interfere with Callister's answer. "I asked for other records," the witness responded, "and was told that they were also missing."

"Told by whom?"

"Reiner."

"What records were those?"

"Records showing the volume of P-2s sold in states adjacent to California." Pausing, Callister added more pointedly, "Also the invoices showing where we'd shipped the murder weapon."

Sarah glanced at Nolan. "What did Mr. Reiner tell you?"

"That no effort had been made to retain them."

"Did you happen to ask Reiner," Sarah inquired with

the hint of a smile, "whether any effort had been made to *destroy* them?"

Callister frowned—less at the question, Sarah sensed, than at the intimation behind it. "Yes," he answered tersely.

"And what did Reiner say?"

"That he had no specific knowledge of what had happened to the records."

The edge of distrust in Callister's voice illuminated for Sarah an unexpected image of George Callister as a man caught in an environment he had begun to suspect was treacherous. "Aside from the disappearance of the records themselves, did you have any other reason to suspect that Reiner might be lying to you?"

"Objection," Nolan asserted. "Lack of foundation. I don't believe the record justifies an accusation of deliberate lying."

Slowly, Callister turned to his lawyer. "No," he said flatly. "I think 'lying' about covers it." Facing Sarah, he said, "Reiner and I had fundamental disagreements about the future of our company."

"Such as?"

"I wanted to discontinue making the P-2 *and* the Eagle's Claw bullet. In both cases, Reiner was adamantly opposed."

Abruptly, Sarah felt her litigator's field of vision open wide. "For what reason did you want to drop the Eagle's Claw?"

Callister paused to frame his answer. "In my view, its lethality exceeded our customers' requirements. Therefore the controversy involved in making such a bullet outweighed its utility.

"Reiner disagreed. In his view, the P-2 and Eagle's Claw were essential to our position in the marketplace. But the fact that I'm sitting here tends to validate my judgment."

The last two sentences hinted at disgust and a certain

weariness. It was the first time, Sarah noticed, that any of Callister's answers had clearly exceeded the scope of her question.

Nolan seemed to notice as well. "We've been going for over an hour," he suggested. "Why don't we take a break?"

It was fifteen minutes before the witness and his lawyer returned to the conference room. When Sarah's questioning resumed, Callister angled his body slightly away from Nolan. The two men no longer chatted about football, or much of anything else.

"Given your concerns about Reiner," Sarah asked bluntly, "did you ever attempt to independently determine what had happened to the missing documents?"

Briefly, Callister glanced at the table. "I made no such attempt."

"Why not?"

Once more his eyes met Sarah's. "Because it would have involved investigating my own vice president of marketing. After the First Lady's family was murdered, I had more pressing concerns—like keeping this company afloat. It wasn't the right environment."

Between the phlegmatic lines lay an answer of startling candor: an internal inquiry which uncovered the truth would have been devastating to Lexington's public posture and, even worse, could have generated evidence damning in a lawsuit like Mary Costello's. "So it was better," Sarah said sharply, "to believe that Reiner was dishonest than to prove it."

The cast of Callister's broad midwestern face suggested both resentment and defensiveness. "The First Lady's mother, sister, and niece had been murdered with a gun and bullets made by Lexington Arms. Aside from the terrible impact on her family, these murders could have spelled the end of a century-old business which employs hundreds of good people. I owed all my energies and judgment to the task of protecting the company and the families who rely on it."

Sarah considered him. Abruptly, she asked, "Do you know a man named Norman Conn?"

"Yes. He's a longtime employee."

"Were you ever told that Conn believes Reiner destroyed a document suggesting that the shipment of stolen P-2s, including the murder weapon, were being sold at gun shows by members of a white supremacist group?"

Callister shook his head. In an emphatic tone which suggested genuine anger, he said, "Not until last week."

Nolan held out his hand between Callister and Sarah. "I will caution the witness not to testify regarding conversations with counsel."

"Outside of conversations with counsel," Sarah persisted, "were you ever told that Mr. Reiner destroyed documents?"

"I was not."

At once, Sarah changed tacks. "Are you familiar with Martin Bresler?"

"I am."

"How are you acquainted with Mr. Bresler?"

Callister sat back, seemingly inclined, as he had not been before, to put her question in a fuller context. "Mr. Bresler," he answered, "was the head of an industry group which included Lexington Arms."

Abruptly, Callister checked himself, as though fighting any tendency toward expansiveness. "What was the purpose of Bresler's group?" Sarah prodded.

"To find a middle way between the gun controllers and the SSA." Callister shrugged, seemingly unable to explain his answer without elaboration. "From the beginning of my time at Lexington, I planned to wean us off the revenue we derived from weapons like the P-2. The idea was to market quality and safety, rather than lethality. To me, that meant things like trigger locks and smart guns—weapons designed to protect the user, and prevent accidents or misuse by folks who shouldn't have them." Pausing, Callister seemed to recall anew the promise of his plan. "President Kilcannon may not have been our friend, but he was a fact of life. The idea was to get him and the trial lawyers off our backs. By far the best way to do it was to unify a number of gun companies in a common approach, then see if we could deal with the President. Martin Bresler was supposed to be our vehicle, and the trigger lock agreement with the White House our first step."

Briefly, Sarah scanned her outline. "After that agreement, did Bresler propose a next step?"

"Yes."

To the side, Harrison Fancher watched the witness closely. "What *was* the next step?" Sarah asked.

Callister grimaced. Tonelessly, he said, "For our five companies to require background checks before our dealers sold any of our weapons at gun shows."

His answer, with its echo of the Bowden murders, seemed to draw the other participants closer to the witness. Even the court reporter cocked her head.

Quietly, Sarah asked, "Did you ever reach agreement with the President?"

"No."

"What stopped you?"

Callister crossed his arms. "All the other CEOs withdrew their financial support from Bresler's group. In essence, they fired him."

"Why was that?"

Briefly Callister seemed to wince at some distasteful memory. "They claimed Bresler was becoming too divisive."

"Did any of them mention the SSA?"

Studiously, it seemed to Sarah, Callister ignored Harrison Fancher's presence. "They all did. They were afraid that the SSA would encourage its members to boycott any company that dealt with Kerry Kilcannon. Four million members, and all of their friends, is a hell of a lot of customers to lose."

Sarah glanced at Fancher. "Did any of them tell you that they'd been threatened by representatives of the SSA?"

"Not directly, no."

"Did you ask?"

"I did not."

Pausing, Sarah replayed the tenor of Callister's answer. "Did the SSA threaten *you*?"

"Objection," Fancher snapped. "However pejorative in tone, the question impinges on the defendants' First Amendment right of political association—including the formulation of legislative and political strategy. Such confidential discussions are *not* subject to discovery."

Sarah did not move her eyes from Callister. "You may answer," she told him.

"He may not." Turning to the witness, Nolan said with quiet emphasis, "The SSA's objection is well taken, George, and the right belongs to Lexington every bit as much as it does the SSA. I'm instructing you not to answer."

Facing Sarah, Callister said, "You heard my counsel, Ms. Dash. I'm under orders not to discuss any conversations with the SSA."

"That's obstruction," Lenihan burst out.

"Mr. Nolan," Sarah interjected with a controlled professionalism she found difficult to maintain, "your objection goes to the heart of our case that the SSA conspired with others to enforce uniform conduct on the American gun industry, in violation of the antitrust laws, contributing to the murders of Mary Costello's family. You've got no basis for your instruction."

"Then take it to the judge . . ."

"You know damn well we can't," Lenihan snapped back. "By the time we get there you'll have passed this unconscionable gun immunity bill."

Nolan smiled. "Acts of Congress are your department, Bob, not mine. My job is to represent my client."

"Which one? The SSA?"

Staring at the table, Callister had seemed to turn inward—most likely, Sarah thought, out of distaste for the whole proceeding. Crisply, she told Lenihan, "Let's call the judge right now."

At once, Sarah rose, took a speakerphone from the corner of the conference room, and placed it on the center of the table. Glancing at her notes, she stabbed out Bond's number, and asked for the law clerk assigned to *Costello versus Lexington Arms*.

"We're in the middle of Mr. Callister's deposition," she explained. "A discovery dispute has arisen—an instruction to the witness not to answer questions essential to our case. We're hoping to speak with Judge Bond, describe the issues, and ask for an immediate ruling."

"Very well." The clerk's reedy voice was pompous with borrowed authority. "I'll find out what we want to do."

He put Sarah on hold. Silent, lawyers and witness gazed at the speakerphone as if it were a line to God. The room felt hot and close.

After a few minutes, interminable to Sarah, the clerk returned. "If there's a problem, plaintiff's counsel should file a motion. The judge says he'll rule in the normal course."

The answer struck Sarah in the pit of her stomach. "Thank you," she managed to say. The obligatory words had never felt more hateful.

When the clerk hung up, Nolan was the first to speak, the softness of his voice betraying his residual tension. "Why don't we have lunch, Sarah? The witness has been going long enough."

Eating a ham sandwich with Lenihan in her office, Sarah tried to bank her outrage. At least Nolan had given her time to think.

"There's something here," she speculated, "that Callister doesn't like."

Lenihan slumped in his chair, a portrait of frustration. "Yeah. Mike Reiner."

Sarah put down the sandwich, gazing out her window at the uneven skyline south of Market Street. "There's something else, I think. I just don't know if I can get to what it is."

Returning from lunch, Callister looked somber, all trace of humor vanished. "After your fellow CEOs cut off Martin Bresler," Sarah began, "did President Kilcannon contact you directly?"

"Yes. We met three times at Camp David."

"What did the President discuss with you?"

Callister hesitated, eyes narrow with thought, as though still reluctant to divulge his private conversations with the President of the United States. "A potential agreement, brokered by the President with the thirteen cities who'd sued us, to end their litigation against Lexington Arms." His tone took on the edge of self-justification. "A single hundred-million-dollar verdict would wipe out Lexington Arms. The legal fees alone could drain us of our profits. If the President could offer a way out, I thought we should explore it."

"What was Lexington's side of the deal?"

"Though I couldn't admit that to the President, he was asking for a lot of what I thought we should do anyhow. Phase out the P-2 and the Eagle's Claw. Require background checks at gun shows." Briefly, Callister grimaced. "He also wanted us to retrofit our weapons to accommodate only magazines with a maximum of ten rounds."

This tacit reference to the murder of Marie Costello prompted Nolan to glance at Callister. "Did the President propose anything else?" Sarah asked.

"Not directly. But he acknowledged that we'd need money to offset the phaseout of the P-2, and suggested that it was possible to obtain a federal research grant from the Justice Department to help us develop smart guns—guns designed to fire only in response to the 'fingerprint' of the actual owner."

"What was your reaction?"

Callister ran a hand through the grey stubble of his crew cut. "That it would be hard to reach agreement without support from other gun companies, but that it was still worth trying." He looked briefly at Harrison Fancher. "I thought if we could agree on the outlines of a deal, in private, I could try to bring in some of the other manufacturers. So I told the President I'd take it to our board of directors."

Gazing at the pen she twisted in her fingers, Sarah pondered her next question. "Before you went to the board, did you discuss President Kilcannon's proposal with anyone at Lexington?"

"I didn't want the negotiations leaking. But I spoke with Ray Stipe, our general counsel." Pausing, Callister added in a neutral voice, "Also with Mike Reiner."

"George," Nolan interjected, "were your discussions with Mr. Stipe for the purpose of obtaining legal advice?"

"They were."

"Then they're covered by the attorney-client privilege and I instruct you not to disclose them."

Callister nodded, then turned back to Sarah. "Mr. Stipe aside," she inquired, "why did you consult with Mr. Reiner?"

"He was our VP of marketing. Much of the implementation of our agreement would have been up to him."

"Did Reiner express a view of the President's proposal?"

"Yes. He was vehemently opposed."

"On what grounds?"

"That the President was asking us to be the canary in the mine shaft." Callister's tone became cooler. "Reiner had helped develop the P-2 and the Eagle's Claw, and thought they were essential to fighting off our competition. He said accepting Kilcannon's plan was tantamount to suicide."

"Were Mr. Reiner's objections the reason that Lexington did not reach agreement with the President?"

"They were not," Callister answered firmly. "In my view the P-2 and Eagle's Claw were a dead end, and my job was to wean us from trying to outdo the other guys in making deadly weapons and lethal bullets. So I told Reiner I was going to the board."

"And did you?"

"Yes. I didn't want to put anything in writing. So I verbally outlined the President's proposal and asked them to consider it."

"What was the board's reaction?"

"There was a lot of uncertainty and concern. But they authorized me to meet further with the President."

"Did that happen?"

Callister seemed to draw a long, slow breath. "No."

"And why not?"

"Because I received a phone call from Charles Dane."

"Concerning what?"

"He said that he'd heard about my negotiations with the President, and requested a private meeting."

At once, both Nolan and Fancher seemed hyperalert, poised to intervene. Pausing, Sarah sought to frame a question which would avoid an instruction not to answer. "How did Mr. Dane learn about the negotiations?"

"I can't imagine it was Stipe." Callister summoned a tight smile, more to himself than for Sarah. "That leaves Reiner, or a member of our board."

"Did you meet with Mr. Dane?"

"Yes. At the offices of the SSA."

At the corner of her eye, Sarah watched Nolan. "Was anyone else there?"

"No." Callister's voice was flat, his features immobile. "Dane said he wanted to work things out alone."

Tensing, both Nolan and Fancher eyed the witness. Sarah glanced at one lawyer, then the other, and calmly asked, "What did Dane say to you at the meeting?"

"Same objection," Fancher cut in, turning to Nolan and the witness. "The question seeks to probe confidential discussion of political and legislative strategy protected by the First Amendment. The SSA requests that Mr. Callister not answer."

"So directed," Nolan told his client.

Sarah kept watching Callister. "Would you classify your meeting with Mr. Dane as a 'confidential discussion of political and legislative strategy'?"

Callister folded his hands, gazing silently at the table. At length he looked up at Sarah with a new aura of equanimity. "Not in the main."

Sarah smiled faintly. "Then when you answer my questions, please leave out the 'confidential discussions of political and legislative strategy.' "

"Objection," Nolan snapped with rising annoyance. "It's impossible to segregate what may be a general discussion from the legislative and political discussions which are intertwined with it. I direct the witness not to answer any questions about his private discussions with Mr. Dane."

Sarah turned to the witness. "Do you think you can separate 'legislative and political discussions' from whatever else you and Dane talked about?"

"I believe I can, yes."

Nolan grasped Callister's wrist. "As counsel for Lexington Arms," he said in a peremptory tone, "I am directing you not to answer Ms. Dash's questions, or to attempt to distinguish what is confidential from what is not."

Callister stared at Nolan's hand. "You've given me your advice, John. I get to decide whether or not to take it."

Removing his hand, Nolan turned to Sarah. "I request a break to consult with my client."

Sarah forced herself to remain low key. "Mr. Callister?"

"You can take a break," Callister told Nolan. "I'm fine."

In a tone of alarm, Fancher interjected, "I protest the continuation of the deposition without time to discuss with Mr. Callister the implications of your questions for the First Amendment rights of Lexington and the SSA."

Shrugging, Callister turned to Sarah. "Go ahead, Ms. Dash."

Ignoring Fancher, Sarah asked, "During that meeting, Mr. Callister, what did Mr. Dane say to you?"

"Several things," Callister answered in a calm, incisive voice. "That anyone who dealt with President Kilcannon was selling out the Second Amendment. That if Lexington made this deal he would use the SSA's newsletter, the Internet, and grassroots organizations to urge every American gun owner to boycott all our products and every gun dealer to bar us from their stores. That the SSA magazine would refuse to run our advertisements, and that other gun publications would follow suit.

"With respect to private lawsuits like this one," Callister

went on, "our defense is financed by the Heritage Fund, which is principally funded, and therefore controlled, by the SSA itself. Dane warned me they wouldn't fund the defense for any company who cut a deal with Kilcannon." Turning to Fancher, Callister said evenly, "At the end of his summary, Mr. Fancher, your client promised me that settling with the President would lead to the destruction of Lexington Arms. I didn't take that to be a 'First Amendment discussion of political and legislative strategy.' "

Sarah felt as stunned as John Nolan and Fancher. Callister's tone suggested a man who was finally and inexorably fed up; that his last response delivered the SSA to the edge of an antitrust violation seemed to concern him not at all. "In connection with his threats against Lexington," Sarah managed to inquire, "did Mr. Dane mention your fellow manufacturers?"

Callister turned back to her. "He asked if I remembered Martin Bresler. Then he wondered aloud if I didn't think the others would be happy to carve up the market share of someone who'd just sold them out." Briefly, Callister's voice betrayed his bitterness. "But just to be sure I didn't strike a deal, someone leaked the negotiations to the *Washington Post*.

"All of a sudden, there were demonstrators in front of our company, and I was getting death threats on the Internet." Pausing, Callister finished quietly, "The day before the President's wedding, the board ordered me to pull the plug."

Sitting back, Sarah surveyed the scene in front of her: Callister, now dissociated from the lawyers, Fancher scribbling notes with the fury of a slasher, Nolan, straining to cope with a loss of control which, in his experience, surely was unprecedented. "George," Nolan said in a strained voice, "your testimony has implications far beyond the concerns of the SSA. You have obligations to your company."

Callister turned to him with a look of mild disdain. "Yes," he said simply, "I do."

"After the Costello murders," Sarah cut in, "did you take any further action?"

"George," Nolan repeated, "I'm imploring you to take a break."

Callister turned from him. "I went to the board," he told Sarah, "and said enough was enough. The shooter had used a P-2, and the eleventh Eagle's Claw bullet in a forty-round magazine had killed that little girl I'd met at Camp David. It was past time for reaching an arrangement with the President, if that was even possible with all that had happened." Callister's tone grew soft. "I knew Kilcannon would do everything in his power to destroy Lexington Arms unless we gave him what he needed, and that was what I told them."

His quiet statement, with its implicit reference to the lawsuit, reminded Sarah of her first call from Lara Kilcannon. It seemed a long time ago. And for most of that time, she had assumed that George Callister was as callous as Charles Dane. Softly, she said, "Why couldn't Lexington reach agreement with the President, Mr. Callister?"

"Lord knows I tried. In fact I told the board I'd resign unless they authorized me to discontinue the P-2 and Eagle's Claw." Callister gazed at the table, as though drawn into memory. "I guaranteed them there'd be more lawsuits coming—if not from the First Lady or her sister, then from the other families, and that the victims had too much public sympathy for us to risk a trial. But before the board could hold a vote, Dane called to ask for a second meeting . . ."

"Mr. Callister," Nolan said formally, "I'm forced to admonish you to consider the legal implications of your actions here today. By ignoring my instructions, you're acting in conflict with the interests of your company."

Callister shrugged. "Someone is. Maybe you should hear the rest before you decide it's me."

Tense, Sarah sensed that what was to follow would dwarf all that had come before. "At the second meeting," she asked swiftly, "what did Dane have to say?"

"That the SSA's objective was to get rid of Kerry Kilcannon. Rather than make a pact with the devil, I should just get out of the way and let them work with the Republicans on a tort reform bill which would get us off the hook."

Sarah heard Lenihan laugh softly. "That conversation," Fancher protested, "is the epitome of political and legislative strategy . . ."

"Did you respond to Dane's suggestion?" Sarah broke in.

"Yes. I said that Congress had never passed a gun immunity bill and sure as hell couldn't now. And that Kilcannon would veto it if they did."

"How did Dane react?"

Briefly Callister glanced at Fancher. "He said that the SSA would commit whatever resources were needed to pass tort reform in both houses of Congress. Then he told me something that I couldn't understand: that Kilcannon could be handled if he got in the way."

The last words of his answer hit Sarah hard. At once, she was intensely aware of the video cam focused on George Callister. "Did Mr. Dane tell you what he meant by that?"

"Not at first." Callister's voice was gentle, his eyes bleak. "I told him he was crazy to think that Kilcannon could be 'handled' after what had happened to his wife's family."

"How did he respond?"

"That I didn't need to worry, because they had personal information which concerned both the President and the First Lady."

The room, and everyone in it, was completely still. In

the silence Sarah noticed the soft whir of the video cam. "Did you ask him to elaborate?"

"Yes. All that Dane said was that they could never survive it, and they'd be foolish to try."

Fancher had stopped taking notes. Absently, Nolan scratched the bridge of his nose. Quietly, Sarah asked, "Do you now know what Dane meant by that?"

Callister nodded. "The morning the abortion story broke I called Dane, demanding to know if this was what he'd meant. He just laughed, and asked me why it mattered when the President had just become a eunuch." At last, the witness turned to Nolan. "You're the lawyer, John, not me. But I always thought that blackmail was a crime."

When Nolan did not answer, Callister told him, "Maybe the board will get rid of me for this. But right now your choice is to represent this company and not the SSA. Or I'll fire you along with Reiner."

When the deposition was over, Callister said to Nolan, "I'd like a word in private with Ms. Dash." It was not a request.

They stepped out in the hallway. Callister stood over her, the briefest glint of humor appearing in his level grey eyes. "If you happen to speak to the President," he requested, "tell him that the Prime Minister worked his magic. And that now we're as square as I can make us. From here on out, both of you are on your own."

TWELVE

SARAH AND MARY sat at opposite ends of Sarah's couch, a cold winter rain splattering against the windows of her living room. Mary listened closely as Sarah struggled to convey the quality of what she had experienced.

"You know by now what it's supposed to be like," Sarah told her. "Depositions aren't a human process. The lawyers object, and the witness gives the answer he's supposed to give. But not Callister.

"At some point he began to expose the whole charade for what it was. Suddenly I wasn't just a lawyer, and Callister was more than a witness. Nolan has never looked so small." Pausing, she tried to translate her sense of Callister's reactions. "Callister had been taking in the entire rancid joke—Bond doing his Wizard of Oz routine through his little twerp of a law clerk, knowing full well that the defense lawyers were screwing us over; Nolan and Fancher working together to conceal the SSA's legal problems until the Senate votes. Given what he knew, Callister couldn't stand playing the role of the good German."

Mary herself looked dazed. "Do you think the defense lawyers knew about the blackmail?"

"Maybe not about Callister's final call to Dane. *Maybe.* But Nolan's too good a lawyer not to have interviewed Callister about everything that happened *before* the lawsuit, pretty soon after we filed it. So the appearance of the abortion story had to raise for Nolan the same questions about blackmail that Callister asked Dane." Contemplative, Sarah sipped from her glass of chardonnay. "If you wanted to be charitable, you'd argue that Nolan decided that his client's best interests lay in sticking with the SSA. After all, the day after tomorrow the Senate's due to bury this case for good."

"So why didn't Callister just keep quiet?"

"Callister's smart—he didn't just do this out of conscience. My guess is that he thinks our lawsuit actually serves Lexington's interests."

"How?"

"Because it may be the only way to break the SSA's control over the American gun industry. With what Callister told us, the SSA would become the principal defendant, and Lexington could cross-claim against the SSA for any damages *you* recover from Lexington." Sarah thought more swiftly now. "Suppose Callister offered to settle with you for a small chunk of cash, Lexington's agreement to the terms the President proposed, and the company's cooperation in prosecuting your case against the SSA at trial. The SSA's power to bully gun manufacturers could effectively be over."

Mary shook her head in awe. "Blackmailing the President of the United States. Imagine what might happen if *that* got out."

"Imagine," Sarah said, and felt again how shaken she was. "It reminds me of that classic conundrum, 'if a tree falls in the woods, and no one hears it, does it make a sound?' What Callister said is a tree in the woods. Outside of the people in that conference room, no one heard a sound."

"Because of the judge's order."

Reluctantly, Sarah nodded. "Callister stuck this in my pocket, and now I know what's happening. But all Callister did was cross his lawyers. *I'd* be violating a court order. I haven't seen Callister showing up on *Meet the Press*."

"He didn't just cross his lawyers, Sarah. He crossed the

SSA, and put his *company* on the line." Pensive, Mary paused. "What does Bob Lenihan say?"

Sarah rubbed her temple with the fingers of one hand. "A couple of weeks ago, he used a loophole in the order to leak some records to the *Times*. Bond can't prove it, but he knows it. Whoever flouts the order now is in Bond's crosshairs, and Lenihan doesn't want it to be him."

Mary studied her. "You've already asked him if he'd leak it, haven't you."

"More or less," Sarah admitted wearily. "He said that maybe after the Senate kills your suit we can petition Bond to open the files. That's as far as Lenihan's willing to go."

Mary's face softened with compassion. "What about your law license, Sarah? It doesn't seem fair that this has to fall on you."

"There's no one else, and no escape." Sarah gazed into her wineglass. "I keep wondering how we got here. I wanted to hold Lexington or the gun lobby responsible for their actions, and help the President change the way this country treats gun violence. But the President and your sister live in a parallel universe, as you well know, and there's nothing they can do for me."

Mary considered her. "Then that leaves me, doesn't it?"

"How do you mean?"

Mary smiled faintly. "Because I'm your client, Sarah. Whatever we do, and how we do it, is for me to decide."

The next morning, at a little before eleven o'clock, Sarah Dash and Mary Costello entered the principal meeting room of the Mark Hopkins Hotel. Set up behind the podium was a table supporting a cardboard box, a television, and a VCR. Gathered in front of it were reporters from newspapers, networks, and local TV stations—intrigued, in light of Judge Bond's blackout, by Sarah's hasty summons to a press conference regarding a "critical development" in *Costello versus Lexington Arms*.

Nodding to Mary, Sarah approached the podium, Mary beside her. Sarah had not slept. Laying her notes on the podium, she felt the slightest tremor of her hands.

She paused, drawing one deep breath. CNN was carrying the press conference live, and she could not be any less than poised.

"I'm Sarah Dash," she began, "one of the counsel for Mary Costello in her wrongful death action against Lexington Arms and the Sons of the Second Amendment. Because of the importance of the information we are about to share with you, Ms. Costello wanted to be here in person."

For a final instant, Sarah hesitated on the brink of defiance. "Yesterday," she continued, "I deposed George Callister, the CEO of Lexington Arms. In the box behind me are copies of the videotape of that deposition, which we will make available at the conclusion of this press conference. In the meanwhile, I have prepared taped excerpts of Mr. Callister's testimony, which I will play in a few moments."

Attentive, the reporters began stirring with surprise and anticipation—those who had followed the case knew at once that Sarah was violating a court order. She saw a reporter from Fox start speaking rapidly into his cell phone. "As you know," Sarah went on, "Judge Bond has ordered us not to disclose evidence revealed in discovery. We do not do so lightly . . ."

Summoned to the SSA's conference room by a hasty call from Carla Fell, Charles Dane found her watching CNN.

"What is it?" he demanded sharply.

"Sarah Dash. She just told the judge to go fuck himself."

Filled with foreboding, Dane mentally replayed the phone call from Harrison Fancher, the sleepless night which followed—spent alone because Dane could confess his involvement to no one—spinning calculations about how to keep the lid on Callister. The best plan he could construct was to make sure Fasano shut down the lawsuit in the Senate, do everything possible to keep the files under seal and, should they surface nonetheless, to claim that Callister was lying—or, at least, had badly misconstrued their conversation.

"What's she saying?" Dane asked Fell.

"We don't know yet."

On the screen, Sarah Dash appeared composed. *One of the principal claims in Ms. Costello's lawsuit is that the SSA controls the American gun industry. Yesterday, we learned how true that was. But we learned far more than that.*

Turning, Sarah walked to the television, and punched a button on the VCR. In close-up, George Callister's image filled the screen.

How did Dane react? Sarah's voice inquired.

He said that the SSA would commit whatever resources were needed to pass tort reform in both houses of Congress. Then he told me something that I didn't understand: that Kilcannon could be handled if he got in the way.

Heavily, Dane sat down. At the corner of his vision, he saw that Carla Fell was watching him. Her eyes seemed to ask the question Sarah's voice was putting into words.

Did Mr. Dane tell you what he meant by that?

THIRTEEN

ON RETURNING TO her office, Sarah was assaulted by phone calls from the print media; interview requests from CNN, Fox, MSNBC, and the evening news and early-morning shows for the three major networks; angry messages from supporters of the SSA; calls of encouragement from friends, including several she had not heard from in years; and—unbelievable to Sarah—a film producer who had rescripted her defiance of Judge Bond as a vehicle for Sandra Bullock. " 'Sarah Brockovich'?" Sarah mused aloud, and told her assistant to keep stemming the deluge. Sarah had done all the talking to the media she intended to or, clearly, needed to. The cable news stations were awash in images of Sarah and Callister; speculation regarding the impact of Callister's revelations on the gun debate, the SSA, the Congress and both political parties; instant polls asking whether the videotape had affected the Kilcannons' standing with the public. Sarah felt tired, worried, and altogether overwhelmed. To have generated such a firestorm by defying the legal system, rather than working within it, deepened her anxiety. She could only guess at how George Callister must feel.

At two-thirty, Sarah left the office, having taken only two calls.

The first was from Lara Kilcannon. With a depth of emotion Sarah had not heard before, Lara told her how grateful she was, even more for the President than herself. "Is there anything we can do for you?" she asked.

"One thing," Sarah answered simply. "When anyone

asks, make it clear I did this on my own. Or the whole situation will be that much worse for me."

The second call was from Gardner Bond. "I'm issuing an order," the judge said with a coldness more daunting than angry. "But court orders don't seem to impress you very much, so I thought I'd deliver this one in person.

"Tomorrow afternoon, at four o'clock, I'm holding a contempt hearing regarding your activities this morning. You may wish to consider attending."

Without awaiting Sarah's answer, Bond hung up.

Paul Harshman was the first of the Republican leadership to reach Fasano's office. As he entered, Fasano was watching a liberal columnist eviscerate the SSA on MSNBC.

"This all could be a smear," Harshman cautioned. "Orchestrated by Kilcannon."

Fasano turned to him. Evenly, he inquired, "Do you really think that?"

Harshman's expression took on an obstinate cast. "What do we *really* know about this man Callister . . . ?"

"Give it a rest, Paul. Let's focus on saving this bill." Fasano's tone brooked no argument. "I'm not taking calls from Charles Dane. I don't want *you* to take any. As soon as we're through here, I'm going to distance us from Dane as quickly as I can, and you'll be right there with me. Just like Sarah Dash and Mary Costello."

Gathered in the Oval Office, Kerry, Kit and Clayton watched Fasano on CNN.

Flanked by Paul Harshman and others in the Republican leadership, he stood in the rotunda of the Capitol. *None of us,* he said, *can know what Mr. Dane intended to convey to Mr. Callister, and its precise connection to the President's own admission of his personal conduct prior to assuming office.*

"Do remind us," Clayton said caustically. "Some may have forgotten."

Only Mr. Dane knows, Fasano continued. *But we cannot be blind to the implications of what we learned today. The blackmail Mr. Callister suggests has no place in our public life. However committed we may be to the protection of unborn life—and, for that matter, gun rights—we in the Republican Party utterly repudiate such despicable tactics.*

"But not their benefits," Kerry said softly.

Senator Fasano, Kate Snow of CNN called out. *How does Ms. Dash's revelation affect the prospects of overriding the President's veto?*

It's too soon to tell, Kate. Frankly, we're still absorbing this. But I can tell you what logic suggests, at least to me. Fasano's expression was grave, his tone measured. *This is, as I've said, a sad chapter in our civic life. But—just as Mr. Dane's alleged conversation should not reflect on the four million members of the SSA—Mr. Callister's charges have no more to do with the merits of the Civil Justice Reform Act than does the private life of the President and First Lady.*

Gun immunity is only a small portion of the comprehensive and badly needed reform of our legal system contained in this important bill. Whatever our problems—including gun violence—in my opinion the current culture of litigation makes them worse. I intend to press for an override as vigorously as before.

Having delivered his message, Fasano left the podium.

"The sonofabitch is smart," Kit told the President grudgingly. "He's put all the daylight he needed between himself and Dane. But he wants to keep the SSA in his debt, and their votes and money in his party's pocket. And if he can override your veto after this, he's king of the Hill."

"Not on my watch." Kerry felt both anger and

exhilaration, the freedom of knowing who was responsible, and what he needed to do. "I've got some senators to call."

"What about a statement?" Kit interposed.

Kerry smiled. "I'll take care of it myself."

At six o'clock in the east, sufficient time to make the evening news, the President appeared as promised in the White House press room. Fasano, Majority Whip Dave Ruckles, and their leadership team watched on CNN.

Earlier today, the President began, *Senator Fasano suggested that "none of us can know what Mr. Dane intended to convey to Mr. Callister." For myself, I find statements like "I have personal information that the President and First Lady can never survive," and "the President can be handled if he gets in the way" less ambiguous than does the senator.*

Let me review the sequence of events. I was threatened through an "anonymous" phone call relayed by Senator Slezak, I nonetheless vetoed the Civil Justice Reform Act, and some very "personal information" promptly became public. Mr. Callister has now identified the source. The President's tone took on a trace of irony. *To be fair, the Majority Leader has found this sequence sufficiently damning to separate himself from Mr. Dane. I also agree with him that the membership of the SSA does not believe in blackmail. But its leadership plainly does . . .*

"Saying isn't proving," Harshman scoffed. "No matter how many times he says it."

Fasano was silent. Of all the men in the room, only he was as certain of Dane's involvement as Kilcannon. But he could never admit this to the others. "There's no reason for Callister to lie," he said at length, "and now the President can unleash the FBI. The prudent thing is to assume that, sooner or later, the President will pin this on Dane."

In addition to his repudiation of blackmail, the President continued, *I offer Senator Fasano this practical suggestion: that his party return the over two million dollars the current leadership of the SSA gave it in the last election cycle—or, at the least, that it refuse to accept such money in the future. That might help them, to borrow the senator's phrase, focus on the "merits" of the Civil Justice Reform Act ...*

"Whoever leaked the story," Dave Ruckles observed, "I sure as hell don't like blackmail. But our quality of life was better when this guy felt more chastened ..."

Consider one compelling fact. If the Senate had overridden my veto a mere two days ago, instead of tomorrow as the senator hopes, this bill would have prevented George Callister from being sworn to tell the truth—about the destruction of evidence, the SSA's unlawful domination of Lexington Arms, and Mr. Dane's use of blackmail to advance the SSA's agenda. From the standpoint of the SSA, the bill's "merits" are now clear: suppressing truth and perpetuating injustice.

Fasano turned to Ruckles. "Where does Palmer stand?" he asked.

At that moment, the senior senator from Ohio had no wish to be on Capitol Hill. He was at home with Allie, refusing to answer the phone. This still was true three hours later, when Charles Dane appeared on *Larry King Live.*

"This," Chad told his wife, "should be one for the time capsule."

Larry, Dane said with deep sincerity, *I share Senator Fasano's feelings of indignation over charges such as these. But however Mr. Callister chose to interpret our many conversations, never once does he claim that I mentioned Lara Kilcannon's abortion.*

What's important here is to examine Callister's motives. Lexington and the SSA are codefendants in an inflammatory lawsuit which is bad for Lexington's image. So he's blaming the SSA instead of the President for its existence, and trying to pass on to us any liability they might have . . .

But why would he do that, King interrogated sharply, *with the Senate about to wipe out the lawsuit altogether?*

"How uncharitable," Palmer observed. "Larry's becoming Tim Russert."

Clearly, Larry, Callister hedged his bets—and it backfired. He *never considered that President Kilcannon and his legal surrogate, Sarah Dash, would use his calculated lies to practice the politics of smear and victimization against American gun owners.*

Kilcannon and his followers smear us because we're the most dedicated upholder of every decent American's right to defend themselves and their families against murderers, rapists and child molesters—the scum of the way-too-permissive society exemplified by the Kilcannons. Then the President tries to advance his true agenda—confiscation—by pretending to be the victim of the big bad SSA.

"Pretending?" Allie said.

Dane's voice filled with scorn. *In the Kilcannons' narcissistic world, everything is about them, everyone is after them, and anyone else is responsible except for them. So let's call a spade a spade. They had the affair. They aborted their unborn child. And now they want the four million law-abiding members of the SSA to pay for their immoral conduct that sickened decent people everywhere . . .*

In profile, Chad saw Allie's eyes brim with tears. "It's hard to watch this," she told her husband. "It's too much like what they did to our daughter."

I call on every patriotic American to reject these ugly machinations, and to urge their senators to support the reform of our civil justice system.

The telephone beside Chad rang. At first he ignored it, and then saw the identity of his caller flash up on the iridescent panel of the phone.

"Watching Larry King?" the President asked.

"Never miss him." Chad hesitated, then added softly, "Dane's making a mistake, Mr. President. More than that, I'm deeply sorry."

"I know that, Chad." The President paused in turn. "I need your help on this. What's at stake transcends the Civil Justice Reform Act."

"That's the problem," Chad answered. "This is way too personal to me, and there are a *lot* of things at stake. I need time to think it through."

The President's laugh was quiet and without humor. "You and I have twenty-four hours. That's how much time Fasano's given us."

FOURTEEN

FOR KERRY, the predawn hours were punctuated by two events.

The first was Lara rising from bed, treading softly to the bathroom and carefully shutting the door. Though muffled by running water, Kerry heard the quiet but unmistakable sound of his wife becoming sick.

He waited until he heard Lara splashing more water on her face. Then he slowly opened the door.

Dabbing her face with a towel, Lara saw him in the mirror. "Can I get you something?" he asked.

Her skin was pale, Kerry saw, and her expression was wan. But she managed to smile at his inquiry. "Maybe a new stomach?"

He tilted his head. "What about a different life?"

Closing her eyes, she gave the briefest shake of her head, swallowing as though she still felt sick. "It's not that," she answered in a weak but insistent voice. "If stress did this to me, I'd have never survived Kosovo. I'm coming down with the flu again."

Perhaps that was all it was. Lately, they had both been more prone to colds. But Kerry felt again the cost to Lara of marrying him, the tragedy, and now the misery which had followed. So much had happened since Slezak's warning; that they had so little time to absorb it, or do anything but cope with its impact on his Presidency, struck Kerry as inhuman.

Putting his hands on Lara's waist, he rested the side of

his face against hers. She smiled again in the mirror. "Don't get too close," she advised. "You'll catch it."

"Are you going to be all right?"

Her eyes, reflected in the glass, seemed to query how he meant this. "You might call down for some ginger ale," she answered.

Kerry left it there.

The second event was the arrival, with Lara's ginger ale, of the early-morning edition of the *New York Times*. The headline "SSA Accused of Blackmailing President" led a spate of articles which confirmed what Kerry already knew—that the body politic was shell-shocked; the Senate in flux; and that the Democratic expressions of outrage had not, thus far, translated into a change of any votes. The problem—as the *Times* pointed out—was that upholding the President's veto was an all-or-nothing proposition. Tort reform remained overwhelmingly popular in the Senate, and there was no longer any way to separate gun immunity from the rest. All that seemed likely was that the President would hold the thirty-three votes which remained after Leo Weller's defection. Though a single senator might set off a chain reaction, on the surface Kerry remained a vote short.

Head propped on a pillow, Lara read along with him, then kissed him on the cheek. "Good luck," she said. "It looks like a big day at the office."

His seven a.m. meeting, with Tony Calvo of the Chamber of Commerce, had been scheduled at Calvo's urgent request. The President had granted him fifteen minutes, and Calvo wasted none of them.

"We'd like to revisit the deal you offered us, Mr. President—with modifications. We won't support an override if you'll support the passage of the Civil Justice Reform Act without the gun immunity provisions."

At once, Kerry grasped two essential facts—that Calvo was uncertain that Fasano's votes would hold, but that Calvo viewed Kerry as so damaged that he could drive a hard bargain. " 'Revisit'?" he inquired with a smile. "What about 'rewrite'? The compromise I offered you did not include the corporate goodies Fasano's trying to jam through."

Calvo nodded. "True, we're looking for some movement. But we're offering to help save you from an embarrassing defeat, at the worst possible time, on the worst possible issue for you. Guns."

Like any Faustian bargain, Kerry thought, the blandishment was seductive—saving the President from a defeat which was, at least in prospect, catastrophic. So it took him longer than he liked to ask quietly, "What do you take me for? However you may couch it, you're piggybacking on what the SSA has done to us—most significant, in my mind, to Lara . . ."

"That's not so," Calvo protested.

"Nonsense, Tony. You think I'm so weakened that I'll sell you the store in exchange for selling out Charles Dane. I can't fault your practicality, or blame you for trying. But don't blame me for being insulted."

"Mr. President," Calvo said more soberly, "I deplore what was done to you and the First Lady."

Propping his face in the palm of his hand, Kerry considered him. "I appreciate that. Though not quite as much as if you'd said it earlier, in public, when these people were dragging Lara through the mud.

"But understand that this is more than personal. I don't think politics should ever be conducted in this fashion. For the sake of the next President, and whoever else comes after, I can't cave in to this. You're asking for too much, too late."

Calvo held his gaze. "If that's true, Mr. President, I'm sorry."

"So am I." Kerry's voice remained even. "Before you tell your coalition that you've failed, I'd like you to take a moment, and think very hard about your support for a Senate leadership team that subordinates your interests to a pack of blackmailing fanatics who may wind up getting your wife or children shot.

"This game so many business interests keep on playing puzzles me. You compromise with fundamentalists who want to outlaw Charles Darwin and put women in their place. You get in bed with gun nuts. You tell yourself that's the only way you'll get what you deserve—tort reform, and all those tax cuts—and that it's okay to let these people dictate our social policy as long as they don't get to come to dinner and fill your children's heads with nonsense."

Kerry's last comment induced, in Calvo, the glimmer of a sardonic smile. "As long as I'm President," Kerry told him, "they're not running anything. On the other hand, I believe the interests *you* represent are essential to the country—just as long as you don't think you *are* the country, or that this yawning wealth gap we've developed is good for you or anyone. The system only works if people are secure and treated fairly." The President's tone grew firm. "No matter what you think, the trial lawyers don't own me. If you want fairness and not your usual wish list, my door is always open. Otherwise you're going to have a very long three years."

Thoughtful, Calvo studied him. Then he asked the question Kerry had been hoping for. "How can we start over, Mr. President?"

Kerry smiled. "For openers? Stop pushing Vic Coletti to support an override."

*

Senator Coletti, Hampton thought, had seldom looked less happy.

They sat alone in Hampton's office, sealed from, but ever mindful of, a Senate tense with rumor and confusion, each side waiting for a break in the other's ranks which might not come.

"It's up to you," Hampton told him bluntly. "This isn't about tort reform anymore, or even about adultery. It's about blackmail, and whether a Democratic President who stood up to it will fail or succeed."

Coletti folded his arms. "I gave you my vote against gun immunity, and you lost in spite of that. There are significant interests in my state absolutely wedded to this bill."

"Vic," Hampton said with ominous quiet, "I don't give a shit about the fucking insurance companies in Hartford. The SSA set out to destroy this President. He's got an extremely long memory, and so do I."

Absently, Coletti rubbed his beak of a nose, eyes focused on Hampton. "You're beginning to remind me of him, Chuck. That's not how you became the leader."

"Maybe not. But I intend to become *Majority* Leader, and for that I need a President strong enough to help carry us to victory." Hampton smiled. "Maybe then your parochial concerns will cut more ice with me. But in the meanwhile, you might want to check in with Tony Calvo. Something tells me that Tony and his friends might give you a little more slack than I will."

Shortly before noon, Senator Hampton went to see the Majority Leader.

With a calm and amiable demeanor, Fasano waved his rival to a chair. "What can I do for you, Chuck?"

"Get out of the way."

Surprise delayed Fasano's smile by fractions of a second. "Just like that?"

Leaning forward, Hampton spoke with more conviction than he felt. "There's a backlash building. What the SSA had going for it was fear. And the residue of fear, when it subsides, is hatred.

"You miscalculated, Frank. You married tort reform to the SSA because you had no choice. Now you're trapped— just like George Callister was trapped. The best thing that can happen to you is for the President to destroy the SSA."

The smile lingered in Fasano's eyes. "Don't you think," he asked, "that it's a little more complex? Or, perhaps, less. Beating Kilcannon is good. Losing to him is bad. Put more artfully, it has adverse implications for my future."

"Getting out of the way," Hampton answered, "is different than getting crushed. Or getting tarred with the SSA."

In the recesses of Fasano's gaze, Hampton glimpsed a disquiet he could not pin down. "Thanks for the advice," the Majority Leader told him pleasantly. "But you should assume that I'm going forward."

With a civil handshake, Hampton headed for his office, intent on phoning Senator Palmer. But the senior senator from Ohio was already taking Fasano's call.

FIFTEEN

TWO HOURS AFTER Hampton's warning, amidst rumors that Senator Coletti was about to switch his vote, Frank Fasano watched impassively as Vice President Ellen Penn recognized the senior senator from Ohio.

"A few hours from now," Chad began, "we are scheduled to vote to uphold, or override, President Kilcannon's veto. A few moments ago, the senior senator from Idaho suggested that we should hold this vote some other day—that in this 'emotional time' we cannot trust our reason." Pausing, Palmer turned toward Senator Harshman, allowing himself a hint of sarcasm. "Is this atmosphere any more 'emotional' than it was four days ago, when the Majority Leader set a vote after the President acknowledged the fact of—and the grounds for— an attempted act of blackmail? Or did it become too emotional only when we learned the identity of the blackmailer?

"Enough of this. Let us vote, and be done with it."

Crowded into the Oval Office, the President, Clayton, Kit, and his legislative relations team watched C-SPAN. No one spoke. No one knew what Palmer would say. Though he held the balance of the Senate in his hands, the senator from Ohio had told them nothing.

Where there is fact, Chad admonished his colleagues, *we need not fall back on emotion. And the facts are clear enough.*

The SSA sabotaged Martin Bresler.

The SSA threatened Lexington Arms with economic ruin.

The SSA—as Mr. Callister has now made clear—asked the Congress under false pretenses to place it above the law.

The SSA attempted to remove the final obstacle—the President—by the most despicable means . . .

"If I were Fasano," Kit ventured hopefully, "I wouldn't like the trend." But the President, intent on Palmer, did not respond.

Now, Palmer continued, *the president of the SSA tells us that the president of Lexington is not to be believed. He tells us, having smeared the President of the* United States, *that an honorable businessman—who finally became too sick of Mr. Dane to cover up for him—is lying.*

For what? *To ruin his own career?*

"He's a turncoat," Dane snapped at the screen. Sitting beside him, Carla Fell said nothing.

We know *better,* Palmer told the Senate. *So let us not pretend that we don't know who the liar is. Or, for that matter, the blackmailer . . .*

He could ride this out, Dane told himself. The SSA would not simply crumble in the face of these attacks, throwing Dane to the wolves to propitiate its enemies. The e-mails in response to his appearance on *Larry King* were proof that its members believed him—the most important "fact" of all.

With knowledge, Palmer went on, *comes responsibility. I was a principal sponsor of this bill. I advanced the interests of the SSA. For me to say now that I dissociate myself from their tactics, but not their goals, would be unconscionable.*

Carla Fell spoke at last. "Palmer's more than a turncoat, Charles. He just stabbed Fasano in the back."

*

Palmer's voice filled Sarah's office. *Tort reform*, he said firmly, *is a worthy goal. Some other day, I will fight for any bill but this. But the principle at stake today is not tort reform, but who* we *are and how we do business. And that moral imperative impels us to tell the SSA—as did President Kilcannon after another ruthless lobby sacrificed my daughter to their aims—that we do* not *do business* this *way.*

Watching, Mary told Sarah, "I think we did it."

Sarah felt a moment of pure elation. Perhaps, in the end, *she* had made the difference.

"I hope so," she answered with renewed trepidation. "But that may only make Bond come down even harder."

"When will this end?" Palmer asked the Senate. "And who will bring about the beginning of the end?

"I say that job falls to us. Like the President and First Lady, none of us are perfect. We all are worse than that, and we know far better than that." Pausing, Palmer ended flatly, "I ask you to join me in upholding the President's veto. *Today*."

As applause burst from the galleries, gaveled down by Ellen Penn, Cassie Rollins slipped over to Fasano. "Is this still a leadership vote?" she asked.

"You'll hear from me shortly," Fasano answered. "But whatever you do, you'll do it today."

"You're not trying to postpone this?"

"No."

As Cassie struggled to decipher this piece of news, Vic Coletti rose to speak. "I won't mince words," he said. "Or use many of my own. Senator Palmer spoke for me."

Across the aisle, Cassie noticed, Chuck Hampton glanced at Frank Fasano.

*

At five-thirty in the afternoon, having ignored his fourth message from Dane, Senator Fasano took the floor.

"I believe in this bill," he said simply. "All of it. It should become law—all of it. It should not be drowned by a sea of emotion, accusation, speculation, charge and counter-charge. And whether or not we support the SSA, the issue of gun rights in America should *never* be placed in the hands of trial lawyers."

Standing straighter, Fasano surveyed his colleagues—their expressions by turn rapt, curious, bewildered, tense, as they awaited the will of the Senate's most powerful member. "Because it is right, I will vote to override the President. I urge you to do likewise. But however you vote, you should do so on the merits, without obligation to the President—or to me."

With that, Fasano sat down.

Shortly after six o'clock, in a hushed chamber, ninety-nine members of the United States Senate began casting their votes. The thirty-fourth vote to support the President, upholding his veto, was cast by Senator Cassie Rollins. The final vote was fifty-six to forty-three in favor of the President.

One senator, Jack Slezak of Michigan, sent word through an aide that influenza had left him too ill to attend.

Leaving the chamber, Chad encountered Frank Fasano.

For Chad, it was a strange moment. He had inflicted a defeat on Fasano and, by doing so, had cemented the enmity of those who controlled his party's Presidential nomination. More curious yet, if their colleagues but knew, was that he had done what Fasano wished—delivered the *coup de grâce* to Charles Dane, for which he, not Fasano, would absorb the ire of the militant right. That Fasano's deal with him on campaign finance reform remained intact was Chad's recompense for doing what, in his heart, he had always known he must.

"Well," Fasano observed, "it's done. Kilcannon's won again."

Palmer shrugged. " 'The luck of the Irish,' " he said dryly. "If you can call it that. But you'll survive." Smiling, he lowered his voice still more. "You just dodged a bullet, Frank. An Eagle's Claw at that."

SIXTEEN

SHORTLY AFTER THE vote, President Kerry Kilcannon returned to the White House press room.

Whether he should do this was a matter of some debate—Clayton, for one, was worried that the potential appearance of triumphalism would ill suit a President who had sustained such personal damage. But it was time to reassert himself, Kerry felt, and he also had a debt to discharge. Stepping behind the podium he felt lighter, more confident than he had since the miserable day when the SSA had forced him to come here to acknowledge Lara's abortion.

With an air of ease and command, he scanned the reporters jammed into their appointed chairs. "Let me begin," he told them, "by publicly thanking the fifty-six senators who voted to sustain our veto of the Civil Justice Reform Act—and, most of all, Senator Chuck Hampton.

"This was a difficult fight. I am fortunate to have the aid of Senator Hampton on the next two legislative battles —for passage of our gun safety proposals, and Senator Palmer's effort to clean up our shameful and corrupt system of campaign finance." Kerry permitted himself a smile. "I'm also grateful to Senator Fasano for his agreement to bring those bills to a vote, without delay."

Kerry paused for emphasis, and his expression became serious. "I also want to express my respect for George Callister. His testimony not only exposed the SSA's control of the gun industry, but meant a great deal to me personally. He is an honorable man, and I look forward to working with him and other leaders of his industry to make our society safer."

Nodding briskly, the President signalled his willingness to take questions, then jabbed a finger in the direction of John King of CNN. "Mr. President," King said, "it seems likely that Mr. Callister's revelations expose the SSA to the risk of a sizeable verdict in Mary Costello's lawsuit. Do you agree, and how will *that* affect the political prospects for the passage of your gun bill?"

Briefly, the President considered his answer. "With respect to the lawsuit, it's not appropriate for me to comment on specifics. Obviously, the recent revelations—and I expect there will be others—will change the dynamics of the gun debate, both legally and in terms of public attitudes.

"The bottom line is this—I believe that my gun legislation will pass, and that thousands of men, women, and children will live who otherwise would have died."

"As of now," King persisted, "do you think that the SSA is a political leper?"

" 'Leper,' " Kerry answered with a smile. "Is that a term of art?" His smile faded. "I'll leave the phrasemaking to you, John. Obviously, this has been a difficult time, both for the First Lady and for me. I hope now there will be a greater public understanding of why we've persisted in this issue—one that transcends our personal history and focuses on the more than thirty thousand people other families lose to guns each and every year."

Glancing about, Kerry spotted the person he was looking for, a young woman from the Associated Press. Pointing in her direction, he said, "Marcia?"

She stood. "Sarah Dash—the lawyer who made public Mr. Callister's testimony—is now facing a contempt hearing. As a former lawyer yourself, do you have any comment?"

Gazing down at the podium, the President feigned

thought. "I need to weigh my words here," he began. "Just as the judge has to weigh the respect due his orders against what one might consider the larger moral context.

"Strictly as a moral matter, I think Ms. Dash acted in the tradition of those who have risked adverse personal consequences to themselves in order to save lives, and expose the wrongdoing of others." Pausing, Kerry finished mildly, "Obviously, the judge did not intend his order as a cover-up for perjury, obstruction of justice, and the attempted blackmail of a President."

When the press conference was done, Clayton greeted Kerry in the hallway. "I hope Bond watches television," he said.

Kerry laughed aloud. "Oh, I think he'll get the message. Just remember we owe a favor to Kit's friend from the Associated Press."

With Lenihan at one side, Mary Costello and the Director of the Kilcannon Center at the other, Sarah Dash stood before Judge Bond.

The benches behind them were full, and more reporters stood at the rear of the courtroom. After weeks of judicial secrecy, Gardner Bond had lost the ability to shut out the press and public. But such was Bond's pride of place that this left Sarah no less apprehensive than before. His posture was stiff, his expression suffused with the offended dignity of an egotistical man to whom his primacy was all.

"Did *you*," Bond demanded of Lenihan, "know what your client and cocounsel intended?"

"I did not," Lenihan answered. "But Ms. Costello wishes me to advise the court that it was *she* who made the final decision."

Briefly, Sarah felt Mary touch her arm, and then Bond glared at them both. "Ms. Dash," he snapped, "is an officer of this court. Her role is to admonish her client to obey Court orders, *not* to foment their violation."

"I understand, Your Honor," Lenihan said agreeably. "But I also think that President Kilcannon put it very well. Ms. Dash acted to prevent a larger injustice . . ."

"Ms. Dash," Bond snapped, "acted to affect the political process in a manner adverse to the defendants."

"Forgive me," Lenihan answered more quietly. "But, given Mr. Callister's testimony, it's somewhat hard to see the difference."

Though visibly annoyed, Bond hesitated. On impulse, Sarah said, "May I be heard, Your Honor?"

Curtly nodding, Bond answered with veiled sarcasm. "Please."

Sarah's own voice was shaky but determined. "I *do* believe that politics and morality should coincide. As should justice and morality.

"As a lawyer, I deeply regret abridging this Court's order. It was a painful choice, and I apologize to you for the offense caused by the choice I felt I had to make." Sarah paused, then decided to take a chance. "As I made it, I could only hope that it was a judgment the Court would have considered making, had it stood where I stood, and known what I knew . . ."

"You're badly mistaken," Bond interjected sharply. "The choice was this Court's, not yours. Your only role was to ask me to dissolve the order."

Helpless, Sarah moved her shoulders. "There was no time," she said simply.

This clear reference to the Senate's pending vote seemed to deepen Bond's annoyance. Behind her, Sarah heard John Nolan's voice. "May I speak on behalf of Lexington, Your Honor?"

Bond gave a slightly more pacific nod. "Counsel."

Stepping forward, Nolan glanced at the piece of paper he held.

"Your Honor," he said in a subdued voice, "in light of my client's reevaluation of its interests in this litigation, our firm may be withdrawing as counsel. However, Mr. Callister has directed me to tell the Court that Lexington does not ask for, or endorse, any sanctions against Ms. Dash. However much or little that may weigh in the Court's consideration."

As surprised as, judging from his expression, was Gardner Bond himself, Sarah saw an indignant Harrison Fancher quickly rise to seek the judge's attention. "I assume," the judge said tartly, "that you don't share Mr. Callister's somewhat gratuitous beneficence."

"We do not." Fancher's tone was one of open anger. "The SSA views Mr. Callister's testimony as slander—a tissue of lies used by Ms. Dash and her client, in blatant disregard of this Court's order, to shift the blame for the shootings to the SSA and to curry favor with the President. Who, as we all know, is the *éminence grise* of this entire travesty of justice."

Fancher shot a venomous glance at Sarah. "For *her* role," he concluded harshly, "we believe that Ms. Dash should face disbarment. That's a proper sanction for a lawyer who can't conform herself to the law."

Beside Sarah, Lenihan prepared to respond. Swiftly, she whispered, "Let it go, Bob."

He gave her a puzzled look, but Sarah was watching Bond. The judge, confronted for the first time with a packed courtroom, was forced to consider how appearances might affect his own prospects of promotion, fully aware that the sole counterbalance to the President's measured comments was the harsh demand of a very besmirched SSA. To Sarah, Bond's stern air seemed newly tempered by a hesitance which betrayed the tacit erosion of his power.

"All right," he snapped. "By their own admission, Ms. Dash and the Kilcannon Center stand in contempt of court. It is not up to lawyers to select which orders to obey. Accordingly, the Court orders that Ms. Dash and the Kilcannon Center each pay a fine of two thousand dollars. The Court will also send a copy of this order to the State Bar of California."

Abruptly, Bond cracked his gavel. "All rise," his courtroom deputy intoned. As the onlookers stood, Bond strode stiffly from the bench, covering his retreat with a last show of judicial dignity.

Glancing at Nolan and Fancher, Sarah suppressed a smile. The jaws of Kerry Kilcannon's trap had shut on them at last. Perhaps she would not have Nolan to kick around anymore, but she intended to nail Harrison Fancher's client to the wall.

SEVENTEEN

THREE DAYS BEFORE Christmas, to be spent with Mary, Kerry and Lara visited the gravesites.

It was morning. Thin sunlight filtered through a dissipating fog, and the grass on the knoll glistened with dew. Holding Kerry's hand, Lara gazed down at the headstones of her mother, sister and niece.

They were President and First Lady. Lara understood, and accepted, that the press, gathered some distance away, would film them, and that the image would linger over the Senate when it debated Kerry's gun bill, as it would over Gardner Bond's courtroom on the first day of trial. She knew that, in part, this was why Kerry had suggested coming. But she also knew that, with all the hurt they had sustained, Kerry sensed that this was a time for Lara to seek peace. Although, she thought to herself, he did not yet know the final reason this was so.

After a time, she banished those watching from her mind. In turn, Lara thought of Inez Costello, then Joan, and then Marie—recalling each not as she had seen them last, but in life, until their memory filled her like a living thing.

She did not know how long this took. When they stepped away, it was because she was done; when they stopped, a short distance from the graves, it was because Lara wished it.

"I can't imagine," she told him, "how this would have been without you."

A hint of pain surfaced in his eyes. "Without me," he answered, "it wouldn't have been at all."

"It wasn't you, Kerry." She hesitated, then touched his face. "All my life I've been afraid to lean on anyone. Now I know that I can. And so can you."

Kerry smiled a little. "Then that's all I could want."

She cocked her head. "All?"

His expression became puzzled. Watching him, Lara felt her anticipation quicken; this moment, before it was strained through the prism of politics and public life, belonged to them alone. She saw his puzzlement change to wonder.

"It wasn't flu . . ."

Lara smiled up at him. "Diapers," she informed her husband, "are the acid test of character. Even for a President."

Afterword and Acknowledgments

Gun violence in America is a subject of daunting complexity, requiring a knowledge of its political, governmental, legal, medical, public health, social, and cultural dimensions. I should start by acknowledging that I approached this undertaking with a distinct point of view: I am a strong advocate of common-sense measures to curb gun violence. This position is buttressed by my presence on the boards of the Brady Campaign to Prevent Gun Violence and the Family Violence Prevention Fund. I am also concerned about the influence of special interest money in politics, which in part accounts for my current service on the board of Common Cause, the public interest lobby. Each of these affiliations has shaped my thinking, and stimulated my concern, with respect to the causes and the toll of gun violence in America. By no means am I a dispassionate, or neutral, observer.

That said, the enormous amount of research required by this novel informed and complicated my view of these subjects in countless ways. To write *Balance of Power*, I tried to probe every aspect of this problem and every point of view. So I am deeply indebted to all those who helped me to achieve the knowledge base necessary to write this book.

I must also make it clear that they represent disparate and often conflicting experiences and perspectives, and that their help does not constitute an endorsement of this book, let alone of any particular opinion expressed herein. As always, the buck stops with me, and any disagreements or hostility engendered by this novel should be directed at me alone.

I am, of course, a fiction writer, and this is a work of imagination. Nonetheless, I have striven for accuracy throughout the book, in ways both large and small, and the story is firmly rooted in the reality of our current political environment. For example, a bill immunizing the gun industry in a manner similar to that portrayed in this novel was pending in the last Congress, and its proponents claimed two hundred twenty-eight sponsors in the House of Representatives, a majority. In the Senate about to be convened, the control has now returned to the Republicans; it is quite possible that a bill will be introduced and voted on by both houses before this book is published. Readers should also know that the general outline—though not all of the details, and certainly not the blackmail of a President—of the problems faced by George Callister and Lexington Arms in settling with Kerry Kilcannon were faced by Smith & Wesson when it entered into a tentative settlement in 2000 with the Clinton Administration which never came to fruition. And the basis and legal theories of the Costello lawsuit reflect, to a considerable degree, the litigation involving the shootings in the 101 California tragedy in San Francisco—including the nature of the weapon, the mode of advertising, and the kind of harm inflicted—and the "flooding" issue appears in lawsuits filed against the gun industry by several California cities.

Finally, the chapter in which Kerry Kilcannon visits a gun show in Las Vegas is rooted in my own personal observations of such a show. Every description in that chapter is derived from that experience. The only alterations are that I took the bumper-sticker aspersions cast on other public figures and substituted the Kilcannons; modeled the "Lexington P-2" and "Eagle's Claw" bullet after other, virtually identical, weapons; and imported a target practice cutout of former President and Mrs. Clinton from a gun store in New Hampshire, replacing the Clintons with Kerry and Lara Kilcannon.

With that, I wish to thank all those who helped.

The Senate is an institution unto itself, and its workings and procedures are as intricate as they are, to me, fascinating. I am deeply indebted to the following current or former members of that body: Barbara Boxer, William Cohen, John Edwards, Edward Kennedy, John McCain, and, in particular, Bob Dole, whose advice has been invaluable for three books now. Others, including current and former Senate staffers, helped with respect to both politics and process: Melody Barnes, Mark Busey, Bruce Cohen, Meredith McGehee, Ed Pagano, Martin Paone, Robin Toone, and Bob Tyrer. Special thanks to former Senate Parliamentarian Bob Dove, who not only walked me through the process, but was kind enough to review the manuscript.

I was lucky to have advice from several scholars, journalists, and public officials and writers who have studied the issue from various perspectives: Ron Brownstein, Dr. Philip Cook, Morris Dees, Dr. Glen Pierce, Dr. Stephen Teret, Dr. Jay Wachtel, and, especially, Matt Bai and Susan Ginsberg. Similarly, I was schooled in the medical aspects of gun violence—from surgery to the public health aspects— by Dr. Beth Kaplan, Dr. Arthur Kellerman, Dr. Robert Liner, Dr. Robert Mackersie, Dr. Irene Marquez-Biggs, Sean Reynolds, Dr. H. William Taeusch, and, in particular, Dr. Margaret Knudson and Dr. William Schwab.

A number of current or former employees of the Bureau of Alcohol, Tobacco and Firearms helped me with the often complicated regulatory environment surrounding guns, as well as with various investigative methods: Dale Armstrong, Terry Austin, Tara Bedford, Tom Cannon, John D'Angelo, Fanny Hasselbacher, Ed Owen, Jack Patterson, and John Torres. Many thanks to all.

Several talented people discussed with me the subject of gun politics at the Presidential level, as well as past legislative and regulatory efforts to reduce gun violence, including Harold Ickes, Bruce Reed, and Max Stier. Special thanks to Bruce Lindsey and Cheryl Mills, not only for their advice but for reviewing all or part of the manuscript, and to President Bill Clinton for his observations about the politics of guns. Still others filled me in on various aspects of gun politics: Rich Bond, Carter Eskew, Peter Fenn, Mandy Grunwald, Ron Kaufman, Joel Klein, Peter Knight, Celinda Lake, Joe Lockhart, Mike McCurry, Bill McInturff, Scott Reed, Don Simon, Tom Strickland, and Michael Terris.

The jurisprudence of gun lawsuits and the Second Amendment was also an important subject. I read every significant legal decision regarding the Second Amendment and lawsuits against gun companies, as well as a number of scholarly articles on these subjects. I am grateful to the following legal experts for their help: Fred Baron, Arthur Bryant, Leah Castella, Owen Cléments, John Coale, Leslie Landau, Linda Lipson, and Dennis Henigan. Thanks as well to Victor Schwartz and James Wooten for their important observations regarding gun lawsuits and tort reform.

I was fortunate to have the advice of a number of prominent advocates of gun safety. I begin with my current and former colleagues at the Brady Campaign: Mike Barnes, Ellen Moran, and Tony Orza. I learned much from the Web site for the Brady Campaign (www.bradycampaign.org; www.bradycenter.org) and that of its grassroots affiliate, the Million Man March (www.millionmanmarch.com). I am also grateful to the following members of Americans for Gun Safety: Jon Cowan, Jim Kessler, Matthew Bennett, Michael Harrington, Lisa Kimbrough, and Meghan Sherman. Finally, I am deeply grateful to two women who, having lost loved ones to gun violence, speak to this tragedy as advocates in the most important way possible: Mary Leigh Blek and Carole Kingsley.

I was not as fortunate with gun rights advocates. My calls and letters requesting time with the principal officers of the National Rifle Association went unanswered; apparently, and perhaps understandably, they did not wish to meet with a novelist affiliated with the Brady Campaign. Nonetheless, that choice was theirs, and I regret being unable to present their thoughts. I did have off-the-record talks with two persons affiliated with the NRA, and immersed myself in NRA publications. Thus the SSA's public rhetoric and positions on gun rights closely reflects that of the NRA. In particular, the article I attributed to the SSA magazine in Chapter Two of Part One includes quotations from or close paraphrases of an actual, much longer article in the NRA magazine *America's First Freedom*. Similarly, Charles Dane's speech at the Washington Monument includes brief passages from two speeches given by Charlton Heston, then the President of the NRA, and Wayne La Pierre, its executive director. I am very grateful to Beth Lavach, who has extensive experience in Congressional relations on behalf of the gun industry, for her advice on legislative matters. Also of great assistance were two gun rights advocates whose efforts at compromise sometimes put them in conflict with the NRA, Richard Feldman and Robert Ricker.

One of the interesting benefits of my research is that I came away with some real sympathy for the executives of gun companies, many of whom value guns for their quality and craftsmanship. These executives face a difficult dilemma, caught as they are between gun safety advocates and the lawyers who represent them, on the one side, and the NRA, which—in addition to its dominant presence in Washington, D.C.—reaches many of their customers. For these reasons, the NRA has an immense power over the gun industry—perhaps even, as has been demonstrated in the past, the potential to create a credible threat of such crippling economic harm that an individual company fears being forced out of business. Special thanks to Paul Januzzo, Ken Jorgenson, Bob Scott, and Ed Shultz for sharing their diverse perspectives as current or former executives of Glock and Smith & Wesson.

Gun violence is the leading cause of death in domestic violence incidents. My outstanding colleagues at the Family Violence Prevention Fund, Janet Carter and Esta Soler, helped me present the dynamic of an abusive marriage, and Esta was kind enough to review the manuscript. Also of great value were several publications by the Fund. And Susan Breall, Sarah Buehl, and Juan Cuba helped me present both the legal and personal aspects of this tragedy.

A number of people advised me on other subjects: Letitia Baldrige, former social secretary to the Kennedy White House, concerning the Kilcannon's wedding preparations; Fr. John Blaker with respect to the religious aspects of the wedding; Katie Couric on the nature of the media competition for the Lara Kilcannon interview; Alan Dershowitz with respect to the intricacies of the Kilcannons' privilege claims; Dr. Kenneth Gottlieb and Dr. Rodney Shapiro regarding the psychological issues surrounding the Bowden's marriage, and the reactions of both Kerry and Lara Kilcannon to the murders; San Francisco Homicide Inspector Napoleon Hendrix on the details of the murders; John Phillips and Mary Louise Cohen on the role of inside informants in complex litigation; and Terry Samway of the Secret Service regarding the problems surrounding the protection of the Kilcannons and the attempts to protect Lara's family. All helped enrich the texture of this novel.

My understanding was also enriched by reading,

including the book *Making a Killing* by Tom Diaz; *The Gathering Storm* by Morris Dees; *Gun Violence: The Real Costs* by Philip Cook and Jens Ludwig; and *Public Guns, Public Health* by Dr. David Hemenway. I also read relevant articles, papers, surveys and opinion pieces by Philip Alpers, Matt Bai, Paul Barrett, Carl T. Bogus, Thomas Cole, Philip Cook, John Donohue, David Grossman, Arthur Kellerman, Abigail Kohn, Stephanie Molliconi, and Garry Wills. Publications by the Brady Campaign, Americans for Gun Safety, and the Violence Policy Center were also immensely helpful.

Finally, I would like to thank my wonderful publisher, Gina Centrello of Ballantine, for believing that there is a place for serious popular fiction on controversial social and political topics; Nancy Miller and Linda Marrow of Ballantine for their discerning editorial advice; Fred Hill, my sharp-eyed and indefatigable agent; and, of course, the wonderful Alison Porter Thomas, my assistant, who comments both conceptually and in detail on every page until the days' work more or less meets her approval. My wife, Laurie Patterson, reads and comments on each chapter; when Laurie has a question about a character's behavior, I've found that it is well to listen. And there is Philip Rotner, who reads every line I write and has been, for nearly two decades, the best best friend anyone could have. This one's for you, pal.

Because this book is also a cautionary tale about the costs of public life, I cannot leave this subject without an observation about those who elect to enter it. Very often, they are far better than we choose to believe; to the best of them, and they are many, we owe the better campaign finance system that we private citizens are often too detached or lazy to insist on. Every once in a while, someone makes us think of that, if only for a time. Laurie and I think often of Paul and Sheila Wellstone.

Finally, *Balance of Power* marks the end of what I think of as the Kerry Kilcannon trilogy, which began with *No Safe Place* and continued with *Protect and Defend*. For me, it's been a wonderful experience, and I can only hope that my readers have enjoyed inhabiting Kerry's world half as much as I.

New Year's Day, 2003

Addendum

It is nearly six months since I completed and edited *Balance of Power*, and fiction and reality have merged in an uncanny way.

In January 2003, survivors of the victims of the Washington, D.C., sniper filed suit against, among others, the manufacturer who noted the adaptability of the weapon for sniper-type activity, and the dealer from whom a juvenile and a man with a record of domestic violence somehow acquired a weapon. In March—following the lead of a majority of the House of Representatives—fifty-two Senators (forty-three Republicans and nine Democrats) introduced a bill that would immunize manufacturers, dealers, and the National Rifle Association from all such suits. As anticipated in my novel, the bill swiftly passed the House, and is now pending in the Senate.

The only material difference from the scenario presented in *Balance of Power* is that this legislation is supported, rather than opposed, by the current administration. But, as in the novel, its fate rests with a handful of swing Democrats and Republican moderates in the Senate—who, because the President will sign such a bill, must join with enough Senators to reach the forty-one required to sustain a filibuster.

As in *Balance of Power,* the gun lobby has deployed its full resources, hiring a large team of lobbyists, generating phone calls and letters to Senate offices, and suggesting to undecided Senators that the intensity of their opposition in the next election may turn on this vote. The resulting

legislative battle has been as tough as my narrative anticipated. In the interest of full disclosure, I should note that
I know this first hand; I have been intimately involved in
this conflict, meeting with Senators to urge support for a
filibuster, and strategizing with opponents of the bill. By
the time this novel appears in mid-October, the outcome
may well be decided.

June 20, 2003